The Gaardian Saga

Four books:

I. Life Before Conception
II. Starlight Adventures
III. The Still Small Voice
IV. Stepping Beyond

James J. Stewart

ISBN: 978-0-9861334-0-4

Online Order Web Site
James-j-stewart.com

Author's Foreword

Although these stories have no basis in fact, the characters reflect the personalities of people that the author has met, both in the United States and in a dozen other countries. The tales are told with these assumptions:

1. Our universe reflects the handiwork of a Creator we call God.
2. God loves all of creation.
3. There is probably intelligent life in places other than Earth.
4. God provides for the salvation of all of God's children, both on Earth and possibly on other worlds.
5. Each planet's savior has followers and fans, as well as detractors and enemies.

In the midst of each of the four sets of tales, there is a story that encompasses all four of the previously published books:

> - *Life Before Conception*
> - *Starlight Adventures*
> - *The Still Small Voice*
> - *Stepping Beyond*

This one-volume edition encompasses all four of the above books with relatively minor changes. In addition to the ongoing characters in each installment, the story that begins in the first volume and ends in the final volume ties all of the stories together.

James J. Stewart

Table of Contents

I. *Life Before Conception*

Prologue

1. Walter

Walter's story begins in Northern California well over a century ago, along a beach on Monterey Bay in California. There was the rhythmic slap of the waves, the smell of the salt air, and the cries of gulls above. Unseen eyes were observing. They were looking for someone who could be trained for the job of policing Earth's sector of the universe. They wanted genetics and temperament to be just right in their next recruit. The recruit's physical, emotional, and spiritual essence had to be carefully considered.

It was on this warm summer evening, as children were playing near the ocean, that people were being watched from the shadows of a large cypress tree. "It is almost time," said Kieya ["k'EYE-yuh"], a four-legged creature with stripes, somewhat like a tiger but with a human-like face. The two of them stood up in the midst of the shadows.

"Yes," said Qaak ["kuh-ACK"], a three-legged humanoid creature. If it were not for the shadows, Qaak's turquoise and yellow coloring would definitely have stood out to those playing on the beach. "The one called James has real potential."

"He will probably meet his mate soon. Perhaps we will use one of his descendents."

"Yes. We will return for more." The two creatures vanished. On the beach, no one noticed their departure, but then no one had seen their arrival either.

+ + +

Two years later, James met a tall brown-haired woman named Prudence. When he told her she had the same name as his grandmother, she smiled. They were both nineteen and quickly fell in love. After their wedding in 1870, they said their farewells to their families in Monterey and moved north to San Francisco, where they started an importing business across from a huge wharf. Together they become successful importers. Just after they returned from a buying trip to New Zealand in 1875, their first child was born – a girl. Two more, George and Earnest, came along later.

+ + +

Ernest was handsome, strong, and tall like his father, but he did not do well in school. He went overseas, and one day at Blenheim, New Zealand, Ernest met the most beautiful woman he had ever seen. The day after they met, he got down on one knee. "Will you marry me?"

"You're crazy!"

"Will you marry me?"

"We have just met!"

"Will you marry me?"

She consented. On New Year's Day 1900, Barbara and Ernest were married at the Anglican Cathedral in Christchurch. The aliens Qaak and Kieya returned from their visit a half-century earlier, and they watched from the shadows of the organ loft, high above the ceremony. "This is excellent. We can stop following the other family lines except as alternates."

"Yes. Neither of these is suitable, but one of their descendents will surely be the one who we want."

+ + +

Barbara and Ernest's first child was a boy. Born just before Christmas in Earth's year 1908, they named him Edward. Two decades later, Qaak and Kieya watched Edward carefully as he courted a beautiful woman named Judi. One afternoon on the Thames River in London, the two aliens looked on from the shadows under a bridge, as Edward asked Judi to marry him. Qaak's eyes glowed subtly as he spoke. "The time grows close."

"Yes," replied Kieya. "Our first Gaardian ["guh-ARE-dee-un"] from Earth probably will be one of their children."

Arthur, born in 1938, was both strong and bright. He was good both at sports and in his academic subjects. His younger brother, the future Gaardian, was born in 1942. Edward and Judi named him Walter.

Kieya and Qaak were now even more attentive. When Edward and Judi brought Walter home from the hospital, two giant stuffed animals were delivered from an anonymous admirer. Edward liked the tiger the best but thought that the three-legged one was ugly. Judi loved them both – particularly the three-legged one. They placed the stuffed animals in one corner of Walter's nursery. After Edward and Judi left the nursery that evening, the two stuffed animals transformed and started to move.

Kieya stalked up to the crib. Quiet and intense, her tiger-like stripes rippled slightly as she walked. "He's going to excel, Qaak. Come and get closer."

Quiet and calm, with his eyes glowing, he simply responded, "Yes." Qaak moved gracefully to the crib and touched the baby's forehead with three fingers. "Sleep soundly, Walter. We are going to give some wonderful dreams to you. When your creativity is in full bloom, and when your mind is ready for the impossible to become possible, you are going to have new friends on other worlds. You will be a Gaardian." (He pronounced it precisely like 'Gu-ARE-dee-un'). "Your dreams will become training for you, but now Kieya and I are going to make sure you are always safe."

A pale blue glow surged through the room. As the glow subsided, they looked back to the corner where they had been posing as toys. Identical stuffed animals appeared. Then the two looked at one another and vanished.

A few days later, Edward got a letter from Berkeley, California. The California State College system was opening a new campus in Long Beach in the fall of Earth's year 1949. Edward was invited to join the faculty as a full professor. The family moved from Christchurch to Long Beach in the summer. It was several decades later that Walter's story as a Gaardian began.

Part One: A Second Beginning

<h2 style="text-align:center">2. Retiring</h2>

Walter's close friends often compared him to Cliff, in television's *Cheers* comedy series. In his bedroom, a clock radio on the headboard said 4:00 AM, and a diploma on the wall identified the sleeper as Walter Stephanopolos. In one corner of the bedroom were the timeworn stuffed likenesses of Qaak and Kieya. The clock radio started to play softly. Walter turned on the light on his headboard and opened a copy of Christianity Today magazine. His cat hopped up on the bed, and Walter stroked the head of the very large mixed-breed.

"Good morning, Tiger. Where have you been prowling all night?" Tiger blinked his eyes sleepily. Walter was now in his sixties and balding, with what is left of his hair streaked with gray. He did some light reading while he woke up, and then he opened his Bible. Tiger continued to purr at the foot of the bed.

After dressing and walking into his kitchen, Walter filled a large plastic mug with filtered water, warmed it in the microwave, and drank it down without stopping. His automatic coffee maker had brewed a pot of herbal tea, so he re-filled the mug with tea.

Going to his front door, he reached out and grabbed the morning newspaper. In the living room, he sat down and drank the tea while reading. He looked down. "I know, Tiger. You want attention, and you want to be fed. Well, there's food in your dish. I'll spend some time with you when I come home for lunch, okay?" Tiger sat back on his haunches and gazed at him.

During breakfast, he indulged himself in a half-hour sermon by a television preacher before leaving for the church. Outside his door, he walked down the hall and took the elevator to the parking lot below. He climbed into his Subaru SVX and drove about a mile to the church.

Walter was always punctual. Arriving around 8:00, there were already other cars in the lot. When first meeting Walter, he can appear to be rather cold, but church members there knew he was warm and loving. It was typical of Sunday mornings. Inside the church, there was vigorous activity. Quincy, slender and tall with slightly graying hair, spoke out with a booming voice, "The boiler is going to need some work."

"What's the problem, Quincy?"

"We had a minor crisis, but it's being dealt with. The heat didn't come on in the early morning as it usually does. We had a pipe burst, and the old asbestos insulation is ruined. We'll talk about it at the next board meeting."

"Okay." Walter liked taking things step by step. "What happens between now and then?"

Quincy just winked in response, turned, and walked away. Musicians were warming up at the front of the chapel. Walter shook his head in wonder as he headed down the aisle.

The rest of the morning was typical. After the early service, filled with rock music and lots of enthusiasm, Walter taught a church school class for older adults. Then he led a more traditional worship service.

It was interesting to Walter how people of different generations paid attention differently when they wanted to worship. He had noticed that the younger members tended to like worship with a fast pace, contemporary music, and lots of rhythm. For them, when things slowed down or there was silence, there was a tendency for them to get impatient or bored. "Why should we have to sing those stuffy old hymns?" some of them asked.

Then there were people like Quincy and his wife. They began to worship before other people arrived, and before the music and visiting with others began. It happened again when there was a time for silent prayer. Unlike the younger generations that used music to shut out other distractions, Quincy's wife said, "I hate it when there is music during silent prayer -- it makes me focus on the music rather than upon God!"

As Quincy and his wife would sit there in silence, they would become aware of the rhythm of their breathing. Quincy could sense the calming and slowing down of the beating of his heart as he began to sense an envelope of warmth and peace. His wife became aware of the inaudible voice of God speaking to them in the quietness. They had found that one particular aspect of the presence and power of God would begin to rivet their attention. It was often healing or other kinds of holy help that their friends and family needed. They enjoyed the contemporary worship with their children, grandchildren, and great grandchildren, but they still hungered for and enjoyed the silences. They became enraptured with the power they experienced when they totally surrendered to the flood of the Holy Spirit enveloping them. Their granddaughter said that in her generation, they experienced some of that spiritual ecstasy by letting contemporary music and rhythm lift them higher and higher.

In both services, some spoke of being in touch with God through Jesus and "the seduction of the spirit." The more they experienced holy joy the more they wanted. As they "put their hands into the hands of The Master," they never wanted to turn back from the exhilaration, regardless of their age.

After the second service, most of the six hundred in worship attended a luncheon. As the program afterwards concluded, Walter said a final prayer, and people hung around and talked as they cleaned up. Walter helped a slender and elderly black woman into his SVX, got in himself, and drove away. The ride home was unusually quiet. "I must admit I'm tired, Margaret. The rock music in the first service really energized me as usual, though. I'm ready for a nap."

She was quiet at first and gazed out the window. "At least the sky's not leakin' today," she said. "Across the bay, the Golden Gate is in its usual cold soup, but over here we're crispy critters, aren't we?"

Walter grunted and smiled as she put her seat back a little more and basked in the sun. "You're unusually quiet today, Margaret - how are you feeling these days?"

"As well as a ninety-one year-old woman can expect. I was just thinking of something you've often said about preaching."

"What's that?"

"You've often said that sometimes you have to comfort the afflicted, and sometimes you have to afflict the comfortable. You keep a pretty good balance, for the most part, between the two. That's one of the reasons I like your preaching so much." She paused.

"And why are you thinking about that today?" Walter turned off onto a smaller street.

"Since the earthquake this last spring you've done a lot of comforting the afflicted both in the pulpit and with individuals. Your pastoral counseling instincts are amazing."

"Thanks. But why are you thinking about that balance today?"

"For the last couple of weeks, I've been waiting for you to shift gears. Too many of us have gotten into the habit of feeling sorry for ourselves since the earthquake. I've been feeling like we need to stop feeling sorry for ourselves, and start getting back to doing some caring beyond our families and friends. I was surprised that you seemed timid about confronting the issues more bluntly. I think they're ready for it again."

"You think so? I guess I could do a little more afflicting of the comfortable, now that we are nearly a year beyond the quake." He paused. "You like organizing parties, Margaret. Would you like to have a party to celebrate the anniversary of the earthquake and our recovery since?"

"That sounds like a good idea. I'll talk to our women's group about it on Wednesday."

The conversation shifted as they arrived at her retirement complex. She spoke again. "I still think though that it's time for us to get off of our duffs and get back to being a mission to our community. I know, some of those we match in marriage end up joining us, but we both know that's not enough." She paused. "I'll get off my soap box now!"

He pulled to a stop in front of her retirement complex. "Thanks for your feedback, Margaret. I guess I'll see you at the luncheon on Wednesday."

She opened the door. "Okay. Are you getting enough sleep, or are you having those dreams again?" As Walter nodded she continued, "If I were younger I'd be your wife sitting here, hen-pecking you!" She smiled, got out, and closed the door.

Walter, also smiling, leaned over to speak through the open window to her. "Thanks, Margaret, but I should be able to catch up on my sleep tonight. If you were my wife, we'd go for a drive tomorrow! Anyway, I'm going to take tomorrow morning off. See you Wednesday!"

"Bye!" Margaret ambled off, hardly using her cane.

Walter headed for his condominium. Driving past the entrance to the condominium complex, he pulled into the secure garage under the building and under his condominium. He parked and headed down the aisle. Hearing laughter and screams from the pool area, he headed for the elevator, punched the '4' button inside, and leaned against the wall while the elevator headed up to his floor.

As the door opened, his neighbor greeted him, and came in as he was leaving. Ann was around thirty-five and average in height. She had a face and figure that confirmed her many wins at beauty contests.

"Hey, Ann, you look great! Is that a new bikini?"

"No. Are you just getting home from church?"

"I'm afraid so. If you want to visit again next Sunday, I'll take you out to lunch afterwards, okay?"

He grinned as she smiled. "I know you're being romantic, and maybe someday I'll take you up on that and more! Meanwhile, I'll check my calendar and let you know! ... Thanks!" The elevator doors closed.

Walking down the hall Walter noticed a lamp out and made a mental note to have it replaced. Unlocking the door to his condominium, he glanced up. "Lord, Ann sure is a beautiful woman. She's incredible. I love her dearly. I wish she was more centered on you."

Heading into the kitchen, he put a few leftovers in the microwave. Then, heading for the bedroom, he saw his cat blinking away the fact he had been fast asleep on Walter's bed. "You've got an easy life, Tiger, don't you, boy?" Tiger purred as Walter scratched his head a bit. Sitting down and taking off his shoes, Walter headed for the bathroom. He splashed some water on his face and ran a comb through his thinning hair. Hearing the faint beep of the microwave, he remembered his dinner and headed back to the kitchen.

As he ate, he surfed the TV's cable channels back and forth between news, cartoons, and an old movie. He watched briefly, but decided he did not have time for it. He settled for some classic Warner Brothers cartoons. Walter had been a Bugs Bunny fan since childhood.

His dinner only partly eaten, Walter set the tray aside, put his feet up on the sofa, and lay down to take a nap. Considering the time of day, he realized he might have to put chores off until tomorrow or Tuesday. "Where have the hours gone, Tiger? Maybe I'll leave you by yourself again this evening and see a couple of the visitors. What do you think, Tiger?" Tiger blinked and hopped up on his lap for a scratch. As he stretched out, he really did not want to sleep very long.

All his life, Walter frequently awakened in the night from extremely vivid dreams. They were not nightmares in the usual sense. When he was very young, he had a nightmare from time to time – until he was about six. After he started taking piano lessons, he began to have vivid and detailed dreams that were often bizarre.

Eyes closed, Walter prayed, "Heavenly Father, this day has been awesome! Thank you! I'm looking forward to whatever you have in store for me tomorrow. It is by your grace that I serve your Son Jesus, and it is in his name I pray. Amen." He drifted off to sleep.

He began to remember some fragments of his dreams from the previous night. He had conversations with science-fiction-like characters. Many had been with him every night, and they even had names. Two of them resembled the stuffed animals in the corner near his bed. When he awakened, he could not remember any details except a few names. Try as he might, he could make no connections between the characters in his dreams and the everyday events in his life.

He consistently knew when he was dreaming because the light always seemed to have a bluish cast. He had tried making notes during the night right after awakening, but it had been gibberish. When friends had stayed the night, he tried waking them up as soon as he awakened himself to tell them what he had remembered. The next morning they could not remember what he had said.

Now, thinking he was still awake, Walter found himself in a dream that was more vivid than usual. He was being lectured by one of his favorite dream characters – the turquoise and yellow humanoid with three legs and huge ears named Qaak. To Walter, Qaak was handsome in his own alien way, resembling his favorite stuffed toy from childhood. Qaak was Walter's teacher and guide, who had escorted him through much of the universe of his dreams. Qaak introduced him to many provocative and fascinating characters in their travels together. They had become friends, as Qaak had shown Walter the beauties of other suns, planets, climates, and cultures. Qaak was amazingly patient when Walter's dreams took them to new places that Walter did not understand. Perhaps the most amazing part of Walter's dreams involved how Qaak taught him to communicate without spoken language.

Before Walter began learning algebra, in his waking days at school, Qaak began teaching him concepts that are far more complex. Long before Walter learned to defend himself in his waking hours through skirmishes with his friends, Qaak taught him how to use weapons that make hydrogen bombs seem like toys. Qaak taught Walter how to measure the time between stars, before in his waking hours, he learned to measure his waist for clothes. While Walter was learning to play the piano and appreciate human music, Qaak taught him the arts and crafts of dozens of other cultures on other planets.

That particular day, his dream was a series of flashbacks to old dreams. Walter was also often amused by how Qaak could fold any one leg like a chair to provide rest for the other two while he is not moving.

That day, Walter dreamed that he had made himself comfortable, lying on his side while Tiger purred at his feet. As Walter seemingly dozed off, he found himself dreaming that he was on the sofa in the same manner, and Qaak was sitting chair-less across from him – in front of the TV. Walter knew he was dreaming because everything has that familiar bluish cast. Qaak seemed excited, and his eyes were twinkling with joy. "Walter, your training is over! We have been training you during your dreams for more than fifty of the years of your planet. The time has come for your dreams to merge with your waking reality."

Walter was puzzled. Usually, his dreams began in some mystical or fantastic place – never in his own living room. Yet, here he was in his living room, with Tiger at his feet! "What do you mean?"

"Right now, while you and I are talking, you're aware of lying on your sofa, aren't you? When you fell asleep and began this dream, you were lying in the same place, only Tiger was lying at your feet. In this dream he is not there, is he? If you concentrate you can still feel his purring through your feet, can't you?" Walter was now intrigued as Qaak continued. "If you can feel Tiger purring, then you realize that there is a subtle connection between this dream and where you are dreaming, right?" He paused. "Now Walter, I want you to try something you've not tried before. This is no different than trying everything else we did in the past together. Keeping yourself focused on me, raise your left arm—your real one."

In his dream, his left arm went up, and Tiger looked up from his feet as his real left arm went up. "Wow! Is this really happening?"

Qaak began to rock back and forth on his third leg, his eyes twinkling even more. "Now that you are aware of your body apart from this dream state, continue focusing on me while you swing your legs off of the sofa so that you are in a sitting position."

In his dream, Walter swung around to a sitting position. As the real non-dreaming Walter brought his legs around, Tiger stood up, stretched, and sat back looking at him quizzically. "This is unreal!"

"Of course! It seems unreal because you are between being asleep and being awake. You are almost awake, but your real eyes are still closed of course. Relax! This will be over in a moment!"

"I must be dreaming all of this!"

"You ARE dreaming this conversation, but your real body really is sitting up. You will see in a moment. I am now going to show you why all of this is both fun and important."

"Fun? It's kind of weird!"

"Quiet now." Qaak paused. "Keep your eyes focused on me and open your real eyes."

"Then I'll be awake! The dream will be over. I need to take this nap – I'm tired! I can't do that!"

"Trust me! Try it!"

Walter slowly opened his eyes. His living room had a soft, warm, and familiar light, no longer a soft blue. He was still in the same place in his condominium – only Qaak was sitting in Walter's recliner! "I must be hallucinating!" He rubbed his eyes. He hit his head with his hand. He looked again. There was Qaak. He looked slightly different in the warm light of the late afternoon, but Qaak was still turquoise and yellow – like the stuffed toy in his bedroom.

It was real! Qaak was real! Walter's head was swimming. "All of those dreams for the last fifty years were more than dreams, weren't they?"

Qaak leaned closer. "Walter, right now you are feeling very confused." He paused as Walter nodded. "I need to integrate you – integrate the past fifty years of sleeping and waking." Walter looked at him. "This will only take a moment." Qaak extended his right hand, putting three fingers on Walter's face. Two fingers were on Walter's forehead, and the third was between Walter's eyes. Qaak looked out the window, and his eyes began to glow. The glow began to envelop first Qaak and then Walter. Tiger looked on, curious but unafraid. Walter had experienced the glow before, although he was asleep the first time when he was a baby. This time it lasted less than twenty seconds.

Walter blinked. "I understand! At first, I thought maybe I was going crazy, but I see it all now! Wow! I've been living two lives simultaneously for most of my life! In my sleep, I was learning things in another part of the universe, wasn't I? Evidently, my five senses have been enhanced with a few more, too. You, Qaak, have been keeping my two worlds separate until my training was complete. Now you've integrated me." He paused. "Now what?"

"First, let's go down to your car in the garage." Qaak faded to invisibility, but Walter could still see him with his enhanced senses. The two of them got up and walked toward the condominium door, which opened without either of the touching it.

Down the hall, as the elevator doors opened, Ann stepped out, her bikini still dripping from the pool downstairs. She stood a bit taller and subtly thrust out her chest before speaking. "Hello again, Walter! Headed back to the church again?"

"Hi Ann!" As they greeted each other again, she smiled and walked right through Qaak. She used her body to flirt, suddenly being very much sexier. He looked back over his shoulder. She paused, standing in a provocative profile as he answered.

"Many women look like drowned rats when they're wet, but you look stunning, Ann!"

"Thanks! I love you too!" She opened the door to her apartment across from the elevator. She again turned and paused to smile. She looked down at herself. "I'm getting a bit chilly. I'd better get inside and dry off. See ya!" She closed the door.

Qaak turned his head. "I liked walking through her. Her spirit is very beautiful. She's starting to get lung cancer though, so unless she stops smoking I don't think her body will last as it should." Walter winced when Qaak mentioned cancer. He tried to get her to stop smoking, but with no success.

The elevator doors opened again at the lower level. In the garage, they walked together down the row of cars. They got into Walter's red Subaru, and he reached to put his key into the ignition. Qaak touched his hand and spoke again. "That isn't necessary unless you want to. From this day forwards, you can do that if other people are in your car. I have made some modifications so that this car is also your first star vehicle. It is your SVX – it is just different from this point on. In your training, you liked to call it a 'hot rod.' Put your hand on the middle of the steering wheel and picture your old 'hot rod.'"

The Subaru SVX dash, steering wheel, and other motor vehicle controls disappeared, as a starship instrument panel and controls appeared. Qaak pointed out the window. "From outside the windows, everything appears and sounds the same, and you seem to be alone in your SVX. Now, let's go."

After turning right out of the driveway, they turned right again and headed down the hill. "Computer, scan for anyone observing us. When clear, cloak us and head for Qaak's planet." Walter turned down the hill.

"Evidently, I need to remind you," said Qaak, "you do not need to speak to the computer." Just converse with it in your head."

"Maybe later! Right now I'm still getting used to all of this." Walter took the on-ramp and got on the freeway.

Qaak adjusted his seat and got comfortable, weaving his three legs like a clumsy braid. "I should tell you now about your ring."

"My ring?" After heading down the hill and turning east, Walter got on the freeway and headed in the direction of Concord. They were beginning to get up to speed, heading up the hill in the direction of Walnut Creek, when he asked, "What about my ring?"

"Do you remember the first one – just like it? You lost it in a movie theater and went back to the jeweler to have it replaced."

"I remember. The first one was a replacement for the one that Aunt Gerri brought back from Hong Kong. She had picked out a manufactured alexandrite for me, but they had mounted it in the wrong mount." Walter took the interchange and headed east on the road to Lafayette and Walnut Creek. "I gave the ring to mom, and she bought me that replacement. Then it came off in the theater. Insurance paid for this one."

Qaak grunted. "That's true only as far as you and your Mom knew. I designed the original ring for the jeweler in Hong Kong, although he did not know it. While it was in transit to your country, we gave it some additional features. I did not anticipate your rejecting the revised version, so the one your mother got was a visual twin of the one you rejected. The ring you got from the jeweler in Long Beach was useless except as jewelry. That would not do. I slipped it off your finger without your knowing it in the darkened theater and re-designed it again. I did another switch at the jeweler's in Long Beach, and you are wearing the result."

Walter frowned. "Why? What's so special about this ring? I've been wearing it for more than thirty years. It seems like an ordinary ring."

"It's supposed to. Without technology far beyond anything native to your planet, there is no way anyone could detect any difference. It appears to be a manufactured alexandrite in a plain mount of seventeen-carat gold. Actually, it is an unusually large and very real alexandrite that we extracted from a spot about thirty thousand meters beneath an area of your planet called Siberia. To Earth's scientists, it is just a crystalline alloy of beryllium and aluminum. Actually, this particular isotope is found nowhere else in your Milky Way galaxy. It is also quite rare among the other galaxies. On Earth's jewelry market, it would be worth millions of dollars because of its clarity, purity, cut, and weight. It's the one substance on your planet that we can use to hide, empower, and enhance Gaardian technology."

Walter smiled. "Do you mean to tell me that this ring that insurance paid about a hundred bucks for is actually a technology portal?"

"Exactly. It is a terminal for your computer, which of course is protected in another part of the universe. It's also the power port that I taught you to use in your dream-state training."

As they approached the Oakland-Lafayette tunnel, Walter made a mental suggestion to his computer, and the ring shimmered. As they entered the darkness of the tunnel, no one in the other cars noticed that they vanished totally. Suddenly, they were airborne, then in space. "It's nice not having to worry about my movements affecting the atmosphere or the planet when we are cloaked. In all the science fiction I read as a boy, the heroes always had to pay attention to such things."

"Why aren't we jumping to my place?" Qaak asked.

"In all of those years, you never let me cruise my own solar system, Qaak. I thought I would take a quick look at my moon and the nearby planets."

"As you said, 'maybe later!' Others are waiting for us. You need some final orientation about your new job."

"New job?"

"You will see. You will like it! . . . Jump!"

Walter complied. In the flash of the jump, Walter understood that the ring was to be a tool, and he gazed at it for a moment. "As you can see," Qaak said, "your ring is a resource, a defense, and countless other things." The light inside seemed to quiver for a moment, and then they were at another planet. "In your dream training, you called this Earth II. Actually, it's Gaardian Planet. The climate temperatures here are similar to that of Earth, but life is very different. The atmosphere contains almost no nitrogen -- it is a rare gas here. In addition to about eighteen percent oxygen, the atmosphere is a mix of rare gases and a small amount of hydrogen. Although Gaardian is slightly smaller, the two planets are in two different galaxies. Gaardian's gravity is much greater. It is also sentient."

"I assume my ring is controlling how the gravity affects me. Otherwise, it would be lethal to most of my planet's animal and plant life, right?"

Qaak grunted.

As they approached the surface, the resemblance between the two planets faded. Down on solid footing, colors were more vivid than generally seen on Walter's Earth except in its oceans. They were nowhere near water. "Not here this time." Qaak motioned upward. Curving into the turquoise sky, Walter brought the SVX to a halt at the Conference Center, miles above the surface of the planet. Walter had been here before in his dream training time. Now it looked a little different due to the more natural lighting. Soon his other alien teachers along with a couple of alien classmates were surrounding Walter. Puz ["P'uh'zz"] greeted Walter in English. "Hey, Walter! I am glad you are here too! I'm glad I'm not the only student attending this integration and send-off party!"

"Your English is excellent!" Walter spoke to him with telepathy. "I always had a hard time with those grunts of yours! Who else is graduating with us?"

"Only the one you call 'Pixie.'"

Walter spotted Pixie at the other side of the center. Except for her golden skin, she could have passed for a human. Genetically she was almost identical to Walter, and she looked enough like him to be his sister. She was very beautiful. Walter called her Pixie because she was very petite, a little busty, and always full of fun. To both Puz and himself, Walter said, "We had some great times together in our mutual dreams. I wonder if there will be opportunities for more of the same in real life." Walter had a slight grin on his face as the three of them sat down near their teachers.

"Let's get started!" Qaak addressed the others, and it was quickly evident he was the convener of the meeting. A map appeared in three dimensions. It showed their location in relation to all the galaxies under Gaardian protection. As a schematic, it revealed few individual stars except if one looked very closely. Walter, Pixie, and Puz listened intently to their friend Qaak.

"When I was still young, my species become extinct due to my planet's collision with another body. As I was about to die, Gaardian made itself known to me through telepathy. It taught me more than words could describe at this time. As years went by, Gaardian and I – mostly Gaardian – came up with a plan for providing Intergalactic Law enforcement. The rest is history. I am now some sixty-seven thousand years old to Walter's way of thinking. Our territory is vast. Look at the map. These are only some of the more than a thousand galaxies where Gaardians currently in place have jurisdiction." Qaak was enjoying himself. "There are of course our continuing attempts to communicate with adjacent areas of the universe. Without being too vague about the rest of our history, let's say it's a story for another time, perhaps when we are younger!" There were some chuckles among the teachers. Qaak paused long enough to offer his equivalent of a smile. "You three have the new jurisdictions that are being monitored by other Gaardians until you can get your operations up and running."

Walter muttered to himself, "Five years maybe?" The presentation was shorter than expected. The map disappeared. Food appeared, and the graduation party began. During the party after the presentation, Walter spoke to Qaak. "Do you think maybe I've five years to get up and running?"

Qaak looked him straight in the eye. "No, you do not have much time, Walter. You should get your base configured as soon as possible. Unless you have another idea, the moon of your planet would be good. Its rotation makes it ideal for putting the base at the edge of its horizon with Earth. That would keep Earth's prying eyes out of your way temporarily. You should also put a few cloaked satellites in orbit to monitor your planet. Let your computer do the monitoring so that you can concentrate on other things. When you get your configuration the way you like it, you will have a basis for placing probes throughout your sector for continuous monitoring. As soon as you get your base configured, you should make your presence known to your planet's leaders – keeping your family roots hidden of course. At that time, you should also communicate with the leaders of the other planets in your sector at a similar stage of planetary development. Then you can start recruiting your staff. Do not spend more than one-half of your planet's regional seasons getting your base configured. You will then need one to two seasons for recruiting staff. You should start training as soon as you can. Make it one of your years, at a maximum. You probably will not have to face your first policing action for at least one of your planet's years, unless the other Gaardians get too busy. In that case, you'll be on your own."

"I'm going to miss our times together, Qaak. Can I still call on you?"

"In an emergency, other Gaardians and teachers will join you in facing that emergency. I will help with some of the advanced training of your crew, particularly those who will go into space with you. Other than that, there's always Gaardian mail."

As the party wound down, Walter said good-bye to Puz. He approached Pixie. "Let's make a date!"

"A date?" She batted her eyes at him playfully.

"As soon as we get our bases configured, let's get together for dinner. We won't have opportunities very often in the future, and I don't want us to lose track of each other."

"Not much chance of that!" She paused to wink. "It's a date!"

Walter saw it was time to go. He beamed into his SVX and headed home. Gliding away from the Conference Center high above the planet, he aimed the SVX just to the left of the planet's sun and jumped across time and space. As the stars flashed by, Walter muttered, "Lord, what have I gotten myself into? Did you plan all of this? I may be headed home now, but how much longer will I call Oakland home?" He paused. "Home? Home will soon be the moon! I'm going to enjoy showing Pixie that!"

The world was no longer Walter's home – he was just passing through – and he was not alone, any more than we are.

3. The Voice

The following Sunday, Margaret greeted a man named Jim as he held the door for her. Jim was a handsome young architect with a large 'afro,' making him appear even taller than his six-foot height. He also had some extra weight around his middle. The man smiled and seemed overflowing with happiness.

Margaret smiled too. "Good morning, Jim! Is Gladys fixing breakfast for Wee Church this morning?"

"As usual! A good morning to you too, Margaret! Isn't it a beautiful day! I think the praise singers are warming up if you want to go on in." Jim's wife Ambur, pear-shaped and average height, waved at her from across the hall, and then went into the ladies' room. As Margaret walked into the worship area, she made her way slowly toward the front. Her arthritis was giving her pain in her left leg that morning, but she did not use her cane, as did some of the other women. Margaret still looked like she was seventy or so and still tried to walk a mile or two each day.

Inside, she saw Walter shuffling papers on the podium, as the musicians were about to start. Sitting down in the pew, Margaret turned to a man sitting next to her and said, "I like the Christian rock and country rock music of the early service. So many of my friends avoid this service because of the music, but I was a nightclub singer up until my late husband retired thirty years ago."

Middle aged, with curly red hair and a few extra pounds, he was dressed in a suit without a tie. He simply nodded.

"Even at ninety-one I still like to help with the children's music and dance programs."

"You're ninety-one?"

"Yes. Up until last December, I helped serve communion and take the offering. My arthritis in my hands stopped me from that pleasure, just as it had stopped me from playing the piano a year earlier." The music stopped, and she turned her attention to the front.

As Walter began to highlight some of the announcements being displayed by the video projector, Margaret's mind wandered back to the day when she bought the projector for the church. Glancing backward at it, she remembered how its being state-of-the-art it crimped her retirement income for a month or two, but she was so glad they were no longer wasting paper and money on fancy bulletins and hymnals. Suddenly, something Walter was saying caught her attention.

Walter's voice boomed out over the crowd. "As many of you know I've begun thinking about what I am going to do when I retire. I love this old church, and when I retire, I want the transition into the future without me to be a smooth one. I have spoken to several of our key leaders this past week about hiring an Associate Minister who eventually will become my successor. During this coming week, a committee will be formed to begin that process, and I'll be calling our denomination's regional office this week to advise them of our plans." He paused. "Now, here's Shannon Marshall to lead us in our call to worship and opening prayer."

As Shannon came up, Margaret watched her pastor and friend carefully. Walter sat down behind the lectern. She noticed the lighting on the stage seemed to change slightly.

A soft glow seemed to surround Walter, and he seemed to be looking off into the distance.

"Walter!"

He clenched his jaw as the sound came from inside his head. He assumed that one of his alien mentors was communicating with him. The glow around him almost obscured everything around him.

"Here I am!" thought Walter. "Who are you? Are you communicating with me from Gaardian Center?"

> "Be calm and do not speak, Walter. The worship service will proceed without you until it is time for you to preach. Do not be afraid. No one else can hear me. You have known me all your life. Search your memory and you will remember my voice. You heard me first when you were four years old, when you almost drowned in the fishpond. You heard me say yes when you professed your love for Jody, though she was afraid and did not marry you. I spoke to you in the chapel while you were in seminary. I have spoken to you at other times, but you have not always been listening. Now hear what I tell you. Your two lives have been integrated by Qaak. Through it all, you have felt and heard me in your heart, without words, though you have not seen me. Your mentors have forgotten me, but that will change when I show you they are ready. The age has come for me to speak to Gaardians directly. Do not be afraid. I will counsel you each day. You shall be my prophet. I am near to you always. Now, preach the sermon that is in your heart."

His heart pounding, Walter got up out of his chair, and the glow subsided slightly. He spoke passionately. "Do you know what it's like when you feel incredible? Sometimes it happens when we achieve a lasting friendship, such as the one between King David and the son of Saul. Sometimes it is when something truly fabulous happens in our lives, like the experiences of the Apostles at the transfiguration. We feel great! We feel connected to all of God's creation in a moment! We have an incredible connection with the God that designs everything well. You get that sense when you feel the presence and power of God, who has known you personally since before you were born! Even thinking about those days when we feel truly blessed makes us feel warm and wonderful -- right now!"

Walter relaxed a bit as he got into his preaching. The words of Walter's sermon seemed to flow from somewhere deep inside of him, flowing from the Bible's wisdom. There was then a closing hymn, a benediction, and his greeting people as they left.

After church, Walter again drove Margaret home. Her voice was strong and clear. "What was wrong with the lighting up there this morning? Before you began preaching, there was more light on you than on the rest of the stage. There seemed to be more light on you than usual as you were preaching, but when you were finished, the lighting seemed like it went back to just as it usually is on Sunday mornings."

Walter hesitated, his jaw clenched. Walter knew how to make tough calls and stick by his decisions. What should he tell her? Would she believe him? "Maybe things seemed a little different because I talked about retiring."

"Nonsense! The whole worship service seemed different this morning – and not just because of your announcement!" Walter sighed. Margaret continued to comment on various parts of the service, but Walter was not listening. He too had noticed some extra light while he was preaching. Could it have something to do with the voice he had heard before he began to preach?

So much was different, and everything seemed to be happening faster and faster.

As they came to a stop in front of her door, she turned to him. "Get some sleep, Walter! ... Bye!"

"Bye, Margaret!" She slammed the door and was soon inside. He drove to his condominium and pulled into his parking space in the garage. As usual for a Sunday afternoon, no one else was there except for a few around the swimming pool. He turned off the engine and looked at his ring. As the stone shimmered for a moment, two hundred thirty-two thousand miles away, the Gaardian base he had planned materialized on the edge of its horizon with the Earth. Getting out of the SVX, he headed out of the garage for his condominium. He could hear noises from the pool area.

In moments, the elevator came to a stop, and the doors opened. He half hoped to see his beautiful neighbor and glanced at her door. This time Ann was nowhere to be seen. He could hear her singing inside though. Down the hall, he unlocked the door. Tiger greeted him with a soft meow. "Hi there, Tiger! Are you hungry?" He fed his cat, making sure there was plenty of food and water for a few days. He also cleaned the litter box. Getting a cold drink from the refrigerator, he sat down in his recliner and relaxed.

Tiger hopped onto his lap and settled down with a purr. Walter scratched his head. "Tiger, tomorrow's a holiday, and I'm going to be gone for a few days. Don't get too lonesome! I'll be back on Tuesday morning and fix us both some breakfast. Meanwhile, you've plenty of food and water." He paused. "Okay?" Tiger blinked and continued to purr. Walter took him to the windowsill, and he set his feline friend in his favorite spot in the sun.

Starring at the expanse of clear blue sky to his right, Walter sighed. "Lord, this is exciting, but this is all so new! I sure hope you're ready to redeem some more of my mistakes!" Tiger turned away from looking at him, lay down, and was soon fast asleep.

Walter gazed out the window, seeing in the distance a piece of San Francisco Bay. On his right hand, the stone in his ring shimmered. In an instant, Walter and Tiger were on the moon.

4. Gaardian Beginnings

Time flew by quickly. Walter configured the base on his moon faster than the others, but not by much. He did not have to push himself to stay busy. His cat, Tiger, particularly enjoyed playing in the lesser gravity of his new home whenever Walter was sleeping.

"Computer, let's do a Gaardian mail to Pixie." She appeared before him as though she was there. "Ready for our date?"

"Sure! I need a few minutes to coordinate things before flying out your way." She smiled, obviously pleased to see him.

"Why fly?" You can be here in an instant if you wish. Qaak taught us how."

"I'm still getting used to this, just as you are. I want to see stars, planets, and other stuff going past me on my way to you."

"Okay. How soon?"

"Not long."

Walter smiled. "Until then." Her image disappeared. Walter moved about on the base, out to the large central atrium with its clear ceiling. In its gentle light, he glanced around at the stars above. Turning to the area just to the left of the lounge, he went into the medical clinic. As its lights dimmed, he turned next to the opening to a large pool and gym area beyond the atrium. Just inside the doorway, there was a whirlpool large enough for a dozen people or more.

His clothing disappeared to a bathing suit as he stepped in. He enjoyed the swirling warmth and steam for a few moments, before a chime sounded, and the steam suddenly disappeared. He hummed with pleasure just before getting out. As he got out, he was suddenly dry. He walked past an Olympic sized pool with both low and high diving boards. There was exercise equipment on the far side in its own area. As he left the recreation area, his ring shimmered, and he was again fully clothed.

Stepping past a hallway that led to another area of the base, he came to a blank area in the wall. His ring shimmered again, and doors appeared. He stepped through into a large room. His ring shimmered yet again, and it became a dining hall with tables, chairs, planters, and indirect lighting. Returning through the atrium to his quarters, Tiger was sitting on the bed watching him. Walter stood at a window and gazed at the Earth on the horizon.

After a few moments, he returned across the atrium to the den. Pixie appeared just as he was sitting down in front of the fireplace. She sat down beside him. Staring at the fire, Pixie smiled with amusement. Walter had created the den to be quite large, with a fireplace and lots of overstuffed furniture, somewhat like a hotel lounge he had seen in New York City.

Pixie was thoughtful. "My planet does not have anything like this! I like it. Does it look like this in your planet's stronger gravity?"

"Yes. Actually, the fireplace is independent and functions in nearly Earth normal gravity. The smoke that would normally go up the chimney is recycled. Right now, gravity is Earth normal throughout the base."

She snuggled up to Walter. "I am beginning to understand what you humans mean by romance. Isn't it interesting that both of our species include kissing as part of romance and mating?"

"Speaking of kissing!" Walter kissed her lightly on the forehead.

"That's not fair!" She took on a mocking tone.

"What do you mean?"

"It's not fair for you to kiss me, unless I've a chance to kiss you back!" She turned to him, and they had a much longer kiss. They separated and looked at each other.

"Let's eat! We can discuss this over dinner. No movie this time though." They both smiled. Walter's ring shimmered, and a table full of food appeared with two chairs just behind the sofa. They strolled over to the table arm in arm and sat down. Walter bowed his head a moment.

Taking a bite, Pixie looked across the table. "Getting started was harder than I thought it was going to be."

"It was the same for me. I've got property in the Southern Hemisphere of Earth where I am officially going to retire from my church in Oakland, but even with computer help it has been difficult to get around the red tape."

"Red tape?"

"That's what we English-speaking humans call legal complications that require lots of written documentation."

She smiled. "We have a term for it too." She said something unintelligible, sounding like 'xraprllposzt.'

"'Red tape' is easier to pronounce."

"Maybe for you! My planet doesn't have just one moon, so I had to choose one if I was going to follow your example."

"Which did you pick?"

"None of them!" She laughed. "At Kieya's suggestion, I created my own satellite. I think you would probably call it 'cool.'"

"I'm going to have to see it!" Walter stared into the fire. "We're both getting impatient to recruit our teams – I think Puz is too."

"We all have our bases, and each has provisions for ample room for expansion as the need arises."

"All of us have put personal touches to our quarters on our bases..."

She nudged him and interrupted, "I assume we can examine your personal quarters in greater detail later?"

He grinned. "Of course – and you'll like my guest room!" He paused while she pouted and then continued. "Anyway, as we have compared notes, I think we've gotten a few ideas from each other. Puz has not been interested in personal comforts or pleasures – he has been more focused on getting his goals accomplished."

"Right!" She gave him a peck on the cheek. "We had better get some rest – or at least try to! In less than ten of your hours we have to be at Gaardian Center." They both got up. The lights dimmed behind them as they walked out of the lounge. Outside, the Earth hung low on the horizon.

The next morning, they chatted animatedly as they settled into the seats of the SVX, and soon they were jumping across galaxies. Walter was thoughtful. "I wonder why we are going back to the Center so soon."

"Qaak said something about new activity on the edges of our sectors. Let's speed this up, shall we?" Pixie's ring shimmered with his, and the stars outside streamed by more furiously and brightly. "I think we just passed through a double star."

"Right! Using both of our rings gets things done, doesn't it?" His voice trailed off as they came to a halt at the Center. There was no party atmosphere now, and there were three other Gaardians – Doff, Kieya, and Waagere ["wah-GEAR"].

Qaak let Doff start the session. His planetary name was nearly impossible to pronounce. Everyone called him Doff. He was a male more than twice Walter's height, with a translucent silicon-based physiology. He had a great sense of humor and a unique deep bass laugh and voice.

"Several integration parties ago," Doff began, "some of us decided that once the shock of new beginnings wore off that it would be helpful to get some pointers on recruitment. None of us supervises our sectors alone. Finding those we both like and can absolutely trust is essential in starting a support staff." There were nods of agreement between the other two experienced Gaardians.

Puz spoke telepathically. "Why not let our computers monitor candidates to see if they are trustworthy?"

Kieya responded, "Short term surveillance profiles are not reliable enough. It is good to monitor all of your staff for an extended time as a precaution, but absolute trust can best be determined through the telepathic tests learned in your early training. For your closest staff, one option is to apply telepathic testing to beings that you have known for a long time. Once you've a small intimate basic staff, you can turn recruitment over to them while you get on with other matters."

"I've a question on another matter." They turned toward Walter. "Just after returning to Earth after the integration party I had a peculiar experience. Shortly before my weekly address at my church, a soft glow began to surround me. The glow continued until I had I finished speaking. I have not seen the glow since. Is this part of being a Gaardian, now that I am integrated?"

Qaak was puzzled. "As Gaardians, you will witness all kinds of interesting phenomena, but this is not something I've heard about before. What about the rest of you?" Qaak and Walter looked around. "Let me know if you see this phenomenon again, or if you figure out what it was. I'll be interested."

Waagere spoke precisely. A biped the size of Walter and Puz, she had a neck almost three times longer than either of theirs. "Before we break into smaller discussions, I need to tell you – and have the word passed to other Gaardians – about a probable challenge. For some time, we have been trying to communicate across the abyss near sector 103-A579-F7813. That is part of Walter's area of responsibility. We have begun receiving logically configured transmissions that we are now able to translate. As they are available, these communications are being uploaded to all Gaardian computers. So far, we cannot determine their exact intentions, but they are not friendly. Basic triangulation determines the source of the transmissions to be possibly within easier jump range in a short time. As a precaution, the new Gaardians need to move as quickly as possible in getting their operations fully functional. Established Gaardians should be on the alert."

Several discussion groups begin to form as other Gaardians arrived at the center. Walter tried to get into a conversation with Pixie, but Qaak intercepted him. "What happened during the time of the glow?"

"The worship service had begun, and I went into a kind of altered state. I experienced a glow around me. One of the members of my church said she thought the lighting was different that day."

"So others noticed it too! Strange! Have you analyzed what happened?"

"I am still working on it. I have isolated an encrypted file on my computer. It is helping me analyze what happened."

"Good! Let me know when you have some results!" The triped wandered off to confer with the other two seasoned Gaardians.

Walter spotted Pixie coming in his direction. "I am going to jump directly back to my base. Did you have a good talk with Qaak?"

"Yeah! I think so...." He paused. "I'm sorry you're not going back with me, but we've both got things to do. I hope to see you again real soon!" They lightly kissed and vanished. Qaak noticed the display of affection and subtly grunted.

In the SVX, the now familiar jumping through the stars was automatic. Walter was in a meditative mood. "Lord, that old song keeps going through my head, 'Precious Lord, take my hand, lead me on....' When I was preaching in Oakland, I often talked about your having plans bigger than any of us could possibly imagine. I am beginning to get some kind of new feel for those much larger plans of yours. I hope I did the right thing in mentioning the glow to Qaak and the others. I didn't want to reveal too much." As the SVX jumped across galaxies, Walter heard the voice as a glow filled the SVX, and Walter gripped the controls tightly.

> "Waagere is your adversary among the Gaardians right now, but she is careful not to reveal it. When you mentioned my glow, she became more wary of you. It is good that you mentioned the glow to them. You said just enough to keep yourself honest. I am pleased. I will deal with Waagere. Do not be afraid, Walter. Everything is unfolding, as it should."

The glow faded, and Walter relaxed. Walter was never alone! Arriving above Oakland, he made his way to a Waffle Hut in Berkeley, a couple of miles down the street from his church, and he had a good lunch.

5. Belinda

The next morning Walter was humming "Amazing Grace" while doing some thinking under a long hot shower. As he dried off, Tiger was sitting on the tank of the commode and watching him. "Who have I known the longest? What do you think Tiger? Who can I absolutely trust? Apart from some of my friends who have died an early death...." Walter hung up the towel as he thoughtfully considered his oldest friends. Tiger blinked and began to wash himself, then jumped down. As he went out of the bathroom, Walter was suddenly fully dressed, including a tie. As Walter sat down on the sofa and Tiger jumped up, the cat sat back on his hindquarters and studied his master. Walter smiled. "I wish you could talk, Tiger."

Suddenly, the glow he had experienced previously began to fill the room, and his jaw clenched as he heard the now-familiar voice, low, like the lower notes of a pipe organ.

> "Walter."

Walter's voice was tense. "Here I am."

> "Belinda is a good choice. You must get her to seek you. She still has initiative, and that will be very important to you. Her body is wasting away with cancer. Heal her. Turn back her clock just as you turned back your own."

Less tense, but curious, his voice was steady. "How do I get her to seek me out?"

> "Let Earth's leaders know of your presence and see you as the young man you once again are. Keep your old self visible in Oakland until you retire. Speak of Earth as your planet. Give the media a glimpse of your larger view of the galaxy. When Belinda sees you in the news, she will write to you. When she agrees, she will become a valuable partner."

The glow began to fade. "Is there anything else you can reveal to me now?

> "You are the first Gaardian to hear my voice. Others will, in time. There are some on my Earth that will see you as their enemy. Do not be afraid. I will lead you to all success. Just follow me."

As the glow faded, things begin to appear normal again. Walter took a deep breath and sighed.

+ + +

On Sunday morning, Walter announced his retirement just before the sermon. "I know this is going to be a shock to most of you, but I have decided to retire immediately. I have talked to our Regional Minister, and he is going to arrange for you to have an interim pastor beginning next month. I will be with you two more Sundays, and then I am moving to New Zealand, where I have purchased some land. I will miss all of you very much. I will take with me many wonderful memories of our life together here in Oakland."

He paused. "The title of my meditation this morning is 'Going to the Mountain.' When we ride on an elevator, we often go into an altered state. It is a form of self-hypnosis. We will look at the numbers flashing by as we go by the floors, and we tune out the rest of the world and just focus on those numbers until we get to our floor. This is not new. We can be almost certain that as the people of God crossed the Red Sea with Moses, they were filled with wonder. They were also so focused on getting across that they probably were in an altered state of consciousness." As he preached, Walter thought about the glow he had experienced the previous Sunday and since. Preoccupied, he did not preach as along a sermon.

The musicians began to play, and the congregation sang a chorus of "The Family of God," while Walter walked down the aisle to the rear of the church. The music stopped and there was a brief moment of silence.

"May the peace of God be with you all."

The congregation responded, "Amen!"

As he greeted people, everyone wished him the best. He told them that it was with both sadness and excitement that he was saying farewell.

Driving away from the church, his SVX climbed into the Oakland hills to a secluded spot, and he parked with a view of San Francisco Bay. He gazed at the fog banks that were drifting about on the West Side of the bay. The sun glistened brightly on the water on the Oakland side, and he glanced down at his ring. He heard his computer voice say, "No one is observing." The SVX vanished.

Reaching for the controls, he slowly began to fly, first out over the bay and then curving eastward. Accelerating rapidly, he headed for the Sierras. Seconds later, reaching the foothills near Modesto, Walter slowed to enjoy the scenery. Deep into the hills, he dropped down to the Merced River and flew rapidly a few yards above the water. He came to a sudden halt near his favorite spot in Yosemite Valley. Invisibly, he hovered just above the water. The top of the SVX disappeared for him, like a convertible.

On his right, Bridal Veil Fall was fairly full. There was a dusting of snow all around the rim of the valley. He began to move very slowly up the river. He felt great as he flew along, and he felt a wonderful sense of freedom. To be free means to have alternatives of course, but Walter felt truly free because he was not locked into making choices. He had the kind of freedom that allowed him to feel a sense of equilibrium, as if part of him was acquiring a sense of being centered.

From the time of his childhood, Walter only felt this way in Yosemite. As the cold evening air flowed over him, he achieved a kind of peace that renewed him. He thought about the Bible verse where God says, "Behold, I make all things new!" In the distance, he could see a small piece of Half Dome illuminated by the afternoon sun that shone from behind him. El Capitan loomed magnificently on his left, and he was surprised by a generous flow of water over Ribbon Fall.

As the SVX made its way eastward, Walter saw that Yosemite Falls had lots of water. Spotting the Ahwahnee Hotel, he began to rise rapidly over Mirror Lake. Curving around he passed Clouds Rest and turned back westward to land on top of Half Dome. There was no one on top, although several people were making their way down.

In high school, Walter hiked here with his family and best friend, Steve. Across the Happy Isles canyon, he could see where the Glacier Point Hotel used to stand. Childhood memories of lunches on the hotel veranda flashed across his mind. Rising again and crossing the canyon, he landed where lightning and a subsequent fire had eliminated the hotel many years earlier. "One more stop," he murmured to himself. The SVX rose a few hundred feet and moved westward to land softly on Sentinel Dome. "Computer, enough for today. Keep this tour in the vehicle navigation log, and save all that I've seen today in a holographic record." His ring shimmered, and he jumped to the Moon.

After landing outside the lounge, Walter vanished inside and stood next to a small table by the window. Tiger was sitting there. Walter's ring shimmered, and his features grew younger. He now appeared thirty, he had all of his hair, and he only had a couple of frown lines on his brow. He stared at the Earthrise, sometimes glancing down while scratching Tiger's head.

"How do you like your new home, Tiger? Your body is regressed back to what you were when I first got you from Friends of Strays. Do you like practically being a kitten again? ... Sorry – you're still neutered, but if I get you a female companion I don't want to worry about dealing with kittens."

Tiger seemed content, and he seemed to enjoy playing with the virtual toys in the "family" room. The age regression had surprised Walter, and he had continued to enjoy stretching, jumping, and flexing his newly young fingers.

"Computer, I need to converse with someone besides Tiger. I don't want you to be just a voice. I want an android. First, let me hear a sampling of voices, reciting random selections from the Gospel of John."

"For God so loved the world that he gave his only son."

"I am the true vine, and my Father is the vine dresser."

"Let not your hearts be troubled. You believe in God, believe also in me."

"If you abide in me and my words abide in you, ask whatever you will and will be done for you."

"This I command you, that you love one another as I have loved you."

"I want you to be male." Walter listened intently to the three male voices again and sometimes glanced upward.

"I am the true vine, and my Father is the vine dresser."

"If you abide in me and my words abide in you, ask whatever you will and will be done for you."

"This I command you, that you love one another as I have loved you."

Walter gestured with his fist up to the ceiling. "Yes! I like that one. That will be your voice. I am going to call you Frank, because you will always be honest.

Let's give you some substance. Let me see a male, about thirty, six feet tall, about one hundred eighty pounds. Give him black hair and green eyes, with European features and complexion." He paused and studied the result. "Good. ... Frank, I'll expect you to be dressed casually except as occasions warrant otherwise. I want you to be physically present whenever I need to talk to you. Also, I want you to give Tiger some attention at least one hour per day until I get him a playmate."

"I can create a playmate for him."

"Good idea! Let's give him a permanently present model of Tammy, the other cat I had. Do you have enough data to create a Tammy?"

"How's this?" A replica of Tammy appeared, hopped down, and approached Tiger. Tiger arched his back and sniffed. Tammy arched her back as well. Tiger started to walk away, and Tammy began to follow, but Tiger hissed at her. "This won't work. Tiger senses that she is an android and does not trust what he sees."

"Okay. Delete her from your program. Give Tiger some regular companionship, and I'll plan on bringing in a companion for him from Earth."

Walter went to the fireplace and sat down in a large recliner chair. Frank took another one nearby. "from this day forwards, Frank, I'll be less visible as my older self at the church in Oakland. I'll spend only a few hours each day there."

"The Middle Eastern threat of biological terrorism is going to provide the stage for your first public appearance as the Gaardian."

"I already have set things up. I've manipulated the terrorists into choosing Washington, D.C. as their target. They were going to do it with lots of flash and flourish in an effort to make a political statement."

"It will be easy to stop them as The Gaardian, and make your first worldwide headlines."

Walter was thoughtful. "The terrorists will want to exact revenge of course. They will probably get further financing from the drug lords in South America."

"We are prepared of course. They will not be a problem."

"No. .... also, I'm sure you've noted that since my integration, I've continued to pray. Evidently, that does not upset Qaak. Let's go to my encrypted file. I don't want any record of the verbal key anywhere in our database except as necessarily attached to the file." He paused. "j-g-l-d-j-r-h-t-o-f-k-g-o-i-6-9-7-u-w-3-9-b-k-5-8-k-m-7-o-c-f-j." He paused again. "My secret advisor was right of course. Belinda will be the best choice as my first recruit. She will see the newscast and telephone me in Oakland. Be sure that you monitor voice mail from my condo."

"Right."

"I want to set up an opportunity to visit her. I don't think there will be any problems. The voice knows her far better than I ever will even know myself, so I am going to trust His judgment."

"Are you confident as to the source of the voice?"

"Yes, but I am not ready to tell Qaak yet. Close the encrypted file." He paused. "Let's talk about tweaking the noses of those terrorists and introducing me to the world." Walter continued to talk to Frank for several hours more, planning in detail Walter's first public exposure to Earth as The Gaardian. When at last he was ready to go to bed, he transported himself and his SVX to Oakland. There were details to wrap up the next morning in his church office.

+ + +

It was easy to deal with the terrorists. The resulting media frenzy was worldwide. Almost everyone on Earth knew there was a Gaardian. Two weeks later, Walter awakened in Oakland to the glow and the voice.

"Walter. Write to Belinda. I'll guide you as to what to say to her."

The glow faded before he could respond. He walked into his living room and sat down in the recliner. "Frank."

The android appeared. "Yes?"

"I know that Belinda is the woman whom I can trust to help me get this venture started.

The android looked at him. "This must be a special kind of trust."

"It is. What's really great is when you find yourself sharing a deep sense of trust with someone, as I have trusted Belinda since we were in the third grade. Although I want to see Belinda in person, because she is terminally ill under hospice care at home, it's better to send her a letter on a disk first. She will have time to read it on her computer before I go to her home. Although it's not necessary, I'll dictate it out loud."

"Go."

"Belinda, using six digits, type the day, date, and year of our first kiss into the box below. Then hit the 'enter' key in order to read the rest of this email.

Dear Belinda,

Two weeks ago, just before I made my first public appearance as The Gaardian, I told my friend Frank that I would be contacting you as soon as possible afterwards. You have a right to be curious. In seeing me on television, you had a shock seeing me so young, but you probably knew I would be contacting you.

Writing to you invites many memories, including the day when I first learned that I was leading a double life, but I need to reflect on some of our mutual history first. In those early years, you were sleeping soundly through the nights that the trainers were at work on my subconscious. The trainers of Gaardians work deep in the mind of the candidate while he or she (or it) is asleep. At the end of each night, they allow a dream to surface so that later the training will connect with the Candidate while awake. Although you were not a Candidate, they sometimes worked with you (and some others in our schools) while you were asleep, because you knew me so well in my "regular" life. Without knowing it, you were sometimes giving me support to my "other" life because the trainers had been working with you.

It is hard to believe that the secret stayed hidden for so long. When you suddenly surprised yourself with doing great stuff you never thought you could, many times it happened because of the "extras" the trainers gave you while you were a sleeping teenager.

You are going to be the first person to know the full story. It's to some extent because of our friendship, to a certain extent because I need to tell it, and partly because of your curiosity. As I said, you have a right to be curious.

The selection had nothing to do with my ethnic background, my sex, my intelligence, or anything else. Once chosen, they began their nightly training ritual while I was asleep. Recently my two lives merged. This message is auto encrypted – only a minor risk at this point, but from this day forwards, any correspondence between us should be encrypted more safely. When writing to me (and I hope you will!) use the day and date of our first kiss – without spaces or punctuation – as the encryption key. I'll use the same key in writing back to you when I get a chance.

All my love,
Walter

"Deliver the letter on a CD-R disk in her mailbox." Frank vanished. Looking around the apartment, he sighed. As his ring shimmered, he vanished to the Moon. Wandering about on the Base, he began making modifications to his original configuration. He enjoyed himself as he put the finishing touches on what would be his home – and the home of his team – for many years to come.

Belinda called three days later. Walter was sitting in a recliner in front of the fireplace, reading Carl Sandburg's *The Prairie Years and the War Years*. Frank appeared next to him, standing in front of the fireplace. "I'm forwarding a telephone call to you from Belinda."

"Okay."

The android vanished, and Walter closed the book.

"Hi, Walter, this is Belinda."

Relaxed, Walter spoke as though into the fireplace or like she was standing in front of it. "Hi, Belinda. I was hoping you would call."

"We need to talk, Walter. Can you come over this evening?"

"Sure! What time would be good for you?"

"How about seven?"

"Sounds good! See you later!"

"See you later! Bye!"

On the way to her home that evening, Walter's head was swimming with memories of their childhood and teen days together. The SVX made the jump to Belinda's community south of Los Angeles, where he materialized on a deserted freeway off ramp. Her home was only a few blocks away. When he knocked, she called out for him to come in.

Walter stepped into a small living room with a love seat and two chairs. She was sitting in one of the chairs next to a fireplace. Her hair was as streaked with gray. To him, she was as beautiful as she ever was. "Come in, Walter! I gave my daycare nurse a few hours off so we can talk uninterrupted."

He went to the other chair, turned it slightly to face her, and sat down. "It's great to see you again! It's been more than twenty years, hasn't it?"

"Yes, I'm glad that you wrote. When I saw you on television, I was startled to say the least. You are five months older than I am, but you look forty years younger.

"How could I forget?"

"I am grateful that you've managed to stay in touch through the years, sending me Christmas cards and church newsletters. When I heard rumors and saw news stories about a Gaardian, I could not have imagined it to be you in my wildest dreams! Then to see you looking like you are thirty, when we are both much older! I'll admit that all kinds of questions have arisen in my mind. My son Michael is about forty, and I seldom hear from him because of his work with the CIA. Karen is a nun, of course. Steve died last year. He was a good man, and I miss him terribly."

"Didn't you get my note of condolences?"

"I didn't see it, but then Michael and Karen opened a lot of the mail after Steve's death. Your digital letter brought back all kinds of memories."

"Remember when we carried our instruments together and talked about classes? I remember how sometimes you invited me in, and we had a Pepsi together."

"We were both growing like weeds, and we had gotten so that we talked about nearly everything -- e-n though we had not yet had our first real date." Belinda paused. "We somehow maintained our friendship -- t- bad more kids could not have been as close as we were at that age."

"In some ways we were closer than so-called 'couples' there at Bancroft." Walter smiled.

"Yes! Now, tell me more about the trainers! Did I actually meet them and not know it?"

"Maybe we can talk about that later!"

"I wonder why they didn't help you excel athletically as well as academically. Am I to understand that you did not even know that you had been in training until recently?"

"There will be time for talking about that later too."

"One more thing," Belinda continued, "I hadn't done encryption before. At first, I wondered why you had attached that software to your note. Then I did a bit of research and concluded that published encryption software probably contains a hidden master key. The password you chose was perfect! It's funny how we both remember the day and date of our first kiss. I can even give you the time – 11:45 PM – within a few minutes or so."

He smiled. "I learned long ago how women are good at remembering such things!"

"I am so glad you wrote! I've read that letter of yours several times in the last few days. I guess you figured you could trust me with all of that because I am dying."

"I know." He nodded. "Let's talk about that. I do appear to be about thirty in public. My physical age has not been synchronized with my chronological age for weeks now. It is part of the technology available to me as The Gaardian."

"We've always liked, loved, and trusted each other unconditionally, haven't we?"

"Absolutely. Once all of me was a single conscious identity, I had a great deal of work to do. I decided to put my primary base on the dark side of our

Moon on the horizon. After configuring my base, I had a ship – *The Grace* -- built to my specifications by the same group that provides for the Trainers, and they delivered it to a relatively convenient holding area. With that busy work accomplished, I began to insert myself into some of the problems of our planet."

He" face brightened. "It "as been fascinating to watch you on television!"

Walter paused. "I know you are facing death from cancer. I also know that what was scheduled for you was risky, to put it mildly. No wonder you decided on hospice. I am curious about what you would do differently in your life if you had a chance to do things over again."

She" began to speak more quietly. "Seeing you so young again has certainly gotten my creative juices flowing in this old body of mine."

Walter chose his words carefully. "Actually, that is something we can talk about."

"Meaning?"

"I know that Steve has been dead for more than a year now, and your two children are expecting you to die any time. Isn't that pretty much the situation?"

She" nodded. "Yes" I'm afraid there's nothing the doctors or I can do about that."

Walter was calm and spoke more quietly. "Belinda, you and I have always been able to talk transparently with one another, so I'm going to lay something on you."

"Shoot."

He spoke confidently but quietly. "I a" going to have to be recruiting and training support staff in a very intensive way over the next year. I'll 'e doing that while doing some appearances as The Gaardian here on Earth and having to make trips beyond our solar system to do problem solving from time to time."

She" smiled. "Sounds like fun! Go on!"

"I want you to help me."

"Walter! I'm....' She" hesitated. "No wait. You know my physical condition, and you look forty years younger than you should." She paused. "What exactly do you have in mind?"

"Do you still trust me, Belinda?"

He" face brightened. "Of "course! With my life - as–always!"

"If you want me to, I have the technology to turn back your biological clock as I have mine, and clear your body of all disease." Her eyes grew big as he paused. "Obviously, I cannot start doing that publicly or there would be riots, as people would want me to cure their every ill. I can only do it for my staff. I'll make that technology available to the public when our world is a bit more ready. Right now, there is too much other stuff going on."

She nodded. "I would not want to undo any of the experiences I've had. I've had a wonderful life, even with all of its ups and downs. Knowing you as I think I still do, however, I suspect you are asking me if I would like to be thirty again and live another life."

"Something like that."

Belinda hardly hesitated. Her face nearly beamed. "Yes" I'll do it. I cannot imagine not doing it!" She paused, and spoke more quietly. "Are you expecting romance between us?"

He paused, then quietly he said, "I honestly don't know. I don't have a romantic agenda."

He" face was sober. "I've" trusted, liked, and loved you since the third grade, and I guess you still feel the same."

He nodded. "Yes""

"Okay! Since I'm going to do it, what happens next?"

"Now that you've made your decision, I'll eliminate your health problems and turn back your physiological clock. The technology is still amazing -- e-n to me."

She" almost grinned. "Once" I'm younger again, then what?"

Walter paused. "I'll" create a body that looks just like yours does now. We'll leave it here so your family and friends can have a funeral or memorial service for you. Once the clock is turned back for your body, anyone who knew you will see you and think that you must be a daughter or close relative of the Belinda that they knew."

He" face seemed to light up. "Why not? I'm certainly ready to face death, but the idea of spending some time with you after all of these years is appealing." She" managed a wink. "I'll" get on the phone this evening and have some final conversations with my children. Then I can die during the night. Want to come back later?"

Walter was relieved, pausing just for a moment. "I didn't know what I would have said if you had said no! I'll 'e back around ten to create your double and make the switch, okay?"

Belinda nodded, picked up the telephone, and started to push buttons. She looked up. "See you later!" As she again looked down at her phone, Walter vanished to his SVX outside.

6. Getting Started

Walter jumped to Oakland, materializing in the shadows of some dense trees in the Oakland hills. He drove down the hill to Broadway and went to his favorite coffee shop. He parked and went inside. On the walls were menus from years past. Sitting down at the counter, he was approached by a server. "Herbal tea as usual, Walter?"

"Okay."

"Blue Zip?"

"Right. The special too." She nodded and moved away. Walter was going to miss Oakland. He loved his church here, and he loved the multi-cultural environment. He found Oakland much more interesting than San Francisco. He lingered over a second cup of herbal tea, and then he had a generous dinner of lamb chops and steamed vegetables.

A short drive then took Walter back to his condominium. Tiger was on the moon, so there was no feline greeting. Looking out his balcony window, he made a quick decision. He had already had his farewell reception at the church, and he had told them he would head for New Zealand in a few days. That connection having been severed, Walter turned and looked at the contents of his apartment.

Looking up he says, "Call the realtor at her home." There was a click.

"East Bay Realty Junction."

"Hello, Joan? This is Walter."

"Hi Walter!"

"I'm sorry to call you so late – I've moved out."

"Really! That was quick!"

"Right. It's all in your hands. Have I signed everything?"

"Yes. I'll take care of everything."

"Good. Go ahead and sell, getting the best price you can. I trust your judgment. When everything is finalized, have the title company do a wire transfer of the funds to my bank in New Zealand."

"New Zealand!" I didn't realize you were moving there. The account number and bank name didn't give me a clue."

"Yes. New Zealand is now officially my home. Thank you for everything you've done. I'll probably call you from New Zealand after the funds have cleared my bank there."

"Good luck to you!"

"God be with you! Bye!"

"Bye Walter!" There was another click.

Walter took a deep breath and looked around the living room. Tiger was already there. His ring shimmered, and everything else was suddenly in place on the moon. Walter walked around the apartment one more time, and then returned to the patio door. He gazed out west at the sunset. In the distance, he could see a piece of San Francisco Bay. With his enhanced vision, he could see part of the Golden Gate Bridge. Walter sighed, and his ring shimmered again.

He was back in the SVX. After scanning both the garage and Belinda's neighborhood for anyone who might observe, the ring shimmered, and he was in front of Belinda's house. The door was open behind a screen door, so he walked in. "Hi! Are you ready?"

"Absolutely! What's first?"

"Can you stand up?"

"Sure! I'm not gone yet!" She struggled to her feet. He took her hand and steered her a few steps to the fireplace.

"Belinda, you're about to see a never alive replica of yourself in the chair. Are you ready?"

Belinda squeezed his hand on her arm. "This ought to be interesting," His ring shimmered, and another Belinda appeared in the chair, with her eyes closed. "Is she human?"

"Chemically, physically, and biologically she is you, but this replica will never be alive." Walter paused as they looked at the duplicate. "Do you want to walk out to my car – and can you?"

"It will be a struggle, but I want to make one more journey in this older version of my bag of bones. Come on." She did not realize it, but Walter had rendered them invisible. Each step was a struggle, but they made it to his car.

"I like your car." She paused as he helped her in, and he then went around and got in himself. "An SVX is more exotic than I imagined as your vehicle. I know we are going to the moon, but how are we going to get there? This is a nice car, but..." Her voice trailed off as the dashboard disappeared and the starship controls appeared. "Wow!" was all Belinda could think of to say.

Not wanting to expose Belinda to too much technology as well as quickly, he got back on the freeway. On a straight stretch going north, Walter let the car pick up speed. When the traffic thinned out, they vanished behind a truck and curved up into the sky.

Seeing that Belinda was speechless, Walter broke the silence. "I'll take you on a tour of our solar system another time. Right now, I want to get you to our new home on the Moon, so that we can make that bag of bones back into the fantastic body that I remember from our teen years." Belinda looked at him and smiled. "I'll make this trip a quick one." The moon suddenly loomed up on them, and the SVX settled into its spot both automatically and silently.

Belinda could see the furniture of the den through a large window. She started to reach for the door handle but Walter said, "That's not necessary." His ring shimmered, and they were inside. "This is the clinic."

"It doesn't look like any clinics I've visited in the last few years."

"I need to have you step behind this modesty shield." He walked her over to a small u-shaped partition. "That's it." It rose to the height of her shoulders. "Now, look at the display panel on the wall across from you."

A rectangle about three meters high and a meter wide first displayed her skeleton, then her muscle system, and then her organs. Walter went to stand by a console and pointed. "Those highlighted areas show you how extensively the cancer has spread. Put your hands on the top of that modesty shield and hold on. You are going to feel a bit weak for a moment."

Belinda suddenly saw every color of the rainbow, and heard a sound like wind through trees, as her knees seemed to buckle, but she held on. Realizing that her eyes were closed, she opened them, and she looked down at herself. She was naked but with the body of a twenty-something. Standing by the panel, Walter smiled. "Do you see why you have a modesty shield?"

"Where are my clothes?"

"You can have them back if you really want them, but the base can instantly fabricate anything you might want to wear."

"How about a bikini?" Suddenly, Belinda was wearing a bikini. "Is this my old suit?"

"No, I replicated it for you from the picture you sent me years ago. I thought you might like to try it on again."

Belinda smiled. "You're so thoughtful!" She stepped from behind the shield and walked over to him.

"I think you look even better than you used to. Let's find out if our little machine has made any genetic repairs. Many people are genetically damaged during their formative years because of environmental influences. I imagine it is fairly common for those who grow up living in the pollution of the Los Angeles basin as we did." She joined him by the console. "It looks like you got a few minor genetic repairs done. Your bronchial tubes are slightly more generous, and your waist is somewhat narrower due to improvements in muscle tone. It looks like your bust is about the same size as it was after Michael was born – ever so slightly larger than it was when we were in high school."

"I like it! Do you?"

"Of course!" Walter grinned. "Now come on, we've things to talk about. We're going into the den where you can meet both Tiger and Frank."

"Tiger and Frank?"

"Tiger is my cat, and Frank is an android that I created to give my computer a voice."

As they entered the den, Tiger jumped down from a table and stroked around their legs. She reached down and scratched his head. "Where is Frank?"

"Here!"

Belinda jumped closer to Walter as Frank appeared over near the fireplace. "If you are going to be suddenly appearing like that it's going to take some getting used to!"

"Sorry!" Frank came over and shook her hand. He turned to Walter. "If you don't need me, I'll go back to my calculations."

"Adjust gravity to moon one please." Belinda, Tiger, and Walter suddenly felt lighter on their feet as Frank vanished. Tiger began jumping high in the air and readily amused himself. "I think we need to get a companion for Tiger. You might keep that in the back of your mind and check an animal shelter or two. How do you like the normal moon gravity?"

She jumped about five feet in the air and floated down. "Wow! That's also something I'm going to have to get used to, but I think I like it already!" They sat down on the large overstuffed sofa that had been in Walter's living room in the condominium. "I like the furniture."

"I brought a lot of this from my condo in Oakland. It's empty now and up for sale. Tiger likes it better here. Later this month, I'll need to finish establishing a residence in New Zealand, as I announced to my church. I have some land on South Island, near the little town of Franz Joseph. I'll let you handle that. My identity as a pastor needs to die there, so I'll maintain a part-time presence there for a few years. Then I will work a way to keep it as a retreat area. Want to go house hunting with me? If we find one we like I'll simply fabricate an identical one for my lot in Franz Joseph."

"Sure, but that's not exactly what I thought we would be doing though."

"That will be for our spare time."

"So we're actually going to have some spare time?"

"Sure! We have to if we are going to maintain our sanity. Let's talk about the work we have ahead of us." Walter paused. "Within the next year, we will need to hire a few hundred people to work with us. As we establish a Gaardian presence on other planets in our sector, we will of course recruit as needed. Initially, I'll be asking you to help me with that. As our organization fleshes out, I expect that you will get some idea what you will want to do on a long-term basis. I'll leave that entirely up to you."

"What do you mean?"

"Getting started is going to be somewhat different from day-to day operations after our staff is in place. Meanwhile, you will just have Tiger and Frank for company part of the time as I attend to Gaardian duties. Once we have some staff in place, things will change of course. As you can guess, my central computer will help us stay in touch via e-mail and Gaardian mail."

"Gaardian mail?"

"Gaardian mail – often just called g-mail – is communication that can reach across galaxies. Sometimes it is a direct three-dimensional video connection, and often it is a video interactive 'letter' from one person to another. From time to time, I will disappear for anywhere from a few hours to several days. Right now, I am assisting another Gaardian with a problem, but I should be back in a couple of days. After I give you a tour of the base, I will take off. I'll trust you to keep on with what you are doing until I get back. I'll show you how to get what you want – anything you want." He paused.

"While I am on this trip, I hope you will furnish the area where you want to live the way you like it. Then you can start scanning the Internet and the broadcast channels to figure out how we are going to recruit staff. I am already The Gaardian for this sector of Gaardian space – my work will not wait until I am fully organized. Frank will give you lots of help. During this organizing time, I will be here on the moon and on Earth as much as I can. Sometimes the other Gaardians will be able to cover for me, but many times they will not."

A tone sounded. "I'll take it here, Frank." His favorite Gaardian classmate materialized in front of them. "Hi, Pixie!"

"Hi yourself! Who is this?"

"This is Belinda. I told you about her."

"Hi, Belinda. Call me Pixie. No human can come close to pronouncing my real name. I thought Walter was exaggerating when he described you, but you are stunning!"

"Thanks! So are you!"

"Walter, how soon can you get back here?"

"How about a day?"

"How about a few hours? I need your creative juices."

"As soon as I can."

"Bye you two!" The image vanished before either of them can respond.

Belinda smiled. "She's quite beautiful! That golden skin is amazing! Is she human?"

"Humans are found only on Earth, but she is very close to us genetically speaking." He paused. "You have no idea how much it means to me to have you working with me. Having someone who at the least will always be my friend will make my work a lot less lonely. I know that you understand that I cannot share everything with you, but since we have trusted one another for so long, I'll share as much as I can. … Frank, Earth normal gravity please." He paused as they got heavier. "Com" on. I'll give you a whirlwind tour of our new home!"

The tour did not take long. First, they went to the atrium. "This is the center of the base." He pointed to the lounge. "We came from the lounge, which sometimes I call the den. Beyond it, through that other doorway is the screening room or auditorium. To the right of that, through the other doorway, is the swimming pool and gym. To the right of the entrance of the lounge is the clinic of course – you started there. Beyond the clinic is anticipated space for nurture, education, and crew support. To the right of the clinic is the entrance to the office complex. Right now, it only has two offices – yours and mine – but it can expand as much as needed. To the right of that is the entrance to the residence quarters. My apartment is the first one on the left, and yours is across from mine. Again, there is space for expansion. The next doorway is to the galley area. There is a large kitchen if we want to do food preparation here, but there are also synthesizers for us to use. As you can see, a door connects the galley area and dining hall to the lounge. That completes the circle around the atrium. Whatever you want, including what you want to wear or want to eat, Frank will fabricate it instantly for you."

Belinda smiled. "Frank, in my closet at home is a red jumpsuit and white blouse that I used to wear when I wanted to be casual. Do you think...?" Her voice trailed off, and she squealed in delight and as her bikini changed into the jump suit. "Fantastic! This is just like the one that was back at my house."

"Actually it is, in this case. I had Frank transport all of your clothing and personal effects from California to your new quarters. He left duplicates behind in your former home." He paused to smile. "Now, Belinda, I've got to go and help Pixie. Frank will teach you how things work around here and keep you company. It looks like Tiger is going to enjoy playing with you too. I should be back in a few days. Then maybe we'll have time to do that house hunting in New Zealand." Walter gave her a peck on the cheek and vanished. A few moments later, the SVX outside the den window vanished as well. In the SVX, Walter heard the voice amidst the glow.

> **"You can trust Belinda with as much as you need to, Walter. I have prepared her for what she must learn and do. I will guide her as I guide you, but she will not yet hear my voice as you do. Stay focused on what I have told you. I am with you both."**

+ + +

After Walter left the Moon, it did not take Belinda long to furnish her apartment. "Frank, I'd like you to create furniture similar to what I had left behind. I know I can change it later if I want to." He appeared next to her. Instantly her apartment was filled with familiar-looking furnishings. "Could I please have my clothing from Earth in a closet over there?" She pointed to an area near the bathroom door.

"I can instantly supply you with clothing, just as I did with what you are wearing now."

"I am still getting used to all of this new technology, Frank. I assume you know my sizes. Just fill my closet with a good selection."

"Mid-western United States current fashions okay?"

"I guess so, at least for now." Instantly the closet was full of clothing. Belinda was tired. "You may find this difficult to understand, Frank, but a woman enjoys trying on clothing. Maybe later I will get used to doing the thing instantaneously. What time is it?"

"Would you like a clock set to your time in California?"

"Please." A clock radio appeared on her nightstand. It displayed 11:00 P.M. "Can I get radio stations up here?"

"You can receive any radio or television broadcasts from anywhere in the world. The monitors on the wall can be adjusted in size to suit your tastes. Just tell me what selections you would like when you want them."

"Thank you Frank." She paused. "I think I need to get some sleep." Suddenly, she was wearing pajamas just like some she had had at her old home. "Thanks again, Frank."

"Good night, Belinda." He vanished.

As Belinda crawled under the covers, the lights gradually dimmed. "Lord, I don't know where all of this is leading to. It isn't fair I know, but I trust Walter even more than I trust you. Please forgive me Lord. He has always seemed to get along better with you than I have. I suppose that's my fault. ... I guess I had better work on it. Good night, Lord. Amen." Soon she was fast asleep.

Seven hours later Belinda awakened to the smell of bacon and eggs. Frank and Tiger ate with her, though she knew it was only for show on Frank's part. Then she got down to work. During the next several days, with Frank's help, she quickly got into her new routine. She took a swim in the pool and tried the whirlpool a few times. Gradually, she began to miss Walter. "Frank, I want to send Walter a Gaardian mail message.

"Walter, I'm not ready to try a video connection with you yet so this is a compromise. I am still adjusting. I just want to send you a quick note to let you know that I am proceeding with the applicant search. I was going to change my name to go with my changed life, but I've decided that would be a little too much, and it's not necessary anyway. I will start collecting the applications from the receptacles beginning at midnight local time in each time zone after the publicity begins. It feels kind of weird to have the computer retrieve them via matter transport. I have to keep pinching myself to remind myself that all of this would be like science fiction to the rest of the Earth. For you of course, it is very real, and for me, it's becoming more real. When you get back, I hope you will have time to relax and join me for a swim. I like -- no, LOVE – swimming in the limited gravity of the Moon! I've learned to have the computer – Frank -- adjust the gravity depending on my mood. Is that self-serving or what?

Love always, Belinda."

Walter responded in minutes via G-mail. "I'll be back on base in about two days unless a crisis looms on Earth. I'll soon be done helping Pixie this time around."

"Are you two romantically involved?"

Walter grinned. "We are very close friends." He paused. "I want to encourage you to proceed with recruitment efforts without me."

"I continue to be amazed at how closely we work together and trust one another, despite the fact that we were apart for forty years. I will send you another note tomorrow. Bye!" The connection ended.

The next day Belinda got busy with her new job. "Frank, send a press release to all the news editors on the World Wide Web, including newspapers, magazines, radio stations, and television stations. Don't send it until you feed it back to me so that I can double check myself. Make it like this ...."

+ + +

The next day, in London, the editorial staff of The London Express had its daily meeting. In a conference room, editors from the various departments gathered around a table, discussing the day's news. The General Editor rapped the table to get their attention. "We've an e-mail for the front page from the Gaardian. It's not that long, so I'll read it to you." As she read, various people seated around the table reacted with startled interest.

Editor:

This announcement is being sent to all media news editors on the World Wide Web that have provision for receiving e-mail. Others are being reached via postal services. The Gaardian will begin receiving applications for employment, to be processed beginning December 1. Please make a careful note of the following:

1. No Earth-based laws bind the policies and activities of the Gaardian.

2. Once fully employed by The Gaardian, an employee may or may not have contact with friends and family.

3. Applications shall include recent pictures of the applicant along with a statement of fewer than one thousand words stating why employment with the Gaardian is desired.

4. National loyalty cannot influence someone working for the Gaardian.

5. Age, health problems, or handicaps will not hinder acceptance of anyone having lived at least seventeen full years.

6. Current skills, talents, experience, and abilities might not be utilized in Gaardian employment.

7. Placement is at the discretion of the Gaardian.

Signed,
The Gaardian.

"All right, until further notice this is our lead story, not only for news of here in London, but around the world. Get on it everyone. Dismissed!"

Everyone began filing out of the room.

On the Moon, Belinda watched the reactions to her press release on the major news networks. Frank stood nearby. As she expected, reactions were mixed. One commentator said, "Many have wondered about future press conferences with the Gaardian. Now that our planet knows it has a Gaardian, people are going to want lots of information."

Another said, "I hope some qualified journalists will provide first-hand news to us!"

Belinda told Frank, "I need to discuss that with Walter as soon as possible."

"Copies of these broadcasts are available to Walter now and when he gets back."

"Good!"

Although Walter's return was delayed, Belinda's work continued at a rapid pace. The next several days were a whirlwind of activity. Belinda had Frank set up an area in her office with a desk and many monitors. She added a sauna and steam room to the pool area. She set up the auditorium to have a flexible seating capacity with a giant video screen. "Frank, let's consider who we might recruit for leadership before we start receiving other applications."

"All three planets?"

"Three planets?"

"Including the Earth, there are three planets in our sector ready or nearly ready for interplanetary travel. Walter's leadership team should include at least one from each planet, even if most on the team are human."

Belinda was thoughtful. "I hadn't thought about that. I'll leave it to you to do some research on the other planets to find possibilities. Let's do some screening for Earth."

"I already have. There are files available at terminals both in your office and in your quarters. For sifting through Earth's possibilities, why don't we utilize the large display in the screening room that you've configured next to the lounge?"

Belinda got up from her desk and followed Frank through the lounge into the screening room.

Frank faced Belinda. "How do you want to begin?"

"We can't depend entirely upon those who are responding to the media, so some might be directly recruited. To start with, let's eliminate those holding government offices, elected or appointed. They will tend to be too nationalistic or provincial."

The large display at the front of the auditorium turned a mottled brown color.

"There are still millions of faces on our display." Frank's voice showed no emotion.

Belinda scowled. "We'll expand our parameters for later screenings, but let's eliminate those without any formal education."

"Done." The display became more granular.

"Now eliminate those whose intelligence is below average."

"Done." The display became coarser.

"Now, let's eliminate those who are not mentally healthy, those whose net worth is in the top five percent of the world population, and all of those who are in upper management in the biggest companies and corporations."

"May I assume you are eliminating them because of preoccupation with status and power?"

"You're getting to know me, Frank! ... Now let's eliminate those who spend more than a fourth of their income on entertainment. They are preoccupied too much with pleasure. Let's also eliminate those who are more than ten percent overweight, those addicted to drugs, and those who smoke."

"Done." The display was now almost countless but tiny discernible faces.

"This is almost fun, but now it is getting harder. How many are still possible candidates?"

"One million, four hundred fifty-two thousand, five hundred forty-seven. I have a suggestion. Eliminate those who have been married more than twice."

"I have an even better idea! It is not fair, but let's eliminate those currently married, and those who are divorced. This is arbitrary, but we can consider at least some of those currently married or divorced in later screenings." The faces in the display were now fewer and much larger. "How many now?"

"Nineteen thousand, seven hundred sixty-three, following the other criteria, and based upon those who have actually applied as of today."

"That's at least manageable. Let's see how many of them apply before the deadline. I have a few more screening ideas to try. Send the profiles to the console at my desk. I'll take it from there."

Frank vanished as Belinda walked back to her office. As she passed one portal, the SVX descended and stopped just outside. She didn't see it. There was a knock on her doorjamb. She looked up and saw Walter.

"Hello stranger! It's been nine days!"

"I just got back a few moments ago. It is great to see you! I always have liked that red jumpsuit." He felt something at his feet and looked down. "Yes, Tiger, it's nice to see you too."

"Have you had a chance to catch up on what has been happening?"

"Frank has kept me posted. It is amazing how many people from public life – particularly those in the fine arts — have applied. That one woman near the top of our list is an interesting development. Go ahead and send her that letter you have composed."

Belinda raised her eyes slightly and spoke into the air. "Frank, go ahead and beam the letter to Debbie Schaffner."

+ + +

An instant later, a letter appeared on the floor next to Debbie Schaffner's front door, below her mailbox. Frank rattled the mailbox flap in the door, and hearing it, Debbie came into her foyer and saw the envelope. Knowing that it was not the usual time for mail delivery, she cautiously opened the envelope and read its contents.

Dear Miss Schaffner,

I know that you and your boyfriend were planning your Beverly Hills Christmas party for many months. Thank you for the invitation. I understand you two broke up yesterday. I can relate!

The Gaardian was surprised that so many people in the fine arts applied for work with us, so thanks again for hosting those invited to your home in addition to your other guests.

I know it is a bit unusual for you to invite some people to your annual Christmas party that are not part of the entertainment industry. I think your non-industry guests will have a great time, and they will enjoy meeting both you and the others.

Also, thank you for not letting on to them that The Gaardian will be there to talk with them. I must warn you that some law enforcement agencies and military personnel will be watching those who come and go from your party. This has happened because several have made public statements that they had applied.

Although you have always known that it would be necessary, I still want to express to you my thanks for trusting The Gaardian with all of this. I recognize that we can trust you as well, and that is no small matter at this time in our relationship. I sense from you a warmth, a serenity, and a special kind of strength. You and all your guests will be safe and protected.

Whether or not you eventually work with us, Miss Schaffner, you will undoubtedly remember this Christmas party for the rest of your life.

Belinda Thomas

Personnel Director

Walter smiled. "The letter has been delivered. Good job! I want to relax and finish reading Carl Sandburg's Lincoln, and then I will get some shuteye. Are you about done for the day?"

"I think so. How about joining me for a soak in the hot and cold whirlpool? I've really learned to love that thing."

"Sounds good. Do you do it at Moon normal gravity?"

"I hadn't thought of that! Let's try it!"

Getting up from her desk, she walked with Walter to the pool area. As they approached the whirlpool their clothing changed to swim suits, and they stepped into the steaming pool.

"Moon normal gravity, normal program." Suddenly the frothing of the pool was much higher, and the steam became almost opaque.

"We float so easily! It's like being inside an angry cloud!"

"Good metaphor!" They linked arms as the froth lifted them higher and higher.

"This is fun!" A chime sounded.

"That's the cool down signal. We'll be done in about fifteen seconds."

"I think I'll pop directly into bed from here. See you tomorrow!"

"Tomorrow!"

He vanished. She stepped out of the pool and walked out into the atrium. The pool ceased its activity.

+ + +

Days later, Belinda was wearing a blue leotard, when she and Frank walked into the lounge from the atrium and begin examining the details of some decorations that were in a miniature three-dimensional display.

She went to a chair by a roaring fire and sat down. Walter walked in. It was December 10. Belinda had decorated the base's den with Christmas decorations. "Thanks, Frank! You did a great job with the Christmas decorations. You've come to understand my tastes very well!"

"You're welcome." Frank vanished.

Walter and Belinda sat in front of a roaring fire. "Walter, do we need to talk about what we need to do between now and the Christmas party?" She paused. "By the way, can I go to the party too?"

"I suppose so, but you'll need to wear this." He paused. "I planned on your being there." Walter reached into a pocket and pulled out a ring that was a smaller and more feminine version of his own. He put it on her right ring finger. "I would not be giving you this so soon if we were not the closest of friends, but you need to understand that this is not just decorative jewelry." Walter paused. He had decided not to tell her everything about the ring. "This is a computer link to Frank. It's also a power portal so that if you get into trouble when I am not around Frank can help you."

Belinda was thrilled. "I prefer to think of it as a friendship ring, and those extra qualities make it extra special!" She winked.

"I assume that you figured I would say yes to your going to the party. Have you told Frank what you want to wear?"

"Of course!"

Right now, I want to go over the plans I have for the evening." He paused. "I need to have you get acquainted with our candidates and develop some rapport. I will be busy with managing the whole evening. Whenever you need Frank's help with anything, just touch your ring, and think of him – projecting in thought what you want to say. Try it right now."

Belinda touched the ring and closed her eyes. Frank appeared and put another log on the fire. "Thank you, Frank!"

"You're welcome." He vanished.

"You don't need to close your eyes to think, Belinda. Actually, you do not even need to touch the ring. I told you to do that to help you focus. Try again."

Belinda was silent for a moment, then a stool slid across the floor, she lifted her feet, and she planted them on top. "Wow! This is fun!"

"I'm glad you're enjoying yourself. Now, more seriously," He paused. "Frank and I have thought through all contingencies. I want you to focus on getting to know our candidates. I know we have done a lot of narrowing, in getting it down to twenty-two. The truth is, some are going to drop out this evening. For most, it is a career decision. One of them is just plain scared. You will discover which ones are a go and which ones are not, but do not do any pushing. Be just as friendly either way – I know you can be. Think of yourself as a stand-in for Debbie as a hostess. Okay?"

"Sounds good. Do I have time to soak in the hot and cold whirlpool before we go?"

"Go ahead. We'll leave in less than an hour." Walter vanished. Belinda headed to the gym.

7. Team Leaders

No one living would ever again go to a party like this one! Walter's personality plus his Gaardian gifts made everything different. Promptly at 6:00 P.M., Walter and Belinda met by the fireplace. Belinda reached down to scratch Tiger's head, and then straightened up. "I'm ready when you are!"

Walter looked at her. In his head, Walter heard Frank say, "All clear." Walter took Belinda's hand and they jumped instantly to the porch at the front door of Debbie Schaffner's house. Belinda looked around. Out beyond the gate to the grounds, there were numerous cars on the street. Both the house and grounds were surrounded by a masonry wall. Near the gate, there was a private police version of Frank.

On the porch, Walter touched the doorbell. "She sure has a nice house!"

A beautiful woman opened the door. Debbie unconsciously stood taller, and greeted her guests with a smile. "Good evening Belinda, Walter! Come in!" She led them inside. As he gazed at her, she was possibly the most photogenic and attractive woman he had ever seen. Debbie was brilliant, talented, and wise. She was not as tall as most of the other women there. Her natural auburn hair was pinned up. In her sojourn as an actress, she learned to walk and carry herself with Hispanic flair. She particularly enjoyed dressing like her Brazilian and Peruvian friends, emphasizing her figure.

Walter smiled as he spoke quietly. "Thank you for your patience as well as your hospitality for the party. I particularly appreciate how you handled yourself in organizing this." His voice was cool and even, but his heart was pounding.

"It's like a movie premiere! It's fun!" She had excitement in her voice.

Belinda smiled. "I am glad you see it that way. I suspect you will maintain your grace, charm, and sense of humor even when events may exceed your wildest imaginings."

"I hope so!" She was energized, walking erect with the manner of a model on a runway, frequently glancing at them. "It is so nice to meet both of you. ... Belinda! You could do modeling like I did if you were a little taller!" She waved at someone across the room. "This is like one of those old 'Keystone Cops' movies!"

Walter smiled. "How so?" He began to relax.

"In the last couple of hours, I have joined my butler in answering the front door to the police, the Highway Patrol, the FBI, the National Guard, and the Army. Thanks for supplying a security guard for the gate."

Belinda feigned curiosity. "Did you have any trouble?"

"None of them had search warrants. It was almost fun telling them that they could not come in because they did not have invitations. That General Grommond! He tried to get in on an invitation I had sent to Clint Eastwood. I do not know how he got it, because Clint had to be in Carmel tonight. ..."

Debbie veered off to the right to talk to one of her staff. Separating, Walter and Belinda began to mingle. Out on the veranda at the rear of the house, the glow of dusk disappeared as the sky grew darker. Belinda and Walter greeted everyone. They explored the veranda, the living room, and the den, and they waved at workers in the kitchen. As they explored, they listened to murmurs of conversation as guests got food from a large buffet.

After the last of the twilight faded, Walter beckoned to both Debbie and Belinda to join him in the middle of the living room. "This has gone far enough."

Belinda looked at him and grinned. Debbie had a wary look as she turned to face him. "What do you mean?"

"Invite your guests and staff out onto the veranda, telling them they are about to see a great show that will never again be duplicated."

Debbie stepped up on top of one of the nearby chairs. Projecting her voice very loudly as though on stage she called out, "Attention everyone!" Everyone grew silent as all turned to face her. "Tonight there is going to be a very special treat for all of us. If everyone will please step out onto the veranda, we will see something that no one on Earth has ever seen before and never will again. Those in the kitchen, please come out and join us for a moment."

Belinda took Debbie's hand, and the three of them walked to the other side of the house. Debbie's excitement could hardly be contained. People were murmuring excitedly as they moved out onto the veranda. Debbie murmured quietly, "What's going to happen?"

Walter responded just as quietly, and with a smile. "I'm going to move your house here in Hollywood, along with everyone in it, to a bluff on the Tasman Sea in New Zealand."

"What?"

Debbie turned to look at him. Walter looked straight into Debbie's blue eyes and continued to speak quietly. "I own the land. New Zealand time is currently about sunset, so the view will be spectacular."

"You're serious, aren't you!"

"You bet! Let's get this show on the road -- just imagine the surprise that awaits the media and military who are gathered outside!"

At Debbie's gate, some vehicles had turned on their headlights, and television crews had set up lighting for their location work. Soldiers and police were milling about on the street in front of the house. Some made gestures in the direction of the house, as officers gave orders. Police cars were coming and going as the media continued to jockey for the best position.

General Grommond, in full-dress military uniform, spoke to a group of reporters. "I have marines stationed all around the property and throughout the neighborhood. We may not be able to interview this Gaardian character, but no one is going to leave without being debriefed by my staff. That house . . . ."

As the General gestured toward the house, it disappeared. His mouth stayed open mid-sentence. Some of the soldiers leaning on the security fence fell down as it disappeared. In addition to the house and fence, a hole appeared where Walter had transported a wedge of Earth underneath the house along with its contents, to include the swimming pool and the basement under the house. Exposed were gas and waterlines along with power conduit, and TV cable conduits, moving slightly as though in a breeze. Members of the press, along with police and marines, scurried all over the vacant lot, as the atmosphere became bedlam.

+ + +

The sun was almost setting, overlooking the Tasman Sea, near the little town of Franz Joseph in New Zealand. A gentle breeze was blowing across the long grass on the bluff. Debbie's house appeared with the veranda facing west just as in California. Everyone saw the sun suddenly appear just off the veranda over the water, the bright hues shining through a few clouds. Beyond the front yard, mountains shimmered slightly.

As he spoke calmly and firmly, everyone turned to Walter. "Wherever I am involved as The Gaardian, I'm always in control of the situation. The military could have launched a nuclear missile at this house, and the energy would have been totally absorbed instantly...." There were a few murmurs from his listeners. "Some of you may recognize where we are. For those of you who don't, we are now in New Zealand on a bluff overlooking the Tasman Sea."

There were a few exclamations. "Behind us in front of Debbie's house are the Southern Alps. Nearby, just south of here is the little town of Franz Joseph. We are going to be here for a few hours and then return to California. You must remain on Debbie's property. Meanwhile, the phones are still connected to California in case of emergency, but I request that you not call anyone. Those attempting to call the house will get a busy signal. Please feel free to enjoy the newly revised scenery, but do not attempt to leave the property. I will have you back in California by 4:00 AM California time. Debbie has seen to it that there is plenty of food and drink. There are musicians if you want to dance. This is something that none of you will ever experience ever again, so enjoy yourselves!"

Walter and Belinda again began to mingle with the guests. After a few minutes, he approached Debbie, speaking softly. "Your party is so well planned that I actually have the time to relax and enjoy it. Since you are one of those joining my team, I would appreciate it if you would invite those on this list to gather in your den at 3:45 AM." He handed Debbie a piece of paper. Her eyes were still showing surprise and a sense of wonder. She glanced at the paper. "Make sure that their calendars are clear for a minimum of six days. If anyone asks, they are taking a break to go out of town for a week. Say absolutely nothing more."

"They already know that, but I will confirm it."

"Though they are going to be gone for a week, I will provide for their needs. Starting now they need to trust me."

Debbie was quiet and curious. "How long are we going to be here in New Zealand?"

"Like I said, we will be here until just before 4:00 AM California time. The house will reappear in California just as the morning news programs are beginning on the East Coast of the United States. Both the media and the military will be focused on who comes out of the house when it reappears. Except for you, they will not notice at first who does not reappear."

Debbie suppressed a quiet laugh. "Everyone out there is going to go nuts!"

Belinda smiled. "That's already true. Let's mingle some more and spend some time enjoying New Zealand."

Walter, Belinda, and Debbie moved about, enjoying with the others the spectacular scenery as well as the unique situation. As Debbie talked, she smiled. She also watched Walter. Debbie murmured to herself, "I could easily be smitten with him." Debbie glanced over at Belinda. "I wonder if they are an item...." The party continued without incident.

Sometime later, after glancing around at the other guests Debbie looked at her watch and stepped up on a chair in the living room. "May I please have everyone's attention?" The few still on the veranda came in to listen, and quiet settled over the gathering. "It is past 3:45 AM California time, though it is still earlier here. We will soon be transported back to California. If you have not been told otherwise, please gather up whatever – and whoever – you have brought with you to the party, and go out to the front lawn." She paused and giggled. "I guess you can prepare yourselves for a breath of fresh smog!" As the others snickered, Debbie got down from the chair and walked into the den. Most of the crowd moved to go out on the front lawn.

+ + +

In California, the police had the property roped off, and the crowds were all across the street. When the house reappeared, there were yelps of recognition from the police and media as they crossed the street to the house. The party guests on the front lawn were warmer in Hollywood, and a few began coughing from the smog. Some laughed and made jokes after they coughed. The media crews broke through the barricades and swarmed onto the front lawn to interview those that were there.

In the den Walter, Belinda, and the candidates were seated comfortably in a circular pattern. All but Debbie, Walter, and Belinda had gray or white hair. Walter took them all in with a sweeping glance. "I want to thank all of you for your courage as well as your willingness to explore possibilities with me. I know you have questions, but it is important that we get out of here, before the police and military begin swarming over this house. Debbie, if there is any damage from that invasion I will take care of it."

Debbie smiled. "Don't worry about it! I'll take it as a tax deduction!" Everyone laughed.

Walter had a keen sense of honor and integrity. "Nevertheless, Debbie, thank you for your hospitality. Now, I want everyone to please stand up." They did so. Those with arthritis did so slowly. All looked at one another with curious expressions and shrugs. "Tonight all of you experienced being transported from here to New Zealand and experienced no real difficulties, and none of you felt the move. Right?"

They all nodded at him and each other. A few murmured an affirmative. "Now we're going to go quite a bit further. We're going to the moon."

Debbie's eyes widened with excitement. "Holy cow!" The others nodded. A few grunted.

"If any of you want to back out, now is the time to say so. Debbie has told you that you have to trust me unconditionally from this day forwards. Has anyone changed their mind?" Everyone shook their heads.

Belinda smiled. "Shall I . . . ." Before Belinda finished her sentence, they were on the Moon.

"I have adjusted gravity here to Earth normal for the time being. You will have ample opportunities to experience the Moon's lesser gravity after you get settled." Walter smiled.

"Shall I take the women to their quarters while you take the men to theirs?" Walter nodded. "Once everyone sees where his or her quarters are, everyone can meet at the pool. You can feel free to look around and explore all you want. We will start our first moon day in about nine hours. By the way, everyone, don't step on Tiger – our cat. He'll probably stay out of your way until he is used to you though!" Several chuckled.

Walter's tone was reassuring. "I want all of you to get used to Moon normal gravity. In thirty minutes, the gravity will be adjusted to Moon normal. I suggest you not try any acrobatics until you get used to it. Just walk slowly and carefully and you will be fine. Tomorrow morning you will awaken again to Earth normal gravity. Men, if you'll come with me." Everyone began leaving the lounge slowly and talking softly. Belinda showed each of the women their own apartment, down the hall from those of Walter and herself. Walter did the same for the men. As people retired for the night, the Moon's quiet became palpable.

The next morning everyone seemed rested. The pool area seemed to be enclosed by a transparent geodesic dome (actually a force field) that sometimes glistened. The resulting visual atmosphere was tranquil. In the shadow of a Moon crater's mountains, everything was lit by Earthlight. They were talking softly in small groups.

Walter approached an older Asian man in his sixties and indicated he was to follow him. "Did you sleep well?"

The old man nodded. The two of them walked out of the pool area, crossing the atrium to the clinic. As they slowly walked toward the clinic the man said, "Debbie was a friend of mine. I met her in China. I went to Harvard Medical School, where people started calling me Butch. Then I returned to China to practice in some of the small villages there. Relatives and old friends saw to it that I also learned the skills of acupuncture, acupressure, and herbal medicine. Debbie and I met five years ago, while she was making a movie. She was injured, and I treated her. As she was leaving, she invited me to join her in the United States. My wife was deceased and my children were grown, so I moved to Los Angeles. I retired from my practice as a physician."

As they entered the clinic, Butch was totally fascinated. Walter led him to the modesty panel where Belinda stood when she first arrived. He spoke quietly. "Stand here and hold onto the top of this modesty panel firmly. You're going to feel shaky for just a moment." The display panel lit up, showing first his skeleton, then his organs. Butch looked intently at what was shown. Suddenly, his clothing disappeared and his body is that of someone about thirty years of age. "Look at the screen in front of you, Butch. Here are the diseases and genetic abnormalities that have been dealt with."

A black swimsuit appeared on him. All Butch can say was, "Amazing!" His head swimming, the two of them went back to the pool area, and at first people did not recognize him in his bathing suit.

"Ladies and gentlemen, this is the newly young Butch Eng." Everyone was as amazed. "Butch understands the complexities existing within people. He does not call a lot of attention to himself. He has the high intelligence required of a physician, and much more." Butch smiled, waved at everyone, and sat down.

"Lauryn, you're next." An Englishwoman with white hair, she was in her seventies and could barely move without her cane. As they slowly found their way to the clinic, Walter tried to set her at ease and asked, "Lauryn, tell me a little about yourself."

"I was Karen Oreskovich's babysitter. Karen is the one sitting quietly in the corner, watching the rest of us. I knew her when she was still in diapers. While a babysitter part time, I was a fashion designer full time. Sometimes I modeled my own creations. I am almost as old as Judy Valez, who is also waiting by the pool, over by the sauna. As you can see, I can barely move without my cane. I lost both breasts to cancer." Her eyes sparkled as she glanced around the clinic.

Walter led her behind the chin-high partition and had her put her hands on the top. "Hold on to this, Lauryn. You probably won't need it, but you may feel a little weak in the knees when you are restored to age thirty."

"Age thirty? Really?" Just as she said it, the machine transformed her. Both she and Walter were stunned. No longer bent over from arthritis, she was a tall, stunning redhead with a body that would make most women envious. "I hope you know I'm naked back here!" As she spoke, she was dressed in a red bikini, with a terry cloth wrap. "Now that's what I call service!" She grinned and laughed aloud. They walked arm in arm back to the pool. There were whistles from Butch and an older man, Ken Lyman.

Ladies and gentlemen, this delightful woman will be a valuable asset to our team. Lauryn sometimes gives the initial impression of being aloof and perhaps somewhat cold, but wait until you get to know her!" Lauryn continued to smile as she settled into a nearby chaise lounge. "Karen?" Walter looked down at an aging Polish beauty.

Nervous, she talked rapidly as they walked toward the clinic. "I've been talking with Debbie. She and I have some things in common. Did you know that in my youth I was a European movie director? I won three Academy Awards in the 1950's." Walter nodded. More quietly, so that only Walter could hear she said, "I guess I'm nervous. That's not like me."

She stepped out of her restoration stunningly and began to dance. "I studied ballet. Before I started making movies, I danced in every major city of Europe! It is great to be able to move again! I eventually became a choreographer." She paused as they began walking. "As I got older, I spent the rest of my career doing film work in Europe and the Middle East. ... I can't begin to thank you!" She gave Walter a quick kiss on the cheek. "I had forgotten until now how much I loved to dance to express my joy. Wow! I've gotten real joy again!" She and Walter waltzed back to the pool, and both took bows to the applause.

"Ladies and gentlemen, I present to you a brand-new Karen. She has a bit of a rebellious streak, and she might argue with you over values sometimes. She can be pretty entertaining, since she sees the world in her own different and special way."

"I'm next I hope!" Judy Valez was upbeat. "I am a retired Brazilian writer. I'm probably the oldest woman— I'm eighty-six! I think John is a little older though!"

"Eighty-six?" Debbie whistled. "I didn't realize you had been retired that long! You look much younger!"

Judy and Walter walked very slowly to the clinic. The results were truly dramatic. Smiling broadly, she boldly stepped from behind the partition. A tank bathing suit covered her, with a towel around her neck. As they walked back to the pool, she effervesced. "Growing up in Brazil, I impressed my teachers with my storytelling. A wealthy farmer sent me to the United States to get a college education and become a teacher. Instead, I wrote a screenplay while an undergraduate and ended up in film school." As she arrived at poolside, she was greeted with applause.

"Our new Judy does best in a flexible situation, where her coworkers take a personal interest in what you do together. Right, Judy?" She laughed. "Judy has both creativity and flexibility." She sat down next to Debbie.

"Can I go next?" asked Stephanie Smith, an obese woman in her seventies.

Debbie smiled. "Stephanie was a CPA. Weren't you the first black accountant at the San Diego Zoo?"

"Yes." She paused and turned to Walter. "Am I to go that way with you?" She pointed at the clinic.

Walter smiled. "Any time you are ready." As they headed to the clinic, they could overhear the others swapping stories about their before and after experiences.

When Walter and Stephanie returned from the clinic, she was as slender and svelte as an athlete. As she sat down, Stephanie told everyone, "I was born in Nigeria. My childhood was centered on my love of running. Eventually, I got a silver medal in the Olympics. When the Olympic Games were over, I managed to extend my visa by doing commercial endorsements while getting my education for becoming a certified public accountant."

"Fantastic!" Butch grinned. He came up and gave her a hug.

Debbie Schaffner was already standing, and she quickly joined Walter in the clinic. "There aren't many years to peel off since I'm thirty-two." She stepped behind the partition. "Growing up in Germany, I had planned on going to law school. – Whoa! Among my brothers and sisters I am the oldest, but in this group I'm the youngest – at least to start." A black bikini covered her as she stepped from behind the partition. "Though I was well-known in the entertainment industry and a rising star, I've now gladly left that to be with you -- and your crew."

As they returned to the lounge, Jody called out, "Hey, Debbie! That suit covers too much of you!" Debbie smiled.

Walter turned to look at Debbie as he spoke. "Most of you have some knowledge of Debbie because of her public image, but there is a lot more to this lady." He turned. "Jody?"

"I was a nude model in the early 1960's." Jody walked with Walter, glancing at him several times, studying his face. He showed her where to stand behind the partition. "Will it hurt?" She yelped with delight at her renewed body. "As a pre-med student at nineteen, I had been spotted by a photographer and asked to model. Within five years thousands of nude images of me were being sold around the world." Walter nodded. She was now wearing a conservative blue tank. "I tried some small acting roles, and eventually settled into doing commercials." She stopped by the clinic door to study Walter's face as she spoke. "I was always bored. Eventually, I used my brains to develop new technology to create and display my art. Have you seen any of my work?"

"Yes, as a matter of fact, I have. I rather like it! Photography is my hobby. I saw your presentation on Frank Lloyd Wright in Oakland."

"Ten years ago, I was diagnosed with Parkinson's disease, which had put a damper on my artistic efforts. It led to complications that had ravaged my body in the grotesque ways you saw. I am now truly a new woman." As they walked back to the lounge, she looked at herself in a mirror in the atrium. "I'll never be able to thank you enough!" She hugged him tight.

Back by the pool, Walter stopped and scanned the group. "In the past, our Jody was easily frustrated by the inconsistencies of others, but that will not typically be a problem for her here. Truth usually wins out over tact with Jody." He paused. "Now, it's time for the rest of the men. Who's first?"

"We've taken a vote. I am. Call it an Indian's revenge!" Toby Ballentine grinned.

As he and Walter walked out to the atrium and into the clinic, Debbie turned to Belinda. "Toby Ballentine is the only Native American writer to have won a Pulitzer Prize. He lives in Carmel Valley and keeps to himself – or at least he did. I understand he has written a couple of novels and some poetry under other names. He evidently does not like publicity." She paused to look up. "Holy smoke! You're one handsome Indian!" Everyone laughed.

Suddenly thirty again after being quiet for years he let out a whoop. "Great great Spirit! I can't remember ever looking this good!" With his genetics now idealized, he had the high cheekbones and handsome good looks of his Navajo heritage. "I'm not sure just why you accepted my application. I didn't think you would -- but I am glad you did." He smiled.

Walter returned the smile. "Glad to have you with us. Toby, you focus deeply on your values and devote your life to chasing ideals. That impresses me. You often draw people together around a common purpose and work to find a special place for each one within a group. That will be very useful. You are creative and seek new ideas and possibilities. The ladies will like that!"

Next into the clinic went Jim Crenshaw, a wiry African-American man in his seventies, bent over with arthritis. Judy watched him with admiration. "He had escaped the ghetto of Los Angeles to a major-league baseball career, until his health failed." Judy paused, looking up at the restored athlete. "Hey! Now that's the body I admired when you were on the diamond!" He grinned.

John Carson approached them. "I'll save you a little walking, okay?" He turned with Walter and started back to the clinic. "You may not know this, but I had barely finished high school in Texas when as a teenager, I was in minor skirmishes with the law. I held down dozens of jobs before going to clown school. Did you know I went to clown school?" Walter nodded. "Eventually, I wrote comedy sketches for television and had opportunities to act in some of them, although I never had the pleasure of meeting Debbie. Once you make me her age maybe I'll give her a shot!" He grinned. "Right now, now I'm in my late eighties – eighty-nine." As the machine finished its work, he whistled. "You've peeled nearly sixty years off of me! I was in pretty good shape, walking five miles a day, but this is fantastic!"

As John and Walter came out of the clinic, Jim Crenshaw got up from his chair and headed toward them. "I have a question. I have noticed that a lot of us either are from the entertainment industry or associated with it. Why is that?"

"You'll have to ask Frank and Belinda. They are the ones who narrowed down the list. It was somewhat easier to get information on all of you because of your public backgrounds, but there was much more to it than that. I think you'll get the most complete answers from Frank."

Walter and Ken Lyman walked silently together to the clinic. With his cerebral palsy, Ken was not talkative until they got to the clinic. With him positioned behind the partition, Walter stepped to the console. "Now, Ken, just stand there behind the partition."

"I guess you know I was a producer for one of the Christian television stations in Los Angeles. If I'm like the others I'll only lose about ten years in this process." The machine hums.

"Ken, it's not just a matter of years, but a matter of physical, mental, and spiritual health." ... The machine did its work. "Now, Ken, stand up straight."

"I can only repeat something that Jim said! Sweet Jesus! I've lost my cerebral palsy?"

"No problem. By the way, I know you were raised in Australia by Canadian parents. ... I also know that you had hesitated in applying."

Stepping from behind the partition in a swimsuit, he smiles. "I had always dreamed of being an astronaut before getting into a television ministry." Ken chuckled. "I guess my prayers have been answered. You can walk, but I'm going to run back to the pool!" He took off in a sprint.

Frank appeared as Walter returned following Ken. "Frank, put out the party food. It's time to relax!" Food appeared, and everyone got into animated conversation. Some jumped in the pool or got into the hot and cold whirlpool. The party lasted for hours.

Finally, Walter brought things to a halt. "It's time for all of you to get your apartments organized the way you want them. All of your belongings have been put there. Separate out what you do not want, and then just say, 'Frank, I need you,' and he will appear. Tell him what you do not want and make requests for anything that you do want. I'll see you in about four hours or so." He vanished. They all began to go to their quarters. In his apartment, Walter saw the glow and heard the voice.

"You've done well. I am pleased. Enjoy your rest. You've nothing to fear."

The glow faded. He stretched out on his bed, and soon he was fast asleep.

A few hours later, Walter, Debbie, and Belinda were wearing sweat suits and sitting in front of the fireplace, which now had a much lower blaze. Walter was mellow. "As comfortable as this is, we have things to do. Come with me to the Conference Room I've configured. I think I need some input from you two -- from a woman's point of view." Together they walked through a doorway. A twelve-meter square conference room was just beyond the lounge, with appropriate food stations, comfort station doorways, and lounge furniture on the perimeter. In the center was a five-meter circular table surrounded by high-backed upholstered swivel chairs. The table was black, and the chairs were white.

Belinda spoke playfully. "Walter, do you mind if I ask Frank to give us a little color?"

"Who is Frank, anyway?" Debbie looked around.

"Let's just say that he and Walter together make things happen. Got any ideas for decorating this place, Debbie?"

Debbie whispered to Belinda.

"Frank, please make it happen!"

Belinda's ring shimmered. The room transforms to a plush conference room like those in the offices of some major corporations just as the others are arriving.

"I like it!" Walter smiled. Moments later, as the others came in, everyone quickly was seated around the table. "We need to get down to business." All around the table, he had their full attention. "After the swim party, I know you have had a chance to get acquainted, but not thoroughly, and not with everyone. There were nods. "Belinda and I know all of you far better than you may think, but it is important that each of us know some details about the others."

Butch was serious. "How is it you know so much about us? Do you mean you know more than what we put on our applications?" The others nodded.

Walter was reassuring. "In time, you'll understand just how much is known about yourselves, but suffice to say I have used some technology from another galaxy that has literally looked at some of your past activities by looking back in time."

John whistled, now dressed as a tanned white Texan. He was tall and slender, with boyish good looks and a bit of a perpetual smile. He was nonetheless serious. "I'd rather forget some of the stunts of my teen years!"

Walter smiled. "Not to worry! You're here, aren't you? Out of tens of thousands of applications it has been narrowed down to this group as our beginning point."

Debbie looked at John then back at Walter. "What do you mean, 'our beginning point?'"

"During the next few months, I am asking all of you to do what Belinda has been doing. As you begin to learn new ways of doing things, you will also be recruiting another couple hundred people who will work under you and with you. When I'm not around, Belinda is Base Commander, or head honcho, or whatever title she wants to use."

She smiled, and took a mocking tone. "I think 'Your Imperial Majesty' will do just fine!" Everyone laughed.

"The point is, she and I are going to train all of you in what you will be doing. Then you will all work together as a team to recruit whoever is necessary to make things run smoothly." There were several low whistles and exclamations.

Belinda smiled an easy smile, shifting in her seat. "I was intimidated by all of this myself at first, but we have resources that are pretty amazing. Believe me when I say that Walter - that's his name, by the way - is probably the only one who is apparently not going to be amazed every day for the next several months."

Walter was relaxed. "I want us to get to know one another so that you know where we are coming from. Before we get to that, however, I have a couple of additional introductions to make. They have been listening in on our comments since we arrived last evening. They preferred it that way. Keeta ["KEY-tuh"], will you and Asayak ["uh-SIGH-ack"] and join us?"

As Walter looked toward the residence area, all turned to see where he was looking. A creature about seven feet tall glided into the conference room. It had smooth translucent green skin that almost seemed to glow. It also had lots of long hair mingling with the glow. It had four arms that swung slightly with an array of finger-like appendages at the ends. Near the top, it appeared to have what seemed to be an eye, but there was no evidence of ears or mouth. It glided across the floor with no legs.

"Ladies and gentlemen, this is Asayak. It comes from a planet from about a third of the way across our galaxy - I use the pronoun 'it' because that is its preference. In a few minutes, I will let it tell you about itself. Go ahead and greet them Asayak."

"Hello!" They all heard its voice but could not tell where it came from. All but Walter nodded greetings or said 'hi.' Asayak glided to where Butch was sitting. "Butch, may I stand next to you?"

Butch nodded and slid his chair over so that Asayak could stand next to him. Part of Asayak seemed to glide under the table as it descended to just over Butch's height.

"I told you that I was introducing you to Asayak and Keeta. Neither Asayak nor Keeta breathes oxygen as we do, but I have equipped both to be comfortable in our environment. Keeta is also here in the room with us. Normally, her species is transparent. Keeta, would you please bring that chair over there and sit next to Belinda?" A chair moved up next to Belinda, who slid hers over to make more room. "Keeta, please greet your new friends."

A silky, soft feminine voice said, "Hello friends!"

"Now that all the introductions are complete, I'll start things off. ... I was a pastor in Oakland, California until a few months ago." As Walter began to speak, three-dimensional images appeared over the center of the table, corresponding to what he was saying. "What I did not know was that throughout my life, each night I was trained by teachers from other galaxies. A few months ago, my sleeping life and my waking life were integrated. I traveled to another galaxy for a celebration for two others and myself - from other planets though -- who had been recently integrated. You will meet one of them soon. My duties as The Gaardian are still unfolding. If you have questions about my life before becoming a Gaardian, you can ask Belinda. Why don't you go next Belinda?"

Belinda took a deep breath and sighed audibly. Similar three-dimensional images appeared. "I grew up in Seal Beach, California, where I went to school with Walter. I got married and started teaching. My husband and I were together for many happy years. I have a son in the Central Intelligence Agency and a daughter who is a Roman Catholic nun. I began to have cancer a few years ago, and decided not to go for the surgery that might have lengthened my life, and I went into hospice. I wrote to Walter, and he visited me. That evening, we left a duplicate of my body in my home, so that officially I died. The rest is history. Asayak, why don't you go next?"

"All of you can hear my voice because I communicate telepathically. When I met Walter a few of your weeks ago I felt comfortable because he communicates with me at a level that is only matched by my progenitors and teachers."

Ken stared. "Progenitors?"

"Yes. We reproduce without what you would call sex in a private process which I will not describe." Three-dimensional images began appearing near him. "I come from a planet that we do not name where the predominant atmospheric gas is carbon dioxide. The carbon is our food. We do not have eyes, ears, or mouth. What appears to you as an eye is an illuminating organ providing radiation both visible and invisible to you. It enables me to sense at many levels. When you speak to me, I hear the words as you are thinking them. When we are young, we are taught it is impolite to read minds beyond what others wish to reveal. My world is less than a generation ahead of Earth in most ways, but in a few, Earth is far ahead. The fine arts - music, sculpture, painting, and other arts fascinate me. Our society is just beginning to blossom on that frontier. Thank you for hearing me."

"Thank you, Asayak. Debbie, you had a question?"

"I am a well-known actress and model. Will that be a problem?"

"One thing at a time. We will probably take advantage of that from time to time. We have not heard from Keeta. Keeta, would you please make yourself at least a little visible so that we can see you as well as hear you?" A pale yellow humanoid appeared. "Thank you, Keeta. Would you please tell us a little about yourself?"

A similar media show accompanied her. "Thank you. My planet is between Earth and Asayak's planet, though a bit in the direction of Gaardian Planet. As my species developed, we focused on wisdom and the arts. A short time ago, our wisest elders realized that since there had to be other intelligent life forms, we had to get ready to meet them. In the last ten of Earth's years, we have established colonies on three planets near our own. Qaak suggested me to Walter as a representative of my planet. Now that I have heard from each of you, I feel comfortable here, and I'll remain visible for you unless circumstances dictate otherwise."

"Thank you, Keeta." He paused. "I briefed Asayak and Keeta two days ago, before the party at Debbie's home. They each know the basic about Earth and its history. Everyone has now introduced themselves, either in this meeting or in casual time. You will not be going back to Earth at the end of the week. Each of you will go back as need arises, but don't worry about that now...." Walter took a deep breath and sighed. "My first challenge is coming in about ten days, but that will not concern you. We need to talk about both your training and the recruiting of the rest of our staff."

Belinda assumed the manner of a teacher. "Since we are going to be the senior staff, we need to think of ourselves in at least two roles – the roles we are going to play during the next few months, and the roles we will want to fulfill after the organization is up and running. I have decided to concentrate on my current job for right now, but keep my eyes and ears open for the future. I recommend that each of you do the same." Everyone glanced around at one another.

Walter stood up. "Butch, I want you to come with me to the clinic while Belinda starts training the others."

As they left, Belinda began. "Frank, it's time to bring out the briefings." Electronic note pads appeared in front of each of the others. "Those note pads are computer terminals though much tougher and advanced than anything you have previously seen...."

Belinda's voice faded as Walter and Butch walked across the central atrium to the clinic. Butch talked animatedly. "I keep expecting to see the moon among those stars and have to remind myself that we're on the Moon." They paused their walking in the atrium and faced each other. "Are you assuming that I want to work in the clinic because of my background as a physician?"

"Not entirely. Your background will help in terms of your medical instincts but not help you in terms of medicines or tools, because the technology is different. If you had not reacted as you did in the clinic yesterday, I might have hesitated before proceeding as we are. You seem to have a hunger to be a new kind of physician."

"True! Very true!" Butch grinned. "What I've seen so far in the clinic goes far beyond anything that I had ever imagined would be possible in my lifetime or that of my children!" They turned and went into the clinic.

"You're not even close. Cultures far more advanced than ours can look at the Earth and predict with some precision how fast our future developments will proceed. At Earth's current rate of scientific discovery and technological development, most of this technology will not be developed for another thirteen hundred years or so. Some will not be available for much longer." Walter hopped up and sat on the edge of a table, and Butch sat down in a chair. "Now that you have met Asayak and Keeta, you already know that you will not be caring just for humans. Frank is available to instruct you. He is better than a written text or even pictures."

As Walter was showing Butch how he was to learn the new technology, Belinda finished getting the others started in learning their new positions. "I want you all to either go to your quarters, or find a place where you can study. If you want to form small groups to study together, that's a good idea, but be sure to stay with the materials. There are monitors, both traditional video and three-dimensional video, throughout the base which you can use as needed."

As they went off to study, Belinda reviewed her own timeline for what was to happen next. "Frank, it's time to dispatch that e-mail I wrote to the media – the one Walter and I worked on before Debbie's party."

Editor:

As with my previous information releases, please inform your readers/viewers/listeners of the following. This information is being sent to all news editors on the World Wide Web that have provision for receiving e-mail. I will continue to communicate with the media in this manner until August 1, when I will begin supplementing news releases with digital audio and video. In September, barring any galactic incidents, I will hold a somewhat limited media conference. The date, location, and circumstances of the media conference will be provided later.

At the media conference, you will get answers to some of your questions regarding events up until that time, including the disappearing house incident, the unscheduled eclipse of the moon, and the temporary elimination of cocaine production on our planet. I hope that your questions about these events will not overshadow any curiosity about my role as The Gaardian or my developing organization and operations.

A Gaardian team member named John, who has had some previous experience with the media, will hold the first media conference after my initial one. It is his intention to set the tone for future media conferences so that those who do them later will have it easier. Questions deemed to go out of the bounds of the following subject areas will not be answered. For the time being, questions by the media will be limited to:

1. Background information about the conference leader prior to his or her deciding to work with the Gaardian.

2. The nature of the leader's decision to work with the Gaardian.

3. His or her feelings, and comments about work, play, love, or worship.

4. The leader's physical, emotional, and spiritual health.

5. Extremely general comments regarding the differences between our planet's most advanced science and technology, compared to the resources available from and through the Gaardian.

Media leaders wising to make specific and brief editorial pleas for expanding these media conferences may do so during the first six hours after midnight on the same satellite transponder frequencies.

The Gaardian

8. Paula

Walter had finished getting Butch started, and Belinda was joining him as he headed to the den to relax and take a break. Belinda spoke quietly. "When you're off the base for extended periods, I think I miss our fireside conversations the most. It is strange how Frank had not previously computed how important fireside conversations can be to people. It is also interesting how he makes improvements on our requests once he gets the picture. I do not think anyone has gotten used to how spectacular a roaring fire is under the moon's limited gravitational pull. The dancing colors seem even more hypnotic!"

Walter was equally enthusiastic but relaxed. "Absolutely! Actually, the fireplace is almost Earth normal gravity in order to control combustion. ... I think John Carson is going to do a great job! I will be interested to see how long it takes the media to figure out that he really is who he is. There will be general disbelief when he reveals that the handsome thirty-year-old they are looking at used to be the old man who retired from show business near the end of the last century."

"Yes! I can also see how well the others are going to do. I understand why you've been so impressed with Debbie, but Ken, Belinda, Jody, and all the others are going to be terrific as well." Walter nodded as she continued. "Jim and Lauryn are also truly amazing – so are Keeta and Asayak. They all will be great assets for us. I am glad we have been able to recruit Butch as our first physician. As you suspected, he has such great creative instincts that Frank is having no problem helping to expand his sense of calling to develop skills useful to other life forms."

"I suggested that to him as I was helping him get used to having Frank instruct him."

"All of this has been great therapy for me, Walter." Belinda paused. "I still miss Steve, of course, but God surely sent you at the right time. Perhaps that could be a topic for one of the larger fireside chat fests with the others."

"Good idea!"

"The work has helped me get my mind off of the past, and it has been great to renew our friendship after all of these years. With my daughter in Rome and my son who-knows-where, I guess I was getting a bit lonely and feeling sorry for myself. These past few months, you have surprised me with how much you have shared with me so quickly. I understand now why my parents stressed the importance of mutual trust so much. Being able to like, love, and trust someone without worrying about being pressed into an agenda gives me a great sense of security and hope in the midst of all of this chaos."

"Chaos?" Walter grinned and offered mock horror.

"Yes, chaos! I continue to be amazed at how easily Frank seems to keep things organized and under control. Maybe someday I will be more able to understand some of the differences between Frank and the rest of the computers that so much of Earth's society seems to depend on. When I consider what Frank can do on a moment-to-moment basis, the Bray computers my son has talked about seem so primitive! Along a similar subject, each time I look over at Debbie, she seems like a kid in a toy factory. She just might become one of our best problem solvers."

+ + +

Over in the clinic, Butch was getting used to talking with Frank like a friend. "I used to dread giving physicals to some of my older patients."

"Why?"

"In some cases, some cases I was virtually certain before doing the physical that I was going to have to give them bad news. It is never easy telling someone that they are terminal, or that they have a very poor prognosis. Missionary parents raised me, so my belief in a God helped, but I did not practice my faith much. Working eighty to a hundred hours a week did not leave me much time to think about church. Debbie was my first American patient after I finished my residency and set up my practice in China. When I returned to America, she never preached to me or harangued me about going to church, yet she has had a subtle influence on me. Even before I met Walter, I began reading my Bible each morning and spending a couple of minutes in prayer. By the time I decided I wanted to work for the Gaardian I was regularly praying for everyone I knew."

Frank turned toward the door as Belinda came into the clinic. "She didn't try to get you to go to her church?"

"No, and in hindsight, I now wonder why she didn't. I guess I will have to ask her the next time I talk with her. Anyway, this is a completely different world – no pun intended! Walter did Gaardian versions of physicals, when Gaardian technology analyzed us medically and restored us on that first evening. For me, it was an interesting turning of the tables to see my physiology displayed on a panel. My world started spinning when I saw what had been a nasty and possibly lethal growth in my groin before my transformation. My world was turned upside down yet again when I realized that Walter had removed it painlessly and completely in less time than it took me just now to tell you about it."

"How bad did it appear to you?"

"The initial thought that flashed through my mind was a six-month prognosis. That is currently so easy to forget, since our physical ages are now all identical."

Belinda nodded. "I agree!" Belinda was emphatic. "I also only had a few days to live, and I had already lived a full life."

Butch nodded. "After Walter removed my cancer and cured a few other minor glitches in my health, he then did the genetic fine tuning, although it all happened in moments. To me that is one of my best tools in the clinic here. I walk more than an inch taller, and I feel a lot more masculine – as well as feeling as if I am in peak health. I guess I am not alone in this. ... I think it is going to be interesting giving physicals to Asayak and Keeta." He paused. "My biggest thrills, however, will be when I am able to give someone a new real arm made of their own flesh and blood to replace one that had been amputated previously."

"So you're looking forward to being our first physician?" Belinda was genuinely curious.

"I want two or three assistants as soon as it can be arranged, but I'm willing to wait until we start getting more recruits in. Speaking of which, we all will probably be impatient for the second phase of this recruitment drive. I know what has to be done, and I am ready for it! I am really looking forward to meeting some of these recruits."

Belinda nodded her head. "In pre-screening, I see real leadership potential in a dozen or so."

Walter walked in. "How soon are you and I going to discuss leadership balance again?"

"Not until we take a good look at our next batch of recruits."

"Leadership balance?" Butch was puzzled.

"The male-female ratio. Let's continue this later at the fireside."

Now both were puzzled as Walter abruptly excused himself, walked across the atrium, and into his quarters. A warmth and glow surrounded him. The voice spoke firmly inside his head.

> **"Everything is proceeding as it should. Do not be alarmed when Belinda finds romance without you. I have plans for her, and for her next husband. Your time to have a mate is coming soon. Stay focused on me. Do not be afraid. I am with you."**

The glow faded, and Walter walked back into the den.

+ + +

In a television studio in San Francisco, Paula Rutledge was adjusting her microphone. Anchoring the NBS Evening News this evening was not going to be easy. In her late twenties, blonde, photogenic, and usually in a form-fitting business suit, Paula had been the permanent anchor only for a month. The day she was hired, she overheard someone outside her office say, "If the Gaardian is not the lead story, what is?" During this first month, the Gaardian was the lead story almost four days out of five. Around the world, speculations regarding the Gaardian were at a fever pitch. Paula and her staff had tried in vain to set up an interview, but then so had all the other media outlets.

Turning from the anchor desk and speaking to one of her assistants, Paula said, "Jane, yesterday I tried to get an interview with Belinda Thomas because she seems to be the spokesperson for the Gaardian. Last week, I spent countless hours trying to set up an interview with Debbie Schaffner, but evidently, not even her publicist knows where she is. Rumor has it that Debbie is making a movie in Australia, but I've not been able to confirm it, let alone locate Debbie."

Jane was an attractive redhead in her early twenties, but she dressed down so as not to show up her boss. "I might have a lead here in San Francisco. I'll do some more digging." She walked away quickly.

A man in his fifties, balding, in a long-sleeved white shirt with loosened tie and sleeves rolled halfway up, approached her with a concerned look on his face. "What is it, George?"

George handed her a raw news printout. "The Gaardian is going to hold a news conference."

Excitedly, Paula scanned the pages for highlights then went back to read more carefully. "George, this needs to be our lead story tonight!"

"Tonight? We're on the air in ten!"

"Tonight! I want copy to look at in five." George ran out. Paula frowned. How should she handle this? Was she going to be able to get to that news conference, or was she going to have to watch it on TV like the rest of the world?

George stuck his head in from the doorway. "Paula! Call for you on line six."

Paula picked up the phone and punched a button. "This is Paula Rutledge."

"Paula, this is Debbie Schaffner."

"Debbie! How are you?! I've been...."

Debbie cut her off. "Paula, I don't have time for small talk right now. Just listen, okay?"

"Okay." Paula grabbed her notebook – the computer was down.

"Paula, the Gaardian is calling a press conference. I'm calling you personally because you and I have known each other for several years, and because I think I can count on you."

"Thanks, Debbie, I think a lot of you too."

"Get to your computer or get your notebook. Ready?"

Her voice became low and cautious. "Of course!" Her face was flushed with excitement.

"I want you to call Tawny Gannon, Barbara Jones Smelter, Deborah Lopez, Tamara Williams, and Jeri Eng. The six of you are going to be able to question the Gaardian at his first news conference."

"Those are all women!"

"Listen carefully. The news conference will begin at noon Greenwich Time the day-after tomorrow. Each of you is to be at your home or apartment at Noon, Greenwich Time that day. You are to be in front of your television sets or monitors in your living rooms, dressed in business attire. At precisely noon, you are to be standing - not sitting. You will first hear from the Gaardian at that moment. You can have no other people, cameras, or microphones present. Is that clear?"

"Yes, but these instructions seem bizarre! Tawny Gannon, Barbara Jones Smelter, Deborah Lopez, Tamara Williams, and Jeri Eng. Noon. Greenwich. At home. Dressed for business. Standing in our living rooms in front of our TVs. Have I got all of that right?"

"That's correct. See you then. Bye!"

Paula opened her mouth to respond but the connection was gone. Paula gave a deafening whistle. "George!" As George came around the corner with news copy she requested, Paula spoke rapidly. "George, that was Debbie Schaffner. I am to be at that news conference with the Gaardian the day-after tomorrow with five other woman journalists. I need fifteen minutes." He started to interrupt. "No! Just listen! Have Jim do the lead story, telling the listeners that I am on assignment with a tag that I will have a personal report later in the newscast. Have him take things at least until the first break. If I am not ready, he may have to take it until the second commercial. Tell Jack ...."

Jack came to her desk as George scurried off. "Jack! Big news! I just talked to Debbie Schaffner, and I am to be part of a news conference day after tomorrow with the Gaardian. I need time during the first part of this evening's broadcast to work out the details. I'll have about a three and a half-minute report at the end of the broadcast - let Jim do the rest of the anchoring." Paula stood up and headed to the door, with Jack walking with her.

"Get going on whatever you have to do! I'll have questions for you after tonight's broadcast."

Paula went on through a doorway as Jack turned to talk to a camera operator inaudibly for a few minutes and others scurried about. She walked into her office, sat down at her desk, and picked up her phone. A few moments later Jane walked in. "I overheard you talking to Jack so I got started on things. Barbara Jones Smelter is in Paris, and she will catch the next flight back to London. Deborah Lopez is in Miami visiting family, and she'll catch a flight back to Mexico City. Tamara Williams is in Cairo, so getting back to Johannesburg is going to be a stretch, but she'll make it. Jeri Eng is in Auckland, but she can get back to Hong Kong in plenty of time."

"Good work! I'm on the air in a few minutes!" Paula absent-mindedly put the phone down, muttering to herself, "What am I getting into?"

+ + +

On the scheduled day, Paula was ready. Her apartment was lit by late morning sun. She walked into the living room, stopped in front of the television, and gazed at the clock. The television was off, and as the clock sitting on top said noon, Walter's face appeared on the screen. "Are all of you ladies ready?"

Paula's face showed surprise as she responded as though to herself. "Yes!"

There was a flash of light. The six of them appeared in the den at the Moon Base, facing the largest window. The Earth hung low in the sky just above the horizon. Some of them exclaimed delightedly, and all were smiling. Walter was standing next to the window and smiling back at them. "Ladies, there are micro-cameras and microphones throughout the base, so all of this is being transmitted live throughout the Earth and is being translated as needed in the various media markets. You arrived here under artificial Earth normal gravity conditions. Most of the people living here prefer it that way while working. Just in case any of you has any doubts about where you are, here is moon normal gravity.

There were squeals, as everyone lost more than three-quarters of their weight. They moved as though coming to a stop at the top of a fast elevator ride. "Welcome to the moon, ladies. I will let you see some of my staff here as you tour the base later. Now, here is Earth normal gravity again." They moved, only as though coming to a stop at the bottom of a fast elevator ride. They groaned as they got their weight back. "Later you can experience moon normal gravity again if you wish. You were all chosen by my computer. I told it I wanted a highly visible media representative from each continent except Antarctica. We are in our den or lounge. My staff and I come here to relax and at times to have informal discussions. Would any of you ladies like to have a fire in the fireplace?"

They all nodded. A fire appeared in the fireplace. "Please be seated." He motioned for them to sit down. "I will begin with background." Three-dimensional images appeared next to him to illustrate as he talked. "I am the product of three continents. I grew up in North America, and I was educated there. I will not be more specific about my early life for the next several years in order to protect the people that knew me. Less than a year ago, I moved into my Gaardian role. Gaardians first started doing their work about sixty-five thousand of Earth's years ago. They are a galactic police force, currently supervising more than a thousand galaxies. My jurisdiction comprises our Milky Way galaxy plus several others. Gaardians do not generally get involved in intra-planetary issues. I have been involved in few minor incidents on our planet simply to make my presence known. In less than three months, there will be beings from another galaxy wanting to enter our solar system. In order to keep them out of our area, I will have to do some things that will be noticed by scientists eventually. For purposes of both information and historical record, I will be providing audio and video feeds when the time comes. To avoid panic I am making my presence known now. Having this press conference is an effort to make the issues and my intentions clear."

The media show next to Walter vanished. "Before you leave I will see to it that you have a complete tour of the base excluding staff quarters. This is supposed to be a press conference and not simply a lecture. Questions?"

Paula spoke as if to a man with whom she wanted a date. "Thanks for the 3-D media illustrations. I assume you will not be telling us how you do that. You say you grew up in the North America. Are there records?"

"You're right in your assumption about Gaardian technology. Certainly, there are records. In addition to the record of my birth there are my educational records."

Tawny, in her forties, with an Australian accent, spoke firmly. "When will those records become available?"

"I need to protect family and friends of my other life for a few decades because Gaardian technology has regressed my age several decades."

Deborah had Paula's attitude and added her own cultural flair. In her late twenties, she was Mexican, stunningly attractive in a feminine business suit that revealed some cleavage. "You took some kind of youth potion?"

"For right now I am not going to reveal the nature of any of Gaardian technology. It is hundreds of years ahead of that of our home planet Earth."

Jeri was proper and reserved but obviously attracted to him. She looked younger than most her age. Her Chinese heritage hid her maturity. She was in fashionable Western attire. "You say hundreds of years. Are you saying that Gaardians pre-date the dynasties of my Chinese forebears?"

Walter smiled. "By many thousands of years."

"Why then did Gaardians recruit you at this time?"

"The development of civilizations tends to follow patterns. Gaardians saw that Earth's inhabitants would soon begin exploring the space around them. They entered into a standardized process, selected my grandparents, followed my parents, and then trained me. There are civilizations on two other planets besides ours in my sector that are at the same place in technological and social development. I am making similar appearances to them."

Some of the women glanced at each other. Walter continued. "All of this has caught the attention of some inhabitants of another galaxy that are intent on colonizing this area of space. It is best that Gaardians become known beforehand to alleviate any potential panic. Even though I am from Earth, there are going to be those who distrust me. It will be even harder for the inhabitants of the other two planets."

Tamara Williams had become very relaxed. In her thirties, she was dressed in a mix of Western European and African attire. "So, many of my third world neighbors are going to have a hard time with this. Many if not most do not have access to modern communications."

Walter nodded. "The word is going to have to be passed. Naturally, there will be those on all continents who attach superstitious or religious significance to what they see and hear. There are still those who believe that Neil Armstrong never landed on the moon and that the Earth is flat."

Barbara was restless and distant. "We British will mostly take all of this in stride - we're proud of such things, but I can't say the same for my European counterparts. Are you going to be doing anything in the next few months that will establish your role as the Gaardian more fully?"

Walter nodded. "Let me tell you about something that is happening even while we are talking – but first an introduction. Frank appeared, and there were glances around as none could see how he came in. "This is Frank." The women all murmured or nodded hello. "He is an android. Think of Frank as my friendly assistant who acts as an interface between Gaardian technology and me. While we have been talking, Frank has been working on a project. Tell them about it, Frank."

Frank talked coolly and evenly, as images appeared to illustrate his response. "Recent terrorist activity on the Earth is diverting world leaders' attention from matters more important. I have been delivering hard evidence to various nations showing who the terrorists are, who finances them, and what their plans are. As soon as the United Nations decides on a place to hold the terrorists for trial, those directly connected to worldwide terrorist activity will be delivered to that holding area. The Gaardian requests that the trials proceed quickly as well as justly. If it becomes clear that the United Nations is unwilling or unable to put the terrorists on trial, then the terrorists will simply be removed."

The journalists responded almost simultaneously. "Removed?"

Walter smiled and was reassuring. "The criminals will simply be removed to a place where they can no longer participate in the civilizations into which they were born. They will live out their lives in another place, which I will not discuss." Frank walked out as the women whispered among themselves.

Paula spoke for the group. "If, as you say, the evidence has been delivered into our leaders' hands, that's a story that others can cover." The others nodded. "We'd like to see more of your base and ask some questions more informally."

"Of course." Belinda came in from the atrium. "This is Belinda. Some of you have talked with her on the phone or had e-mail correspondence with her. She knows almost all that is going on here at our Moon Base, and if any of you asks a question that she cannot answer, Frank is available. I will leave you in Belinda's capable hands." Walter vanished.

The women all stood up and blinked, but then they shifted their attention to Belinda, who led them out, talking as she walked. "As a teenager I was a tour guide at Disneyland. This is old hat!" They laughed.

In his quarters, Walter lay down on his bed, staring at the ceiling. The familiar glow filled the room, and Walter tensed up.

> "Watch Paula Rutledge. She will become a valuable member of your team and a trusted friend. Encourage Debbie Schaffner to maintain their friendship. Be a pastor to Keeta

and Asayak. Your friendship will be important to their planets. Do not be afraid."

Walter relaxed. As the glow faded Walter's eyes closed, and he drifted off to sleep.

+ + +

In her San Francisco television studio a few days later, Paula Rutledge was sitting at her desk. The cameras were on her, and the director gave a cue. "This is NBS Evening News, coming to you from San Francisco. I'm Paula Rutledge. Less than a week after The Gaardian had his press conference with six of our world's journalists including myself, two attempts are being made today to attack The Gaardian's Moon Base. Tonight we have reports from the other five journalists who spent a day with me with the Gaardian last week. Our coverage begins with Jeri Eng in Hong Kong. Jeri?"

On a balcony in bright sunlight, Jeri Eng stood next to the railing holding a microphone. "Thank you, Paula. At 2:00 AM Hong Kong time, a missile was launched from China's mainland, and an hour later the media relations office for China issued a statement announcing the launch. For more than four hours, tracking stations in Australia and the United States confirmed the trajectory. Three hours and forty-seven minutes after the launch of the first missile, radar stations in five countries reported the launch of a second missile, launched from somewhere in the Southern Hemisphere. We do not know its exact origin. Reactions from leaders of NATO and SEAPAC were swift. ... Jeri Eng, reporting from Hong Kong. Now to Barbara Jones Smelter in London. Barbara?"

With Big Ben illuminating the night sky behind her, Barbara was standing in the midst of a park on the river. "Thank you, Jeri. Here in London there was an initial alarm until it was learned that the two launches were anticipated because of a top-secret briefing distributed through diplomatic channels yesterday. The briefings were necessary so that no one would make the mistake of thinking an attack was being launched against another nation here on Earth. Britain's Prime Minister, Matthew Ferguson, offered only a brief statement."

The Prime Minister was seen sitting at his desk, talking to Barbara in an adjacent chair. "We were informed early this morning that these two launches would be taking place against the Gaardian. Some of our world's leaders were not satisfied after the Gaardian's press conference that the Gaardian is an asset to our world's security. They think he is a threat, and they are acting accordingly – but independently from other nations. That is all I will say at this time."

In the park, Barbara continued her report. "We have other reactions from around the world, beginning with Deborah Lopez in Rio de Janeiro. Deborah?"

Deborah was in a sundress on a beach, squinting at times from the sun. People were moving back and forth in the background. "Thank you, Barbara. Here in Rio reactions are mixed. Government officials in Rio, Santiago, Lima, and other capitols are generally subdued, but a surprising reaction came from Columbia's largest drug cartel leader. Julio Castro arranged for financing of the Southern Hemisphere launch. No one is sure, but it is rumored to be related to the sudden drop in cocaine availability. Elsewhere there were voices of surprised concern. I am Deborah Lopez in Rio de Janeiro. Now to Tamara Williams in Cape Town, South Africa. Tamara?"

In a small studio, Tamara was seated, talking casually. "Thank you, Deborah. Anglican Bishop Christopher Long offered a powerful protest today to the news that missiles had been launched against the Gaardian. In a hastily called news conference, Bishop Long offered a strong protest on the steps of the Church of the Nativity."

A tall middle-aged man was in clerical robes, and he was speaking quietly. "I am deeply disturbed by the launching of these two attacks. For the past week, there have been Anglicans fasting and praying in dozens of countries. The universal observation is clear that God is using the Gaardian for humanity's benefit. We are confident that nothing will come of this attempt."

Tamara Williams continued her report leaning forward slightly. "It appears that these Anglican Church leaders are right, as news came moments ago that the missiles have disappeared from radar. Tamara Williams, back to Paula Rutledge in San Francisco."

Paula appeared relieved both in her appearance and in her voice. "We had been waiting to see what would happen as these missiles headed to our moon. Our wait is over much sooner than expected. With late-breaking news, we turn to Tawny Gannon in Sydney, Australia."

In front of the Opera House, afternoon traffic could be seen with a few cars in the parking lot. Tawny was standing near the entrance. "Thank you, Paula. Here with me in Sydney is Dr. Malcolm Ruggeridge, who is in charge of deep-space telemetry and observation at the new digital optical telescope installation twenty kilometers north of here. Dr. Ruggeridge, tell us what we have just learned about the two missiles."

A short, slender, handsome man with white hair now spoke excitedly. "With our new optical telescope array with digitally enhanced imaging, we have been able to watch the two missiles in real time with extremely high clarity. On this monitor you can see what happened." The two of them turn to a monitor next to them as he continued to speak. "Video of the missile from China shows that it disintegrated, simply coming apart into a dust cloud. Switching to the second video, we can see the other missile meeting the same fate. We have traced the second missile's trajectory now, and we know it was launched from South America, from a valley known to be controlled by one of the drug cartels."

Tawny Gannon turned back to the camera. "As we saw, the missiles simply disintegrated into dust. Dr. Ruggeridge told me a few minutes ago that their analysis indicated that the missiles were carrying multiple warheads. ... Tawny Gannon reporting from Sydney. Back to Paula Rutledge in San Francisco."

Paula was looking directly into the camera, which had moved in closer. "As we come to our first commercial break, stay tuned for reactions from Washington, Paris, and Moscow." As the transition music began to play, Paula's face showed her to be deep in thought. She muttered to herself, "How can I get back to that base on the moon?"

Jack spoke from the studio's darkness. "Figure out a way!"

"Jane!"

The assistant came running up to the desk. "Yes ma'am?"

"I've got a new priority for you. Try every day at least twice a day to reach Debbie Schaffner. She is my one connection to all of this. Maybe she can get me back to the moon. Got it?"

"Done!"

Paula thoughtfully tapped a pencil on the desk.

9. Challenge

The team was becoming unified. They were going to experience their first challenge. Walter was standing in front of the fireplace in the den, muttering absentmindedly, and staring at the flames. "This isn't working! There is no way we can have these people prepared for Gaardian work by doing it all here on the base."

Belinda walked in. "What are you mumbling about?"

"There's no way I can get everyone trained for the challenges we are facing by doing all the training here on the base. You and Frank have done wonderful jobs recruiting additional people – much faster than I expected. As fantastic a job as you and the others have done, however, we need to push up the schedule."

As she approached the fireplace, he turned to face her. "Why the rush? What about the other nearby Gaardians that have been helping you up until now?"

"They have their own agendas. I can't keep on asking them to help out here just because we are not ready yet."

"But didn't you say things were proceeding as expected?"

"Yes, as expected, yet I didn't expect to feel this much pressure to get up and running. Somehow, reality has set in with a speed that I didn't imagine."

"For instance?"

"There is a species that Gaardians have never dealt with approaching the edge of our jurisdiction. They will be here in just a few weeks. Before I go out to meet them, I've to have our team ready to respond."

"What are we going to do?"

"How quickly can we get our core group in here for a meeting?"

"Now?"

"Now! Frank!"

He appeared. "Yes?"

"Let them know I want them in here in no more than ten minutes."

"Done." Frank disappeared.

Walter sat down at the slightly oval-shaped table in the middle of the conference room, and with a shimmer of his ring arranged the chairs around it with a space for Asayak. As they arrived, Walter greeted each of them and told them to relax. Then Walter got down to business. "We've got to move at least some of the training off of the base."

"Off base? Where? I've a couple of decent doctors in training, but where would I take them?" asks Butch.

"You're getting ahead of yourself. There is just so much training that can be done here on the moon, even with artificially created three-dimensional environments. The time has come for at least some of you to step into space."

There are a few low whistles. "When?" Debbie asked. "How? Where?"

"The when is in ten hours. The where is on *The Grace*, and the how is by taking a few field trips or practice runs together."

John was intense. "I take it *The Grace* is some sort of space ship. When did it get here?"

"It has been here all along, invisible, orbiting the moon for months. I mentioned it when all of you first got here. We also need to have some of you maintaining a Gaardian presence here, continuing the training and research on the base, and policing minor events on Earth and the other planets in our sector. By 'minor' I mean minor by Gaardian standards."

There were a few chuckles. "So who goes and who stays?" asks Toby.

"Since most of you were getting ready to call it a night anyway, I want all of you to go to your quarters. Frank will visit with you there. Talk to him about whether you want to stay or go, and what you would want to do in either case. At 2400 hours, everyone is to meet back here. ... Go!"

Frank appeared to all of them at once in each one's quarters. Walter 'listened in' as he sat by the fire and stroked Tiger. The cat's purring testified he had really begun to enjoy his life on the moon.

+ + +

At midnight, everyone returned to the den. Walter addressed them cordially. "All right, I want to hear from each of you. Let's be chauvinistic and let the women go first. You first this time, Keeta!"

"To state the obvious, I am naturally suited to intelligence gathering. When technology does not suffice, my transparency helps. I can see myself useful on Earth and the other planets, but I would be far more useful in space. Besides, I want to see more of what is out there."

"I agree. You will be with us on *The Grace*. Judy?"

Judy Valez spoke softly but firmly. "I don't think I am ready to go out into space. I think the Moon is quite enough. I would like to stay here and find some use for my writing talents. Maybe I can do some police work among the millions on Earth who might identify with me as Hispanic."

"Good choice, Judy. ... Lauryn?"

"You may think this a strange answer, Walter, but I want to be wherever you need me to be. Just name it!"

"Fair enough, Lauryn. For starters, I would like you to take care of new recruits here on the base and policing from time to time in Europe and Asia." Lauryn nodded. "Karen?"

"I can see myself dancing with beautiful creatures from other planets, but if you need me here I'd like to be in charge of physical training."

"I might need you later to do physical training here on the base, Karen, but your experience as an organizer and administrator I can use aboard *The Grace*. I appreciate your honesty about staying here on base, but I need you elsewhere. You will be our chief executive officer, and you will be in command of communications and personnel. Stephanie?"

"I think I would rather work here on the base and do some policing work on the planets. My accounting skills can be used in areas other than money."

"Another excellent choice. Jody?"

"Part of me wants to start over and make a difference on my own planet, but I've got this cockeyed notion that I can use my artistic instincts for more than just art, if I get a chance to go into space. I know you probably do not see me as the space type except as being a bit spaced out, but I would like a shot at being out there. Okay?"

"Jody, I overheard what you said to Frank a while ago. Up until you talked about it with Frank, I thought you would stay here on the base. I have changed my mind, because I've gotten a cockeyed notion too. Over the next few days, I want you to spend a whole lot more time with Frank. I am going to make you chief engineer on *The Grace.*"

John grinned at her. "Now I'm sure I want to go into space!"

"Thank you! You won't be sorry, Walter!"

"I'm sure I won't be. Belinda?"

"In our first life, you wanted me to be the woman you came home to, but I married someone else. I think this time I will be the woman – or one of the women – you come home to. I have gotten used to helping you run things around here, and I like it. It's kind of like being a combination of a tour guide at Disneyland and being a cross between Roy and Walt Disney. I'll stay here at least for now."

"You don't look a bit like either Roy or Walt, but 'Viva la difference!'" They all laughed. ... "How about you, Debbie?"

"There's no way I want to be on Earth in a new identity as the Gaardian, and I think I would get bored and feel confined if I had to spend all of my time here on the base. I think I could be a good space cadet." She smiled.

"You will not be a cadet. I want you to get some extra training from Frank in the next few days. I've decided to make you science officer."

"Fantastic! However, I didn't do well with science even in high school."

"This is a different ball game, Debbie. Frank will help Butch expand your intelligence level and then give you a scientific knowledge base that is light-years ahead of Earth's. Welcome aboard. ... Now! What about you, Asayak?"

"Walter, I know you don't worry about your own personal safety. The power available to you is amazing. The rest of us, however, will want to have a sense of personal security when you are not around. I would like to be responsible for weapons and security. There is some technology from my planet that might be useful to all of us. With Frank here this base seems secure enough for now, so I'd like to go into space with you."

"I think you're on target, Asayak." Walter looked around the room. "Now then, men! Who's first?"

"How do I increase Debbie's intelligence, so she can be the science officer? That's impossible, isn't it?"

"I have a surprise for you, Butch. Have you stopped to think about how easily you have understood the new technology here – technology that is many generations ahead of what you spent a dozen years learning before getting into medical practice? As a matter of fact, when each of you went through your physical reconditioning, your intelligence levels went up dramatically, though you did not notice it. All you and Frank will do is give Debbie's intelligence an extra push. Besides, Qaak has ways of training key personnel that will amaze you." He paused. "Now, having said that, and since you've spoken up first, do you want to stay here or go into space?"

"Are you kidding? Any of these women and men I have been training can manage the base clinic stuff. If you're offering me the chance to go into space,

I'm going. I want to meet Pixie and all the others you come across – particularly Pixie!" He smiled.

"Okay, Butch, you've signed on. Now how about you, John?"

"Like Debbie, I am still all too well known on Earth, even after peeling dozens of years off of this carcass of mine. Can you use another former entertainer in space?"

"I don't need an entertainer, but you had valuable experience in working for the circus back in your teens and twenties. You will not be intimidated by the unusual, and you keep your cool in dangerous situations. I am glad you decided you want to go into space. You will be trained as a pilot and navigator. Ken?"

"I think you can guess. Before I became a Christian TV producer, I wanted to be an astronaut. I don't know what I can do up there though."

"You have good people instincts, Ken. With a little extra training from Frank in addition to the experiences you've had already, I think you can make a decent counselor to work with Butch. He might even turn you into a pretty good nurse. What do you think, Butch?"

"Sounds good to me! I actually thought at one point he would make an excellent doctor."

"Then that's settled. ... Jim, how about you?"

"If I went into space I think I would naturally gravitate in the direction of the typical science fiction role of security officer."

Debbie giggled, and he smiled.

"But I can see already that security is not really an issue with Gaardians. Besides, I think I would like to be available both here on the moon and on Earth for wherever I am needed – kind of like Lauryn."

"Sound's good, Jim. ... So, Toby, I guess you're the last one to choose."

"The last of the something-or-others!" They all laughed. "When I was a child, I had a vision of going among the stars with the Great Spirit. I am not trying to lay religion on you, but I see that as kind of prophetic. I want to go."

"It may well have been prophetic, Toby, but not in the way you may think. I think you will be a valuable asset to the crew. You'll be our ombudsman and troubleshooter." Walter paused, looking around. "Right now, now I want you to work out with each other which of our new recruits are going on *The Grace* and which ones will stay here. In the process, you will need to assign each person his or her duties, at least for the short term. After this first shake-down cruise, we will evaluate and see if any jobs need to be reassigned." Walter paused again and looked at them all. His gaze landed on his old friend. "Belinda, the base will be in very capable hands with you – you will continue to be in command of course when I am not here. You will have help from Judy, Lauryn, Stephanie, and Jim. I would like you to stick around for a moment. The rest of you can work out crew assignments. For those of you going out on *The Grace*, Frank is now transferring your belongings there."

They all stood. Belinda and Walter moved to their favorite chairs by the fire in the den. The others formed small clusters of quiet conversations throughout the den and conference room. Belinda reached over and put her hand on Walter's. "What's on your mind?"

Walter gazed both thoughtfully and lovingly at Belinda. "I know you don't want to go on *The Grace* right now, but you and I have not taken that little stroll around the solar system I promised back at the beginning. Would you like to take a couple of hours to do that – and to take a quick look at *The Grace*?"

"I'd love to!" They got up and walked together to the window and the SVX. Butch noticed them leaving and smiled after them, but the others seemed not to notice. As usual, the red SVX was 'parked' adjacent to the den. They vanished, appeared inside the vehicle, and made themselves comfortable.

"The last time you and I rode in this I was forty years older," Belinda mused. "This is going to be a new experience!"

"Unlike when we were in high school, I won't take you up on Signal Hill to see the city lights. We're going to see the 'solar lights.' We only have time for a quick tour I'm afraid." The SVX rose and headed toward the Sun. "I am going to have to be back in about five hours to take the others for their shakedown cruise."

"I would love to go along, Walter, but there is too much to do at the Base."

"I agree. Time permitting however, I may have a surprise or two for you. I'm swinging around the Sun here so you can take a look at Mercury. As you can see, it's a rather strange-looking blob of gases and rock." Walter continued the tour, showing her all the planets before docking the SVX at the bridge of *The Grace*. As they came to a halt, the SVX disappeared and their bucket seats became chairs on the bridge of *The Grace*.

"That's quite a trick! ... Yes, yes, I know it's not a trick, but it's like magic to me!" Walter and Belinda stood up, watching the monitor as they cruised past the planets. From time to time, one or the other pointed out features of the planets and their moons but both remained otherwise silent. They got onto the trans-lift and did a quick tour of the other decks.

"Walter, as much fun as this is, how much time do we have before you pick up the others for the beginning of the shakedown cruise?"

"We've a couple more hours. Would you like to go up to the bridge for a surprise?"

Belinda smiled. "As much fun as this is, I assume that we can do more of this when you get home from the shakedown cruise. What's the surprise?"

Walter's ring shimmered. They were on the bridge.

"I never get tired of that! – instantly having things change."

"I must admit I like it too. Now, how would you like to meet my mentor?"

"Qaak? Where? How long will it take to get to where he is?"

"In *The Grace*, no time at all! Sit with me here at the helm and watch the view screen." They sat down as stars begin to streak by faster and faster, until it was all a multicolored blur. Suddenly, everything was still. There were three bright stars nearby. A large translucent sphere was ahead of them on the left. "Qaak will be here in a moment. He's dismissing his class for a break while we talk."

"How do you know? Are you talking with him telepathically?"

"Yes." Walter's mentor appeared.

"How do you do, Belinda? I've been looking forward to meeting you!" He ambled forward to grip her hand. "Walter was right! You are probably the sexiest human I've ever seen!"

Belinda blushed. "How do you do, Qaak? You're a more handsome dude than I expected!"

His eyes glowed slightly for a moment. "You are very kind. Walter chose well in choosing you to help him with his beginnings as a Gaardian."

"He's told me a little about you. Are you really more than sixty thousand Earth years old?"

"I'm afraid so. It is probably time I retired."

Belinda giggled. "No way! I've just met you! I've got to have a chance to get to know you."

"I have not had a mate in several thousand years. I would welcome another friend, however." He paused. "Walter, she is quite charming. I want you to bring her back again when you have more time, and when I can give her the attention she deserves. I will probably have a new leg before I see you again."

"New leg?" Belinda stared.

"Yes. Body parts do not last forever. On the other hand, I might go back to having just two legs for a few hundred of your years. I enjoy it. The third leg is always my oldest, and folding it under me when resting extends its life." He paused. "Belinda, it was a delight meeting you. I look forward to our next meeting. Perhaps it can be more intimate." The triped vanished before she could answer.

Belinda looked at Walter. "Fantastic!" They both smiled.

"Time to head home." The View screen flashed streaks of stars until suddenly they saw the moon.

They hugged good-bye. Walter stayed on the bridge while Belinda vanished to her quarters. Walter beamed everyone including himself to the hanger deck for an initial meeting of the crew.

10. Quzaks ["COO-zacks"]

Aboard his ship, Qaak was thoughtful, the glow of his eyes surging from time to time. As he began jumping across galaxies, he spoke to his computer. "Memo to Gaardian Center. Our three new Gaardians are ahead of schedule in their adaptations to their new lives. Their bases are well equipped, and their staffing efforts are better than we hoped for at this stage in their new journeys. Puz is having some difficulties with acceptance by his own, but Pixie's acceptance is adequate, and Walter's is both adequate and sometimes amusing. Walter has ample time to prepare his crew for their encounter with the Quzaks."

He paused, closing his eyes momentarily while his whole body seemed to glow. "The probability of love developing between Walter and Pixie seems virtually certain. As previously discussed and analyzed, such a development is unlikely to interfere with their duties. If Walter and Pixie form a union as anticipated, the likelihood of superior offspring is high. If discussion of any of this is desired, I have additional data for our next plenary meeting in two time periods. Walter's friend and Base Commander is a treasure. I shall spend more time with her at the first opportunity. I am arriving now at the Center and will rest."

Qaak was always happy to be at Gaardian Center. It was home for him most of his lifetime. With his ship docked, Qaak beamed to his quarters, which were very spacious. Spherical in shape and poised several miles above the planet's surface, Qaak's apartment faced all directions. The outer "wall" was entirely transparent. When he needed privacy, he moved closer to the core. Resting on the outer wall on his third leg, Qaak watched the arrivals and departures of various ships around him as he thought about Belinda and Walter. "Personal File. I hope that Walter's growing love for Pixie does not come into conflict with his established love with Belinda. Walter's Base Commander is very capable. In time, she may become a Gaardian herself. I am impressed with her. I wonder how we missed her family as we were searching for new Gaardian candidates. I must discuss this with Kieya. End entry."

Qaak paused. "Computer, display waiting messages."

Kieya appeared in a Gaardian mail. "Qaak, as soon as you return, come to the Conference Center. The Quzaks have accelerated their approach. Time is of the essence."

Qaak's eyes glowed as he telepathically surveyed Gaardian Center. Kieya was in the Conference Center with several others. A ring on Qaak's smallest finger of his left-hand shimmered, and Qaak was with his friends. "I just got your Gaardian mail, Kieya. What has happened?"

Qaak looked at the galactic map that was displayed before them as Kieya responded. "As you know, on their original course, they would have arrived in about two thousand time periods from now, two sectors away from Walter's. Two time periods ago, they disappeared from our scanners. Less than a time period ago, they reappeared just a few time periods beyond Walter's sector. We have been discussing alternative responses. It would be best if Waagere could help him, but he is not available. What about Pixie and Puz?"

Qaak's eyes glowed for a moment. "In that time frame, Pixie and Puz are also unavailable. I shall make myself available to Walter and his crew. I want to get to know his crew better anyway."

Waagere moved to the three-dimensional map, studying it carefully. "We have discussed that before you got here. It will be best if you assist Walter in training the crew on his ship, *The Grace*. Then you must leave and let Walter confront the Quzaks. He may be afraid, but the danger to him is minimal. His crew needs to see him acting alone."

"Agreed." Qaak paused. "I will probe train his key crew leaders. Strategy?"

Kieya spoke cautiously. "Let Walter use the procedures with which he has been trained. We have beamed some additional hidden relays to the edge of known Gaardian space adjacent to Quzak space. You should assist the Quzaks with interpretation of their encounter with us after Walter completes his mission. Once you've interpreted Gaardian policy to them, the relays will of course no longer be necessary."

"Good!" Qaak moved to join Waagere closer to the display. "Are you sure you won't join me in visiting *The Grace*? I know you like Walter and see some potential in him that I've not seen yet."

"Very well. I will go with you and observe from the ship. My presence aboard *The Grace* might add to their stress. I will come aboard only if necessary. All agreed?" After a pause, all except Waagere and Qaak vanished to their quarters. "Qaak, I'll meet you in three time periods at your port."

Qaak grunted. "Let's use your ship. I want to examine some of the artifacts you told me about."

"Very well." They vanished almost simultaneously.

+ + +

In orbit around Earth's Moon preparations were complete. As *The Grace* took off on its first cruise, there were fifty-four people on the Moon Base. With Frank's help, Belinda set up a video conference call in her quarters. "Hi Michael! Hi Karen!"

"Hi! Wow! This is terrific! I've so many questions!" Karen was jubilant. In her mid-twenties, she looked a lot like her mom.

"Yeah, Mom. Where did this equipment come from? How did it get into my apartment? I've got first-rate security." Michael was in his late twenties, and though he looked a lot like his sister, he was tanned and very rugged in appearance.

"Stop it, Michael." His younger sister had a voice that demanded respect. "I've got stuff in my room here too that just appeared out of nowhere. So, what's the story, Mom? You sure look young, and I guess you are healthy."

"Okay, you two! To save time let me tell you a few things, and then you can ask questions, okay?" They both nodded. "All right. First, I have to ask both of you something very important. Can you both promise me that you will keep it a secret that I am alive and that you are in contact with me? It is very important, because both of you would be in great danger if anyone makes a connection, between me, as one working for the Gaardian, and with you two. Do you understand?"

They both nodded. "Michael, in your intelligence work, this will be the biggest secret you will ever have to maintain, and you and Karen must be the only ones who ever know. I cannot stress that enough. Karen, with you working for the Vatican, I doubt that you will have any problems or even temptations in this regard, but Michael you could have problems. In the CIA's records on you, they have pictures of me when I married your father. They will obviously see that the way I look now and the way I looked on my wedding day are virtually identical. Michael, you are going to have to practice affirming the resemblance and dismissing it as a coincidence. Got it?"

"Right!" Michael was half smiling. "The prospect of successfully denying that you are my mother is an amusing idea, but I know how serious this is. Would you be endangered if the connection is ever made?"

"No, Michael. Both of you can rest assured that I will probably never be in any danger. On the other hand, I am officially dead anyway. If they exhume the body, they will confirm that the body is me – it's an exact duplicate except for having never been alive in the first place. Karen, do you still keep that antique hairbrush that I used to use?"

"Yes Mom."

"Good! What did you do with it after I gave it to you? Did you clean it up or wash it?"

"No, Mom. It's in a plastic bag at the bottom of my bureau. It's a keepsake."

"That's fine! Do not do anything with it. There are still a few of my hairs on it. For DNA purposes, the brush might come in handy some day, okay?"

"Okay."

Her son's CIA instincts kicked in. "What about this equipment you've sent here, Mom?"

Belinda smiled. "Don't you think I've already thought of that? Come on! As soon as we end this conference call, the equipment will disappear and return to me. Everything will come back except one thing. Do not look now, but I have placed a new digital watch on top of your pillows on your beds. It looks just like a Chronex that you would buy in a jewelry store. There is even a receipt with it, to show that you paid cash for it at a store near each of you. Wear those watches at all times from now on, okay? Anytime you want to talk to me, just tap the crystal three times, and say Belinda. I will answer as soon as I can, usually within a few seconds. If I do not answer right away, don't worry. I have the Gaardian's version of call waiting service. You can also tap it twice, say message for Belinda, and talk as long as you want. When you are finished, tap it twice again. One more thing. Do not ever try to open the watch. If anyone without your permission tries to open it, they will think it is an ordinary watch. When you get it back, however, it will no longer work as I have said. I'll know, however, that it has been tampered with, and I will replace it as soon as I can."

"Mom, there's someone at my front door. I had better answer. The Agency has me on tap today."

"Okay. Kids, I'll end this call for now. By the way, there are electronic bugs in both of your apartments. Be aware, okay? They are not from The Gaardian or me. Bye kids!" She severed the connection, and the equipment on Earth disappeared. As she got up from her chair in her apartment, Belinda went to the door and called out, "Jennifer?"

"Right here." Belinda's favorite assistant, a petite redhead in a white jump suit, was patiently waiting just outside Belinda's quarters. "You've a Gaardian mail from Qaak. In addition, I have everyone busy on that crime control project for Mexico. How was the call?"

"Just fine, Jennifer. Tell Judy I want to see her before dinner, okay?" Jennifer nodded and walked away. Belinda headed for her office.

Judy had five people to assist her in whatever tasks are assigned to her. Her office had two adjoining offices for her five assistants. Standing in the main doorway, she saw Jennifer approaching. "Yes, Jennifer?"

"Belinda says she wants to see you before dinner, okay?"

"Okay. I'm just about ready to go down and confront that drug lord in Brazil." Jennifer nodded and headed to Karen's office.

As Jennifer walked in, Karen Oreskovich was at her video console. "Hi Jennifer." Jennifer waved absentmindedly to the screen. "I'm aboard *The Grace*. Need anything?"

"I just have a question. Will we have a constant video link with *The Grace* while it's in space?"

"Most of the time there will be just one video and audio channel. Walter says that there will be 'richer' communications between the base and *The Grace* after I get used to the new equipment. I don't know how long that will take."

"Thanks! Bye" Jennifer turned and headed down the hall. As she went, she waved at Stephanie and Jim in their offices as she walked by. At the end of the hall, she stepped into Lauryn's office. It was a beehive of activity.

Lauryn had taken over some of Belinda's duties for personnel recruitment. She liked a group atmosphere, so her office space consisted of one large room with her desk and other equipment on one side, and the ten desks for her staff scattered throughout the room. She called out to Jennifer. "Hey, Jennifer, are you here about the next batch of recruits to consider?"

"Not really. I was just passing by and thought I would say hello. Why, have you got something for Belinda and me?"

"Almost! I know that we are not going to take in any newer people for six months at least, but I want to do some preliminary sorting. I should be ready in a few days. Tell Belinda that when I see her at dinner...."

Jennifer interrupted. "Wait! Belinda told me yesterday that you might say something like this. She said to remind you that Walter does not want us discussing Gaardian business during meals. Remember?"

"Right!" She stuck her tongue out at Jennifer playfully. "Okay, tell her that I'll catch her after breakfast tomorrow!"

"See ya!" Jennifer walked quickly out the door and down the hall to the office, which she shared with Belinda, and she walked up to her desk. "Have you any idea how much fun it's to work here? Lauryn just stuck her tongue out at me!" They both giggled.

+ + +

Aboard *The Grace*, Karen had fifteen people assisting her with communications and personnel issues. She was giving them a brief tour to acquaint them. "Here, next to the bridge we have a communications center where most of you will work at least part of the time. We monitor communications on all three of the planets that are aware of our Walter's existence. We also monitor the more primitive communications on several dozen other planets. Over here," she pointed, "we monitor our scanning satellites. All of them are automated to provide us information only when either it is crucial or when we request it. After the meeting on the hanger deck, your shifts will begin as scheduled. Each shift will have one person doing routine checks of the satellites. We should be checking every satellite at least once every ten days." She paused to look out the doorway. "Hi Jody!"

"Hi!" On her way to the bridge, she paused. Jody had the biggest staff. "When you see Walter, will you tell him that I'm almost ready, and that I'll be down in engineering?"

"Okay. See ya later!"

Jody waved and kept walking. On the bridge, Jody approached Debbie quietly. Debbie was obviously concentrating on something in her display. "Debbie?"

Debbie, as the science officer, had forty-six people to assist her both with research and with analysis of data. "Hi Jody! What's up?"

"Sorry to interrupt! Once we are underway, would you have Karen feed me a sampling of the data you're gathering? There is a monitoring section on the port side of engineering that could receive it. I'd like to see more than just where we're going and where we've been, okay?"

"Sure! I'll set up a rotating sampling of all of our sensors. Is that enough?"

"Great! I've got to get back to engineering. I am supposed to meet Walter down there before the meeting on the hanger deck, and that starts in about eight minutes. See you there. Bye!" She got on the trans-lift, and the doors closed.

In the medical clinic, Butch had a staff of eight, including five nurses and two excellent physician's assistants who could eventually become doctors. "After the meeting, I want all of you back here. We need to work out our shift schedules." As they went down the corridor, Butch stopped to pick up John at the astral-navigation center. John had a staff of twelve. "How are things going, John?"

"Great! A couple of weeks and we should be a well-oiled machine. Right now, I see another Gaardian ship approaching. I wonder if Walter is expecting them." John beckoned his team to follow them out into the corridor. Together they headed for the hanger deck.

"Walter knows everything that's going on. We may not have a couple of weeks, John. He tells me he is accelerating the training schedules. Even Qaak is going to help. That's probably Qaak's ship we saw on the monitor."

John whistled as they turned a corner and went through large automatic doors. Just inside they spotted Ken and Toby, and they walked over to join them. Ken and Toby both were independent operators with no staff assistants.

On the hanger deck, Karen tweaked the controls of the three-dimensional video projectors as they all watched. "This short multimedia presentation showing star charts, galaxy pictures, and a description of our initial shakedown journey are self-explanatory. It lasts only a few minutes. As you know, we are already underway. The growing red line on the star chart shows our journey thus far. The pictures being displayed are of the galaxies we have already passed through."

She paused as the display changed. "Now you are seeing pictures of galaxies we're going to pass through during the next twenty-four hours. Our officers are stationed throughout the hanger deck. As the show continues, please feel to approach any of the officers with questions you may have. This is an informal meeting, so feel free to ask anything you wish from any officer."

Walter circulated and heard parts of the questions and answers. He approached Debbie and listened with a slight smile on his face. "Yes, gravity is controlled throughout the ship. The default gravity for all areas is Earth Normal. Some of you may wish to try sleeping in Moon Normal -- particularly when we are on our way home to our Base."

Walter moved on to listen to Butch. "You can come to the clinic at any time. There will always be someone on duty. Most of the time, however, you just have to touch your badge and say, 'Medical please.'"

Against one wall, Walter listened to John as he pointed to a viewer. "The 3-D viewers throughout the ship will normally display the ship's view forward, but just touch the control, and you can request almost anything."

Ken was in his element. "Yes, I am the ship's counselor, and I double as chaplain."

Walter began to make his way to the platform where Karen had stood. As he passed Toby, he smiled. "... You will find me almost everywhere. I'm the troubleshooter and ombudsman."

Walter stepped up onto the platform previously occupied by Karen and held up his hand to get their attention. The three-dimensional display vanished. Conversation faded quickly. "I am sure that everyone will have more questions as we get under way. For the next five days, all one hundred eighty-six of us are going to get used to working with each other here on *The Grace*." Walter paused, and the three-dimensional display reappeared, showing an almost bizarre-looking sector of space. "Less than one hundred twenty hours from now we will be confronting our first adversary." Walter paused again for murmuring. "We are not returning to the Moon base after a short cruise as originally planned. Additional data coming in means that time is short. I know I can depend upon all of you. During the next fifty to sixty hours, we are going to need to work to become a cohesive team. This is no longer a shakedown cruise or a pleasure cruise. I am confident that we will handle the situation with no significant problems. You will be working long hours. Keep alert. Your schedules are now posted in your quarters with my apologies to the junior officers. Initially at least, senior officers are the only ones that have private quarters. On average, I expect everyone to get six to seven hours of sleep out of every twenty-four. Be patient with *The Grace* and with each other. That's all for now."

Karen and her team headed for the bridge. She turned aside and entered her cabin as the others continued on. She sat down at her desk before her view screen. She murmured, "I wonder if I could arrange to get Qaak to help me understand this stuff?" In a normal voice, she continued, "Computer, connect me with Qaak."

"Connection in approximately forty seconds."

"Dim cabin lights to forty percent." The lights dimmed as Karen gazed intently at the screen. It remained blank.

Qaak appeared less than a meter away. "What can I do for you Karen?" He seemed comfortable leaning on his third leg with his other two crossed.

She stared. "I was not expecting you in person! You surprised me!"

"I suspected you would be seeking my help, so I anticipated your request. Tell me, Karen, do you trust me?"

She smiled. She definitely liked Qaak. "Do I trust you? Of course! If I couldn't, I should not be on this ship! I thought you were going to ask me what my questions were!"

"I know you have many questions, but answers would lead to more questions. That would not be good use of our time. I'll teach you through direct mental contact - it is much faster."

Karen's eyes grew slightly larger. "Direct mental contact? How?"

"Lie down on your bunk with your knees and head elevated." Karen moved to the bunk and reclined as instructed, using pillows to make herself more comfortable. "You are not going to sleep, but you need to close your eyes. Do not try to analyze what happens. Just go along for the ride."

Karen closed her eyes as Qaak's fingers touched her face. In a dream-like state, Karen saw thousands of images, heard a jumble of sounds, and experienced tastes, smells, and other sensory experiences as well.

"Open your eyes." Karen seemed almost surprised she was still in her cabin. Qaak reassured her. "Do you have any questions?"

"I feel like I have just graduated from seven or eight years of college! Actually, everything is quite clear! I understand even better than I thought I could! How long did I have my eyes closed?"

"In your time, one hundred ninety-two seconds. How do you feel?"

"One hundred ninety-two seconds? Wow! I feel great!"

"If there is nothing else for now, I shall go. Walter has made an excellent choice in choosing you - I am going to enjoy working with you." Qaak smiled.

"Thank you! Would you join me in the view lounge for some refreshment?"

"No, thank you, but perhaps some other time. God be with you. "Qaak vanished.

Murmuring, she replied, "God be with you too, Qaak. That was an odd farewell for an alien. Alien? No! I'm the alien out here." Getting up, she left her cabin and turned to her left. As she got into the trans-lift, Jody was there. Excited, Karen could hardly contain herself. "Where are you headed, Jody? I'm taking a break from a session with Qaak and headed for the view lounge. You?"

As the doors of the trans-lift closed, Jody's face and voice showed surprise. "Me too! I had an absolutely thrilling experience from Qaak, and I am digesting it. I called for Qaak just before the meeting in the hanger. How long did you take with him?"

"He said about a hundred ninety-two seconds. Seconds! How about you?"

Jody giggled. "I was almost late for the meeting. My session lasted for more than eleven minutes, but it seemed like an eternity."

"Wow! And I thought I had learned a lot!" The trans-lift doors opened at the view lounge, and they stepped out.

Jody responded as they entered the lounge. "I asked Qaak if Walter knew all the stuff I knew. He said that he had taught me enough to get me started, and I that I had learned about six percent of what he had taught Walter in my field of expertise."

The two women stopped for drinks at the synthesizer station and went to a window where Debbie, Stephanie, and Toby were already sitting back and watching stars go by.

Debbie was mellow. "Hey, strangers! What have you two been up to?"

Jody was still excited. "We've been having meetings of our minds with Qaak. I met with him before the meeting with Walter in the hanger, and Karen just now finished."

Debbie laughed. "Isn't Qaak a trip? If he weren't a few thousand years too old for me, I think I might try to seduce him!" They all laughed. "Well! Look who's coming to join the party!"

Butch was approaching with a chocolate sundae, grinning. "Easy, Debbie! You and I can flirt another time! Right now, I want to indulge myself for a few minutes before getting back to the clinic."

"Speaking of getting back, I'd better get back to engineering. Now that I have Qaak's training to back me up, I need to start rehearsing various scenarios. See ya later!" Jody ambled off to the trans-lift.

Debbie was still mellow. "I'm still thinking about what Jody said. If she knows only six percent of what Walter knows regarding engineering, his training must have been long and rigorous."

Butch paused between spoonfuls of his chocolate sundae. "You've got that right. Walter's training was all night while he was sleeping every night, starting when he was a little boy until a short time ago."

Debbie whistled softly and smiled. "The more I hear about that man the more he interests me - and not just as our leader."

Karen smiled too. "You'd better get in line. Belinda has known him for most of her life. They met in grammar school and did not separate until after high school. If she wants him, she has the edge."

Debbie was thoughtful and had a wistful smile. "Maybe, maybe not. Belinda is not out here while we are on *The Grace*. That could give one of us the edge - at least while we are out here. I don't have time to think about that right now though. I have organized teams for basic scientific research, astral navigation, and biological research. Butch, I need to talk to you about coordinating my biological research team with your department."

Butch looked at her thoughtfully. "Maybe we can do that after we have our encounter with the armada in a few days. Right now, I am rehearing my staff for various emergency scenarios." Butch got up, dropping his dish and spoon into the disposal slot next to the table, where there was a subtle flash of light. He turned before going. "I'm getting back to work."

The others nodded, indicating they needed to get back to work as well. They all got up and headed for the trans-lift. One by one, they got off at three different stops. Finally, the trans-lift stopped at the bridge. As Butch stepped out, John was at the helm, nodding and answering questions from the other pilots. "...as I observe each of you getting better I will allocate time with Qaak for those who are doing the best work." John paused as he saw Butch. "What's up, Butch?"

Butch came to a halt at the helm, joining the others. "I think I have a way to help both of us accomplish some of our objectives. I have assembled a simulator in the clinic that tests how input from our senses is processed in our minds. I was thinking that if you and I design some flight plan simulations designed to stimulate all the senses, maybe we can accomplish some Qaak-style training right here aboard *The Grace*."

John grinned. "Great idea! Let me get a few hours sleep so I am fresh. How about meeting in the clinic at 0400?"

"Great! I need a few hours as well. See you then." Butch turned and headed back to the trans-lift.

As John got up from the helm, he turned it over to one of the others, indicating to her to sit down at the helm. "I'm going to get some sleep. I want all of you to study up both on your navigational skills and, if you have time, your knowledge of our weapons systems."

She nodded, and John headed for the trans-lift. He waived at Toby in the Captain's chair.

Toby touched a spot on the chair's arm. "Bridge to Ken Lyman."

"Hey Toby! I'll be up there in a few minutes!"

He paused, and then he touched the same spot. "Toby to Qaak! Have a safe journey!" In the main viewer, Waagere's ship began to pull away. After a short distance, it vanished.

11. Relocations

Inside his ship, Waagere was intense in his enthusiasm. "I am glad I have been here, watching! Walter has a terrific crew! While you were doing the probe training, I scanned the rest of Walter's crew. He has chosen some humans I would never have dreamed of choosing. I want to study Walter's gifts. He has a way of seeing potential in his fellow beings that is remarkable."

"Yes." Qaak shared his enthusiasm, though more subtly. "Walter calls them his pastoral instincts. Those so-called instincts may be related to his profession in his first life, but it's more than that."

"How so?"

"He is future-oriented, and directs his insight and inspiration toward understanding himself and thereby, human nature. His work mirrors his integrity -- reflects his inner ideals."

"But he is quite pragmatic, isn't he?" Waagere talked as he touched the controls.

"Yes, but there is more to it than that. He understands the complexities within people. His inner circle of leaders aboard *The Grace* and on his base reflects the fact that he would rather have a few close friends than be part of a big party."

"But Walter is not anti-social."

"No. Definitely not." Qaak was thoughtful. "He is quiet yet persistent, and determined in his efforts toward long-term goals. That sense of vision is useful to him as a Gaardian."

"How so?"

"When he works toward his vision, he wins cooperation rather than demands it. That is crucial to his leadership style, and it's very productive, as you've seen with other Gaardians."

"Yes. I see the same quality in Pixie and in you, but not in Puz, or in other Gaardians like Kieya and myself."

"Yes ... and speaking of Pixie, when Walter becomes attracted to someone special, he prefers this one deep relationship to many superficial ones. That was true of his relationship with Belinda when they were much younger. This depth is only partially communicated outwards. I think ...."

Waagere interrupted. "I've been studying Belinda's file. Walter's life would have been very different if they had formed a union."

"True. If Walter had married Belinda, he probably would not have had the same sense of what he calls pastoral vision. Paradoxically, Walter tries to watch out for becoming blinded by the idealism of his vision or focusing only on his ideas."

"He has done as well in that respect as in choosing his crew." As they came to a halt above Gaardian, Waagere turned away slightly from the controls, looking both at Qaak and at the planet below. "Let's talk about some of his crew."

"Yes, but first let me make two more points about Walter. First, he is loyal and instills loyalty in others. His crew aboard *The Grace* and at his moon base can depend upon him to be patient and fair with them. He seldom loses control of his emotions, and when he does, it is usually quite productive. Also, he can lose out if he doesn't act assertively, and he's reluctant to intrude on others with his ideas, but as a Gaardian, he seems to be able effectively to control that tendency." Qaak paused. "Do you have a particular crew member in mind for discussion?"

Waagere was thoughtful. "The one called Debbie Schaffner is an astonishing choice as the science officer. It is usually better to go for wisdom -- by choosing those that are older, and regressing them. By human standards, she is very attractive. Obviously, Walter sees beyond that. She is one of his best choices."

Qaak chuckled. "Actually, Belinda was largely responsible for that choice. Belinda saw her on what humans call television – two-dimensional video with audio – and Belinda's intuition led her to choose Debbie as an early choice.

Interestingly, Debbie is one of two people on the crew who have a chance to supplant Pixie in terms of romance."

"Who's the other one?"

"The other one is Jody Dunn, the chief engineer."

Waagere turned to face Qaak more directly. "She is extremely interesting. If she were galactically and genetically closer, I would really take an interest in her. According to her profile, when Walter and Belinda first saw her, her physical and mental capacities were severely diminished by disease. She is a most remarkable choice."

"Yes, she is. There are circumstances that may occur to put her in line for Gaardian training. I suspect Walter has a similar idea."

"I'd like to study two others that we haven't discussed. The ones called Keeta and Butch." Waagere looked out at the planet below. "Was Keeta's species not sufficiently ready when you were considering candidates on Walter's earth?"

Qaak responded softly, almost gently. "Keeta is the result of a genetic accident."

"I've not studied her file yet." Waagere turned back to face Qaak fully. "What happened?"

"About the time that Kieya and I were observing Walter's birth, the last war on Keeta's planet was raging. Both sides were sure they were right. One side decided to use biological warfare."

Waagere stared. "I didn't know her planet was so primitive!"

Qaak continued to speak quietly. "Actually, it was not primitive at the time – it was more advanced than Walter's planet. A mentally unbalanced leader developed and launched the biological warfare. Ironically, and somewhat predictably, it backfired. Both the leader and everyone on his side of the conflict were wiped out. Only a few of their enemies were killed. On the side of Keeta's forebears, everyone had ingested a protective agent that worked throughout their systems. The warfare agent and the defense agent combined in their systems in an unexpected way. There was a genetic transformation of the entire population, making transparent pigmentation dominant and intellectual genius dominant as well. Keeta is the product of two generations of genius parentage combined with a perfection of the ability to control pigmentation."

"Gaardian records show that combination to be extremely rare. No wonder you recommended her to Walter."

"Yes, but the man who calls himself Butch is rare in another way."

"I see his work in *The Grace*'s clinic." Waagere almost seemed to purr. "He may be a doctor I can turn to if I've symptoms – however rarely. Though he does not speak of it, he sees body and mind as functions of the spirit. That is a special genius."

"True. Interestingly, it was the one called Debbie Schaffner that made him stand out in Belinda's sorting. A good happenstance."

"Let us continue this tomorrow."

"Yes." They both vanished.

+ + +

Aboard *The Grace*, it was almost time for the confrontation with the Quzaks. As the trans-lift's doors opened, Ken Lyman stepped out onto the bridge. "I must have read your mind, Toby! What's up?"

Toby was thoughtful. "I've been circulating throughout the ship, lending a hand wherever needed. Walter sure has me pegged – I love the variety."

"So what's the problem?"

"I'm seeing several. You may have noticed some of them. Everybody has been pushing hard, and that has to be expected. One of my concerns is Jody."

"Is this a personal interest?"

They both smiled. "Not at this point. I know she has her eye on someone else. The thing is, she is a workaholic, and friction may develop if she pushes her team as hard as she pushes herself. You might want to keep an eye on her – in your capacity as the counselor." They both grinned as he emphasized the last point. "You might also check in with Butch from time to time. It is hard to tell just how tired he gets because very little shows in his face. I've not seen him show interest in any recreational or diversionary activities so far."

"That's true for most of us. One of the things I am doing these first few days is help people develop a balanced routine, and it is not just the officers who have this problem. ...I found one interesting item in the astrophysics lab. Walter has a game up there. It's some kind of racing through the galaxy thing, but I cannot figure out how he controls it."

"I'll take a look – it sounds like it might be a fun way to get inside his head a bit!" Toby touched the button on the chair's arm again. "Bridge to the Captain."

Walter's voice was calm. "I'm on my way. Your shift is up in about forty seconds. I'll be there." As Toby turned the chair to look at the trans-lift, suddenly Walter was beside him. Toby jumped as Walter said, "You're relieved, Toby."

"Captain on the bridge!"

"As you were." As Toby got up, Walter eased into the chair. "Get some sleep, Toby. You too, Ken. I am going to need you both at your most rested and sharpest in a little over nine hours. We will be encountering a species that calls themselves the Quzaks ["COOZ-acks"], or at least, that is the best way we can pronounce it.

Toby was intense. "Anything more we can know right now and pass on to the crew?"

Walter paused. "Okay. Briefly." Everyone on the bridge turned to him. "A galactically short distance away the invading armada is approaching in Earth's direction. The flagship is about twenty times the size of most of the other twenty-three thousand ships that are traveling with it. It is a lot more massive than *The Grace* in almost every respect. While most of the ships have a crew of eight, and a few larger vessels have crews of five hundred, the flagship's crew is nearly two thousand. The Quzaks are remarkably similar to humans in appearance except most are not over five feet tall. They have gray skin, with males distinguished by a slightly blue tint and the females having a slightly green tint. The females tend to be slightly stronger and more aggressive than the males and have three breasts."

Toby whistled. "Wow! We're up against all of them?"

"Absolutely." Walter was calm and relaxed. "From what we know of them, we should have no problem sending them back home. For our crew, we need to observe and record everything. The whole crew needs to learn how Gaardian police actions work." He paused. "Now get yourselves something to eat and hit your bunks – no detours, okay?"

"Right!" They said it almost together.

The stars on the main viewer continued streaking by.

As Toby and Ken were getting off the trans-lift on the bridge a few hours later, Walter's ring shimmered to change the main display. Quzak leaders were gathering in a conference room of the flagship. They had no way of knowing that their meeting was being seen and recorded on board The Grace. At Walter's direction, Karen was also broadcasting the meeting to Gaardian Base on Earth's moon. On the bridge at her station, Karen touched a key. "Belinda, is this coming through as expected?"

On Earth, Belinda was acting as commentator and host, broadcasting the intergalactic feed to Earth. "Loud and clear. Translating circuitry is carrying the signal to every country on Earth in their native tongues."

+ + +

On the invaders' flagship, dozens quickly filed in and took chairs around a large table. The Commander slapped the table to get their attention. "We're expecting to reach the inhabited planet called Earth in nine paks. We have detected the approach of one ship, and their approach will intercept us in three paks." About fifty officers nodded acknowledgement of what they all knew. "The little ship is no threat to us, of course, but it will be interesting to see what they have to say when they get here." There was some laughter. "Does anyone have any questions about our strategy? This conquest should be just as easy as that of Kippa or Alaadda. We will let this little ship that is approaching us say what they have to say or make their feeble attempt to slow us down, and then we will destroy them." There were nods and grunts of enthusiasm.

Walter suddenly appeared beside the commander. "That is not likely."

In the sudden turmoil, several of the Quzaks advance toward Walter but find themselves back in their seats before they can take more than a step. The Commander spoke: "Who are you?"

"I am the Gaardian of this sector of space. Think of me as an intergalactic police officer. You have two choices. You can voluntarily turn your armada around and go home under your own power, or I can send you home in disgrace and dishonor. The choice is yours. Contact your home world if you wish."

"Do you think that you and your puny ship can overpower our twenty-three thousand ships?" The Commander and several of the others laughed.

Walter showed no emotion. "As of right now, I am halting all of your ships right here. If you attempt anything other than to turn around, you will have made a serious mistake." Walter vanished.

Aboard The Grace, Walter reappeared on the bridge. Karen had the conference room still on the bridge display. She allowed the transmission to continue to the Base and on to Earth. When Walter reappeared on the bridge, Toby, in the captain's chair, stood and said, "Captain on the Bridge!"

"At ease, everyone. This is not a military vessel, though thank you Toby for the recognition." Walter turned to look at the three-dimensional view screen.

Aboard the flagship of the invasion force, the Commander and the other leaders were furious. "Return to your stations, target that puny little ship, and wait for my orders." He turned to the female seated next to him, his recently acquired consort. Ooza ["OOZE-uh"] was slightly taller with refined classic features, light blue hair, and a slender figure accentuated by a form-fitting uniform. She gazed affectionately at him as he spoke to her. "Ooza, there is no way that puny little ship has the power to keep us from proceeding. As soon as most of our ships have that creature and his crew targeted, tell them to fire!"

Aboard *The Grace*, Walter turned to his chief engineer at her station. "Jody, have *The Grace* absorb and store all of their weapons' energy, then dump it into that blue star we passed earlier."

"Right."

On the viewer, the Quzak female gestured with her hands within a display in front of her. "Fire!" She paused. "Strange! Our weapons do not affect it. All the energy was absorbed."

"What?" Send a message that we all will proceed at the maximum speed to our destination when I give the signal." The female touched the display in front of her.

"Ready!"

"Now!"

The commander never could have imagined what happened next. Aboard *The Grace*, Walter's ring shimmered.

For the Quzaks, space around them blinked.

Seen on *The Grace*'s viewer, a line appeared and expanded to become a door into blackness. The twenty-three thousand ships seemed to fall into the blackness. Then the door closed to a line again before the line shrank to a dot and disappeared. It all happened silently in about ten seconds. Walter and his crew watched the armada vanish.

"Where'd they go?" John was dumbfounded. "This is almost surreal!"

"Yeah, what happened?" Debbie stared at the screen.

Walter was calm. "They're home, adrift without fuel near their home planet. Even if they decide to come back, it will take them months to refuel, and three more years to get back here at their highest speed. They will probably think twice before coming back here."

Mouths were open, but few sounds came. Finally, Debbie regained her composure. "Walter, am I going to know how you did that?"

Walter was thoughtful. "I must admit that even with my Gaardian training, I am amazed at how quickly things have gone down. I can explain some of it over dinner. Some of it I must analyze. The short version is that Gaardian technology opened a portal in space-time, and we let them fall through it. Debbie, it was a variation on what we do when we jump across galaxies rather than travel through them. The difference was that it happened not just to our small ship and us, but also to more than twenty-three thousand ships, many of them larger than ours. Many times, Qaak has reminded me that size and distance are relatively unimportant, but this was amazing even to me." Walter paused with an amused smile. "Now, anybody else hungry? I am starved! John, you have the bridge. Toby, relieve him in an hour so he can get some dinner too." At that point, Karen cut the transmission.

+ + +

At the Moon Base, Belinda giggled before making some final comments. "This concludes this Gaardian broadcast for the planets in this sector of Gaardian space." In the auditorium, all the crew on the base had been watching on the giant view screen, and they let out a cheer. Comments were numerous.

Lauryn was enthusiastic. "That was better than the best movie I saw last year!"

Jim laughed. "Funny too!"

It was getting late. Some went for a swim, but most headed for their quarters.

+ + +

At Gaardian Center, Qaak observed events from his apartment on a three-dimensional display. "Memo to Gaardians. We have unexpectedly stepped up to a new level of involvement in intergalactic affairs. We have all observed what happened to the Quzaks. I am doing the follow-up interpretation. ... We know that Walter was the only Gaardian in position to accomplish what happened. The results, however, are beyond his training and experience. It is illogical. Our analysis must be accurate. I will welcome observations when the interpretation is complete. End memo."

+ + +

In another galaxy, thousands of Quzaks were recovering from shock and rushing to deal with the unexpected crisis. The Commander was dumbfounded. "Where are we?"

His consort touched a disk below her ear. "About twenty-five thousand argeets from Base One." His consort, agitated, tried to hug him.

"What?"

"We seem to be back where we started, my love, only with one difference."

"What's that?" He collapsed into a chair next to her.

"None of us has any fuel." She gazed at a view screen in front of her. "Reports from the sub-commanders say that all the ships are running on battery power and drifting toward one of our two suns. If we see that ugly 'Gaardian' again let me eat him piece by piece until he dies. I'll throw the rest to our gomands!"

The Commander grunted. "Not before I cut out his eyes. We are doomed! Without fuel, we have no way to get back to base. Battery power won't transport five percent of our troops back to base."

She touched the disk below her ear again. "There's a message coming in from Base One, love."

"Put it through." He gazed at the screen in front of them, and three Superiors appeared. "I do not know what has happened!"

The one on the left, a male with many decorations on his uniform, spoke soberly and solemnly. "We do, commander. We have had a conversation with what is known as Gaardian Center. We were told that our mission to that little planet called The Earth was unacceptable. A creature named Qaak told us that our armada would be returning shortly."

"How did we respond?" said the Commander, edgy.

The one on the right, also a male, but with fewer decorations, spoke angrily. "We told this creature calling himself Qaak that after we conquered The Earth that we would come after his Gaardians. His answer seemed peculiar. He simply said, 'Not likely.' When I started to respond, I suddenly found that I could not breathe. I looked around at the others here and found that they could not breathe either."

"What happened then?" The Commander's voice was lower.

The superior in the middle, a female with high and prominent cleavage provocatively displayed, had cold fury in her voice as she shook her fist. "The creature Qaak told us he would count to three before letting us breathe again. He counted, and then as we began to breathe, he told us that our armada would be returning without fuel. When we told him that was unacceptable, he said it was not negotiable." She looked at the others. "Then he gave us instructions."

"Instructions?"

"We have reopened Base Seventy-two. All personnel will be transported there in a micro-pak or two by these beings who call themselves Gaardians."

"What? Where are they?"

The female superior looked at the other two, before speaking with the superiority of command. "Based upon our preliminary calculations, we could reach them at your flagship's maximum speed in about Fifty-four thousand paks. We will see you at Base Seventy-two in twelve mini-paks. That's all." The screen went dark.

"I'll be culled!" The Commander was furious and paced back and forth. "Pass the word, Ooza, to the other ships. Tell them to shut down all unnecessary systems and wait for transport." His consort snarled, touched his cheek lightly with her fingers, and vanished through a nearby doorway. The Commander stared out the portal into space as one of their suns slowly came into view. Aloud he said to himself, "What's next?"

As if on cue, space vanished. The huge flagship, along with the entire armada, appeared on the ground at Base Seventy-two. The Commander's mouth dropped open.

Back at Quzak's Base 1, Qaak was on a view screen, speaking again to the three Superiors. "We are placing your armada on the ground at Base Seventy-two. Their fuel has been placed in Base Seventy-two storage. In this particular operation, you have not lost one Quzak or one piece of equipment. We have also conserved your fuel. We owe you nothing. I must warn you, however. If you make any attempt at reprisal, you will lose everything in your attempt." A small rectangular object appeared on the desk in front of the Superiors. Qaak spoke again. "In front of you is a summary of Gaardian guidelines for acceptable intergalactic behavior. In the future, you may encounter us again. It makes no difference if you run into either the same Gaardian or another one. That Gaardian will know that you are now informed of these guidelines. We do not have any desire to take away the freedoms you enjoy as a species. Since you have the ability to travel between galaxies, there are limits prescribed by Intergalactic Law. Someday one or more of your species will be sufficiently ready to become Gaardians. Meanwhile, you are expected to respect Intergalactic Law, regardless." Qaak paused briefly. "Each Gaardian is carefully and thoroughly trained. Their word is law. All Gaardian activity is monitored carefully. If one of them acts in an inappropriate manner, we punish our own. Do you have anything to say in response?"

The Superiors looked at one another. "We will study this."

"Do that." Qaak severed the connection.

The Superiors looked at each other quizzically. The female spoke. "Let's transport to Base Seventy-two. We need to know exactly what happened out there!"

+ + +

At Gaardian center, Qaak was thoughtful as he talked to Kieya. "That's a new record! More than twenty-three thousand ships and crews over a distance equal nearly to the breadth of Gaardian territory!"

"How did he do it?" asked Kieya.

"I don't know. I'll not press for that now. He is still new and needs to finish getting organized." Qaak paused and reflected. "Soon – yes, soon!"

"Could he have already succeeded in improving Gaardian technology?"

"Walter is very creative. The two sides of his brain are relatively balanced, but he has a larger node near the rear at the center. Few of his species have ever had that kind of brain configuration. Do you remember watching those musicians Johann Sebastian Bach, Wolfgang Amadeus Mozart, Ludwig van Beethoven, and Claude Debussy? Do you remember observing Leonardo da Vinci and Albert Einstein, George Washington Carver and Martin Luther King Jr.?"

"Yes – they all had that enlarged node. It is an interesting feature in human development. It must be genetically recessive. It does not happen very often. Remember when we first started recording humans in detail, we saw the same enlargement of that node in Socrates, Confucius, and – most astoundingly – Jesus."

"Yes, Walter may have improved Gaardian technology. When though?"

12. Christmas

Belinda enjoyed setting up the banquet. She had planned to expand the conference room for such occasions, but Debbie had offered her home in Hollywood – it had been mostly empty since she had joined the team. As they appeared with Frank in the large living room and looked around, Debbie ran a finger through the accumulated dust on an end table. "It's been about a year since I was last here. Ugh! Frank?" He had it spotlessly clean in a blink.

Belinda was thoughtful. "Debbie, if we move some of the furniture we can make room for most of the tables, but I have an idea. What do you think of temporarily removing the wall between the living room and the study? It would give us more room. We could put the head table next to the fireplace."

"Frank, can you do your magic here in my house?" The air seemed to shimmer briefly as the wall disappeared. Then the furniture seemed to melt to the sides of the newly created larger room and round tables appeared with white linen tablecloths. "Thank you, Frank, I like the white linens."

"Frank, did Walter have China and stemware in his apartment in Oakland? Did he keep the things I remember him inheriting from his parents?" Belinda smiled as eight place settings of China and crystal appeared at each table, and fourteen identical place settings appeared on a large head table near the fireplace. "Wow! Walter has good taste! I should not be surprised - his Mom loved to entertain. When we were growing up, I was over there for dinner a number of times - dinners were really special in that house."

Frank turned to her. "What about candles, salt, pepper, and sugar?"

"If I know Walter he had those things to match the crystal." The tables were then completed with candles and other necessities.

Debbie began smiling. "I just had another idea! I just realized that this is to be a Christmas Eve party!"

"That's right! We've been so wrapped up in the confrontation with the Quzaks that I forgot!"

Debbie was emphatic. "Let's make this a Christmas celebration. Frank, how about decorating with variations on Walter's parents' Christmas decorations?" There was a shimmer, and the entire house was transformed with copies of the original decorations and place settings.

Debbie whistled. "Wow! I'm impressed!"

Belinda moved about, looking at the tables, and was equally awed and grinning. "This brings back memories of Christmases when Walter and I were kids! It's great!"

"If you don't mind I would like to have this catered. I know we can synthesize the whole thing, but I have friends who have a fabulous restaurant about two miles from here, and it would definitely be special for Christmas Eve."

Belinda turned to the android. "Frank, will you see to it that anyone not belonging to our teams have mental blocks so that they don't look at the people that they are serving?"

Frank nodded. "They will look at faces in the kitchen but nowhere else in the house. I will also plant substitute memories."

"Debbie, call your friends and set it up for tomorrow night. Will that be too soon?"

"I don't think so - the chef I am thinking of owes me a favor. Besides, I will pay them triple their normal rates."

"Triple?"

"Yes. Double can keep most people silent. Triple is special. She will only ask people that she can absolutely trust."

"She?"

Debbie turned to a nearby telephone. After punching eleven numbers, she paused before speaking. "Can I speak to Dawn please? It's Debbie Schaffner." Debbie turned to Belinda and Frank. "Her name is Dawn. You will never again have better food!" She glanced down at the telephone. "Dawn, this is Debbie!" She listened to her friend. "Thank you! Could you fix dinner for me tomorrow night? I know it is short notice. Figure on about two hundred fifty people, plus your crew. They will have their own tables and their own dining room. I will have the recreation room fixed up for them. I will leave the menu to you. I want a banquet of your very, very best, and I am paying triple." She winked at Belinda. "Yes, we both know what that means. The house will be open at noon. Dinner is at 7:00." She paused, as her friend confirmed the date and time. "I really appreciate it, my dear friend! Bye!" Debbie suddenly looked thoughtful.

"What are you thinking, Debbie?" Debbie hesitated. "Come on, what's on your mind?"

"I was just thinking of inviting outsiders."

"Outsiders?"

"Yes."

"Who do you have in mind?"

"I think we ought to invite at least Paula Rutledge. She has just recently gotten engaged to a nice guy, and he could come along. I think the other reporters we had at the base could come with their husbands or boyfriends. We could tell them that there will be no cameras or recordings allowed. We can also give each of the women the option of bringing another reporter and escort with them, so long as they understand the rules." Debbie turned to the android. "Frank, you can see to it that hidden cameras and microphones or any other recording equipment they bring doesn't work."

Frank nodded. Belinda was thoughtful. "Fantastic! Go ahead and invite them." She turned to Frank. "I think we're done here for now, Frank." She turned back to Debbie. "Let's get back to the base."

Their surroundings changed, and Frank vanished as the women walked across the atrium and into the communications center. Lauryn was sitting at a console when they walked in. "Lauryn, pass the word to everyone on base that the crew of *The Grace* will be here tomorrow morning. Make sure that everyone knows there is a Christmas Eve banquet tomorrow evening at Debbie's house on Earth. Dress is casual, but sharp and festive."

Lauryn nodded, typed at her keyboard, and then began to stare blankly.

Belinda paused for a moment and then continued. "Also, get a hold of the reporters who were here for the interview. They can come with their husbands or boyfriends. Tell them that there will be no cameras or recordings allowed. Each of the women has the option of bringing another reporter and an escort with them."

Lauryn continued to stare. "They're coming back tomorrow? It will be Christmas Eve! When will they get here?"

"Walter wants the crew joining him in a bit of star gazing and planet watching on the way back. It could be as early as midnight and as late as noon!" Sounds of a commotion came from the pool and recreation area. Belinda and Lauryn headed that way. As they entered the lounge, Walter appeared. Belinda smiled and walked over to him. "Walter! You're early! Welcome home!" Belinda gave Walter a hug and a quick kiss on the cheek.

Lauryn waited patiently. "We thought you were not going to be here until tomorrow!" She also gave him a hug and planted a very brief but moist kiss on his lips.

Walter smiled, first at Lauryn and then at Belinda. "Everyone was anxious to get back, so I showed John how to hop across a galaxy or two a little faster. Right now, I am glad to be back on solid ground again. I'm sure going to sleep tonight!"

Belinda took the tone of a doting mother. "How about a swim?"

"I'm not in the mood for a swim, but I think I'll go for a soak in the hot and cold whirlpool." They walked to the pool area. As they walked to the whirlpool, their clothing instantly changed to swimsuits. Around the corner came Debbie in a black bikini, with Jim in white trunks.

"Can we join you?" They walked over to a large pool of whirling steamy water.

As they got into the warm water, Walter turned his face upward to speak. "Our usual program."

They all found places around the perimeter of the pool as the water swirled more vigorously. Some of them closed their eyes.

Debbie calmly called across the swirling waters. "What program is this thing following?"

"Over the next few minutes the water temperature increases. When you hear the chime sound, in less than ten seconds, the water drops to five degrees centigrade." They enjoyed the soothing warmth, and some of them were smiling. Then the chime sounded. All of them murmured expressions of satisfaction and pleasure as they got out and were instantly dried off. They headed for their quarters.

+ + +

Christmas Eve evening, the Hollywood police were on alert because of activity at Debbie's home. Through their binoculars, the only person the police recognized was Debbie. Frank was invisibly watching the perimeter. The police kept their distance, even when the journalists and their escorts arrived.

Belinda greeted the reporters as they arrived in the foyer and pointed the way to the expanded living room. In the kitchen, Debbie talked to Dawn, who in turn gestured to others on her kitchen crew. "I brought about half of the restaurant's menu with me. There is prime rib, rack of lamb, halibut, lobster, and crab, along with smaller amounts of poultry and vegetarian fare. I think you will like it. I assume your special friend is here, so in his honor, I fixed some mincemeat pie with rum sauce. I also arranged for some pastries from Franz American bakery in Santa Barbara.

"I have learned that the bakery was founded by one of Walter's forebears on his mother's side, though it's owned by others now." Debbie reached into a pocket and pulled out a slip of paper. "Here's $25,000. Let me know when you have a final tab."

"Thanks Debbie." She folded the check and put it in her apron without looking at it. She smiled. "I had better get back to work." She turned, business-like, and began to supervise a sauce on the stove.

Debbie left, crossing the living room to the patio. Quite a few were gathering to watch the sunset. Debbie approached Paula Rutledge and her beau, and Paula was effervescent. "Debbie, this is a fantastic party. I would have liked to bring along a camera crew, but that would have ruined it. We have all agreed to behave ourselves. Will interviews be possible soon?"

Debbie laughed. "You'll have to ask The Gaardian! By the way, you can call him by his first name just this evening. His name is Walter. Tell all the others that if his name is released, none of them will ever have access to him again. Okay? On the other hand, if they behave themselves, they'll get a periodic moon visit."

Paula nodded, as did her fiancé, who stood close beside her with his arm around her. "The threat's not necessary, but I'll go pass the word. The moon visit is a nice incentive though." They walked off arm in arm.

John Carson moved through the crowd, listening in on various conversations. He approached Jim and Toby, who were speaking animatedly. "Aboard *The Grace,* there were surprisingly few real problems once we got underway. There were a few minor glitches in engineering."

Jim was thoughtful. "How so?"

"Jody is a real workaholic! She has to be careful not to come across too pushy."

He smiled as Jim nodded. "At the base, it seems like Belinda never sleeps, although Frank says she gets about seven hours a day. When she is awake, she is encouraging and prodding people constantly. She's very supportive of everyone's efforts, and all want desperately to please her."

"Maybe she can give a few pointers to Jody. I'll arrange a conference." John started to move away without speaking. "See ya later, John."

John smiled as he moved away, and he headed toward Karen, Judy, and Lauryn. They were standing over on the north side of the patio. As John approached, Karen gave him a sly wink and spoke in a falsely seductive voice. "Hi, John."

He nodded at each of them in greeting. "Hi, Karen. Judy. Lauryn. What was the wink for, Karen?"

Coyly she moved closer. "We were just talking about some of the most attractive men here. Were your ears burning?"

He grinned, taking her in, head to toe. "I was just trying to picture the three of you working as bunnies at that forerunner of all gentlemen's clubs -- the Playboy Club in Hollywood -- the one on Sunset Boulevard."

"Didn't the first one open in Chicago?"

"Yes, but none of the other clubs ever measured up to the one on Sunset. I think the clubs would have never closed if women like the three of you worked in them!"

Lauryn acted seductive. "Flattery will get you everywhere, John!" She playfully put her arms around his neck and planted a kiss on his lips. "Shall we find our own hutch to play in after dinner?"

John grinned again. "Any one of the three of you would be too much woman for me!" He looked past Lauryn to Judy. "Judy, has anyone gotten your Latin blood pumping since you regained your youth?"

"Pumping?" She thrust her hips first one way, then the other, then did a little dance in place. "Some of you guys seem bent on keeping me from doing my work!" She looked beyond John and nodded, pointing. "Here comes Walter. I wonder if any of his romantic juices are flowing!"

The others all turned. John moved in Walter's direction, while the others went back to quietly conversing among themselves.

John caught Walter's eye, and he responded, "What's up John?"

"You sure put on a good party."

"The credit goes to Debbie and Belinda - and Frank, of course. The chef's name is Dawn. You will want to speak to her after dinner I think! You met her a long time ago."

John nodded. "I haven't seen Frank."

"He's pretty much staying out of sight."

"Any security problems?"

"None. Excuse me. I need to speak to Jody."

As Walter moved off toward Jody, who was on the far south side of the balcony, John spotted Ken and Butch talking by the juice bar. Ken was intense. "So you take into account a person's spiritual side when you evaluate their overall health? Hey, John!"

John smiled as he turned to hear Butch's reply. Butch nodded. "Hi, John." He smiled. "Yes, Ken, in China I was taught to be aware of someone's religion as a factor in a patient's health. Frankly, however, I was quite surprised when Qaak emphasized it."

John's eyes grew wide. "Qaak thinks religion is important?"

"Qaak?" Ken stared.

"Yes. He says most sentient species usually come to recognize that logically, one ultra intelligent and ultra powerful being created everything. Most thinking species have, as part of their history, an event in which The Creator of the universe lives out a life as one of the sentient beings on that planet. The result is a more solid relationship with The Creator which lasts indefinitely beyond the natural planetary lifetime of that one being."

Ken's eyes were wide. "That sounds like Earth's experience of Jesus!"

Butch nodded. "I suppose so. After that conversation with Qaak, I began reading The Bible a bit more. Frank has included it in my study schedule, along with parallels to The Bible from a couple dozen other planets."

John was impressed. "I've got to ask Frank for some of those sources to read. I am more or less a generic Christian. Right now, I want to check in with Belinda to see if I can be of any help. I see her over there with Stephanie."

John moved away toward the two women, who were standing near the doorway into the kitchen. He stopped for a moment, took in a bushel of air through his nose, and licked his lips as he exhaled and smiled. Then he approached the women. Stephanie and Belinda were working on a budding friendship. Belinda spoke nonchalantly. "When I lived in Orange County, my husband Steve and I knew a wonderful black family that lived next door to us. Eddie, Lawanda, Steve, and I used to have dinner together. Lawanda introduced me to soul food - my favorite was her recipe for turkey necks."

Stephanie and John responded together. "Turkey necks?"

John shook his head. "I'm sorry, but that idea just does not appeal to this Scotsman's palate."

Stephanie giggled. "Don't knock it 'til you've tried it, John! I love turkey necks too! I went to a mostly white church when I was living in Oakland. My pastor, a colorblind white man, used to come over to my house in North Oakland for turkey necks every few weeks. I'd cook them all afternoon."

John was impressed. "Really!" John smiled, excused himself, and headed to Jody and Walter. Other people were milling about, some taking a dip in the pool, and some attempting croquet on the back lawn. A few simply wandered about in the garden, which included more than five acres of the back yard. On the south side of the balcony, Jody Dunn and Walter were talking quietly and intimately. Before John got close enough to join their conversation, however, the sounds of a string quartet began to be heard above a voice that John recognized as Dawn's.

"Dinner everyone!"

Everyone came in from the yard and patio to the tables. At first, Walter's team leaders sat down at the table next to the fireplace. Quietly he spoke to them. "Let's make this a bit less formal. Everyone go and sit at separate tables. Try to sit with some people that you do not know."

"I like this idea!" Debbie headed to another table.

Walter approached some reporters and their escorts. "Join me at the big table, and let me tell you a little about a three-legged friend of mine named Qaak..."

As the rest fanned out, the mood was festive and relaxed. Soon there were a lot of conversations and occasional laughter.

At Debbie's table, she quickly sensed some rivalry in the adjacent tables occupied by Belinda and Jody. Debbie looked across to the Base Commander at the other table. "How long have you known Walter, Belinda?"

"More than a half century. We dated in junior high school a couple of times, but somehow seldom had classes together in high school. When we graduated, Walter tried to connect with me, but my Mom was getting a divorce and never passed on his messages to me. I married a wonderful man named Steve. I know that Walter is very fond of both you and Jody. He's also fond of Pixie."

Jody's eyes were wide. Debbie's face had a hint of a smile, as she remained silent. The others at the table snickered. Jody's surprise was evident. "Really? How about this! Why don't the three of us form a pact and be Walter's harem?! We'll include Pixie too!" Everyone laughed, and several of them looked over at Walter's table.

Belinda continued to smile. "If that were to happen, I know one thing. He is the most loving man you will ever know, and he does not have a jealous bone is his body - and a terrific body it is at that!" Jody giggled. "If he sees jealousy in someone, it is a turn off for him. Even-handedness and fairness are integral to his personality. He has been that way since we were children. One more thing – he is a Christian. Qaak seems to accept Walter's Christianity as part of who he is."

Jody looked across at Belinda. "Tell us more about Qaak!" The dinner and conversations went on into the night. Belinda launched into discussing her conversations with Qaak, and what Walter had told her about him ....

13. United Nations

Subtle changes were taking place in the mindsets of individuals and governments on the planets in Walter's sector. Politicians and diplomats, regardless of species or planet, always had their own point of view, depending upon whom they represented. Activity at the United Nations building reflected these changes. With hard evidence that there was more to life than what was on the Earth, there was renewed pressure upon governments for progress. After Walter dispatched the Quzaks on worldwide television, radio personalities of all stripes were beginning to clamor for changes in the ways governments related to one another. Newsmagazines were doing the same, both in print and on television. There was renewed interest in the effectiveness of the United Nations as a body.

A few days into the new year, Walter accepted an invitation to speak to a special session of the United Nations General Assembly. As Walter was beginning his initial presentation, several three-dimensional displays appeared throughout the Assembly Hall to illustrate what he was saying. As he talked about his early years, images appeared of Qaak, Waagere, and Kieya.

After taking about five minutes to discuss some background about himself and about his encounter with the Quzaks, he paused. "I want to thank you, ladies and gentlemen, for being patient in hearing a bit about my background as well as hearing about what happened after my encounter with the Quzaks. Do any of you have questions?" He paused. "Yes, the ambassador from Italy."

The Italian ambassador began asking his questions in Italian. "I've two questions. Is this friend of yours, Qaak, related to the Quzaks that you sent back to your home world? My second question is: what does their being sent back home mean for us here on Earth?"

Walter did not wait for a translation but suppressed a smile. "My mentor and friend, Qaak, is more than sixty-five thousand Earth years old." There were hushed murmurs in the crowd. "The Quzaks had not begun to become civilized when Qaak was born. Not only is there little genetic relationship, but their planets are so far distant from each other, that the light from each other's suns hasn't reached the other's planets yet during Quzak history. Regarding your second question, the return of the Quzaks to their home world simply means that they shall not be a threat to Earth, either now or soon.

"I broadcasted to you from my base on our moon, so that you may know that my primary concern as the Gaardian of this sector is beyond the immediate sphere of my home planet, Earth. When I am not on Earth or in the area, a member of my team will always be readily available in case a problem develops that is of a planetary or near-planetary scale. I have no interest in getting involved in national or international politics. In fact, our planet Earth will not be ready to get involved with species of other planets so long as nationalism is prevalent. Many planets of advanced civilizations still have regions or provinces that are distinctive in some ways but have worldwide governments. All planets of advanced civilizations also either have eliminated monetary systems, or have planet-wide currencies. On those planets, law enforcement, defense, and governances in general are worldwide in scale. At Earth's present rate of international social development, we probably will not see those kinds of changes for at least two hundred years." He paused. "Yes. The Russian ambassador."

The woman's tone was crisp and direct. "I also have two questions. What is the extent of space that is policed by Gaardians? In addition, you have spoken about your team. I would like to hear about the others you've selected."

Walter was firm and direct. "Most of you will need the help of a mathematician or two to decipher my answer with regard to the extent of Gaardian space. To understand you need to comprehend some very large numbers. A googol is the number one followed by a hundred zeroes. A googolplex is the number one followed by a googol of zeroes. The number of suns that occupy Gaardian space numbers several googolplex." Walter paused for quiet murmuring, and then continued. "Considering that huge number, there are relatively few Gaardians – less than two thousand – so Gaardians are always recruiting and training." Again, there was murmuring.

"You are probably asking yourselves about why there are so few Gaardians for such a huge expanse of the universe. The answer is a combination of percentages and technology. The percentage of stellar bodies with significant amounts of life on their surface is exceedingly small. The percentage is seven pi times ten to the minus one hundred ninety-seventh power. The percentage of those stellar bodies that has intelligent life present is even smaller. Most bodies do not have life at all, but we have one sentient planet in Gaardian space." He paused. "The other factor is technology. Gaardian technology is highly protected and more advanced than that of any civilization in Gaardian space." Walter paused again.

"Now, regarding those on my team. My current crew complement is under three hundred. One hundred eight-six are currently assigned to serve on *The Grace*, which is the space vehicle you saw us occupying on video. The others serve mostly on the moon, although small crews are being formed on each of two other planets in my sector. I do not anticipate recruiting any additional people for at least five to ten months, probably longer. The base team includes team leaders whom I will take in random order. Lauryn, responsible of Personnel and Recruitment, is a former fashion designer. She could barely move without her cane when I first met her. She lost both breasts to cancer. Her restored body is stunning. No longer bent over from arthritis, she is a tall redhead. Jim, one of my Gaardian ambassadors for Earth, is a former baseball player. He is a Brazilian raised in Cuba. In his second life, he is quite satisfied with getting his athletic body back after having suffered from arthritis and a host of other ailments. Judy, another Gaardian ambassador for Earth, is a retired Hispanic writer who is actually the oldest chronologically at eighty-six, and her restored body is dazzling."

The United States ambassador spoke. "What do you mean by restoring their bodies?"

"When we restore someone's body, it has the physiological age of about thirty. Over the next several decades, parts of this technology will be made available here on Earth and two other planets in my sector. The same technology is related to interplanetary and intergalactic travel. Our planet is not currently ready for this technology, either scientifically or socially." He paused briefly. "Now, let me finish describing my leadership team as was requested by the Russian ambassador. Stephanie, another Gaardian ambassador, is a black former accountant from Nigeria." Pausing again briefly, he continued. "Belinda, my Base Commander, was my first recruit. I visited her while she was in hospice and dying. I have known her since childhood. There are others on the base, and they come from all six normally inhabited oontinents on Earth. Yes sir?"

The British ambassador's relaxed manner belied his intense interest. "Is your moon base visible to the Earth if we have adequate telescopes?"

Equally calm, Walter said, "If you knew where to look for my Moon Base, you would not see much of it. Earth is just above the horizon as viewed from our base. Most of my base is hidden from Earth's view by the natural rock formations. Yes, madam ambassador, I am going to finish answering your question."

"Thank you." The Russian ambassador smiled.

Walter smiled back. "Please do not bother asking me about the technology or even about the speed of *The Grace*. Since it moves using technology that avoids the physical laws of mass, motion, and time, there is no point in my even beginning to discuss the technology or the science involved." He paused briefly.

"Debbie, the chief science officer, grew up in Germany. She planned on going to law school. Among her siblings, she is the oldest, but in this group, Debbie is the youngest chronologically, and she is well-known in the entertainment industry. Many of you have recognized her in videos of Gaardian activities. She does not intend to return to show business. John, our pilot and navigator, held down dozens of jobs before going to clown school put on by a circus company. I met him when he was in his late eighties. John was thrilled to have nearly sixty years peeled off by Gaardian technology.

"Toby, our ombudsman and trouble-shooter, is a Native American writer, who says he cannot ever remember looking as good as he does after restoration. He has the high cheekbones and handsome good looks of his Navajo heritage.

"Karen, our communications officer, had studied ballet in Europe, including Russia, and was retired and living in southern Portugal when she applied.

"Ken, our counselor and spiritual advisor, only lost ten years in his restoration, but he also lost his disability from a genetic disorder. Raised in Australia, Ken hesitated in applying but always dreamed of being an astronaut, which he now is.

"Butch, our very capable chief medical officer, is from China. Although he had gone to medical school in the United States, he returned to mainland China to practice in some of the small villages there.

"Jody, the chief engineer, had been a medical school student when she was asked to model. She had Parkinson's disease when I met her, which had put a damper on her artistic efforts and had led to complications that had ravaged her body in grotesque ways. Restoration for her also meant that her intelligence was enhanced."

"Are there other questions for the Gaardian?" the Assembly's leader asked.

The Greek ambassador spoke with a deep bass voice. "You said that there is a sentient planet in Gaardian space. What do you mean by that?"

Walter smiled with a kind of boyish grin. "It is very beautiful. Gaardian Planet Headquarters hovers like a satellite high above the surface. Direct conversations with it are somewhat rare. During my training, I got to converse with it a couple of times. The data gathered in Gaardian controlled space is much too massive to keep in any one Gaardian computer, as advanced as they are. Gaardian Planet itself stores the largest accumulation of data and does the most complex calculations. It is not merely sentient. Its intelligence is incredible. I have a dream that someday we will find Gaardian a companion planet with which it can converse. I genuinely enjoy its company when I am on the surface. I think it very interesting that one of Earth's science fiction writers created an entire story revolving around a sentient planet several decades ago."

After a pause, Walter finished his presentation. "Thank you for your kind attention. Soon I will visit some of the leaders of our world's nations. I will not tell them beforehand that I am coming, however. Until then, farewell." He vanished.

+ + +

On Base, Belinda greeted him with a hug. "I think you won over most of them, but some of them are still wary."

"That's to be expected." He paused. "I'm going to pray and get some sleep. See you in about seven hours." He walked to his quarters.

Belinda called out. "Hey! Am I ever going to get to visit or meet your planet friend?"

Walter laughed. "Maybe!"

Inside, Tiger and Tammy were on the bed, and they both got up to greet him. Absent-mindedly, he scratched their heads. His ring shimmered, he was in shorts, and he crawled under the covers. Walter stared at the ceiling for a few moments. "Lord, I'm tired. I think I'll get some sleep and pray after I've rested for a few hours." The cats came up to his shoulders and burrowed under the covers. The bulges of their bodies could soon be seen on the other side of the bed near the foot. Walter's eyes grew heavy.

"Walter."

"Yes." Walter was wide-awake again. The room had the familiar glow.

> "I am pleased. There is much more to be done. You must trust me to accomplish it. It was not you and Gaardian technology that sent those ships home. I know your thoughts. You must not assume that Qaak and the others were there nearby to help you. They were not, but I am always with you. I multiplied your efforts and sent the Quzaks home. Qaak and Kieya believe that you have improved Gaardian technology. They will not ask you how you did it for some time. You must use that time to your advantage. I will show you how. Now you must sleep."

The glow subsided, and Walter slept deeply for hours.

+ + +

The team leaders and officers gathered in the den a few days later to reflect on their first few months together. Belinda led off. "When you pulled me out of hospice, I was not sure what to expect. I guess I envisioned some kind of adventure like those I'd seen in science fiction movies." Thoughtful, she held up her hand when Walter started to speak. "I suppose I was expecting to have to adjust to strange devices and little green men, but even Qaak seems a normal part of our environment. I suppose I could be disappointed, but I am not. Not long ago, I told you that I felt God had brought you back into my life at the right time. I still think that is true."

Walter was looking at the fire. He turned and smiled. "I remember you saying that. Since being integrated, I've often thought about something. When I decided in my twenties that I was going to be in full-time Christian service, Qaak never talked about it with me. That seemed peculiar at first, because Qaak and I have talked about everything and everyone else, both in that dream world and in now my real world. Qaak has only told me a little of his species' history. Thousands of our years ago, most of his species came to believe in God, and in someone who had lived on his planet a long time earlier. I understand that Gaardian scientists currently are unanimous in their acceptance of God's existence. The existence of God is even built into their logical systems. Add to that mix my own convictions about God, and I believe that the timing of all that has happened these last few months looks like God's handiwork. Yes Belinda, I think you are right. Like the old song goes, someone has been watching over us, and I don't mean just Qaak and the other Gaardians."

"You've made this seem so natural, Walter, and I'm looking forward to many years of this."

"Thanks. I have been amazed at how fast all of you have adapted to this new life. Any regrets, anyone?"

Everyone shook their heads. "I was not expecting this sense of friendship and family." Jody's eyes were moist as she glanced around. "It has been only a few months, and already I feel like I am closer to all of you and to a few others than I've ever been with anyone else. Walter, you have helped me experience something I would not have dreamed possible. You have set an example for all of us that I think most of us want to emulate. I've no doubt that you genuinely love us, fully and completely, and I don't understand why."

Belinda nodded. "I do – I know that part of it comes from the fact that for more than thirty years, you were a pastor. You seem to be a pastor to us, loving us as your flock, as it were, but I think there is something more that you have not told us – and I am not talking about technology or science. I am not even sure that you've told Pixie or even Qaak."

"You've known me a long time. What you are suggesting is true, although I referred to it obliquely to Qaak and to the others that were gathered for my integration celebration. When I am ready to tell Qaak more about it, I will share it with all of you. I promise." He paused and turned his head. "Debbie, any reflections?"

Debbie was thoughtful. "I suppose like Belinda, I didn't know what to expect, but maybe I came at this in a different way because I am chronologically younger, and because I come out of show business." She paused. "A lot of people in the business are Jewish or claim they are Jewish. Recently, I read about the prayer of Jabez, and afterwards I started attending a Baptist church in Alhambra. As I prayed about whether or not I wanted to be part of this, I decided that I would treat this like the biggest and most important acting role I would ever play. That just didn't work."

"Why not?" Belinda was amused.

"In my house, it was like acting on my own home stage. When we got here to the moon, however, I left acting behind. I was so fascinated and thrilled, I did not think about acting or even about fear. I also agree with Jody, in that I have felt so encouraged and supported by you and Walter that I have never even wanted to look back at where I had come from. Does that make sense?"

Everyone nodded. They all stared at the fire in the fireplace for a few moments, deep in thought.

"Walter?" said Butch, "I think I have an insight. Qaak gave me texts to look at from other civilizations, where they had come to a faith similar to Christianity. Much of what I had observed in Christians through the years began to make sense. That isn't all though. I wanted to see what Pixie looked like, so Qaak showed me a video of your integration celebration. When we get a chance I'd like to talk to you about something you said that day." He paused. "As for expectations and disappointments, I've had no disappointments. It seems as though every week I have at least one day just like my first day of medical school. It has all been so new and exciting I've forgotten if I had any expectations or not!" He grinned.

"Thank you, all of you. Now, on to some business. Butch, Asayak, Jody, and I are going to respond to a catastrophe threatening the entire population of a planet roughly equal to Earth in the mid-twentieth century. Jody, you will need to work with scientists and engineers to design some new technology for them using their level of science. Asayak, they are not humanoid, so seeing you will be no more of a shock than seeing us." He turned to focus on Butch. "Butch, I will have you along to teach their doctors how to use the medical technology we give them to save their species. You will have to invent some things that don't go far beyond their science."

He turned to look at Debbie. "Next week, Debbie, you and I are going to analyze and document some phenomena that has never been seen before - not even by the other Gaardians in all of their history. It is happening in our own galaxy. We will take the SVX and set up a temporary base on an asteroid. We will bring back holographic video, and everyone will be amazed. Belinda, now that we have recruited the people we need and have given them basic training, your job is just beginning."

"I had a feeling you were going to say something like that!"

"You need to integrate *The Grace* crew into base life when here. We will leak out scientific knowledge strategically to accelerate scientific progress for Earth, and for Keeta's and Asayak's planets – and to others when appropriate." Walter looked beyond her to Karen, who was sitting closer to the fireplace. "Karen, you need to appoint a skeleton crew for scientific ventures like these. The rest of the crew can work with Belinda."

Butch smiled. "Sounds like fun!"

"Definitely. In addition to our guidance of scientific advancement, we are going to need to begin guiding our planets away from nationalism and provincialism. We will exile to another planet the criminally insane and those condemned to death or life imprisonment we have confirmed as guilty."

Ken's interest was piqued. "Exile? You mentioned it in that news conference."

"They will be able to talk with family via video periodically but will fend for themselves. We are also going to continue destroying large stockpiles of illegal and destructive drugs on Earth, and we will take similar actions on Asayak's and Keeta's planets. Frank and I are making plans to do something innovative with our world's nuclear arsenals." He paused. "I know at least some of you are tired and want to turn in. Go ahead if you wish." Most got up and headed for their quarters.

Butch turned just beyond the doorway and returned. "May I talk with you?"

Debbie stood up, stretched, and moved in the direction of the door. "I have some reading to do before I go to sleep. Good night!"

Jody stood up, touched her toes, became erect, and looked up at the stars as she stretched. She followed Debbie. "Me too! Good night!"

Butch waved with a smile. Walter nodded. "Good night ladies!" Walter and Butch headed for the fireplace and stood with their backs to the flames.

Butch spoke quietly. "Qaak has shown me a pattern."

"Shoot."

"He gave me material to read, about dozens of civilizations that have developed Christian-like religions. It amazes me that so many of them are hundreds of years more advanced scientifically than Earth."

"Right."

"Do you think Qaak is a Christian?"

Walter laughed. They moved away from the fire and sat down in two chairs nearby. "No! Qaak has observed Jesus and many other historical figures. His species had someone who lived out a story similar to that of Jesus on his home planet."

"Have you been talking with Jesus?"

Walter had a small smile and a twinkle in his eyes. "Maybe I'll come up with a good answer when I figure out my prayer life."

Butch stood up. "Okay – good night, Walter."

"Good night, Butch." Walter stared at the fire for a few moments. Then he got up and walked to the window. He looked out at the SVX and at the Earth hanging on the horizon. "Now what?" he muttered.

Turning to the door, he wandered out as lights went off behind him. He crossed the atrium, glancing around. As he entered his quarters, he flopped onto his bed and watched a rapid three-dimensional video of his confrontation with the Quzaks. It stopped just after he disappeared from the command ship. The lights faded, and he closed his eyes. A glow filled the room.

"Butch is almost ready to meet me."

Walter turned to lie on his back, eyes closed.

"I will tell you when it is time. Don't be afraid."

Walter opened his eyes.

"Pixie will awaken you after you have rested. She will soon know me through one of her own. She and you will bring Qaak to me."

Walter started to speak, but the voice continued.

"You have much more awaiting you. Tonight I am giving you complete rest for your body, mind, and spirit. You have done well."

His eyes slowly closed. The glow faded.

<u>Part Two: Unconditional Love</u>

14. Aegeene

Walter awakened to the music of the third movement of Tchaikovsky's Sixth Symphony. The night had been uneventful, and he had slept soundly. As he awakened, the bedroom lighting began to glow brighter, as the classical music continued to play. He enjoyed awakening to music like that of The Pathetique because it begins softly and gradually develops more volume. The second theme began as he turned and looked at the wall of his bedroom. His ring shimmered. Suddenly, the wall disappeared to reveal the lunar landscape beyond a transparent force field. As usual, the Earth hung low on the horizon. He could see several tropical storms – two in the Atlantic near the equator, one in the Caribbean, and one just north of the equator in the western Pacific.

Walter felt movement at his feet. Tiger moved across the bed to look out the newly created window. "Where's Tammy, Tiger? Why is she out prowling the base while you lounge here at my feet?" Whenever the cat heard his name, he gazed at Walter as though understanding. This time, however, Tiger looked at the door, as Tammy walked in with a subtle purr and hopped up on the bed. "Good morning, Tammy! What have you been up to this morning?" Tammy flopped down next to Tiger and began to clean herself. Both cats had adapted well to the Moon Base environment, and Gaardian technology kept them both healthy and content.

Following his daily routine, Walter quickly read four chapters from his Bible. The monitor went blank as Walter said his silent prayers, which that day lasted only about five minutes.

He swung his legs out of bed. With casual indifference, the cats looked on as he headed for the shower. Stepping into a chamber made of black marble, he closed his eyes as more than two gallons per second of warm water cascaded over him from all sides. He could hear the sound that scrubbed within the waterfalls, though any other human could not have heard it. The automatic cycle completed, the water stopped, and he was instantly dry and fully dressed.

Turning to look in the direction of the bedroom, he saw the two cats as they lay on the bed silently watching him. "Why is it you two always like to watch me take a shower? You aren't interested when I soak in the tub!" They both lay down and closed their eyes.

Walter walked past them. A monitor appeared in a corner, and Walter stopped to take in high speed compressed headlines first from San Francisco, followed by Tokyo, Auckland, Bangkok, New Delhi, Moscow, Athens, Rome, Paris, London, Johannesburg, Rio de Janeiro, and Mexico City. In less than a minute, he 'heard' about three hours' worth of newscasts. After a pause, he watched compressed news capsules from most of the inhabited planets that had electronic communications. Then he watched a three-dimensional summary of activity in his sector of the Gaardian space. Stepping up to a slight indentation in the wall, he stretched out his hand and closed his eyes as the Gaardian computer brought him up to date on everything else of significance in his jurisdiction. Finally, he checked for Gaardian mail from Gaardian Center, but there was none.

Walter was about to head to the mess hall for some breakfast when the glow began to fill his quarters. Walter stopped and almost absent-mindedly fell to his knees as the voice began to speak.

> **"Walter. Butch Eng's heart has melted and is seeking me. Leave him alone until the time of your second meal today, when you are with Xpraepostq. ["eggSPRAYpoST'kuh"] Butch will approach you to share his joy. Help him build substance to his new faith and be patient with him."**

"Is there anything special I should do for him?"

> **"I will give you the words you are to say as you speak, and I will illuminate his way as I do yours. Just be yourself."** The voice paused briefly. **"Also know that the one you call Pixie is seeing on her world what was seen by the apostles Peter, James, John, and the others on Earth. When you next see her, she will experience salvation as you have. Learn from each other."**

The glow faded. "How are we to learn from each other?" Walter heard no answer. Heading out to the mess hall, he greeted several members of his crew along the way. Some were arriving for breakfast while others had been there for varying lengths of time. Food replicators supplied most of what was desired, but some were requesting that a real team of chefs and bakers be recruited for base life. It was on Walter's agenda.

Debbie Schaffner was sitting at a table by herself near one of the view ports facing Earth. She looked up as he approached.

"Mind if I join you?"

"Not at all! I just got here. Would you save me a trip to the food port and get me whatever you're having?" Walter smiled as his ring shimmered.

The table was suddenly filled with bacon, sausage, country fries, honeydew, muffins, grapefruit juice, and herbal tea. "Is this okay for you?"

"Wow! I forgot how much you eat! If I were not working for you and under Butch's care, I could get fat eating meals like this! What's up today?" They began eating, and conversed between bites.

"It looks like I am heading out to Aegeene to visit Pixie."

"Really? I like her. She is so beautiful inside as well as photogenic outside. If I could work with her for a while, I would like to seek a friendship with her. You two seem fairly close."

"We are the best of friends I guess. We trained together of course and have spent a lot of time together."

"Just friends?"

"For a while we both thought there was going to be much more. Her life is now going through another radical change."

"Tell me about it."

"I'll let that be between you and her. I am grateful for all the fine work you are doing. I'm almost as comfortable with you as with Belinda."

"Thanks!" She smiled.

He looked out at the Earth, low on the horizon, the Pacific Ocean now centered in their view. "Have you noticed that one storm -- the one just north of the equator off of San Diego?"

"I have been watching it." She paused to take a forkful of country fries. "When I went to bed the computer had not come up with a prediction with enough accuracy. I will check in after breakfast this morning – this honeydew is better than any I ever got in restaurants in Hollywood!"

"The eye of the storm will not touch land, but your old stomping grounds are going to get a couple dozen inches of rain."

"You're kidding! The flood control system is going to be loaded to the max!"

"Worse! San Bernardino and Riverside Counties are going to get a one hundred year flood that will come down the wash near Mentone. The geological plug created by an earthquake will not hold. The Army Corps of Engineers has been recommending an upgrade of that flood control system for decades, but politicians have been unwilling to face the situation and assess the taxes. The result is going to be far more costly."

"How soon?"

"Within nineteen hours. Be today's friendly Gaardian. I do not want them to question that we know what we are talking about. Prepare a Gaardian-mail."

"A Gaardian-mail? That will get their attention!"

"I hope so. Be yourself but dress professionally. Have Frank send it to all the mayors, law enforcement heads, and civil defense people. Be sure to include impressively illustrated and accurate data, with the standard avenue for contacting us with questions. Frank will help you provide impressive three-dimensional graphics integrated into video. Do it as soon as we finish breakfast to provide time for evacuation."

"Is that going to be necessary?"

"If that geological plug lets go, a wall of water will come down that canyon near Highway 30 at least fifteen meters high as it passes Mountain Home Village. It will grow there because of another flash flood that will come down Loch Leven Canyon. Evacuations will be necessary to avoid loss of life, and the damage is going to be in the billions."

Debbie whistled. "Suddenly, I'm not interested in food! Maybe I will have a big lunch. Join me?"

"No - I'm going to be with Pixie on Aegeene, remember? Get going! I'll see you later."

Debbie smiled and reached across the table to squeeze Walter's hand. "See you later." Walking quickly, she was nearly out the door in seconds. Walter watched her leave with a slight smile on his face, as she looked back to give a short wave.

As Walter watched, Ken Lyman walked up. "Mind if I join you?"

Walter looked up and grinned. "Not at all. I have just given Debbie a major project for the morning. Better be careful! The same might happen to you!"

"I'll take my chances. Those muffins look delicious!" He paused to take a bite. "Any special instructions for me?"

"Keep a watchful eye on Keeta. Be available to her - she needs a friend. Keeta's doing a terrific job, but she feels out of place being one of only two non-humans on the leadership team."

"Okay."

Walter paused to take a bite and looked straight into Ken's eyes. "I know you are attracted to her."

Ken turned red. "Come on!"

"Don't worry about it. She is attracted to you too. Do not worry about the species differences either. Just be her friend – and more if you both want."

Ken was thoughtful. "I don't know...."

"Now, I'm headed out to Aegeene. See you soon!"

"Take care!" Ken watched as Walter simply vanished from the table. Looking beyond where Walter had been standing, Ken saw Keeta come in from the crew quarters area. Her face lit up as he waved to her. She walked toward him, her eyes locked to his. He invited her to sit down where Walter had been sitting.

15. Savior

Pixie's base was a space station circling around her planet, Aegeene. If it were not for Walter, Pixie would have had her work area in her own quarters. When watching Walter and asking him questions, she saw the advantage of compartmentalizing her life. Her quarters were much more comfortable than they had been when she was a child. They contained reproductions of art decorating her walls as well as a fireplace.

Her quarters were a stark contrast to her work area – Walter called it her 'office.' It was utilitarian in every detail. The walls were all plain except for the one opposite the door, which had a large portal. It looked just like a window. From time to time, however, what appeared on the other side of this 'window' changed. Pixie monitored her planet on this display. It encompassed nearly the entire wall. Much of it was automated, covering the planet in general but automatically focusing in on areas of concern.

She was sitting in a padded chaise. Her ring shimmered from time to time, as she took an interest in something she saw, and the display focused in on what piqued her interest.

Sitting next to her in another chaise was Oxza ["OGG-zuh"]. Pixie liked Walter's use of Frank as a physical representation of his computer, so Pixie had Oxza. She looked enough like Pixie to be her sister, and was an adult representation of the sister who had died when she was much younger. Pixie had a team slightly larger than Walter's.

Most of her team preferred to sleep on the space station that Pixie had created where they could sleep at the gravity level of their choice. It also had extensive recreational facilities. They liked working on a planet's surface as much as possible rather than at the base. Hundreds of observation posts were scattered all over both her planet and others in her sector. They were invisible to all but Gaardian technology. Pixie's team members moved from post to post, monitoring the activities of the planets and interfering only with Pixie's authority.

High above in the space station, Pixie was watching the conflicts on her planet with keen interest. "Oxza, it's sure tempting to get more involved in these wars and skirmishes!"

"You have already pushed a few Gaardian rules to control some of the fighting. Do you plan to do more?"

"No, I've done too much already. Team members need the experience. All of these conflicts are good experience for them and for me. I'm fascinated by the comparative lack of violence and turmoil in the second hemisphere on Salts Sea."

"Yes. The center of the tranquility is one individual called Eiraynay ["eye-RAY-nay"]. In our most ancient tongue, that name means 'peaceful one,' an appropriate name."

"I'm going down there! Keep vigil." Pixie vanished.

She arrived invisibly in the midst of some shady overgrowth next to a large clearing. In the middle of the clearing was something that on earth would gather many tourists but was common on Aegeene, where large crystalline formations were a frequent part of the landscape. This could best have been described as a monolith. Approximately three meters square and five meters high, it was composed of almost pure beryllium aluminate – alexandrite. In this case, it was an isotope different from the stone in Gaardian rings. Pixie made a mental note to bring Walter here to see it. Crystal artisans had shaped it into a useful platform for public speaking and had worked with masons to create a stairway to the top made of translucent stones of various colors. There was almost a mystical respect for the clearing and its monolith. Soldiers had never fought there, and law officers had never made an arrest of anyone occupying the clearing. It was a place of sanctuary and peace.

This particular day, Eiraynay was seated cross-legged on top and teaching people about The Maker of Everything. "Consider the smallest creatures that we see every day. They do not have to plan for meals, or for storing food for the future, and yet The Maker of Everything is like a loving parent who sees to all of their needs. If the Maker of Everything cares so much for the smallest of creatures, will He not care far more for you? How many of you have increased your life span by worrying? Look around you! Look at the beauty of the fruit and the flowers that surround us! Those plants do not do any physical labor the way we do, to see to their own survival, yet they thrive. So if the Maker of Everything sees to the health and beauty of the plants around us, does He not care that much more about you? You will find great happiness through trusting in The Maker of Everything. He alone is truly God. Trust in the Maker of Everything brings power, peace, and fulfillment. You only have to admit that you have done things against His will and resolve to never do them again."

Pixie listened to Eiraynay for a long while, but then Oxza appeared next to her. "You told me to remind you when it was time to intervene on the other continent."

"Yes. Thank you, Oxza." They both vanished.

+ + +

On Earth, Butch's life was about to undergo a radical change. Coming from the Base, he appeared in a restroom stall on the beach in Santa Monica. Using tokens Frank had supplied, Butch took a bus east for several miles, and then got off. Walking briskly, he followed Santa Monica Boulevard for a number of miles. Nearing Hollywood, he cut over to Sunset Boulevard, and he continued until he reached his destination. The Medical Center west of Hollywood was an imposing complex, but Butch had been there before. As he approached the main entrance and went up the steps, he was conscious of Los Angeles' smog, in stark contrast to the pure air at the Moon Base. Inside the entrance, he noticed the air was cooler and less irritating and took in a deep breath before he approached the information desk.

A rather pretty middle-aged woman greeted him. "May I help you sir?"

"Carl Dennison, please."

After just a few keystrokes, while gazing at her monitor, she reached for a pad next to her and wrote. "He's in room fourteen twenty-six, sir." She handed him the slip. "Just take one of those elevators over there to the fourteenth floor. When you get there, take the corridor to your right. His room is just beyond the first nurse's station."

"Thank you." Butch stepped into an elevator that opened just as he got there. He pushed 14, and the doors closed. A few moments later, Butch made his way down the hall and into Carl's private room.

As Butch was entering the room, a balding man with white hair greeted him with a crooked smile. "Hello! You must be Butch's son! I would recognize you anywhere! You look just like your father did when he was your age!"

"Hello Mr. Dennison!" Butch struggled not to give away his Gaardian connection. "My father wanted me to look in on you if I was ever in Los Angeles. How are you doing?"

"I'm blessed, of course! I won't be on this Earth much longer, but I'm looking forward to the larger life." The old man's obvious joy mixed with the euphemism for death brought a slight smile to Butch's face.

"What's the prognosis, if you don't mind my asking?"

"Oh, they have some fancy name for the tumors I've got, but let's not talk about me. That is what everybody else here does with me! Tell me, how's God blessing you these days?"

Butch smiled. He knew he could not tell him as much as he wanted to, so he chose his words carefully. "I think most people would say I'm blessed. You were one of Dad's oldest friends, and he told me more than once that you are a Christian. Your reference to God gives me a question for you. As you perceive it, did this God you referred to create everything – the whole universe?"

"Absolutely! Why not? Since he created everything, including space and time, He obviously can't be limited by them." Butch started to respond, but the old man held up his hand. "Let's shoot straight with each other, okay?"

"Okay, but why do you ask?"

"You're not Butch's son; you're Butch, aren't you? I'll bet you're working with the Gaardian now. Don't worry! I won't live long enough to tell anyone!"

Butch looked at him seriously and lowered his voice. "Okay, my old friend. You've got me! We've got to keep it a secret, right?"

"Of course! And don't worry! I would not want to do what you're doing."

"What I'm doing?"

"Live my life over again in a new capacity. I've enjoyed this life, but I am ready to meet Jesus in person."

"What do you mean?"

"Listen, Butch! When you leave here, go to Sunset Boulevard, and turn west. There is a small church not far from here that has a chapel open every day. Just go in there and talk to God. I think you're finally ready to hear the answers to your questions."

"I'm still not a religious man, Carl."

"I know, Butch. I am not asking you to get suddenly religious. I'm simply telling you that the answers are ready for you, if you simply talk to God."

"You mean pray? I don't know how."

"Just talk to Jesus, as though he is invisible but there. You may be surprised at what happens."

"What will happen?"

"You'll see. Listen, just before you came in, they gave me a pain shot, and I'm fading fast. It's been good to see you!"

"It's been good to see you too, Carl."

"Have a nice forever – I'll see you later." The old man closed his eyes.

Butch left the room, thoughtful. His friend Carl had always been religious and had invited him to church a few times, but Butch had always managed to excuse himself. At the entrance of the Medical Center, he paused and looked around. Making a quick decision, he took off, heading south down a side street at a brisk pace.

Less than a half-hour later, Butch paused in front of a little church. A small white sign on a red-brick base said Chapel of the Good Shepherd. On a door was a sign that read "Chapel Open." Butch went in. As the door closed silently behind him, Butch found himself in a small cool foyer. Two old leaded stained-glass windows gently lit it. Hanging from the arched ceiling was a small crystal chandelier that reminded Butch of one he had seen in a theater in Hong Kong. Butch spotted a door that evidently led to a larger room. Thinking aloud, he said, "This must be the chapel."

"Yes, it is." A voice to his right startled him. "Can I be of service? My name is Paul."

"No, thank you. It's nice to meet you, Paul. My name is Butch. I just visited a friend of mine who is dying over at the Medical Center. He is a Christian, who has tried to get me to church for many years. I decided that to honor him, I would find a church and try to do some praying."

"A lot of people come here to pray. The chapel is always open."

"How do people pray?"

"Some stand, some sit, some kneel, and a few pray with their faces on the floor. I doubt that it makes much difference to God in most cases. God meets us where we are."

"Meets us where we are?"

"Yes. For instance, did you grow up in a good family with loving parents?"

"I'm from a traditional Chinese family. My parents were very caring."

"Many people find it helpful to think of God as Jesus does – as our loving Heavenly Father."

"As Jesus does? You believe that He is alive?"

"Of course. He lives forever. He is like a window on the eternal." He paused. "At home, my bedroom has a large oak tree right outside the window. If I stand at the door, pointing to the window, and I say, 'That's an oak tree,' the person I am talking to knows that I am not talking about the window, but about the tree outside. In the same way, when people refer to Jesus and say that He is God, it's simply an affirmation of something Jesus said long ago: 'He who has seen me has seen The Father.'"

Butch nods. "I think I understand. So you're saying that Jesus is like a window, through whom we can see God."

"Yes. The closer you get to a window, the more you see of what is on the other side of the window. In the same way, the closer you get to Jesus, the more you understand and see God."

"If you don't mind I think I'd just like to sit here a while and think about my friend, okay?"

"That's fine. I am the pastor. My office is through that door on the right if you need me. It was nice meeting you, Butch."

"Thank you. Thank you for your help." The pastor turned, and in a moment left Butch alone.

Butch took a seat about midway to the altar at the front. His first thoughts were of Carl. "I'm going to miss him," muttered Butch softly. "I wonder why he's tried so hard to get me to a place like this. What has it been that has made him so peaceful and joyful in almost every situation?" He looked up at a large cross, suspended overhead. "He has always spoken of Jesus as being alive. So does a man I just met – Paul. I have read from Qaak about religions of other cultures, and I have read the Bible's gospels. They seem to point to how important His being alive is. If He is alive, there are many questions I want to ask Him. If He is alive, it solves many the mysteries I have been struggling with. If He is alive I need Him."

Butch closed his eyes. Softly, he prayed, "Jesus, if you're real I want to know it. If you're real I want you to be part of my life the way you are part of Walter's and Carl's lives." A glow began to surround him.

> "Carl's life is with me now, Butch. You will not join him in heaven for many years."

It was not a voice Butch could actually hear, but deep inside him, the voice was unmistakable. "Is that you, Jesus? Is Carl with you in heaven?"

> "Of course, Carl is with me. He looked forward to being with me for a long time. From this day forwards, you will know me too. You have read how some of my followers have known me. Now is your new beginning. I want you to be born again in my spirit. Ask Paul to baptize you before you leave. I'll be with you always."

Later, Butch was finishing drying his hair after being baptized. "Thanks for baptizing me on short notice." He was pleased. "I didn't want to wait until Sunday."

"I always consider it a privilege. Will I be seeing you on Sunday?"

"Probably not. I am going to be out of the country. I'll be back though."

"I'll look forward to seeing you again. I want to introduce you to others who worship here. It's good to have a church family you can turn to."

"I know. My friend Walter has taught me that. He has been a Christian most of his life. I want to show my gratitude to God and to this congregation." He paused. "I'll see to it that the congregation receives a donation in a day or two."

"That will be appreciated of course, but we don't charge for doing baptisms."

"I know – but I have the need to give. Do you know what I mean?"

"Yes I do. I know the feeling. Be safe in your travels." A telephone rang on his desk. "I need to get this – my secretary is off today. Hope to see you soon!" He picked up the telephone.

Butch turned and strode out of the office. He stopped to look at a statue of Jesus embracing children, with a shepherd's crook at his side. He also went across the hall to the men's room to double check and make sure he had not left anything behind after getting dressed after his baptism. Coming out of the restroom, he went through the door into the worship area, and Butch looked around in the little chapel. There were no people around. He looked at the ring on his right hand. "Frank, please beam me directly to my Moon Base quarters."

In an instant, he was standing next to his bed. He looked at his baptismal certificate that the Pastor had given him. "Frank, would you please put this in a plain black wooden frame and put it on the wall above my headboard?" The certificate disappeared from his hand and reappeared above his bed. "Thanks Frank." He headed for the door.

Butch left his quarters knowing that he had been 'born again.'

+ + +

At her orbiting base, Pixie stood in front of the giant display with her arms crossed. About thirty armed soldiers awaited Eiraynay as he left the clearing, and they put fetters on him. Forced into a waiting vehicle, Eiraynay was taken quickly to an assembly of political leaders in a large structure that probably used to be a theater before being damaged and taken over by the army.

Pixie watched a brief interrogation, which was followed by the placing of a red hood over Eiraynay's head. "This is ridiculous Oxza! First, they arrest him on a trumped-up charge of treason." She spun around turning her back to the display. "Treason!" Pixie fumed. "How could he be a traitor when none of his activities were the least political? This is so bizarre!"

She turned back to the display. "For all of our scientific and technological advances, why does injustice run rampant on my beloved planet? The people of Aegeene make foolishness a planetary art form!"

"You have a valid point."

She looked at Oxza. "I thought we had gotten past this when we merged all the nation states. Nationalism has been dead for more than two hundred years. Even ethnic disputes were outdated until this mess. I will be so glad when my world progresses to the point that it does not need a monetary system for everyday life. Greed is running rampant – worse than at Walter's Earth stock markets. This is almost a civil war in many ways, but with at least a dozen different groups trying to force their agendas on everyone else."

Oxza's voice was calm. "It's even more strange. Some so-called leaders consider peace a threat to their agendas, and those who are peacemakers are seen as a special enemy. Each leader seems to be behaving like an animal – like a terrorist or some other kind of sociopath. This so-called 'Peaceful One' called Eiraynay is going to be executed in moments. Why? It is illogical."

"I don't know. I can stop his execution, but Gaardian guidelines prohibit me."

They both stared as 'The Peaceful One' was dismembered. Pixie winced, and tears rolled down her cheeks. "Are you okay, Pixie?"

"I think so." She paused. "Oxza, set up a Gaardian mail to Walter." The display shimmered for a moment, and Walter's face appeared. "Walter!"

"Hello, Pixie! What's the matter?"

"I just watched an execution that should never have happened. I am not sure why, but my heart is breaking. I have watched other people die, but this was special. This is a time when I do not like being a Gaardian. Can we get together and talk in person?"

"I've been expecting your call."

"How soon can you get here?"

"I'll be there as soon as I can."

"Expecting my call?"

"I'll explain later."

"Good. Maybe you can help me sort out some of what is going on here. See you soon." She smiled.

"Soon." He returned her smile, and the image disappeared.

"Oxza, how could he have been expecting my call? Have you been in communication with Walter or Frank?"

"No. This too is illogical. That man has gifts that are unique within Gaardian records. I am supposed to function with the pure logic of your Gaardian computer, but this does not allow for a logical conclusion."

"Why not?"

"Logic has two universal parameters. The first is, nothing can both be and not be simultaneously. The second parameter is more complex in application. It says that all conclusions are always based upon both facts and assumptions.

I cannot form a logical conclusion because I do not have an assumption with which to work that is reasonably valid. I am looking forward to finding out how he came to be expecting your call."

"I'll find out soon enough." She headed for her quarters. As she stepped through the door, her pet Qaquk greeted her. On her planet below, Qaquk would have been considered much too dangerous to be a pet, but as a Gaardian Pixie enjoyed his company. Other than having six legs, Qaquk would have seemed like a Russian wolfhound on Earth. His hair was extremely fine. His teeth were small and sharp, and he was stronger than three or four men. He had real affection for Pixie and was never a danger. Her Security Chief saw Qaquk as a kind of guard dog.

Pixie reached down and stroked his head. She began to relax. Reflecting on the events of the day, she began to float in the center of the room and was soon fast asleep.

+ + +

Elsewhere, Belinda was studying her computer monitor when Walter walked in. "Hey Walter! Sorry I could not join you for breakfast this morning – I've been up for hours!"

"That's okay. I am taking off, and I do not know how long it will take. Pixie G-mailed me early this morning and asked me to meet her at her space station. It sounded important. I don't know what's up yet. I'll keep you posted."

"It can't be a Gaardian crisis – I've not seen anything posted by The Center."

"No, I think this is something personal for her, and perhaps involves her planet. I will see when I get there. I'm going to take the SVX and do some cruising and thinking on the way. Bye!"

"Bye!"

Walter's ring shimmered, and he was in the SVX. The vehicle quickly took off, as though on its own.

+ + +

Leaving his quarters, Butch went looking for Walter. He went down the hallway into the office complex and saw Belinda coming out of Debbie's suite. "Belinda, where's Walter? I need to talk with him." He paused as she looked up.

"Sorry, Butch! Walter just left for Aegeene. You might try Gaardian mail. Is it important?"

"I'll say! This afternoon I said farewell to one of my oldest friends, became a Christian, and got baptized!" He grinned.

"Wow! That's great! I became a Christian as a little girl. This must be a major change for you, old man!" She smiled.

"Old or not, my body is young, and I feel young. Now I have been 'born again,' and feel like I am starting a completely new life! Again! Thanks for the word of encouragement." Butch headed back to his quarters.

"Frank, can you get Walter for me on Gaardian mail?"

Frank appeared about a meter away. "Sorry, Butch. Walter is in privacy mode. I'll only interrupt him if this is an emergency."

"It's not an emergency – in fact, it's kind of the opposite – but I really want to talk with him."

"Walter has not indicated when he will be back, but I don't anticipate his being gone more than a few days."

Butch is thoughtful. "Frank, how can I get to Aegeene?"

"I won't beam you there under these circumstances. I will create another SVX for you. You've been trained for the controls."

"Great! Thanks Frank." Frank vanished.

Butch headed to the conference room. He saw Belinda through her office doorway and called out, "Belinda, I'm headed out to see Walter. I don't think I'll be gone long. The clinic has not been busy, and my team can handle almost anything."

"Have a good visit! Get some digital pictures of Aegeene for me, okay?"

"Right! Bye!"

Belinda touched her control pad and rang Walter in his SVX. Frank appeared next to her. "You'll have to wait a moment Belinda. Walter is making an entry in his journal. I'll then put you through."

"Thanks Frank." The android vanished.

The SVX was actually flying in response to Walter's thoughts. "Personal journal." Walter paused about five seconds. "The voice said – and it's never wrong – Pixie is having or is about to have a life changing experience. This seems strange yet familiar. I remember when I first became a Christian, and I have walked many people through the so-called 'born-again' process, but this has to be a little different. After all, her planet has a very different environment, and has a very different culture. I can only wonder how my experiences can help her, and I'll be darned if I can figure out how I am going to learn anything from Pixie in this. That is what the voice said was to happen, so I guess this will be a new adventure for both of us. End journal." Walter watched the stars flash by for several moments. A chime sounded.

"Yes, Belinda?"

Belinda's three-dimensional image appeared suspended beside him over the passenger seat. "Butch was just looking for you. I told him where you have gone. With Frank's help, he is going to meet you a little later at Pixie's. He is coming in another SVX. Is that okay?"

"Of course. Thanks. See you when I get back."

She disappeared. "Okay," he thought aloud, "enough slow cruising for today. On to Pixie's!" Suddenly, the stars lurch faster and into a blur past the SVX. Just as suddenly, the blur was gone and the SVX was hovering near Pixie's space station.

+ + +

Just outside where Walter usually had his red SVX at the base, there was now a blue one. Butch strode from Belinda's office to the conference room, where he saw the blue SVX parked. In a blink, Butch was inside, seated comfortably in the driver's seat. After refreshing his memory of the controls, Butch took off. "Aegeene, pace eight when appropriate," he said aloud to the controls. The SVX rose from the Moon's surface, accelerating rapidly until he was just beyond Saturn. Then suddenly the SVX went to pace eight. Although he had experimented with traveling to pace ten and beyond, Butch liked the stars going by slow enough so that he could enjoy the view.

The SVX computer's voice said, "Arrival at Aegeene in sixty-three minutes." Tipping the seat back, Butch closed his eyes. Soon he was fast asleep. Sensing his loss of consciousness the SVX accelerated silently to decrease travel time to just minutes. The SVX sat suspended above Aegeene until Butch awakened.

Meanwhile, Walter's trip was uneventful, and he beamed onto the space station and into Pixie's quarters as soon as he arrived. Pixie and Oxza were standing in front of her display. Walter appeared next to them.

"Hi, Walter!" Pixie greeted him with a hug. There were marks where tears had run down her face.

"What's wrong, Pixie?"

"Don't you know? You seemed to know when I Gaardian mailed you."

"In prayer, God warned me that you were going to need me. What's up?"

"You know how my planet is going through a period of more wars and skirmishes than usual? Sometime ago I noticed an area that was visibly calm in the midst of the most violent turmoil. It turned out there was an individual called Eiraynay, which in our Ancient Tongue means 'The Peaceful One.' Everywhere he went, everything was peaceful. The violence came to a halt whenever he was in a particular area. Not long ago, Eiraynay was arrested on a false charge of treason, and just before I called you, I watched him being executed. I could have stopped it of course, but Qaak so often stressed our staying out of the way of such events. Right now, I am questioning my role as a Gaardian."

"I understand how you feel. I have had to stay out of a number of conflicts on Earth for the same reason. It is not easy. I suppose..." Walter's voice trailed off. A blue SVX appeared next to his. "That's Butch. Belinda G-mailed me, to tell me he wanted to talk to me, and he could not wait until I got back. I hope you don't mind."

Butch appeared a meter or so away from them. "Hi, Walter! Hi, Pixie!" He was smiling.

"You look happy, Butch! What's happened?" Pixie asked.

"It's just that I need to talk to Walter. Maybe you would like to hear it too. You two look so serious though. Is anything wrong?"

"Pixie watched the execution of an innocent man and is struggling with her role as a Gaardian – as I do in these cases. What's going on?" Pixie and Walter sat down on a large chaise.

"Well!" Butch paused a moment. "Yesterday I visited an old friend, Carl, who was only hours from death. I asked him about his Christian faith, and he urged me to visit a little church on Sunset Boulevard there in Los Angeles. I was not going to go at first, but I went to the little chapel anyway. I was all by myself. At first, I just looked around. I had been in churches before, but I guess things felt different because I was there because of my friend's urging."

"How did you come to know Carl?"

"He was one of the first people I met when I moved from China to the United States. He re-introduced me to Debbie." He paused briefly. "Anyway, I sat down and began looking carefully at all the artwork in the windows and the other Christian decorations in the chapel. Up in front, there was a large cross suspended over an altar."

"A cross?" Pixie asked.

"Yeah, a cross. It was the form of execution for Jesus of Nazareth about two thousand Earth years ago. Anyway, for some reason, that cross seemed to hold my interest. I do not know why. There was nothing particularly unusual about it.

Anyway, suddenly a glow seemed to fill the chapel. I looked around, but the lights were all turned off. Up until that moment, the only light was from the colored windows."

"What was the glow like?"

"Strange. The light seemed to not only penetrate the darkness but everything else as well."

Walter smiled. "Then what?"

"I heard a voice." Walter started to say something, but Butch held up his hand. "I know, I know, it sounds very strange."

"Actually, it doesn't. I have experienced this glow and heard this voice myself. I told the other Gaardians about it at the celebration of our integration as Gaardians. I didn't tell the other Gaardians about the voice – only about the glow."

Pixie touched Walter's arm with a curious look. "Why didn't you tell me then?"

"I couldn't at the time, Pixie. Now is a good time to talk about it. Nevertheless, this is Butch's turn to talk. What happened, Butch?"

"I'm still thinking about what the voice said. It was Jesus though."

"Jesus?" Pixie asked. "I thought he died thousands of years ago!"

"Yes, but Christians believe that he was resurrected on the third day after his death. Now I know they are right – actually, I guess I mean we are right. I am a Christian now."

Pixie got up from her chaise. "Butch, I can tell you have more to say, but I need some time to think. What you are telling me is just too strange for me to take in right now. You two go ahead with your conversation here. I will be back in a little while. I am going to go for a jog. There is a nice park near where Eiraynay used to teach. I need to work off some energy. See you two later!" She vanished before either of them can respond.

"You think she's okay?" asked Butch.

"For now." Walter gazed at the planet in the display.

As they continued their conversation in the satellite far above, down below Pixie was beginning to jog by herself in a large park. Remembering the marks on her cheeks, her Gaardian ring shimmered, and the streaks from her tears disappeared. Unlike the clearing where Pixie had first seen Eiraynay, the park was filled with all kinds of plant life and many kinds of animal life. Some of what Walter would call trees were more than a hundred meters tall, though there was a tinge of blue in many of the taller ones. It was a beautiful day. The two suns provided nice warmth in the midst of the light purple sky.

The park was a blaze of color. Many of the plants were bearing fruit. Her ring shimmered, and Pixie spoke. "Personal journal. I know Walter is a Christian of course, but I do not know much about that religion. Now his Chief Medical Officer has become a Christian. I would not be concerned except for this business of resurrections. Even as a Gaardian, it seems pretty fantastic." Pixie began to hear the footsteps of someone jogging nearby. "End journal." She glanced to her left as another jogger was pacing her. She saw his feet and legs but did not look at his face. He was matching her stride for stride.

"Good day!"

"Good day! I've not seen you jogging here before." He was tall and slender, his chest at her eye level.

"No, I've not jogged here before, but I've admired the park." They continued jogging in silence.

"You seem troubled. Is something bothering you?"

Pixie was struck that this stranger could sense her distress when she was trying so hard just to appear normal. "I didn't think it showed." She slowed down slightly, and he matched her pace. She still did not look at his face. "I watched as an innocent individual was executed. It must have been politics, but that whole situation baffles me."

"Have you read much of the writings of the ancient ones?"

"Not really. In school, I read some, of course, but it never really interested me. Why do you ask?" Pixie's mood was quickly changing, though she did not know why. She glanced sideways again, noticing that his slender arms had hands with long and slender fingers.

"The ancient ones wrote that someday there would be a time of great turmoil in which one individual would bring peace in that part of our world. They also predicted that this individual would be unjustly accused and executed, but in about a solar cycle, that individual would come back to life and live forever."

When he mentioned the prediction of new life, Pixie began to think about Butch and Walter. Her face seemed to light up as Pixie had momentary mental flash pictures of them in her apartment. "There's a fountain over there. Would you join me for a piece of fruit and liquid refreshment?"

"Certainly." As the two of them jogged to the fountain he said, "When I mentioned the prediction of resurrection your face seemed to light up. Why is that?"

They stopped, and each took a drink. "I have these friends...." As Pixie drank, she looked at his face for the first time. He vanished.

"Eiraynay!" she murmured.

16. Melding

She shouted at the sky. "Oxza! Who was that jogging with me and where did he go?"

Oxza appeared beside her. "The individual was the one called Eiraynay. When he vanished, there was nothing to trace."

"Nothing?"

"Affirmative."

"That's impossible! Gaardian technology can trace any kind of matter transport. There is no trace whatsoever?"

"None. It is as though he has never been here. However, digital record shows him here with you."

Pixie stared. "I've got to talk to Walter and Butch." Looking around, she was still alone. They vanished back to her Base.

Walter and Butch were reclining next to the large window and talking quietly while looking at her planet.

"Walter! Butch!"

"Hey Pixie!" they said almost simultaneously.

"I just had the strangest experience!"

"What?"

"I was jogging in a park I had previously visited, and making a few notes in my audio journal. I became aware of someone jogging near me, so I concluded my journal entry, just as I noticed this individual jogging beside me. After greeting each other and jogging a few meters, he told me I looked troubled and asked what was wrong. I told him I had seen the execution of an innocent man, that I assumed it was political, and that it bothered me. He asked me how much of the ancient writings I knew. I know very little, except a few passages I learned in early schooling. He told me the ancient ones had predicted someone would come along, who would be falsely accused and executed, and that within a solar cycle later, he would become alive again and live forever. It sounded something like your Christian tradition."

Walter and Butch smiled as Pixie continued. "I was getting tired and asked him if he would like to join me for some refreshment at a fountain we were approaching. As I was drinking, I looked directly at his face for the first time. It was Eiraynay! The one I had seen executed! As soon as I recognized him, he vanished!"

Walter continued to smile and nodded as Butch exclaimed, "Wow! Are you sure?"

"Yes! I would recognize that face anywhere. I asked my computer to tell me where he went, but Oxza said it was unable to trace his whereabouts. That is doubly strange."

"Not really. You are going to find that He will stick around for several more of your solar cycles before leaving for good. What do you think, Butch?"

"This is following the pattern that I discovered through those extra sources I've been reading with Qaak's help. Do you think we could go down and meet him?"

"What? Meet him? How do you know we can find him?" Pixie was incredulous.

"It's not a matter of us finding Him, but a matter of His finding us, Pixie." She stared at them both, as Walter turned and spoke to Butch. "Do you mind if I create a bit of visual disguise for us so that we can look like Pixie's people?"

"Go ahead!"

Walter's ring shimmered, and instantly they had the same skin and similar features to those of Pixie. Their clothing also changed in keeping with Pixie's culture, and they got shorter. Walter produced a mirror behind them. "Take a look."

"I like it Walter! Pixie, your people are certainly stunning!"

"Thank you. Walter, you had better prepare Butch for the differences in gravity and atmosphere."

"Not necessary, but perhaps a reminder is needed." Walter pointed to the ring he had previously given to Butch. "Butch, your ring that I gave you last week is an interface with Frank and my computer, and it will help you deal with the increased gravity as well as the atmosphere."

Butch nodded. He paused and looked at Pixie, remembering protocol. "Thank you, Pixie, for letting us visit your planet."

"Oxza, is Eiraynay visible on my planet's surface?"

The android appeared next to them. "Affirmative."

Pixie paused for just a moment as she closed her eyes. Then she opened them. "Shall we go?"

Their rings shimmered, and instantly they were on the planet's surface in the midst of some dense foliage. Pixie pointed. "He's over there – I see him next to the lake. Please let me do most of the talking – you don't know the local idiomatic expressions." She walked slowly and deliberately toward Eiraynay. There were some others with Him, about a dozen of them, with equal numbers of males and females.

Eiraynay greeted them as they walked up. "Hello Xpraepostq," He said, using Pixie's real name.

"How do you know my name?"

"Perhaps later your friends can explain that to you. I recognize them as well, so you need not identify them. I am glad all three of you have come. We were just going to have something to eat. Please join us."

They all sat down on what appeared to be brightly sparkling sand – composed primarily of quartz crystals. Eiraynay talked easily as they ate. "For those who know me well already, remember what I've taught you. You must cover the foolishness of others with silence. Forgive others as you ask The Creator of Everything to forgive you. Have faith in our Creator and His creation, and trust Him. He loves you, so seek Him with your whole heart. You must persevere with all the happiness you can. Never take pleasure in the mistakes of others, and find happiness in pursuing the truth, no matter what the cost."

"Why?" Pixie's eyes were focused totally on Eiraynay.

"It's the loving way. You must also do your best to be courteous, focusing on the needs of others more than your own needs. Do not let others prod you, or control you through your anger. Think in terms of what is best for all."

One of the others, a taller female with darker features cleared her throat before speaking. "That sounds hard."

"Yes," said Eiraynay. "Loving requires a great deal of patience. Love is something you do, more than something you feel. You cannot waste your time wanting what others have, either. If you compare yourself with others as though you are the better one, you will have failed your created function of peaceful love."

A male, appearing much like a brother to the female, followed up with another question. "After you have left Aegeene, how far are we to go with your teachings?"

"I will never leave you. I have conquered death, so just follow me. It is true, you will no longer see me physically, but I will be with you always. For this reason, you will never run out of real and genuine love because you are not the source. I am. My source is our Creator. You simply have to decide whether or not to let my love flow through you to others. If you nurture your relationship with me, you will never be lacking in my presence and my power." There was murmuring among all of them. Butch gazed at him as if transfixed.

"Since I have eaten with you as well as touched many of you, you know that I am real and not just some vision. I will appear to you for several more solar cycles. Then, even when I am no longer appearing as I do now, I will still be with you. I will always be with you. I will see some of you during the next solar cycle. Until then, farewell." He smiled, and then vanished.

Slowly, the crowd began to disburse. Pixie looked at Walter and Butch, and both were smiling at her. She stepped a bit closer to them. "Let's return to the foliage. I am ready to go home. You?" They nodded. The others did not notice that, after the three stepped into the shadows, they vanished.

Back at Pixie's space station, they reappeared where they left, but Walter and Butch had their normal appearance. They were quiet but not somber. "Walter, you and I need to go to Gaardian Center. I want to talk to Qaak. How about you?" Pixie smiled.

"Okay, Xpraepostq." He pronounced it very carefully, with the help of his Gaardian ring.

Her smile broadened. "That's the first time you've ever attempted to pronounce my real name. Not bad for a human!"

"I thought medical terms were sometimes difficult to pronounce, but your name beats all." Butch also smiled. "Say it, Pixie, and I'll listen carefully."

"Xpraepostq."

Butch shook his head. "I don't want to insult you by pronouncing it wrong. If you do not mind, I will continue to call you 'Pixie.' I am glad I came today. It puts some unusual substance to my new Christian faith."

Walter smiled. "I can well understand why. I too have a new perspective on the Christ I have followed for most of my life. Maybe you and I can discuss this more when Pixie and I get back." Walter paused. "How do you like flying an SVX?"

He was enthusiastic. "It's fun! We ought to keep one or two of them handy on *The Grace* for short trips and training flights. I'm going to suggest it to John when I get back."

"Good idea, Butch." Walter reflected Butch's mood in his own voice and face. "Pixie, want to join me in my SVX? I can drop you off here when we return."

"Good!" Her golden skin seemed to sparkle slightly. Let's go!" The three vanished into their vehicles. Butch headed for the Earth's moon.

"Computer. Gaardian Center. My alternate route and speed." Walter and Pixie flashed out of sight as they headed for Gaardian Center."

As stars appeared and disappeared, Walter and Pixie looked at each other and outside. From the passenger seat, she gazed at her friend. "I perceive you're not in any hurry."

"I know you're a little confused with regard to Eiraynay. I've some perspective on him that I think might be helpful to you."

"Really? You just met him today, and all that you know about him before today is what I have told you. What gives?"

"Let's stop and talk." They slowed down to sub-light speed and halted. Except for a small amount of space dust, the nearest celestial body was millions of miles away. Walter's ring shimmered, and the passenger compartment grew to the size of a small room with two chairs. Stars could still be seen beyond the windows.

"Are you getting romantic?"

Walter smiled. "I'll admit it's tempting, but not this time." Walter looked off into space for a moment and then turned back to face her. "Pixie, there're a lot of things I could simply tell you or export as data to your computer for you to study. It would be easier to help you understand my understanding of Eiraynay if we mind melded. Are you game?"

"Of course. Let us do a total mind meld – my species does body melds for intimacy, but this would not be the same. We can meld our heads, instead of simply transferring information in certain areas as Qaak and others do. I will understand if you do not want to. If we totally meld, then you will know all that I know, and I will know all that you know. We will share not only our memories but also our ideas, thoughts, and training. You will be able to speak my language and understand my people's culture – and vice versa."

Walter nodded. "There is one condition. I know we can trust each other with things we have not yet told each other, but we have to agree not to reveal to anyone else that we have melded. We may even have to lie and say that we have not. We both treasure the truth very highly, but this you and I would have to protect with our lives. Okay?"

"Agreed. All you have to do is lean over and put your face into mine when you see me transform."

Pixie's body seemed to glow and become almost translucent. She moved toward him. As he leaned over, his head melted into hers, and Walter's body began to glow as her head melted and flowed like golden honey over his. In a matter of about a minute, their bodies glowed brighter and brighter until both were almost pure light. After about ninety seconds, their bodies emerged from the light, and her body took a normal form again.

Pixie was excited. "I was not sure how well it would work, because I had never done it with a different species before. It was both different and better with you than anything I could have imagined." She paused. "Eiraynay is my personal savior! He's my people's savior!" Pixie began to giggle and then to laugh. "Now I understand why Butch was so excited! The joy is infectious!"

"I don't know what to say. I know one thing – that I'll see my life, you, Xpraepostq – all of life and creation – a bit differently now."

"Yes. You pronounced my name perfectly for the first time. Try my language!"

In her language, he said, "The Lord is my shepherd. I shall not want."

"Perfect!" She smiled and looked out into space for a moment. "How shall we report this to Gaardian Center? They know we are coming."

"How about a mental video presentation? We can confine our report to the facts. I can share my experiences with the voice, and you can share both of our experiences with Eiraynay."

"No argument here – how could there be after our meld?" She giggled.

"Let's get back on our way. You can assemble the mental video while I fly." The 'den' became the passenger compartment of the SVX again, and soon they were flashing across the sky, arriving at Gaardian Center in moments.

As Pixie and Walter walked across the giant atrium at Gaardian Center, Kieya met them. "Walter! Xpraepostq! I am looking forward to your report. We will not meet for three time periods. Qaak is on the planet to think and reflect. He told me to tell you, Walter, to join him at Canyon of Red Falls when you got here." Walter vanished. "Xpraepostq, I'd like to walk a while with you myself. Would you join me at Blue Water Park?" The two of them vanished.

Kieya continued. "You and I can enjoy ourselves here, while Walter talks with Qaak." She paused. "Long ago the Gaardians had moved all of their operations off of the planet's surface and had let the planet return mostly to its natural state of beauty." She and Pixie walked together along a river that was similar in color to the best of the Adriatic Sea on Earth. "This water contains no salt of any kind. It cascades amidst these brilliantly colored crystalline stones from a dozen different directions into larger streams and rivers until all the water reaches a whirlpool near the center of the park. From time to time, creatures of various species will slip into one of the rivers to glide into the whirlpool, where after spinning around several times they will drop through the center. Below, they will be separated from the water, which is pumped to lakes high above us in the hills. Most creatures are almost immediately returned to where they started."

Pixie and Kieya enjoyed the scenery and an approaching sunset, and shared trivia that nourished their friendship, while on the other side of the planet, Walter was enjoying the colors of the rain forest near Canyon of Red Falls. It was an entirely different environment, just after sunrise. The rainforest there reminded Walter of a park in the southwest corner of South Island in New Zealand on Earth. The main difference was in the colors. The rainforest on Gaardian looked like it was in Earth's equivalent of autumn – only these colors were permanent. Walter did not look long before finding Qaak. The ancient three-legged creature was in his favorite spot in the rainforest, next to a geyser that almost constantly spewed water one hundred meters into the air – almost as high as the adjacent red waterfall that cascaded into the canyon.

"Hello, old friend!" Walter greeted Qaak with a clumsy hug.

"Hello, Walter!" It is good to see your handsome human face. Did Kieya send you down here?"

"Of course! You know she did. You still share a mental link part of the time don't you?"

Qaak cackled quietly. "Yes, but only once or twice a day. We each need our privacy." Qaak leaned back on one folded leg like a chair. "I wanted to speak to you before the conference. This is a conversation that I'll not share with Kieya and the others unless you tell me to."

"What's up, old friend?" Walter continued to smile but less brightly.

"If you're willing, I want you to tell me what happened on your first mission – the one where you sent the Quzaks home."

"Have you not studied my report?"

"Of course! However, we both know that you did not accomplish that feat by yourself. In addition, I suspect you know it was not other Gaardians that helped you send those ships home. If you are not ready yet to tell me I'll wait, but I really would like to know."

Walter looked intently at his friend. "Qaak, my friend, let me begin by saying that the information you seek is somewhat related to what Pixie and I are going to report at Gaardian Center."

"Really?" Qaak's eyes glowed for a moment. "Indeed! That did not occur to me! Does it all have something to do with what you call 'the glow' of which you have previously spoken? Is the glow that of The Creator?"

"Yes." Walter answered softly and carefully. "It's important, Qaak, that you draw your own conclusions. I will tell you this much more. The material you gave to Butch to read is also related to all of this."

"Are you talking about the history of religions in other cultures on other planets?"

"Yes."

"Indeed." Qaak's eyes continued to glow as he closed them. He hummed softly to himself, as the glow of his eyes seemed to pulse slightly in intensity. Walter had seen this many times before and knew better than to interrupt Qaak's thoughts. Suddenly his eyes opened as he laughed. "Yes! It is logical! It's fantastic!" He paused and heaved a sigh.

Qaak cackled. "Those who haven't met your Jesus, as you have, necessarily scoff. I remember when training you during your dreams, you developed a fondness for dinners of prime rib. I thought it was interesting you had a passion for a food, because it was not otherwise part of your personality. I had never thought of food as anything other than necessary nourishment, so your interest in prime rib made no sense to me. I had to find out what you were so passionate about, so I went with you on your birthday. I slipped my mind inside of yours for your trip to the restaurant, so that I could experience all of your normal human life. There were several surprises."

"Surprises?"

"Yes. Your human family was bonded with a level of love that I had seldom seen in any species. In addition, there was a level of emotional intimacy that was very refreshing. The biggest surprise, however, was the prime rib dinner you ate. From then on, I understood why so many affluent humans have a problem with their weight. Through you I experienced culinary pleasure that I had previously only been told about."

"What does experiencing my birthday on earth have to do with understanding of The Creator or of Jesus?"

"Simply this: ... Until I actually tasted – through you – what prime rib tastes like, I scoffed at the idea of food that could bring pleasure. In the same way, until someone actually meets The Creator through that planet's savior, a logical person may scoff at the idea of that kind of intimacy with God."

"I see what you mean. Until Pixie met Eiraynay, and until Butch met Jesus, to both, God was mostly an intellectual idea with minimal substance. Meeting God in that way was for them – as for everyone else – a life-changing experience."

"Yes! Exactly! Until now, your encounters with the glow were intellectual curiosities for me. Now I think I am ready to meet The Creator. Perhaps it will happen soon. We will have another time to discuss this when we again have privacy. Now, let's get to that meeting!"

They both vanished from the surface of the planet and reappeared in the Center's atrium. As if on cue, a moment later Pixie and Kieya appeared nearby. The four of them walked into the Conference Center.

As the senior Gaardian, Qaak ambled to the platform and led off the discussion. "Walter and Xpraepostq have witnessed something on her planet that was truly remarkable. It was a pre-religious event. Seldom have Gaardians had the opportunity to witness the beginnings of a new religious faith. The event sequence was a striking parallel to similar religious beginnings on many other planets we have studied, including the Christianity of Walter's planet."

"Yes," Kieya responded, "Xpraepostq – that's 'Pixie' to Walter – has given me a detailed report. They have a series of edited event records to show us. Walter, since this is all so new to Pixie, would you like to introduce what you are going to show us?"

Walter nodded. He stepped onto the platform and turned to face the gathering. "As Qaak has indicated, what Pixie and I have witnessed is remarkably similar to the early records of my own faith. Of particular interest to me is the fact that the given name of Pixie's Savior, Eiraynay, is a close approximation of Earth's ancient Greek language word for 'peace.' As you will see in the records we are about to show you, Pixie's first encounter with the resurrected Eiraynay is also a remarkable parallel with an event recorded in Christian scriptures."

Walter and Pixie then show the edited three-dimensional records of Eiraynay and their encounters with him. As the records played, there was quiet murmuring among the Gaardians. Qaak rocked back and forth on one of his legs folded under him. His eyes sometimes gave off their telltale glow. He was obviously content.

As the recordings conclude, Kieya stood to speak. "What we obviously have here is an example of how legends are sometimes formed, and how sometimes these so-called legends are actually the stories of legitimate religion centered on The Creator."

The Gaardians gathered into small groups. Kieya and Qaak, having talked with Pixie and Walter, realized that this was not simply the beginning of legendary material. They talked with Walter on into the night.

17. Piatek ["PIE-uh-tek"]

Hours later, the SVX was flashing through galaxies. "I know it now! Eiraynay is the savior of my world! Since I have shared it with the other Gaardians, it is no longer like a dream! It is real!" Pixie talked excitedly with Walter as they cruised back to her world. Suddenly, the vehicle came to a halt at her satellite home, and both vanished from the ship to her living quarters. "After our mind merge, I have come to understand the parallels between Eiraynay and Jesus."

"Yes. The night before Jesus was executed, He had a final meal with them. At that time, He passed a loaf of bread to His closest followers and told them that it represented His body. A bit later, He passed a cup of wine to them to represent the blood He was going to shed for them. The afternoon after He was resurrected, He met some of his followers as they walked along a road near where Jesus had been executed. They did not recognize Him at first, but that evening when they were sharing in some bread they suddenly recognized Him. Then He vanished."

"That is very similar to what happened to me when I was jogging with Eiraynay in that park. I am going to have to record that story for His followers."

"Sounds good! Such a story might eventually become part of the scriptures of your species."

"Be sure to Gaardian mail me a copy of your scriptures. I've a feeling it will be helpful to me as I begin to understand what happened with Eiraynay."

"For me, all of this is not a surprise because of the voice that I told you about. Let me show you." Walter's ring shimmered, and each of Walter's experiences with the voice was played back. Pixie totally immersed herself in what she was seeing and hearing.

"So you knew what was about to take place on my planet with Eiraynay?"

"Not exactly. As you saw in our mind meld, the voice only tells me just enough to guide me. I did not know any details except that, as the voice said, I had to be here for you as all of it unfolds. Our being in each other's lives is part of The Creator's plan."

Pixie was thoughtful. "At Gaardian Center only Qaak and Kieya truly believed what we showed them. The others were skeptical."

"I don't think we need to worry about that. In forty years of full-time Christian service, I learned that there would always be skeptics. It seems you and I will be going to have vital roles in the lives of Kieya and Qaak – particularly Qaak."

Suddenly, the satellite around them seemed to fade, as a glow began to surround them. Pixie started to speak. "Walter…" He motioned her to be silent. For the first time, they listened to the voice together.

> "I am pleased with both of you. Do not be afraid. Both of you know from your forebears what it means to be faithful to me, though one of you has had less practice. Xpraepostq, you know me through Eiraynay as Walter knows me through Jesus."

"What about Qaak and Kieya?" Walter's tone was serious.

> "Kieya's time will come soon. Qaak is ready to listen to your faith journey in your voice. He knows the facts and knows you, but now needs to know you in terms of your faith."

"We'll need your help as usual, Lord."

> "Speak from your heart. I will guide you." The voice paused briefly. "Xpraepostq, go with Walter, but not just because you love him. You can learn a great deal about following me and learning from me by watching Walter. He has much to teach you before you meet the one who is to be your mate. Your mate is among those who have been pursuing Eiraynay's followers. He has now met me, and I am molding him into the servant I want him to be as he walks with you."

"Who is he?"

> "Be patient. Everything is unfolding, as it should. He is almost ready for you, just as Walter's mate is almost ready for him. The two of you can still be as close as you are even after you have your mates."

"When do we seek out Qaak, Lord?"

> "Qaak is ready to seek me, and soon I will lead him to you for instruction. Trust me, and let me be God. I will be with you."

The glow faded. Pixie was the first to speak. "I've never had an experience like that! Experiencing God makes Gaardian technology almost seem primitive. Is it always that way?"

"Whenever the voice has spoken to me directly, it has been like that – peaceful, serene, powerful, and sublimely comfortable beyond pleasure, although at first I also found it un-nerving, as you know, since our meld. Prior to hearing God's voice directly the first time my experiences of God were as varied as all my other experiences." Walter paused. "This has been a full day, Pixie. I think I will head back to my Moon Base and wait for Qaak's call while catching up on some work there. Gaardian mail me or drop in if you need me, okay?" Walter kissed her lightly and then vanished to his SVX. Walter's brow was furrowed, deep in thought as he flashed back home.

+ + +

In another galaxy far away, the Quzaks had not learned their lesson. The mates of the military leaders were actively making plans for their next encounter with the Gaardians. The Quzak Commander's mate was speaking to a group of children on a beach, not far from her home.

Ooza was looking out at the twin suns, low on the horizon of her planet's sky. "My mate has been forced home from a military mission in disgrace by some species called Gaardians." The children with her on the beach were listening in rapt attention. "Now our leaders are talking about an alliance with them. They are also talking with some of our oldest enemies about an alliance. So far, I do not know what this means. My mate needs to know, so I am going to find out." She paused, looking up at the suns again, and then turned her gaze back to the children. "That's all for today, children. Thank you for inviting me to be with your class today."

Ooza rose from the sand, nodded to the children's teacher, and walked to a vehicle hovering nearby. A door opened automatically. She got in and touched a blue triangle. "Supreme headquarters, level fourteen." The craft moved automatically, and she sat back and silently studied the buildings as they passed by. Touching a small disk on her chest, she leaned forward to the transparent front of the craft and said, "Personal note. I do not understand why we are in talks with our enemies. We never negotiate for power – Quzaks take it." Her expression was grim. "It was bad enough that we come home in disgrace. Now we are talking with our bitterest enemies. What is next? End note." She touched the disk again and sat back.

As the vehicle came to a halt, Ooza got out and confidently strode to the nearby doorway while the craft zoomed off. Inside, Ooza spotted several friends on a raised lounge having drinks. As she approached, she greeted each of eight females with a hug. "I need to know what we are doing!" she said. "Our mates may control the military, but if we are going to maintain coordinated control of them, we are going to have to get our thinking congruent, and our intimate contact speeches well honed. Why are we letting them talk to our enemies?"

Zahrahted [ZAH-rah-ted"], a green-haired beauty next to Ooza, was the mate of the highest-ranking general in the military. "The sisterhood is not in danger Ooza. You missed a lot while you were being debriefed. We do want your input because the plan we have put together is almost as complicated as it is powerful."

"Go on."

"We have decided to work a double agenda, so that whichever way the plasma flows, we Quzaks maintain power. We have decided that these so-called Gaardians have more power than we can even imagine. Our first priority is to have that power either working to our advantage, or at least not working against us again."

"Agreed!" Several of the females nodded.

Zahrahted continued, "We are briefing our best negotiators on coming up with a working relationship with the Gaardians. That is the first of two strategic fronts, and it is the one that is public. Behind the scenes, our best intelligence officers are telling their counterparts among our enemies that the Gaardians are a danger to them too. They are exploring possible alliances based on 'my enemy is your enemy.' This strategy is being done in unofficial channels. If it fails only our agents are at risk." Ooza nodded in agreement.

Zahrahted continued, "Here's where you come in, Ooza. Since your mate is the most influential among the largest number of troops, what do you think should be his stance in all of this? What would be of the greatest advantage to you, to your mate, and to the rest of the troops?"

Ooza furrowed her brow. "I must admit I was angry when I first heard the rumors. Now I see the wisdom we can use for our mates. Right now, he passionately hates the Gaardians, particularly the one that disgraced us. On the other hand, he is very practical. He has hated the Gaardians for only a few dozen paks, but he has hated the Paqazitpis since his father taught him to hate."

Piatek ["PIE-uh-tek"], one of the older and wiser females, was shorter than the others and had light green hair. She said, "My father taught me to hate the Paqazitpis ["PAH-uh-zip-eez"] before I started formal schooling." Her voice exudes wisdom. "Your mate became a High Commander not only because of your guidance and wisdom, but because he inherited some of his own. I am sure you do not underestimate him."

"No, much of my passionate support for him comes from appreciating that wisdom as well as his physical assets. I think because he is such a public figure, it is best that I guide him toward support of a working relationship with the Gaardians over against our other enemies. I am not sure he needs to know yet of the other strategy."

Zahrahted nodded. "That is very wise. Are you continuing to guide him while approaching sleep?"

Ooza smiled. "Usually, I would. This is different. I am suggesting a romantic getaway, to help us leave our troubles behind. He has wanted to get away for a long time, but we have not had a chance. When he is the most relaxed, I can then lead him in the right direction. I will not use our sleep cycle for this unless absolutely necessary. I want to save that strategy for more critical situations." Ooza smiled again.

"It sounds wise. I like your strategy." A small triangle on her wrist chirped. "It is time. Our mates are finishing their physical training period and will be hungry. Let us stay with the plan and meet back here in twenty paks to discuss any complications."

"Agreed." Ooza and Zahrahted hugged first, and then the others followed suit as they headed to their homes. There were a few short conversations, as all said their farewells, and soon the lounge was empty.

Ooza strode to the door. Both suns were almost below the horizon, and the sky was a rainbow of colors. "Much better," Ooza mumbled as she got into a nearby hovercraft.

"State destination again please."

"That was not the destination. Take me home." The craft moved.

+ + +

At Gaardian Planet in her quarters, Kieya was seeing Ooza traveling in the hovercraft on a view screen. Watching the Quzaks, she was relaxed. She grunted, rose, and vanished. She appeared in the atrium at Gaardian Center.

Qaak materialized a few moments later, and they strolled into the conference hall together. Most of the other Gaardians -- nearly two thousand - were already in their places. Qaak strolled up onto the platform. A three-dimensional display showed the female Quzaks in their meeting as Qaak began to speak. "I have been talking with the Quzaks about a working relationship. Even without my good friend Kieya's report, I know that the Quzaks cannot be trusted. I operate on the assumption that they do not know about our surveillance. I see nothing to be gained by a working relationship with them other than perhaps recruiting a resident Gaardian at some future date. I do recommend we put personnel on the planets in question that are in Quzak space. Kieya, would you please make your presentation?"

Without a word, Kieya launched a full three-dimensional report with rapidly flashing scenes beginning with scenes of what happened when Walter encountered the Quzaks and sent them home. When the other Gaardians saw the Quzak armada transported back to their home solar system, there were quiet murmurs. Qaak's memo regarding Walter's training and ability being exceeded in the operation was heard as commentary while the three-dimensional video shows the Quzaks drifting without fuel before being transported to the surface of their home world.

Next was a visual of Ooza, Zahrahted, and Piatek, planning the Quzak strategy for their mates. Kieya spoke with quiet authority. "The Quzak alliances with their enemies are potentially an ongoing minor nuisance. Even if the alliances were all fully functional, their efforts can be contained with little effort. It is recommended that since their crews are now both in place and functionally effective, Walter and Xpraepostq should handle Gaardian responses initially. Their sense of teamwork rivals that of Qaak and me. Qaak, I believe now is the time to add the other report."

Qaak spoke confidently. "I've been talking with Quzak leaders about a treaty. The duplicity of the Quzaks - holding treaty talks while secretly talking with their enemies regarding an alliance against the Gaardians - was expected. I agree with Kieya that such an alliance would be a minor problem, but it nonetheless must be dealt with. I submit that, in light of how effectively Walter handled the Quzaks the first time, that he continue the work. I also agree that Xpraepostq should work with him. They work well together, and the experience of working with the Quzaks would be valuable to her. Are the two of you agreeable with that plan?"

Pixie spoke with confidence equal to Qaak's. "My team is really beginning to function as a team. I think it would be good for them to work without me for a time, and I am very interested in exploring this Quzak challenge - even if it is a relatively minor one."

Walter responded, nodding. "I have two teams that work well together. My base team has excellent administrative and policing abilities. My mobile team, which primarily works on my ship, has all the skills necessary to do scientific, exploratory, and if required, military work. I know I can trust them to be on their own. I have equipped several of them with subsidiary rings that access Gaardian power when necessary. Having Pixie come along is a great idea, and I think my crew would enjoy getting to know her and working with her." Walter paused thoughtfully. "As for the Quzaks, I'd like to see if a productive diplomatic relationship can be achieved."

Qaak's eyes closed briefly, and when he opened them again, they had their signature glow. "Good! Unless others have objections, it is settled. Proceed immediately. Meanwhile, it will be necessary for all of us to meet here again early tomorrow. I will have another issue to discuss with all of you at that time. Agreed?"

There were murmurs and nods of assent throughout the hall. "Very well. Tomorrow then. Walter, Pixie, I want to see you in my quarters. Refresh yourselves first - I need a short rest. Then we shall meet." The Gaardians disbursed and begin disappearing – some like Kieya and Qaak to their permanent quarters at Gaardian Center, and others to guest quarters. Pixie and Walter beamed to the planet surface to enjoy the park directly below.

In his home later, Qaak was the perfect host. They had always found Qaak's apartment very comfortable. He was warm, hospitable, and gracious. "Make yourselves comfortable, my friends. Make furniture that is the most comfortable to you. Walter, how do you like the fireplace I have created? I enjoyed yours on your moon so much I made one for myself."

Walter grinned. "It's terrific, Qaak."

"I enjoy fireplaces too, Qaak. I have not created one for my quarters yet, but you have given me a good idea. Walter and I've had many great conversations in front of his fireplace in his base's den."

Qaak spoke gently and quietly. "Walter, again I ask, did not The Creator help you to send the Quzaks home?" The old teacher looked at him intently.

"Yes, Qaak, He did. I use the pronoun 'He' because I know The Creator through The Creator's fully human Son, Jesus."

"Yes, of course. I have studied your Bible and the other books that I gave to your physician, Butch. I have been searching what remains of the records of my own species and have discovered a similar phenomenon. Last night, I searched my childhood memories. It was difficult because so much time has passed. I vaguely remember my parents telling me..."

Pixie interrupted. "Your parents? You've never spoken of your parents!"

"Yes. I have thought of them only rarely in recent thousands of years. Last night I remembered something that had not occurred to me for so long that I do not know the last time. My parents told me about one of our own named Qapoku ["kah-PO-coo"]. The more I analyze those early memories and scan my records, the more I realize how the life of Qapoku was a remarkable parallel to those of Eiraynay and Jesus."

Pixie's eyes gleamed. "Did you know that I've accepted Eiraynay as my savior?"

"Ah! Walter, are you aware of this?"

"Yes, she asked about my teachings regarding the Christian faith, and somehow The Creator moved her heart. A little later, she and I heard from The Creator."

"Indeed! She heard the voice at the same time you did?"

"Yes." She spoke quietly. "I heard the voice as Eiraynay, and Walter heard it as Jesus. The voice spoke to both of us at the same time, and I heard it in my language while Walter heard it in his."

"I wonder...." Qaak's voice trailed off as the glow familiar to Pixie and Walter began to fill the room. The fireplace seemed to disappear along with the rest of Qaak's quarters as the glow filled their space.

"It has taken many millennia for you to be ready to hear my voice Qaak. You have called Walter and Xpraepostq here to discuss your retirement, but there is yet much for you to accomplish before I call you home."

"Home? Are you The Creator? Did my parents know you as Qapoku?"

"Your parents know me as Qapoku, Creator, and many other names. There is more for me to accomplish through you before I call you home. Go with Walter and Xpraepostq as they work with the Quzaks. Walter will teach you about me. Pixie will grow with you. You will offer them wisdom that I will give to you when the time is made perfect. Be at peace, Qaak. Your retirement will last longer than you have expected. Then I will call you home, and you will see your parents again. I am with you Qaak. I make everything new. The three of you will see many new things."

The glow faded. At first, the three of them were silent, staring into the flames of the fireplace as it reappeared. "I would not have thought it possible." Qaak spoke quietly, but with evident excitement. "How could I have known that I could see the universe as differently as I do now? To say that this is incredible creates a new standard for understatement!"

"So you've decided to retire?" asked Walter.

"Yes. The Gaardians will need to establish a new convener. Kieya does not want the honor. She too is nearing retirement."

Pixie was pensive. "What will happen to the Gaardian leadership team? What will we do without you?"

Qaak chuckled. "Evidently, I am still going to be around for a good while. You can't get rid of me easily." His eyes twinkled. "I am glad that you and I have become intimate with The Creator at the same time. It gives us a kinship, Xpraepostq." Qaak chuckled again. "You and I will be classmates with Walter as our teacher!"

Walter laughed. "Yes! Teacher and student trading places! I did not think of this! You spoke of needing to get another convener. Do you've someone in mind?"

Qaak was quiet as he looked at Walter intently. "You."

"Me?" Walter stared. "I've not had nearly as much experience as the other Gaardians! Why would you want me to do it?"

"You have gifts that make age and experience less important. Kieya and I have already discussed it."

Walter was not pleased. "I'm not ready to be the convener!! Isn't there someone more qualified? Someone with more experience? Who has the same gifts?"

"No."

Pixie had a sly grin on her face. "Can we still snuggle in front of the fire after you are crowned king?" They all laughed.

"Tomorrow I'll tell the others of my retirement and make my suggestion. The decision will be made slowly and deliberately. When the voting was done to elect me the convener it took more than fifty meetings." Qaak paused. "On the other hand, somehow I suspect that The Creator is ready for all of this and has planned accordingly."

Walter nodded. "You're right. All that God does, God does well." Walter stood up, and so did Pixie. "Get some sleep my friend. Tomorrow is a big day for you. Good night!"

"Good night Qaak," said Pixie.

"Tomorrow," murmured Qaak. The other two vanished.

+ + +

Meanwhile, the same Quzak females who had gathered previously were seated on comfortable furniture in a circle. Piatek was shifting on her sofa. "The Gaardian called 'Qaak' will be here in twenty-two paks. I believe we should launch the attack at least five paks before he gets here."

"I agree." Zahrahted leaned forward and spoke intensely. "The combined armada is almost overkill. We planned on attacking and conquering sector 9-V-47 soon anyway. It would have taken at least twenty mutapaks before we gained full control with just our own ships. With our ships combined with those of our six worst enemies, it can be done in twenty-five to thirty paks."

Ooza almost interrupted. "Yes! My mate says we have a fleet five times as large as the one we took almost as far as the planet called 'Earth.' He does not think the Gaardians can stop us. If they try, the battle will tell us much about Gaardian strength."

"The Gaardians are centered in the opposite direction." Piatek was enthusiastic. "I estimate that for our ships to travel the distance from the planets we are about to conquer to the Gaardian headquarters it would take more than my lifetime."

"Fantastic!" Zahrahted and the others nodded. "If this 'Qaak' creature is on his way here he will not be focused upon our armada far on the other side of us."

"I've a new twist my mate has added to this." Ooza was conspiratorial.

"What's that?"

"The commanders have decided to split off about a fifth of the forces to attack four other planets in adjacent sectors. We have already conquered them, but this will be an opportunity for plunder."

"Excellent!" Piatek stood up. We shall meet here before meeting Qaak. Agreed?" All murmured assent. Each went off to join her mate.

+ + +

At Gaardian Center, the Gaardians watched the meeting on their giant three-dimensional display. "What is your pleasure?" asked Qaak. Will you leave this to our best judgment?"

Waagere walked to the podium. "This nuisance can be handled in several different and simple ways. Gaardian shields can stop these ships from going further, but of course, if they are determined enough they will eventually find ways around the shields. Walter's previous strategy can be used – returning the ships and crews to their home planets without damage or loss."

As Waagere spoke, Kieya began walking forward. "I believe our action should be more punitive. The Quzaks have been previously warned, and they have passed on that warning to their former enemies, who are now their allies."

"What do you have in mind?"

"I do not think we need to destroy any lives, but some sort of destruction of their property would seem to be in order. I do not think simply separating them from their ships will solve the problem. When they recover their ships, they will try again. We need to slow them down. What do you think, Qaak?"

Qaak stood where he was and spoke. "These are all reasonable responses. We have previously decided to let Walter and Xpraepostq use their best judgment. I will be with them. Please let us do our jobs. Agreed?" Assent was telepathically vocal. "Very well. With that out of the way, I wish to announce my retirement, effective as soon as we Gaardians select a new convener." There was silence. "I recommend Walter. We will convene for discussing this as soon as I return from my journey with Xpraepostq and Walter. That is all." They all vanished.

Arriving at Earth's Moon Base, Walter, Pixie, and Qaak lost no time in briefing the crew of *The Grace*. In the lounge, they gathered around the fireplace. The entire crew was sitting in chairs or on the floor, facing Walter, Pixie, and Qaak, who were standing next to the fireplace. Walter's face showed the seriousness of the situation. "All three of us are here because something important is happening. The Quzaks are up to their old tricks."

Butch was more casual. "Last time we didn't have to do much. What's different?"

Debbie's tone was light-hearted. "Unless things are a lot different it should not take much effort to send them back again."

Jody's attitude was similar. "Yeah! How hard can it be?"

"This is a different sort of challenge." Walter smiled.

"How?" Karen asked.

"The Quzaks have formed alliances with their worst enemies to face their common foe – us. They've formed an armada a couple dozen times larger than last time and have a much bigger arsenal."

Butch lost his casual attitude. "Then what –"

Walter interrupted. "I don't want to waste time giving everyone all the details right now. John, we need to intercept the armada shortly after it gets underway. Program the navigation accordingly. Butch, work out a rotation for your staff aboard *The Grace* so that the majority is on duty at all times. Keeta, I am going to have a special assignment for you. Asayak, I want you to do an assessment of their weapons as soon as we intercept the armada, so that you can provide that information to all personnel as needed. Jody, Karen, and Debbie, you are going to get some extra training in the next few hours. I want everyone on board and ready to go within thirty minutes. Qaak, Pixie, and I will be in my quarters until we get underway. That's all."

Walter, Pixie, and Qaak vanished. Some of those nearest appear startled for a moment, and then everyone started moving out of the conference room fast. A few hours later, *The Grace* departed from orbit around Earth's Moon. John set navigation programming to have them intercept the new Qaak armada shortly after it got underway.

In his quarters, Walter discussed the situation with Pixie and Qaak. "What did you think of Kieya's suggestions? I don't think we need to consider those of Waagere."

"I agree that we need a bigger demonstration of Gaardian power." Pixie was adamant. "Confiscating their ships, even if done with a flourish, won't impress them."

"Correct." Qaak fixed his gaze first on Pixie then on Walter. "When you and The Creator transported the Quzaks back to their planet, it was impressive, and all of us here know that the power it took to do that was greater than anything Gaardian technology had previously done. The problem was that the power was not obvious. There was insufficient sophistication among the Quzaks to recognize the extent of The Creator's power that was used." Qaak paused, and his eyes glowed for a moment. Walter started to speak, but Qaak interrupted. "Let's look at the locations of the Quzaks and their enemies. Let us consider seven civilizations on five planets. Let's also consider the psychology of what we do."

"I think I know where your thoughts are leading us." Walter's ring shimmered, and a map of the affected sectors of space was displayed three dimensionally. "Perhaps we can make this as simple as one-two-three."

"Meaning?" Pixie looked at him intently.

"Since the armada is on the move already, we first need to return them to their home planets. It is important that we begin our actions before they split off part of their armada to do plundering. All of this will be a little old for the Quzaks, but for their allies, it will be impressive. This time, let us return only the crews to their planets and not their ships. We can get help from Gaardian Center to do DNA mapping, so crew members can be transported to their own homes. My crew here on *The Grace* can gather the data and transmit it to Gaardian Center for analysis, mapping, and programming."

Qaak's voice was animated. "Yes! It is not a small order for your crew, but it can be handled fairly quickly. The challenge will be good for us! What do you have in mind for step two?"

"This is much easier technologically, but we will need a vote from Gaardian Center. Once everyone is on their home planets, we extinguish their suns."

"Ahh!" Pixie was excited. "I know we can do it fairly easily. I also know that the reaction on those planets will be extremely powerful, no matter how well their societies are developed. They cannot last long without the heat of those suns. What's the final step?"

Qaak's voice was now animated even more. "This too will require power and calculation. Gaardian Center must do the calculations. We will put the five planets in orbit around five different suns in five different sectors of Gaardian space. We will choose stars of approximately the same magnitude, color temperature, and mass. Waagere has done two before, and Kieya has done one. Our teamwork will pay off in the favor of these civilizations."

Pixie was excited. "Fantastic! That is one of your words Walter, but it fits. Let us do it! But...." Her voice trailed off.

Qaak looked at her intently. "You've something to add?"

"Yes." Pixie spoke more quietly. "What about giving the planets that are used to two suns just one sun and vice versa?"

Qaak's eyes glowed. "Indeed." He paused. "Yes! It is good psychology, and it will be a permanent reminder that they are in Gaardian space."

Walter also spoke more quietly. "I like it. I will brief the crew's officers tomorrow morning. They can pass the word. It should not take more than a couple of sleep cycles to gather the data – I've got a great crew."

"Good!" Qaak's eyes had a characteristic glow. "Let's get some sleep." Qaak vanished to his quarters.

Pixie leaned over and gave Walter a light kiss on the lips. "Good night my dear friend. See you in the morning." She too vanished. The familiar glow began to permeate the room.

> "**Very good. Everything is unfolding, as it should. Tonight as you sleep, I will teach you what you need to know about the days ahead. Be courageous. I am with you.**"

The glow faded quickly, and Walter fell asleep.

+ + +

The next morning's briefing began in its usual tone. Walter turned to his Science Officer on his right. "Debbie, before briefing your science team, query the ship's computer regarding DNA mapping. That will fill in your knowledge gaps. You already know how to set up most of it – Qaak has already taught you most of what you need to know. It's just a matter of putting things together." Debbie nodded.

He looked across the conference room table to his right. "John, the armada is going to rendezvous at star 12A-5-G15, the one I showed you earlier this morning. We need to be there before they get there, and they will get there in less than seventy-two hours. You can make it happen – there's time." John touched his electronic notepad a few times, as he nodded.

His communications officer at the other end of the table caught his gaze. "Karen, you already know most of what you actually need, but you need to query the computer regarding continuous ultra-stream data transfer."

"What's continuous ultra-stream data transfer?"

"Think of it as sending Gaardian mail at a rate multiplied by two googol." He smiled. She whistled. "Jody, you will need to put together extra power and controls for Karen's data operations. You don't need my help with that."

In the corner near the door was Walter's security officer. "Asayak, I want you to monitor all life forms continuously within two jumps of us. Before we arrive, I want you to see to it that we are ready to be under cloak regardless of the needs of the other departments."

Walter turned to his physician friend on his left. "Butch, I want you and your team to monitor the entire crew for emotional overload. Do not let anyone even come close. Make sure that everyone gets enough sleep and that their sleep cycles are complete."

He scanned everyone with his gaze. "Questions?"

"What about the billions of people – I use the term loosely – that are going to be affected by what we do? Most of them are not in the military. What is going to happen to them emotionally?" Ken was very serious.

"Good question, Ken. It will, in fact, be a psychological shock. That is intentional. We want pressure from the masses to restrain the military. Once this operation is done, each planet will be monitored by the Gaardian of their sector for any problems that may develop in the aftermath. If you want details on how that is done, send a G-mail to a Gaardian named Waagere. She can brief you on what has happened when this kind of action has been taken previously by the Gaardians. Other questions?"

He noticed the quizzical look of his intelligence officer sitting next to Debbie. "Keeta, get plenty of rest – I've a mission I want to discuss with you later." Walter paused and turned to look at Qaak, sitting behind him on one leg. His eyes were closed, and his body had a faint glow.

Walter turned back to the rest at the table. "Okay. Dismissed."

Everyone went to their posts. As Qaak, Pixie, and Walter walked to the bridge, Qaak's voice was colored with amusement. "I see the Quzaks are led by the same Commander whom you met the first time. Do you want to speak to him before we act?"

"I've been thinking about that." He paused. "It might be good in terms of the histories of these peoples that they were given the opportunity turn around and go home. Some of their historians will portray them as heroic for not giving in to the Gaardians, and some will portray them as foolish. The three of us know that they will not consider seriously anything I might say to them – I am the enemy."

"I agree." Pixie was thoughtful. "I think that we ought at least to confront them before acting. On the other hand, what would we do if they actually took us seriously?"

Qaak chuckled. "Little chance of that. Even if they give in this time, there will be another time. Our work will not have been wasted, because there will be less preparation later – it will only have been a delay. Both of you should appear to them. It's best if we allow them to assume that I am not with you, and that I am on my way to the Quzak planet."

"Sounds like fun!" Pixie was enthusiastic. "I have a suggestion. Why not have Keeta go along. Remaining totally transparent, she could do some useful intelligence work and get some good experience as well. We could retrieve her just after extinguishing the suns, and before we transport their worlds to their new locations."

"Pixie and I think alike. That's what I was referring to when I spoke to Keeta a moment ago."

"Indeed!" Qaak seemed almost to purr. "Excellent. She can get a feel for the Quzaks that we cannot get from simple monitoring. She is a valuable asset, Walter. You can use her more. Let's get some sleep." Qaak vanished, and Pixie and Walter followed.

The next morning, the three were again meeting with the officers in the starboard conference room. Walter made it clear that he was pleased with their work. "I'm proud of all of you, and everything is on schedule. Keeta, I want you to join Pixie and I when we go to the command ship."

"Yes, sir."

"I want you to be totally transparent – the Quzaks are not to know you are there. You will stay on board the command ship until just before we transport the planets to their new locations. You are to stay with the Quzaks and get a feel for who they are beyond the basic observable data. You must avoid being detected. Here is something for you." Walter extended a small ring. "As you put it on it will stay the same shade of yellow as you are. When you go transparent it will go transparent." She put it on and vanished along with the ring. A moment later, she reappeared. "Listen carefully Keeta. That ring will respond to your thoughts. If you need to return to *The Grace* just think it. Debbie, go to the monitor over there and tell me – do sensors show that Keeta is here?"

Debbie walked over to the panel and touched a keypad. "Wow! As far as normal sensors are concerned, she's not even here, yet I can see her here and with Gaardian technology."

"Good. That is the way it should be. Have a seat Debbie." Walter paused while she returned to her chair. "Keeta, to the best of my knowledge, it's impossible to design a sensor to detect you when you choose to be totally transparent while wearing the ring, except for Gaardian technology. I want you to know, however, that I will never let you be lost. The ship's computer, Pixie, Qaak, and I will always know where you are along with your status. You need not understand how, any more than you can understand how the ring works. It is simply true." He paused. "Jody, Karen, any problems with the data flow?"

Karen spoke first. "We finished transmitting the DNA data just before the meeting. If Jody and I had not been trained by you and Qaak we would never have dreamed that such a feat was possible."

Jody was enthusiastic. "I agree. I've a feeling that my work is not done, however."

Qaak laughed with his characteristic cackle. "You're as brilliant as you are beautiful, Jody. If only I was a few thousand years younger!" They all laughed. "Jody, you are going to have the honor of extinguishing the suns."

"What?"

"Yes! Walter, Pixie, and I have other tasks, so you get to do the honors. It requires a bit of preparation."

"You've never taught me how to extinguish a sun! Neither has Walter!"

Ken cut in. "Ah, come on Jody! If you can extinguish the passion in a man's heart, you can surely handle this!" There was more laughter.

"Easy Ken!" Walter smiled and paused while the laughter subsided. "Actually Jody, you already know how – you just don't realize it." He paused. "Picture in your mind how we convert energy into mass, such as the replication of food and anything else that we need on board *The Grace*. The principles are the same only on a larger scale. On board you use specially designed conduits and conversion modules. Now picture in your mind how we travel through space faster than light by folding the space around us. When I sent the Quzaks home, I folded space to let the Quzak armada fall back into the space of their own planet. In this case, you are going to fold space so that the energy feeds back upon itself to form matter – no conversion module will be necessary. The result is a cold mass, not unlike a typical 'dead' star. Get the idea?"

"I think so. Qaak, is there time for me to talk it through with you before you, Pixie, and Walter take off?"

Qaak spoke quietly. "Talk is not necessary. Come over here." Jody got up and moved her chair, to sit next to Qaak. "Now Jody, trust me again." Qaak put three of his fingers on Jody's face. A green glow enveloped the two of them for about five seconds. "Now you know how. Just remember a most important fact. This cannot and must not ever be done without the approval and participation of the Gaardian Center. Do not ever try doing it without a Gaardian either assisting or approving. You've seen what would happen."

Jody was quiet. "Qaak, it's not just a matter of me trusting you. You've shown me that you trust me, and I'll never violate that trust."

"I know." Qaak touched her nose and chuckled. There were smiles all around the conference room. "Debbie."

"Yes, Qaak."

"It's crucially important that you and your science team monitor very carefully every scrap of data as it comes in. When Walter is not on board and

Karen is Captain, she and John are going to be depending upon you for accurate input. You and Karen must monitor carefully the overall reactions on the surfaces of the five planets. You are going to be doing it from a remote location, so be sure the data streams are not interrupted." He paused. "Anything you want to add Walter?"

"Yes. I trust all of you. Just do the jobs you've been trained to do and all of this will go like clockwork."

"Clockwork?" Pixie smiled.

"It's an old human expression." Walter paused. "Okay, everyone, let's do it."

18. Moving Day

In the Quzak armada a few kilometers away, Ooza was massaging the shoulders of her mate as he barked into his communicator. "Tell everyone that all ships will come together as planned in one pak. Tell them to be in synchronous orbit around the star until all are assembled." He paused as Ooza rubbed his temples. "That's great, Ooza. We must massage each other more often – perhaps tonight before sleep. Today is important – we must delay the fun until later."

"Yes my love." Ooza was thoughtful as she remembered her last conversation with the other females. "We should be in orbit at the meeting place momentarily."

"Good." He looked at Ooza with love. "Let's look forward to that massage." They made their way to the meeting room where leaders of the other planets were waiting. "Greetings! We should be ready to proceed in three paks. Any problems?" The others were silent. "Display!" All turned to look at a display of the sun they were orbiting, showing thousands upon thousands of ships in orbit with them. "In two paks we shall be ready to proceed. Are there any...." His voice trailed off as Walter and Pixie appeared. "You!"

+ + +

Moon base personnel were observing the giant screen next to the conference room showing the Quzaks in their meeting room aboard the Quzak ship. Belinda was sitting at a console. "Ladies and gentlemen, this is Gaardian headquarters. We are sorry to interrupt your other programming, but you need to see what is happening with your Gaardian in another galaxy. Communications are being translated into your own language, so please disregard lip movements."

As the audio feed began, Walter was speaking. "After your last military experience with the Gaardians, you should have learned your lesson. Evidently, you did not. To make matters a bit more complicated you are involving others in your pointless effort."

"Pointless!" There were murmurs around the room, but Walter and Pixie were not letting any of them leave their places yet.

"You have a choice." Pixie's tone demanded their attention. "The Quzaks have informed the rest of you of what happened to them when they tried to invade a planet protected by the Gaardians. In launching this expedition, you do so with full knowledge that the Gaardians would not allow it. You now have the choice of either returning to your home planets or suffering the consequences. You measure time in paks. You have two of your paks to get underway back to your home planets. If you attempt to move in any other direction, you will all suffer the consequences." She paused very briefly. "There is more. The first encounter of the Quzaks with the Gaardians resulted in intentionally minimal discipline. If you attempt to complete this new mission the results will not be minimal by any definition." Walter and Pixie looked at each other, nodded together, and vanished simultaneously. Silently and invisibly, Keeta remained in one corner of the room.

+ + +

On Earth's Moon, Belinda highlighted Keeta's presence with commentary for both Earth's viewers and those of the other planets in Walter's sector. "The Gaardian wants the audiences in our sector to understand that the person being highlighted can be seen by us due to Gaardian technology, but she cannot be seen or in any way detected by the others."

+ + +

As soon as Walter and Pixie disappeared, there was pandemonium. Ooza climbed onto the table in front of her, opened her mouth wide, and made a sound of sixteen hertz – somewhat like the lowest note on a pipe organ – so loudly the table vibrated. There was silence as she climbed down and her mate rose to speak. "I do not like what they said any more than you do. I would not have thought of what happened to me and my soldiers as 'minimal.' Nevertheless, we cannot turn back now. We have far more troops this time – there will probably be more than just the one Gaardian ship to contend with, but we have fought fierce battles before." He paused. "We are ready. Return to your ships. We should proceed as timed. Agreed?"

A large Zargadete ["ZAR-guh-deet"] stood up at the other end of the room. Over six feet tall, with piercing eyes, muscular build, and crude but beautiful armor, he spoke with fury. "I don't like it either! Nevertheless, what choice do we have? We cannot let these Gaardians control our destiny!" There were cheers. All began disappearing to their ships.

+ + +

Aboard *The Grace*, Walter and the others were watching all of it on their bridge display with keen interest. "This was expected." He paused. "Karen, do you have Kieya standing by?"

"Yes. She says that as soon as their ships start to move all of their personnel will be transported to their homes on their home planets. She says she will signal us when it's done." She paused as they all wait about thirty seconds while staring at the display. The command ship began to move. "Kieya says they're all home." She gulped as Keeta appeared next to Walter.

"Wow! That was quick!" Karen's eyes were wide.

Walter turned to Keeta. "Keeta, did you learn a lot? Are you okay?"

"Yes sir. That was a fantastic experience! It will all be in my report. Thank you for letting me be there!"

"You're welcome." He turned to his Security Officer. "Asayak, as soon as you and Jody are sure that all the ships are headed into that sun give me a confirmation."

"Yes sir."

"Karen, transmit the message I gave you to all five planets in all languages. Make sure the data stream is clear so that there are no misunderstandings.

They must understand that what is about to happen will not be fatal, but it will be permanent."

"Right!"

Asayak's voice seemed to boom out. "All ships will be incinerated within fifteen minutes."

"Jody, are your preparations ready and complete?"

"Anytime."

"Karen, has the message been received as planned?"

"All frequencies and venues have been covered."

"All right, ladies and gentlemen, to use an old human expression, 'it's show time!' Jody, we will wait a few moments, and then you can do your thing. The stars should totally be extinguished in less than a minute using the method we have chosen."

"There's another way?"

"Yes, Jody. Actually, there are several ways. It all depends on how quickly you want to do the job and how messy you are willing to be. The method we are using is the most common. In the thousands of years of Gaardian police work, we have extinguished less than a hundred stars. We do not do it often because of the long-term consequences. In this case, we are going to be conservative."

"Conservative?" Toby stared. "How can extinguishing a star be conservative?"

"Actually, Toby, it's rather simple. You'll see." He paused. "Okay, Jody, snuff them out cold."

Jody's hands begin moving rapidly over her console. "As Qaak told me, it's really easy as … one … two … three!" She paused. "Wow! It is done! I just snuffed out their suns!"

"Well done, Jody." Walter paused. "Now, John, set course for transplant sector number one. Make it fast."

At the helm, John had previously set the course. "We should be there in a moment." Stars on the bridge's display go by too rapidly to be seen separately. "Okay, we're at the coordinates you gave me, but is that the sun that the planets are going to revolve around?"

"One of them. The Quzaks will see this sun in just a few moments. Every one of the five planets will get their own sun. The Quzaks had a double star, so they are getting a single sun. Those planets that had single suns will now have double suns." Walter smiled. "When the Quzaks look up, they will see their new sun where they are used to seeing a double one. Their greater shock will be at night. Look out there and notice what you see in our viewer. They will see very few stars at night, and the one's they can see with the naked eye will be very dim – very unlike the sky they previously had. Their scientists will find none of the stars familiar to them. They are now in a new galaxy – a galaxy that is so distant from their old galaxy that it would take them years at maximum speed to get there with their current technology. Both the Quzaks and their old enemies have new galaxies to get to know."

Karen caught Walter's eye. "Kieya with Gaardian mail for us. Shall I put it through?"

"G-mail? Sure!"

Kieya appeared on the bridge, as though she was actually there. "Well done everyone! You and your crew can be very proud, Walter!"

"Thanks, Kieya."

"This was much easier than the last time we moved a solar system. At Gaardian Center, it was almost routine."

"Good."

"Walter, I want you and your crew to come to Gaardian Center." She turned to John. "You might like to make it a sight-seeing cruise, John. There are some interesting sights to see between here and Gaardian Center."

"Where's Gaardian Center?"

"Walter will tell you." She turned to Pixie. "I am pleased, Pixie, that you worked so smoothly with Walter's crew – I'm impressed."

"It was easy. These are great people to work with." She cast a smile to everyone on the bridge.

Kieya turned back to Walter. "I suggest that you and your crew take at least three of your days to get to Gaardian Center. Check on the other planets that we have put in orbit around their new suns. On the way, you and Pixie can equip everyone on your crew with at least minimal ring support so that all of them can enjoy Gaardian Planet while we do a review at the Center."

"Sounds good. See you then."

"In three days." Kieya vanished.

+ + +

On Earth and at the Gaardian Moon Base, everyone was cheering. The other planets were reacting in similar ways. Belinda signed off saying, "This concludes our special Gaardian broadcast."

On Earth, Paula Rutledge was sitting at her anchor desk in the studio. Getting her cue that she was on camera, she was stunned. "I'm almost speechless! Here on Earth, we have just witnessed another Gaardian broadcast, sent to us from a great distance. I have here in the studio with me Dr. Mervin Eddison, an astronomer who works at Palomar Observatory in California, and who was one of the designers of the Abeen Telescope in orbit above us. Dr. Eddison, do we have any idea about where our Gaardian was during any of this broadcast?"

"Actually, yes! During the beginning of the broadcast, we were allowed to see the Quzak armada through the viewer of the Gaardian ship. I noticed that as the camera scanned the armada, it paused at one point. I was not sure why at first, because there was nothing unusual about the ships within that view."

"I think we have a repeat of that video available. Do we have it?" Paula paused and looked at her monitor. "Yes. Here is the scene to which you were referring."

"All right. Notice that in just a moment, the camera will pause from panning for a moment. There! Can you hold that? Yes! Now, can your technicians zoom in on the upper left there?" He paused. "Yes! There! Do you see that pattern of five stars, with two of them greater, one of them much larger and having a bluish cast? We have seen that cluster. I do not know the distance off hand, but I can do some checking and provide you with information in less than an hour."

"That would be fine, Dr. Eddison. We will look forward to that report. We now go to Deborah Lopez, who is at the Grande Cielo radio telescope just outside Mexico City." As her camera switched off Paula got up from her anchor desk. "I need a break, John. How much time do I have?"

"Twelve minutes, maybe a few more."

"Make it twenty. I'll be in my office." She strode quickly into her office and closed her door. Sitting at her desk, she leaned back and closed her eyes. "I've got to talk to our Gaardian more. I've got to!"

+ + +

Above Gaardian Planet, Walter offered a smile to all of his bridge crew. "Everyone has Gaardian rings. Without them, you would die in seconds on the surface. Enjoy yourselves. Gaardian Planet is sentient, so talk to it all you want, just by thinking what you want to say. Pixie, Qaak, and I will be at Gaardian Conference Center or at Qaak's apartment." He paused. "That's all! Have fun everyone!"

All of them vanished, leaving the bridge empty. The crew appeared on a level area near the red falls on the planet. Pixie and Walter beamed directly to Qaak's apartment above Gaardian. Murmuring greetings to their old friend, they quickly made themselves comfortable in chairs that appeared.

Walter looked at Pixie. "I've given base personnel rings as you have. She is ahead of me in some things, Qaak." The triped nodded.

"I'm still a little ahead of you in that I am already assigning people to duties on other planets in my sector." Pixie smiled.

"I know. We are getting started with that. I've got to ask Belinda to speed that process up."

Qaak took his usual stance on his third leg. "Doff, Kieya and Waagere have briefed me on their work. This conversation is just for the three of us."

Pixie became more serious. "Why the secrecy?"

"This is about discretion, not secrecy. I do not think it wise that this conversation be part of the debriefing tomorrow."

Walter was quiet. "What's bothering you my old friend?"

Qaak's eyes glowed for a moment. "The crew of *The Grace* did its part, and the team at Gaardian Center did its part, but what was sent by your crew was not what was received here at The Center. The transfer was direct - there was no opportunity for an adversary to intercept it."

Pixie's curiosity was palpable. "What was the problem?"

"Not a problem, a mystery. Previously, DNA mapping received at the Center was raw and had to be processed before it could be applied."

Walter's voice was soft and steady. "That's what we sent to The Center - the raw data. We did not have the personnel to process it in a timely way."

"I know - I was there. The Center received data already prepared to be applied. Waagere and the others assumed that we had help, and they were grateful."

Pixie stared. "Wait a minute! You're saying that nearly thirty trillion DNA profiles and locators were processed instantaneously?"

Qaak grunted. "Exactly. . . . Walter, did the voice tell you that He was going to intervene or help?"

"No, but that is what happened."

"You know this? You have proof?"

"I know by faith. A man named Paul once said that 'faith is the substance of things hoped for, and the evidence of things unseen.' As sure as I am sitting here and enjoying your home, Qaak, I know that it is what happened."

"Indeed."

Pixie spoke softly. "Don't scriptures say that nothing is impossible with The Creator?"

"How can you logically say that?" Qaak's eyes glowed subtly.

Walter got more comfortable in his chair. "The Creator created matter, anti-matter, energy, space, time, and everything else. In order to create all of that, The Creator would have to exist apart from creation."

Qaak's eyes closed as he began to glow. When he started to speak, his eyes were still closed at first. "This makes me different."

Pixie smiled. "How does it make you different?"

"For almost as long as I can remember, my identity has been that of a Gaardian. I have belonged to the Gaardians. Gaardian and I assembled the Gaardians. I have existed by and for the Gaardians. No longer. Not because I am retiring. Not because I am old. I am The Creator's child, and Qapoku is my brother - my living brother. I am different because now I have more than simply those with whom I work. For the first time in thousands of years, I have family. I belong. I have hope beyond this life. I have meaning beyond being a Gaardian. I am different."

Walter was thoughtful. "What are we going to say when we meet with the other Gaardians?"

Qaak chuckled. "Somehow I think The Creator has plans for that." Suddenly, he stopped, as the room began to glow.

"Yes."

"Is that you, Qapoku?"

"Yes, Qaak, and more."

"Forgive me if I am skeptical, Qapoku, but I have been a scientist all of my life. I am not used to accepting things strictly on faith."

"You are who you are, but you need to step beyond science in order to know me."

"How can I step beyond science?"

"Nothing is too hard for me. Walter and Xpraepostq, each of you put a hand upon Qaak."

Pixie and Walter stepped forward to either side of Qaak and put their hands on his shoulders. A chronometer could be seen on a wall, marking seconds as well as minutes and hours. It said 07:44:55.

From their perspective, their existence became surreal. They saw more than sixty thousand Earth years all at once. There were fleeting images, sounds like that of wind through treetops. They saw how Qapoku, Eiraynay, and Jesus affect their entire lives. The glow was suddenly gone, they were back in Qaak's apartment, and the digital clock said 07:44:58. For a few moments, they just breathed deeply.

Walter was thoughtful. "This gives new meaning to the word 'confirmation.'"

Qaak spoke quietly. "Yes – indeed! Time to meet with the others." They nodded, and all vanished.

At Gaardian Center, Qaak appeared on the podium, and Walter and Pixie appeared nearby.

Qaak spoke forcefully. "It is indeed rare when every Gaardian is here simultaneously. While I am going to serve as an advisor for the foreseeable future, the time has come for the Gaardians to select a new convener. You have heard my recommendation. It is not made lightly. Being the convener is not so much a matter of having experience as having a perspective. Walter's perspective is unique and important." Qaak paused as he folded one leg to sit on it. "As we enter the first phase of discussions each of you is going to be called away for a moment of education. We will reconvene for the next phase of selection when we are convened either by me or by Waagere. That is all."

Well over a thousand Gaardians began gathering in small groups all over Gaardian Center. From time to time one would disappear for a moment. When they reappeared, they had a slight glow and excused themselves from the group they were in, quietly finding their way to others that had the same glow. Gradually, the tone of the small groups began to change. Soon all were glowing.

Waagere spoke telepathically. "Let us return to our sectors of responsibility for a time of refreshment. We will then call for phase two and reconvene." All began to vanish.

+ + +

Walter and Pixie appeared on the bridge of *The Grace*. After pausing to look at Gaardian Planet on the viewer, Walter turned to his friend. "I'm going down to send the crew up here. Would you program navigation for return to Aegeene and then on to Earth? I want to get under way as soon as everyone is on board."

"Easy. It'll be done before the first one gets back."

Walter vanished. At Red Falls on the planet surface, Walter reappeared. He approached one small group after another, speaking to them softly, and they vanished.

Pixie was just finishing her navigation instructions for the computer when John appeared. "Hi, Pixie!"

"Hi, John. I have programmed navigation to take us to Aegeene. Upon arrival, another program will appear for you to return the ship to Earth."

"Thanks." John smiled.

Walter appeared next to him. "As soon as Karen says everyone is on board, let's get under way. Make it at least pace twelve, faster if you are comfortable with it."

"Right."

Karen spoke firmly. "Everyone is here."

Walter turned his head to look at her. Then he turned back to John. "Okay, John."

Suddenly the stars in the viewer were a blur. "We're at pace nineteen. We'll be at Aegeene in fifty seconds."

"Good."

Walter went to the captain's console and sat down. As Aegeene popped into view, Pixie spoke softly, smiling. "A better sight than a thousand stars. Walter, see you soon!"

Walter smiled. "Soon, my friend!" She vanished. "John, take us home."

"We're there in five seconds."

Suddenly, they were in orbit between the Earth and its Moon.

Walter stood up. "I'll be in the den for a while. If anyone joins me, I do not want to talk shop. John, you've got the bridge until everyone else has disembarked."

"Yes, sir."

Walter vanished. Coming from the bridge of *The Grace*, Walter reappeared near the sofa in front of the fireplace where the perpetual fire was blazing. The same sofa used to be in his condominium apartment in Oakland. "Frank."

The android appeared. "Yes Walter."

"Update the base computer with my memories of the last few days." Walter sat down.

There was a pause. "Fascinating." Frank looked in the direction of the fireplace, and then he vanished.

"Yes." Walter paused as his favorite team leader appeared on the other side of the fireplace. "Hi Debbie! Come join me. Make yourself comfortable."

"Thanks. I was hoping I'd be welcome!"

"Definitely. Are you tired?"

"Not really. Maybe I'm still wired from all that has been happening."

"That's part of it. Another factor is the ring you're wearing."

"Really?"

"Yes. It's boosting the filtration of your blood and boosting your body's recovery mechanisms." He paused. "Let's not talk shop, okay?"

She sank into the sofa next to him. "Okay. Let me ask you this: Do you have any desire to go back to Oakland?"

"Definitely. I would have to disguise my appearance of course, but I am fond of both the city and many of the people there. It used to be the stepchild of San Francisco, but not anymore. It avoided most of the struggles with civil rights because a ship builder integrated the town during World War II. It was able to achieve urban renewal early in the movement. The people I knew there did not have a prejudicial bone in their bodies. They were loving and caring. Of course, I want to go back."

"What about New Zealand?"

"I love all of New Zealand. I would be willing to vacation there any season of the year "

"I loved what I saw of it when you took my house there that night. Would you take me with you the next time you take a break there?" She smiled sweetly.

"When did you have in mind?"

"Well, it would be a matter of getting my boss – I think you know him – to give me some time off at the same time you get time off. Do you think that could be arranged?"

"I'll send a memo to Frank. How about that?" He smiled.

"You do that. Why did you ask if I was tired? Do I look tired?" She grinned.

"Is this your way of fishing for a compliment? I cannot imagine a situation in which you would not look fine." He smiled back.

"Why, thank you, kind sir."

"Do you miss your days in the industry?"

She looked up and then looked out at the Earthrise. "I loved acting, and I loved modeling. I also loved working behind the camera. It was work that was both satisfying and at times heartbreaking. Having said that, would I go back to it, as long as I could be Science Officer for the Gaardian? Not on your life! I seldom have time to think about it, and when I do I've no regrets and no longings to go back." She paused and snuggled closer to Walter on the sofa. "My primary frustration with working for the Gaardian has arisen out of my desire to seduce my boss." She looked at him out of the sides of her eyes.

"Sounds ominous! Are you sure that seduction is necessary? The word 'seduction' implies getting someone to do something that they don't otherwise want to do." Walter smiled and looked at her out of the sides of his eyes.

Debbie got very red. "I think that it's time for me to say goodnight." She leaned over and gave him a kiss on the cheek.

As she stood up Walter asked, "Don't I get to kiss you back?"

Again, she turned red. "I guess so."

"Would you consider it sexual harassment?"

She grinned. "Of course not! I started this!" She paused as he stood up. "So are you going to kiss me back?"

Walter kissed her. She kissed him back.

Walter looked into her eyes. "As much as I would like to continue this, I think we should get some sleep. What do you think?"

"I'm enjoying this too, but I agree – we've another long day tomorrow." She gave him another short kiss and walked out into the atrium. "See you in the morning!"

"Good night!" He watched her leave and then turned his eyes back to the fireplace. He murmured, "Lord, what's going on here? Is this part of your plan?"

19. Wedding

After some sleep, all the team leaders were gathered in the den with Walter, who was standing by the fireplace. "Frank has told me that all of you are well informed regarding what has happened with Pixie, Qaak, and the other Gaardians. None of our discussion here is to be shared with the rest of your teams until either Frank or I give you clearance. I'd like to say a few things and then we'll open things up for discussion." Walter paused.

Butch spoke wistfully. "I wish Pixie could be here."

"I agree. She is having a similar meeting on her station. Butch, in a few minutes, I am going to ask you to share your perspectives on what happened on Pixie's planet in light of your own recent experiences. First, I want all of you to look at a display I've prepared for you." The ceiling of the den was suddenly tapered steeply so that the wall across from the fireplace was more than ten meters high. Walter gestured to the area behind them, on the other side of the den. They all stood up to watch. A three-dimensional sphere appeared, about ten meters tall, made up entirely of stars.

"This represents Gaardian supervised space." A yellow line appeared with an arrow pointing to a spot near the center of the sphere. "That is the location of Gaardian Center and its sun. You are only seeing the brightest of the suns." Another line and arrow appeared to the far upper left of the display, with a small area shaded orange. "This is our sector of Gaardian space. As you can see, our sector is relatively small." As they watched, the sphere was broken up into hundreds of other sectors depicted with various colors and sizes. "Does anyone here remember what a googol is?"

Stephanie smiled. "I suppose I know this because it's a number, though it has nothing to do with accounting. A googol is the number one followed by a hundred zeroes. A googolplex is the number one followed by a googol of zeroes."

"Yes Stephanie -- and I'm glad you mentioned the googolplex. I mentioned both the googol and the googolplex when I spoke to the United Nations some months ago. As I indicated to them at that time, in Gaardian space, there are several googolplex of stars, plus planets, moons, comets, and smaller bodies."

Butch whistled.

"In our sector, there are thousands of stars and hundreds of planets with various forms of carbon-based and silicon-based life. There are a few planets in our sector with life that does not fit those parameters. You can be seated again." The display vanished, and everyone turned back to Walter and sat down.

As they got settled, he continued. "Until now, now religion was seen by Gaardians simply as a way of experiencing reality from another perspective. Religion was of course a vital part of lesser developed societies and cultures, but as science and technology began to dominate those societies and cultures, religion usually took a secondary role. The Gaardians have seen themselves as the most scientifically and technologically advanced group in the known universe for thousands of Earth years. For most Gaardians, religion has been only a minor part of life, little more than a footnote to their biographical files."

Walter smiled with a broad grin. "Now, all of that has come full circle. God has taken each Gaardian individually out of the universe momentarily, so they could experience life apart from time and normal dimensions. Now, every Gaardian is living and working with an awareness of God actively at work. All of us have returned to our own sectors to live with all of this for a while, and to digest all that has happened..."

"Now, I am asking Butch to tell more details of what has happened in these last few weeks. I must excuse myself." Butch rose and approached the fireplace. "I need to talk with Pixie before she and I go to Gaardian Center. Qaak is retiring. He has recommended me as his replacement as convener. I do not feel comfortable with that, so it must be discussed. I'll see all of you when I get back." As Butch began to tell his story, Walter vanished, and in a moment, the red SVX outside the den vanished as well.

Walter stared blankly at the stars flashing by as he made his way to Pixie's quarters. He did not go slow enough to enjoy the scenery this time. Soon he appeared outside Pixie's quarters and signaled his arrival. On a tiny display in front of him, she appeared. "Come on in!" He vanished from the SVX and reappeared to greet her with a light kiss on the cheek just seconds after her welcome.

"Hey there, handsome! I am glad you came! I'm beginning to assimilate all that has happened, and I want to bounce some of it off of you."

"Okay. I want to talk to you about Qaak's proposal."

Pixie grinned. "Yes, your future highness!" Walter grimaced and then smiled as well. "Let's go below to that park where I met Eiraynay." They both vanished from her quarters and reappeared in the park. They walked slowly as they talked. Pixie was quiet and thoughtful. "It's been exciting, meeting with other people who knew Eiraynay and talking about our experiences. He's appearing less frequently now, and I suppose he will be returning to The Creator permanently soon."

"Has he talked about what is to happen after He leaves?"

"Yes, but that is what I want to talk to you about." She paused. "He has talked to us several times about leaving some kind of presence behind when he leaves. Is that what you followers of Jesus call The Holy Spirit?"

"Yes, I assume so. Why don't you ask Him?"

"I did, and He just smiled at me. He said that I could talk to you about your experiences with Jesus and the Holy Spirit."

Walter smiled. "The Holy Spirit provides counsel, wisdom, and power."

"Power? When we mind melded that did not make sense to me."

"Yes. As time goes on you will discover that the Holy Spirit will help you accomplish things far beyond Gaardian power as we know it."

"Really!"

"Yes. I suppose the wonders of Gaardian power have affected me differently because I am a Christian." Walter and Pixie stopped to watch some children playing a game nearby, and then they continued walking. "On Earth, there are some people who call themselves Christians as a kind of default religious description in their communities. Then there are those who label themselves Christians because they go to church. Obviously going to church does not make one a Christian any more than regularly going to a supermarket would make that person a grocer."

"I see what you mean. I gather that a person's faith is a constantly growing and developing process."

"That's right." Walter stopped and pointed down at the paved trail they are following. "Think of it like this path, where one's faith begins as one gets on the path and does not end until one either leaves the path or goes on to join The Creator in the larger life.""

"The larger life – I liked that expression when we melded."

"It's one of my favorite euphemisms for eternal life in heaven. Some Christian leaders say there are four signposts along one's faith path that mark our progress."

"Spectator, seeker, disciple, and kingdom-builder, as I recall."

"Yes." Seekers are the people who decide that they want to be more than merely spectators, and they seldom remain seekers very long. They almost immediately became both His student and a follower. In my native language, the term for that is 'Disciple.'"

"That makes a lot of sense. In any spare moments I have apart from my Gaardian duties, I find myself wanting to know more about this strange and wonderful friend that I've known only a short time."

"Right. The last path marker, kingdom-builder, means that the person of faith is trying their best to work under the guidance of The Creator toward increasing everyone's awareness of God's role in creation."

"I've met with others who have met Eiraynay several times now, and He's not there as often as He was at first. Yet at the same time, we feel as though He is there even when He is not. It's so strange."

"That's another way of describing the presence of the Holy Spirit."

"Oh!" Pixie smiled. "That makes sense!" Pixie raised a palm to Walter and spoke more quietly. "That's enough about me. You wanted to talk about Qaak's retirement, didn't you?"

"Yes, and more than that." Walter paused as they both listened to a brief musical signal.

"Looks like a Gaardian mail coming in – priority."

Qaak appeared before them. "Hello my friends. Xpraepostq, I planned to visit you in person this time but so much has changed since meeting The Creator. I am glad you are there Walter. I would like the two of you to join me immediately in my quarters. Agreed?"

"Agreed." Walter and Pixie spoke simultaneously.

Instantly they were in Qaak's quarters near the center of Gaardian space. The three of them were suspended and relaxed, facing each other.

"I know that young Gaardians like you like to use vehicles for travel, but I sometimes like the speed of instant transport. I hope you did not mind. I sent the SVX to your base."

"It takes some getting used to I guess," mused Pixie, "but I didn't mind."

"Neither did I. What's up, my old friend?"

"Xpraepostq, I want to know more about this Eiraynay of yours. May I touch your mind?"

"Of course." She closed her eyes as he reached out with three fingers to touch her face.

A moment later, he withdrew his hand and softly cackled. "Seeing your Eiraynay and listening to him through your memories has stimulated some old memories of my own childhood long ago. Walter, I need to look at your memories from another perspective. May I?"

As Walter nodded, Qaak reached out and touched him. His hand stayed with Walter longer than with Pixie. "Does that help you, my old friend?" Walter smiled.

The old Gaardian grunted. "I'm disappointed with me."

"Why?"

"Yes, why?"

"I was with you nearly every night for more than fifty of your planet's years Walter, and for some reason, I never understood what I now understand." He grunted again. "Your experience of Jesus is like looking through a portal to The Creator. Like any portal, the closer you get to it, the more you see of what is on the other side of the portal." Qaak's voice got slightly louder and more animated. "During all of that time I was so focused on your seeing things through Gaardian eyes, I never really tried to see things through your eyes. I apologize."

"No apology necessary, my friend. You were doing your job exceedingly well."

"Xpraepostq, I apologize to you as well. Thank you for letting me see Eiraynay through your eyes."

"You're welcome. It is incredible! With this, I may be able to help my new friends who are becoming Eiraynay's followers."

"Be careful. You must not reveal his culture or yours."

"I understand. Walter's culture is quite different from mine, but I can adapt. Meanwhile, what is going to happen with your retirement?"

"I decided it was time to retire when I saw my life apart from time as a dimension of my living. You were there." Qaak walked over to Walter, bringing his face up close. "The Creator said that I should nominate you." Walter's face showed little surprise as the whole room began to glow.

> **"Everything is unfolding, as it should. You shall be the convener, Walter. You are my prophet. I am with you. You shall teach the other Gaardians what they need to know about me. Be a brother to him Qaak and encourage him. He still needs you. Xpraepostq, your new path will be a difficult one. Do not be afraid, for I am with you."**

The glow faded quickly before any of them could respond. Qaak's glow did not fade as quickly. "It's time. We must meet now with the other Gaardians at the Conference Center." The three of them vanished from Qaak's apartment and reappeared in the lobby of the Conference Center.

As they walked in, both the audible and the telepathic chatter ceased. Qaak stepped up onto the platform. "This may be the last time I convene the Gaardians. I have announced my retirement, and I have made a nomination. All of us have had time to ponder my retirement. We have also had time to consider our impressions of seeing all of creation through the eyes of The Creator. Who wishes to speak first?"

Kieya slowly walked forward. "It appears you've nominated Walter to replace you because of his wide experience with conversations with The Creator. The rest of us are just getting started. I believe the convener should have experience with seeing things through the eyes of The Creator. The term on his planet for a person with such a perspective is 'prophet.'"

Kieya returned to her former place as Waagere came forward. Her voice rang out telepathically with a strength that belied her years. "I agree. I also believe that The Creator has led us to this point with the assistance given to Walter's service as a Gaardian."

Puz spoke quietly from his seat. "At first I thought I would have a problem with Walter being the convener because we had gone through training together. In the last couple of time periods, I have come to see the opposite. I personally will be more confident in being able to appreciate Walter's leadership because I know him so well."

Walter stood up at his place. "On my planet, the nominee for a position often leaves the assembly so that the others may have a more thorough discussion. I think I'll go to the planet below until at least this part of the discussion is completed."

"No. That may not be necessary Walter." Waagere paused as she walked to the platform. "Gaardians, when Qaak was nominated previously for a second time, I offered my services, and I do so again. We may be already at a consensus. Let each Gaardian telepathically cast their vote to the Gaardian computer. Please cast your votes."

There was a pause, and then there were some soft murmurs of conversation. The voice of the computer sounded remarkably similar to Qaak's. "Walter has been unanimously voted to be the convener.'" Several expressed their congratulations. Qaak glowed.

Pixie's face had a broad smile. "Let's take a break for a couple of days."

"Do you have something specific in mind?"

"You'll see."

A moment later, they were in an entirely different environment. "This is a great spot for a vacation, even if we only have a short time." Walter and Pixie were floating on the surface of a turquoise colored liquid. Actually, it was not a liquid but a colony of fluid animals. "Our friends here are certainly accommodating."

"See that black mass coming in our direction? We had better get to higher ground. There are thousands of animals that want to get to the soil beneath us for food." Walter and Pixie beamed over to a nearby hill and got comfortable in the midst of the foliage. From their vantage point, they could see the pool below as well as the rugged mountains in the distance.

Pixie was deep in thought. "You know, we owe a debt of gratitude to the Quzaks." She stood up. "I'm hungry. Can you duplicate some of that food at your first Christmas banquet at Debbie's?"

"Frank?" The android appeared. "Frank, do you have enough in your memory of the food from the first Christmas banquet to set a table for us?"

"Yes, although I did not do a detailed analysis of the shellfish. The sauce was very complex. I may not be able to do it properly."

"Give it your best shot." A large table appeared with two chairs. There were samples of all the Christmas fare on the table – enough for several meals.

"Thanks Frank." The android disappeared, and Walter stood up. "How's this?"

"It looks wonderful!" She looked up. "Thank you, Creator, in the name of Eiraynay."

"Amen!" Walter paused to take a bite of the rack of lamb. "What did you mean when you said we owe the Quzaks a debt of gratitude?"

Pixie looked across the pool below as she took another bite from her plate. "You got to have your first Gaardian challenge with them, but my sector was kind of quiet. When the Quzaks chose to take a second lesson from the Gaardians, it gave us an opportunity to work together. Somehow, I have the feeling that Eiraynay knew what I was facing. Several of your Earth days before we confronted the Quzaks together, I had an interesting conversation with him. He told me that I would learn a lot from you and from Him because you and I will work together from time to time."

Walter was thoughtful. "At first I was a bit envious of you because you've gotten to meet and get to know your planet's savior in person. In hindsight, I think otherwise. A man named Thomas once said that he would not believe that Jesus had risen from the dead unless he put his fingers where the nails went through Jesus' hands. When he saw the risen Christ, he was enthusiastic in his faith, but Jesus said something very important. He pointed out that Thomas' faith would have been much stronger if he had believed despite the fact that he had not seen Jesus. Would you have so quickly come to believe that Eiraynay is your planet's Savior if you had not seen him after he had been resurrected?"

Pixie looked into Walter's eyes. "I honestly don't know. I would like to think so though. At the same time, now that I've confronted the Quzaks with you and Qaak, I feel more confident as a Gaardian."

"I think maybe that's why Qaak wanted you to join us. I'm glad you did."

"I think it's going to be a while before the Quzaks or any of their former allies will be building empires. It will be interesting to see how long it takes any of them to get to know the part of the universe they are in well enough to both explore and accomplish anything beyond their own planets."

"I talked to Waagere about that. She said that when the Gaardians have transplanted planets previously, it has usually taken two to three generations to get back out into space in any kind of effective way. Usually, they are less war-like the second time around." A large bird flew overhead and landed nearby. To Walter, it looked a little like a cross between a peacock and an eagle. Its wingspan was over three meters, and its plumage was very colorful.

Pixie's gaze followed Walter's. "Do you think that's a male or a female?" Her ring shimmered. "Interesting! It is nonsexual. I was hoping it was female. I have been thinking about the female Quzaks. I was far more impressed with them than with the males."

"How come?"

The bird took off, and she and Walter watched as it soared higher and higher. "I liked their strength and confidence."

"I did too. That's one of the things that made me interested in Belinda when we were much younger."

"The Quzak women are more aggressive and vindictive than the men. On the other hand, they are very protective of their mates and very loving."

"Now we are referring to them as women and men. Genetically they are virtually identical to humans. If I were not so tall I would like to go in there and live incognito for a week or two."

Pixie smiled. "Even though I'm shorter than you, I'd still be too tall compared to most of the Quzaks." She studied her food for a moment. "There's someone on my team who is very short. With a Gaardian ring, I could make her look just like a Quzak. What do you think?"

"Sounds like a good idea. I've got a man on my base team that is also quite short but as strong as an ox."

"An ox? What is that?"

"It's a beast of burden used in less-developed countries on earth. The two of them could pose as mates and blend right in. By the way, I called you 'Pixie' because your name was so hard for me to pronounce. I suppose your friend's name is just as bad?" He grinned.

"Actually, I think you humans could pronounce her name in a way fairly close to our language. Transliterated to your alphabet it is spelled Daie-ahnn ["diee-ANN"]."

"Wow! In English, we would probably distort it into 'Diane.'" Walter's ring shimmered, and Belinda's image appeared beside their table. "Belinda! How are things going back home?"

"Hi, you two! Fine! Our planetary patrols are becoming almost routine. What's up?"

"How tall is Steve over in communications?"

"Just over five feet."

Walter laughed. "Perfect! Tell him that Pixie and I will have a special assignment for him when I get back on base. After you tell him, I'll have Frank fill in the details for him."

"Great! How are you, Pixie?"

"Incredible! We are having a repeat of the dinner you and Debbie put together. Now I need to call on my friend – you will call her 'Diane' – who will be working with Steve. See you later!"

Belinda vanished, and Pixie took a more serious tone. "Walter, Daie-ahnn has been mostly working at my base so far. I need to approach this carefully to motivate her."

"I trust your judgment."

Pixie's ring shimmered, and a strikingly beautiful woman appeared beside their table where Belinda's image had been moments before. Though probably no more than four feet ten inches tall, she was even more stunning than Pixie. "Hello, Daie-ahnn." They spoke in their native tongue, but Walter heard them clearly because of the mind meld.

"Hello Xpraepostq. You are looking well. Is this the Gaardian you call Walter?"

"Hello, Daie-ahnn." Walter greeted her in her own language and decided that he would continue to use her tongue for this conversation. "I am pleased to be able to meet you."

"Likewise, Walter." She turned slightly to more fully face Xpraepostq. "May I assume this is not a social Gaardian mail?"

"Correct. I've made a suggestion to Walter, and he would like to cooperate if you will."

"What is it?"

"Did you watch the proceedings of the last encounter with the Quzaks?"

"Yes, Xpraepostq."

"I believe because of your size you would be ideal to infiltrate the Quzaks. I would equip you with a ring that would disguise your real appearance and provide language conversion."

"Is there more? Perhaps through Walter?"

"Yes, Daie-ahnn. He has a man named Steve, who is only a little taller than you are, and who is willing to help. I would like Steve to pose as your mate. The two of you would then work together to provide information to the Gaardians on what is going on in that culture. If this works well, we will do the same with the other transplanted civilizations."

"Do you think I'll have any problem working with this being named 'Steve?'"

"Walter?" Pixie had a formal tone.

Noticing Pixie's tone of voice Walter assumed a very diplomatic tone. "I've seen a number of the men on your planet. I believe that you will find that Steve is quite attractive physically. He is also both very capable and completely honorable."

"Very well. Xpraepostq, how soon will I begin?"

"I'll fill you in on the details when I return the next time period. I'll talk to you then."

"Good. Farewell Walter, Xpraepostq." Daie-ahnn disappeared.

Walter had a wide smile on his face. "So now we are being matchmakers?"

Pixie giggled. "I don't think so. But maybe. They will have to work together for an extended period of time."

"Yes, maybe so. Right now, I am thinking about what the voice said to us. I wonder how soon you are going to meet your mate."

"What about yours? I wonder if it is going to be someone on your team – perhaps someone in your inner circle. I know that my mate is someone who has changed from battling against the followers of Eiraynay to defending them. He should not be too hard to find. I think I am going to check that out when I get back."

"Sounds good. For myself, I am beginning to get an idea, but of course you know since we have mind melded." He paused to wipe his mouth with a napkin. "Had enough to eat?"

"Yes! It was delicious! I've had enough." Walter's ring shimmered, and the table disappeared. They both stood up, and then they hugged. "Walter, I know that our relationship is going to be a little different from now on, but somehow I think we don't have to worry about our friendship."

"I agree." Walter kissed her lightly. "I love you Pixie, and I know our friendship will endure." They kissed again, still lightly, but for a bit longer.

"We had better go back to our bases. I've got to work with Daie-ahnn, and you need to get Steve ready." They stepped apart from each other, and almost simultaneously, they vanished to their respective bases.

+ + +

In Walter's quarters, Tiger and Tammy were sitting on the bed and licking themselves, as he stepped into his sonic shower. His clothes vanished briefly while the shower did its work, and then they reappeared. As he came from the bathroom, Belinda was standing by his bed. "Welcome home! Are you and Pixie rested?"

"For now, I think. We've got work to do."

"Frank has briefed Steve, and he's excited about the assignment. Do you want to talk to him?"

"Yes! Frank?" The android appeared. "Tell Steve I'll meet him in the den in a few minutes. I need to talk to him about Daie-ahnn." Frank nodded and vanished. "Belinda, after I send Steve on his way I want to talk to the team leaders."

"Okay." She reached up on tiptoe and pecked him lightly on the cheek. "I'm glad you're back. I'll see you in the den."

As Belinda walked out, Walter touched his cheek where she had kissed it. He looked down as Tiger stroked around his legs and purred. "Tiger, things sure would have been different if she had kissed me like that more often when we were in high school! Ah well!" He stooped down and scratched his cat's head. "Somehow I think one of these women is going to become my wife. I am beginning to get an idea, but nothing seems clear yet. Which one?" Walter sat down on the bed, swung his legs up, and stretched. Tiger hopped up and crawled up on his stomach. "Tiger, I hope you won't get jealous when it's no longer just you and me and Tammy!" He closed his eyes, and when he took a deep breath, Tiger hopped down. Walter swung his legs down to the floor and walked out, down the corridor, and into the den.

Steve was standing there, waiting. He was short, athletic, and strong, with handsome good looks. "Hello Steve! I'm glad you're willing to do this."

"It sounds exciting. Frank has given me a pretty good picture of what Diane and I will be facing."

"Daie-ahnn is who I want to talk to you about. Before we recruited you for Gaardian work, you used to have quite a social life. You really liked the ladies, and seldom had a steady relationship. Working with Daie-ahnn you are going to have to re-think how you relate to persons of the opposite sex."

"I'll be on my best behavior."

"Your best behavior by past standards will not be good enough. You are going to be facing several problems that you have never faced before."

"Meaning?"

"First, her name is properly pronounced Daie-ahn. She probably will not object if you call her Diane when alone. You will both have to take Quzak names when you get there. She is very courageous but is also very wary of humans – she has had no experience with our species, and she will be probably on the defensive at least emotionally. Second," Walter paused, "picture in your mind the most beautiful woman you ever dated." Walter paused again. "Got someone in mind?"

"Sure -- easy!"

"Okay. You will probably find Diane far more attractive."

"That's a problem?" He grinned.

"Yes." Walter paused to intensify his look at him. "Because if you make any early romantic overtures of any kind, it could create problems far greater than you can imagine, and Gaardians or other people will not be there to help you solve those problems. You will only have each other. You won't be able to trust any of the Quzaks."

Steve whistled. "This might be harder than I thought."

"Right – and there's no 'might be' about it. There is one more thing. This is essential. You must, under all circumstances, unconditionally trust one another. She has capabilities that you do not have and vice versa. You will be a team. You cannot be macho. Worse, in public with the Quzaks, you will have to learn to appear to let your wife – Daie-ahnn – provide leadership in the relationship. Now Steve, do you trust me?"

"Of course."

"Okay. I am doing to do a mental transfer. Stand closer to me and close your eyes." As Steve stepped forward, Walter spread his fingers across and against Steve's face. In about four seconds, Walter stepped away. "Now you speak Quzak and understand Quzak culture. You also speak Daie-ahnn's language. You also know what you need to get started in their main city."

"Incredible."

"Give me your right hand." Steve extended it, and Walter slipped a ring on his fourth finger. "Steve, look at me." Steve looked up from the ring. "Those on the crew of *The Grace* already have these. This ring is a terminal with Frank. He will always know where you are, and he will monitor your vitals. If you get into a bind, he will appear, so do not be surprised. Do you understand?"

"Yes." Steve was solemn.

"Now my friend, I am going to transport you to Pixie's planet, where you will meet Daie-ahnn. Pixie will send the two of you on from there. Do you've any questions before you go?"

"I'm going right now?"

"Yes. Is that a problem?"

"I guess not. I've almost gotten used to the fact that Gaardians don't waste time."

"God be with you!" Steve's mouth started to open in reply, but he vanished as Walter's ring shimmered.

Walter turned to the fireplace and saw that the others had already assembled, and they had probably overheard his instructions to Steve. Butch called out from a chair by the fire, "Sounds like Steve and Daie-ahn are going to have quite an adventure!"

"You've got that right!" Walter smiled. "All of us have adventures ahead as well. That's why I've called you together." Walter walked to the fireplace while the others turned to face him. "Even though I am not going to give individual assignments for your teams tonight, we're all part of a larger team, and we can help one another. For instance, Paula Rutledge on Earth needs us. Ken, you and Butch will be working together on this. She has stated on the air that she would be willing to give up her career in order to be part of the Gaardian team. Later, she was interviewed by another network, and it appears she is sincere. We can use her talent, but we must proceed very carefully just in case this is a journalistic ploy to find out more about our operations. Toby, she did not meet you when she was here, so she does not know you. I want you to work under cover in her office, and coordinate with Karen on all of Paula's communications. Understood?"

Toby cleared his throat. "How am I going to get a job in her office? Have we got an in?"

"Actually, I think you'll like the 'in' as you put it. Your Native American background will be used to advantage, along with that other very special talent that only you and I know about."

Toby grinned. "I get the picture. I think I can feed her curiosity very well – very well indeed."

"I agree." Walter turned to his left. "Keeta, you and I are going to be working together on a project that may also involve Pixie. I will tell you more about that tomorrow, but suffice to say I have not done enough for your planet yet. I want you to help me establish some priorities and perhaps a tentative time line for assisting your culture."

"Yes, sir."

Walter turned to his security officer in the corner. "Asayak, I want you to be thinking along the same lines, because when Keeta and I get back I want to spend some time with you on your planet."

"Good. Thank you."

"You're welcome." Walter turned his head. "Jody, I want you to spend enough time with Asayak to get a feel for his planet's technology, and how we can help them make some useful advances. John, I want you or someone on your team to be available to take Asayak and Jody wherever they need to go to do their assessments."

Looking down at the sofa in front of him, he addressed his Science Officer. "Debbie, there is a double star that has changed and, from Earth's viewpoint is getting ready to turn into a super-nova in Earth's time frame. So far, Earth's astronomers are not aware of what has happened or, more correctly, what they can see has already happened. I want you to figure out a way to give them some better views of that special event without revealing Gaardian technology. Work with Jody on that. This is to be a gift to earth's scientific community – and those of Keeta's and Asayak's planets as well."

"What about helping them modify and improve the research equipment on satellites or space stations?"

"That's okay so long as you only use Gaardian technology to tweak theirs. Do not give away any new scientific advances yet. That will come as trust is built between us and the planets in our jurisdiction. By the way, you and Jody have a project that will take up some of your time next month. Planet 2-AM-5063-C is just beginning its pre-scientific age developments. They are in peril from a comet that is going to collide with them in about two of our years. We need to adjust trajectories so that it does not happen until such a time as when they can re-readjust trajectories themselves."

Walter paused and looked around the den. "That's all for now except for this. Since I am now the convener of the Gaardians, there will probably come a time when I move permanently to Gaardian Center and place someone else in my position here. I do not anticipate that happening this year or next year, but it will happen. Good night, everyone." He put his arm around Belinda and gave her a hug before heading for his quarters. He left behind animated conversations in the den that lasted into the night. As he flopped on his bed, the two cats jumped down to do some exploring.

Debbie appeared at his door and knocked on the doorjamb. "Care for a cup of tea?"

"Absolutely! Come in!" His ring shimmered as his door closed. Debbie and Walter walked to the larger wall of his apartment as it seemed to dissolve and reveal Earth low on the horizon. Walter's ring shimmered again, and a double width recliner appears. Soon they were snuggled together and enjoying the view.

"How much can I read into the way you responded when I kissed you?" Debbie turned to him, her eyes sparkling.

"Why read anything into it?"

Debbie smiled. "When other men have said things like that I was always waiting for the other shoe to drop."

"Would you like to step out in faith with me?"

"Logically, I should hesitate, but. . . ." Her voice trailed off.

Walter looked at her straight into her eyes. "Are you open to a simple and dramatic solution? In a way that I learned from Pixie?"

She looked at him quizzically. "How does this solution work? No! Just do it!"

"Watch!" Walter began to glow. Following what he learned from Xpraepostq Walter grew brighter and brighter until his body began to become fluid and flowed over Debbie's. Her body began to glow as well. Their bodies became one unified glowing body without human features and remained within one another for several moments. The entire apartment also began to glow with the characteristic glow of the voice. Then Walter's body flowed back to where it had been.

> "Walter, Debbie, you have chosen well. I will greatly bless your choosing each other. Your union will be long and fruitful, for I will make your union last many lifetimes. If you wish, I will bless you with children. Long ago, I gave Gaardians authority and power, and they have made good use of what I have given them. Now, they again know who has given this responsibility. Wherever the Gaardians expand their authority, I will be with them, so long as they continue to listen for my voice. Work together, and I will multiply your efforts and glorify myself. I will be with you wherever you go. Lean on Walter's faith, Debbie, and learn from him. In turn, he will greatly value all that you are and all that you can be together. Have courage. Your journey will be blessed."

The glow faded. As they closed their eyes, their bodies melted and flowed together, their human features became a blur, and together they glowed softly as before.

20. Party Times

Qaak was lonely. The triped awakened and reached out mentally to Gaardian planet, far below his orbiting apartment. Qaak had known his friend the planet for nearly all of his life. When his home planet was destroyed, Gaardian rescued him. Qaak did not think often of Gaardian's beauty, but he was acutely aware of the importance of their friendship.

"Gaardian. I am feeling isolated. Since I retired, I have felt the need to have someone as my companion, perhaps as my mate, though I have not had a mate in thousands of years. Any wisdom?"

The planet hesitated before answering. "As Walter pointed out when you retired, you are about sixty-seven thousand of Earth's years old. Perhaps a mate is what you will need eventually. For now, why not invite your closest friends to your apartment for nourishment and conversation?"

Qaak's eyes glowed for a moment. "Indeed. Good. Send a text invitation using your best media. I will await the results."

"Very well."

Qaak chuckled, and his eyes glowed. "This just might be fun."

+ + +

Several days later, the living room of Qaak's apartment was lit by the soft light of the planet, along with the flames in the fireplace. Qaak had placed comfortable furniture throughout the room, but most of his guests were gathered around the fire. They were enjoying their favorite beverages, as the murmuring of their voices was at times punctuated by the crackling of the flames. Qaak sat on his third leg, at one edge of the semicircle of friends, next to one of the windows. Walter and Debbie were sitting in a recliner across from him talking quietly while snuggling close. Xpraepostq was sitting next to them with her husband Saahmn ["SAY'am"], and they were simply listening. Doff's deep bass voice rumbled with laughter from across the room, where he was pouring a steaming liquid into a mug while watching something on a view screen.

Kieya lounged cat-like on a plush pile rug in front of the fire, her stripes seeming almost three-dimensional in the flickering light. She deftly grasped her steaming mug with her paws. In front of her, Waagere also sat on the floor with Kieya, legs crossed, while her head bobbed from side to side as she listened and watched.

Qaak beckoned to the new convener. "Walter, do you remember bringing *The Grace* here so that Belinda could meet me?"

"Of course! That seems like a long time ago."

"I know. She is a special friend to you that you have known since your childhood. How is she doing?"

I think she's made that job into something she loves to do." Walter paused and looked at Debbie. He gave her a light kiss, looked around the room, and then spoke a little louder. "While we're all here, I want to invite all of you to join me for a celebration. I received a letter in New Zealand inviting me to an anniversary celebration at the last church I served. I would enjoy having all of you there, even if invisibly, and I think all of you would enjoy it as an interesting change of pace. In anticipation of your agreeing to come, I am having John Carson set up transportation arrangements. He's going to configure a special vehicle that can look like a tour bus when it gets to Earth and near the church, but will transport our guests from various parts of Gaardian space."

Qaak's eyes glowed subtly. "I wouldn't miss it. Perhaps I will see that former neighbor of yours again. Ann is a most interesting and provocative woman."

Debbie smiled. "Why Qaak! Do I hear romantic interest in your voice?"

Qaak's eyes again glowed for a moment. "I have not had a mate in thousands of years. It's an interesting thought that has not escaped me."

Pixie grinned. "I wouldn't miss it! I'll bring my beloved Saahmn here -- he'll enjoy it too!"

Her new husband nodded and looked at her. "Xpraepostq, seeing Walter's old church just might be helpful to all of us, what do you think?"

"I think so too. Doff, what about you?"

His deep voice was full of amusement. "It sounds like fun. I always enjoy the celebrations of other species."

Kieya purred subtly, "I too will be there. Waagere?"

"Of course! I have heard so much about Walter's first life from Kieya and Qaak. It ought to be interesting."

Debbie hugged her husband as Walter smiled broadly. "Thank you all. It will be eight Earth days from now. When you get to the church, go to the seldom-used balcony of the worship area."

Debbie looked at him and nodded. "Debbie is reminding me that we need to be getting back home to the base. It has been enjoyable everyone. Thanks for your hospitality Qaak."

"You're welcome." Walter and Debbie vanished.

Waagere stood up. "It is time I, too, returned to my work. Excuse me, old friend?"

"I too must be going," Kieya purred.

Saahmn and Pixie rose as their chairs vanished. "We've got to be going, too." They vanished. The others all indicated they too were departing, and they vanished one by one. Qaak stood up and turned to one of the windows. His apartment began to glow softly, and he heard the voice speak in its low rumble.

"It is time. You will be a better source of wisdom when you have a helpmate again. Trust me, and I will guide you."

The glow faded quickly, and Qaak's eyes glowed as he pondered what all of it meant, staring out the window.

+ + +

In their apartment, Walter and Debbie appeared in their bedroom. Walter sat down on the bed to stroke the cats. Debbie walked to a nearby door, beyond which a bathroom sink could be seen. He heard her voice from within. "I've been thinking about something ever since we got that invitation to the celebration in Oakland."

"What's that?"

Her voice almost echoed around the corner. "Ever since God blessed our union, and our bodies merged the first time, I have known we are married. Have you ever thought about our needing an actual public wedding ceremony with guests and festivities?"

"Not really. After the way God blessed our union with both a voice and a powerful presence, it just did not seem necessary. How about you?"

Debbie came out of the bathroom and sat down beside him on the bed. "Same here. A wedding ceremony would be an anti-climax of sorts. As a little girl, I had detailed plans for my wedding day, but I never considered how God could be involved in such a direct way."

"Do you still want a ceremony anyway?"

"No way! Our merging with each other anytime we want is a special gift." A chime sounded.

Walter looked puzzled. "I wonder who this will be. Frank, put the call through."

Qaak appeared. His apartment could partially be seen in the background. "Hello Walter, Debbie. Walter, were you planning to convene the Gaardians before your celebration or wait until afterwards?"

Debbie waved at Qaak, as Walter responded. "I am convening the Gaardians after the celebration. What with another graduation celebration soon, I do not want other business to mix with that. Frank is now transmitting an agenda to you and all the others. We'll use the conference center."

"Good." He looked down at a pad, and then looked up again. "I see on the agenda that the recent developments on Quzak planet need study and visioning. I can provide some suggestions to you before the meeting with the others."

"Thanks, Qaak. I was hoping you would. Anything else?"

"No. See you in Oakland."

Debbie waved again. "See you in Oakland, Qaak."

Walter nodded. "Until then."

"Until then." Qaak's image vanished.

Debbie put her arm through the slight curve of Walter's. "Shall we relax for a while?"

"Good idea!" As the two got on the bed, the cats jumped down. Walter and Debbie embraced and snuggled together. The cats jumped back up at the foot of the bed. They kissed lightly and closed their eyes. Their bodies begin to glow softly.

+ + +

When they arrived in Oakland, Walter's old church was almost glistening in the afternoon sun. Modeled after a cathedral in Mexico, its red tile roof and gleaming white plaster were a striking physical presence just north of downtown. After becoming a Gaardian, Walter had given them a departing gift, though they did not know just how valuable it was. Walter had an android man come to the church and offer at no cost a special insulating and protective coating. All the church had to do in return was allow them to use pictures of the church as publicity. The new pastor and the Church Board readily agreed. A team of androids showed up the following week and put a coating a fraction of a millimeter thick all over the outside of the church, including the roof and (secretly) the underside of the building. The congregation did not know it, but the church would never need painting or insulation again. Though the coating was very thin, it had an insulation value of one hundred inches of spun fiberglass. In the middle of one night, the crew also coated the newly re-paved parking lot.

This day the parking lot was full, and there were cars parked in the street. Many people were walking to the front entrance. Walter, once again with balding gray hair appropriate for one in his sixties, was standing on the landing at the top of the steps while greeting some of the people as they arrived. Debbie was standing next to him, but nobody recognized her. For the occasion, she had snow-white hair, and she had weathered skin appropriate for one in her sixties. Her voice was a bit coarse and higher than usual as she greeted people that Walter introduced to her. A very frail old black woman, walking with a cane and slightly bent over, approached slowly on Debbie's side.

"You must be Debbie! Walter wrote to me about you! You must be very special to snag this crusty old bachelor! My name is Margaret."

Debbie responded as the doting homemaker that was thoroughly enjoying herself. "Margaret! It is so nice to meet you at last! Walter has told me so much about you. You have been such a dear friend to him I feel like I know you!" She smiled broadly.

"You're very kind. Walter is a fine man, so you must be incredible. Would you walk me in, and help me get a pew a few rows down?"

"Certainly! I would be glad to! Walter, I'll sit with you up in the balcony, okay?"

Walter returned her smile. "I'll join you up there after the service starts. I have to do some official greetings down front at the beginning of the celebration."

"Okay! See you later!"

As Debbie and Margaret started walking through the door, Walter looked down the street to see a tour bus pulling up. From the outside, it looked like any other tour bus. Inside it was a fully equipped but compact space vehicle. The first person out was his oldest friend, and he greeted Belinda with a continuing smile. "Good afternoon! I'm so glad you and the tour group could make this part of your tour!"

Belinda had a full head of white hair and wrinkled skin. She smiled an impish smile. "Hi! Yes, as you can see, the bus is unloading the rest of our New

Zealand friends who have decided to join the celebration. John is a most interesting driver, and he took us on a bit of a sightseeing tour! Where do you want us to sit?"

"I think Debbie wants all of us to sit in the balcony. I think that's a good idea, don't you?"

Belinda winked. "Yes! Will it hold all of us?

"Oh yes, the ushers have reserved the entire balcony just for our New Zealand group."

Various people from Walter's Moon Base smiled as they walked by. Many of them looked considerably older than usual. John waved as he pulled ahead and parked in a space on the far side of the parking lot that had been reserved for the bus. Some of the women were wearing wigs or other disguises, while some of the men had beards. Keeta looked completely human as she walked up the steps arm in arm with Ken, and Walter followed them into the church. Inside, while the others went up the stairs, Walter walked down the center aisle to the front row. He turned to look up into the now full balcony and saw Asayak, Qaak, Waagere, and other aliens invisibly occupying some of the open spaces.

He took a seat on the aisle next to a man in a clerical robe. They smiled at each other as he sat down. "You've only been here a short time, but already it looks like you've made this pastorate uniquely your own. Thank you for inviting me."

The pastor, a tall African-American man with graying hair at the temples, smiled warmly and shook his hand. "How could I not invite you? You were here for so long! You are the only other person who has pastored this church that is still alive!" They both chuckled.

Walter looked around at the chancel. "Whoever restored the old pipe organ has done a good job. Does it still have five divisions and four manuals?"

"Yes. Pedal, great, swell, and choir, with antiphonal trumpets in the balcony as an extension of the choir division. Who thought of the trumpets?"

Walter smiled and looked up wistfully at a memory. "A previous organist had a husband who repaired and maintained organs."

Up in the balcony, as the pipe organ began to play softly, Asayak conversed telepathically with Qaak. "I have been studying Walter's religion and its history. His Christianity has had a profound positive influence on what his species calls the fine arts. My planet could learn from this!"

Qaak's eyes glowed subtly and briefly. "Yes. Now that Walter has appeared with you a couple of times because of the Quzaks, will you introduce some of Earth's fine arts to your planet?"

John Carson sat down nearby and whispered. "I've just placed our vehicle in a parking place at the back of the parking lot. Can I listen in on this conversation?"

Qaak's thought voice came through to him clearly. "Certainly." The pipe organ began to play more loudly "Lift Every Voice and Sing," and the words to the hymn appeared on a large screen in the church's chancel. While others around them began to sing, Qaak and Asayak continued their conversation.

Asayak stirred to the rhythm. "Can I introduce Earth's fine arts to my planet? I do not want to violate Gaardian rules regarding the intermingling of cultures."

Qaak looked around at the people singing before responding. "There are guidelines to be followed, but yes. It is important that you not use contemporary art that has not weathered the tests of time."

John's thoughts were intense as he watched the worship service on the main floor below. "This is fascinating."

Asayak also looked around. "I understand. I am enjoying this. Even though I do not hear the music the way humans do, I experience the pipe organ in a wondrous way, particularly the lower frequencies and upper harmonics. It is a most pleasant difference from some of Earth's more contemporary musical instruments. Through you, John, I am experiencing the music as others on Earth do as well."

Kieya walked silently over to where they were conversing. "Hello friends. May I join in?"

Qaak grunted.

Asayak extended an appendage and stroked his friend. "Of course. Thank you for joining us."

"Since our lives have been transformed by our new knowledge of The Creator, I am seeing Walter's church and its music differently."

Asayak stopped swaying to the music. "How so?"

John turned to face Kieya with a quizzical look. "Yes, why?"

Kieya purred rhythmically to the music for a moment. "I no longer simply watch and absorb. Now I experience Walter's worship with my own sense of worship."

Asayak again swayed with the music. "Yes!"

"Indeed!" The music stopped. Qaak's eyes suddenly glowed brightly as he turned his attention to the podium, where Ann stepped up to speak.

"For years, I lived down the hall from Walter Stephanopolos, our former pastor. Although he is fifteen or twenty years older than I am, I constantly flirted with him. He never gave up trying to get me to join this church. I loved him -- and still do, but I could not see myself married to a pastor. I wish I had joined when he was here. Walter, I hope you will not join your friends in the balcony, but will play the piano so long as you're up here! Now I see that you have married a fabulous woman. I have never been impressed with anyone more than I have been impressed with you, Debbie. I missed my opportunity, but you two certainly bless each other."

Asayak stirred. "Qaak, why didn't Walter recruit Ann for our Moon Base?"

Qaak responded without taking his eyes off Ann. "Belinda was his necessary first choice, and she helped make the other choices."

Ann stepped down from the podium, and music began again. Walter was at the piano and electronic keyboard as the organ played. A drummer began playing at her trap set, and others stepped up with guitars and other instruments. The music became loud, rhythmic, and energetic, and people began clapping as they sang.

Waagere's head swayed back and forth with the music. "I'm glad I came for this!"

Asayak's illuminating organ pulsated with the beat. "I did ...not ...want ...to ...miss!" Everyone in the balcony swayed, clapped, and enjoyed the music, though not all could be seen by the rest of the congregation. From time to time, people on the main level looked back and up to see the "party from New Zealand" singing with them.

+ + +

The next day, most returned to their homes. In the base's atrium, Walter and Qaak were talking quietly as Belinda came out of her quarters. Walter waved at his childhood friend. "Good evening, Belinda! It was a long day yesterday, wasn't it?"

"Good evening! Hello, Qaak! Yes, it was a long day, but I am glad I got to meet some of your old friends. That is a beautiful church!"

Qaak chuckled. "Yes. It was quite enjoyable. I saw the church differently this time because of knowing Qapoku again. What are you doing this evening Belinda?"

"I'm working with Jody and Butch on a project of theirs." Belinda's head turned somewhat as her eyes shifted to the far end of the hallway in front of her. Sounds from the mess hall could be heard slightly, as Paula Rutledge and Jim Crenshaw came through the doorway. Belinda waved and motioned for Paula and Jim to join them.

"Good evening, Paula, Jim!"

Paula sparkled. "Good evening, everyone! "

Jim grinned. "Good evening!"

Paula paused to give Qaak a hug. "Good evening, Qaak! Did you enjoy Walter's church yesterday?"

"Absolutely."

"I'm just getting used to this new life. I heard Keeta and Ken talking in her language at dinner. While you're here could you give me some mental training in linguistics before you leave?"

"I'll do it now -- it won't take but a moment." Qaak touched her face with three fingers, and his eyes glowed for a moment.

"Thanks, Qaak! That is amazing! Now I can even understand what I overheard Keeta saying!"

Jim was more serious. "Qaak, maybe later you can give me the same treatment in a dozen or so Earth languages."

Qaak grunted as his eyes glowed a moment. "An interesting request. You would use it in your role as goodwill ambassador?"

"Yes. I've spent a lot of time talking confidentially to old friends from my first life as an athlete. Now I'd like to use their contacts to introduce me to some of Earth's leaders, and make bridges between Gaardian activities and my planet's future."

"Indeed. That will be very worthwhile. I will visit you in your apartment in a few days after I return from other pressing matters."

"Thanks, Qaak. Paula, didn't you have something to talk to Walter about?"

"Yes. Walter, are you going my way? I've got a couple of things I'm working on that I'd like to run past you."

"Okay. Let's head for your office -- I'm going that way anyway. Give me a moment first though to say hello to Tammy and Tiger in my apartment. They may feel neglected because Debbie and I haven't been home much in the last few days. After the meeting on Gaardian tonight, Debbie and I are heading to New Zealand. It will be some time before we get back. Maybe we should take the cats with us!"

Paula paused to look at a plant and smell some of the blooms while Walter went into his apartment. Walter walked to the bed and sat down. The two cats jumped up on the bed and began stroking their heads and bodies against him. "Hey, you two! Want to go to New Zealand with Debbie and me tomorrow? You haven't been off of the moon for months!" The room began to glow, and everything faded into the light except Walter. The Creator spoke in the characteristic low rumble.

> "I will be with you as you lead the Gaardians. I will be on your lips to help you. Open the eyes of your heart. See Qaak's desire for a mate and help him stay close to me. After your meeting, make time to see Ooza on her planet. She does not yet know me, but soon I will reveal myself to her. I will show you how to help her. Trust in my ability to achieve whatever I reveal to you."

Scenes of Qaak, Belinda, Ann, and Jody together and separately flashed before Walter. Then scenes of Ooza, her mate, and the other female leaders flashed by. The vision faded, as did the glow. The features of Walter's apartment and the two cats reappeared. "Wow! Did you two see any of that? Walter reached down and stroked each one of them briefly. He got up and headed to the door, which opened automatically. "Okay, Paula, let's go to your office, but let's stop and see Butch first."

"Thanks, but I'll meet you back here. I see Toby over there near the mess hall, and I want to speak to him." Paula headed to Toby, as Walter walked quickly to the medical clinic. As he entered, he saw Butch leaning over a console.

"Good evening Walter."

"Good evening Butch. I have a project for you."

"What's that?"

"How much data have you gathered on Asayak and his species?"

"Funny you should ask. I was just studying some material that I acquired from his planet. One of his progenitors is supplying me all kinds of information."

"Good. As you familiarize yourself with his species, I want you to observe Asayak with as much instrumentation as you can without being intrusive. Tell it you want to study its telepathic abilities scientifically, and that I asked you to do so."

"What's this about?"

"I think Asayak has gifts that it does not know are gifts, and some of its abilities are more extensive than either Asayak or any of its species realize. This is not a secret project, so tell it that, and if it has questions to ask me.

"Right. By the way, I think it is good that we maintain a more or less twenty-four hour day clock here on the moon, even if the sun does not rise and set. It's good for our health."

Walter turned to go. "Thanks for saying so. I'll see you later." Walter headed back into the atrium, where Paula was waiting. Stephanie and Judy wave at Paula, and she returned the wave. They approached her just as Walter rejoined her, and Belinda and Qaak turned to listen to what they had to say.

Stephanie talked with her hands as much as with her lips. "Judy and I were just comparing notes about our Gaardian adventures. My Nigerian roots make it easy to fit in when I talk to leaders in Africa and South Asia, or work with the military in various countries."

Judy smiled. "Yes! In addition, my Hispanic roots help me in most of our Western Hemisphere in the same way. We are looking for ways we can build more political bridges that cross national boundaries."

"You need to spend some time with Qaak and Jim. Next week Qaak will have the time to give you some perspectives from other cultures on other planets. He is training Jim later today or tomorrow to speak in more than a dozen languages. After you talk with Qaak and Jim, do some experimenting. Invite Jim along on some of your visits. Post your reports to Frank, and I'll keep track of your work as usual. You are both doing fine -- I'm proud of you."

Stephanie had a wide smile. "Thanks Walter."

Judy turned with Stephanie as they started to go back to their quarters. "Thanks! We'll see you later!"

As Paula and Walter headed to her office, Belinda turned back to Qaak, still standing there. Belinda spoke quietly. "I'm wondering about something that Butch said the other day. Jody says it should be easy to do as he suggests, but that's not the issue." Qaak's eyes glowed for a moment as he looked at Belinda. She took his arm, and they walked to the lounge, talking quietly.

21. Franz Joseph

The Conference Center orbiting Gaardian was glistening in the sun. Partially in the shadow of the planet, it looked like a giant geodesic sphere or Bucky ball. Walter appeared in the atrium outside of the auditorium and began walking to the entrance. Qaak appeared nearby and approached him. "Walter, I suggest you have Frank give you a flash update on what has been happening on Quzak planet. They are responding to their new situation in a new galaxy as expected. Ooza is emerging as having significance for the future."

"How so?" The two of them arrived at the front of the conference stage.

They continued talking as others entered and took their places in the amphitheater. "As you will see in the briefing, she has some special gifts and qualities. In addition, she has an old friend who is supportive and has a unique gift of her own."

"I'll have Frank give me a level two briefing."

"That is wise. I see it is time to start. I will take my new place." The triped walked to a place nearby. A lounge chair appeared, and Qaak relaxed into it.

Walter went up the steps of the stage, and went to a spot just left of the center. "Attention everyone! As this is my first experience as convener, I have prepared for you both an agenda and flash briefings. All of you are thus equally prepared. Kieya, would you please share your remarks and additions with regard to the Quzaks and the other species that we relocated recently."

The large tiger-like Gaardian made her way to the other side of the center of the stage as a three dimensional image of Quzak planet appeared at the center. "As you know, we recently relocated five planets along with their respective civilizations to five different galaxies far from their original locations." Images in the display shifted to show five different planets going through the changes that Kieya described. "Planets that previously had but one sun now have two, and those that previously had two suns now only have one."

The Gaardians murmured as she continued. "Although the Zargadetes are now embroiled in a civil war, that war was already in its beginning stages when we relocated them. All five planets are adapting to their new locations in predicted and expected ways. Once the shock of seeing a different number of suns in their skies wore off they went back about their lives with few differences. It is both an acceptable and pleasing outcome." Kieya paused as the display disappeared.

Waagere rose and went up on the platform, as Kieya returned to her previous place. "From our briefings you know that we have been observing interesting developments on Quzak. After we pause for food and refreshments, I expect responses from many of you as to guidelines. Please give all input to Walter as soon as possible. I will be working with him on an ongoing basis with regard to the Quzak situation. If you will turn your attention now again to the display I would like to show you a few key Quzaks in that planet's future."

As Waagere continued to speak, Ooza appeared in the display. "This is Ooza, the mate of a military commander. She has unusual gifts. Females on Quzak organize to provide guidance for their mates while ostensibly allowing the males to be the leaders." The display changed. "This is Piatek. She sees beyond what others hear and see. She is old and wise, and she must not be underestimated." The display changed repeatedly. Waagere continued his lecture until it was time for a meal.

+ + +

Two days later, the little town of Franz Joseph in New Zealand was enjoying a warm afternoon. Sheep were grazing in the adjacent fields, with the Southern Alps rising nearby. Seagulls and other birds were flying about. Down the street from a gas station, Debbie was loading groceries into the back of her SUV wagon. She closed the rear hatch, got in, and drove north down the left side of the highway. She turned onto an unmarked road going into the trees to the sea. Periodically, morning sunlight flashed through the branches of the trees. Coming out of the trees at the top of a grass-covered hill, a small log cabin was visible in the distance, and she stopped. Looking around, sheep and the birds were in abundance. Thoughtful for a moment, she smiled broadly, as she looked out in front of the suv. Ahead, she saw what appeared to be a small red glowing insect on a small tree beside the road. As she drove past it, her ring shimmered.

The scene changed. Suddenly there was a large sprawling complex visible, much larger than the one she had at her home in Hollywood. There was a swimming pool and spa area under a transparent geodesic dome. A large assortment of animals roamed about. Most were native to Earth, but a few were not. Following the road to the sea, she turned into an opening in the complex. As a door closed behind her, the groceries vanished from the back of the vehicle.

Passing through the kitchen, their visiting chef, Dawn, greeted her. "Hi, Debbie!"

"Hi! Where's Walter?"

"I think he's on the west porch. Thanks for picking up these groceries. Some of these local vegetables and fruits I cannot get in the states, and they're fabulous! Thanks for the MediHoney too – I will take it back to Los Angeles with me when I go home next week.

"Hard to believe your vacation's almost over. I'm glad you joined us!" Debbie started to the door.

"I'm always willing to cook for you and Walter. Besides, this kind of working vacation is not really work compared to my restaurant." As Debbie moved to a doorway, Dawn called out, "Later!"

Debbie walked into a great room about the size of a hotel lobby, furnished with overstuffed furniture and a large fireplace in the round with a fire blazing. Veering to her right, she walked out onto the porch.

"Hi, gorgeous! I sure like how you have given our place the feminine touch." Walter greeted her with a kiss.

"Thanks. I liked the rustic log cabin look, but I am glad you invited my input. Just now when I was driving back from Franz Joseph with the groceries, I came in on our little access road. When I saw our home I almost burst out laughing."

"Why?"

"For just an instant I thought I had taken the wrong turn. Then I remembered that what is seen from outside our property is a hologram. It's fantastic how you make it appear that you've built a small cabin on the edge of a bluff, leaving the rest of the property intact. When Qaak was convener he mostly stayed in his little apartment above Gaardian, didn't he?" Walter nodded. "I'm glad we decided to make this our second home. How soon will Qaak get here?"

As if on cue, the triped appeared just to their left. "Good morning! Those aromas from the kitchen are wonderful!"

As Qaak took a deep breath, Debbie smiled.

Walter greeted him almost simultaneously with Debbie. "Good morning, Qaak!"

"I was just wondering when you would get here, and I asked Walter."

"I am glad to be here. The two of you have made a fine home here. It is all beautiful."

"Thank you. Some of the furnishings are from the home I used to have in Hollywood. Other things Walter and I have picked out and created together. How long can you stay this time?"

"Only for a couple of your days. I want to wander about for a while in the rain forest of the Te Wahipounamu World Heritage Park near here. It has plants and animals native there that are found nowhere else on Earth. Tell Belinda she can join me if she wishes. I'll be back before that fragrant food is ready." Before either of them could respond, Qaak vanished.

Debbie looked to where Qaak had stood. "I have really learned to enjoy Qaak's company."

"He enjoys you too. He was impressed with you before you and I became one. He and Kieya talked about you when we were on our second mission against the Quzaks."

Debbie giggled. "I like Kieya too. If we go camping, and we sleep on the ground, we can use her soft body for a pillow! Her fur is amazing!"

Belinda's voice came from the great room. "Hey! Where is everybody?"

"Out here Belinda! On the porch!"

Belinda came through the doorway. "Good morning! Did Qaak get here? Did he tell you I was coming?"

"Yes. He has gone to wander around in the rainforest near here in the Te Wahipounamu World Heritage Park. He'd like it if you join him."

The three headed into the great room. Walter took a playful tone with his old friend. "I think Qaak's a bit smitten with you, don't you think?"

"I like him, too. I think, though, I would like to walk to town and see some of the local sites. I'll be back before lunch, okay?"

"Sure! Have fun. If you go out this door, you will find a portal to the women's rest room at the service station. Bye!"

"See ya later!" She went out the door and closed it behind her.

Dawn came in from the kitchen. "Lunch will be ready shortly. Do you want it on the porch or here in the great room?"

Debbie was thoughtful, and then she replied, "Let's have it here, Dawn. Okay?"

The chef nodded and stepped out. Walter's ring shimmered, and a table appeared with several chairs around it between the fireplace and the door where Belinda previously left.

Qaak appeared next to the fireplace. "Those kiwis are amazing. In the darkest part of the forest next to the cliffs, I remained visible, and they ignored me. Neither of you ever saw them, but there used to be carnivores native to New Zealand. I saw one when I was visiting some of your forbears, Walter."

"You never told me about that. Were they the bakers?"

"Indeed. Their pastries were amazing."

Debbie was upbeat. "Glad you had a good time in the park, Qaak. Belinda has gone for a short walk. Lunch will be served soon."

The doorbell rang, and Walter looked puzzled. "I wonder why Belinda is ringing the doorbell."

Walter opened the door, and Ann was standing there. "Hi, Walter! I hope you don't mind my dropping by unannounced, but I'm here on South Island on vacation and decided to –"

Ann's mouth dropped open as she saw Qaak. Walter turned to see what she was looking at, and Ann stepped inside.

Qaak ambled forward and extended a hand. "How do you do! My name is Qaak."

"How do you do! Who – or what – are you?"

Walter's ring shimmered, and a chair appeared behind her as her legs began to buckle. She sank back into it. Walter spoke reassuringly. "As he said, his name is Qaak. I know you are a bit surprised to see someone like him. Do you trust me, Ann?"

Ann stammered slightly. "Of course!"

"You have already shaken his hand, so you know he is real. I suggest you let him touch your forehead, okay?"

Ann was very quiet. "Okay."

Qaak stepped forward and put three fingers on her face. His eyes glow briefly, and then he pulled back.

Ann stared. "Walter! You are the Gaardian!" Her head turned. "And you are his friend and trainer!" Her head turned back. "Debbie! You knew all this!"

Debbie extended her a hand to get up. "Yes, Ann. Come on. Let's have some girl talk. The powder room is this way." The two women walked hand in hand through another doorway.

Qaak chuckled. "She sensed me before she saw me. I decided it was time to become real for her."

Walter was upbeat. "I thought maybe Belinda had changed her mind about taking a walk."

The door opened again, and Belinda came through. "Did I hear my name? I decided there was not enough time before lunch and came back. Where's Debbie?"

Walter smiled. "She's with Ann."

"Ann? Ann Cotter? What's she doing here?"

"It was a surprise for all of us – especially for Ann – when she saw Qaak inside a house that is not the small cabin she thought it was."

Belinda giggled. "Is Ann okay?"

"She's fine. Debbie has her in the bathroom for girl talk. Why don't you go and see if you can help?"

Belinda nodded and headed to the bathroom.

Qaak's eyes glowed briefly. "This is all good – not planned, but good."

"How so?"

"I've wanted to get to know her. Now it is possible." Qaak closed his eyes, and his whole body began to glow. The others watched silently, curious. Inside his head, Qaak heard the low rumble of The Creator's voice deep within him.

> **"Everything is unfolding, as it should Qaak. I will redeem Ann's coming here today. Be patient, Qaak. Trust me. I am with you."**

Qaak's glow faded, and when his eyes opened, the others seemed to start moving again after a pause. "Qapoku says he will redeem this. I am glad. I am also hungry. Is lunch ready?" As he asked the question, the three women came back in from the bathroom, and lunch appeared on the table. They all took chairs and sat down.

Walter smiled. "Ann, are you okay?"

"The shock is beginning to wear off."

Qaak touched her arm with a finger. "The first time I saw you was at Walter's condo, and you walked through me. You are wondrous inside as well as out, but you absolutely must stop smoking."

Ann smiled. "Maybe you're walking through me was why I shivered a bit when I saw Walter that day!"

Walter smiled. "Let me interrupt for a moment to bless the food." He looked up. "Heavenly Father, thank you for this food, for friendship, and for your presence. In Jesus' name, we pray. Amen." They ate silently, passing various dishes to each other.

Qaak put down his fork as the others continued to eat. "This food is wonderful." He called out, Dawn?" The cook came in, wearing an apron. Qaak beckoned to her. "You're food is exquisite as usual." The others nodded.

"Thank you. I see we have another guest. Will we be having dinner here again?"

"I think its best that we all head back to my base, now that we're about finished. Our new guest is going to need some orientation. If you wish, you can stay here a few more days as we talked about, but I have an alternative for you – a surprise."

"A surprise?"

"I've flown your fiancé here. He will be at the hotel you love so much in Queenstown in a few minutes. What would you like to wear when you greet him?"

"Wow! Thank you! I don't have anything here to dress up in. If I were in Los Angeles I'd wear a scarlet sheath that he likes." Walter's ring shimmered, and suddenly she was transformed, wearing the sheath, with her hair and makeup exquisitely done.

"Is this what you had in mind?" A mirror appeared next to her. Everyone was smiling.

"Fantastic! How will I get there?"

"You know how I do things. I have a large suite there for you. I will transport you to the suite, and you can go downstairs to meet him. Are you ready to go?"

"Thank you so much!" She took a deep breath. "Yes! I'm ready!" The ring shimmered again, and she vanished.

Belinda's tone was playful. "Walter, I've always liked your style!" They all laughed quietly.

Walter looked around the table. "Is everyone about done? If so, let's get going!"

Ann looked puzzled. "Go where?"

They all vanished and reappeared in the Moon Base's atrium. When they reappeared, Ann looked around silently with her mouth slightly open. She followed automatically as they went into the lounge.

Paula walked in from the pool area wearing a red one-piece swimsuit. It changed into a jump suit. "I thought I saw people arrive! Who's this?"

"Hi, Paula. I recognize you from television. You used to be a network anchor, but now you have become an independent journalist. I'm Ann Cotter."

"Hi, Ann. Actually I'm working for Walter. People on Earth do not know that. I hope you can keep that a secret. Are you a new recruit?"

Walter interjected. "She's not really a recruit, Paula. She is an old friend who accidentally discovered my identity. By the way, now that you are on the Gaardian team, I want you to introduce Toby to some key people you know, so that he can use his special gift that you found so fascinating. As far as Ann is concerned, don't worry about our secret."

Paula smiled broadly. "Okay. I will work Toby into some of the inner circles of the diplomatic corps. I can take him with me when I post that story Frank gave me yesterday."

"Good. Keep me posted." All of them went into the lounge, and they took chairs and couches to make them comfortable. Butch and Jim walked in and joined them.

Qaak moved toward Ann to make introductions. "Ann, this is Butch, the base physician, and Jim is the goodwill ambassador to Earth. This is all very sudden for you. We hope you will join us, but we will not force you. Other arrangements can be made."

Ann spoke softly. "How do you do?"

They smiled. "Hi, Ann." Butch shook her hand.

"Frankly, I had never really considered working for the Gaardian. Of course, I did not know it was you, Walter."

"Understood. If you want to, you can just wander around here on the base looking things over for a few days."

Qaak's eyes glowed briefly. "I have an alternative. I would like Ann, Paula, and Belinda to join me on Gaardian planet. We can have some very relaxed conversations in its low-key environment."

Paula scowled. "Qaak, I'd like to join you, but I think I'd better make it another time. I've some other things on my mind and a few things I need to do here on base."

"Belinda, Ann?" The two women looked at each other and nodded.

Belinda was animated. "Sounds good to me – I've wanted to see Gaardian ever since I heard about it. Let's go!"

A chime sounded. They all paused as Waagere appeared in front of Walter. "I hope I'm not disturbing anything important, Walter."

Walter was serious. "What is it, Waagere?"

"The Quzaks have decided to launch an exploratory expedition despite the fact that they have not yet mapped their sector of space."

Qaak grunted. "Do they not see that this is foolish?"

"The military is determined to save face with their people. We anticipated this possibility, but they have moved more quickly than expected."

Walter was quiet but intense. "Qaak, I want you to go there." Qaak nodded as Walter continued. "Ladies, it appears you and Qaak will have to make it another time."

"Agreed. I have been following through with the Quzaks anyway. I'll keep you posted."

Waagere gestured by stretching his head forward. "Come to the center first. I have a strategy."

"Very well."

Waagere vanished. Jim Crenshaw spoke seriously. "I've always liked what I've seen of Waagere. Qaak, before you go, I want to thank you again for the language training. I used it today when visiting friends in Belgium. They told me my Flemish was flawless."

"You're welcome. I must go now!" Qaak turned, raised a finger to the group, and vanished.

Butch approached Walter. "I have a preliminary report on that project you gave me."

"I appreciate that, Butch, but just have Frank add it to my briefing for tomorrow morning. Right now, there are other things more pressing on my agenda." As others sat down in the lounge, Walter headed across the atrium.

+ + +

Above Gaardian, Qaak appeared in his apartment. He went to a console nearby and studied it for a few moments. Then he went and stood by a window. "Personal journal. The Quzak challenge was resolved before Waagere could get there. Daie-Ahnn and Steve are doing an excellent job in their covert surveillance. They did not need to reveal their identities in order to thwart the Quzak mission. I believe Qapoku guided them and helped them. Both are gifted, but even with their gifts combined they could not have done this without help."

Qaak's eyes glowed briefly. "Their strategy was to befriend the Quzak Commander and his mate, Ooza. All went smoothly. I intend to record Ooza's activities for future reference. It appears she might be an excellent prospective Gaardian. Note to myself. I am considering romance with both Belinda and Ann. I am also attracted to Jody and Paula. End journal." The apartment began to glow, until the furnishings disappeared.

> **"You must not forget your parents' teachings or mine. Do not choose your mate based upon the chemicals that are generated in your brain in response to what you see and hear. That chemistry will deceive you as it did the first time you chose a mate."**

"I remember."

> **"Learn from your history, Qaak. Follow the teachings of my Son, Qapoku."**

"Yes. Who shall I choose?" The glow faded quickly.

Belinda appeared in front of him. "Hi, Qaak. Nice apartment! I'm never disappointed with doing g-mails."

"Thank you. Is there something that Walter wanted you to tell me?"

"No, Qaak. You, Ann, and I have been invited to join Pixie and her mate, Saahmn, for a picnic."

Qaak's eyes glowed momentarily. "Where? How soon?"

Belinda smiled. "I hope that twinkle in your eyes means something good! The picnic will be in the park where Pixie first met Eiraynay when jogging. Pixie is already there setting things up. Ann and I are leaving now. Pixie wants you to come as soon as it is convenient."

"Tell Pixie I will be there before the mid-day."

"Good! See you soon!"

+ + +

A few hours later, in the park on Aegeene, both suns were shining brightly. The park's foliage was vivid, and the trees seemed to reach forever into the sky. In a clearing near some fountains, Xpraepostq and her mate were standing in the shade of some of the colorful trees.

Her ring shimmered, and a large quantity of food appeared, spread out on a cloth about three meters square that hovered about a meter off the ground. Some of the food was steaming, while some of it was in trays of ice. "That will get us started, Saahmn."

Slightly taller than Pixie with similar coloring and longer and darker hair, her husband reached out and hugged her. "This is another reason I'm glad I mated you! You do put on a fine meal! How soon will the others get here?"

"They should be here any minute. When we get back tonight let's just take some time to relax and enjoy one another."

"You don't have to convince me." Saahmn kept his arms around his mate and gave her a kiss. As he stepped back, Belinda and Ann appeared just outside the shaded area.

She waved. "Here are two of them. Hi, Belinda! You must be Ann!"

The two women smiled. Belinda took Ann's hand and stepped forward. "Pixie, I'd like you to meet Ann. As I told you via g-mail, she is an old friend of Walter's that accidentally discovered his identity.

"Hello!" She smiled.

As Ann shook Pixie's hand, Belinda shifted her focus to Saahmn, who responded with a warm smile and took her hand. "Hello!"

Pixie put her arm around him. "Saahmn, these are Belinda and Ann."

Ann looked about in wonder, shading her eyes as she looked at the two suns. "Hello! Seeing two suns in the sky is amazing! And those trees! I am new to this Gaardian reality, and I am not sure I can pronounce either of your names correctly. Can I call you Pixie and Sam?"

Xpraepostq and Saahmn laughed, and Pixie spoke with assurance. "Of course! Walter called me Pixie until recently, and most from Earth still do. I warned my mate you'd probably like to call him 'Sam.'"

Her husband was also calm and reassuring. "'Sam' is fine. The two of you are remarkable. Except for being taller than our species, and except for the slightly more opaque skin, you Humans look remarkably like us."

Ann now had an impish smile. "I was going to say that you look like an ex-boyfriend of mine except that you are a lot shorter."

Belinda showed surprise. "Are you talking about that guy named Paul that you almost married?"

"Yes, but let's leave that alone, okay?"

Qaak appeared next to Belinda, and before she could speak, he gave her a hug. "Hello again, Belinda!"

"Hi Qaak! Now we are all here! Have you met Sam?"

"I've not had the pleasure. Pixie has chosen well I see."

"Hello Qaak. Actually, my name is Saahmn, but Sam will do. I believe the food is ready. Qaak, I understand there's a beverage you want us to try, is that correct?"

"Yes." His ring shimmered, and a tray holding beverage containers appeared, floated forward and stopped adjacent to the cloth with the food.

Pixie reached out and took a container. "Thank you, Qaak."

Her husband looked up. "Thanks Eiraynay for friends and food. Please be present, even invisibly, as we eat and enjoy one another. We want you to be glad you came and joined us."

Pixie touched her mate on the cheek. "Thank you, Saahmn."

Each of them took a beverage and put portions of the food on a plate, then chairs appeared in a circle, and they all sat down to eat. Qaak sat on his third leg. "I will take all of you to Gaardian Planet soon. Aegeene is beautiful, but it is very different from Gaardian. Saahmn, what has it been like, living with your local Gaardian as well as your mate?"

Saahmn smiled and looked at Pixie. "I have had to shift the way I think about things again."

"Again?"

"Yes. I changed my way of looking at life when I met Eiraynay in the spirit. Then I fell in love with Xpraepostq, and began to think in terms of my responsibilities as her mate. Then I had to shift my thinking again, when she revealed to me that she was the Gaardian of Aegeene and of this galactic sector. I first saw Walter on g-mail, then in person. Now I have met two human females on the same day, and I have met someone who is special to my mate, but looks a lot less like us. All of this has been happening while telling others on Aegeene about Eiraynay. There have been a lot of things to get used to!" They continued to eat silently.

Belinda swallowed what she was chewing and took a sip of liquid. "Pixie, why don't you, Ann, and I take a walk? If we were on Earth, we would excuse ourselves to go to the ladies' room, but let's go for a walk."

Ann was eager. "Good idea! I want to see more of this place. Come on, Pixie! Show us around!" The three women got up and walked down a path into the forest.

Pixie's husband watched them leave and then turned to Qaak. "Qaak, there are some multi-liquid fountains nearby. Would you like to see them?"

"I'd be honored." The pair started walking across the clearing to a more rocky area.

22. Summer Christmas

The pool area at the Moon Base was almost crowded, with many people taking time to exercise and relax. Belinda suddenly appeared in the pool area between the swimming pool and the whirlpool, and she changed instantly to a bikini. In the whirlpool were Keeta and Ken, cuddling very close together.

Ken smiled at the Base Commander. "Hi, Belinda! Did you just get back from Aegeene?"

"Hi, lovebirds! Yes, Aegeene is beautiful. I want to relax for a few minutes before getting back to work. I have a lot to do. Toby is now working several hours each week in the State Department in Washington, and he also works at the House of Commons in London. I am helping him coordinate his efforts with Stephanie and Judy." Belinda stepped into the whirlpool.

On the other side of the recreation area, she saw Ann and Stephanie gazing in rapt attention at Asayak while he gestured. The three moved to the conference room. Ken pointed to the conference room doorway. "Asayak has been explaining his planet's culture to Ann and Stephanie for the last hour or so. It used to seem a bit spooky to see him conversing telepathically with people, but I've gotten used to it."

Keeta nodded. "I don't think I would want telepathy as one of my gifts. I would be tempted to snoop into people's private thoughts. Being able to be transparent brings enough temptations for me. Look -- there are Paula and Butch! She seems to be fitting in pretty well now."

Paula and Butch walked into the pool area together and dove into the pool. Coming out of the water, they talked intimately.

Belinda watched it all with amusement. "Butch is enjoying Paula alright, and she's continuing to be intrigued by everything here on the base. I think she's beginning to find her place." Ken, Keeta, and Belinda continued to watch the others at the pool and saw Ann in the distance through a doorway.

Ann sat relaxed in an overstuffed chair as Asayak stood nearby. She spoke with him with the conviction of one who has struggled with Earth's social problems, particularly those in the United States where she lives. "During the previous quarter century, the rise in the crime rate was directly proportional to the drop in funding for the fine arts in our public schools."

Asayak gestured with an appendage. "Understandable. It appears the fine arts provide structure and context for values. Are things improving?"

"A few visionary politicians are waking up to the trend and are trying to make changes." Qaak appeared near the fireplace, ambled over, and then rested on his third leg. She gave him a warm smile. "Hi, Qaak! It's good to see you."

Asayak reached out with one of his arms and touched the triped, who responded with a subtle glow in his eyes. Qaak was enthusiastic. "It's good to see you both. May I listen in on this conversation?"

Asayak gestured again with the same appendage. "By all means."

Ann too was enthusiastic. "Of course! I have been telling Asayak about the rise and fall of fine arts education in my country. Asayak is looking for ways to further the fine arts on its planet. As you observed, for hundreds of years the inspiration for fine arts in Earth's western culture was dominated by its primary religion, Christianity. In our eastern culture, there were slightly different trends, but they sometimes ran parallel. Asayak, I cannot even imagine your culture's development without fine arts."

"We did not have written records of our thoughts until a few of your centuries ago. As our recorded language developed, our need for non-verbal illustration developed. We have what you would term photo imagery, but we recognize the need for other kinds of creativity."

Qaak shifted two of his legs to get more comfortable. "Your culture has a few parallels on other planets. My I transfer those thoughts to you?"

"Of course." Qaak touched Asayak for a moment as his eyes glowed briefly. "Thank you. Ann, do you think that our society will have greater structure and stability as we develop our fine arts?"

She was thoughtful. "I would think so. On the other hand . . ."

Qaak got up off his third leg. "Forgive me for interrupting, Ann. Duty calls. I must be going. Excuse me, my friends!" He vanished before either of them could respond.

Outside the base on the barren landscape, Qaak reappeared on the far side. The slight glow of a force field surrounded his body as he walked across the moonscape, bouncing slightly in the weaker gravity. A larger glow began to surround him. The low rumble of The Creator inside of Qaak's head caused him to pause with a sense of peace.

> **"Everything is unfolding, as it should, Qaak. Do not allow yourself the temptation of jealousy. It will bring you great unhappiness. Your path and Ann's are not congruent. Let her find her way and find my preparations for her. There is yet greater love for you in store. I am with you."**

The glow faded. Qaak grunted and turned back to look at the base. His ring shimmered briefly and he vanished.

+ + +

Meanwhile, in her office Debbie was tapping a finger or her desk as she was staring at her console screen. Belinda walked in, and she looked up. "Hi, Belinda! What's up?"

"Not much. I just want to thank you again for your hospitality when I went skiing near your place in New Zealand. The Southern Alps are certainly different than either the Sierras or the Rockies."

"Walter and I were glad to have you stay with us. I know how much you love the area. Have you thought about acquiring some property there by the slopes?"

Belinda's voice became slightly distant. "I wondered if I was still welcome there, since Walter and I have known each other so long."

"You're always welcome in our home, Belinda."

"Thanks. I have to go. See you later."

"Okay. Bye!" Belinda turned and left. Debbie looked up, tapping her finger on her desk again. She looked back at her video console. "Personal journal. I wonder if Belinda is in love with Walter, or if she ever was. Does she have regrets? Did she expect Walter to replace her deceased husband now that she has a second life to live? Is she jealous of me? I hope not. I like Belinda a lot, and have a great deal of respect for her. End note." She paused. "Frank, transmit a copy of my last journal note to Walter along with a g-mail of this last conversation with Belinda."

Debbie got out of her chair and went to the window. She turned and faced her desk. "Frank, put me in that red gown and prepare the following as a g-mail." Instantly she was in a glamorous red dress, with every hair in place. She smiled. "Hi! Let me be the first to wish you a very merry Christmas! Walter and I want to invite you to our big Christmas gala at our house in Franz Joseph. The party will be on December twenty-third. If you want to come a day or two early, there will be plenty of room. You can also stay through Christmas if you wish, although Walter may not be with us the entire time. There will be lots of food, fun, music, and worship. Let us know as soon as you can! Okay?" She paused. "Frank, send that g-mail to everyone on our list. Thanks."

She changed instantly back to her office outfit, as she went back to her desk. "Frank, ring my friend Dawn in Hollywood. She's probably at the restaurant."

There was a pause, and then Dawn's voice could be heard. "Hello?"

As the phone connection was made, Debbie spoke into the air. "Hi, Dawn. This is Debbie."

"Hi, Debbie! Good to hear your voice!"

"Good to hear yours, too! Congratulations! I'm sorry I can't be there for the wedding!"

"I am too. We're still working out the details of when and where."

"That's the reason I'm calling. I want to make you an offer and ask a favor."

"Shoot!"

"I'd like to fly you and your new husband down to New Zealand for your honeymoon. I know you both love to ski, but even if it is mid-summer in New Zealand at Christmas, Walter and I can see to it that you have plenty of snow for skiing. If you don't want to stay with us, we'll put you up at that terrific hotel in Franz Joseph."

Dawn's voice was excited. "Wow! I will have to ask James and see what he thinks. What's the favor?"

"Would you and your husband be willing to cook for us at our Christmas party on the 23rd?"

"James just walked in. Hold the line for a minute!" Debbie turned her chair to look out the window. When Dawn came back to the phone, she turned back to her desk. "Debbie? James says that since you're paying for the honeymoon of our dreams, how can we refuse to cook? We'll stay in the hotel -- if you don't mind -- until the day of the party. Then after we clean up from the party, we will spend the night with you. Okay?"

"Fantastic! You'll have first-class air reservations to fly down. You will get them by messenger tomorrow morning. You'll also get the best room in the little hotel. Walter and I look forward to seeing you both!"

"Thank you so very, very much! This is fantastic! See you then! Bye!"

"Bye!" Debbie touched her console. "Karen?"

In a moment, Karen Oreskovich appeared in the doorway to the hall. "Were you calling me?"

Debbie turned and smiled. "Yes! You came by just in time. We need to set up an enriched communication link with Quzak Planet. There are things going on there that need closer monitoring."

"Do you want enriched video as well as audio?"

"Yes, and I want more scientific data coming in on what's happening there. I think Belinda would like to keep track of our two undercover ambassadors more effectively. You're the communications expert. I'm hoping you can come up with something."

"I'll see what I can do. Right now, Lauryn has me working on something too. I'll try to get back to both you and Belinda later today."

"Thanks. See you later." She looked up at the ceiling. "Frank?"

As Karen disappeared down the hall, the android appeared next to her desk. "Yes?"

"Let Walter know about these latest arrangements. Right now, I want you to walk with me to the lounge. I have some ideas I want to run past you." The two of them walked out of her office.

+ + +

On the twenty-third, it was bright and sunny in Franz Joseph. In Walter and Debbie's New Zealand home, there were traditional Christmas decorations throughout the house, with special emphasis on the Christian roots of Christmas. All of Walter's key crewmembers were seated around the room, along with Qaak, Kieya, Puz, Pixie, Doff, and Waagere. Dawn and James, in chef's outfits, were standing next to the patio door. There were numerous conversations going on throughout the great room.

Walter raised a hand to get their attention, and quiet ensued. "As I said earlier, it's hard to believe that this is our third Christmas together! That was a fantastic dinner, Dawn and James!"

Debbie shared his enthusiasm. "Yes! You two surpassed yourselves!" There were murmurs of agreement throughout the room.

Dawn did a mock curtsey. "Thanks. Thanks for our dream honeymoon! Now all we have to do is clean up!"

Walter's ring shimmered. "It's done!"

"Wow! I wish it were that easy at our restaurant!" Everyone laughed.

Debbie turned to Belinda to speak quietly to her. "Are we okay, Belinda? I don't want anything to come between us."

Belinda responded quietly. "Neither do I. Everything's fine as far as I'm concerned. I'm happy for you and Walter. I'm beginning to see the possibility of a new love of my own! Don't worry about it. Everything's cool."

"I'm glad."

James cleared his throat. "Walter? Are Dawn and I the only ones here that are not part of your crew?"

Walter nodded as Qaak's eyes glowed for a moment. "Yes you are. I have talked it over with some of the crew and a few of the other Gaardians. Would the two of you like to join us on the Moon and become part of the crew?" The newlywed couple's eyes grew wide. "You would help us expand our menu in the mess hall, and prepare special meals from time to time, but we also will find other roles for you."

The newlyweds looked at each other. James nodded. "In the kitchen, while we were preparing to serve dessert, we talked about what we would do if you asked us something like this. We agreed we'd say yes."

"Great!"

Dawn held up a finger. "There's a catch though. I think I'm pregnant." There were expressions of congratulations from all around the room. "Thanks. Will that be a problem?"

Qaak cackled, his eyes glowing. "Not at all! Your baby may be the first on Walter's base, but we can be sure it won't be the last!" There was quiet laughter.

Dawn was thoughtful. "Maybe I can be a home teacher!"

"Why not?" Debbie was enthusiastic. "Qaak can give you a college education in five minutes -- a doctorate only takes a few seconds longer!" More laughter erupted.

Dawn's husband was more serious. "Sounds like I have my work cut out for me as well."

John Carson spoke from a far corner of the great room. "You've got that right. You have the temperament to be a pretty good clown. I have both training and experience. It would be fun working with you if you're interested."

"I don't know about being a clown, but I do enjoy entertaining."

Debbie nodded. "We might even put together a local drama troupe!"

Walter turned to look at her. "The skills of your first life might come in handy after all! Let's go upstairs for a few minutes."

"Okay." The two of them got up and walked to the spiral staircase at the far end of the great room. Conversations broke out among the others. Jody approached Qaak. They walked to a far corner of the patio, sat down, and talked quietly.

In moments, Debbie and Walter were coming up the stairs and heading to the first doorway, which led into a very large bedroom. As they entered the bedroom, they saw their two cats playing in one corner. The cats saw them coming and went through a doorway into an adjacent room. Debbie and Walter went to a large window that looks out on the Tasman Sea.

Debbie put her arm around him. "What's up?"

"You and I have not had much time just to ourselves these last few days."

She hugged him and gave him a short kiss on the lips. "I know. When we've headed to bed, we've fallen asleep almost immediately, and when we've finished with morning devotions, there are always things to be done."

"We need a vacation from our vacation!"

She smiled. "Yes! Got any ideas?"

"Where would you like to go, even if it's just for a couple of days?"

"We could stay here, but there are too many reminders of what we need to be doing. How about going to Gaardian?"

"Sounds like a good idea. The planet can shield us, give us some privacy, and screen our g-mail calls."

"When can we – or shall we go?"

"Let's make it the day after tomorrow. Meanwhile, be thinking about how we can help Qaak. He's lonely, now that he is no longer convener."

"Lonely? I guess he is. He needs to get away for a few days too. Why not suggest he visit Yosemite?"

"Good idea! He has never been there, though I have told him how special a place it is for so many humans. Since it is winter, it won't be a challenge to achieve privacy. Let's plan on some time just for ourselves this evening, okay? Meanwhile let's get back downstairs."

"Right." They hugged again. Then they walked to the door.

Downstairs, there were small conversations going on throughout the room. Jody and Qaak were in a far corner. Jody spoke earnestly. "Qaak, I'd like to have your help in improving my knowledge of Gaardian science and technology. When we were on Gaardian Planet after our last mission, I had an interesting dialogue with it. Gaardian said that despite our species differences that you and I have complimentary personalities. I'd like to learn more from you."

"Definitely. There are some things that perhaps I can learn from you as well."

"Really?"

"Yes." He paused as they saw Walter and Debbie coming down the stairs. "I have been a Gaardian so long that I have had little time for leisure pursuits. I have almost forgotten how to get to know others on anything but a professional basis. Now that Walter is convener, and I am officially retired, I need to learn how to enjoy The Creator's creation again."

"I never thought of myself as someone who can be of help to you."

"Indeed. Shall we try a brief mental contact again?"

"Sure!" Qaak reached out and put three fingers on Jody's face for about ten seconds. His eyes increased their glow.

Jody's eyes grew wide, and then she smiled. "We have far more in common than I realized!"

"Yes!"

"Since you want some advice I'll say this too you right now. Speaking as a woman, I think you ought to resolve your feelings for both Ann and Belinda – for their sake as well as for yours. I suggest you create a low-key opportunity or two to make that happen."

"Agreed. Thank you, my dear friend!"

"You're welcome!" His eyes glowed. They hugged.

23. A Retreat

Important lessons can be learned in remote places. At more than sixty-seven thousand of Earth's years, Qaak had a natural tendency to think there was little left to be learned. Several days after their affirmation of friendship, there were some unusual visitors in Bridal Veil Creek Campground in Yosemite National Park. Since it was winter, there was no one around except for occasional cross-country skiers. The mid-afternoon sun was going in and out from scattered clouds. The winter snows were very deep, making access to the campground appear to be impossible. Walter, Qaak, Belinda, and Ann appeared there in winter clothing, and they began walking along the creek toward the fall. Walter pointed ahead. "I think you'll enjoy walking from here. If you did not have Gaardian ring support I would not recommend the Pohono trail in the winter, but the snow will give you excellent privacy. Yosemite is my favorite place on Earth. I hope the three of you enjoy it as much next few days as I have all of my life."

Belinda looked around with a sense of wonder. "Thanks for suggesting this as a location for our retreat."

"I want this to be a relaxing time for the three of you. As Qaak knows, I have some personal things to follow up on."

Qaak floated above the snow and rotated in all directions. "I'm glad to be here. I have experienced it previously only through your mind. Now I will find out for myself what makes this place special to your species."

"Have fun! I'll see all of you in a few days!" Walter vanished.

Walter reappeared on Gaardian near Red Falls, and walked toward a structure that seemed to blend into the landscape, except for windows facing the falls and a doorway. Walter stepped inside and saw his wife standing by the windows.

Debbie turned, approached him, and gave him a hug. "This is incredible! I had images in my mind of a landscape out of one of the science fiction movies, but this is much more surreal! It's stunning!"

"I'm glad your first impression of Gaardian is so positive. Would you like to hear Gaardian's first impression of you?"

"First impression of me? What do you mean, 'Gaardian's first impression of me?'"

"Gaardian is sentient."

"Sentient?"

"Sentience means having the ability to think and to reason."

"This planet can think?"

"Absolutely. Its presence is at the core of how the first Gaardians became who they were, and how all Gaardians continue to be who we are."

"You're serious aren't you?"

"Absolutely!"

"Okay. I'll play along. How do we communicate with Gaardian?"

"Easy – Gaardian, will you please communicate with Debbie and me through telepathic contact?"

"Hello Debbie. Hello Walter."

Debbie's mouth dropped open. "Hello Gaardian! Walter, I truly, humbly, completely apologize! I thought those stories you told me about Gaardian were just tall tales for entertainment! Don't get me wrong, I truly enjoy your stories! However, that's all I thought they were, well – stories! Gaardian, I apologize to you too!"

"No apology necessary! My first impression of you was that you are a perfect match for Walter. I am not an adequate judge of physical appearance, but in your mind and spirit, you are truly beautiful."

"Thank you, Gaardian. Walter, this gives me a whole new perspective on who you are and who the Gaardians are." Debbie turned away from Walter and looked out the window again.

"Gaardian, Debbie and I need a break from our regular environment and activities. Please screen our calls and visitors for at least three of Earth's days. I don't want us to be disturbed except for real emergencies."

"Very well. I will withdraw from your minds until you again address specific thoughts to me. Enjoy your vacation."

Debbie smiled. "Thank you, Gaardian. It was nice meeting you!"

"It was most pleasant meeting you as well."

Walter hugged Debbie with one arm. "Thank you, Gaardian. Now, love, do you want to stay here for a while, or would you like a whirlwind tour of the planet?"

Debbie turned back to Walter. "Let's take a whirlwind tour. Have we a vehicle of some kind available?"

"If you wish." An oblong vehicle appeared just outside, hovering over the ground. Walter and Debbie stepped outside and got in. As the vehicle began to move, Walter pointed out various features of the planet's surface. Debbie pointed at the distant sparkle in the sky of the Gaardian Conference Center. The vehicle rapidly rose and approached it.

+ + +

In Yosemite, Qaak and the women were walking on snowshoes alongside a nearly frozen riverbed. Qaak was amused. "It is good that ring support keeps us warm this afternoon, but I like our clothing."

As they began walking eastward, Ann looked at her own outfit and at Belinda's. "Thanks, Qaak. Are there any skiers nearby that can see us?"

Qaak's eyes glowed for a moment. "There is no animal life for several kilometers except for non-humans. Their minds are centered on survival. Winter here is very quiet. I like walking on this frozen water, but I am glad we are near the falls. I expected more sound this time of the year."

Belinda paused to look around. "I love the quiet too. I just saw a fox -- or maybe a coyote. I've never been to the top of these falls, though I've been to Taft Point."

"Taft Point?" Ann pointed. "There it is! It's a coyote."

Qaak turned to look. "An interesting animal."

Belinda started to move again. "Coyotes are scavengers. Though they sometimes kill, they often eat the meat of animals already dead." She pointed. "Taft point is a few miles east of here, and Dewey Point is just west of us, over there." She pointed to the left.

Later, they came out of the trees and approached the cliff. Qaak was enthusiastic. "This is stunning! It is very different from anything on any other planet I have visited."

Ann nodded. "It's beautiful!"

Belinda pointed again. "I think I like Sentinel Dome east of here even better, but this is nice."

"I did not choose Sentinel Dome because I like the vegetation here in this area." Qaak's arms swept around. "Let's get comfortable." A transparent shelter appeared around them with overstuffed furniture. It had a fire in a fireplace but no smoke. "The shelter is invisible, and so are we." Qaak sat down in a recliner and stretched out his legs in a relaxed braid. The women sat in swivel rockers that appeared. Food appeared on tables next to them, and they began to sip hot liquids while eating finger food.

Ann turned to Belinda. "Why is it called Bridal Veil Fall?"

"It has to do with an old Native American legend."

"Native American?" Qaak was curious.

"Those descended from the original inhabitants of this continent use that ethnic label. The original inhabitants had migrated from the continent on the other side of the Pacific Ocean, probably over a land bridge at the northern end."

"So, what's the legend?" Ann shifted and got more comfortable.

"The legend is called Pohono, which is also their name for the falls and the name of the trail we'll follow from here to Glacier Point. A Native American man and woman wanted to get married in the valley, but their parents disapproved. On the day that she was supposed to marry the one selected by her father, she went with her lover to the top of the falls, and they jumped off."

Qaak grunted. "Those kinds of romantic legends are found on almost every planet. A romantic notion or two led me to ask the two of you to join me here today."

"How so?" Ann turned to face Qaak.

"The first time I saw you, you did not see me. I had just integrated Walter, and we were approaching the elevator across from your apartment. You got off the elevator in a wet bikini and walked through me as you passed Walter. I saw both the beauty of your spirit and the lung cancer that was afflicting you."

"Lung cancer? I had a cough, but I did not know I have cancer."

"You no longer have cancer. The Creator healed you when you gave your life to Jesus before you were baptized. The voice has said He has great plans for you. For a time, I have wondered if you are the one who is to be my new life companion."

Ann smiled. "I really care about you, Qaak. You're a terrific and unique friend. I treasure your role in my life -- you have made a profound difference that I could never have imagined. My life is now new and more securely centered in Oakland, where God is using me through Walter to do a special ministry there. Asayak has helped me find new ways to do things that no human could have imagined. He too is a valued and trusted friend now."

Belinda smiled also. "I'm glad. How has Asayak helped you?"

"It's fascinating. I am not telepathic as Asayak is, but he has taught me how to tune into people's emotional base and help them connect with their own potential. It's hard to explain."

Qaak chuckled. "Asayak has gifts that it does not recognize as gifts. This suggests to me that I can mentor it with some interplanetary perspectives through our direct mental contact. I will discuss this with him."

Belinda turned to Qaak. "When you have trained me, I have felt an interesting kinship with you."

Qaak's eyes glowed for a moment. "Indeed. I have sensed it too. When we encountered the Quzaks the first time, I told Waagere that I wanted to spend more time with you and get to know you better."

"I've enjoyed getting to know you too, Qaak. I told Walter that I halfway expected to be uncomfortable around aliens, but I never have been uncomfortable around you." She paused. "Look at the eastern end of the valley! Isn't the sunset's pink glow on the clouds and peaks beautiful?"

"Mmmm..." Ann simply stared. "Yes! It is wonderful! It reminds me how long this day has been though, Qaak, though let's sleep up here for a few hours."

Qaak's ring shimmered for a moment as the furniture turned into beds with blankets. "We can all use some sleep. Let's do so." The shelter's transparent shell became darker. "I've darkened our shelter. It will allow the sunrise to awaken us. Pleasant dreams."

All three had vivid dreams, with rapid and colorful images. Ann saw herself working with people in Oakland and continuing her connection to Asayak and Qaak. Belinda saw herself in a romance with a man whose face she could not see, who worked with her both on the moon and elsewhere. Qaak saw himself talking with Jody, telling her about his visit to Yosemite. All three of them had the sense that these were prophetic dreams.

The next morning there was bright sunshine, and Qaak created a path through the snow as they approached the base of Sentinel Dome. They began to climb upward. Belinda stopped on her snowshoes and turned around. "This has been a great hike, Qaak. I have not taken this trail in the winter before -- probably few if any people have, because in winter it is so dangerous. The views have been breathtaking."

Ann stopped. "Speaking of breathtaking -- let's stop for a moment."

As Qaak stopped, he was puzzled. "You should not be tired -- ring support keeps you going."

"I'm not physically tired, but emotionally I find it thrilling to stop and enjoy the scenery. Last night, I sure had a vivid dream!"

Belinda was excited. "Me too!"

Qaak was amused. "I did as well. When I wished you pleasant dreams I did not realize that The Creator was up to something!"

"Really? I dreamed I said farewell to my new Gaardian friends and returned to Oakland. I am going to make a difference in thousands of people's lives, and that I will seldom see my Gaardian friends. I will miss Asayak. And Qaak, I love you like a brother, and I hope that you will continue to be available to me when I need you as I pursue my new calling."

Belinda was serious. "I think Qaak will be keeping track of us whether we are aware of it or not. Right, Qaak?"

Qaak's eyes glowed for a moment. "Indeed. Tell us about your dream Belinda."

"I can't recall anything specific except that there were vivid and colorful images. I am not sure now I know this, but I am confident that God is leading me to romance with someone I would never have otherwise considered. I do not know what that means yet, but I will marry again. Like Ann, I treasure your friendship, Qaak, and I look forward to working with you for many years."

Ann started to move again. "Let's go on over the dome and on to Glacier Point, okay?"

Belinda followed. "Let's go!"

They began to move on. Qaak was silent as he created the trail ahead. The women continued to converse, but Qaak's eyes had begun to glow. Soon he could no longer hear them. He saw his surroundings take on a slight glow as he heard the voice deep within himself.

"You have done well, Qaak. You have helped them pause in their lives long enough to catch a glimpse of their futures. Neither of them will be your new mate, but both will remain close to you. Be at peace, Qaak, everything is unfolding, as it should."

As the slight glow faded, he again heard the crunch of snow beneath their feet. Qaak glanced behind at the women. "Were either of you up here at Glacier Point when you were younger?

Ann responded quietly. "My parents brought me to Yosemite when I was a child, but we only visited the valley. My first time up here was just a few years ago. How about you Belinda?"

"As youngsters Walter's parents and my parents brought us up here, and we spent the night at the hotel here a couple of times in order to watch the fire fall be pushed over the edge."

"I remember seeing the fire fall a few times, but I didn't know there was a hotel up here!"

"Indeed." Qaak paused. "I have done some research and have seen detailed pictures and plans of that old hotel. It was quite rustic, but beautiful by human standards. I need to ask Walter about the fire fall sometime. I am confused by some of the things I have read about it – particularly why the tradition was started. I know it was stopped due to environmental damage by the people watching below and because of public safety." They approached Glacier Point, crossing the empty parking lot covered with snow.

As they got to within a few yards of the eastern cliff, Belinda stopped and gestured. "Right over there is an amphitheater that is used in the summer sometimes. The hotel sat there." They walked down an incline to the edge of the valley. "The veranda was about here, overlooking this part of the valley. Down there on the right are Vernal Fall and Nevada Fall. Further over there to the right is Illoette Fall."

Ann looked around, amazed. "The view from the rooms must have been fantastic!"

"Yes! Even when there was not much water in the waterfalls in the late summer, I still loved to look down there."

Qaak gestured at the amphitheater area. "The hotel was evidently difficult to maintain in its latter years. It seriously needed upgrading, but those in charge were not willing to go to the expense."

Belinda was pensive. "I wonder . . ."

Qaak turned to look at her. "What do you wonder about?"

"What would happen if the hotel reappeared up here for no apparent reason?" She giggled.

Ann burst out laughing. "Wouldn't that be a trip for the Park Service?"

Belinda laughed. "They would stumble all over themselves trying to come up with an explanation for the return of the hotel!" She paused, looked at the site, at Qaak, at Ann, and back at the site. "Seriously though...."

Qaak's eyes glowed for a moment. "Indeed. If I follow your logic in a more serious vein, this could be a good location for Gaardian retreats in the winters here. Each time we need it, we could create a center that is configured somewhat like the old hotel but with Gaardian conveniences."

"Yes! We could do what Walter and Debbie have done in New Zealand to protect their home there -- create a holographic image of the way the area is supposed to look. We could create natural snow boundaries and barriers to keep cross-country skiers away."

Ann looked over at a nearby building. "Let's go over by the building there and relax. I think it is the gift shop in the summer and ski shelter in winter."

"Good idea! There's no one else here today." The three of them walked back up the hill and over to the gift shop. Belinda's ring shimmered, and chairs appeared. They sat down, and steaming cups of hot chocolate appeared on tables next to them.

Qaak sniffed the chocolate and then tasted it. "This is the first time I've had hot chocolate. It is – it is delicious! I now understand why this place is so special to Walter and to other people of Earth. It is truly one of The Creator's masterpieces."

Belinda pointed back to the amphitheater. "I'm trying to remember how big the hotel was. Qaak, wasn't it about two stories high?"

The triped chuckled. "Closer to three and a half. I want to try something, but first let me assemble my thoughts." His eyes began to glow, and as he closed them, his entire body began to glow. "Yes! I am ready." His ring shimmered. A replica of the old Glacier Point Hotel appeared in the same place where the original had stood.

Belinda whistled. "Wow! Fantastic, Qaak! That's just as I remember it as a child! Is it a hologram?"

"No. It is real. There are no other humans at this altitude for several kilometers right now, but I cannot leave it there for long. I have updated its building materials and technology. We can go inside for a short visit. Shall we?"

The women responded almost together. "Yes!" They moved rapidly down a short incline on a path cleared of snow to the front door. Inside it was warm, with a fire in the fireplace. They wandered about the main level almost silently except for low expressions of pleasure.

Then they stepped out on the veranda, where Belinda looked around with delight. "Thank you, Qaak! This has brought back some wonderful memories." She kissed him lightly on the cheek, and his eyes glowed briefly.

"Me too! This is wonderful!" Ann kissed him and gave him a hug.

His eyes again glowed briefly. "I will save this configuration for future use. Walter may wish to use it and make variations of his own. It is too small an area for all the Gaardians but perhaps for all of Walter's crew. It could be used for other small gatherings as well."

Belinda was enthusiastic. "Yes! This will handle well over a hundred of us easily, perhaps three or four times that with some minor changes." The three of them stood at the railing of the veranda, gazing silently at the valley.

"Ladies, the rest rooms are functional and well supplied if you wish to freshen up before returning to the Moon. I will soon need to join Jody and Asayak on a planet where they are engaged in a rescue mission. After you leave, I shall withdraw this hotel for future use before going there."

Belinda turned to go inside. "Sounds good, Qaak. This has been an incredible outing! I'm glad the three of us could do this."

Ann turned to follow. "Yes! These last few days I will never forget. I am glad Walter suggested all of this. I'll thank him when we get back."

"Do that! Express my thanks to him for me as well."

They opened the door and went inside the hotel. Qaak veered off to the right, while the women went to the left.

24. Bending Time

A good friendship will refresh your soul. It is the best basis for deep, long-lasting relationships, regardless of where you are. Soon after the three left Yosemite, on another planet several galaxies away, there was pale green light diffused throughout the landscape. Jody and Asayak were working with some equipment in an open field.

The pale glow of a force field surrounded Jody as she worked. "Asayak, we're going to need help in getting this planet prepared for that meteor shower."

"Qaak is coming to help." It paused. "This planet's culture is just beginning its time of scientific and technological development."

"It's hard staying out of sight to do all of this."

Qaak appeared nearby. "How did you do that Asayak? You touched my mind on the other side of Gaardian controlled space. No one has ever done that before."

"It occurred to me that if I can touch your mind when in each other's presence, why couldn't I use ring support to enhance the distance? It worked."

"It did. I told Gaardian. It is considering ramifications and possibilities. How is progress?"

The three of them moved about among the equipment as the conversation continued. Jody gestured to one large piece of equipment. "We've configured field generators to deflect the meteor shower utilizing the planet's volcanic energy converted to a gravitational diversion matrix. There's enough energy available, but we need to increase the size of our efforts geometrically."

Asayak extended an appendage to the sky. "The shower will begin shortly. We are running out of time."

Qaak spoke more loudly and with authority. "Time is the key! Asayak, Jody, hold your rings adjacent to mine." Asayak and Jody approached Qaak. One of Asayak's appendages was extended with a ring, and Jody extended her right hand.

There was a brilliant flash of light. Jody looked around. "This may seem like a strange question, but what did we just do?"

Asayak turned all the way around. "Yes. . . . I am confused."

Qaak spoke more softly. "Your confusion will subside in a moment. My species is not strongly affected when we bend time." Qaak's eyes glowed for a moment.

"I see! In bending time, the planet was in a different place in its orbit when the shower passed through. The shower's time function was accelerated until it was beyond the planet's orbit." Asayak pointed to the sky. "In another sense, the shower had already passed by when the planet was where it is or was supposed to be. Time is now back to its normal shape and parameters."

Jody was amused. "That was almost as much fun as snuffing out those stars! You taught us what we had to do in a modified instant. In a parallel instant you slowed down the planet while in another parallel instant I speeded up the shower."

Qaak chuckled. "Correct. Look -- the meteors are showing reflected light off the planet's sun as they leave." Qaak folded one leg under him to relax, and Jody relaxed in a chair that appeared. Asayak stood between them as they watched the shower move away. "You may be interested to know that I took a hike with Belinda and Ann a few time periods ago. We all had vivid dreams while sleeping in those mountains."

Asayak stirred. "I have been helping Ann discover new ways of helping people."

"She told me. I think, Asayak, that you have abilities that you do not realize are gifts."

"Gifts?"

"Yes. If you permit me, I can mentor you with some perspectives from other civilizations."

"Do so!" They touched each other as Qaak's eyes glow more intensely, and a glow of the same color enveloped Asayak. Then it subsided. "Remarkable. I did not realize. I did not comprehend. I am -- how would Walter put it? – humbled. Amazing."

"You mentioned Belinda earlier." Jody turned to Qaak. "I have seen her working with someone on the base, and judging from what I saw, there are romantic possibilities. I'd like to see her find love again."

"As would I. Before going to Yosemite, I considered her a romantic possibility for myself, but while hiking one afternoon, the voice told me He has other plans for her. Ann also has a new path to follow with The Creator's help."

"Really! I want to hear all about it! Our work here is done though. Let's get rid of this now useless equipment and get back to the Moon Base." The equipment vanished. Then the three of them vanished as well.

The three of them reappeared at Walter's base, and they stood there, looking around for a moment. Jody pointed to the gym. "I'm in the mood for the hot & cold whirlpool."

Asayak concurred. "Yes! My spirit needs to warm up."

"Indeed." They began walking to the gym.

Karen and Lauryn came into the gym from the lounge as they arrived. Lauryn called out, "May we join you?"

The triped's eyes glowed. "Of course! We are going to relax in the hot and cold whirlpool. Ring support makes us warm enough, but the thought of the hot whirlpool is indeed appealing."

Their clothing changed, and they wore swimsuits as they approached the whirlpool and stepped in. Asayak seemed to flow into the water. "This is stimulating!"

"Why stimulating, Asayak? Don't you find this relaxing?"

"My body does not have muscle tissue, as you know. I do not need to relax in that sense. Stimulation such as this is refreshing."

Jody murmured softly. "When I relax like this, it helps me let go of emotional issues."

Qaak's eyes glowed briefly. "Indeed. I can get past current mental turmoil in this pool and see things more clearly."

Asayak gestured with an appendage. "As I have conversed with each of you telepathically I have concluded that the two of you should try forming a limited mind link that is focused on personal as well as professional issues."

Qaak shook his head. "That is not something I can accomplish, Asayak. When I form a mind link, it only communicates facts and assumptions. There is no emotional content."

"I offer myself as a link for the two of you, Qaak. You would not meld your minds as can be accomplished by Xpraepostq or Walter. I would simply provide a complete but temporary and passive conduit for your minds to exchange what you choose to exchange."

"This sounds worthwhile. Jody?"

"I trust you both. I'm game."

Asayak sank more deeply into the water. "So we shall begin. Just continue to do your relaxing." Karen and Lauryn watched as Asayak's body glowed slightly pink, as Qaak and Jody closed their eyes. Qaak's eyes, though closed, glowed intensely. After a few moments, they opened their eyes.

Jody was quiet. "Thank you, Asayak."

Qaak nodded. "Indeed. Thank you. That experience was unique."

"Yes! I feel as though my friendship with you, Qaak, has moved to a much deeper level."

"Yes. I wonder why I have not before realized the importance of our friendship." The three continued to enjoy the pool. Lauryn giggled.

+ + +

Several days later at the Moon's recreation area, a few dozen base personnel were lounging around and near the pool. Qaak was also by the pool, but he now had only two legs. Walter was looking Qaak up and down. "Now that you've shed your older, third leg, how long before you grow a new one?"

"In the past, I've sometimes gone for an extended period without a third leg."

"Really! We're going to have to get used to seeing you this way!"

"Eventually, I will need to grow a third leg at least temporarily in order to discard the oldest leg. It is the way of my species. Furthermore, my balance is better on three legs."

Jody touched Qaak's shoulder. "Can you swim with three legs?"

"I have never tried swimming as you know it. With three legs, I can do things that make swimming unnecessary."

"Since you now have just two, why don't you try learning to swim? It can be lots of fun, Qaak!"

"Are you volunteering to be my teacher?" There was laughter.

"Sure! Let's jump in. This ought to be fun!"

They jumped in. The others watched.

Ken slid into the water nearby. "Hey Qaak! Are you getting water in your ears?"

Qaak chuckled. "Yes! Large ears provide ample opportunity for water to enter."

"That's tough!"

Qaak floated on his back for a few moments.

Jody spoke seriously. "Does the water in your ears bother you?"

"No, but I can do something about this." His eyes started to glow. "Gaardian. Will you assist me?" As the glow continued, his appearance changed. His ears grew smaller, and his skin color became more like Jody's.

Walter whistled. "That's amazing, Qaak. I didn't know you could form a mind link with Gaardian at this distance."

Jody hugged him. "You look terrific, Qaak! I like your new look!" She gave him a light kiss on the lips.

"Thank you. A few hours ago, something Asayak did suggested to me that such long distance mind links are possible. There are future ramifications which are still being analyzed."

Walter stood up and began to leave. "Let's go to the lounge." He looked up. "Frank, tell Keeta to meet us there."

They all got out and were instantly dry. Everyone became fully dressed and headed for the lounge. As they entered from the pool area, Keeta walked in from the atrium.

"Did you send for me?"

"Yes, Keeta. I have an intelligence project for you. It may take you several weeks, but I will have you return here daily, so it won't interrupt your base life here."

"What do you want me to do?"

"Each morning, call for Frank, and he will transport you instantly to Quzak planet. Daie-Ahnn and Steve are doing a great job in their covert surveillance, but I need you to see things with another set of eyes and ears. Use all of your instincts and abilities. Do not just observe Daie-Ahnn and Steve's activities. Pay particular attention to a Quzak female named Ooza, and check on her close associates in her social circle."

"Do I check in with you each day?"

"No. Just report to Frank. I'll ask for further details as you accumulate data."

"Okay. Do I leave now?"

"Yes, in a moment. I want you to get started. Frank, ask Karen to join us."

A moment later Karen walked into the lounge from the atrium. "You sent for me?"

"Yes. Debbie asked you to set up enriched communications between here and Quzak planet. Now I want you to do even more. I am having Keeta spend time there each day for the next few weeks, doing some intelligence work. I want you to track Keeta and make a link available to her anytime she needs us. Okay?"

"Just like we did, when we confronted the Quzaks the second time?"

"Yes. Now, Keeta, ready to go?"

She nodded. As Walter's ring shimmered, she vanished.

+ + +

On the other side of Gaardian controlled space, Ooza was once again talking to a class of school children while on a beach outing. Keeta arrived invisibly. A sun was fairly high on the horizon on a clear day. The children's teacher was standing nearby.

"The last time I talked with you children, we had two suns in our sky. Now we have only one. Things are very different now in many ways."

A young female called out. "Why is that? What happened to our other sun?"

"Actually the sun we see now is not either of the suns we saw before. We are in a different part of the universe."

A young male raised his hand. "What happened?"

"As your parents probably told you, our planet has been moved to another place in the universe as punishment for something our military tried to do. We do not need to talk about that now. What you children need to understand is that we are all safe."

The first child called out again. "Who did this to us?"

"It is a group of intergalactic policemen that call themselves Gaardians. They are very different from us, because they have no interest in war and conquest."

The boy was puzzled. "No interest in conquest at all?"

"Not as far as I can tell. Personally, I find them most intriguing."

"Why?" The girl asked.

"Conquest generates waste and bloodshed. Gaardians control far more space than we have ever dreamed about, yet in my experience, they have wasted little, gained much, and shed little blood. That is profoundly unique."

The teacher spoke out with authority. "Children, Ooza always answers all of your questions, but she has other duties. Let us go back to our classroom and prepare for tomorrow's test." The children groaned.

Ooza smiled at the children. "Thank you for letting me talk with you again. I look forward to seeing all of you at your graduation. Bye!"

The children said good-bye, as Ooza headed for a nearby hovercraft and got in. Keeta invisibly sat with her in the hovercraft.

In his apartment orbiting Gaardian, Waagere was monitoring Ooza and the children on a view screen. "G-mail to Walter. "

On the moon, Waagere appeared to Walter in the lounge. "Greetings everyone. This is for you, Walter, but the others can know what I tell you. I have been monitoring the Quzaks, particularly Ooza, as we discussed. As anticipated, she has not responded to the Quzak tragedy as have the rest of her peers and Superiors. Her mate is puzzled."

"She is thinking creatively?"

"Yes, and more. We will know more in a short time. She is going to have lunch with Diane and Steve. They have made a connection with her. She is attracted to Steve, and she respects Diane. Most interesting. I now see Keeta sitting invisibly with Ooza in her hovercraft. Did you send her?"

"Yes. I have given her an intelligence assignment. Keep me posted, and make sure that Qaak and the others know what is happening."

"Agreed. Until later."

The connection was severed. In his apartment, Waagere returned to watching the monitor. Ooza was entering a restaurant. Diane and Steve were sitting at a table, and Ooza walked in and came over to join them. Keeta sat down invisibly on a nearby planter box.

Ooza extended a hand. "Hello Diane! Hello Steve. It is good to see you both. May I sit down?"

Diane gestured for Ooza to sit down and join them. Steve was silent. "I'm glad you could join us. I was just telling Steve about what we have learned about the galaxy we are in, and where it is located."

Steve shifted his eyes from Diane to Ooza. "It is fascinating. My research group has been scanning space for communications and has found little more than background noise. The exception of course is that we know the direction of the Gaardian base, and are waiting for future communication."

Ooza nodded. "My mate is still angry with the Gaardians, but he is practical. He is not wasting energy thinking about the Gaardians, but is looking to the future in our own new area of space."

Diane put down a utensil and looked at Ooza. "That sounds very good. He is a good leader, so you must be doing your part."

"I hope I am doing enough. I was going to stay and eat with you, but I must meet with my peers this afternoon. I may have to leave prematurely. In that case, can we meet again next week? Steve, if you connect with one of the Gaardians I hope to get an opportunity to speak."

Diane nodded. "Steve will do his best, won't you Steve?"

"Yes. I will keep what you have said in mind."

Diane continued her focus on Ooza. "Tell us a little about your mate, Ooza. How long have you been together?"

"We have been together many planetary revolutions around our previous suns. I understand that with our new sun, the number of days in a year are only a few more. From the beginning, we decided not to have offspring of our own. We may nurture those of others if the occasion arises. In our private moments I call him Com -- his real name is not something we use or discuss."

Steve looked up from his food to Ooza. "I understand he is very intelligent."

"Yes. He is far more intelligent than most of his superiors, but he must hide it. I am paving the way for his advancement through the wives of others. One of the reasons I always go to the meetings of my peers, such as the one today, is that I do not want to miss an opportunity to open a door to advancement for him. I may have an opportunity today."

Diane tried to control her enthusiastic interest. "Really?"

"Yes." A chirp came from a small triangle on Ooza's chest. She looked down. "I see that the meeting is about to start. Farewell, you two! Until next week!" She got up, and was quickly gone. Keeta followed.

As Waagere had been watching the restaurant conversation on his view screen, he now shifted his gaze from the screen to Gaardian planet, through a nearby window. Walter appeared next to him.

"Hello Walter. I am glad you could come. Xpraepostq should be here any moment."

She appeared next to Walter. "Hello Walter, Waagere. I understand there are developments with the Quzaks."

"Hi, Pixie! I'm glad you are here too."

"I have been watching Diane and Steve as they met with Ooza over a meal, with Keeta watching nearby. Ooza has just left. Diane and Steve are doing better than expected. Their friendship with Ooza may be more than simply a good development."

They all turned to the screen, where Diane and Steve are continuing to eat. There was no sound. Walter turned to Waagere. "What do you mean?"

Waagere gestured at the screen, and Ooza could be seen getting out of a hovercraft in front of a building with Keeta following closely. "I am shifting our view to follow Ooza and Keeta now, because Ooza is going to what may be an important meeting. She is proving to be an exceptional Quzak, with some characteristics not unlike those of you two. I am impressed, as I think you will be as well."

The display now began to include sound, as Ooza entered the building. She walked down a hall and through another door into Zahrahted's apartment. Zahrahted was a gray-haired beauty who was the mate of the highest-ranking general in the Quzak military. Inside the apartment, Ooza was the last to arrive of the group, which was her pattern.

Zahrahted stood and greeted Ooza with a hug. "Pleasant afternoon, Ooza. You are not late. We are about to begin." Ooza sat down in a deeply plush chair. Keeta moved invisibly about the room, looking at each Quzak face carefully as they spoke.

Ooza spoke coolly. "I'm glad. It is good to see all of you again. Much has happened since our beginning the age of one sun. It seems imperative that we now plan using new strategies, using new language, and we must establish new types of goals. Some nodded their heads. Others shifted positions in their chairs.

Zahrahted showed intense curiosity. "New types of goals?" There was murmuring between some of them.

"In the past we focused primarily on our mates' advancement goals and upon military strategies, both at home and in space. It seems that now we must also set goals for our society as a whole, in light of movements within our population on both the east and west continents."

All began nodding and murmuring agreement. Zahrahted was serious. "These additional goals will be much more difficult to develop, and even more difficult to implement, don't you agree?"

"Of course, but we have no choice."

Piatek cleared her throat. She was the oldest and wisest of the females, and her hair had lost most of its green color. "The young one speaks good wisdom. I am the oldest here, but in my considerable lifetime there has never been a greater challenge for Quzaks."

The old woman shifted her gaze around the room to everyone, and then focused on Ooza. "Ooza, you have special gifts that the rest of us would wish we had if we considered it. You know my special gift, however. I see beyond what is soon by others and sometimes hear what will be. This is one of those times. . I have a question for you Ooza. Think about the two encounters you have had with the Gaardians, and consider the one you saw both times. Can you still hear his voice?

Very quietly and in a trance-like voice Ooza responded. "Yes."

Keeta placed herself invisibly between Piatek's gaze and Ooza's face and looked back and forth between the two of them.

Piatek's voice became softer and lower. "Listen to his voice not with your head but with your heart. What do you hear?"

Ooza stared straight ahead, and her eyes gradually became wider. She blinked several times. The last time slowly. Keeta turned and looked Piatek and back at Ooza.

Ooza was very serious. "Thank you, Piatek! I can see! I can hear! It is a male with extraordinary gifts that exist apart from his being a Gaardian! There is wisdom behind him and power! There is – what is that word – yes, joy! But, wait! There is more! He loves! Differently than we love. It's . . . ."

She blinked, and then turned to Piatek, who responded. "I know. This is a creature that does not fit any category we have in our history or our databases."

The group's leader was incredulous. Zahrahted is almost indignant. "Why is this important? We must plan for our mates and for our planet with its new sun. Why consider this horrible creature?"

Piatek was firm. "Precisely the point. This creature is not horrible. We have assumed this creature to be horrible because he – yes I know he is a male – because he and his Gaardians thwarted our plans. We need now to consider, as Ooza has now seen with my help, that all of this may have unfolded as it should."

Ooza was calm, and her voice was firmer and louder. "Yes. If we approach things that way, we can move beyond our anger, and make the most of what we have been given."

Zahrahted was still incredulous. "What we have been given?"

"We have new history to begin because we have been given a fresh start, without losing any of our past assets except our location in space – and our two suns." There was nodding and murmuring throughout the room. There was silence for a moment.

The old female spoke clearly and firmly. "Ooza, you must now consider new priorities."

"New priorities?"

"Please do not be offended by what I now offer you. Your mate, as wonderful as he is, must now be secondary as an individual to the future of the planet. It is also true for the rest of us. What will consume us in the near future may cost some of us our mates and bring pain."

Zahrahted was angry. "No! We cannot! This must not be!"

Piatek was firm. "We must! It must be!"

Ooza nodded. The others began to nod, murmuring 'agreed' to each other. Keeta again moved quickly around the room to listen to the various females gathered there. Ooza continued to nod. "For my mate, the emphasis will be on comfort and encouragement. I will encourage his ideas and give him fewer of my own. I want him to begin to shape his own new destiny, even if he departs from me. I love him too much to hold him back, if that is what he will choose."

The old woman was calm. "How sad!"

Zahrahted was beginning to hear the wisdom in the conversation. "Perhaps in the short term. But both Ooza and her mate have greater destinies now."

The old woman spoke more softly. "I must now ask that we end this meeting early. These old bones need some rest, and I must use my gift in preparation for our next meeting."

The leader was genuinely curious. "Preparation?"

"Yes. I must listen to all of you and see beyond what you tell me. I must listen to our news capsules and see beyond what is reported. My remaining days must be used wisely. Enjoy today's twilight all of you!" All of them nodded and got up, ready to leave.

In Waagere's apartment, the sound was muted as Walter & Pixie turned to face one another. Waagere was serious. "We must not underestimate Piatek and her gift. I look forward to Keeta's observations. I suggest the two of you Gaardian mail Steve and Diane with what you have seen here, and give them your reflections on possible implications. Perhaps I should commune with Qaak. Perhaps he and I can commune with Gaardian itself."

Pixie looked at her wise friend. "Do you commune with Gaardian often?"

"Seldom. I myself have only done so periodically. Qaak has a different kind of relationship with the planet."

Walter nodded. "Qaak does not speak of it often. Debbie and I communed with Gaardian recently for a short time when we took our mini-vacation."

"Since The Creator has awakened us, Qaak has invited me to join him in such conversations more often. The planet's awakening was just two rotations ago. Things already seem a little different on the planet's surface, though I cannot exactly say how."

Pixie stared. "Fascinating! The Creator did not awaken Gaardian when he awakened the rest of us?"

"Evidently not. What do you think about that meeting? Have you some idea with regard to what you want to say to Diane and Steve?"

She nodded. "I think before Walter and I talk to them about these developments, we ought to provide them with a secured recording of what we saw."

"I agree. Let us give them a recording of the conversation. It may be all that is necessary for them. They are proving to be quite capable as a team. Afterward, let us take them off Quzak to the surface of Gaardian to discuss it. I've just had a thought, though." Walter's ring shimmered. "G-mail to Lauryn."

Lauryn Backstrand appeared in front of them. "Hello, Walter, everyone!"

"Lauryn, I need you to do some special recruiting."

"What kind?"

"You know how we recruited Daie-Ahnn and Steve to do intelligence work on Quzak?"

"Of course!"

"I want you to recruit some others for the other planets we relocated."

"This will take some time."

"I know. I want you to get started on it immediately. Keep me posted. I'll see you when I get back."

"Okay, see you later," She vanished.

Waagere spoke firmly. "I suggest you bring Daie-Ahnn and Steve here to Gaardian but far enough from Red Falls for you to have some quiet, so that they can reflect."

Pixie smiled. "Agreed. Waagere, if you will provide them the recording of Ooza's activities, Walter and I will set up a meeting time in a few days."

"I'll do it right away. Go back to your planets now. Get some rest!"

"Yes, my old friend. So we shall." Walter and Pixie looked at each other and vanished.

25. Memories

The best and only true love is unconditional. Walter knew this well, after observing his parents' long marriage. When Qaak's planet was destroyed, such love became less common. There is still hope for Earth.

In the atrium of his base, Walter appeared adjacent to the door to his apartment. As he walked to the door, it opened. Debbie was relaxing on the bed, watching an old Bugs Bunny and Daffy Duck cartoon, "Rabbit Seasoning." As Walter entered, the video paused. Debbie got off the bed, crossed the room, and greeted Walter with a hug and brief, moist kiss. "Welcome home! Anything new?"

"It's good to be home! I've missed you! Pixie and I have been talking to Waagere about the Quzaks. Keeta is doing exactly what I expected of her. She is a treasure! Now, I need to freshen up. Do you feel like joining me in getting a shower?"

Debbie smiled. "That's tempting, but you go ahead." She gave him another peck on the lips. "Maybe we can get together in the whirlpool later. Some of the gang in the inner circle have asked me to talk about how our romance developed. We're having a bull session in the lounge. Why don't you join us, after you get that shower?"

"Sounds good! I'd like to hear what you have to say about us!" He winked. Then he turned and headed to the bathroom doorway.

Debbie turned away and headed out of the apartment and across the atrium. She came across from the center of the atrium and into the lounge where Ken, Keeta, Jody, and Qaak were gathered around the fireplace.

Qaak turned from warming himself. "Good evening, Debbie. Will Walter be joining us?"

"In a few minutes. He is freshening up a bit. I gather he has some interesting things to tell us. He and Pixie have been talking with Waagere about something." Qaak's eyes glowed for a moment.

"Indeed. Excuse me for a moment." He vanished.

Jody suppressed a smirk. "The first time he disappeared like that I thought I had done something wrong. When he got back, I told him that I was concerned, and he apologized. Then he touched my face and transferred all the sights and sounds he had experienced while he was gone. Ever since, I've known that I can always trust him completely."

Qaak reappeared, just as Walter entered from the atrium. "Good evening, Walter. I have just checked with Waagere and Gaardian. We will meet with Diane and Steve in a few hours. Debbie, I want to hear about how you experienced the development of your friendship and romance with Walter."

Ken was playful. "Yes! How did Walter pursue you?"

Debbie laughed. "He didn't! I've thought a lot about this as I have watched the love develop between Jody and Qaak. When their friendship blossomed into love, it was a surprise to both of them and all of us. As for Walter and I, ... I was curious about Walter from the beginning – as many other people were. Once I sensed my own attraction to him, I was not sure how to handle my emotions. That was a new experience for me."

Keeta snuggled close to Ken while speaking softly. "What was new?"

"A good actress manages her emotions, particularly when she needs to perform. The entire first party, when we transported to New Zealand, I felt like I was performing. Yet, I was experiencing emotions that were new. Walter is unique for me in ways that have nothing to do with his being Gaardian."

Jody's arm was around Qaak, and she squeezed him. "How's that?"

Walter smiled and had a playful tone. "Yes! Do tell!"

Debbie grinned. "I had never before met someone who loves everyone unconditionally. I understand now that in church life the better pastors are that way. It was not part of my experience. I decided to focus on Belinda, and that helped."

Qaak was surprised. "Belinda? Why?"

"Theirs is a relationship of unending love, involving everything a successful intimate relationship should have, except for romance and sex. It was something new and different for me, so I decided to focus on understanding it from Belinda's perspective. The more I understood Belinda's relationship to him, the closer I got to Walter. In the end it was like we were two magnets that finally got close enough that we snapped together." Everyone was smiling.

Walter continued his playful tone. "So we're like two magnets?"

"Exactly! When we kissed the first time it was a surprise to both of us I think."

"True!"

Momentarily, Keeta was almost transparent. "It was almost like that for Ken and me."

Ken smiled and put an arm around her. "Yes. Walter told me over breakfast one morning that he knew I was attracted to Keeta. I was embarrassed momentarily, until he told me that Keeta seemed to find me attractive as well. That was a bit scary."

Keeta giggled. "We have always talked about everything with each other openly, so we talked about our mutual attraction too. We decided that since the attraction might lead us in the wrong direction, we should focus on friendship."

"Indeed." The triped's eyes glowed for a moment. "The voice reminded me not long ago to ignore my attraction to possible mates, because that had been my mistake with my first mate."

Keeta turned to face Qaak more directly. "Really? Ken and I just decided to take the logical approach and spend time getting to know each other. One day, just like with Walter and Debbie, we just clicked together."

A chime sounded as Frank appeared. "Waagere has a g-mail for you, Walter."

"I'll take it here." Frank disappeared as Waagere appeared nearby.

"Walter – Diane and Steve want to meet with you and Xpraepostq. They will meet you at the other side of the ridge not far from Red Falls on Gaardian. Should Keeta be there?"

"I'll save Keeta's reporting for later. Thanks Waagere. Will you be there?"

Keeta smiled. "No. I am continuing to monitor the behavior of Ooza. Also, I must return to my sector to catch up on my duties there."

"Thank you, my friend." Waagere disappeared. "Debbie, I think you should go along. I am going to suggest to Pixie that she bring along Saahmn with her. We'll make it a picnic."

"Sounds like fun! How soon shall we leave?"

"Let's check with Xpraepostq. Frank, g-mail to Xpraepostq."

Pixie appeared nearby. "Hi, Walter! Hi, everyone. What's up?"

"You and I need to meet with Steve and Diane. I'm going to bring along Debbie. Can you get Saahmn to come along?"

"Just a moment." She turned to the right, and Saahmn came into view with her.

He was apologetic. "Forgive my listening in. I knew Daie-Ahnn before I met Xpraepostq. It will be good for us all to be together."

"Good. How about thirty Earth minutes?"

"Good. Until then." Xpraepostq and Saahmn vanished.

"Okay. We still have a little time to continue our conversation here. Jody, we haven't heard from you yet."

"When I first encountered Qaak I was amused."

Qaak's eyes glowed intensely for a moment. "Amused?"

"Yes! You were so very professional, it took me a few days to comprehend that the glow of your eyes reflects your emotions more than your voice does. I really have had fun learning to read the glow from your eyes." Qaak chuckled as his eyes twinkled. Jody became more animated. "Once I figured out how to read your eyes, I began to see you as someone whose professionalism hid a secret loneliness. When I heard of your attraction to both Belinda and Ann, I decided that it was important as your friend to nurture that."

"I'm glad you did. Going on that hike in Yosemite helped resolve those feelings. But as you know, that same hike also left me a bit confused. My emotions kept me from seeing clearly the role of your friendship."

Ken was curious. "So what happened then?"

Jody grinned. "I was confused too, though I didn't know it. I kept telling myself that romance simply was not possible with Qaak, not only because of our age difference, but because of so many things we see differently."

Keeta was mostly opaque. "What changed?"

Jody giggled. "I guess you could say that with Asayak's help we made a detour. He connected us with emotions as well as facts, and in so doing each of us made an end run around what stood between us."

Walter was incredulous. "A detour? An end run?"

Jody smirked. "Each of us saw our paths as leading in a very definite direction on a very definite route. Each of us had detailed expectations in our minds as to how our lives were supposed to go. Asayak built a bridge over and around our expectations, and we found ourselves arriving in the same place, having the sense of fulfillment that we both wanted."

"I'm going to have to think about that metaphor for a while!" There were murmurs of assent.

"Ken and I have some plans for this evening on my planet. If you'll excuse us, we're going to take the blue SVX and take a cruise to my planet."

"Yes! I am looking forward to spending a few days there. It will not be all vacation though. She says she needs my skills, and I'm more than willing to comply." He grinned. The others around the room smiled.

Ken and Keeta stood and held hands. "We're off! We'll see the rest of you in a few days!" They waved and vanished. A moment later, the blue SVX could be seen leaving outside the lounge's large portal.

Debbie had a romantic tone in her voice. "Walter, let's take a dip in the whirlpool before we leave, shall we?"

"Good idea!" As Walter and Debbie got up to leave, a chime sounded.

Frank appeared. "We have another g-mail from Waagere."

Walter and Debbie stopped and turned.

Waagere appeared. "Hello again, everyone. Walter, are you leaving soon?"

"Yes. Debbie, Xpraepostq, Saahmn, and I will be on Gaardian shortly."

"Good. Qaak, I think you should come to Gaardian as well. I would like for us to commune with Gaardian."

"I was going to bring Jody to my apartment. Will she be welcome at our meeting?"

"I had not considered it, but of course she will be welcome. Soon?"

"Soon." Waagere vanished.

Jody took Qaak's arm. "Let's take a stroll in the atrium, shall we?"

His eyes glowed. "Good." They moved to the doorway and on through. Qaak looked almost human as he and Jody walked in the atrium, stopping from time to time to enjoy the stars or various exotic plants growing there.

She squeezed his arm. "With all of your sixty-five thousand years of Gaardian experiences, where do you see our new path going?"

"Thousands of your years ago, my last mate asked me a similar question. I cannot answer in the same way because things have changed. I am different, because The Creator has made me new again. In the past, my mate would follow in my path. The Creator helps us to see that our new path is as much yours as mine."

"Yes. When Walter made me Chief Engineer aboard *The Grace*, it was as though my life had taken a turn back onto the path that God wanted for me from the beginning. When I modeled, I could not stimulate my mind. Becoming an artist helped, but I always felt something was missing. It turns out there were two things missing."

"Two?"

"I needed challenges for my mind, and I needed you."

Qaak's eyes glowed for a moment, and then he chuckled. "The Creator told me that there was still much for me to accomplish after I retired as convener. I never imagined it including the fulfillment of my heart." A glow began to surround them, causing their surroundings to fade into a bright mist.

> **"You have chosen well in choosing each other. I will lead you to new and exciting adventures as I bless your union. I have given you a glimpse of your future together. I am the one who saves, redeems, and makes new. Trust me, and I will never let you down. Seek me, and you will accomplish far more than either of you can imagine."**

The glow faded. "Indeed."

"Wow!"

"Let's go to Gaardian. Waagere is waiting for us. Are you ready?"

She put her arms around him and gave him a hug. "Of course!" They vanished.

In his apartment with Jody, Qaak looked around his apartment. He then closed his eyes as they began to glow. "Waagere. Jody and I are in my apartment. You are welcome." He opened his eyes and looked at Jody.

Waagere appeared a few feet away. "Hello again. Have you seen my report on the Quzaks?"

"I have seen it. Ooza shows promise. It is late to be starting her dream training."

"It is not without precedent."

"True. Have you discussed it with Walter?"

"He suggests we begin by inventorying her memories. He also suggests that, by beginning where she is, we can save much time."

"Excellent. Give her nocturnal protection. In her next sleep cycle, bring her mind here. I will give her some initial dreams and then evaluate. Putting his arm around Jody, Qaak's eyes glowed for a moment. "The conference for Steve and Daie-Ahnn has begun. We are not needed there. Go to Ooza's home and help her make her beginning with us. I am going to take Jody to the other side of Gaardian." Waagere vanished.

"The other side of Gaardian?"

Qaak reached out and took her hand. "Yes." They vanished.

In a deep forest, the sun was low in the sky, rising slowly off the horizon. Jody looked around transfixed. "It is beautiful here."

A low voice rumbled inside their heads. "Thank you."

"Who is speaking to my mind?"

Qaak's eyes glowed subtly. "It is Gaardian."

"Gaardian?"

"Yes. As you previously learned, I am sentient. Like Asayak, I do not have a voice, so I speak to you telepathically. Don't be afraid."

"I'm not afraid. The Creator's voice speaks to me as well. I let God be God and let Christ be King."

"That is why I wanted Qaak to bring you here. I experienced The Creator initially only a short time ago. I want to experience your mind as Qaak does, for I have known Qaak most of his life. I am glad you have come."

"I'm happy to be here as well."

"If you desire it I will give you and Qaak a quick aerial tour."

Qaak chuckled. "You'll like it. It's fun."

"Okay! Let's go!" Qaak and Jody were sealed into an intimate force field as they rose above the ground. They began to fly all over the planet at rapid speed, faster and faster. Both smiled and looked at each other frequently. Then they landed. She beamed. "How large are you compared to the Earth?"

"I am slightly smaller, but being much denser I have much greater gravity. Time grows short. Here is a g-mail from Walter."

Walter appeared. "Hi, you two! Are you having a good time?"

"Fantastic! What's up, Walter?" Jody smiled.

"I need you back here at the base. You need to get started on those special projects for Keeta's planet and Asayak's planet."

Qaak's eyes glowed briefly. "Understood. I will send her in a moment." Walter vanished.

"You're sending me? Aren't you coming?"

"Later. I must help Waagere with the initial sleep training for Ooza." He wrapped his arms around Jody in a warm embrace and gave her a kiss.

"Will I see you tomorrow Qaak?

"Tomorrow." His eyes glowed intently for an instant, and his ring shimmered as Jody vanished. Qaak paused a moment, then spoke again to the planet. "You spoke of experiencing The Creator for the first time."

The planet's voice seemed tender. "Yes, You have known me most of your life. Before encountering you however, I had wandered for immeasurable time amongst the stars. Until I encountered you, I had never experienced any other being that could think. I thought I was alone in the universe."

Qaak's eyes closed as they glowed intensely. "You've been a good friend."

"As have you. Knowing you and other thinking beings has given my existence meaning. I now understand that, even when I thought I was alone in the far reaches of The Creator's creation, I was not alone. I now know there are other planets like me, but it is unlikely that I will meet one. It does not seem to matter."

"After experiencing creation apart from time, I told Walter and Xpraepostq that I am different. Are you now different as well?"

"Yes. A moment ago in the conference for Steve and Daie-Ahnn, Walter's mate Debbie spoke of their having a guardian angel. I touched Walter's mind with a question. He flashed me thoughts and images that intrigue me. Will you please discuss guardian angels? I want to know more about angels."

"Indeed. As do I. Perhaps it is time for me to return to Walter's base for that, and for communing with Jody."

"Yes. She is good for you, Qaak. You now have more peace and joy within you, than I have known you to have since you were young."

Qaak chuckled. "The joy of which you speak began when I encountered the voice and experienced all of creation apart from science. Sharing our faith with each other has added much fuel to that joy for Jody and me. As for the peace of which you speak, perhaps it is now the wholeness and completeness I experience in knowing her."

"Perhaps. Let us commune again soon."

"Soon." Qaak vanished.

+ + +

A few days later, coming from the atrium at Walter's base, Qaak and Jody were walking into the lounge. Walter and Debbie were already enjoying the fire.

Walter looked up. "Hey, you two! Qaak, have you seen Butch's reports on Asayak?"

"No. Are they significant?"

"Yes! Frank, have Butch join us for a moment, will you?"

They heard footsteps as Butch crossed the atrium and entered the lounge. Butch greeted them with a smile. "Hi, everyone. What's up Walter?"

"I asked Qaak if he had seen your reports on Asayak. He has not. Would you please allow Qaak to do a direct read from your memories?"

"Of course."

Butch walked over to Qaak, who stood up and placed three fingers on Butch's face. Butch closed his eyes as Qaak's eyes glowed for a moment, first softly, then intensely. Qaak withdrew his fingers. "Indeed! Thank you, Butch!"

Walter spoke quietly. "Butch, I know you've got lots to do, so you can get back to the clinic."

"Thanks. Thank you, Qaak. Good evening everyone!"

Butch walked back to the clinic. Qaak sat down again by Jody. Qaak was thoughtful. "Butch's findings are truly remarkable. I must spend more time with Asayak. Also, never underestimate Butch's gifts!"

Walter smiled. "I don't. He is a special asset to this team. Debbie, why don't you and I turn in so that Qaak and Jody can be alone?"

Debbie smiled. "Sounds good to me. She winked. We have some special things to talk about."

Walter returned her gaze and her smile. "As Qaak would say, 'Indeed!' Good night, Qaak, Jody!"

Debbie waved. "Good night, you two!"

Jody waved back. "Good night!"

Qaak's eyes glowed for an instant. "Good night. Frank, give us a bigger fire in the fireplace."

Logs appeared and began to burn brightly as Walter and Debbie left. Qaak and Jody got out of their chairs, walked over, and stood in front, warming themselves.

"Does watching a fire like this have the same effect on you as it does on humans?"

Qaak's eyes glowed for a moment as he chuckled. "Do you remember the shifting colors on Gaardian near Red Falls?" She nodded. "The effect is similar, though without this warmth. Earth's anthropological history lays the groundwork for the human fascination with fire. Other species on other planets find phenomena for themselves that assist the focus of their thinking or of their creativity. I must ask Gaardian if it uses any phenomena in that way."

"For me the phenomenon does not have to be moving -- at least not perceptibly. Look at the Earthrise out that portal."

They walked to the giant portal facing Earth. "What is looking at your planet on the horizon making you think about Jody?"

Jody smiled a wistful smile and sighed. "Several things come to mind, all blending together. There is an old Sunday school song that goes, 'This world is not my home, I'm just a-passin' through.' From a Christian's point of view, that is true I guess. It is literally true for you, Qaak. On the other hand it is my home, or at least where I come from, but you are now a part of my life, and you make up a part of my sense of 'home.'"

"Indeed. That world is not my home, and this base is not my home, yet I feel at home here, because it is where I have found you."

"Where is your home planet, Qaak?"

Qaak was motionless and silent for a moment before answering. "It no longer exists. I am the sole survivor of my planet's destruction. I will tell you about it someday. Gaardian found me, and for most of my life, that beloved planet has been home, parent, brother, and friend."

Jody's face brightened. "Let's toast our planets, each other, and our new beginning!" Champagne glasses appeared in their hands.

"I understand the concept of a toast, but what shall we use?"

"Frank?" asked Jody.

The android appeared. "Yes, Jody?"

"Search Earth's databases and find the best and/or the most rare of all the champagnes ever made on Earth."

The android paused only briefly. "The one that was considered the best by many is no longer available. The last bottle was drunk several years ago."

"Wait a moment." There is a brief flash of light as Qaak vanished, and another less than a second later as he reappeared holding a bottle of champagne. Frank disappeared.

Jody stared. "Is that a bottle of that champagne?"

"Indeed. Remember when you, Asayak, and I put our rings together? This was easier." Qaak suspended the bottle between his hands without touching it, and frost began to form on the bottle. The cork popped out, and the bottle poured into the glasses with no apparent help from anyone.

Jody had a broad smile. "That's cool, Qaak! Here's to our planets, our homes, our love, and each other!"

After sipping the wine while looking at each other, their wineglasses disappeared. They embraced. Their bodies glowed and merged together into an almost blinding light that became pure white.

+ + +

Nearby in their apartment, Walter and Debbie were standing at a portal looking at the same Earthrise. Debbie came up behind him and hugged him, pressing her body to his. She then let go and moved beside him, and they put their arms around each other. He looked into her eyes. "Do you realize that we're coming up on our first anniversary?"

"Of course! Don't you know that all women remember those things?" She smiled, tickling him a little.

"My parents were married more than sixty years ago. This reminds me, I've been thinking you ought to have another ring besides your Gaardian ring."

Debbie's surprised smile made Walter smile as well. "A wedding ring?"

His voice became softer. "Actually, a wedding set. It was my mom's."

Debbie's eyes grew wide as she looked down at a little green velvet box that appeared in his hand. "That's the set?"

"It's the actual set, in the same box that they came in, when I inherited the set, after my Mom went on to the larger life. You wear your Gaardian ring on the ring finger of your right hand, so if you want, this set can go on the ring finger of your left hand."

Debbie opened the box, and tears welled up in her eyes, as she smiled and put the wedding set on her left ring finger. "It's beautiful! Thank you, thank you, thank you, my darling Walter!"

They kissed. When they separated, Walter pointed at the ring. "You should know that there's a bit of history that goes with this."

"History?"

"This was purchased just before the beginning of World War II. The central diamond is of a cut that is no longer used."

"I don't care what a jeweler would say it is worth, but to me it is priceless!"

"To me as well, just as you are priceless!"

Debbie smiled. "You said 'a couple of things!'"

I suppose I should wait until tomorrow to give you your anniversary present, but it is the only other thing I have left that was my Mom's. He extended a little blue velvet box to her. She opened it and took out a cross. "This cross is only costume jewelry, but I gave it to my Mom as a Christmas present the year I entered the cub scouts."

Debbie put it on. "I love it! Now, I'll give you my anniversary present to you!"

"Now? Really?"

"It can't wait, but you can't see it right now."

"Let me get this straight." Walter looked puzzled. "It's my present you're giving me now, but I can't see it?"

"Right! I'm pregnant!"

Walter's eyes got very wide. He wrapped his arms around her. As they embraced, the familiar glow filled the room. The low rumble of The Creator's voice resonated around them.

> "I am pleased and share your joy. For the two of you, this is yet another beginning. The two of you will face great challenges as my children and as parents, but I will be with you. Debbie, you will be nurturing a child with a special gift, and that will be difficult when Walter is away. ... Walter, you will be teaching both Ooza and Gaardian how to love, each in a way that I have made unique for them. I will continue to bless you both. There is the great glory ahead that is yet to be revealed. Never be afraid. I am with you."

The soft glow grew brighter into a brilliant all-consuming light.

26. Deadly Secret

The originator of "tough love" was The Creator. The scriptures of many species on many planets are full of illustrations of the importance of discipline and justice, exercised with love. Now Walter was seeing this in a new way.

Under his base's atrium, part of the Earthrise could be seen above the doorways. Dawn was in a kitchen apron, moving about from plant to plant, humming to herself as she trimmed exotic plants here and there. Personnel were moving back and forth between the entrance to the mess hall and the entrance to the gym and recreation area. Walter and Debbie came out of their apartment and walked over to Dawn.

Walter smiled. "Good morning, Dawn! Are you used to puttering in a garden?"

"Good morning, Walter, Debbie. No, I'm just thinking I'd like to grow some herbs and spices here in the atrium."

Debbie grinned. "That sounds like a great idea! They don't have to all be from Earth, you know."

"I know. I'm hoping Keeta and Pixie can give me a few suggestions."

"Go for it! Come on, Debbie, let's get some breakfast."

Dawn called after them. "If you want to try something different, try my eggs au buerre noir. I read about them in a Rex Stout mystery, and I've followed the recipe."

Walter and Debbie walked down a short hallway to the mess hall. They sat down at a small table in one corner, then Walter's ring shimmered, and food appeared on their table. They began eating.

Debbie took a forkful of the eggs Dawn had recommended. "Wow! The eggs that Dawn recommended are sure different, but they are delicious! ... It was good to hear the voice again last night. Do you have any idea what's in store for us in the immediate future?"

"I'm a bit curious too, but I've learned to trust God with the process. We are beginning to do dream training with Ooza on Quzak. Both Waagere and Kieya see things in her that are unusual."

"Like what?"

"I think as the dream training continues we will get a better idea. We know that she is brilliant, and she sees her life and her gifts differently than most females on her planet. We also know there is something unique about the way her brain is configured."

A tone sounded. Qaak appeared next to them, seeming to sit on his third leg next to their table as though he was joining them for breakfast. The faint glow of the g-mail surrounded him. Debbie greeted their friend with a smile. "Good morning, Qaak! Should I excuse myself while you and Walter talk?"

"Not necessary. Good morning to you both."

"Good morning Qaak."

Walter and Debbie continued to eat breakfast as Qaak spoke. "There have been significant developments in the last few of your hours. Ooza's dream training has set a new record -- it is almost complete after only five sessions."

Walter put his fork down. "Incredible! How is that possible?"

"Incredible, indeed. We have talked previously about how Jesus, Einstein, and others from your planet had unusually large bridges between the two sides of their brains. For Ooza, instead of having one larger bridge she has more than a thousand small bridges -- almost like my brain. While she slept last night I melded minds with her and transferred the rest of the basic knowledge she needs to be a Gaardian."

Debbie swallowed and paused from her eating. "Amazing, to say the least!"

"Indeed. Walter, today she has a special challenge, because her mate is leaving on some sort of secret mission that he will not discuss with her. Males always discuss major things in their lives with their mates."

Debbie was thoughtful. "It sounds like I'd better get *The Grace* ready to go just in case."

Walter nodded. "I agree. Talk to John and the other officers, and muster the crew right after breakfast. We'll take a precautionary trip to the vicinity of the planet."

"Right."

Qaak got up off his third leg. "I will continue to monitor developments. Kieya has said that if you are going to Quzak, she would like to join you."

Walter nodded. "Good! We'll take a short detour and pick her up at her planet."

"Very well. I shall inform Kieya. Until later." Qaak vanished.

Walter's ring shimmered, and the table in front of him was cleared leaving Debbie's area alone. "I've had enough to eat for now. Position *The Grace* so that there is Earthlight shining on her as she orbits. There are some monitoring stations on Earth watching for activity, and I want them to see. Have Paula prepare a g-mail to go to the major news outlets."

"This is the first excitement we've had in several weeks. I'm no longer hungry either!" Her ring shimmered, and their table was clean.

They got up, and Walter turned to face the rest of the mess hall. "Attention, everyone!" People in the mess hall turned to look at him. "We are going into mission mode. All crewmembers for *The Grace* report on board in thirty minutes. Everyone else needs to add mission support to their duties until we return. That's all."

Walter and Debbie turned and headed to the door where they entered. The rest of the people in the mess hall began leaving as well.

+ + +

Kieya's planet, as seen from space, was orange-red in color. It revolved around a double sun. Kieya's apartment and base were in a secluded part of the planet. Inside, Kieya was sitting on her haunches looking out a window. Her apartment sat on a rugged bluff overlooking a lush green valley, and she was watching the movements of several of her species.

A tone sounded. Qaak appeared next to her, and immediately sat down on his third leg to relax. "Hello Kieya."

"Yes, hello. Have you talked to Walter?"

"Indeed. He will call for you here in a short time. He and his crew will depart his base in less than one of his hours."

Kieya purred subtly. "Yes. Good. I look forward to being with his interesting crew. What about Ooza?"

"She will return from a meal meeting with her female strategy group in a short time. I will generate fatigue, induce sleep, and following regular procedures, I will integrate her. If she chooses not to be a Gaardian I will induce sleep again, delete the training, and hold her in sleep until the next day."

"Good."

As they spoke, *The Grace* was moving rapidly through space, with stars streaking by. On the bridge, John was at the helm, and others were at their posts. The trans-lift doors opened, and Walter stepped onto the bridge.

John saw him and spoke with a firm voice. "Captain on the bridge."

Walter nodded to John and looked around. "At ease, everyone. John, Kieya will transport directly here to the bridge. As soon as she is on board, set course for Quzak using the route and speed I gave you earlier."

"Right! Is Debbie ready to get data on that supernova we'll pass?"

"Yes. She'll format it in several versions and transmit it to all the planets in our sector that have the scientific abilities to appreciate it."

John glanced at a screen on his console. "Kieya should be here in a moment."

Kieya appeared next to Walter. "Hello, my friend."

"Hello, Kieya. I'll leave it to you to introduce yourself to members of the crew as you see fit."

"Good. I will take the trans-lift to engineering and speak with Jody." Kieya moved to the trans-lift doors, which automatically opened. After she stepped inside, they closed.

At his station, Walter touched a panel. "Jody, have you finished preparing the long-observation equipment?"

Jody's voice could be heard clearly from his console. "I'm still working on the modifications that work with Asayak's special cloaking configuration."

"I'll send Asayak down there." He turned to his security officer. "Asayak, take the trans-lift to engineering. Help Jody in any way you can."

"I can help her from here with a mind link."

"Perhaps, but you might be able to help her in other ways if you are there."

"Yes." He glided to the trans-lift, the doors opened, he entered, and the doors closed.

Down in engineering Kieya was standing next to Jody at a console and gesturing with paw. "You have done very well. This seems almost complete. When Asayak gets here it may have suggestions."

"This is the most complex piece of equipment I've designed yet."

"You can be justly proud. It will work well, of this I am certain. We need to observe the activity out here without being detected."

The trans-lift doors opened, and Asayak glided over to them. Its voice resonates in their heads. "This will work, though not perfectly."

Kieya looked at Asayak. "What are the chances of our being detected?"

"Less than two percent."

Jody shook her head. "Two percent? Can I fine tune my layout to fit your cloaking, so as to narrow the gap?"

It gestured. "Negative. You have already done better than I even imagined."

The cat responded emphatically. "We must do better. Alternatives?"

There was silence for several moments. Asayak's voice was more thoughtful. "There is another way."

The cat's head turned. "Yes?"

"Jody, your setup is perfect if we are only monitoring one being. There are two alternatives to this setup."

"Two alternatives?"

"Why two?" The cat turned back to the machine they have been working on.

"We can monitor the commander with no chance of detection, but our data would be limited to what Ooza's mate experiences. The alternative is to place Keeta on board and monitor her. She can give us data on the commander, the ship, and every other being on board."

Kieya subtly purred. "Asayak, please tell Walter what you have just told us." There was a pause of just a few seconds.

Asayak gestured. "Walter likes the second alternative. Keeta will be here in a moment. Kieya, she will need your special care."

Kieya purred subtly. "Yes. ... I shall not fail."

The trans-lift opened, and Keeta could be subtly seen crossing over to the group. "Walter tells me you have a special mission. I thought I was going back to the moon base today, but here I am instead."

Kieya turned to face her. "We need you to monitor Ooza's mate on his secret mission. Since he has already left I will transport you directly to his ship."

"Sounds exoiting. When do I leave?"

"In just a moment. Jody?"

"Keeta, remember how, when you went invisible on his other ship, even your Gaardian ring was not detectable?"

"Of course! I always wear it."

"Right. I have set up some additional data links. You need to be very thorough as you gather as much information as quickly as you can. Kieya will monitor your safety. Asayak and I will see to it that you are totally undetected. Understood?"

"Understood. ... Kieya? I'm ready." She vanished.

The cat spoke softly but firmly. "I will be in my quarters so as to stay focused on her. The two of you can do the rest from here. I suggest you keep Walter informed every few minutes."

"Agreed." Jody turned to her controls.

Kieya vanished. In her quarters nearby, she reappeared, went to a cushion on the floor near a portal, and lay down. She stared out the window with great intensity in her eyes, which had a subtle fire at the center of her dark pupils.

The Quzak ship was much smaller than Walter's, but the spy was undetectable. On the bridge, four Quzaks were at workstations. Keeta moved about rapidly but transparently. She touched each work panel on the bridge, and her ring shimmered as she did so. The Commander got up and went to a doorway. She went with him as he left and went down a corridor. Touching a panel on a door jam, a door opened and they stepped inside. The door closed behind them.

The commander touched a badge on his shirt. "Com to Ooza. For security reasons this is voice only."

Ooza's concerned voice was heard from an unseen speaker. "Where are you, my love? Where are you going? Why haven't you taken me with you?"

"Please forgive me for not telling you of this mission. Only two others on our planet know about this."

"Who are they?"

"It is too risky for you to know that. Again, please forgive me. If I am successful, the Quzaks will regain their former glory. If I am not, you will never see me again."

Ooza's voice was much lower and quieter. "This is that dangerous?"

"Yes. This has never been attempted before. It involves new science. It should work as predicted."

"What is supposed to happen, Com?"

The Commander hesitated for a moment. "There is no time for that now. If I am successful, you will know everything. I must close this link, my love." The Commander touched the panel in front of him. He got up and headed back to the doorway. Keeta's ring shimmered. She nodded and touched the Commander. As she did, he froze. As she pulled her hand away, he continued through the doorway and she vanished.

In Kieya's quarters aboard *The Grace*, Keeta reappeared next to her. "Why did you pull me out?"

"It is too dangerous for you to remain. We know now what he is attempting."

Walter appeared next to them. "You have done very well, Keeta. Thank you Kieya."

That cat purred. "Keeta is remarkable. You are a pleasure, Keeta. I hope we work together again."

"Thank you. Am I missing something? I didn't observe anything that I thought was useful."

"Jody's data links through your ring told us a great deal. When you touched the Commander, Asayak touched his mind, and we learned what we needed to know. Quzak scientists have learned how to convert regular matter to dark matter on a small scale. They want to convert dark matter to energy and jump across a great distance in space. There are two problems."

The cat nodded. "Yes. Dark matter cannot be converted to energy as they intend. Also, the conversion to dark matter does not allow for the inclusion of life. They will all die."

"Won't we try to stop them?"

"It is too late. A few seconds after we snatched you back, they made their attempt. Their ship no longer exists."

The cat spoke softly. "Shall we include this information at the time of Ooza's integration?"

"No. Daie-Ahnn and Steve will do that. Keeta, I want you to go find Ken, and join him for dinner. Then after you've had some rest, we will send you back to continue your surveillance."

"Okay. Thank you for letting me share in this."

"You're welcome. Enjoy your dinner." Keeta left Kieya's quarters.

+ + +

The next day Walter came out of his quarters into the atrium at the moon base. He turned to speak through the doorway. "I love you, too. See you this evening!" The door closed, as Walter walked across the atrium to the mess hall. He went down the short hallway, and as he entered, he heard the usual sounds of people eating and conversing. On the far side, Ken waved, and Walter went over to join him.

"Good morning Walter! Join me for breakfast?"

Walter sat down. "Good morning. Thanks. Keeta did a great job yesterday. I'm proud of her."

"She told me it was an interesting adventure. What will it all mean for her continuing work on Quzak?

"It's too soon to say. Steve and Daie-Ahnn are meeting with her today for an evening meal at Ooza's home, after Qaak integrates her later this morning.

"Integrates her? Didn't it take you a half century to learn to be a Gaardian?"

Walter nodded. "Yes. Her brain is configured differently -- it is remarkably similar in structure to Qaak's though he sees it as coincidence."

"Could there be a genetic link?"

"Qaak will be consulting Gaardian, but it seems highly unlikely."

Keeta approached them. Ken smiled and stood to greet her. "Good morning Keeta."

They both smiled at her as she kissed Ken, and then she sat down. "Good morning to you both. I have been thinking about Com's last conversation with Ooza. I wonder about the emotions she must be going through as she waits to hear from her mate who won't return."

"Qaak told her during her final dream training last night." A tone sounded twice. "That's a priority message. I must take it in my quarters. Please excuse me." His ring shimmered, and he vanished.

Walter reappeared in his small living room. He could hear Debbie singing in the shower adjacent to their bedroom.

Kieya appeared as a g-mail. "Walter, I made this a priority g-mail because two separate items must be attended to with dispatch. Qaak believes you should be there for Ooza's integration. Also, the Zargadete civil war is taking an unexpectedly destructive direction because its military is preparing to use its weapons on its own people."

Walter nodded. "I agree – this is serious. Tell Qaak to do the integration without me. If Ooza agrees to become a Gaardian, I want a special integration party with just you and the other most-experienced Gaardians, along with Pixie, Steve, Daie-Ahnn, and myself. We will have it on the surface of Gaardian at the shelter near Red Falls.

Kieya purred audibly. "Excellent. I will inform Qaak. What about the Zargadetes?"

"I'll muster my Grace crew and deal with it right away. Since the Zargadetes are on the far side of Puz's sector, tell Puz I will pick him up on my way."

"Done. I will see you on Gaardian tomorrow. Until then."

"Until then." The cat-Gaardian vanished.

Walter's apartment began to dim and take on a familiar glow. The characteristically very low rumble of the voice was heard throughout the apartment, and Debbie stopped singing.

> **"Ooza will be an excellent Gaardian. She has unknowingly met her new mate, and her grieving will be overshadowed by her new life. Xpraepostq is recalling Daie-Ahnn to Aegeene today. I will guide you and empower you to deal with the Zargadetes."**

The glow faded quickly. Walter muttered to himself. "I wonder why Daie-Ahnn is returning to Aegeene. There is no time to ask Pixie now. What does God want me to do with the Zargadetes?" Walter looked at his ring, and it shimmered slightly. "G-mail to all Grace personnel. We have an emergency. Report to *The Grace* immediately. This is not a drill. All remaining base personnel go to support mode until we return. Make haste everyone! That is all." Walter's ring shimmered again, and he vanished.

Walter reappeared on the bridge aboard *The Grace*, and took his place in the captain's chair. John appeared at the pilot's console, and others begin appearing as well. John was intense. "Where are we headed?"

"Zargadete. As soon as everyone is on board, head there at pace twenty."

John whistled as he touched his controls. He paused to look at a hidden screen, and then he touched another panel. "We're underway. What's the rush?"

Walter looked around the bridge and spoke louder. "The Zargadete military is making preparations to use its weapons on its own people. Their leaders think this is the best way to stop the war."

The security officer's voice telepathically rumbled throughout the bridge. "That's preposterous. Such a strategy is never effective, and it is almost certainly counter-productive."

Keeta had appeared nearby as Asayak spoke. She shuddered. "To say the least. On my planet it led to the destruction of nearly half of my species."

Walter turned to John. "John, we're picking up Puz on the way in a moment." John nodded and worked his controls. "Normally we would not intervene in planetary affairs like this. Gaardian regulations preclude our interference. Since we recently relocated the Zargadetes to another galaxy, there is at least a statistical chance that our action contributed to the severity of their civil war."

Debbie looked up from her console, where her hands were moving rapidly. "The data coming in shows massive energy building up on several of the military bases. What's the plan?"

Walter looked up at the ceiling for a couple of seconds, and then he smiled. "John, we should be at Zargadete in less than thirty seconds, now that Puz is aboard in engineering. Put us in low orbit about the equivalent of half the planet's diameter above the surface. Debbie, if there's any change at all send the data to my console. Asayak, put us under complete cloak, right now."

It stirred. "Done."

Walter touched his control panel. "Jody. Get ready to deploy a tight grid of class-one control satellites around Zargadete. I know Puz is there, and he can help you as needed. He does not have eyes but he can see far more than we can. We will be in orbit in a moment. Do it as fast as you can."

Jody's voice could be heard from Walter's console. "Right. How much of a control matrix should we create?"

"One hundred percent. We are going to intervene on every energy level except life functions. Don't worry, Jody, you can do it. Just relax and stay focused. I'll be down there in a few minutes."

"Right!"

Walter turned to his executive officer. "Karen, you'll be in charge when I'm on the surface. Debbie, Keeta, and Asayak, go to engineering, and have Butch meet us there in three minutes." Walter vanished.

Debbie, Keeta, and Asayak moved quickly to the trans-lift.

In engineering, Puz gestured to Jody near one of the technical stations as Walter appeared next to them. Walter smiled at his friend. "Hello, Puz! Jody, are we ready?"

Puz gestured, as his tenor telepathic voice was heard by all. "Hello Walter. Jody has done an excellent job. All energy on the planet is under the grip of dampening fields. There can be no surges of any kind of energy, and no build-up of energy from sources that are above the levels at the time we established the fields. The inertial dampening fields are working perfectly, so that there can be no sudden occurrences of motion or sudden changes in direction of motion beyond the gravitational acceleration rate."

Debbie, Keeta, Asayak, and Butch came through a nearby doorway, and walked up to them as the conversation continued. Walter nodded. "Excellent. Are the rest of you familiar with how the dampening fields work?" They all nodded. "Good. Jody, since the Zargadete sleep cycle has no unusual features, be ready to add a hibernation field, targeting all military installations, but with provision for the entire planet if necessary. You've never done any of this, but Qaak trained you, I trust you, and I know you can do it."

"Thanks! It is more than a bit scary. But if this weren't so serious I think it could be almost fun."

Walter smiled. "It is serious, but I like your attitude. As for the rest of you, here is the plan. We stay cloaked at all times -- not just Keeta. All of you will be feeding any data you gather to Karen, so that the rest of us can access what we need as we need it. Frank, Qaak, and Kieya started making preparations for us before we left the base. They've laid ground work, now the rest is up to us, with God's help."

Walter looked around. "Each of you has a separate assignment. As soon as I give you your assignment, beam to the planet surface and get to work. Asayak, use any ring functions necessary to visit the military installations. As necessary, probe the minds of military leaders to determine their plans. If you see an opportunity to divert or thwart their plans, you may do so without my permission. I have trained you, and I trust you to use good judgment. You can go."

"I will not fail." The hairy one vanished.

"Butch, as with Asayak, use any ring functions you may deem necessary. Use your good judgment. Visit all major medical installations. Fine-tune their medical technology as opportunity arises. Perform some invisible miracles to lend aid to serious medical emergencies. Craft a message and leave it with the leader of each medical installation, saying that their technology has been upgraded with the compliments of their Gaardian. Be sure to remain undetected. You can go!"

"I like this! I won't let you down!" Butch vanished.

"Keeta, just as Asayak is covering the military leaders, I want you to cover middle-grade officers. Use the skills taught you by Asayak and Qaak to do some emotional guidance, to shape attitudes. Use your ring to generate a blanket of tranquility as needed. You can go now!"

As Keeta vanished, Puz's voice was firm. "I have some things that I can do. May I touch your mind for a moment?"

"Of course." Puz reached out and touched Walter's cheek, then stepped back.

"Excellent! I did not think of that! Go for it Puz!" Puz vanished. "Jody, one or more of us may make ring contact with you to ask for special assistance. Since you know what the others are up to except for Puz, have your staff prepare for some possibilities."

"What are you and Debbie going to do?"

Walter smiled. Debbie put her arm around him and gave him a questioning look. "Yes, what are we going to do?"

"The Zargadetes are not like the Quzaks for one very important reason. Zargadete politics are military politics, though that is beginning to change. This is different, because the Zargadete politicians have an iron grip on the military. I am giving you a Zargadete identity so that you can move about as a lobbyist in their capital. With Frank's help from back at the base, you already have virtually instant power, knowledge, and influence that will amaze them. You will be there on the sidelines when I arrive at The Suppla's ["SOO-plus"] office as the Gaardian. He will recognize me from records of their aborted mission to Earth."

Jody turned from her console. "What's The Suppla?"

"He's the supreme planetary leader. He wields great power but has to answer to a governing council."

Debbie let go of Walter. "How will I get to the Suppla's office? And when?"

"You'll spend the rest of today and tonight becoming the new and powerful lobbyist that everyone wants favors from. Tomorrow morning, one way or another, you will have an appointment to see The Suppla. It's a dream role for an actress, don't you think?"

Debbie grinned. "I wondered if I'd ever get to use my acting chops again. As Jody has said, this just could be fun!"

"It's also dangerous, in that we don't want to make things worse by making our Gaardian manipulations too obvious. Be careful to stay within your identity, particularly when I arrive. You must show no sign of recognition when I get there. Follow my lead and use good judgment."

"Right."

A tone sounded. Qaak appeared as a g-mail. "Walter, Debbie, I have a bit of data that will help you. The Suppla appears to be a male but is secretly a female."

"Excellent! That gives us an edge."

"Indeed. I see the others are already at work. I suggest a Gaardian council meeting to digest this, and to introduce Ooza to the others. She has accepted."

Walter was enthusiastic. "Fantastic! The meeting we discussed for her with Steve and the others will have to be delayed for a short time. I will keep you posted."

"Good. I look forward to watching you and Debbie work."

"Yes. Until later." The g-mail ended.

Debbie was thoughtful. "Ooza as a Gaardian already! That is going to take some getting used to! What are you going to be doing while I get set up to meet the Suppla tomorrow morning?"

"I'm going to invisibly work with their scientists to divert the direction of their research. I will make it more advantageous to use their developing technology to improve their quality of living rather than to use it for military purposes. They have made some discoveries recently, I can help them use to their economic and social advantage. To put it another way, I'm going to bribe them with power."

"Will you stay invisible?"

"I intend to, but I'm keeping my options open. Debbie, you'd better get started."

She put her arms around him and kissed him. Without letting go, she looked into his face. "See you tomorrow morning!" She vanished.

"Any questions, Jody?"

"If I think of any I'll let you know."

"Good." He vanished.

+ + +

In his apartment, Qaak had been watching the conversations on a view screen. As Walter disappeared, Jody turned to one of her crew in engineering and gestured for her to come over to where she was. Qaak turned away from the viewer.

"G-mail to Kieya and Waagere. If either of you are available please come to my apartment." Qaak turned to look out a portal down on Gaardian planet below. Waagere appeared and came over near the viewer. Kieya appeared a moment later and joined them.

The cat subtly purred. "I too have been watching developments at Zargadete. Perhaps we should invite our newest Gaardian, Ooza, to be here as well."

"No. It is too soon. We must allow her to meet with Walter, Steve, Debbie, and some of the rest of us first."

Waagere nodded. "Agreed. She is truly gifted, but we must give her time to accept her integration and her new life. Walter's plans are better."

"Understood. Why did you call us here, Qaak?"

The triped's eyes glow briefly. "Just after I integrated Ooza I learned that Xpraepostq has recalled Daie-Ahnn back to Aegeene. Did either of you anticipate this?

The cat was thoughtful. "No, but it makes little difference. Daie-Ahnn and Steve have been excellent working together and have become friends, but their work is no longer as critical, since Keeta has been at work there. With Ooza now becoming one of us, that operation is now redundant."

Waagere craned her head forward slightly. "Did romance develop between Daie-Ahnn and Steve?"

"Negative. Their friendship is platonic and very supportive, but not romantic. Let us change subjects, Waagere. What were you able to do on Zargadete in anticipation of the arrival of Walter and his crew?"

"Not as much as I wanted to. As you know, I had pressing matters in my own sector. Nonetheless, I planted data in several hundred places establishing Debbie as an up and coming lobbyist. I created written, voice, and video communications that make her appear to be one who prefers working in the background. I inferred in several ways a fiction, that her little-known rise to power had taken place before their relocation to a different galaxy. I established the idea that much about her was somehow lost in the confusion of the new political realities, but that her enormous economic power had survived the transition."

"Indeed. Kieya?"

The cat purred. "My sector duties were not quite as pressing, so I was able to plant a larger volume of data. I created files and resources that are not part of the mainstream of scientific thought on Zargadete. I gave them new verifiable data that will enable them to accelerate their technological progress. Regarding the one scientific breakthrough we previously discussed, I gave it to them in such a way there will be far better use of their military tools for peaceful purposes."

Qaak's eyes again glowed for a moment. "Excellent. Walter will be pleased, as am I. Gaardian told me how I could change their weather patterns slightly to our advantage. They are now finding their entire planet plunging into a severe winter that their meteorologists cannot explain. There will be no long-term effects to these temporary weather phenomena. Just a moment."

The triped's eyes closed, and his eyes glowed intensely for about five seconds. The glow subsided, and he opened his eyes. "Indeed! Asayak just reached out to me. He says he has discovered the material that you planted, Kieya, and says he can use it to advantage."

The cat purred. "Excellent! Asayak's gifts are truly remarkable. Might it be a good Gaardian?"

"It sees its role working with Walter very clearly. It wants to focus on helping its own planet to grow in the area of the fine arts as an extension of his duties with Walter. That is true for the foreseeable future."

Waagere's head bobbed from side to side slightly. "I would have liked to observe the current operations on Zargadete, but we must not take a chance on Zargadetes detecting Gaardian presence."

The cat nodded. "It will be different when Walter meets with The Suppla and Debbie."

"Indeed." The triped's eyes glowed for a moment. "Meanwhile I intend to commune with Gaardian down below. Thank you for coming. I will see you again at the meeting with Ooza, Walter, and Steve. Until then." The triped vanished. The others looked at each other and then vanished as well.

27. Intervention

Events sometimes do not unfold as we expect them to. Walter was expecting confrontation, but there was a twist or two. Aboard *The Grace* in engineering, Jody was moving about from station to station, gesturing directions to various members of her crew. Asayak appeared nearby. The deep resonance of its voice could be heard by all. "Hello. I have completed my work. I have conferred with Walter by mind link, and he concurs that you should put the military installations into hibernation until after Walter and Debbie meet with The Suppla in four hours. We should also put up force fields so that others may not enter the military installations until after the meeting. Understood?"

Several in the crew nodded. Jody looked at it. "Will you be in your quarters?"

"No. I am returning to my station on the bridge. I will mind link with others there as well as with you to bring everyone up to the moment as to progress." It glided to a nearby trans-lift, and soon it was gone.

Jody spoke loudly. "All right everyone! Let's get that hibernation cycle started." People started moving about rapidly.

On the planet below, late afternoon sunlight was shining on the front of a large imposing building. There was a large sign with lettering in the front, in the midst of plants of many colors. Inside, Butch was visiting this hospital's intensive care ward. The ward appeared both futuristic and rather cold and crude. About twenty patients were inside of private areas that were mostly transparent. Butch transparently moved about, looking at the records and medical equipment. He stopped near one patient as several Zargadete personnel tried to keep the patient from dying. They failed and began disconnecting equipment. Butch stepped forward, and his ring shimmered slightly. As the patient opened his eyes, he cleared his throat. There was suddenly a great deal of commotion. Butch moved from patient to patient, healing each one.

As the commotion became more intense, all the Zargadete personnel were running from patient to patient, leaving the central equipment console empty. Butch placed a rectangular object on the desk, smiled, and vanished. The commotion continued after he left.

On the other side of the planet, Keeta arrived transparently in a military mess hall and listened to conversations between the soldiers. She looked directly into the faces of several of them, but they saw through her and went on conversing with their friends. After visiting several tables, she went to a corner. Her ring shimmered, and suddenly the mess hall conversations were quiet and peaceful. She vanished.

In the capital city, the Zargadete governing council chamber was a very large room with a high ceiling. There was a round table at the center, with a hundred chairs around it. No one was seated, however. Conversations went on all around the room in groups of various sizes.

Puz appeared transparently and moved into a group of three Zargadetes that were in a heated conversation. One counselor spoke in an ominous tone. "This sudden cold weather may be an omen, I tell you. It may delay our use of the weapons to stop the war."

Another nodded. "Nonsense! The weapons are not affected by weather. Our military has engaged in far more difficult battles under far colder conditions."

The third counselor nodded as well. "Discretion may be our best course. We need not be hasty. I - - - -"

As the first two waited for him to continue, Puz transparently stepped into the third counselor's body. Puz's glow could be seen in the pupils of the counselor's eyes. "... have done some research. I cannot find a single instance in our records of other planets in our previous galaxy wherein the use of the military against its people ever achieves the desired result."

Puz stepped out of the counselor and moved into another group.

The second counselor who had spoken was extremely interested. "I, too, am uneasy with regard to this action."

+ + +

Meanwhile, in a nearby office building on the top floor an imposing figure looked out the window of a very plush office. Debbie looked like a Zargadete. As she stood at the window, a knock was heard on her door.

"Come!"

A tall, slender Zargadete entered. "A message for you. The Suppla wants to meet with you. It is a great honor of course, but how do you wish to respond?"

"Tell The Suppla I will be there in one time period."

"That is short notice. You must prepare."

"Do as you are told! Leave me!"

"As you wish." The aide left and closed the door. Debbie turned to the window. She smiled.

Across town in the Suppla's apartment, he was sitting at a console, intently studying a screen. He reached forward to touch it, and it went dark. Standing up, he went to a window, where he looked out at the city, with the red light of dawn in the distance. He walked through a nearby doorway, a light came on, and he went around a corner where he could no longer be seen. Water was heard running, and steam could be seen.

Walter appeared next to the doorway, and stepped to the console where The Suppla had been sitting. He touched it, and the glow of the console resumed. Walter's ring shimmered, and the glow began to flash rapidly and more intensely as Walter watched. He reached forward and touched the console again, as the sounds from the adjacent room ceased. Walter vanished just before the Suppla reappeared in a fluffy yellow robe that reached the floor. He briefly looked around furtively as though sensing something might be amiss. Going to the window, he again looked out over the city. Turning back into the room The Suppla crossed his arms across his chest. As "he" did so, the swell of The Suppla's bust became evident. She looked down at her robe and released her arms.

+ + +

Aboard *The Grace*, bridge crewmembers were at their stations. John was studying the view screen, which showed Zargadete planet below. "Karen, I've got to admit I'm restless. I guess that in waiting I want to see something happen."

Karen smiled. She walked over and stood next to John, joining him in watching the view screen. "I don't like the waiting either, but I've learned to trust Walter to know what he's doing."

A tone sounded. Kieya appeared as a g-mail. "Hello, friends!"

Karen liked the cat. "Hello, Kieya."

"Do you have any word from Walter?"

"No. We were just talking about how hard it is for us just to wait. Debbie is meeting with The Suppla in a few minutes. Walter will show up there a few minutes later. It should all prove interesting. I think Walter will clear us for monitoring as soon as he arrives."

"Good. Keep me informed, Karen. You are doing an excellent job."

"Thanks. May I ask you a personal question?"

"Of course."

"On Earth there are creatures without creative thought that are similar to you. They keep their fur coats clean and shining by licking themselves. How do you keep your coat so beautiful?"

Kieya purred. "Thank you for the compliment. My forbears licked themselves. I have a sonically enhanced steam shower when I am at home. Elsewhere I have my ring support to maintain all aspects of my appearance. Thank you for asking." She paused. "Tell Walter I will speak with him tomorrow when we meet. Until then."

Karen smiled. "Until then, Kieya." The cat vanished as the g-mail connection was severed. Karen returned to her console. She looked down and touched a button. "Walter is clearing us for video. I'm putting it on the screen."

The screen changed to show the interior of The Suppla's office. Debbie, as a Zargadete, entered from a doorway.

In her office, the Suppla rose from a desk and walked across to greet Debbie. "Welcome! Please avail yourself of a comfortable place."

"As you wish."

With a sober face, Debbie took a lounge seat near the desk. She leaned forward slightly, showing off her figure.

The Suppla was officious. "I've asked you here because, although previously you were little known to our Council leaders, you are now talked about as one who accomplishes much for the benefit of your clients, and is becoming a more visible and powerful influence in our planet's capital."

Debbie was silent for a moment. "And...?"

"I'm searching for ways in which you can be the greatest help to our planet."

"And I'm always open to new ways to be the greatest help to my clients. Do you want to become one of my clients?"

The Suppla roared with laughter. "Do you not know that I have the power to either help you or destroy you?"

Debbie remained calm and sober. "I know far more about you than you do of me."

"You know what I have my staff reveal about me."

"I know that of course, but I know more."

The Suppla chuckled. "Tell me what you think you know!"

Debbie sat further forward on her cushion, looked intently at The Suppla, and spoke with a lower voice. "I know about your Zargot squad, I know about your anti-matter manipulator, and I know that you are not male but female."

Suddenly there was cold fury in The Suppla's voice. "How do you come by this knowledge? Tell me, or I will have my Zargots extract it from you!"

Debbie smiled. "Not likely."

Walter appeared next to her. The Suppla's eyes grew large. "You! What are you doing here? Guards!"

Walter smiled and sat down next to Debbie, who had not looked at Walter, but continued to look intensely at The Suppla. Walter was calm. "The guards can't hear you. If you will look outside you will see no motion of any kind anywhere."

The Suppla hesitated, then got up from her desk, and went to the window. She then went to a door, which opened automatically. She looked into the outer office area at several Zargadetes, but none of them was moving. She returned to her desk and sat down.

The Suppla addressed Debbie with almost a sneer. "You have not spoken since this Gaardian creature appeared. That is illogical."

Debbie's appearance suddenly changed, so that she again looked human. "I'm with him. This appointment with me was arranged so that meeting The Gaardian would become part of your morning's agenda. Your staff knows you are meeting with me, but we both know now that there is a more important agenda."

"I determine my agenda."

Walter nodded. "I respect your office, but I must alter that agenda slightly."

The Suppla set her mouth into a straight line. She nodded. "Proceed."

Walter continued to speak calmly. "After the Gaardians relocated your planet to a new galaxy, your military became restless and had no focus or agenda. They have made the mistake of creating an agenda that includes attacks on your own people. This is not acceptable to us, and if you think about it clearly, it should not be acceptable to you or to your council."

"The council is in favor of bringing the war to a quick conclusion using the military."

"Check your historical records of other peoples in your previous galaxy. Such actions never produce the desired result."

"Never?"

"Correct. Some of your council members have discovered this historical data, but they are reluctant to speak contrary to what you have been supporting."

The Suppla nodded. "I did not like the military's proposal at the beginning, but they have been persistent."

"They are not of one mind as you have been told. There are many who are against the proposed attacks. As Gaardians, it is not our practice to interfere with the internal affairs of a society unless their activities affect peoples other than their own. That was the reason for the previous interventions about which you already know."

"And now?"

"Now we are speaking to you in your best interests. You are an unusually brilliant and capable leader, so I am speaking directly to you. I am here to help you in an advisory capacity. In your personal private journal, which I inadvertently accessed, you have observed that The Gaardians achieve their goals without waste or aggression. That is amazingly astute for a leader of a species whose history is that of conquest and plunder."

The Suppla was silent, looking back and forth between Debbie and Walter. "If I could politically afford to have a mate, I would care for him and protect him simply because he is my mate. The Gaardians seem to be caring for my people in a similar way. This is unexpected."

Walter reached forward and placed a rectangular object on the desk of The Suppla. "You are living in Gaardian space. As I have told you, we will not interfere with anything Zargadetes choose to do, so long as they stay within Gaardian guidelines of acceptable movement and activity with regard to other planets and their leaders. Gaardians are primarily intergalactic police, but then you already understand that. This is a copy of those guidelines. It also enables you to contact The Gaardians if you choose to do so."

"Understood. What happens now?"

Walter and Debbie smiled. Debbie was warm and understanding. "I came here to provide you with an avenue by which you could meet with the Gaardian and talk with him. I do not currently have any plans to return unless invited. The wealth that I have accumulated here is being diverted as we speak into places that will be helpful to your people. I will simply disappear."

Walter nodded. "You have the time to stop what the military is planning, but to do so you must act immediately. There is one who will act without your permission if you do not stop him, and you know who he is. As we speak, he is planning to proceed with or without your order. A good leader like you cannot tolerate this. The council will support an alternative plan to end the war. There are two suggested plans that have worked in similar situations on other planets. Those plans are attached to your personal journal in an encrypted file. The encryption key is your true name that only you and I know."

"What about my identity?"

Walter and Debbie stood. Debbie smiled. "Your secrets are yours. You need to make some changes, but it is not for us to force you to make those changes."

Walter again nodded. "One more thing I must say to you. We can be of help to you if you ask us as far as your professional work is concerned. I have a suggestion with regard to your personal life."

The Suppla stood, came around the desk, looked at Walter directly, and spoke quietly. "I can hear a suggestion."

Walter again nodded. "Your personal journal is not and will not be a matter of Gaardian records. I accessed it only accidentally, and I will not disclose its contents to others. That male you love both secretly and passionately knows you are a female, and he loves you too. You might consider promoting him, making him your personal assistant, and thus your constant companion. You do not know it, but he is actually your equal in capability and intelligence. You need not ever tell him that. He has one essential quality that you need in a mate: he will never betray you. You can trust him unconditionally, just as he also trusts, likes, and loves you."

"You know this and do not use it against me?"

"It is not my way, nor is it the way of the Gaardians. We knew you were female only by genetic scan. The information in your journal is yours and yours alone. When we leave, your staff and the rest of your planet will return to normal. Do you have any questions?"

The Suppla pointed to the Gaardian data card on the desk. "If I have questions, I may contact you?"

"Yes. ... Until then."

Debbie and Walter looked at each other. Debbie looked at the Suppla. "Until then." They vanished.

+ + +

As Walter and Debbie appeared on the bridge of *The Grace*, the Suppla's office was still on the view screen. They watched as The Suppla touched a button on her desk and barked an order. "Tell my Zargots to dispense with my adversary as specified in order B-78-C. And tell the Council I will meet with them immediately." She paused and looked out at the city. She turned back to the desk and touched the button again. "Tell Arooda I wish to see him in my office as soon as he finishes with his morning assignment." The Suppla smiled.

On the Bridge, Debbie smiled. The picture on the view screen turned back to a view of the whole planet. Walter also smiled. "Karen, is everyone else back on board?"

"Everyone but Keeta. ... Now she's here."

"Good, John, take everyone home – drop off Puz on your way. Karen, I want you and Belinda to debrief everyone. I want detailed video records of the last seventy-two hours and video records of those debriefings except for my dialogue with the Suppla regarding her personal life. Debbie and I are beaming directly to Gaardian. We'll be back on base tomorrow."

Debbie stepped closer to Walter and took his hand. "See y'all tomorrow!"

"Until then." Walter nodded. They vanished.

+ + +

At Gaardian, the planet rotated slowly amidst an array of stars. Walter and Debbie loved Red River Falls, which were thundering in the midst of the colorful foliage that stretched as far as the eye could see. Near the falls was a small structure. Inside was a plush retreat center. Debbie and Walter suddenly appeared next to a window that looked out on the falls. Walter turned back into the room. "Gaardian? Tune in to us please until further notice."

"Good. I have been expecting you. Steve is landing nearby and will be inside soon. Qaak is beaming Ooza and himself directly from Quzak. The other senior Gaardians will be here momentarily."

Debbie turned toward Walter. "Since you've brought me along, it would be nice if Jody could be here too. Qaak would appreciate it."

"Good idea. Gaardian, tell Frank to talk to Jody and have him beam her here."

"Excellent. ... Debbie, I will supply you and Jody with a vehicle, and you can explore not only my surface but the Gaardian Conference Center as well. There is a museum and library there that both of you will enjoy."

Jody appeared. She immediately looked around, and then she stared out the window at the falls. "Wow! This takes getting used to! I've been instantly transported to the other side of the Milky Way!"

Walter and Debbie laughed. "A lot farther than that! We are many galaxies away from the Milky Way."

"That's not what I mean. I know where Gaardian is in relationship to the base. It is the instantaneous part. No travel time! It's amazing, even though I've gotten used to a lot of things as Qaak's wife!"

Debbie giggled. "Come on, Jody! You and I have some window shopping to do!"

"Window shopping?"

"Kind of. We are going to play tourist and take in everything we want to. Our Gaardian-style limo is waiting outside."

Walter laughed. "Have fun, ladies. We'll see you in a little while."

The women went outside and got into a vehicle that appeared there. They took off.

Ooza and Qaak appeared a few feet away from Walter. Ooza was very curious about her new surroundings. "Hello! I remember you! You're now the convener of the Gaardians!"

"Yes. Since we last met, I have taken this role. In a moment you will meet some other Gaardians -- the most experienced of all of us. We are celebrating your becoming the newest Gaardian."

Qaak's eyes glowed for a moment. "That vehicle that is leaving includes both my wife and that of the convener. You will get to know them better."

Steve walked in the door and came to stand beside Walter. Ooza's eyes grew wide. "Steve! You're a Gaardian?"

Steve laughed. "No Ooza. I work for Walter. Daie-Ahnn, the one you thought was my mate, was my partner. She and I were sent to Quzak to monitor your planet's recovery from its relocation."

Ooza smiled. "Daie-Ahnn is not your mate?"

Steve shook his head as he smiled broadly. "We have become very good friends, and we will continue to be friends. Just after we got to Quzak, we decided that romance would never be part of our relationship. We have kept that pact, and we're both comfortable with it."

Steve reached into a pocket, took out a small disk, and extended it to her.

"What's this?"

"Daie-Ahnn made this for you. She said to tell you that this is a personal and private message only for you, and that you are to view it after you return to Quzak. The encryption key is her Quzak name spelled backwards."

Ooza studied the disk in her hand for a moment. Then she stuck it into a pocket in the center of her shirt. "Thank you. When do the others you mentioned get here?"

As if on cue, Kieya and Waagere appeared. "Hello Ooza. My name is Waagere." Waagere stepped forward with an extended hand and craned her head forward slightly.

"Hello!"

She turned to Kieya, who silently padded over and lifted a paw. "My name is Kieya. This is a distinct pleasure."

Ooza took her paw. She smiled broadly. "Hello, Kieya! You are truly a stunning creature!"

"Thank you. The beauty of your spirit is a match for your appearance."

"Thank you!"

Walter looked at Ooza directly. "There is one more introduction to make. Gaardian, please make yourself known to Ooza."

The rumble of Gaardian's telepathic voice is heard by all. "Hello Ooza. I am the planet on which you stand."

Ooza's mouth dropped open, speechless for a moment. "Amazing! Until my Gaardian training I never dreamed a being such as you could even exist."

Walter kept his gaze steady. "Gaardian can communicate telepathically over quite some distance, but it does not listen to our thoughts or intrude on our thinking unless we give permission. Today it has been told to be part of all of our conversations here at this little retreat center."

Ooza turned and smiled at Steve. His eyes were sparkling. "Steve, did you know that Gaardian is sentient?"

"I knew, but this is the first time I've been here, and also the first time I've heard its voice. I am as amazed as you are."

Walter looked around the room. "This party is mostly about conversations and refreshments, but first I need to show you something." Walter's ring shimmered, and a three-dimensional image of Gaardian space appeared nearby, reaching the tall ceiling. A yellow outline appeared on one side, and a red glow appeared at the center. "Ooza, as you know, Gaardian space includes several googolplexes of various kinds of bodies. The red glow at the center shows where we are at Gaardian planet. The small yellow outline indicates the sector of Gaardian space that includes the galaxy containing your people as well as fifteen others.

The triped's eyes glowed for a moment. "There are many planets in your sector that have sentient species. Five of them have species that are as advanced as yours. I am retired, but the rest work mainly in their sectors. As needs arise, as skills are available, and as time allows, we all help each other."

Walter nodded. "In a short time I will be convening a special meeting of all Gaardians to discuss what has been happening on the planet of the Zargadetes. For the record everyone, they call their planet Pzalop ["Zah-lup"]."

Ooza turned to face him. "Has their civil war gotten worse?"

Walter smiled. "Until yesterday I would have answered yes, but their primary crisis has passed. You will have a report waiting for you when you return to your home world. Qaak will be helping you organize your Gaardian team, but this gathering is mostly for us all to get better acquainted."

Everyone began relaxing and smiling. The cat purred. "That aroma tells me that Gaardian has prepared food for us."

A nearby door opened. Jody and Debbie came in. Jody's voice was playful. "Did I hear someone mention food?"

Everyone laughed. Jody went to Qaak, hugged, and kissed him. Debbie did the same with Walter. They went to a buffet that appeared. Carrying food, they began conversing in small groups. Ooza took Steve aside and began talked to him quietly.

+ + +

The next evening Walter and Debbie were in their apartment on Earth's moon. Walter was watching a video flash rapidly before him, and Debbie was in the bedroom, turning back the covers and fluffing the pillows. Walter touched the video screen, and it went dark. His clothing changed to a robe and slippers, as did Debbie's. They got up on the bed, and they leaned back on the headboard with Walter's arm around her.

Debbie cuddled against him. "I think Ooza will be a terrific Gaardian, don't you?"

"Yes. In the future we may need to call on her to help us with the Zargadetes." A familiar glow filled the room until almost everything other than each other faded away.

"I am pleased. You have done well. You must continue your support of Ooza. Let her take Steve as part of her crew. Encourage her to ask Piatek to join her in her adventures. She must not take Zahrahted into her confidence. Let Butch monitor your pregnancy, Debbie. I have given him skills that he has not yet discovered."

"What about the Zargadetes?"

"Their path is going to be difficult, but Ooza is the key. Encourage her to use her gifts and instincts. I will make myself known to her and guide her. The Quzaks' savior will be born soon, but the time is not right for the Zargadetes. Trust me. I will guide you."

The glow faded, and Tiger and Tammy hopped up on the bed with them, purring. Debbie reached out to scratch a feline head. "I guess it is logical for Ooza to want Steve to be part of her team. I wonder why she is the key for the Zargadetes."

Walter smiled. "I haven't the faintest idea, but I know that all that God does He does well."

"Amen to that!" She snuggled closer, and their bodies began to glow.

Part Three: Amazing Grace

28. Ooza

At her base that orbited over Quzak, Ooza moved about in her compact apartment, and then headed to her sleep chamber. She reached into a small pocket in the center of her shirt and withdrew the disk that Steve had given her. She pondered it for a moment, and then she placed it in a slot in a console.

Daie-Ahnn appeared as a three-dimensional video. "Hello, Ooza! I am glad you are looking at this. It means that you have accepted your call to be a Gaardian, and I know you will be a good one. I prepared this little video because I wanted to talk to you as one female to another. Since you now know that I am not a Quzak, let me tell you a bit about my real background. I am from a beautiful planet called Aegeene. My people are all small in stature, compared to most of Walter and Steve's people. One of my gifts is that I can read other's emotions very accurately, and that is the main reason for this video. I know and understand your attraction to Steve. Until your recent tragedy, you could not allow yourself to consider the depth of your attraction to him. You need to know something important about him. You can trust Steve with anything and everything, including your life. He loves you unconditionally and passionately. I know you will be a terrific Gaardian. Steve can help you. I hope to see you again one day soon."

The video ended. Ooza stared into the space where the video had been for a moment. She then reached forward and touched the panel again. Daie-Ahnn appeared. "You can trust Steve with anything and everything, including your life. He loves you unconditionally and passionately."

She touched the panel again, and the video disappeared. She looked upward, then around the room. She got up and went to a window that looked out to a large garden. Looking down at her Gaardian ring it shimmered. The scene suddenly changed, and she was looking down on her planet. She touched a small triangle just below her right shoulder. "Personal journal. I like the way Walter has his large base set up on his planet's moon, but Quzak has no moon. I have not met Xpraepostq, the female that Walter calls "Pixie," but I have decided to follow her lead, and create my own invisible moon base in orbit above my beloved planet. Up here, I don't even miss having two suns instead of one."

She paused and looked around at her apartment. She walked through a doorway into a large atrium similar to one she had previously seen down on her planet outside her previous apartment. Walking through the garden, she passed through a doorway into a large, comfortable lounge. Her ring shimmered, and several pieces of furniture in the center were replaced with a large, triangular fireplace with a fire burning.

"Computer, I want a physical representation of your voice. Give me a female, my height, and my age."

Another female Quzak appears. "That will do. Any voice will do. You will answer to the name Bahna. I am following in the new tradition of Gaardians and including a fireplace in my lounge. I hope to visit Walter's base soon and see the original that started this tradition. I like it."

"Where do you want to begin, now that you've furnished your apartment?"

"I need to choose a crew. Do you have suggestions?"

"Steve is an obvious choice. I also suggest Piatek, if she is willing."

"She is dying. I will speak to her shortly. What about Zahrahted? She is brilliant and very capable."

"She would undoubtedly like to be with you, but she is not a good choice. She is too ambitious and self-serving."

Ooza was thoughtful. "I had not considered that. Where is Piatek?"

"She is in her bed. She is failing."

"I will go directly to her." She vanished.

+ + +

On the planet's surface, there was a tall, triangular building with an open triangular center. In a hallway inside, Ooza appeared next to a door. She placed her palm on a sensor, and the door opened. Walking several steps, she turned to the right into a bedroom. Piatek was in her bed. Another Quzak female, dressed in a bright red uniform, stood nearby.

"Good day, Piatek." She turned to the other Quzak. "Leave us."

The female in red nodded and went out into another part of the apartment.

Piatek's voice was weak. "Come closer dear friend. Let me look into your eyes."

Ooza went to her bedside, and knelt beside the bed. "Look into my eyes and you will know one of the reasons I am here."

The old female turned her face to Ooza and looked at her intently. "You are truly Ooza, but you are so much more now. You have love. You have riches. No, you have power. You have transmuted."

"Transmuted?"

"In your case, your outer form is little changed, but your inner nature has changed phenomenally."

Ooza looked over at the door, and it closed. "I have become a Gaardian."

The old female smiled. "Of course! I should have known. If you are a Gaardian, why do you need me?"

"I need your support, your encouragement, and your gifts."

"I am an old one. How can I give you these things?"

"You can if you are young again."

Piatek started to laugh, and then coughed. "Young again? This is possible?"

"Yes. You would lead another life, but you must leave our planet."

"I've not always lived on our planet, so that would be acceptable. Are you earnest about this?"

"Yes. I trust you more than anyone else on Quzak does. I did not know that you had lived on another planet."

"Of course. I have never told anyone on our planet until now, but we trust each other. My father was a Zargadete. He was the grandfather of The Suppla now leading the Zargadetes on Pzalop."

Ooza's face showed genuine surprise. "Your grandfather?"

"Yes. We can talk more about that another time. If I am to be with you, what will be my role?"

"I want you to help organize and supervise a support team that will work with me in our sector of Gaardian space."

Piatek chuckled. "I once posed as a male and was a general in our army, but that is a story for another time. Right now, this sounds far more exciting. What do we do now?"

"I have medical equipment on my base that can restore your body to its peak and perfect health. I will transport you instantly and directly to my medical unit. I will place a clone of your body where you are now. When your nurse comes to check on you later it will lead to great sadness."

"Proceed."

Ooza stood, her ring shimmered, and Piatek disappeared. The ring shimmered again, and the cloned replica appeared in Piatek's place. Ooza went to the door and on through In a larger room beyond, she found the nurse. "She is sleeping. I suggest you let her rest – she seems tired." The nurse nodded. Ooza turned and went back outside the apartment door. Once in the hallway again she looked around. She vanished.

Ooza appeared in her atrium garden and walked directly through a doorway, where she found Piatek lying on a cushion.

The old woman spoke softly. "That didn't take long."

"No. I told the nurse you were sleeping and suggested she let you rest. She nodded. Now we'll get you back to your youthful self that I have never met!" Ooza went to a nearby control panel. Her hands flew rapidly over controls. A panel on a nearby wall first showed Piatek lying there, then showed flashing images of her physiology, and then showed a young Quzak female.

Piatek sat up. "That's amazing! I think I look better now than I ever did!"

"You no longer need that sleep attire. What would you like to wear?"

"How about something current for the young?" Immediately her clothing changed. Piatek looked down at herself as she got off the cushion. "I don't need to get used to this!"

"Let's go somewhere comfortable. Bahna? Introduce yourself to Piatek."

The android appeared, and the three of them walked across the garden and into the lounge. "Piatek, my name is Bahna. I am an android simulation of Ooza's computer."

"Hello Bahna. I am going to have to get used to you. I cannot read your spirit, because you haven't any."

"I understand, Piatek. Ooza, is there another reason why you want me here now?"

"Yes. Piatek is going to help me put together a beginning team, and then she will work with you to assemble the fuller compliment of personnel. I will ask Steve from Earth to join me, but I need your input as to possibilities from planets in my sector of responsibility -- not just Quzak."

Piatek's eyes were wide. "Are there other planets with thinking species in our sector?" I thought we were totally isolated."

"In terms of Quzak technology we are isolated. It would take us many years to get to the first planet that has advanced as far as we have. Gaardian technology makes Quzak technology seem completely primitive."

"I surmised as much. I will have much to learn."

"This is not a problem. ... Bahna, see if we can establish a direct g-mail with Qaak."

"He is available." As Qaak appeared, Bahna vanished. "Hello Ooza. Piatek, it is a distinct pleasure for us to meet. I have seen you before, but without your knowledge."

"The pleasure is mine."

"Qaak, I would like some help in getting my team organized. It would be useful if you could give some basic training to Piatek for me."

"Indeed. One moment."

The g-mail ended. A moment later Qaak appeared over near the triangular fireplace. "Training takes place in person. Piatek, I need to touch your face. Would you please step closer?"

Piatek walked over rather timidly to the triped. He reached out and touched the now younger Quzak.

"I must tell you I am only half Quzak."

Qaak's eyes glowed for a moment. "Indeed. This explains much. You are one half Zargadete, aren't you?"

"How did you know?"

"I am familiar with both species. I cannot train you with the speed or depth with which I trained Ooza. Nevertheless, I can touch your mind in a wholly different way. This will seem like an intimate moment to you. Will you permit me?"

Piatek smiled broadly. "I think I like you, Qaak. You are not like any other being I have ever met. I know I can trust you. Please proceed."

Qaak placed three of four fingers on her face. His eyes closed, and they glowed intensely for about twenty seconds. As he did so her eyes closed, and they glowed slightly as well.

Qaak withdrew his hand, and he sat back on one leg to relax. "I think it best you both sit down as I have." With curious looks on their faces, they did so. "You will probably find this even harder to believe than I do, but I have drawn a conclusion now that is inescapable. The three of us are genetically related."

The two Quzaks gasped. Ooza stared. "How is that possible?"

Qaak's eyes closed and glowed for a moment. He opened them and looked directly at Ooza as he spoke. "As I have examined Quzak records, your recorded history goes back about three thousand Quzak years. I am nearly fifty thousand Quzak years old. A few hundred of the years before I was born, one of my forbears gave his life for the advancement of the science of my species. In a crucially important experiment that led to transport travel through space, my ancestor had his body converted to energy and beamed toward a place in space where there were no detectable bodies. I now know where that beam of energy ended up."

Piatek's eyes shone and glistened. "Of course! All that Ruach ["ROO'awk"] does, Ruach does well."

Now Ooza's eyes were wide. "What do you mean? I seldom hear you use The Creator's name or that ancient saying. Do you know what Qaak is saying?"

"Yes! Obviously the beam struck our planet."

"Not exactly. I previously have traced the movements of both planets through that passage of time. Twenty-two thousand Quzak years ago, that beam gradually broadened and weakened considerably. It passed a bit closely to a supernova. Eight thousand Quzak years ago, the beam combined with a meteorite shower, which struck Quzak. Evidently, a reaction occurred in the Quzak atmosphere that resulted in a slight altering of the genetic code of your forebears, combining their code with that of my forebears. As you put it, Piatek, 'Ruach does all things well.' I know The Creator by another name, as do Walter and others. That is what I know thus far of the blending of our genetics. It will take some time to research it more fully."

Ooza shifted on her cushion. "We can talk more about Ruach later. Will Piatek need more time for training?"

"No. She knows enough now to do the initial job you want her to do. I have given her the same knowledge I have given you with regard to the other sentient species in this sector. When future needs arise for additional training, it will be accomplished at that time."

Qaak got up off his third leg, turned, and rubbed his hands in front of the fire. He turned back to the Quzaks. "Before I leave I will tell you one thing more."

Piatek smiled. "I thought you were holding something back."

"Indeed."

Ooza was also curious. "What?"

"As you are working to put together the key leaders of your Gaardian team, watch your planet closely. On the southern continent, there is a rapidly growing area of happiness, fulfillment, and great calm among the residents there. Under Gaardian regulations, you must not get involved as the Gaardian with what is happening there. Simply watch. It is the turning point of your planet's history, and everyone on your Gaardian team will learn from it."

"What is happening?" Ooza was puzzled.

Qaak's eyes glowed for a moment. "You will see. It is not my role to tell you exactly what will happen, but the results are already known. You shall see, and you shall be changed. I must go now. Call on me when you need me. Until then."

"Until then."

Qaak vanished. Piatek's curiosity continued. "What did he mean when he said that the results are already known? Can Gaardians see into the future?"

"Not really. I think this was more like a prediction based upon past experience."

Piatek closed her eyes. "No, I read his spirit. It is a prophecy, and when he says that we will be changed, it is said with certainty. I must ponder this."

"Do so."

"There is more. We both know now what I suggested to you, when we first pondered Walter at the meeting of our peers."

"I remember. We talked about how Gaardians achieve their ends without conquest, and how Walter is a creature of peace and of love."

"Yes. We will succeed because we are learning to love -- to love as no Quzak has ever loved."

Ooza's eyes glistened. "No! This kind of love I have seen, but not in myself or in you."

"Where?"

"Every forty cycles I have met with school children on the beach near my apartment down below. I will miss them. As I consider the days when I taught them, I know that it is their love that teaches me."

"Of course! Of course!"

Far away, in his apartment above Gaardian, Qaak was sipping hot pink liquid as he stood by a portal and looked down at Gaardian. "Personal journal. It was because of the combination of Zargadete and Quzak minds within the brain of Piatek that I was able to discern my genetic kinship to both. Somehow I think that either Ooza or Piatek will be the key to peaceful futures on both Quzak and Pzalop." A familiar glow filled Qaak's apartment.

> **"You have done well. You spoke for me faithfully to prepare Ooza and Piatek for what is to come. Everything is unfolding, as it should. Soon you will learn from Walter of a great disaster to be faced by the Zargadetes. I hid the approach of this disaster from Gaardians to remind you that I am God. Remember, Qaak, that I make all things new."**

The glow faded quickly. "Personal journal continued. As I leave to meet with Walter, I wonder: What will be so new, as described by The Creator?"

+ + +

On Earth several days later, it was winter in the Sierra Nevada Mountains of California. Unusually heavy snows were on and around the trees. Two cross-country skiers were making their way down a steep slope in Yosemite near Glacier Point.

Bob was a ski instructor from Badger Pass, the only ski resort to be found in a national park in the United States. He spoke as they moved along. "Jim, I'm glad we made it to Badger Pass before the road was closed with those downed trees. I've never seen so much snow in late December here."

"We seldom get this much snow at any time of the winter season. Climate change or not, this promises to be the coldest and heaviest snowfall in all my years of skiing." The two skiers came to a large clearing on a steep slope. "Is this the parking area? I can hardly believe it!"

Bob pointed to the right. "Look at that! That little ridge must be the roof of the gift shop. It looks like there may be damage."

"Let's get closer."

The two skiers made their way down the hill, until they were a dozen yards or so from what appeared to be the roof of the gift shop.

Bob stared. "It looks like part of the roof is damaged right over there. And, wow! It looks like Half Dome has a bigger lid of snow on it than in all the years I've been coming to Yosemite."

Jim pointed to the east. "Look at this! It is as though there is no slope downward for the amphitheater at all. The snow must be thirty or forty feet deep there."

"At least!"

The snow was partly holographic. Behind the hologram was a replica of the old Glacier Point Hotel. Inside, the entire lower floor of the hotel was decorated for Christmas. Walter's entire team was gathered there, along with Qaak, Kieya, and Ooza. The tables were set in the same way as at the Christmas banquets previously held at Debbie's Hollywood home, and at Walter and Debbie's New Zealand home. There was lots of conversation at the various tables.

Walter stood up at his table. "Attention everyone!" The conversations died down quickly. "Debbie and I have made this our annual tradition. A few of you have been with us before. For most of you, this is your second Christmas with us. For Ooza, this is her first. Ooza, please stand up so that those who haven't met you can recognize you."

Ooza stood up briefly, waved, and sat down again. Walter continued. "Dawn and James have outdone themselves this year. They tell me they have added a few new items to the menu. The buffet is over there by the windows. For those of you who have never been to Yosemite, the big monolith on the left is called Half Dome. The slightly higher ridge just beyond it is called Clouds Rest. In the valley directly outside and below us are Vernal Fall and Nevada Fall. For those of you who want to spend the night, the beds are ready upstairs. Now, for the banquet. Use your Gaardian rings to secure portions from the serving tables, so that we do not have to crowd around them." He paused. "Please pray with me." He paused. "Heavenly Father, with this meal we remember the birthday of your Son, Jesus. Bless this food and bless us in your Son's name. Amen. ... Enjoy!"

Walter sat down. Debbie's and Walter's plates were immediately filled with food. Next to Debbie, Jody and Qaak's plates were not quite as full, and had a few different selections.

Ooza looked at Steve. "I don't know enough about Earth food to know what to choose. I'll try anything you're having, so why don't you select our food?"

"Okay. We will start with the things I always had when I was younger. Then maybe we'll try some different things."

His ring shimmered. Their plates were filled with food.

Ooza looked at Walter and Debbie as she took a forkful of food. "I've asked Steve to explain what the Christmas holiday is about, but I must say I don't understand it completely. Everyone on my planet knows that one ultra-intelligent being created everything. Our scientists accept it as a logical assumption even though there can be no empirical evidence. In our language, God's name is Ruach. Walter, before you became a Gaardian you were some kind of priest. Can you explain what Christmas is about from an Earth perspective?"

Walter paused to chew and swallow a bite of food before answering. "For Earth there is no planet-wide perspective on God as there is with yours. The existence of God is not an automatic assumption on the part of Earth's scientists."

"Forgive me for saying so, but that sounds quite primitive."

The triped's eyes glowed for an instant. "Indeed. Scientists in the vast majority of advanced civilizations in Gaardian space assume the existence of God in some way."

Ooza nodded. "Okay. But why do Christians celebrate the birth of one man named Jesus?"

The triped chuckled. "Walter's is Earth's salvation story. On my planet, we also had a savior. In our case his name is Qapoku, Jesus is Earth's equivalent of Qapoku on my planet and Eiraynay on Aegeene, the home planet of Xpraepostq. Gaardian records show The Creator's promises becoming incarnate for thousands of planets in Gaardian space. In each case, The Creator's promises are embodied as one just like the other intelligent creatures on that planet. That Savior is born there, grows there, dies there, and is resurrected there."

"Resurrected? Do you mean they actually die, and then they become alive again?"

Walter nodded. "Yes. In the case of Jesus, he was resurrected on the third day. The same was true of Eiraynay on Aegeene, who was dismembered, and then two days later appeared alive and unharmed."

The triped was thoughtful. "In every case on the planets I mentioned, the resurrected being speaks, eats, and sleeps with them, and remains with them for several weeks before returning to The Creator."

"Quzak has not experienced this. Do you think it will someday?"

"I am sure of it." Walter spoke almost forcefully.

"So today is the birthday of Jesus?"

Walter smiled. "When Jesus was born, it was not recorded on a calendar. This is the day we traditionally celebrate His birth. It is a tradition that goes back a long time."

Steve put his fork down. "How did Christmas trees become part of Christian tradition?"

Debbie put her fork down. "Walter, you eat. I think I can answer this one."

Walter smiled and nodded. "Thank you, dear."

"Throughout Christian history the church's leaders have brought their knowledge of Jesus to people who did not know Him. They would begin by pointing to local customs and traditions and adapting those traditions for Christian use by redeeming them. In the case of Christmas trees and wreathes, it goes back to the days when Christianity was introduced in an area called the

British Isles. In December, there was a fertility festival in which decorated trees and wreathes were used as male and female symbols. Church leaders redeemed those symbols, by saying that trees pointed to heaven, and that wreathes were endless circles symbolizing eternal life with God in heaven."

The new Gaardian was thoughtful. "You've used two words that do not translate in Quzak: 'Redeemed' and 'eternal.'"

Walter stopped eating. "I'm almost ready for dessert, so I'll take this one. When something is redeemed, it means taking something worthless or nearly so, and turning it into something of much greater value."

Ooza scowled. "That's a foreign concept to Quzaks. Our history is that of destroying that which we see as having no value and then moving on. Does 'eternal' mean the same thing as 'everlasting'?"

"For many, the terms are equal and interchangeable, but that is not logical. Everlasting means having permanent and unlimited resources of time. By comparison, if something is eternal it does not have time as one of its components."

"That's illogical."

"From our perspective in the created universe that is absolutely true. Quzak teachings as well as Christianity's say that God created everything -- matter, energy, space, and time. Since God created the entire universe, God has to exist apart from the universe. God is spirit -- God is not made up of matter, energy, space, and time -- God exists apart from all of it, apart from the entire universe."

There was silence around the table for several moments. People were eating their dessert. "When will Quzak get its savior?"

"Soon." Everyone looked at Walter in stunned silence.

+ + +

Far away on Pzalop, the capitol was buzzing with activity. The Zargadetes were in a panic. The Suppla was staring out the window at the capitol city. Arooda, a male slightly taller than The Suppla, entered from an open doorway. "I have an update for you."

The Suppla turned and smiled. "I'm especially glad you're part of this office right now, secretly or not. What is the update?"

Arooda came closer and spoke more quietly. "The comet we've been watching seems to have changed course slightly as it entered our solar system. It is going to collide with us."

The Suppla sat down, and Arooda pulled up a cushioned seat nearby. "Do we know more about the comet? Can we survive the collision?"

Arooda spoke intensely. "The comet's mass is less than one ten-thousandth of our planet's mass, but its velocity is high. If we actually survive the collision, and there is no guarantee of that, there will be considerable loss of life. Our planet will be forever changed."

The Suppla turned and stared out the window for a moment. She turned back to her mate. "There is something I must do, and you cannot know about it. I need absolute privacy for a time. When this time is over you must not ask me what I did. Please honor me and do as I say."

Arooda got up, leaned over, kissed her on the cheek, and walked out the same door he entered. He closed it behind him. The Suppla stared at her desk for a moment, and then placed her hand on a colored panel near one edge of her desk. A light shimmered under the panel for a moment, and then a little rectangle appeared on the center of her desk. With two fingers, she reached out and touched the rectangle near the center.

29. Comet

The sun was low in the sky. A pink glow bathed Walter's and Debbie's home in New Zealand. Inside, in the large 'great' room, they were on a plush leather sofa near the fireplace. They were facing an open area near the fireplace, where "Les Miserables" was playing in three-dimensional video, and the room was filled with music. Suddenly the sound was muted and a tone sounded. "Put it through, Frank."

The performance they were watching disappeared and they saw The Suppla in a g-mail, sitting at her desk. "Greetings!"

"Hello! What is your concern?"

"There is a comet coming to Pzalop. It will collide with us. If we survive the collision, our planet will be forever changed."

"What is your estimate of how soon the collision should take place?"

"Less than three of our planet's revolutions. It will strike Pzalop's most densely populated area. We do not have the time to evacuate."

Debbie looked at Walter and then back at The Suppla. "I will have my science team analyze your situation and give you even more accurate data."

Walter looked directly at The Suppla. "Do you trust me?"

The Suppla hesitated, and then looked at him intently. "It's strange you ask, for until you asked, I was not sure. Now I am. I do not know why. I am trusting you with my future, along with the future of all my people."

"Thank you. Here is what I want you to do. In a short time, Debbie will let you know the exact place where the comet should strike. When she does, I want you to go there immediately. Take your family and closest advisors. Take your council and their families. Center yourselves at the center of the strike zone. Surround yourselves with your military leaders and as many of their troops that they can muster on that short notice."

The Suppla was incredulous. "You're asking all of us to give up our lives?"

"No harm will come to anyone there. God is faithful."

"God? Our religion is very private. We do not speak of it in public."

"Nevertheless I tell you the truth: God is faithful. In surviving what is about to happen, all of you will triumph."

"This is illogical!"

"I'm not asking you to be logical. I am asking you to trust God. The Gaardians will be there to witness and to serve. When this is over, your planet will indeed have changed, but for the better."

Debbie looked directly and intently at The Suppla. "I suggest that you tell Arooda everything about this meeting. It will help you in the future to have another witness."

"Yes." Walter was emphatic. "Now we must go and prepare for what God will do. You will hear from Debbie shortly. Until then."

Debbie smiled. "Until then."

The Suppla was grim. "Until then." The image vanished.

"Frank?"

The android appeared in front of them. "Yes?"

"Analyze this last conversation."

The android blinked twice. "Fascinating! What is first?"

"Two things. First, assemble the crew aboard *The Grace* and brief the bridge crew so that they can brief the others. Then get the most accurate data you can on that comet. Debbie will need it, when she and I return to the base in a few minutes. That's all."

"Done." The android vanished.

Debbie put her hand on Walter's. "I'm going directly to *The Grace*. What are you going to do?"

"First things first. When you get aboard, go straight to the clinic, and have Butch check the current status of our pregnancy. If he recommends you stay on base, I want you to do so."

"I'm only four months along."

"Please! Just do as I ask. Before I go aboard, I am going to see Qaak and possibly commune with Gaardian. I will see you in a while. Tell John to set course for Pzalop and be ready to go as soon as everyone is on board. If I'm not on board by the time *The Grace* reaches Pzalop, they should assume a standard orbit and wait." Walter took Debbie in his arms. They kissed. Their bodies glowed briefly, then they separated and both vanished.

In his apartment above Gaardian, Qaak was sipping a hot liquid and looking out a portal to Gaardian planet below. A tone sounded twice.

Qaak's eyes glowed for a moment. "Welcome, Walter."

Walter appeared next to him. His ring shimmered, and he began sipping a cup of tea with his friend. "There's a major development at Pzalop, Qaak."

The triped's eyes closed and glowed intensely for a few moments. "Indeed! We did not know of this comet."

"We couldn't. The Creator hid it from us."

"You know this by the voice?"

"Yes. The voice told me that it was hidden so that The Creator's glory may be seen."

"I wonder why." The triped closed his eyes for a moment and swayed a bit. He opened them. "What are your plans?"

"*The Grace* is on its way to Pzalop. They will orbit there until I arrive."

"Do you wish me to accompany you?"

"I've considered it, but not this time. Go to Quzak. Tell Ooza to join me aboard *The Grace* as soon as she can."

"I can g-mail her."

"True. So could I. She needs your help to beam directly – she has not done it before. Also, I have something else I want you to do."

The triped's eyes glowed very briefly. "Indeed. Piatek?"

"Yes. She needs additional training. Also, she needs to spend time with you and Jody. I will send Jody there as soon as we are done at Pzalop. Agreed?"

"Yes. Good. I have a suggestion."

"What is it?"

"I suggest we ask Pixie and her husband to join us at Ooza's base. Ooza is following Pixie's example with an orbiting independent satellite base. Pixie can be helpful to her."

"Good idea. I will leave arrangements to you. Now I must get aboard *The Grace*. I had considered conversing with Gaardian on its surface, but there is not time. Keep me informed."

"Indeed."

Walter vanished.

At Pzalop, *The Grace* was in orbit. Instead of going to the bridge, Walter appeared in his quarters. He went to a portal that looked out into space, with Pzalop at the lower side of his view. "I hunger for your presence, Lord. I could easily dispose of the comet, but it seems as though that is not what you want me to do. Please let me hear your voice."

He glanced around his quarters and then back out into space. "Since you're not speaking to me with your audible and visible presence, I have to proceed on faith that you are guiding me. Please help me to continue to be faithful to you."

Walter went to a panel and touched the wall next to it. The panel glowed with an image of Pzalop. Under his hands, a subtle glow began to dance. The view on the panel changed rapidly until he was looking down on thousands of Quzaks gathered in a valley. Then he saw The Suppla and The Council members standing around her. Walter saw a nearby cliff. He put down his hand, and the panel went dark. He walked to the door, which opened for him. His face showed that he was lost in thought. He walked down the corridor and into a trans-lift, and the doors closed. "Bridge."

The trans-lift's movement could be seen in undulating panels of light around him. The doors opened onto the Bridge.

John saw him. "Captain on the bridge!"

"As you were, everyone."

Jody looked up from her station. "How and when are we going to dispose of the comet?"

Ooza appeared near the view screen, nodded at Walter, and waved at the others.

"Hello Ooza. Jody, in answer to your question, we won't.

Karen stared. "What? We won't?"

Walter sat down in the captain's chair and looked at the view screen, which showed Pzalop. Ooza came and stood beside him.

"No, Karen, we won't deal with the comet at all."

Jody was puzzled, and understandably so. "So does that mean we're going to move Pzalop again?"

"No. It will stay where it is."

Ooza was quiet but excited. "Pzalop will be destroyed – or at least devastated!"

"No. It will not be touched. I hope you all trust me, but more than that, I hope at least some of you trust God. We're going to let God be God."

Karen was perplexed. "Forgive me for saying so, but that isn't logical."

"I know. In this case it is more important to be faithful than to be logical. We're going to witness God's glory."

John was trying to be calm and understanding. "So we're going to sit out here, watch the comet approach, and see what God will do?"

"Not exactly."

Walter's ring shimmered, and the view screen rapidly zoomed in on the planet until they are seeing The Suppla and thousands of others gathered in the valley below. "Look at the view screen. I told The Suppla to gather with her leaders and her military in that valley, which is ground zero – the place where the comet is headed. Since I asked them to be there, I am going to stand there with them to witness God's glory. I hope that some of you will join me, but that is not an order."

Karen nodded. "We all have Gaardian ring support, so why not?"

Walter shook his head. "Gaardian power and ring support will have nothing to do with what happens. I will expect everyone to restrain themselves from using their rings –" The trans-lift doors opened, and Butch stepped onto the bridge with Ken. "Glad you're here gentlemen. It will be difficult because we will be seeing that comet hurling at us, and our natural instincts will be to defend ourselves. If you join me on the planet's surface, I expect you to let God be God. If you do not go to the surface with me, it does not reflect on your relationship with me. Everyone has their own faith journey to make at their own pace. Besides, I expect some to remain aboard to run things!"

They all smiled. Debbie looked around the Bridge. "I'm going with Walter, both because I'm his wife and because I'm confident of my faith."

John shook his head. "I'm not ready to do what you're doing."

Ken nodded. "That's understandable, John. I for one would not expect you down there. When I was a Christian television producer, I knew many people who were where you are in their faith. Your faith will get stronger, but you need to be patient with yourself. Count me in, Walter."

"Good. Anyone else want to join me?"

His medical officer spoke quietly. "My faith us relatively new, but I got to meet Eiraynay on Aegeene before he ascended back to The Creator. Because of meeting Eiraynay face to face, I have no problem letting God be God. I'll stand with you there, and I'll keep my ring hand in my pocket."

Walter smiled. "Excellent."

Everyone was silent for a moment. Jody cleared her throat and spoke softly. "I think I'm ready to go with you. For me it is kind of a self-imposed test that I want to put on myself."

"A test?"

"Yes. Having melded minds with my husband Qaak, I have seen the universe apart from science and time through his eyes. In my head, I have a strong faith. This will be my way of cementing what I know in my head into my heart."

"Qaak will be pleased, I'm sure."

"I will go down. I will abide by your wishes Walter, with regard to Gaardian power, but I am sure it will be difficult. I will not fail." Asayak's voice was almost timid.

Walter nodded. "

Karen shook her head. "I'm not ready. I am doing my best to follow Jesus, but I am still struggling. I'm not sure enough of my faith. I might be sorely tempted to use my ring and obliterate that comet when it arrives."

"I understand. Does anyone know of others on the crew that will want to join us on the surface?"

Ken spoke firmly. "I can't speak for Keeta, but I want her to have the opportunity to decide."

"I think that's a good idea for the whole crew. Karen, after we leave for the surface, provide a ship-wide video of everything we've said here, including what I'm saying now. If any want to go to the surface and join us, they can do so. For those of you here on the bridge, give Debbie and me one minute on the surface with The Suppla before you join us. The others can come down at their convenience. See you there." Walter and Debbie vanished.

On the planet below, The Suppla and all the Zargadetes that Walter suggested to her were in the valley. Some were seated on rocks, but many were standing. Walter appeared a few feet in front of The Suppla and faced her. The Suppla stepped forward with Arooda and spoke seriously. "Greetings. I knew you would be here. Why did you ask for the others?"

Walter smiled. "Greetings. It is important that the key leaders of Pzalop witness what happens here today."

A Zargadete council member standing nearby approached. "Forgive my intrusion, Suppla. Are these the Gaardians that created this mess?"

The Suppla glared at him until he looked down. "The Gaardians are not responsible for this situation. We created it ourselves by our aggression toward a little planet called Earth."

Debbie looked at the council member. "You don't recognize me, but I have spoken to you on other occasions as a Zargadete." Debbie's appearance changed and she grew much taller until she again looked like the Zargadete that first entered The Suppla's office previously.

Another Zargadete council member approached. "I remember you! We had a meal together not long ago! You care about our planet! You're a Gaardian?"

She nodded. "Yes." She became shorter as her appearance returned to normal.

Walter addresses The Suppla. "When we moved your planet to this galaxy and placed it around this sun, the approaching comet was hidden."

Other members of Walter's crew began appearing, creating some commotion. As the conversation continued, even more crewmembers appeared. The Suppla looked around. "These are other Gaardians?"

"No, these are simply with me, and they wish to be with us here on your beautiful planet."

The Suppla was grim. "What happens now?"

"We wait for the comet to arrive. May I address your council and the others?"

The Suppla smiled at the deference to her position. "Proceed."

Walter went to some nearby rocks and climbed up on a large flat boulder. Pzalop's two suns were setting in the distance. As he addressed the crowd, his voice seemed amplified, though not by any detectable means. "Greetings everyone! I am the convener of the intergalactic police group known as The Gaardians. We are the ones who moved your planet to its new galaxy as a disciplinary action."

There was murmuring in the crowd. Walter held up a hand, and silence ensued. "I'm sure that many of you hate the Gaardians for what we did. That is understandable. We are here again now in support of your best interests. Having moved your entire planet over a distance traversing several galaxies, destroying the approaching comet would not even be a minor challenge to our power. That is not why we are here."

Again, there was murmuring, and again Walter held up a hand. "There is one that has far greater power than all the Gaardians combined. We are here to simply witness with you what will happen."

The Zargadete council member who first approached Walter spoke to him incredulously. "Are you saying that you're going to do nothing?"

"That is correct."

The Suppla stepped up onto the rock and stood beside Walter. She noticed that her voice was also amplified and glanced once at Walter as she spoke. "Some time ago I met with this Gaardian. He gave me information which leads me to believe without question that he wants to help us, and he wants what is best for our planet."

Ooza climbed up and joined them. Her voice was also amplified. "Many of you in the military recognize me. I was the mate of the Quzak Commander that led the expedition with you to conquer Earth. Those of you that know me know that I do not lie to anyone for any reason. Com, my mate, is now dead, and I recently made the decision to become a Gaardian. For countless solar revolutions, my people were your enemies. We joined forces against the Gaardians and failed. Though I am now a Gaardian, I am not your enemy, and neither are the other Gaardians. Read my heart, Zargadetes! Starting tomorrow, when this is all over, I will do anything I can within Gaardian guidelines to help you have a productive and prosperous future. That is my promise." Ooza stepped down off the rock.

Walter looked up, then back at the crowd. "The comet is approaching. The Creator of the universe is in charge! Look!"

As Walter faced the reddish glow, where Pzalop's two suns had just set, high and off to the left a huge fiery ball seemed to come out of nowhere. There were cries of terror in the crowd. Suddenly the comet came to a halt several miles above the planet. As Walter spoke, his voice thundered out over the crowd. "Don't be afraid! Watch The Creator of the universe work for you!"

From the direction opposite from the sunset, a fiery hand appeared. It grew larger and larger until it wrapped its fingers around the comet. As the hand became a fist, it glowed brighter and brighter until the light enveloped everything, and all the landscape disappeared. The voice thundered at a pitch like the lowest notes of a pipe organ.

> "Do not be afraid. I am The Creator. I created all that science knows, and all that science ever will know. I forgive, I redeem, and I make new. All of you are my children, and I love you as a parent. I have guided your growth and disciplined you because I love you. For generations, Zargadete parents have failed to teach their children about me. You must not forget. I am love, I am peace, and I am your hope. Make the most of what I have already given you, and I will be pleased. My servants the Gaardians can guide you toward fulfillment and joy. Learn from them. Teach your children and all future generations about me. I reward those who love me with life that is real and everlasting."

The brilliant glow faded, the landscape reappeared, and there was a hushed silence across the valley. Neither the hand nor the comet was seen. Walter spoke kindly. "The Suppla knows how to reach the Gaardians. I ask The Suppla to pass on that information to the Council members. My crew and I shall depart now. I will have Ooza return to visit you in seven of your solar days. She will introduce you to the Gaardian in charge of your sector. Your regular Gaardian, named Puz, is attending to another emergency in your sector today." He turned to The Suppla. "The Gaardians will return as needed. Until then."

"Until then."

Walter, Debbie, and Ooza vanished. All the rest of Walter's crew returned to *The Grace* as well.

Those remaining on the bridge were watching all that was happening below. Walter, Debbie, Ooza, and the others appeared on the bridge and went to their stations. Walter sat down in the captain's chair. He stared at the view screen, which showed The Suppla and her council conversing in small groups. Her military were pulling away in their vehicles. Walter touched a colored spot on the arm of his chair. "Attention all crew members. Those of us who went down to Pzalop have all now returned. Everyone is to meet on the hanger deck in ten minutes. There will be a holographic recording available of what has just happened on the planet's surface. Those of us who were there will be available to answer questions as best we can. That is all."

Debbie looked up from her console. "I'm looking at all the scientific data we've gathered here, and a lot of it is contradictory."

Jody nodded. "That's not surprising. All the instrumentation I've designed and implemented for this was functioning normally, but the data is mostly illogical."

Debbie smiled. "We can confirm that what we saw was real, but none of it fits within the established parameters of science."

Jody was perplexed. "I'm trying to apply the principles of quantum mechanics, and the results are problematic at best, paradoxical at least."

Walter smiled. "All of that is expected, ladies. You can have fun with what you have learned – or might have learned – later. Right now we each need to get some refreshment before heading to the hanger deck." Debbie walked over to the captain's chair. He got up, they embraced, and they vanished. The others headed to the two turbo lifts.

+ + +

Ten days later, there was abundant activity at the Gaardian Conference Center. In the foyer, Gaardians were appearing and moving to the large auditorium. Qaak moved to a seat in the front row, and he sat down. Kieya came in and sat down next to Qaak, quietly purring. There were hundreds in the auditorium.

Walter came in and went to the stage. "Usually, we gather as an entire group only for major challenges or crises. In this case a crisis has already passed. What happened was very unusual. All of you have received detailed briefings and data files. I am calling for discussion."

Puz came to the platform and turned to address the group telepathically. "I wish I could have been there. A short time ago, Ooza and I went to Pzalop, and she introduced me to The Suppla. We have the beginnings of a good relationship. I see remarkable change in the attitudes of the leaders who were there."

Qaak stood up at his seat. "I do not wish to sound pessimistic, but many of them will probably forget and revert to their old ways."

Puz bowed slightly. "This is probably true, but I believe The Suppla is an adequate and capable leader. During her lifetime, she will keep her people on course. Zargadetes live a long time, and her office is for life. She will probably continue to be in office for another three hundred of Walter's years."

Qaak nodded and sat down.

Kieya sat up on her haunches to speak. "Ooza has made a difficult commitment to the Zargadetes. Puz, will this be challenging for you?"

"No. Ooza and I have had long conversations. She will assist me in the same way that Xpraepostq assists Walter from time to time."

The cat purred. "I would like to hear from Ooza."

Ooza walked forward from the middle of the auditorium. "I have spent some time analyzing why I made that commitment. Previously it was not part of my character. It seemed completely natural, however, to say what I did."

"All that God does, He does well, Ooza. The changes in your heart began when Piatek opened your mind to what I represented to the Quzaks."

Ooza nodded and smiled. "I think you are right. In recent times I have developed a much broader sense of what it means to love than I ever dreamed possible."

Doff stood up at his seat. "I do not see anything in our briefings with regard to what happened to the comet."

The big cat got to her feet. "I did a detailed analysis of the comet when we first detected it. Unlike most comets, it was actually like a vagrant moon and was of considerable density. If it had struck Pzalop in the valley, there was a high probability that the planet would have split or shattered. When the hand disappeared so did the comet – as though they never existed."

Pixie stood up. "That's somewhat logical. When I first looked at Eiraynay in person, he disappeared. When Eiraynay disappeared, it was as though He was never there. The disappearance of the hand and comet are on a much larger scale, but the phenomena are the same." There were murmurs throughout the auditorium.

Walter stepped forward again. "I see indications that we need to break up into small groups for discussion. As we do so, please make records of your conversations that will become part of the Gaardian database. We will not reconvene as the larger body. Disburse to your sectors as necessity, or as need arises."

As the Gaardians formed small groups, Doff walked over to Ooza. She was intrigued by this tall, translucent being with the deep bass voice. Doff spoke gently. "I have read much about your people and have wanted to meet you. I am fascinated by the makeup of your head and heart."

"How so? I would like to know more about your people as well."

Doff offered a deep chuckle. "My people are simple to know. They will not be ready for interplanetary travel for a long time. I was recruited by Kieya because intellectually I am a genetic accident, and because I fit the other criteria usually used for Gaardian recruits. Also, there was no other planet in my galaxy that was even beginning to advance scientifically."

"Yet here you are!"

Doff laughed. "Yes! In addition, here you are – trained in a very short time compared to Walter and most of the rest of us. Neither of us are ones who fit a mold, are we?"

Ooza smiled thoughtfully. "No! Are you hungry? Would you share a meal with me?"

"I'd be honored."

Doff beaconed to Qaak, who ambled over. "I see you two are getting acquainted. What, as Walter would say, is up?"

"Is that little retreat center on Gaardian available? We were thinking of having a meal there."

Qaak's eyes glowed for a moment. "Of course! Help yourself."

The very tall Doff took the petite Ooza's hand, and they vanished.

Kieya softly padded over to where Qaak is standing. "Is another kind of Quzak love forming?"

Qaak chuckled, and his eyes glowed briefly. "Possibly. Indeed! I should tell Walter."

Qaak ambled over to the stage, where Walter was talking with a couple of the other Gaardians. Walter nodded, and the others walked away as Qaak approached. "I just saw something interesting."

"What's that, Qaak?"

"It appears that there may be real friendship developing between Doff and Ooza."

Walter smiled. "It's probably too soon to say, but it seems like a likely friendship. She will of course share everything with Steve. They make an interesting pair."

Qaak chuckled. "Interesting, but not surprising. Doff and Ooza are both adept at seeing beyond the obvious. Though they are different culturally, they think alike."

"I agree. Debbie is waiting for me in New Zealand. I think I'll head there now. I'll see you soon. Until then?"

"Until then."

Walter vanished.

+ + +

In the great room of his New Zealand home Walter appeared near the kitchen door. He called out, "Honey! I'm home!" Then he grinned.

Debbie's voice came from the other side of the doorway. "I'm in the kitchen!"

Walter turned and went through the doorway, and Debbie was standing in front of a microwave. "Cooking dinner the old fashioned way?" He put his arms around her from behind and kissed her on the neck.

She smiled, turned, kissed him on the lips, and then turned back to the microwave. "Sometimes I just want to cook so as to give myself some time to think."

"What are you thinking about?"

"Frank showed me what happened at Pzalop. Have you seen it from the viewpoint of *The Grace*?"

"No. I'm still thinking about what I saw from the planet surface."

"Let me show you something."

Her ring shimmered, and they are looking at Pzalop from *The Grace*. God's hand seemed to come through an unseen opening in the darkness of space. "Fascinating! It's like we were inside a black balloon, and God stuck is hand through the side of the balloon."

"Exactly. What happened to the comet?"

"It was inside God's hand and never reappeared after the hand was gone." The room became enveloped in a familiar glow, and the entire house disappeared into the glow.

> "I am pleased that you invited so many to witness my glory. The Zargadetes will remember for a long time. You have done well. The two of you will soon nurture both a child of your own and a planet."

Debbie's eyes grew wide. "How can we nurture a planet?"

> "You will know when the time comes. Everything is unfolding, as it should. I am faithful, and will help you deal with the challenges I give you. Be at peace. You have more new beginnings ahead."

Walter was puzzled. "New beginnings?"

> "I will show you what you should do. You are mine. I will care for you."

Walter and Debbie held each other more closely. Their embrace began to glow, and their glow merged with the glow of God.

30. Special Pregnancy

At the recreation area on Walter's base, Ken and Keeta were relaxing in the hot and cold whirlpool. Steam was rising from the frothing water, and they were both obviously enjoying themselves.

"Ken, I am pregnant!"

Ken's eyes grew wide, as shock and surprise set in. "You are? Fantastic! We have only been married for four months. Butch said we are genetically compatible, but I was not sure we could have kids. How soon?"

Keeta smiled and momentarily disappeared. She reappeared. "With my species the gestation period is normally about twenty-five weeks in Earth time. I understand humans have a longer gestation period. Butch says it's too soon to say when we will have our child."

Ken was beside himself. "This is exciting!

Keeta smiled again. "It's fantastic! There will probably be challenges that would not occur with a one hundred percent human child. I'm really enjoying babysitting Dawn's little girl, Amanda."

"What might be different for us?"

"Children on my planet are born transparent, unless they get sick. They have to learn to control opacity. Also, our children can walk on the first day. They reach adolescence in about three Earth years and are fully mature physically in four. It is hard to say how fast our child will develop. We do know the sex. He will be a male."

Ken smiled broadly. "A son!"

A voice was heard behind them. James came through a doorway with Dawn. "Did I hear you say you're going to have a son? Congratulations!"

James and Dawn joined them in the whirlpool. The water began to froth subtly. Ken bubbled over with excitement. "Thanks. Yes! Keeta has just told me we are going to have a son. Where's your daughter, Amanda?"

"Belinda is babysitting her. She treats Amanda like a grandchild. She tells me that her daughter-in-law is pregnant, so babysitting Amanda is bringing back memories."

The gourmet cook had a broad smile. "Congratulations to you both! When are you due?"

"We're not sure. Since our baby is half human and half biyae ["BYE-yay"], we can't tell yet."

James was curious. "Biyae? Is that the name of your people?"

"Yes, but we seldom use the term on our planet since the genetic change. Raising a transparent baby can be a real challenge for those not used to it. Fortunately, the formative years for my people are brief. Knowledge is passed on genetically, but wisdom of course takes time."

Dawn was perplexed. "What do you mean, knowledge is passed on genetically? Does this mean your planet has no schools?"

"Not entirely – we have special schools for a particular focus, but general knowledge is passed on in the womb. If I were a fully trained Gaardian, my children would be born with all Gaardian knowledge. That is probably one of the reasons that Walter was chosen over me for this sector. Well, hello, Qaak! Jody!"

Qaak and Jody approached from the lounge, instantly changed into swimsuits, and joined the others in the whirlpool. The triped's eyes glowed subtly. "Hello, everyone! Congratulations, Keeta and Ken! I overheard part of your conversation here. You're right, Keeta, it is unlikely one of your people will ever get full Gaardian training unless we can find a way to keep that knowledge from being passed on through the womb."

Jody added her encouragement. "Add my congratulations! Do Walter and Debbie know?"

"Walter probably knows only because Butch examined me a while ago, and I assume Walter knows everything that goes on with his crew."

Qaak chuckled. "Gaardians do not pry into the private lives of their teams, but this kind of knowledge affects everyone, so Frank passes it on. Does anyone know when Debbie will be full term?"

"Debbie is due in three months. This base is going to need a fully equipped nursery and school. It's going to be interesting to see what Keeta and Ken's baby will need."

"Indeed."

+ + +

On the other side of Gaardian space, at Ooza's base in her apartment, she was sipping some hot liquid as she walked into the living area. She went to a portal to look down on Quzak planet below.

"Bahna?" The android appeared. "This is for my personal journal. Both Steve and Piatek are great as my first teammates. I have fallen in love with Steve, and I think he is in love with me. The three of us have narrowed our list of candidates for our inner circle of teammates to fifty-seven. I am leaving the final choosing to Piatek and Steve, because Gaardian duties are pressing."

Steve entered from another doorway. "End journal. Good morning!"

Bahna disappeared as Steve came to the portal, took her in his arms, and kissed her deeply. "Good morning!" He got down on one knee. "Ooza, it never occurred to me that I could ever love someone as much as I love you. My love for you is both unconditional and passionate. Will you marry me?"

Ooza's eyes grew wide, and tears started rolling down her cheeks. "You want me to be your mate? We have only known each other for a short time! And why are you down on one knee?"

"I think I've been waiting for you all my life. I knew you were the one I wanted to marry the first time I laid eyes on you, in that restaurant on Quzak, when both Daie-Ahn and I both looked like Quzaks. Will you marry me?"

"I must admit I have had feelings for you since that day as well, but Com was my mate at the time. He has only been dead a few months. Why don't you get up off your knee?"

Steve smiled broadly. "I'm waiting for you to say you'll marry me!"

Ooza smiled broadly through her tears. "Yes! I'll gladly be your mate!"

Steve got up off his knee, took her in his arms again, and looked into her eyes. "I want us to be more than mated. That is too easy. I want us to be husband and wife. Walter is a pastor. I'd like him to perform a wedding ceremony for us."

Ooza kissed him lightly. "What's a pastor?"

"At Glacier Point you referred to him as a kind of priest. Your Quzak planet-wide religion has no priests, but you know about the Zargadetes on Pzalop. They have priests."

Ooza has a look of sudden recollection. "My people used to have priests. When our scientists reached the inescapable assumption that there has to be one god who created everything, organized religion became integrated with the rest of our society. Do you think Walter will do this for us?"

Steve smiled. "Let's ask him. Bahna?"

The android appeared. "Yes, Steve?"

"We need to connect to Walter via g-mail. Is he available?"

The android paused a moment. "He is in his quarters with his wife, Debbie. Do you wish to connect with them both?"

Ooza was enthusiastic. "Yes! I'd like to see Debbie too."

Bahna disappeared as a tone sounded and a g-mail appeared of Debbie and Walter in the living room of their quarters at the moon base.

"Hello, Steve! Hello, Ooza."

"Hi, you two!" Debbie's smile lit up the room.

"What can we do for you?"

"Steve asked me to marry him. I responded after some discussion by saying I'd accept him as my new mate."

Steve smiled. "I told Ooza that I want more than to be mated, that I wanted us to be husband and wife. We'd like to know if you'd marry us."

Debbie looked at Walter as they both smiled. "How soon? Can I be there and stand up for you, Ooza?"

Walter nodded. "In a wedding ceremony there is usually a witness for the bride, and a witness for the groom. On Earth there can be anywhere from one witness to hundreds or even more."

"Ooza and I have not talked about how soon we would do this, but we just wanted to know if you would do the ceremony. I want God to be part of our marriage."

Ooza looked at Steve. "How is that possible?"

"You'll see." He smiled.

"Let us know when you decide on a time. Congratulations!"

"Yes! Congratulations! See you soon! Until then."

Ooza nodded. "Until then." The connection was severed. She looked at Steve quizzically. "What did you mean by saying that you want God to be part of our marriage?"

Steve smiled. "There's an old saying on Earth that goes, 'They that pray together, stay together.' What many have observed on my planet is that when a husband and wife make God an unseen partner in their relationship, the marriage is stronger, more fulfilling, more peaceful, and happier.

"Are you saying that God can be real and personal?"

"Definitely."

"How is this possible?"

"Do some research of Gaardian records, as we talked about at Glacier Point. You will find that eventually, with all planets that have sentient species, The Creator becomes personal to that species by becoming one of them. The Creator does this so that all The Creator's children can have spiritual life with The Creator without the limits of time."

Ooza was thoughtful. "I will check those records."

+ + +

On the other side of Gaardian space the next day, Walter came out of his quarters and walked across the atrium into the lounge. He stopped, warmed his hands by the fire for a moment, looked around, and then went through another doorway to the recreation area. Several crewmembers were gathered by the pool. Seeing Qaak and Jody, he approached them.

"I have interesting news for you. I am soon going to be performing a wedding ceremony for Steve and Ooza."

Qaak's eyes glowed for a moment. "Indeed! Did you anticipate this?"

"Actually, the voice indicated to me that Daie-Ahnn was being recalled to Aegeene. With that, I came to believe through faith that this was a strong possibility."

"As you like to say, 'All that God does, God does well.' I hope I will be invited to the ceremony."

"It seems likely. Meanwhile, I have another concern. I would like you to help Puz on Pzalop. The entire planet has been a military-industrial society for many generations. One option is to help The Suppla give the military a mission or series of missions. Another is to convert most of the resources of the military to other uses. Historically, Earth has had a number of instances where countries had this problem, but I don't know of an entire planet faced with this dilemma."

Qaak closed his eyes, which began to pulsate, and then glowed steadily with greater and greater intensity. "Indeed! Twenty-two thousand of your Earth years ago, Waagere's planet had a very similar problem. Frank?"

The android appears. "Yes, Qaak?"

"Where is Waagere right now?"

The android gazed directly at Qaak as he answers. "Waagere is in his quarters, sleeping. Do you wish to have him awakened?"

"No. Give him an audio g-mail that is triggered ten seconds after he arises from sleep. Tell him I would like to confer with him at my apartment at his earliest convenience."

"Done." The android disappeared.

"Waagere and I will assist Puz in helping The Suppla. It seems probable that they will shift to a bartering economy as a transition to the future. By the way, are you aware of Keeta's pregnancy?"

Walter smiled. "Butch told me a short time ago. Things are going to get very interesting around here."

"More than interesting. In comparison to the growth and development of purely human children, it is likely that this child will develop at a rate of one year every three weeks.

Walter could not contain his surprise. "That's fast!"

"Yes. Think of a human's so-called 'terrible twos' and multiply that by a thousand. I suggest we talk with Butch."

"Good idea!"

The two walked to the medical clinic and went in. Butch was talking quietly with Keeta, who was sitting on a transparent table. Ken was standing at the other side of the table. Butch looked up and saw them as they walked in. "Hello! I am glad you are here Walter. I was just going to send for you. Keeta is probably going to deliver in less than five weeks. Her rapid weight gain began this morning. Keeta will have to become constantly transparent in order to prepare the child for the outside world. Both will be transparent, so I am installing special monitoring equipment in Ken's and Keeta's quarters."

"Sounds good. Qaak, tell Butch what you just told me."

"Once born this child will develop at the rate of one Earth year every three weeks. It will be your "terrible twos' multiplied a thousand fold."

Butch whistled. "I had not anticipated it being quite that bad. We had already decided that it would not be fair to the child to keep him in Ken's and Keeta's quarters."

Qaak grunted. "They can raise him during the two or three most formative years on Keeta's planet."

Keeta shook her head. "That is not an option."

Walter was surprised. "Why?"

Keeta disappeared. "Keeta?" Ken was puzzled.

She reappeared. "I'm sorry. I could not help it. This is embarrassing. I have been reading Earth's history, looking at news videos of human struggles with prejudice and bigotry. On my planet, it is just as bad, if not worse. Our child would not be accepted there."

Qaak's eyes glowed for a moment. "Indeed. It had not occurred to me. Forgive me for embarrassing you. Isolating him from the other children being born on the moon also would not be good for him or for them."

"Are there precedents?"

Qaak gazed steadily at Walter. "Only one." He paused. "Excuse me. I will return in a few moments." He vanished.

"Frank, where did Qaak go?"

The android appeared. "He's gone to Gaardian."

"To his apartment?" Keeta was surprised.

"No. The planet."

The android vanished.

Qaak reappeared moments later. "Thank you for your patience. My solution involves a long story, but I will simply tell you the conclusion."

"Can we hear the story another time?" asked Ken.

"Yes. Gaardian raised me in a way, and it has agreed to help you raise your son. As we speak, Gaardian is creating a home for the three of you that is slightly larger than this base. A small portion will be your quarters, configured just as they are here now. The rest will be quarters for your neighbors and for guests."

Keeta was surprised. "Who will our neighbors be?"

Qaak chuckled. "I was telling Gaardian that I would move my quarters to the surface just as Waagere arrived for our consultation. While we were discussing this, there came the silent and unexpected arrival of Kieya, who came to commune with Gaardian."

Walter laughed. "Kieya can be wonderfully silent at times! What happened?"

"All of us are moving our quarters there, each for our own reasons. It will be a second home for Jody -- she likes it there."

Debbie walked into the clinic. "I heard laughter. What's going on?"

"The short version is that Gaardian Planet is creating a giant nursery for Ken, Keeta, and their son. Qaak, Waagere, and Kieya are moving their quarters there to be neighborly. What do you think? Should you and I have a vacation home there on Gaardian?"

Debbie laughed. "It will be great. When we want a few days off from being just parents we can go there and let Gaardian babysit!"

Walter grinned. "Great idea! Gaardian can become the premier vacation spot for families with young children!"

Qaak chuckled. "In my sixty-seven thousand years I've never heard Gaardian laugh. Perhaps it will find this as amusing as we do!"

+ + +

Far away in The Suppla's office, two suns could be seen rising outside the far-left side of the windows behind her desk. Her mate, Arooda, was pacing back and forth.

Puz appeared. His telepathic voice touched both of them. "Good morning!"

"Good morning!"

Arooda had turned to face them. "Good morning! Did you come alone?"

"No. I appeared first to make sure we would not unnecessarily disturb your plans for the day."

The Suppla suppressed a smile. "Your courtesy is appreciated, but I have set aside the entire morning for this."

"Good."

Ooza appeared. "You already know me. I'd like to introduce to you two others who you have not yet met."

Qaak and Waagere appeared. "My name is Qaak."

"I am Waagere."

Ooza smiled. "I am here only to introduce them. You know me rather well. I have never lied to you. I tell you that these Gaardians can be trusted. They are among the oldest, wisest, and most experienced of all the Gaardians. I will return if you need me, but you will not. I bid you farewell until next time. Until then."

The Suppla nodded. "I trust you Ooza. Until then." Ooza vanished.

As Waagere began to speak, both The Suppla and her mate focused solely on her. "I am here because many seasons ago, my planet's people were aggressive and possessive, having many of the characteristics of your people. After becoming part of Gaardian space, about the time I became a Gaardian, my people shifted from being a dominantly military society to that of a more internally productive bartering society. There have been many changes since then of course, but that change was the key first transition to what my planet is today."

The Suppla's mouth was set in a straight line. She responded quietly but intensely. "You are talking about a transformation of my entire planet. Where would we begin, and what is bartering?"

The triped's eyes glowed briefly. "That is why I am here. I am a teacher."

The Suppla laughed. "Are you suggesting I send all of my people back to school and take classes?"

Qaak chuckled. "My method is easier and faster than that. I propose to demonstrate. Will you trust me, as Ooza asked you to do?"

The Suppla's gaze on Qaak was steady and intense. "You ask a lot, but I trust Ooza. Proceed."

"A question: If as the leader of your people, you miraculously had time to go back to school and spend several years learning something to be a better leader, what would it be?

Intrigued, she stared upward for a moment. "I would want to learn wiser insights into how to lead my people, and to better understand how changes in our society happen."

"Very well. Please allow me to approach you. I need to touch your face."

The Suppla scowled. "A peculiar request. Proceed."

Qaak moved over to the Suppla and placed three fingers on her face. He closed his eyes, and they began to glow. The Suppla's eyes slowly closed. After about ten seconds, Qaak withdrew his hand. "That is enough to demonstrate."

The Suppla opened her eyes, normally at first, then wider. "Amazing! I feel like I have just been given a lifetime of education in politics and social dynamics! Incredible!"

+ + +

A few days later, in her apartment newly relocated to Gaardian, Kieya was sitting at a console. She got up and walked to a portal that looks out upon the Red Falls. "G-mail to all Gaardians. As you know, part of my duties in my sector near the center of Gaardian space is to monitor unusual phenomena of suns, planets, and other bodies of matter and energy in Gaardian space. In the area where Quzak was located before we moved it to its present location, there was a supernova. From the viewpoint of the surface of Quzak, it was poised directly over its southern rotation point. In their new sector of Gaardian space, Ooza has noticed that there is another supernova in precisely the same location of the night sky of Quzak. We did not notice this at the time we relocated the planet. The odds against this happening are beyond computation. I am investigating with Ooza, and I will have another report soon."

Kieya stared out at the Red Falls. "G-mail to Ooza."

A three-dimensional image of Ooza appeared next to her. "I've been expecting this. Your general g-mail was succinct and included information I had only surmised. How soon would you like to pursue this?"

"How about now? I can have my vehicle outside your base in a matter of moments."

"Good. Until then." They both vanished.

Moments later Kieya reclined on her stomach, facing forward on a sloped cushion, her paws manipulated the controls of her space vehicle. The stars blurred as she got underway. A few moments later, the stars came to a stop as Ooza's large space station appeared above Quzak planet. A vehicle seat appeared next to her, and then Ooza appeared.

"I've told Steve and Piatek that they are on their own until I return. They're ready to begin actual recruiting of the rest of my team."

"Understood." Kieya again manipulated the controls, and they began moving rapidly. All the stars streaked past them except one in the center of their vision. "It appears you are getting your crew together at a typical pace. Right now we need to focus on that supernova."

There was a brilliant flash of light, and Ooza reflexively raised a hand to her eyes. "I think we just passed through a solar flare headed right for Quzak. I don't think it is a threat however."

"No. The distance is significant."

The stars stopped streaking past, as they came to a halt to observe the supernova. "This star seems to have an unusually short life span."

The cat nodded. "Yes. It has gone to supernova much more rapidly than I anticipated. It is not a threat to your planet or any other planets in your sector, but I have to wonder why this is happening."

"Except for the life span, there does not seem to be anything unusual here."

"Agreed. Tell me about the southern continent on your planet."

As they continued to watch the supernova, Ooza scowled. "It is a frozen wasteland. Our scientists have not explored it for a long time. Occasionally there are rumors of Quzaks living there, but our military flies over the continent from time to time on training missions, and no life forms are observed amidst the ice."

"None whatsoever?"

"None. I admit that seems strange in light of my Gaardian training."

Kieya purred subtly. "Exactly."

Ooza looked over at her. "What are you thinking my friend?"

"Something is amiss. We should investigate."

Ooza's voice was suddenly soft but intense. "Definitely!"

Kieya's paws manipulated the controls. The vehicle came about, and the stars again streaked by as they headed for Quzak. As the planet came into view, Kieya took the ship to the small, frozen southern continent. As they descended to the surface, there were the whiteout conditions of a blizzard. "We are a few meters above the surface. I'm going to land on the snow."

"Wait!"

"Yes? What is wrong?"

"Let me try something."

Ooza extended her right hand forward and rested it on the console just below the forward window of the vehicle. Her ring shimmered. The blizzard and the snow disappeared. They were in the middle of a lush green clearing. On both sides of them were tall plants. There were small animals scurrying about, and there were a few larger ones looking at them several meters away. In the distance ahead of them, they could see tall buildings.

The cat touched her controls. "The snow and blizzard were not holographic projections."

Ooza smiled. "Correct. As you know, my planet – this planet – has three continents. Two of the continents are near our rotational equator. We are now on the third. I'm not sure how it is done, but evidently as any vehicle approaches this continent they are transported to a frozen ice mass on the northern end of the planet."

Kieya purred. "Walter told us that you have some special gifts. One of them has now revealed itself."

Ooza smiled. "Evidently so. I instinctively knew that I was not where I thought I was. I do not even know how I used my Gaardian ring to get us here, but here we are. I will speak to Piatek about it when I return to base. She will understand."

"Until then, I'm putting us under cloak, and we will proceed." The vehicle moved slowly forward toward the buildings in the distance.

"It's very different than what I expected. The sun is very low on the horizon of course, seeming to move around us rather than over us as at the equatorial continents." Ooza craned her neck to try to see all around their vehicle.

Kieya gestured with a paw. "Yes. There is perpetual sunset or sunrise, since there are not seasons on your planet. The stars are always out here, but they are dim because of the sun."

"It is not natural for it to be so warm and almost humid. The solar flare is creating a narrow area of brighter light. Let's go to that area at the rotational center."

"Agreed." The cat manipulated the controls. The vehicle rose and moved further south. The large plant life diminished as the sun got lower on the horizon. Where the sun had almost set, they came to a small town. Children were playing, and adults were moving about. The vehicle stopped just outside of the town, hovering several meters above the ground.

"If you will disguise yourself as a Quzak, we can proceed on foot."

Kieya's sloped cushion disappeared, and she shrank to Ooza's size. Then she took on features similar to those of Ooza. "How's this?"

Ooza giggled. "Except for the hairy arms you look like my colleague Zahrahted!"

The hair disappeared from her arms. "Better?"

"Much better!"

"It always feels most peculiar to become a biped." She purred subtly.

"Don't do that! Quzaks don't purr."

"Understood. I will restrain my instincts."

Someone approached from their left. "We will need to provide gifts."

Ooza's face brightened. "Qaak! Except for your eyes and voice, I would have assumed you were a Quzak! Very well done."

"Thank you."

"Hello, Qaak. You just said we would need gifts. Why?"

"The Creator told Walter that this was to happen soon on Ooza's world. We need to humble ourselves and recognize this privilege."

Ooza was puzzled. "I don't understand."

"You will. What is the most precious form of spices on your planet?"

"Spice crystals. They have a multitude of uses but are very costly."

Kieya nodded. "I now understand what Qaak is telling us. Do you have fragrant oils here?"

"Yes. This is all so mysterious. I will go along. What else do we need?"

"I remember watching your female support group talk about the virtues of spun gold."

Qaak looked directly at the new Gaardian. "Ooza, I want you to think back over your lessons in Quzak history. In the age when leaders were born into their legacy, how were these children approached?"

Ooza was quiet and thoughtful for a moment. "We are bringing three gifts. We bring three especially rare gifts." She looked into the faces of Qaak and Kieya, and tears began running down her face. "I now know." She paused. "The Arkaynee ["are-KAY-nee"]! There have been prophecies. Piatek spoke of it recently. We fit the prophecies. This child will bring the quiet but controversial revolution to Quzak that it has awaited during countless generations. This child will rule the hearts and minds of Quzaks for countless generations to come, even after returning to The Creator." She paused again, and she dried her eyes. "To answer your question, we must approach with humility and reverence. After leaving our gifts, we must back out and leave instantly, vanishing and leaving no trace."

Qaak nodded. "I did not come in a vehicle. May I join you in yours, Kieya?"

"Of course. It will adapt. The precise center where the solar flare pointed is that small building over there. Ooza, please provide the appropriate gifts."

Containers appeared in their hands, and they walked quietly to the small building. Going inside they saw a young mother nursing a child, with her mate standing nearby. They approached and began opening their gifts.

Qaak's voice was unusually soft and low. "I come from a planet far away. I bring you spun gold."

Qaak backed away, and Kieya approached. "I too come from a planet far, far away. I bring you spice rocks."

Kieya backed away, and Ooza approached. "I come from the eastern continent, north of here. Have no fear. The Creator, Ruach, has brought us. The knowledge of this special event will not reach the other continents for many years. I bring you precious oil."

She backed away, and the three of them backed out the door. On the outside no one saw them exit, for they vanished instantly back to Kieya's vehicle.

As they reappeared inside, Kieya and Qaak no longer looked like Quzaks. The cat purred audibly and almost powerfully. "We are almost exactly at the rotation point of Quzak. If, instead of moving, we transport directly to Gaardian, no one could detect our departure."

"Agreed. Proceed."

There was a brief flash outside, and suddenly they were in orbit around Gaardian. The interior began to glow. All of their surroundings faded into the glow.

> "I am very pleased with the three of you. You have done well. As my special child grows, you will be tempted to offer protection. Leave that to me. Everything is proceeding, as it should. Ooza, you have seen your planet's Savior. Watch my special child grow as you wish, but do not return to that continent while my child is there. Authority and power are mine."

The glow faded, and their surroundings returned to normal. After a few moments of silence, Kieya touched a small panel. The newest Gaardian pointed. "Look! The supernova has disappeared! How is that possible?"

Qaak chuckled. "Kieya, take us there quickly."

"Agreed." The cat's paws moved over the controls, and the stars were a blur for a moment.

Then stars appeared normal. Qaak pointed. "Indeed! Look over there! That which had been a supernova is now an inert mass. It is as though Gaardians had snuffed it out, but we did not."

Kieya purred. "The Creator amazes us once again. I am in awe." They stared at the dark mass that had earlier been a star.

Ooza nodded. "All that Ruach does, Ruach does exceedingly well!"

31. Nursery

God's love appears in unexpected ways and places. As convener, Walter recognized more of God's activity than most Gaardians. All of this did not entirely insulate his feelings. Several days after the sudden death of the star, activities at Walter's base had calmed down somewhat. Butch came out of the medical clinic, walked across the atrium, down a small hallway, and into the mess hall. He looked around, and he saw Walter over in a far corner eating breakfast with Debbie. Smiling, and waving at several people as he crossed the mess hall, Butch approached their table. "Good morning! May I join you?"

Debbie looked up and smiled. "Of course! Sit down and have some breakfast. Dawn and James have cooked up some unusual waffles today. They're wonderful!"

Butch sat down. Walter paused between mouthfuls, took a sip of grapefruit juice, and greeted the medical officer. "Butch, I have a feeling you're not here for breakfast."

"Right. The waffles are delicious, Debbie. I had one a couple of hours ago. I am here about Keeta. She will give birth in a matter of hours. I want you to move her – and Ken – to Gaardian right away, so that she can give birth there."

Debbie put down her fork, curious. "Why not let her give birth here, and then move them?"

"It's going to probably be an unusual birth. Gaardian can handle things just as well as I can -- perhaps better in this case. There are things going on that no one has ever seen before."

Walter put down his fork. "Like what?"

"I have never seen, heard of, or read about an unborn child having this much activity. It is very uncomfortable for Keeta even with ring support. I tried to help with a bit of conservative acupuncture and got an electrical shock of thousands of volts!"

Debbie's mouth dropped open. "You're kidding!"

Butch smiled. "Actually, it was kind of interesting – it was like touching a Tesla coil or a Van de Graff generator. It tingled more than anything else."

Walter looked up. "Frank?" The android appeared. "Frank, what is your assessment of Keeta's child?"

"There is more energy of all types contained within Keeta's womb than has ever been recorded in a womb in Gaardian space."

"Thank you. Inform Gaardian that its new residents will arrive shortly. Also notify Waagere, Qaak, and Kieya."

"Done." The android vanished.

"Butch, I agree with your assessment. You are the best medical officer a Gaardian could want, but Gaardian can handle this. You have other pressing needs here on base. In addition to your usual tasks, including Debbie's pregnancy and Dawn's daughter, Amanda, in a few days you will have to deal with three other pregnancies, as well as detailed analysis of something that I will tell you about later. You'd better get going. I'll take care of Ken and Keeta."

"Thanks. What other pregnancies?"

"I'll tell you later. Get going."

Butch grabbed a donut from a nearby plate, got up, and headed back to the clinic. Debbie picked up her fork and looked at her husband. "What other pregnancies?"

"The voice told me earlier this morning that more children will be with us soon." She smiled as he continued. "G-mail to Ken and Keeta." A three-dimensional image of them in their apartment appeared.

"What is it Walter?"

"Are there any things either of you need to do before going to Gaardian?"

Keeta and Ken shook their heads. "No. Butch told us he was going to ask you to send us to Gaardian right away."

"Good. Your new neighbors will join you today or tomorrow."

Debbie smiled at them. "God be with you two!"

Keeta smiled a wry smile. "Thanks."

Walter's ring shimmered, and they vanished from within the image. Then the g-mail ended.

On Gaardian, Ken and Keeta appeared in the middle of an empty apartment. A moment later, all of their belongings from the moon base appeared as well. Ken looked around. "How do we communicate with Gaardian?"

Keeta looked at him. "Like this: Gaardian, please be present to us."

"Hello Ken, Keeta. Welcome to your new temporary home. It should be identical to what you had at Walter's moon base. Is there anything you need?"

Ken spoke clearly and slowly. "I don't think so right now, thank you. Do we just address a thought to you when we need something?"

"Yes. I will not read thoughts you do not address to me. I will honor your privacy. It is my intent to be your friend, companion, and physician."

The mother to be was puzzled. "How will the doctor part work? Is there a clinic here?"

"There is no clinic necessary. I will supply your needs. If you look outside your apartment door, you will find an atrium just as you do at your base. You will find also connected to the atrium are the apartments of Qaak, Waagere, and Kieya. There are also several furnished sets of guest quarters. Would either of you like to have an android to speak to like Frank, instead of my telepathic voice?"

Ken and Keeta looked at each other. Ken shook his head. "I think we'd like to try it this way for now."

"Very well. Waagere has arrived and is resting. The other two should arrive soon. I will leave you alone now, but I will monitor your medical vital signs."

Keeta tried to smile. "Thank you, Gaardian."

"Yes, thank you for your hospitality in advance."

"You're welcome."

Ken and Keeta walked hand in hand out of their apartment into the atrium. She walked carefully but enjoyed all she saw. "It is so beautiful! There's plant life both outside and inside of the atrium."

"It's fantastic! Let's explore! It looks like that is a small lounge." Ken pointed.

"It even has a fire in a fireplace. That's a familiar touch." Keeta pointed through another doorway. "That looks like a recreation area. Let's go see."

They walked into the recreation area, where there was an Olympic sized pool, hot and cold whirlpool, and exercise equipment. Around the perimeter several feet up was a walking and jogging track.

"Excellent!" Ken smiled.

A tone sounded. She looked up. "We'll take it here please."

Belinda appeared in a g-mail. "Hello, you two. How do you like it?"

Keeta smiled. "It's fantastic! It has many familiar touches of home. Waagere is here, but we have not seen her yet because she is resting."

"I like it too. What about our work at the base?"

Belinda smiled. "That's the reason for this call. I want you to take a week to get used to your new digs. Make it a mini-vacation. Then we will improvise, both before and after the birth of your son. Check in with me as often as you wish."

"Okay. Thanks Belinda."

"See you later." Her image vanished. The two of them started walking into the lounge. They sat down on an overstuffed sofa facing the fireplace and enjoyed it for a while. Keeta squirmed to get comfortable. "Butch said that Gaardian can be just as good a physician as he is, and perhaps better. I'm going to be interested to see how all of that works."

"What are we going to name our son?"

Keeta smiled. "I've thought a lot about it, and I'm sure you have too. We have both looked at lists of possible names for males on our planets. I'm not happy with any of the names, are you?"

Ken was thoughtful. "Not really. I'm intrigued by some of the biyae names from your planet, but so far I've not found a name on either list that I really like."

"Maybe we should come up with a name that reflects both biyae and human cultures."

Excited, Ken said, "Maybe we could combine our own two names in some way. Kenta? Keeken? Kenkee? Kenkeeta? KeetaKen?" He smiled.

She giggled. "I like Kenkee. What do you think?"

Thoughtful, he smiled. "Kenkee it is then. Kenkee!"

"Good! I am glad we have decided. Ouch! He is really getting active inside me! Gaardian, how close do you think I am to giving birth?"

"He is almost capable of survival outside of your womb. It will probably be only a few days more. When the time comes I will transport him directly out of your body into the special nursery I've prepared next to your bedroom."

Ken nodded. "Thank you."

"Call if you need me again."

They looked at each other and then snuggled closer to each other as they watched the fire. She put her hand on his knee. "After we get settled, in a few days let's invite Dawn and James over for a visit."

"Good idea! I assume that Walter and Debbie will be dropping in from time to time."

"At least Debbie will. Walter's duties may keep him occupied. Since Qaak is retired, I expect he and Jody will visit us pretty often."

+ + +

Far away in her office on Pzalop, The Suppla was standing behind her desk. She came out from behind and went to a conversation pit of comfortable furniture on the other side of her office. Already seated there were Qaak, Ooza, and Puz. She took a large comfortable chair. Arooda came in from an outer office and sat down beside her. She glanced at her mate, and then she looked at the rest of the group. "Before we get to present issues I have a question for either Ooza or Qaak. When The Creator took away the comet that threatened Pzalop and spoke to us, what were your personal reactions? Video of what happened is played nearly every day in one part of my planet or another. My council members and military leaders have talked about it constantly. Have the Gaardians been discussing it?"

Qaak's eyes glowed for a moment. He looked at her directly. "This may surprise you, but no. For quite some time now, Gaardians have had varying degrees of experience with the presence of The Creator. Not long ago The Creator showed each of us our existence apart from matter, energy, space, and time."

She stared at him. "How is this possible?"

"With The Creator all things are possible. Think of it this way: Since The Creator created all matter, energy, space, and time, The Creator has to exist apart from all of those things."

"I must admit I can barely comprehend such a thing."

Her mate shook his head. "I am the same."

Qaak chuckled. "Without The Creator's help none of us can. I can only suggest that you think about what The Creator said that day and try to take it into your heart. That is a challenge. Sometimes the longest journey anyone ever makes is from their head to their heart."

The Suppla nodded. "I will ponder that. Now, as to progress here on Pzalop. I want to tell you what I see happening here and get your suggestions. After issuing a general order to all military personnel, the leaders gave each one in their commands the option of becoming an independent contractor, using the skills that they had learned. A few have gone into agriculture. Some are exploring natural resources. A few are going into manufacturing and construction. Many are going into business, acting as agents for bartering. Many are attempting various kinds of services. The ranking officers seeming to prefer supervisory and policing work."

Qaak nodded. "All of this is normal. Some planets thrive for virtually unlimited periods of time using systems like the one that is developing here. Some planets use a medium of exchange called money to enhance the commerce between sectors of their societies. These mediums of exchange are not always helpful, however."

The Suppla nodded. "The sample training you gave to me not long ago -- I would like you to give the same training to ten of my council members."

"Agreed. How soon can you get them here?"

"Arooda. Please bring the chosen council members in here." Arooda got out of his chair and went out the door into the outer office.

Qaak pointed to an open area in a corner of The Suppla's office. "Have them stand in a circle over there, leaving an opening for me. I request that Arooda join them."

Arooda and the council members began entering the room. "Arooda, I want you and the council members to form a circle over there, leaving an opening for Qaak."

They did so. Qaak got up and joined the circle. "I want the two of you next to me to put your hands on the heads of the ones on the other side of you. The rest of you put your hands on the heads of those next to you."

The Suppla stood and drew closer. "I know this is a strange request, and it crosses our cultural boundaries, but do it as an order from me."

They did so. Qaak then placed three fingers of each hand on the faces of those next to him. "Everyone relax. This will not take long." Qaak closed his eyes, and they began to glow intently. The others' eyes slowly shut. A glow enveloped Qaak, and the others glowed slightly. After about twenty seconds, Qaak lowered his hands. "It is done. I have just put each of you through the equivalent of ten years of classes that meet all day every day." The other counsel members dropped their hands and looked at each other. Many of them began to smile.

The Suppla was pleased. "You are all now dismissed. Meet with me here tomorrow at this time. That is all." The counselors filed out of the room, and Arooda and Qaak returned to their previous seats.

Arooda spoke quietly. "That was amazing! No, incredible! Where did you get all of that knowledge?"

"It is not all contained within me. I simply am a transfer node where knowledge can come to a focus and flow through me."

Ooza looked at the Suppla. "I am learning from you and from your council leaders. My planet is making a transition also. I'm glad we can help each other."

"As am I, Ooza. Do any of you have any suggestions?"

Puz's voice could be heard telepathically. "Those who just received training should form an advisory council to the rest of the council and to you. Your society is making rapid changes, and a smaller group can make decisions easier."

The Suppla nodded. Qaak raised a finger. "You should have Puz monitor all meetings of the full council – but not as a spy. Let his presence be obvious as an observer. Puz may be able to help you see things from a fresh perspective on difficult issues."

The Suppla nodded again. Ooza sat forward on her seat, and she spoke confidently. "This will seem like a strange request, but I suggest that you talk over your day out loud each evening with The Creator, just as though The Creator is another person in the room. I also suggest that you remind yourself each morning that all that The Creator does, The Creator does well."

The Suppla stared intently at her. "That last suggestion was a provocative one."

Qaak's eyes glowed for a moment. "Yes, but a good one. It is a variation of the favorite saying of the convener of the Gaardians. Do you have any other requests of us while we are here?"

"No."

Qaak nodded. "Very well. Until next time."

"Until then."

The Gaardians vanished. Arooda turned to his mate. "I am pondering Ooza's first suggestion. I am going to try it. As for the other suggestions by Ooza and the others, I need to ponder further."

"Of course. Let us go and discuss it while enjoying a meal."

"Let us enjoy a meal and each other. Then we will need rest."

"Agreed."

+ + +

Back in her apartment, Ooza appeared, and she walked over to the window looking out over Quzak. Steve entered with two cups of steaming liquid. "Welcome home. Would you like some green tea?"

"Thank you. What have you been working on today?"

"If you agree, Piatek and I want to begin working with our inner core of team leaders in ten days. I have been considering where to have our wedding. I think we should have it at the Gaardian Conference Center. We can have everyone on Walter's moon base along with all the Gaardians as witnesses. What do you think?"

"This is an even bigger event for us than I thought! How soon?"

"How about the day after tomorrow?"

Ooza smiled broadly. "Great! Being a special ceremony, do I wear a special costume? What do you suggest?"

Steve hesitated, and then he smiled. "Normally the bride makes those kinds of choices, but since this is primarily an Earth-style ceremony, I'll make a few suggestions. Bahna?

The android appeared. "You have a request?"

"Yes. Access your Earth databases and obtain some stills and videos of brides at their ceremonies during the last twenty years. Also, obtain some videos of female entertainment personalities dressed up for the Oscar and Emmy awards. Pay particular attention to the dresses by the most famous fashion designers.

"One moment. Shall I show them here?"

Ooza nodded. "Yes. I want to see this! Show the dress designer's name below each dress."

Images begin flashing by rapidly. Steve smiled. "I must admit this is fun!"

Ooza nodded as she watched. "Stop! Go back to that white dress by Bob Mackie. The dress reappeared.

"Do you like that one?"

"Do you?"

Steve grinned. "Definitely! Bahna, can you modify that gown to fit Ooza's figure?"

"I can do better. I can create an android re-creation of Bob Mackie and let him make the adjustments."

Ooza grinned. "Not now, but I like the idea. We will do it tomorrow. Tomorrow after breakfast, Steve, I want you to go back to Walter's moon base while I get the dress fitted. Then on our wedding day, you are not to see me until I enter the auditorium for the ceremony. That's your Earth tradition, isn't it?"

Steve smiled broadly. "Absolutely. I hope you are having as much fun with this as I am. Bahna, set up a g-mail to all Gaardians, Piatek, and all of Walter's base crew."

"Ready."

Steve and Ooza put their arms around each other and then turned to the window. Ooza waved. "Hello, everyone. Steve and I would like to invite you to our wedding! It will be at the Gaardian Conference Center auditorium the day after tomorrow at midday Gaardian time."

Steve smiled. "Since this is short notice, some of you will not be able to come. We understand that completely."

"Please come if you can! Dress in anything you like that you think is for the occasion. We hope to see you there. Until then."

"Until then." Bahna vanished, and for all on the guest list Steve and Ooza vanished.

Meanwhile, at Ken and Keeta's quarters on Gaardian, Ken and Keeta were smiling at each other. The mother-to-be was beaming. "I want to go to that wedding!"

"I hope we can. Gaardian, how is Keeta's pregnancy coming along?"

"Everything is ready. If you wish, you can give birth tomorrow."

"I'm so glad! I want – Ouch! Ouch! Maybe I should give birth now!"

"Is that what you wish?"

Ken smiled at Keeta, who nodded. "Yes! Yes! Yes!"

Suddenly Keeta's stomach was almost flat, and they heard sounds coming from the nursery. Keeta looked at Ken questioningly, and the two of them went to the door of the nursery, which was enclosed by a force field. There were sounds of running and jumping, grunts and squeals, but they saw nothing.

Ken looked up. "Gaardian, we can hear Kenkee, but we can't see him."

"I have diapered him. I will modify your vision."

Suddenly they could see a gray image of Kenkee, running around the nursery, jumping over some of the furniture, and squealing with delight. He stopped in the middle of the room and let out a wail. Keeta smiled. "He's hungry. I can take care of this."

Keeta stepped through the force field and sat down in a chair. As Kenkee climbed up on her lap, Ken stepped through the force field to join them. Kenkee stuck his head into an opening in Keeta's shirt and began to nurse. The young mother looked down at her son. "He's nursing furiously, which is pretty typical of biyae infants."

Ken was smiling broadly. "I can't begin to describe to you how I'm feeling!"

"I know. I feel the same way."

Kenkee pulled his head out of the opening in Keeta's shirt and looked up at Ken, extending his arms. Ken reached out and picked him up in a gentle hug. As Ken relaxed his hug and looked at his son, Kenkee looked around the room. His inherited memories from Ken and Keeta, added to what he saw around him in the nursery, made him look about in wonder. Unlike his father, Ken, who was born without motor skills or sensory references, Kenkee's inherited memories enabled him to move about with uncanny skill. Like all biyae children, Kenkee was born with a skeleton and muscles that were well defined and solid. The electrical activity in Keeta's womb had been the result of the conflicting genetics of two species.

When Kenkee saw the doorway, he broke free from Ken and ran right through the force field. Ken and Keeta looked at each other in surprise, and then they ran to the door. They heard a wail. Kenkee came, slowly flying through the doorway, wailing his complaint because obviously he was being flown against his will. Ken and Keeta stepped aside as Kenkee flew on back through the doorway into the nursery.

Ken was puzzled. "Gaardian, what just happened?"

"The child has gifts neither of you have. I stopped the little angel in your bedroom and brought him back to the nursery. Until tomorrow, you must ask me to adjust the field for you to be able to enter and leave. Tomorrow I will make adjustments to your Gaardian ring parameters so you may have more control."

"Thank you, Gaardian." The mother smiled with relief.

"The little angel is asleep now. I suggest you take advantage of this and sleep yourselves. I will awaken you when he is hungry."

The new father looked at his son, who was now sleeping on a cushion. "Thank you, Gaardian. I am delighted that you refer to Kenkee as 'the little angel. Good night."

"The term seems appropriate. Good night."

Ken and Keeta embraced, and then they walked hand in hand to the bedroom.

+ + +

The next day, in their apartment above Quzak, Steve and Ooza walked into the living quarters holding steaming cups of liquid. Steve turned and kissed Ooza. As they broke, he pointed out the window. "Walter has loaned me an SVX to travel in today. I am first going to the Gaardian Conference Center auditorium to configure some decorations for tomorrow. Then I will go on to Walter's base. I will see you tomorrow at mid-morning, when you make your grand entrance. See you then, my love!" He kissed her.

"See you then, love!"

He vanished. The SVX outside the window pulled away. Piatek entered the room. "I want to watch. Is that okay?

Ooza smiled at her old friend. "Of course! Bahna?"

The android appeared. "I would like to introduce you to an android approximation of Bob Mackie, the designer of the dress you will be wearing."

A Bob Mackie look alike appeared. "Thank you for asking me to fit you. It is good to have one of my dresses used again. My! You are built like Linda Evans, except for being shorter and having three breasts of course. This will be fun!"

"Who is Linda Evans?"

"She's a fine actress who is no longer as young as you are. She wore the dress you are going to wear when she was about your age. Now, let's have a platform for you to stand on as I work. It should be about half a meter high I would think."

A platform appeared, and Ooza stepped up on it. "Here's the dress." It appeared on her, much too long for her.

"Amazing. I have to keep telling myself that I am not on Earth. Now, the dress must barely touch the tops of your shoes in front and flow to the back. It should fit you quite snugly, as though molded to your body." The dress changed as specified.

"How's this?"

"Something's wrong. What kind of bra are you wearing?"

"What's a bra?"

Bob grinned. "So that's it! Bahna?"

The other android appeared. "Yes?"

"Access your Earth database and look at Earth lingerie. Do Quzak women have anything like bras, corsets, and such?"

"No. Quzak clothing usually has a disposable liner, but supports and enhancements are built into each article of clothing."

Bob scowled, touching his face with a finger and tapping his foot. "Okay. Bahna, consider the way this gown made the natural curves of Linda Evans look best. I need to have those enhancements built into the dress for Ooza."

"Like this?"

The dress suddenly was form fitting, typical of Bob Mackie creations. The bodice had been adjusted for Ooza's body.

"Now, what are we going to do with your hair tomorrow?"

+ + +

In Ken and Keeta's quarters at Gaardian, Ken came out of the bedroom rubbing his head and yawning. He went to the nursery door and looked in. Keeta was sitting in a lounge chair nursing Kenkee. To his left he heard a knock on the door. "Come in!"

The door opened, and Jody and Qaak stepped in. "Good morning Ken. You look like you just got out of bed!"

Qaak chuckled. "I think he did. Did you and Keeta have a long night?"

"Good morning to you both. We got up twice because Kenkee needed to nurse. That's what Keeta is doing right now."

Jody went to the door. "That's so sweet. I cannot even get in with my Gaardian ring functions. What's going on?"

"Last evening Kenkee escaped the nursery just a few minutes after birth. Gaardian brought him back. We were told that today Gaardian will adjust our ring functions so that we can go in and out of the nursery freely without letting Kenkee escape."

Qaak's eyes glowed for a moment. He closed his eyes for about ten seconds, and then reopened them. "Indeed. Kenkee has been born with a very unusual ability. He can temporarily transform himself into pure energy. That is how he got through the first force field. Now the nursery is no longer surrounded by a normal energy barrier. It is a gravitational matrix that is unique to Gaardian."

Finished with nursing, Keeta put Kenkee on a cushion and approached the door. Suddenly Kenkee flashed toward the door, but he bounced back to the other side of the room. Keeta was instantly through the door. "Good morning all!" She yawned. "Forgive me. I am still sleepy. He is now hungry nearly every waking moment. Gaardian, did you explain to Qaak and Jody what happened yesterday?"

"Yes, I have explained it to Qaak, who has interpreted events to the rest. The little angel will only have this lack of control for a few weeks. I am providing the traditional discipline of a biyae nanny."

"You're better than a biyae nanny because you can communicate directly to his brain and bypass his undeveloped language skills."

"Are you going to be able to go to the wedding tomorrow morning?"

"We wouldn't miss it. We don't want to be away too long from Kenkee, but we want to go."

"Gaardian is already storing some of my milk so as to have it available while I am at the wedding. I told Gaardian I did not want Kenkee to have synthesized milk. When I am not nursing, Gaardian transports some of my milk into storage for later use. Gaardian is a great nanny."

There was a scratching sound at the apartment door. "Come in, Kieya!"

The door opened, and the big cat quietly padded in. "A distinct pleasure. Greetings all." They all nodded welcome to her. "Where is the little one? Ah!" She padded over to the doorway. "A gravitational matrix barrier. I cannot remember when I last saw one. May I go in?"

"Of course, but Gaardian has to...."

Before Keeta could finish her sentence, Kieya flowed as a blurred mass into the nursery.

Qaak chuckled; "I had forgotten that she can do that. She only rarely has occasion to use that gift." Kieya went to the middle of the room. Kenkee walked cautiously toward her. Kieya purred softly. Her fur rippled almost hypnotically as she settled down onto the floor. Kenkee put his head against Kieya's chest to hear the purr. Kieya's eyes closed slowly. His eyes started to droop, and soon he collapsed in a heap against her. Kieya opened her eyes, put a paw around him, and continued to purr. Outside the nursery's door, the others watched in wonder.

Gaardian spoke to all of them. "I can lower the gravitational matrix now. Kenkee is in a kind of stasis. Remarkable."

The force field at the door dissolved, and all of them entered. Keeta led the group to their side. Kieya spoke softly as she purred. "The best way to explain it is that I have put him to sleep with love. His life functions are essentially normal, but in terms of power he is on standby."

Jody giggled. "That's quite a trick, Kieya!"

Kieya purred softly and spoke softly. "Not really. My species never feeds at night. Parents love our children to sleep, and we keep them asleep until the parents have had enough rest to deal with their children again. I have shown Gaardian how to do it now, so the two of you can join us at the wedding."

Qaak's eyes glowed as he spoke softly. "May I touch your mind to understand?"

"Of course."

Qaak stepped forward and placed three fingers on Kieya's face. He closed his eyes briefly, and then opened them. "Indeed. I cannot do what you do because I do not have your gift. Keeta does however, but she does not know it. Keeta? Come, let me help you."

As Keeta got closer, Qaak placed three fingers on her face.

She blinked. "Amazing! I see it now. Kieya, let me take Kenkee."

Keeta reached down and took her son into her arms. His eyes opened briefly, but then they shut again. "It is so easy! It's amazing none of my people have learned this."

The father nodded. "Maybe when Kenkee is weaned you can teach it on your planet to others."

"Yes. It just might be a door past the prejudice of my people." She began humming softly, and sat down in the lounge chair.

Kieya padded softly out of the nursery, and the others followed. In the living room, Kieya turned. "Tomorrow is a long day for all of us. I am going to get some rest in my apartment." She turned and headed for the door, which opened.

Jody spoke softly but firmly. "Qaak, I think we should get some rest too. Ken and Keeta need their rest as well."

His eyes glowed briefly. "Indeed. Good night everyone!" Qaak and Jody follow Kieya out.

Ken looked at Keeta through the nursery door. "Keeta, do you want to bring Kenkee to bed with us? We can surround him with pillows." Keeta nodded, and brought Kenkee out of the nursery and into their bedroom.

+ + +

The next morning in the Gaardian Conference Center auditorium, Steve had decorated the arena for the wedding with elaborate splashes of white and green. A large pipe organ was arrayed across the front of the stage, with thousands of pipes ranging from the size of a pencil to sixty-four feet. The stage was lit by thousands of candles.

Quzak music began softly, playing in the background. Late arrivals were filing in from both sides of the arena. The music shifted to contemporary Earth-style praise music, some of which had been heard at the celebration at Walter's church just a few months earlier. Then the pipe organ began to play a J. S. Bach prelude. Walter entered, followed by Steve, Butch, Saahmn, and Qaak. They slowly walked across the large stage. Walter was wearing a white dinner jacket, and the others black tuxedoes. They stood there quietly as the Bach prelude concluded.

There was silence for a moment, and then the pipes of the pipe organ parted to reveal a one-hundred-piece symphony orchestra playing the finale of the third movement from Tchaikovsky's sixth symphony. Jody started down the long aisle from the rear. When she reached the front and turned to take her place, Pixie started down the aisle. Finally, Piatek came down the aisle. As Piatek took her position, the orchestra got louder with the final musical sequence. Ooza appeared wearing the Bob Mackie dress. The murmurs in the audience were drowned out by the sounds of the orchestra. Slowly she came down the long aisle. Ooza arrived at the front and took Steve's arm just as the music concluded. Tears were streaming down her face.

Walter's voice seemed to almost thunder across the arena. "Let us pray: Eternal God, creator of each of us present here, as well as the universe around us, Source of the love which grows among us; we seek you. This time is so very special to Ooza and Steve. We pray that as they join their hands, and bind their hearts to one another, that you will bind them together into your eternal love. In the name of Jesus, Amen. You may be seated."

Steve and Ooza looked at each other, beaming. Walter continued as the orchestra disappeared again behind the organ pipes. "Gaardians and Gaardian team members, we are gathered together here to join together Ooza and Steve in holy matrimony. Marriage is an estate of honor, instituted by God and carried through on nearly countless planets. We wish to impress upon Steve and Ooza the importance, the significance, and the sacredness of marriage, and to invoke on their behalf the blessings and love of God. With God as the third party in their marriage, Ooza and Steve will have a prayer-empowered partnership that can truly endure all that challenges them."

Above them a three-dimensional image of Earth appeared. The image zoomed in on the Middle East, and then zoomed further in, to focus on a town in ancient Israel. Walter continued. "On the planet Earth, Jesus the Savior performed his first miracle as He blessed a marriage in Cana of Galilee by turning water into wine. A wise teacher known as the Apostle Paul tells us that marriage should be entered into reverently, discreetly, advisedly, soberly and in fear of God." The image of Earth disappeared.

"Steve, will you have Ooza to be your wedded wife, to live together according to God's will in holy matrimony? Will you love Ooza, Steve, comfort her, honor, and keep her in all circumstances, and be totally faithful to Ooza so long as you both shall live?"

"I will."

"Ooza, will you have Steve to be your wedded husband, to live together according to God's will in holy matrimony? Will you love Steve, Ooza, comfort him, honor, and keep him in all circumstances, and be totally faithful to Steve, so long as you both shall live?"

"I will."

"Steve, will you please take Ooza's hands and offer your vows to Ooza."

"I, Steve, take you, Ooza, to be my wedded wife. I pledge and promise before God and these witnesses to be your loving and faithful husband -- in every circumstance, whether in joy or in sorrow, to love and to cherish you, Ooza, according to God's will."

"Now, Ooza, please offer the same vows to Steve."

"I, Ooza, take you, Steve, to be my wedded husband. I pledge and promise before God and these witnesses to be your loving and faithful wife -- in every circumstance, whether in joy or in sorrow, to love and to cherish you, Steve, according to God's will."

Walter looked up. "Eternal God, our Savior, giver of all that is good and creator of all, bless these, your servants, Ooza and Steve, that living faithfully together they may keep their vows and covenant. Let your love and peace go with them always. Look mercifully upon them, that they may love, honor, and cherish each other in a home that is a haven of blessing and peace." A glow began to fill the arena, which soon caused everything but those gathered there to fade. The thunder of the voice dwarfed that of the earlier sounds of the orchestra.

>"I am very pleased. Nearly everyone here sought me. Steve, you know me through my special child, Jesus, just as Qaak knows me through Qapoku, Xpraepostq knows me through Eiraynay, and others here know me by other names. Ooza, you brought a gift to my special child on the southern continent of your planet. In the years ahead, you will learn to know me through my child there. Steve, Ooza, choose to make me part of your marriage, and I will bless you beyond your imagining. Never be afraid, for I will always be with you."

The glow faded. Steve and Ooza embraced with tears running down both of their faces. Walter looked out over the rest of those gathered to witness the wedding and saw that they were all equally moved.

32. New Routines

A child's love can teach us many things. A month after the wedding, Ken and Keeta were watching Kenkee play in the nursery. The new mother beamed proudly. "He's on solid food after only a month! That's incredibly fast even for one of my species."

Ken agreed. "Yesterday he ate seven times. According to Gaardian, he is consuming about seven thousand calories a day! He is already up to forty-five pounds – how is this possible? Gaardian?"

"Light energy not only passes through him -- he utilizes it to build his body. The combined genetics of your two species have created a new being that includes the best of both and more. There is one negative aspect to his life -- he is sterile."

Ken and Keeta looked at each other. "Are you sure?" The young parents were stunned.

"Might that change as he grows?"

"It is certain and permanent. He does not have the necessary organs to produce adolescent sexual development of either species. He cannot reproduce."

Ooza was thoughtful. "Can Gaardian technology modify his genetic makeup while he is still young?"

Ken smiled. "Yes! I know that when some of Walter's crew were restored to their younger selves that in some cases adjustments were necessary."

"It would be extremely risky and probably fatal. I could attempt it, but it is very likely that he would lose the characteristics of a living sentient being."

Ken and Keeta were silent as they continued to watch Kenkee play.

Suddenly Kenkee stopped and walked to his parents. "Not bad sterile. Love you and life. May play outside?" Kenkee struggled with his grammar. The combined memories of his parents and their differing languages were a challenge to him.

Ken and Keeta looked at each other. Gaardian was reassuring. "It is safe for him to go outside. I will watch with you."

Ken shook his head. "I don't know . . . ."

His mother was more practical. "We can't keep him in the nursery forever, Ken. Kenkee, will you let your father and I hold your hands for a while as we take you outside?"

"Okay! We go now?"

Ken and Keeta got to either side of Kenkee and started walking with him to the nursery door. Together they walked on through the apartment and out into the atrium. Keeta looked down at her son. "You can play here in the rest of the complex for a while. We will go outside tomorrow. Okay?"

"'Kay!"

They released his hands, and he began running rapidly throughout the atrium. Kieya came out of her apartment. "Hello, Kenkee!"

"Auntie Kieya!"

"Auntie?" Kieya purred.

Kenkee got onto Kieya's back. He was so big his feet almost touched the ground. "Daddy had auntie he played with. You be auntie for Kenkee!"

Kieya began to purr as Kenkee rode her and she walked about in the atrium. Ken and Keeta were smiling. Kieya enjoyed herself. "Let's go see Uncle Qaak and Aunt Waagere."

"'Kay! Giddyap!"

Kieya walked through a nearby doorway and into Qaak's quarters. Qaak was looking out a portal onto the Gaardian landscape and sipping a cup of hot liquid. He turned. "Uncle Qaak! Uncle Qaak!"

Qaak's eyes glowed for a moment. "Hello, Kenkee! It is good to see you. Welcome to my home!"

Kenkee jumped off Kieya, ran over to Qaak, and gave him a hug. Qaak's eyes glowed again for a moment. "Kenkee want Qaak to take him outside tomorrow. Kay?"

Qaak looked directly at Kenkee. "I want to. I really do. I have to help another Gaardian tomorrow. Maybe Waagere or Kieya can go with you and your parents."

Kenkee let out a deafening wail. Qaak closed his eyes. Kenkee ran over to Kieya and got on her back. "Waagere! Waagere! Please! Fast!"

Kieya winked at Qaak, turned, and went out the door into the atrium. Kieya trotted rapidly to another doorway and went in. Waagere was coming into the entry area from another room. "What was that horrible sound? Was that you, Kenkee?"

Kenkee got off Kieya, and went and hugged Waagere. "Aunt Waagere, Qaak can't play outside tomorrow. Can Waagere?"

Waagere craned her neck forward to look down at Kenkee. "I'm very sorry, Kenkee! Waagere will be with Qaak tomorrow."

Kenkee wailed again, only softer this time. Waagere hugged little Kenkee. "Kenkee has his parents to play with. That's even better!"

Kenkee whimpered. "Really? Better?"

Waagere stroked his head and smiled. "Yes. Mommy can take you around and tell you about different things on Gaardian. Daddy can bring along food to share with you."

Kenkee began to smile. "Food? Really? Kenkee hungry now!"

Waagere's ring shimmered, and food appeared on a nearby table. "Let's eat something together, shall we?"

Keeta and Ken were standing at the doorway. "Daddy and I have to go to work for a while. Will you be good and stay with Waagere, Qaak, and Kieya? Gaardian will talk with you, too!"

"'Kay. Tonight?"

"We'll be home tonight." Ken and Keeta each gave Kenkee a hug.

His mother spoke softly to him, looking directly into his eyes. "We'll see you later, okay?"

"'Kay! Later!"

"Later!" His father smiled. Ken and Keeta vanished.

+ + +

In the atrium of Walter's moon base, Belinda was walking across the atrium from the mess hall to her office when Ken and Keeta appeared.

"Hi, Ken! Hi, Keeta! How's Kenkee?"

"Right now he's out visiting his aunts and uncles." He smiled.

"Aunts and uncles?"

Keeta giggled. "His aunts Kieya, Waagere, Jody, and his uncle Qaak."

Belinda laughed. "That's quite an extended family. I have jobs for both of you today. Ken, circulate in all parts of the base, and do an assessment of the emotional and spiritual health of the personnel. Keeta, when Walter comes out, he will send you to Pzalop. We want you to spend the next several hours with The Suppla and her mate, to get an unbiased picture of how things are going there. Ooza wants you to do the same at Quzak later in the week, with their leaders on both the equatorial continents. Next week we want you to visit the southern continent of Quzak to determine who the leaders are, and what's going on there."

"I'd better get started. See you later!" Ken kissed her lightly and headed for the mess hall.

Walter came out of his quarters. "Keeta! I am glad you are here. Hi, Belinda. Did Belinda tell you what I want you to do?"

"As I see it, surveillance of The Suppla. Should I check out the governing council?"

"Good idea, but make The Suppla your priority. I will leave it to your judgment. Gaardian will snatch you out of there after ten hours. Just record a g-mail report for me each day. I want you to do this for the next three days, possibly four. You and Ken will arrive home about the same time."

"Okay. How about I turn transparent and you send me straight to the Suppla's office?"

"Good." She faded, Walter's ring shimmered, and she was gone. "Debbie will be out in a few minutes. She wants to check on a few things with you before heading out to Aegeene. She's going to help Pixie there with a project today."

"I'll watch for her." Belinda turned and headed to her office.

"Thanks." Belinda waved behind her as she went. Walter headed down a hallway into the mess hall. In the middle of the hall to the right, Walter saw Butch and Paula.

As he approached their table, Paula looked up. "Good morning, Walter! Won't you join us?"

"Yes! Join us!"

"Thank you." Walter sat down at their table. His ring shimmered, and some food appeared in front of him.

"I was just telling Paula that she needs to think outside the box in terms of finding a calling here on base."

Walter smiled and nodded. "I agree. Almost everyone here is doing things that they had never done before. Ken and Toby would be two good people to talk to in that regard." Walter took a bite of food. "Butch, what's your assessment of Kenkee? Do you think that things are going well for him?"

Butch was thoughtful. Paula put her fork down to speak. "From what I hear that child is truly unique."

The medical officer nodded. "True. Biyaes naturally grow much faster than humans of course, but Kenkee is outpacing even his own species. I learn new things each day about him. Gaardian is excellent as a nanny, but I need further input."

"What about getting him a biyae doctor?"

Walter nodded. "That has occurred to me. Pixie might have an idea. She has two inter-species marriages in her crew, and some of them are turning into real genetic challenges. Keeta says she does not know enough about medical science on her planet to choose a doctor for Kenkee. On the other hand, she now knows that her species is capable of something she discovered on Gaardian. That might be the key to getting cooperation with her people."

Butch cocked his head. "What did she learn?"

"She watched Kieya put Kenkee to sleep with love. Qaak transferred the knowledge so that Keeta can do it. It is a gift even Qaak cannot duplicate, and it is rare among all species known to Gaardian space."

Butch was incredulous. "Puts him to sleep with love?"

"Right. I am not sure how the gift works, but you may want to study it scientifically. She or Kieya can hold Kenkee and put him into a kind of stasis. All bodily functions continue to be normal, but the brain is put in a kind of standby mode."

"Wow!"

Across the room at the doorway where he came in, Walter saw Asayak standing there. "Hello, Asayak. Do you need me for something?"

"Please."

"Butch, Paula, if you'll excuse me."

They looked over at the doorway. Butch nodded with a mouthful of food.

"Of course." Paula smiled.

Walter went to the door. Asayak turned and went down the hallway and into the atrium. Walter caught up with it as it paused near some tall plants.

"Please forgive the interruption. I asked Frank for the latest on Kenkee. Perhaps I can help. I am not sure about the ethics."

"Go on."

"I suggest that Keeta contact her planet's leaders for the best medical researcher they have. Then she can g-mail that researcher to ask for permission to form a mind link between that researcher and Butch. I can provide the link."

Walter smiled. "Brilliant! Let's give it a try." Walter looked up. "Frank, provide a record of this conversation to Keeta and Ken when they return to their quarters on Gaardian."

"Good. Now I would like to go to my planet and tell some of my own about what I have learned about my species by being part of the Gaardian team."

"Of course. I will let you go for a day or two any time, as often as needed. Be sure to come back tomorrow morning though. I think Ken and Keeta will take you up on your offer."

"Until tomorrow morning." It vanished. Walter was thoughtful.

+ + +

Meanwhile, in their apartment on Gaardian, Qaak and Jody were hugging. "I'm enjoying you both with two legs and with three, but I'm curious. How soon will you grow a third leg again?"

Qaak chuckled. "I guess you have not noticed. My new third leg is developing within the flesh of my oldest one. They will separate when development is sufficient. Hadn't you noticed how one of my legs has become heavier than the other?"

Jody giggled. "Actually I had, but I was not sure what it meant. That's why I asked."

There was a scratching at the door. "Come in, Kieya!"

As the door opened Kieya walked in, and Kenkee was right behind her. "Good morning! Kenkee wants to go outside. Ken is at Walter's base, and Keeta is secretly watching The Suppla on Pzalop. I have gotten a little behind in my duties. Would the two of you go outside with Kenkee?"

"Sounds like fun!" Jody grinned. "We were hoping we could! Is there anything outside on the planet's surface that we need to worry about?"

Kieya purred. "Not at all. Gaardian will keep Kenkee safe. More than anything, Kenkee wants others to watch him play.

"Not true! I can play by myself!"

Qaak chuckled as his eyes glowed for a moment. "I'm sure you can, Kenkee. Jody and I enjoy watching you play. That is what we want to do today. Maybe you can play by yourself tomorrow, okay?"

"'Kay!"

"I'll leave now. See you later, Kenkee!"

"Later!" Kieya vanished.

The triped extended a hand. "Come on, Kenkee, let's go outside. Gaardian, please monitor all three of us until we come back in."

"Agreed."

Holding Kenkee's hand, he led him outside. Jody walked beside them.

"Wow! This is great! Can I go over there to the falls?"

"Go ahead Kenkee."

Qaak released Kenkee's hand, and he began running toward the falls. He ran faster and faster, dodging among the plants, sometimes jumping over them.

"There's something you should know." The planet seemed mysterious.

"What's that?"

"Kenkee can fly."

Jody's eyes grew wide. "Really?"

"Yes. I can hold him here indefinitely of course. He's been flying around in his nursery for the last two days while others were asleep. I have never spoken to him, so he does not know he can communicate with me."

As they watched, Qaak addressed a question aloud to the planet rather than through his mind. "How is he able to fly?"

"His mother has always been able to adjust her mass in order to be totally transparent. His father is an excellent swimmer. Kenkee is learning to create inertia and adjust his mass. The result is that he mentally swims through my gravitational energy."

Qaak's eyes glowed for a moment. "Indeed. You need to inform Ken and Keeta this evening. What about the rest of his development?"

"He appears to be healthy and developing at a rate which is natural for him. I have no more experience with his new species than you do. Walter is taking steps to remedy this."

They watched as Kenkee waved and then dove into the large whirlpool at the base of the falls. They waved back.

Jody spoke aloud as well. "What is Walter doing?"

"Asayak has proposed a mind link between a medical researcher on Keeta's planet and with Butch. It is being arranged. I will report it to Ken and Keeta upon their return. Keeta already has her new use of an old gift to consider. Asayak can help her develop her gift further."

"Excellent! Asayak's gifts are amazing."

"Yes. Today Asayak is on his planet telling others about the gifts he has discovered within himself with the help of Walter, Butch, and you."

Jody waved at Kenkee as he reappeared at the top of the falls, ready to dive in again. "Hi, Kenkee!"

Kenkee waved back, and then he dove. He did not reach the whirlpool. Instead, he swooped up into the air like a glider. "Whee!"

Qaak and Jody stared in disbelief. Jody spoke quietly. "Gaardian, be sure to save a video record of this."

"Of course."

Kenkee swooped directly at Jody and Qaak. Jody started to duck, but Qaak's eyes glowed as he raised a palm toward him. Kenkee came to an abrupt halt and barely landed on his feet in front of them. "Why did you stop me Uncle Qaak?"

Qaak looked him straight in the eyes. "You can have fun with your flying, but you must not threaten anyone with it. Understood?"

Kenkee dropped his eyes. "Yes, Uncle Qaak."

"You can go back to playing. Just remember the Golden Rule."

"Yes, Uncle Qaak." Kenkee ran off, faster and faster, until he began gliding again.

"It's kind of like being a grandparent, isn't it?"

Qaak cackled. "Yes!"

+ + +

Several days later, Walter and Debbie were walking arm in arm out of the lounge to their apartment. She was in her last month of pregnancy, "It's been a long day. When are we going to take a couple of days off again?"

Walter was thoughtful. "Well, tomorrow Butch is going to get a mind meld with a medical researcher on Keeta's planet, but I don't have to be there --

Asayak's taking care of it. Ken and Keeta are going to spend the day hiking the panorama trail in Yosemite. It's mid-May on Earth, and Yosemite's falls are very full."

"What are Jody and Qaak up to?"

Walter smiled. "Today they were babysitters for Kenkee. They saw him fly."

Debbie is awestruck. "Fly! You're kidding!"

Walter grinned. "No. I saw some video a while ago with Butch. He can swoop up and down kind of like a glider."

Debbie smiled. She patted her stomach. "That's incredible! I wonder if our boy will be envious."

He smiled. "You want to hear something even more fantastic?"

Debbie looked at him quizzically. "What?"

"Earlier today Steve took Ooza to Alaska as the kind of grand finale to their honeymoon. They walked into a Tlingit village."

"What are Tlingits?"

"They're Native Americans. Ooza neglected to disguise her body, and the women there expressed appreciation for her figure. They assumed she was simply an unusual human woman since she was with Steve. Steve and Ooza are spending the last night of their honeymoon tonight in a yurt."

Debbie laughed. "A yurt?"

Walter laughed too. "A yurt!"

They walked into their apartment. Debbie spoke quietly. "Getting back to earlier in this conversation, I'd like to go to Gaardian for a few days. Now that Kenkee is flying, maybe we can do a little babysitting ourselves and get a break at the same time."

"Sounds good. Let's get some sleep and go first thing in the morning." A glow began to fill the room, and the features of their surroundings disappeared.

> **"You will not go to Gaardian tomorrow. The time has come for your first baby to be delivered, Debbie. He will be strong and wise, and will need nurture from both of you. Enjoy this time together. There will be only one demand of you as Gaardian convener for the next eight days. Be at peace. I am with you."**

The glow faded.

They looked at each other. Debbie's face grimaced. "Ow! I think I just had a contraction!"

"Frank?"

The android appeared. "First contraction?"

Debbie nodded. "Yes."

"I'll have Butch to meet you in the clinic."

Walter shook his head. "No. Have him come here. She can have the baby here at home. The clinic's less than fifty meters from here."

"Very well." The android disappeared. Walter and Debbie walked to the bedroom.

33. Haydzees ["HAYd-zees"]

Walter had been battling evil in many forms during both lifetimes. He was now to be challenged with something new. At Ooza's apartment and base, Piatek was staring at Quzak planet below. She looked up at the ceiling. "Bahna?"

The android appeared. "Yes?"

"I don't like this. We do not have anywhere near close to a full crew, few of them are trained, and Ooza and Steve will not be back for half a day. Is there another Gaardian available?"

Bahna paused. "I'm connecting you via email to Kieya. She is on her way back from a mission to Gaardian in her vehicle."

A g-mail image appeared showing Kieya at the controls of her vehicle. "Hello, Piatek! What's the problem?"

"Long range sensors show a fleet of ships approaching from just outside our sector of Gaardian space. They are of unknown origin. They appear to be headed to Quzak. At their current rate of speed they'll be here in less than three solar cycles."

"Good work, Piatek. I will investigate and be back to you within one time period."

"Thank you. Until then."

"Until then." The feline vanished.

In her vehicle, Kieya manipulated her controls. The stars streaked by more and more rapidly. "Priority G-mail to Walter, Qaak, Waagere, Xpraepostq, and Ooza. A fleet of unknown vehicles is approaching from outside of Gaardian space and appears to be arriving at Quzak in three Quzak solar cycles. I am investigating. I will be at the conference center in one-half time period. Meet me there if you can. End g-mail."

Working the controls, she put the vehicle under cloaking and went to sub-light speed. As her vehicle slowed, she saw thousands of spacecraft moving in her direction. Her ship passed through them undetected. She came about and followed them. "Personal journal: Propulsion technology is level three. Scanning shows weapons level four, the same as Quzak weapons. Beaming to conference center after passing through a few stars. End journal." There were flashes of light, and then her ship came to a halt outside the conference center suspended over Gaardian. She vanished from her vehicle.

In the atrium, Kieya appeared in the foyer and padded quietly to the auditorium. She saw Walter, Waagere, Xpraepostq, and Ooza. Qaak was not there. Puz appeared and walked beside her.

Walter nodded at the cat as she arrived. "Tell us what you saw, Kieya."

They sat down in a circle near the entrance of the auditorium. As Kieya spoke, a three-dimensional display appeared in the center of the circle, illustrating her flight. "As you can see there are many space craft, but their propulsion technology is level three and weapons are level four."

Walter nodded. "Discussion?"

Ooza was intense. "I don't like this. Based upon their heading, we should have seen them coming a long time ago. Either they are not on a straight trajectory, or they have higher than level three propulsion."

Two chimes sounded. A g-mail of Piatek appeared. "Good! I am glad to see so many of you. Those ships are now less than one solar cycle away."

Kieya slowly blinked. "Not at level three! This is truly strange!"

Qaak appeared, walked over, and joined the circle. "Not strange, Kieya. ... Haydzees."

Waagere stared. "Haydzees? The last time we encountered them, they disappeared without a trace. We haven't seen them in hundreds of Gaardian years."

"Not hundreds. More than three thousand. It was like trying to catch a plume of gas. Not this time."

"What is different, Qaak?"

His eyes glowed intensely for an instant. "Me! I knew they would be back eventually. I have prepared for that eventuality. What is our complement?"

"My crew will have *The Grace* here soon. Pixie has her crew, and her ship is already here. Waagere?"

"My crew is handling that environmental disaster we discussed. They can handle it without me, but none of them can be spared."

"Kieya?"

"I have my full crew."

"Excellent. Ooza, I know you do not have a working crew yet. You and those you have recruited thus far can join us aboard *The Grace*. You can join me on the bridge and have Piatek and the others go where you think best. Waagere, you go with Pixie. Qaak, you go with Kieya and her crew."

"Good. Glad to have you join us, Waagere."

"Qaak, what preparations do we need to make?"

Qaak's eyes glowed for a moment. "I will teach you. Make the circle continuous." They all held hands or in some way touched one another. Qaak closed his eyes, which began to pulsate in their glowing. The others' eyes drooped and closed. It lasted about twenty seconds.

"That's truly innovative, Qaak! I'm sure it will work."

"It should. They have probably changed since we last encountered them. Be on guard. They are creatures of nearly pure energy and very dangerous. They cannot harm Gaardians and those with Gaardian ring support, but they can deceive us or trick us. Keep focused. With The Creator's help we will succeed."

Walter looked up. "Jesus, we don't have to hear your voice to know you are present to us. We trust you. Help us to be faithful to what you have called us to be." Walter looked around at all of them. His ring shimmered. "All right! Kieya and Pixie, issue your orders to your crewmembers. Mine were just issued." Everyone else's rings shimmered for a moment. "We all know what we have to do. Let's do it. Ooza, we'll grab Piatek, Steve, and the others on the way." Almost simultaneously, they all vanished.

On the bridge aboard *The Grace*, everyone was at their stations. Walter and Ooza appeared. As Walter went to the captain's chair, Ooza joined Asayak at the weapons station.

John looked up from his pilot's controls. "How soon do we get under way?"

"Now, John!"

"Right!" He touched his console a couple of times, and the stars in the main view screen quickly blurred.

"Karen, keep me posted on Debbie – check with Belinda periodically. We now have a son, Joseph, who was born a couple of hours ago."

"Congratulations!" Congratulations were expressed by others on the bridge.

"Thanks, all of you. I wish I could be there right now, but Debbie understands. Karen, Ooza has the bridge when I leave. Tell engineering and communications not to concern themselves with the status, position, or activities of either Pixie's ship or Kieya's. We each have a job to do. If one of them gets into difficulty they will notify me."

Karen was incredulous. "What kind of difficulty can we have? I didn't think Gaardian ships got into difficulty!"

"This is different." Walter touched a panel on his console. "Attention everyone. We are facing a different kind of adversary. They cannot harm Gaardians or those with Gaardian ring support, but they are masters of deceptions and lies. They are composed of almost pure energy, and they can assume virtually any form. Be very careful. Go over your orders again now if you must, then do not look at them again until the mission is over. Follow your orders. Stay with your orders, and things will turn out fine."

Karen spoke succinctly. "Steve, Piatek, and the others in Ooza's crew just came on board. They're at their stations."

"Good. Asayak, let Ooza take over your station. Ooza, put us under cloak until the mission is over. Asayak, I have a special task for you. It is something you don't know you can do."

The creature stepped aside and let Ooza take over. "This sounds interesting. How may I serve?"

"In a moment I want you to go to your quarters. There, I want you to use your telepathic prowess to erect a barrier just under the ship's cloak so that sentient energy cannot penetrate it."

"Sentient energy?"

"Yes. You will have to think about it before you do it. I want you to stop any energy that is associated with coherent thought." Walter closed his eyes for a moment.

"Yes. I think I understand. Yes! I do understand. It shall be done!" The creature vanished.

Walter touched a panel. "Walter to Jody."

"Yes sir?"

"John is going to keep us about two kilometers from the Haydzees. Stay with your orders no matter what, understood?"

"Understood."

"Proceed. John, the same goes for you. It is critically important that you stay with your orders."

"Right."

"Karen, we'll be at communications shut down in about two minutes. Stay with the script. Do not be tempted. You've got your orders for when I leave the bridge."

"Absolutely."

Walter looked around the bridge and up at the view screen. The Haydzee fleet was coming into view. "All right everyone. You have your orders. I trust you to abide by them. Go with God." He vanished before anyone murmured back 'Go with God.'

Ooza spoke firmly. "All right everyone. All communications inside as well as outside of the ship are shut down. As Walter puts it, 'stay with the script!' Walter knows I will back anyone up who needs help here on the bridge. I've had more battle experience than any of you, but this is going to be different -- very different!"

In his red SVX, Walter's vehicle was cloaked, and he and the ship were semi-transparent. Walter saw the three Gaardian ships positioned around the Haydzee fleet. There was a much larger space ship just in front of him. A pair of crosshairs appeared on his console view screen, which he centered on that larger ship.

"Personal journal. Everyone is in place. I am about to plunge my SVX through the Haydzee command ship. As it becomes energized and follows me, I will plunge through all the other Haydzee ships. Ramming the command ship signals the other Gaardian ships to fire Qaak's special weapons. This should work. May God be glorified by what we do today. End journal. Here goes the whole shooting match!"

Walter touched a control. At high speed, he rammed into the Haydzee command ship. It bloomed into brilliant energy, and it attempted to envelop Walter's ship. On cue, the other three Gaardian ships fired Qaak's specially designed weapons throughout the Haydzee fleet, but none of the weapons seemed to strike their targets.

As Walter's speed increased with the penetration of each Haydzee ship, a growing plume of energy gathered around Walter and trailed behind him like a comet. Several streaks of energy broke away from Walter's ship and streaked toward the other three ships. They bounced off Walter's ship but penetrated the other two. Suddenly *The Grace* turned and plunged between the other two Gaardian ships. As it did, streaks of energy left the two Gaardian ships in pursuit of *The Grace*, which began to parallel the course taken by the SVX.

Suddenly and simultaneously, *The Grace* and the SVX came to a complete stop. The Haydzee energy plunged forward, and as it slowed to a stop formed a huge brilliant ball.

Inside his SVX he was smiling, Walter reached into a dark container and brought out a large pale purple crystal, about two hundred carats in size. Walter's ring shimmered, and the crystal disappeared. A plume of energy erupted from the Haydzee energy ball and headed for Walter's SVX. The plume formed a sharp point as it shot into the crystal outside of the SVX. The Haydzee ball became more and more brilliant as it shot its energy into the crystal. It rapidly shrank until all the Haydzee energy was within the crystal.

Walter simply watched. When all was complete, Walter's ring shimmered, and the crystal reappeared in his hand. This time there was a tiny shimmering point of light at the center of the crystal. "G-mail to all three ships that have been battling the Haydzees. Concluding message to initiate normal communications and fully normal status: 'We have gone with God. Mission complete.'" He paused. "Well done! I want to see Qaak and Asayak in my quarters aboard *The Grace* as soon as possible." Walter and the SVX vanished.

The SVX reappeared on the hanger deck of "*The Grace.*" Walter disappeared from within the SVX.

In his quarters, Walter appeared with the crystal in his hand. He took a seat in a recliner near an outside portal.

Qaak appeared. "Well done indeed! We had The Creator's help. Ooza will send Asayak momentarily."

Asayak appeared and glided over to the two Gaardians. A recliner appeared that was similar to Walter's, and Qaak sat down. Asayak oozed down to their level, leaving part of its body behind it, away from the other two.

Its voice could be heard by both. "A unique experience. Are all the Haydzees and their ships within the alexandrite crystal?"

"Indeed. Walter, do you have a plan? Gaardian rules preclude our destroying the Haydzees. Apart from destruction, what do you suggest?"

The hairy one stirred. "Is their no exception so that we can destroy them?"

"No. Using a combination of our gifts and those of Gaardian, we could beam the crystal to the center of a very large inert body for nearly permanent entrapment. We could also put the crystal into functional exile by beaming it to a distant spot several googol times the size of Gaardian space away from here."

"We can do this?"

Qaak chuckled. "Indeed. With teamwork, we can. Both are interesting ideas. Which to choose?"

Walter's quarters began to glow. The hairy one grew to its full height. "What is happening?"

"Just wait, Asayak." The glow enveloped the room and everything disappeared except the three of them.

> "Asayak, I am The Creator of all. Do not be afraid. The others know me as Jesus or Qapoku. You may call me Creator. I am pleased that you choose to stay within the Gaardian guidelines I gave long ago through Qaak and Kieya. I know you would destroy the Haydzees if I told you to. You are mine. The Haydzees are also mine. I will deal with them according to my plan. Trust me. ... I am God. ... I forgive. ... I redeem. ... I make all things new."

The glow faded. All were silent for a moment.

Asayak oozed down to his lower height again. "I do not know what to say."

Walter smiled. The crystal in his hand disappeared. "Just report what you have seen and heard."

"Agreed." Walter and Qaak vanished. The creature rose to its full height, and then it disappeared as well.

On the bridge, Asayak appeared near its weapons station. Ooza was in the command chair. Asayak's voice could be heard throughout the bridge. As it spoke telepathically, all turned to it.

"I now report to the bridge crew. This is also a g-mail to the bridges of the other two ships. I have met and heard The Creator along with Walter and Qaak. Walter has gone to be with Debbie. Qaak has returned to Gaardian. The Creator is in command of the Haydzees. With The Creator's help, our mission has been accomplished. Let us go home. End g-mail."

The bridge crew looked around at each other. Ooza stepped down into the command chair. "You heard Asayak! Let us go home! Drop Steve and me along with our crew at my base on your way."

John's hands rapidly flew over his control panel. "Right! Course laid in and executed. We'll be at your base in less than thirty seconds." On the view screen, stars streaked by.

+ + +

Some time later in Ooza's apartment, Ooza, Piatek, Steve, Kieya, and Waagere were sitting and facing each other.

Ooza was smiling. "First, thank you to all of you for your work out there. From the time I became of age, I have been in military operations. That was a battle – however short – beyond my wildest dreams!"

Piatek sat forward in her chair, the way she used to when she appeared to be much older. "This is a very different world for me. To engage in battle without destroying your adversary had only been a thought I would discard. Now I understand the concept of discipline without conquest. One of the texts that Walter loaned me calls it 'tough love.'"

The others nodded. Kieya began purring before she spoke. "Your crew, Ooza, is still small, yet performed very well. I am impressed with their quality. Steve, what has been your role in this?"

Steve smiled and nodded at Ooza. "Ooza put me in charge of recruitment. I depend upon Piatek and her gifts to help me read what is in the minds and hearts of candidates. Our crew includes members of three species, and the balance of male to female is about even."

"That has been a challenge for Piatek, the other Quzaks, and me." Ooza was calm. "It is very different being a Gaardian. We are used to having the males at the center of activity, while the females plan in the background. Equality is a worthwhile challenge, but a challenge nonetheless."

Piatek nodded.

Waagere craned her neck forward before she spoke. "To change subjects, I was at first concerned that Kieya had miscalculated the propulsion and weapons levels of the Haydzees before they were identified."

Ooza nodded. "Yes, I'm curious. What happened?"

"A video file will illustrate. Bahna, show us a video of Walter's SVX colliding with the Haydzee mother ship in extreme slow motion."

In the middle of their rough circle, a three-dimensional video appeared. As Walter's ship appeared to shatter the hull of the Haydzee mother ship, hundreds of beings were exposed within. Slowly the various parts of the ship seemed to be absorbed into the beings, and then they came together into one cohesive ball of light that pursued the SVX. The video ended.

Kieya purred. "An amazing sight even for one who has seen them do it before. Their ship does not exist separately from them. They exercise large-scale teamwork to create a ship that is actually an extension of them."

Waagere's head swayed back and forth, as she nodded. "Yes. This was a new technique on their part. In our previous encounters, they had created ships separate from them, that they only discarded when they were no longer needed. Previously, when they discarded their ships they turned them into energy and absorbed them. Since this looked new I did not recognize them at first. It was excellent camouflage."

"What did Walter do with them?"

Kieya continued to purr. "As you know, it was part of Qaak's plan to absorb them into a Gaardian alexandrite crystal similar to the ones in our rings. Once inside the oversized crystal they continued to live, but in stasis."

Waagere nodded. "According to Asayak, the discussion in Walter's quarters was over what to do with the crystal. They considered two types of exile for the Haydzees."

Piatek stared. "Could they not be sent back to their home planet?"

"No. They have no home planet. Their species developed on the surface of a blue star, but we do not know how. One exile option was to place the Gaardian stone at the center of a very large and cold planet. The other was to send the crystal a great distance across the universe. Neither option was chosen."

"Yes. The Creator intervened. Since the Haydzees are children of The Creator just as we are, The Creator took them."

"Took them? Where?" Piatek's gazed intensely.

Waagere laughed. "A wonderful but paradoxical question. It is true that The Creator can place them anywhere -- and at any time -- in the universe. The Creator could place them so far away from us that they could not make a journey to us in thousands of Gaardian lifetimes."

Piatek nodded. "So why is that paradoxical?"

Kieya rumbled a low laugh amidst the purring. "Simply this: Since The Creator created all of life, matter, energy, space, and time, The Creator exists apart from the entire universe. The Creator is not limited by having to take the Haydzees to any 'where', or even any 'time.' The options are infinitely endless from the point of view of all of us in The Creator's creation."

Piatek's eyes closed, and her body began to glow slightly. She opened her eyes suddenly and stared. "Yes! It is beyond our logic. It is true! It is real! ... I can't explain it!" Ooza smiled.

Epilogue: Coming Full Circle

34. Pause

It has been affirmed many times on Earth and elsewhere, "No news is good news." That is not always true.

In their apartment on Earth's moon, Walter and Debbie were on their bed, leaning against many large pillows. Debbie had their son, Joseph, in her arms as she nursed him. Walter constantly shifted his gaze from their son to Debbie. There was a chime at their apartment door, outside of their bedroom.

Walter called out. "Come in!"

Butch walked through the outer living area and into the bedroom. As he saw them, he smiled. "Good afternoon! How's Joseph?"

Debbie smiled. "He was a bit fussy until I started nursing him a few minutes ago."

"How about his daily scan now?"

"Sure!"

Butch stepped forward, and a dim beam of light came from his Gaardian ring and swept first over the baby, and then over Debbie. He smiled. "It appears that both mother and son are doing fine. I have my ring set up so that it not only records images and data for the clinic but also sends samples directly to my visual cortex. It was Frank's suggestion, and I like it."

Walter looked up at Butch. "That's great. What's the latest on the other children?"

"Amanda is doing fine. James and Dawn are excited with her growth, and Belinda is enjoying being her godmother."

Debbie looked up from the baby. "Fantastic! What about Kenkee?"

Butch laughed. "Kenkee is flying all over Gaardian. Jody told Qaak that he reminds her of a cherub, flitting about from place to place. Gaardian calls him its little angel. He will not be that little very much longer. He is in Ken's equivalent of adolescence and having a growth spurt. I figure he will be over six feet six in five months or so. He not only eats with his parents, aunts, and uncles, but he also munches constantly on the plant life on Gaardian. He will be very muscular and strong."

Walter chuckled, and then he was more serious. "There's a down side, isn't there?"

Butch was thoughtful. "Yes. Two actually. He is sterile, so Ken and Keeta will not have any grandchildren. I think more offspring will produce the same result."

"The other down side?"

"All my test results confirm that he needs strong gravity to be healthy. One day Qaak was playing with him and had Gaardian reduce gravity to zero in the nursery. Immediately Kenkee's vital signs began to deteriorate. When Gaardian increased gravity in the nursery to several times normal he got stronger and stronger."

Debbie spoke more softly because the baby was asleep. "Really! What about ring support?"

Butch nodded. "I thought of that and suggested it to Qaak. He said that when Kenkee is an adult we can try it, but he has his doubts."

Walter scowled. "Why?"

"Qaak says he's encountered a couple of other beings that have been gravity dependent. For some reason, Gaardian ring support provides only limited and temporary help. On the other hand your son Joseph not only is a normal and healthy human, I'm beginning to get clues to his special gift."

Debbie's and Walter's eyes grew wide. "Really?"

"How so?"

Butch grinned. "Ever since I learned that The Creator said he would have a special gift I've been comparing Joseph's physiology to a large database I've created from the medical records of millions of humans. Gaardian technology makes that easy."

"And ...?"

"Two clues have emerged thus far. First, his nervous system is similar to those of quite a number of professional artists. Second, his brain configuration is similar to that of thousands of humans whose occupations require them to have excellent memories."

Debbie smiled. "Among artists, the better actors have excellent memories."

"As do concert pianists. So do comedians who do stand-up work."

"It's also true of surgeons and others who do highly skilled creative work."

Debbie was thoughtful. "We can provide guidance, but all of this has to develop as God wills."

Walter nodded. "True."

"Listen, I've got some other clinical work that has to be done today. I promised Paula that we could take a few days for a delayed honeymoon."

Walter nodded. "Good idea. I didn't tell you before, but Debbie and I really enjoyed invisibly watching you two get married in that old historic chapel in Yosemite."

Butch grinned. "I'll pass that on to Paula. The people you saw there were some of her old friends who know how to keep a secret."

Walter and Debbie laughed. "We recognized Tawny Gannon, Barbara Jones Smelter, Deborah Lopez, Tamara Williams, and Jeri Eng. We will always remember their first visit here to the moon. I saw them all there with escorts. Are they all married now?"

Butch laughed. "Those men were the ones you let come to the Christmas party the following year. That party turned out to be a catalyst for all of them. Barbara Jones Smelter is getting married to her fiancé next month at Saint Paul's cathedral in London. The others have all gotten married within the last year. Even Paula's ex-fiancé is now married."

Debbie smiled. "Fantastic!"

"Anyway, Paula and I decided that since this time of year is so beautiful in Greece, that we're going to take a little cruise of Crete, Santorini, and a couple of other islands, and then end up on Patmos."

"I've been to those islands. I'm sure you'll have a great time. Tell Paula not to be afraid to use her debit card I gave her to buy some things she wants for herself and for you."

Butch smiled again. "She does love to shop! Thanks again. I'll see you in a few days."

"Until then."

See ya later!" Butch turned and went on out. Debbie passed Joseph over to Walter, and they snuggled together. The room began to get the familiar glow.

> "I am very pleased. Walter, tomorrow you will again be asked to address the United Nations. I will be on your lips and in your heart. You have led Qaak to both romance and usefulness in his retirement. Ooza and her crew are learning the value of love. The Zargadetes are discovering a treasure of creativity. Gaardian is developing a relationship with Kenkee. Your son will help humans find new life for their lost souls. My creation continues. I forgive. I redeem. I make things new again."

+ + +

A week later, the United Nations General Assembly hall was buzzing with excitement. A little before ten in the morning the representatives began taking their places and putting on their earphones. Everyone kept glancing up at one of the clocks. At precisely ten, Walter appeared at the podium. Applause began. It grew louder as people begin standing. The ovation lasted almost a minute. Walter nodded in several directions, smiling. Then he motioned for silence. Everyone took their seats, and there was almost total silence.

"I want to thank all of you for inviting me to address this body today. A lot has happened since I was last here. When I was asked to come a week ago, I was told that there were three particular questions of general interest to all of you. I will address those questions first, and then I will respond to particular questions." There was quiet murmuring among several of the delegates and in the gallery.

"The first question I will address is regarding the disappearance of thousands of criminals." There was scattered applause. "My associates and I scanned Earth's records of many individuals who had engaged in various sorts of anti-social behavior that were particularly damaging to society. Most of these individuals were in prison at the time of their disappearance, but admittedly, some were not. As I am speaking, disks are appearing before you that provide essential information about all of these individuals." A disk appeared in a platinum case in front of each United Nations delegate. There was louder murmuring, then quiet ensued again as Walter continued speaking,

"Gaardian technology is able to confirm any and all evidence against criminals, but as usual I will not reveal how. All of these individuals have confirmed records of criminal violence. None of these people will incur any further expense to Earth society. All of these individuals are alive and well, but they are in permanent exile on another planet in another galaxy." The assembly burst into applause, and Walter got another standing ovation. After about fifteen seconds, Walter motioned for silence. "At the end of the disk in your possession there is information on how each criminal may be contacted by family or friends once every three months." There was scattered applause.

"The second general question was regarding the production and distribution of illegal drugs. Some of you may recall the women journalists visiting my base on our moon. At that time, I told them that this problem was being addressed. My associates at the base are addressing this continuing problem. We will only assist you to a certain point. You delegates, along with law enforcement leaders in your countries, must address the problem as well. If you have specific requests for help, we will consider those requests, but only up to a point. If Earth's leaders do not have the political courage to address the problems effectively, then my continuing to help will be a waste of time." There was strong applause.

"The third general question was regarding nuclear weapons." There was total silence in the room. "I will make this offer to you. If there is a unanimous vote by this body – unanimous with no abstentions or exceptions – that I dispose of all nuclear waste and all nuclear weapons stockpiles, I will do so with this clear understanding: I will make absolutely no exceptions and play no favorites." There was silence for a few seconds. Then there was a thunderous standing ovation. It lasted for over a minute.

Walter motioned for silence. "Now I will answer a few questions for individual delegates. ...Yes, the gentleman from France."

The French ambassador stood up and spoke in nearly flawless English. "A few minutes ago you talked about criminals who have disappeared. There have been some prominent people who have disappeared, who were not convicted of any criminal activity. Will you speak to this issue? Also, may we know your given name?"

Walter smiled. "Of course. My given name is Walter. It will be a few more years before I reveal my family name. With regard to your primary question, I believe you are speaking of the over three dozen political leaders who suddenly disappeared." There was total silence in the hall. "I believe that it was their disappearance that precipitated the request for my appearance today." The ambassador from France and several others nodded. "I can understand your concern. As I told you just moments ago, on those disks, you will find evidence on all those who have disappeared. I also said that while most that disappeared had been in jail, that some had not been. Thirty-seven political leaders from twenty-three countries had overwhelming evidence gathered against them by independent non-governmental organizations around the world. After confirming that evidence, those people were put into exile." There was murmuring among the delegates. "I will also tell you another thing that is confirmed on the disks. There were seventeen assassins put into exile who had never been convicted of a crime. The evidence of their crimes is on those disks, and that evidence will provide resolution to hundreds of unsolved murders."

The United States ambassador stood up. "I would like to ask about your offer to rid our planet of nuclear weapons. How can you –and we -- possibly be sure that all weapons are removed?"

Walter nodded. "I will not reveal Gaardian technology, so I will give you a metaphor. When you prepare pasta, you use a sieve to separate the pasta from the water in which you have been boiling it. Last year, when all the cocaine on the planet disappeared I used a tool that is somewhat like an atomic sieve. The sieve was configured to only recognize and remove the combination of chemicals that make up cocaine. That particular sieve passed through everything from fifty thousand meters above the Earth's surface to twenty thousand meters below. There was no cocaine on Earth again until growers again produced it. Gaardian technology can do the same thing with radioactive isotopes, only I would pass the sieve through the entire planet." There was stunned silence. "I repeat what I said before: I will only do this upon a unanimous request by all of those present at the vote. It is against Gaardian regulations to interfere with the affairs of individual planets unless requested, or unless that planet's activities interfere with the welfare of other planets. Are there other questions?"

The Russian ambassador stood. He spoke excellent English but with an accent. "We work with several other countries to maintain a space station in orbit above the Earth. Will you assist us in our efforts and explorations?"

Walter smiled. "Our planet's scientists have done very well in this latest effort. I have been justly proud. My staff has strict instructions not to interfere with your efforts unless there is an emergency. We will not give new science or technology to you, any more than we will give it to scientists of other planets. What I can do is help you fine tune what you have, and sometimes point you in productive new directions for discovery. This is a good question with which to end this visit for me, because I will close with an announcement."

Walter paused. "Over the last several months my engineering team and science team have been gathering some very interesting data. There have been some events in other galaxies that have been very provocative. At the speed of light, Earth's telescopes would not see these events for several thousand years. In a few hours, high definition video with audio narration will be provided through satellite feed. The video and audio will be accompanied by a high-density data stream. That is all for now. I will appear here again as need arises." Walter disappeared.

+ + +

In their apartment, Debbie was watching the United Nations event on a screen when Walter appeared. "Well done! What do you think, Joseph?" She looked down at their son in her arms.

"Thanks. What do you say we take a break? Where would you like to go?"

Debbie was thoughtful. "Shall we take Joseph along?"

"Why not? He can go wherever we go. On the other hand, if you want it to be just us, Belinda has been waiting for you to ask her to babysit."

Debbie grinned and looked across the room blankly. "Frank, ask Belinda to come to our apartment."

"Okay, so if Belinda is babysitting, you still haven't answered where you'd like to go." There was a knock at the door. "Come in!"

"Hi! What's up?" Belinda walked over to them to look at Joseph.

Debbie looked at her. "How'd you like to babysit for a while?"

Belinda beamed. "Sure! Take all the time you want! Where are you going?"

"I'm not sure. Debbie hasn't told me."

Debbie gave Joseph to Belinda. "I just fed him a few minutes ago. He should be taking a nap soon." She turned to Walter. "I'm going to surprise you. Take my hand. We'll use my ring."

Walter smiled and waved at Belinda. "See ya later!"

Debbie looked at Belinda and Joseph. "Mommy will be back in a while Joseph! Bye, Belinda." Debbie's ring shimmered, and they vanished.

A moment later, they reappeared in the midst of some large and colorful trees. Walter looked at Debbie and smiled. "Aegeene, huh? I wouldn't have thought of this!"

"This is not Aegeene."

Walter looked around. "No, I guess it isn't, though it looks a good bit like it. Where are we?"

"Walk with me." Arm in arm they walked amongst the trees. They came to a clearing, and about fifty meters away they saw some homes. A sun was very low on the horizon, and stars were twinkling overhead. "Look over there, Walter. That will give you a big hint. Is the sun rising or setting?"

Walter looked off into the distance with a puzzled look. "Strange. It's moving sideways!"

"Walk with me." She put her arm around him, and they slowly walked to a playground where a number of very small children are playing. "Look at the children, Walter. They are growing to maturity four times as fast as human children. Does one of them seem even more different?"

Walter studied them one by one until he came to one that moved his spirit in an intangible way. Walter's eyes began to get larger. He looked at the child more carefully. "Debbie! Amazing! That child is no different than any other here, except . . . ."

"Yes, my darling. You aren't the only one who looks at Gaardian video streams from other sectors."

Walter spoke quietly. "After all that I've been through as a Gaardian! I am … I am … awed! … This is the savior of Quzak – their Arkaynee!"

She smiled and spoke quietly. "Yes!"

They watched the Arkaynee silently for several minutes. Walter turned to Debbie. "We have to resist the temptation to get involved." He looked back at the child. "It will be especially hard for Ooza – harder than it was for Pixie. This is Ooza's Savior, and her heart is already bonded to the Arkaynee. All that God does, God does exceedingly well!"

She nodded, her eyes sparkling. The scene faded before their eyes as the familiar glow replaced it.

> **"Yes. This is my beloved child. Share this with the other Gaardians. All of you must keep your distance until His time here is full. I am faithful and forgive. I save and redeem."**

The glow faded, and the scene reappeared. An older Quzak male appeared in a doorway in a nearby structure. He opened his mouth and made a low rumble. The children began leaving the playground through the doorway.

Far from their home many galaxies away, Walter and Debbie watched invisibly as the children went inside. As the Arkaynee entered with them, Walter and Debbie looked at each other, smiled, and vanished.

And creation continues . . . .

II. *Starlight Adventures*

Gaardian Beginnings

1. Semaj ["seh-MADGE"]

There used to be a planet that was the home of billions of species of carbon-based plants and animals. The outer surface was divided into five continents, with four of the continents surrounded by mineral-rich water that covered more than half of the planet's surface.

It was larger than Earth, and intelligent beings inhabited most of the surface. Since all of these beings were telepathic, schools were seldom needed. They were humanoids with three legs and huge ears, and the entire population had a collective memory. Near the planet's equator, their skin was mostly yellow, with turquoise edges to their ears, nose, and lips. Further from the equator, their skin was less yellow and had more green.

Unlike humans, they did not express their emotions through the tone of their voice. Instead, their anger, sadness, joy, and other emotions were expressed through a glow that came from their eyes. Also, though they had three legs, most of the time they kept their oldest leg folded up out of the way, as they walked or used it as a counterbalance when necessary. Sometimes they would unfold that leg as a stool when they sat down, if there was nothing else to sit on. As they grew older, they would replace their oldest leg and grow a new one.

All of this was about to end. A large asteroid slowly entered their solar system several years earlier. Now it was on a direct collision course with the planet and could not be diverted. Billions of families were waiting in their homes for the final moments. The father of one such family was named Semaj.

With great effort, Semaj was amazingly calm. He sat with his family in their gathering room. The children, normally full of fun and energetic, were very quiet. All of them were staring at the view screen, listening to the voice of their Prepal ["PREE-pul"] – their country's leader. Semaj and his mate glanced at each other every few moments as they conversed telepathically.

"They understand this is important, but that's all."

"Indeed. They do not understand that our planet will soon cease to be, and so will we."

"I love you."

"And I truly love you."

Qaak spoke aloud to the children. "Soon, children, our planet will cease to exist, and so will we. Do you understand?"

The three children's faces turned towards their father. The oldest asked, "Really, father? We're all going to die?" The others began to whimper.

"Yes, I'm sorry to say. An asteroid will strike on the edge of our continent. It is large enough to split or perhaps shatter our planet." His eyes glowed as they turned back towards the view screen.

The Prepal had tears running down his cheeks, and his eyes glowed brilliantly as he spoke. "It is but moments now. I hope The Creator will call all of us home, where we will see each other in spirit."

There was deafening noise, searing heat, and blazing light as the planet was struck by the asteroid. As Semaj had predicted, the planet was shattered. In little more than an instant, seventeen billion lives ended while their minds hovered in black emptiness – for all but just one life.

+ + +

Semaj tried to cough as his entire body was suddenly crushed by gravity many times greater than he had always known. He struggled to breathe, but all he could barely do was make a hacking sound as he struggled for breath. "Kuh … kuh … aaccckk! Kuh … aaaacck!" The thoughts in his mind were chaotic and confused, as with a nightmare.

Suddenly, there was no crushing weight. He breathed easier. "Where am I?" thought Semaj.

"You are on my surface." A voice spoke in his mind.

"What?"

"You are on my surface. I have helped you deal with my gravity and atmosphere."

"Who are you? How?"

"In the language of your planet, which has been shattered, I am Gaardian. To me, you are Qaak, for that is the first sound you made when you arrived on my surface, Qaak. As for how you got here, I simply converted you to energy and transmitted you here just as your planet died."

Semaj's eyes began to glow subtly. "Did you save anyone else?"

"No." It paused several seconds. "That did not occur to me. Yours is the first mind that has ever touched mine since I became aware."

Tears began to flow down Semaj's cheeks. "Your mind touched not only my mind but those of billions of other beings."

"Yes. Now I understand," thought the planet to Semaj.

"Did you note that my planet revolved around a sun?"

"Yes."

"Can you tell me approximately how many times my planet may have traveled around its sun since you became aware?"

"That is hard to estimate, but many thousands of times. I believe that you call those revolutions years. Until your mind touched mine, I did not know what 'alone' meant, but now I know that while I appear to be unique, I am not alone. You are here, Qaak."

"Indeed." His tears continued to flow. Semaj was at a loss for words.

"When I encountered your mind, I scanned it fully. I now understand the need and the importance for privacy. From this day forwards, I will not enter your mind unless you invite me."

Despite his tears, Semaj was fascinated. "How large a planet are you?"

"I am much larger than your planet was, and more dense. That is why my gravity seemed to crush you at first. My atmosphere was limited, but I am increasing my atmosphere's density and depth. Meanwhile, I have supplied you with assistance. It is on one of your appendages."

Semaj looked at his hands. On the middle finger of his right hand, there was a gold ring. In the center at the top of the ring was a shimmering purple crystal. "I did not notice the ring until now. Thank you."

"You are welcome. When scanning your mind, I learned of other intelligent life in another solar system. We are now going there. I want to encounter other minds that can touch mine."

"How long will it take us to get there?"

"You and I need to spend time touching minds. Yours is my first friendship. I am moving slowly, and I plan to have us there in three of your years. Is that acceptable?"

"Indeed. Yes."

"In your mind, I noticed images and descriptions of plant and animal life. As we travel, you and I can harvest samples to populate my surface to give it beauty. I want to be beautiful in your eyes, Qaak."

Semaj was momentarily amused. "I have previously heard females on my planet say that, but you are neither male nor female."

The planet again paused for several seconds. "I must learn to understand humor. It is a new experience."

Semaj tried to wipe the continuing tears from his face. "I can imagine. I must tell you that I am getting hungry."

"I understand. Consider the ring on your finger and think of what you would like to consume."

A table and chair appeared, and on the table were servings of some of Semaj's favorite foods. Semaj spoke aloud. "Indeed. This is excellent!" He sat down at the table, and he began to eat when utensils appeared.

"Good," said the planet. May I touch your mind as you consume your food? I want to experience what you experience."

"Of course." Qaak continued to eat until he was amply full, occasionally pausing to wipe tears away. He looked at an area nearby, and his ring shimmered. A bed appeared.

"Your ring will maintain your body so that you do not need to sleep," said the planet.

"Perhaps, but I want to have normal sleep cycles so that I can process what I learn from you in this new environment."

"Very well."

Silence ensued as Qaak made himself comfortable on a bed identical to the one left behind on his planet. He did not notice that there was less light now. He closed his eyes, but his sleep was mixed with waking painful images. Suddenly, Semaj's eyes silently screamed from the pain of seventeen billion minds torn away from his. Despite the darkness provided by the planet, the light from his eyes would have lit a stadium if there had been one. His eyes screamed and screamed, repeatedly, as pain and sorrow enveloped Semaj. Aloud, he screamed, "Why? Why, Qapoku, Why?"

"Who is Qapoku?" asked the planet. The planet did not understand, and Semaj did not answer. As thoughts from those nearly countless minds swept over Gaardian, it tried to understand but simply recorded the thoughts for future consideration. It tried to comprehend Semaj's pain but only sensed it through its new friend.

"Why, Qapoku, Why? Why?" Semaj's eyes at times glowed so brilliantly that the planet wondered if Semaj would consume himself. The cries of 'Why, Qapoku, Why?' -- along with the brilliance of Semaj's eyes – continued for a long time.

The ring Gaardian had provided sustained Semaj physically, but neither the ring nor the planet could do anything for Semaj's pain. All the planet could do was wait patiently. It began measuring time in terms of his new friend, and it learned about emotions – particularly pain and sorrow.

After dozens of days, Semaj began walking about, exploring and observing in order to take his mind off his sorrow. Gaardian provided cycles of light and darkness while waiting for his new friend to talk again. Days turned into the equivalent of many lunar cycles. Gaardian decided not to take Semaj to the other planet until its new friend was ready. As it traveled, Gaardian collected samples of plant and animal life from passing planets. In its own way, Gaardian decorated itself while it waited.

Gaardian discovered that when his friend slept longer, that he awakened with less pain, so it tried an experiment. It kept Semaj asleep for twenty of Semaj's normal sleep cycles, and the result was encouraging. Healing began to proceed more rapidly.

Finally, after an extended sleep cycle, Qaak awakened hungry. "Gaardian?"

"Yes."

"I am going to eat again now. I am still somewhat sad, and I am not sure that you understand my sadness." He looked down at his ring, and as it shimmered, food appeared on the table he had used previously.

"I now understand emotions, because as I have scanned your mind, I learned that they are part of your being – a part of who you are."

"Indeed." He got up off the bed, went to the table, and sat down. He took a bite of a fragrant meat similar to what we on Earth would call bacon. "I have sensed that you have emotions, but that they are limited because you have no physical outlet for them."

After hesitation, the planet's telepathic voice was not as firm as it had been. "You are correct. I am experiencing what you call emotions for the first time, and I am learning how to process them."

Semaj began to eat more. Listening to the planet helped him forget his sadness. "You have been learning the value of humor and joy from me as well as sadness." His ring shimmered, and a mug of hot liquid appeared. He drank. "Emotions have their place. You will understand them more fully as we go to different planets and encounter distinctive sentient life forms."

"Yes. I anticipate that." The planet paused. "Who is Qapoku? When I scanned your mind, a being named Qapoku did not entirely seem to fit in with your planet's culture."

"Yes. In the future, when we discuss our awareness of The Creator, I will discuss Qapoku. In the meantime, you have my memories for reference."

"Very well."

"Indeed. I have made a decision."

"A decision?" The planet was puzzled.

"Yes. I have decided that Semaj died on my planet. From now on, I am Qaak, as you have labeled me."

"Would you rather I call you Semaj?"

"No. That is now history. My pain is subsiding. I will never forget, but as time passes other things will be more important."

"Very well, Qaak." It paused for nearly a minute as Qaak ate. "Talk to me about virtues, Qaak."

"Indeed." Qaak paused. The planet did not waste time discussing his decision regarding his new name. He liked that. "That is an interesting request. The most overrated virtue is predictability. Virtually all advanced cultures like consistency. We want our friends and coworkers to be reliable and dependable."

"Are there not other virtues?"

"Yes." Qaak's eyes glowed subtly as he took another bite of food. "Your questions are difficult for me to answer because on my planet, we had a communal mind. Adults were interconnected to form a planet-wide database of information. Now my planet is gone forever..." Qaak's eyes glowed and were filled with tears. He wiped them away before he continued. "Now I can no longer depend on those other minds but must try to remember." He paused. "I will do the best I can for you from what I remember."

"Understood. As the thoughts of those who died began to fade I recorded them, but they are not yet organized. We can work on that together. I will be your communal mind from this day forwards as we gather information from other worlds."

"Indeed. Until then, here is what I remember of some of the basic virtues. These virtues do not function separately but intertwine. First, there is justice. I have already scanned your enormous mind and believe that you have some basic understanding of justice."

"Yes."

"A second virtue is sagacity. It means controlling oneself in terms of thinking and behavior using basic reasoning and logic."

"This is wise."

"Yes, wisdom is a large component of this. Wisdom and sagacity are virtually identical. It is not the same as intelligence. Beings with low intelligence can be wise, and beings with high intelligence can be foolish."

"Understood."

"A third virtue is moderation of thinking and behavior, which appears similar to sagacity. It is related."

"I perceive that they are not identical but complementary."

"Indeed. The other important virtue I remember is courage. This will be hard for you to understand. Scan the memories you have recorded from my mind regarding fear."

The planet was silent for several minutes. "I have never been afraid, but I now understand fear. Is courage the absence of fear?"

"No. It is not." Qaak paused. "Consider this for a period of time before discussing it with me: Courage involves a decision in the midst of fear, believing that something else is more important than the fear. In such a case, a being will proceed to act despite its fear because there is something more important."

"I will consider this for a time as you request. I would like you to talk to me about the cultures of your planet, but not if it is too painful for you."

"No. I think it would help to talk about my lost planet. Throughout our history, many cultures rose and fell. From what I know of the planet we are going to visit, I suspect that the rise and fall of cultures follow patterns that we will be able to anticipate."

"Please give an example."

"Indeed. When an advanced culture collapses apart from war, the most frequent root cause is disrespect for the truth and for logic. When we observe such disrespect, we will be able to predict with some accuracy what will follow."

"That is logical." The planet paused. "Was there something in your history that you can now use to illustrate?"

"Yes. Indeed." He took a bite of food and sipped more of the hot liquid. "Very well. When we were first venturing beyond our planetary atmosphere, we carried our then violent cultural problems with us. Our military wanted to conquer the cultures we encountered on other planets, even if they were non-aggressive. In the case of the planet to which we are heading, they were more advanced scientifically and technologically than we were. Our military simply wanted to steal what they could for our use."

"Changing the thinking of an entire culture would be highly inefficient."

"Indeed. Ideally, we would find the power and the ability to relocate such aggressive cultures to a location where they could do less damage."

"I can now use your favorite word, Qaak, 'Indeed!' We must discuss this more before we arrive at our first destination."

"I must ask you about my ring. The appearance of the purple stone is unlike anything known on my planet – my former planet."

"Yes. That particular crystalline compound I have found on many other planets in a different form. Normally, isotopes are variations of an element."

"Yes," replied Qaak, "The isotopes of an element all have the same number of protons but a different number of neutrons."

"Correct. Though this crystalline compound is found commonly on other planets, the crystal in the band on your appendage is an exceedingly rare variation, where the two elements in the crystal share neutrons."

Qaak's eyes glowed more intensely. "Indeed! So the crystal is, in and of itself, an isotope."

"Yes. Nearly half of my core is composed of these crystals. They enable me to be aware. They also enable me to manipulate matter and energy."

Qaak began to understand his new friend's abilities as they conversed in the days that followed. Qaak and Gaardian took three more years to get acquainted. They gathered plant and animal samples as they traveled to the planet with sentient life that they had discussed on their first day together.

+ + +

When they arrived at their first destination, Gaardian adjusted its gravity so as not to affect the trajectory of the planet or its moons. Then it hid itself behind an energy matrix.

Gaardian was analytical as it spoke to Qaak. "On this planet, the sentient beings have four legs, unlike your three. The females tend to be stronger and larger than the males. They are usually fearless, and they care very little about their appearance, apart from keeping their fur well maintained. The females nurture, teach, and defend their young. They are often aggressive, and usually hide their emotions when faced by a challenge. Females tend to be very practical and rational, and they are in the majority in the fields of mathematics and the sciences. Unlike your planet, Qaak, these females tend to be strong leaders. They dominate relationships, and they are highly disciplined. These planet's females tend to be quite independent, and individualistic."

Qaak's eyes glowed subtly. "In my planet's culture, females were expected to be nurturing. On this planet, this quality is most commonly found in males. It seems that this planet's males are typically involved in the family tasks of routine offspring care after their tats are weaned. For those with limited resources, this continues to be the goal even while males are occupied outside of their lair. The occupations that are attainable by them, however, used to offer less remuneration than those available to females. I understand that males are expected to be well educated now, so they are increasing their participation in their culture's creative workforce, and they are getting equal remuneration."

"Yes," the planet rumbled. "Now I am interested in a male creature named Legere."

"I am also," Qaak said as his eyes glowed subtly. "I will go down and observe him on the surface."

Qaak went down, and he invisibly watched Legere for several days. The creature was very proud of his appearance, and correctly so. His paws were large, and his build was muscular and well defined. His coat was smooth with good highlights. His face was evenly colored, with no blotches, and his whiskers were well controlled. His ears did not droop, and his tail had enviable curvature. Qaak learned that artists loved using him as a model, and his success appeared to be well established planet-wide.

Qaak scanned Legere's mind. As successful as he was, Legere was not happy with his appearance. His total rewards were more than for any other. Still, he decided to try to improve his appearance. Up until that time, he had assistants helping him maintain and improve his build. He had cosmetic experts grooming him several times each day. He had the rewards to pamper himself or maintain himself as much as he wanted, but he was not happy. He decided to make a few cosmetic changes, and he began with his paws.

Qaak reported this to Gaardian telepathically. "This species uses their claws the way I use my fingers, though more subtly With them, their claws are not merely appendages, but they also have appeal to those of the opposite sex."

Qaak could see that Legere understood this appeal, but he had become almost obsessed with having the most appealing appearance. He was thankful that the first surgery had little adverse effect upon the grace of his walking.

Qaak reported, "Recently, Legere bonded with his first mate. When the family gathered to celebrate, they forcefully debated each other's accomplishments. His sister named Kieya took him aside to tell him her thoughts. I am sending you my memory images of that conversation," thought Qaak. The thought images were vivid and clear for the planet.

> "I am surprised at your choice, Legere," she said. "I did not anticipate your choosing a mate so much smarter than you are."

He purred subtly. *"She chose me and pursued me. I am grateful."*

"You did not choose her for yourself?"

His purring grew louder. "I was attracted to her, but I did not think she was interested. I approached her on a path through the forest near my lair, but she snarled and batted me powerfully. I was licking my wounds for days." He paused as he looked out a portal towards her. *"Many days later, I was posing for a new client, and when the session was over, I saw that she had been sitting behind the lights. As I went to my preparation area, she followed me."*

"Truly!" Kieya was surprised. *"What happened?"*

"As one of my assistants was prepping me for the next session, she approached me from behind and licked behind my ear. When my sessions were done for the day we walked together for hours."

"So you were then bonded?"

"No." He paused. *"I did not trust her and told her so. It was many long lunar cycles before I realized I could trust her."*

"How did she teach you to trust her?"

"She did not." He purred a bit. *"I finally realized that I could trust her because she demonstrated that she trusted me. We have never talked about the day she attacked me. We do not have to. We both know now that there will never again be violence between us. We are one."*

Qaak then commented on the images with his thoughts. "Just before they returned to the others, Kieya asked him about his first surgery. 'Does she know?' she asked." Qaak paused. "He stopped purring after saying that they were one. 'Yes, he responded,' 'she does not like it that I do alterations to my body, but she leaves it up to me. In two moon cycles, I am going to adjust the curve of my tail. She is against it, but we do not argue,' said Legere.

Qaak asked Gaardian, thinking, "If he trusted her so much, why did he not trust his sister's advice? If he loved his mate so much, why did he ignore her concerns?"

"It is not logical," the planet rumbled.

"Indeed."

2. Kieya

Qaak began following Kieya instead of Legere. On one occasion, Qaak invisibly followed her to see her learn from a highly intelligent male teacher.

In their session in a large structure on her planet, Kieya's spiritual director was intense. His student needed to see the larger picture, beyond the planet and its diverse problems. "Please understand this: The Creator made all we can comprehend. Everything was nothing, an endless dark emptiness without matter, energy, space, or time. The Creator's Spirit floated above it all, declaring light, darkness, time and space. From then they existed because The Creator said it. Pleased, The Creator declared sky, sea, and land, and they were so. Again pleased, The Creator declared life, and plants were the result. Needing to nurture the plants, darkness and light were organized into night and day, suns and moons."

As he continued, he noticed that Kieya's purr was less pronounced. "Now The Creator was very pleased. Excited, The Creator wanted there to be animated life, so animals were declared. The Creator was filled with joy and loved all that had come into being. Wanting to relax and enjoy, The Creator declared that all life was to reproduce. It did."

"What's this got to do with me, with my mate, or with my lair?" asked Kieya.

The director began to purr. "The Creator had peace, but things were not complete. The Creator had given much thought before beginning. There had to be some form of life that could think freely, hope fully, and love completely, just as does The Creator. To be superior and have authority, such life had to be free to make decisions. To be free meant that such life had to have choices. However, to be truly free, this high form of life had to be able to function in the midst of difficult choices. The Creator thus made felidacas [fel-uh-DAH-kuhz] like us."

"I know all of this," said Kieya. "I know how we bring grief to the Creator. I have taught it to my tats. You have given me nothing new to teach them. This session has not been helpful. I will visit again – and perhaps learn more – after a few lunar cycles." She padded out.

Leaving the school, Kieya sought the quiet of a nearby forest. As she walked, Kieya made mental pictures to be rendered on the walls of her lair when she had time. For now, she chose a longer route back to her home.

+ + +

While on the planet's surface, Qaak gathered data on the world as a whole. It was equal to Earth in size, beauty, and climate, but it revolved around two suns and had three moons. There was an abundance of clean atmosphere, clean water, and varieties of plants and animals. Many of the plants grew much larger and taller than those of the Earth, but most of the animals were smaller. Felidacas like Kieya were superior to all the other animals. Their intelligence was comparable to that of humans, though on average slightly more so.

In appearance, felidacas were four-legged creatures with stripes, having bodies somewhat like Earth's tigers. Though they had ears similar to those of Earth's cats, their faces had no snout or even a nose. Their faces were otherwise similar to those of humans, only with fur overall and two small openings instead of a nose. Just as humans worked, played, loved, and worshiped in an organized society, so felidacas also had roads, structures, and organized lairs or cities with places for worshiping the Creator. While humans on Earth were consuming both plant and animal life, felidacas ate only meat, using plants for medicines as appropriate.

Kieya was brilliant. She was reliable and dependable, which was excellent for her relationship with her mate, Tabobi ["tuh-BOB-ee"]. He frequently praised her for being trustworthy as well as being loyal.

+ + +

Qaak watched invisibly watched early one evening, as Tabobi padded towards the entrance of their lair. Kieya called out to her mate. "Do you have everything you need, Tabobi?"

"Yes, Kieya. Do you?"

"I suppose I am spoiled. I can and do surround myself with the things I want. Unlike you, love, my life is not defined at all by where I am, what I do, or what I have. My life is defined by who I am, and you are very much part of my life. That's why I asked."

Tabobi turned and paused. "Then why do you ask?"

"We have taught good values to our tats, and they have mates of their own now except one, but lately you seem restless. If I may help, I am willing."

"No, Kieya, I am simply restless. I will be back before dawn. Let us converse more then."

"Very well."

Tabobi padded out, never to return. That night he died in a senseless fight. Larger than most felidacas in their city and much stronger, Tabobi could have avoided the battle, but after his conversation with Kieya, he was overconfident. He could have dispatched any three of them easily, but not all five. They left none of their fur behind for the authorities, and they disappeared into the much larger numbers of the city.

When Kieya learned of her mate's death, their families closed ranks around Kieya and her tats. She and her remaining tat in her lair continued to be safe. Qaak invisibly observed everything with keen interest. Because of Tabobi's large size, it took two of Kieya's sisters and three of Tabobi's brothers to bury him deep enough to satisfy both families.

"Tabobi liked to stretch his paws on these trees."

"Yes. We will bury him here. These trees will then be well fed. We will remember him in the foliage."

The five of them carefully put the soil back over Tabobi and rearranged the mulch over the soil. The trees over the grave were its markers.

For seven lunar cycles, the families were together half of every day to remember Tabobi. The families worked out a rotation of emotional support for Kieya and her tat.

Eventually, Kieya's life regained a new sense of normal. Highly talented as well as smart, Kieya found ways to be rewarded for her skills, so she managed to provide for their needs. Qaak reported events telepathically to Gaardian. They constantly discussed and evaluated their data.

Months later, Qaak watched when Kieya's last tat was weaned. The now svelte and beautiful tat took her own mate. Kieya was still somewhat young, yet romance was far from her mind. She simply was not interested in finding another mate, and she wished them well.

After a few more moon cycles, Kieya sought another teacher, and the teacher was excellent. In a short time, she had several new skills. Working with a large company, she rose in rank and authority rapidly. Still, she seldom purred.

Gaardian found this interesting. While Qaak was eating near Red Falls one day, the planet asked him about Kieya's purr. "I have noticed that Kieya's purr varies considerably. Have you noticed this?"

Qaak swallowed. "Yes. I have scanned her mind from time to time, and I have tried to correlate Kieya's purr to her thinking. I cannot read her emotions. It seems, however, that Kieya's purr reflects her emotions in the same way as the glow in my eyes reflects mine."

"Yes. Since you have compared the two, it seems logical. At this time, it seems that as she has grown in influence with her work, she is purring less."

"Yes. Part of her power was given by her supervisors because she continued to be dependable and reliable as well as brilliant. She has been also very consistent in the results of her labors. She has been very productive and has great courage. She was what most humans would call moral as well. She was honest, diligent, and generous."

The planet's voice now seemed lower. "She has also been bored! When today she decided to walk away from the new work she has trained for, her supervisor was very angry." The planet replayed the conversation in three-dimensional video for Qaak.

"Kieya! What is razing your purr? You are intelligent and self-assured. What has happened? Why?" He was right. Her purr was now almost gone.

"I cannot do the same things every day," Kieya said. *"Nothing is original! Nothing is unique! I have lost my creative edge!"* She was almost snarling. *"It is not your problem – it is mine!"*

Qaak's eyes glowed subtly "Kieya has left the company, but she does not realize that she has to walk away from her past in order to embrace her future. The rest of the night she wandered the forest outside of her lair." Qaak's concern was very real and would have to be resolved.

On her planet several sleep cycles later, Kieya was wandering in the forest instead of working in her lair. She sharpened her claws on a number of large plants, and it felt great to her. She rolled in dirt and snarled until she had vented her frustrations and restored her purr. She even chased a few defenseless agabeets ["AH-guh-beets"] just for fun.

Later, Kieya let a few young tabbas chase her. They should have known better. When she was beginning to tire, she turned on them and slapped them off a ridge and into a river. She did not use her claws, however. She did not really want to hurt them. As she walked away, she encountered the essential turning point of her life. With the fun behind her, Kieya was hungry. As she padded back towards her lair, she heard leaves rustling nearby, and she crouched, waiting.

"You handled those tabbas adequately, but a felidaca of your quality and nature does not usually lower herself to such things." He was as beautiful as his voice.

She had never been fascinated by a voice, where as she listened to that voice, it seems to penetrate deep within her. She hesitated before responding. "I thought I was alone."

"So it would seem. May I walk with you?"

"As you wish."

Kieya did not end up at her lair – or his. They walked and talked through the sunset, through the night, and into the morning.

"I see now why you quit," he said. "You need to be doing something unique. You are inventive. You are also imaginative and creative."

"Yes. However, where will it lead me?"

"Go to your lair. I must labor. Before the next sunset, you will have an answer."

Kieya was suddenly wary. "An answer to what?"

"You will know tomorrow." The beautiful male paused. "It has been real." He padded off into the forest.

She looked around, and she saw that she was a short distance from her lair. Once inside, she found herself purring. She was famished, but there was plenty to eat in her chilled dispensers. After eating, Kieya curled up on a corner of her pad and closed her eyes. She was never to see that walking companion again.

As she slept, Kieya had an unusually vivid dream. She was walking along a trail in a deep valley. With her was a tall two-legged creature who in the dream she thought of as her friend. On their left was a thin but high waterfall, and to the right of it was a gigantic piece of bare rock with other two-legged creatures climbing on it. In the dream, a voice spoke to her.

> "Some day, Kieya, this human will be a close friend. You will have many adventures together. Trust me, Kieya, and I will guide you. I will help you do far more than you could ever do by yourself."

Suddenly, Kieya was awake. "Who spoke to me?" she asked. She looked around her lair. No one else was there.

+ + +

On Gaardian, Qaak spoke to the planet with confidence. "Kieya is ready. I think she should be our first recruit."

"Agreed. Kieya focuses on her values and pursues her ideals. This is excellent. When she was working, she would draw other felidacas around a common purpose and worked to give each one under her a productive place."

"Indeed. Kieya is creative and seeks new ideas and greater possibilities. She pushes for what is important and rarely gives up. She is gentle and has a good sense of humor. She has her own vision of perfection."

The planet was silent a moment. "I sense that Kieya is fundamentally a peaceful creature. She likes to interact with others, but she is also independent. She does not let details overwhelm her."

"Agreed. She wants her work to be fun, but it also has to be meaningful."

"It is interesting that she does not wish to draw attention to herself."

"Yes. Watching her, I see that she is a gentle and subtle leader. She likes to lead indirectly and include others in her decision making. This is most interesting. I have not encountered any other felidaca like her."

"Yes." The planet paused. "Kieya does not like conflict. She prefers to let situations work out without her interference. We will have to give her careful training in this area."

Qaak's eyes glowed. "Then we are agreed that she shall be our first recruit?"

"Yes. Kieya seldom finds perfection, but she relentlessly pursues it. She will be a great asset."

+ + +

When Kieya awakened from sleep, she went to the entrance and looked out. Her planet was a beautiful place, and she loved exploring it in her leisure time. Whenever she did, doing so would restore her purr. This was particularly true when she had been through a great ordeal. Thousands of years later, Kieya would invisibly walk with her friend Walter in Yosemite Valley on Earth, and they would enjoy such strolls together. Now, walking in the area of her native lair affected Kieya in a profound way, and this particular day Kieya needed no sleep.

Soon enough, the suns had both set. Suddenly, in the twilight, the fur along Kieya's spine stood out. She sensed something or someone behind her.

"Have no fear."

Kieya turned and thought perhaps she was dreaming. Sitting nearby, against a wall, was someone who made no sense. She was looking at a turquoise and yellow creature with two legs instead of four, a face similar to hers, but with huge ears. He was sitting down, but she could not see how. Kieya had seen a creature like this in her dreams. She even told bedtime stories to her offspring using a creature like this one as one of the characters in her stories. Her purring stopped.

"Kieya, please relax."

"You do not exist."

"Obviously, you are mistaken."

Kieya crouched on the floor, facing him. She was not as tense, but she had no purr. She was wary.

"I know you are probably feeling confused, Kieya. Is this not true?"

"Yes," she almost whispered. "You know my name, but I do not know yours."

"Perhaps." He paused. "You are much larger and stronger than I am. Will you permit me to touch your face?"

Kieya blinked. She blinked again. "Very well."

The creature stood up. She now saw that the creature had a third leg that he had folded and used as a stool. He ambled a few steps towards her and reached out. He touched her with three fingers on her face. Kieya's eyes closed for a moment, and she saw bright lights, flashing colors while hearing a sound like wind in treetops. When his hand was withdrawn, she opened her eyes.

"You are Qaak!"

"Yes, Kieya. Indeed." His eyes glowed for a moment.

"I remember you from my dreams!" She was purring as she had never purred before. "You and I have been together in my dreams for a long time!"

"Indeed, Kieya." He paused. "I have a question for you. I sent a messenger last night to talk with you, so I know you are ready. I want you to do something with me never before done. It will be new every day. Most would call it an adventure. If you do this, we will have to trust each other no matter what happens from now on." His eyes glowed subtly.

She was now purring intensely. "Your messenger was correct. This is the answer I was seeking. I am ready. Where or how do we begin?"

"Indeed." His eyes were glowing as he extended one hand, holding a ring. "Slip this ring over the third claw of that front paw and onto the finger. It will fit."

Kieya did so. It was almost hidden in her fur. "This is a power portal, is it not?" She continued to purr loudly.

"Indeed, and much more. Now look at me and into my mind."

As she did so, there was a flicker of light, and then they were on another planet. Because of a lifetime of dreams, she knew this place. "We are on Gaardian." She pronounced it carefully.

"Indeed. Gaardian, I think Kieya would welcome conversation with you."

"Hello, Kieya," said the planet inside her head. "It is good to meet you at last."

She purred softly. "I feel as if I know you because we've had conversations in my dreams."

"Yes. I understand. Now that your waking knowledge and your sleeping knowledge are one, I suggest that you explore me. We can talk and really get to know each other."

"Yes! I would like that," she said as she purred. "I sense that your intelligence is greater than the combined intelligence of all the felidacas on my planet."

The planet hesitated. "I do not find it useful to compare myself with others. Elsewhere in the universe, there are undoubtedly greater and lesser minds than my own. Thus far, it does not matter."

"I will return soon enough," said Qaak, and he vanished.

Kieya began to pad across the stunningly different terrain. "Gaardian, I find that to maintain my purr, I must speak truthfully and peacefully, but most importantly I need to listen to what others tell me. I think that with you I can do this," said Kieya thoughtfully.

"That is interesting. I have observed your mind as you stretched your claws and rolled in the dirt on your home planet. I have learned from this, just as I have learned from Qaak's emotions. I am learning to maintain contentment by grooming my surface."

"How do you groom your surface?"

"Learning from observations of Qaak's former planet and yours, I have adjusted my mountains and created new rivers and waterfalls. I also adjust these things when I acquire new plant and animal life from other planets. I told Qaak on our first day that I wanted to be beautiful for him. He found that amusing. I want to be beautiful for you also, Kieya."

The big cat purred. "Thank you. There are many things that all of us must learn in the vast time ahead of us."

"Yes. As we begin to police the galaxies, we must focus on learning because it may well be easy to get lost in the challenges."

"Are we going to police galaxies?"

"Yes. I have perceived heroism among some of the thinking creatures on the planets we have observed and explored. On those planets, there seem to be always those with ideals and good values. I understand this because Qaak has taught me much about civilized societies."

"Good." She paused. "I am comfortable talking with you. I am *totally* serene when I talk with The Creator. Whatever challenges face us, within the noise and chaos, we must be tranquil in spirit. With all of life's pretense deceptions, toil and fruitless dreams, life is always still worth living."

"The Creator? Qaak and I have not discussed this in detail, though I know Qaak's mind well. He associates The Creator with one of his fellow creatures called Qapoku." It paused. "Indeed." If the planet could show emotion, it seemed to be in this word. This time it sounded louder in Kieya's mind. "It is logical that one being has created all that I have experienced and observed. It fits the science that we have learned thus far. That there is a Creator is consistent with the science findings of both Qaak's planet and yours. It also fits my findings. When I became aware, I learned to manipulate gravity, energy, and matter to suit my own needs. This is logical. There is an intelligent being responsible for all the galaxies that I have seen." It paused. "Indeed." The planet paused much longer. "I am at the moment giving you solitude now with your thoughts." Kieya spent the next several sleep cycles simply walking all over Gaardian, sometimes talking with Qaak, and sometimes just being with Gaardian.

The planet was moving more rapidly through space now, surveying suns and planets for intelligent life. While Qaak and Kieya rested in their sleep cycles, sometimes the planet traveled great distances. Though Qaak and Kieya did not know it yet, Gaardian could traverse several galaxies in just a few moments.

It was good for Kieya to walk the planet in reality, when she had previously walked it only in her dreams. In conversing with Gaardian, she learned how many planets had sentient species in the particular galaxy they were in or in adjacent galaxies. As Gaardian traveled about among the galaxies, it acquired vast amounts of knowledge of science and technology. With Qaak's assistance and guidance, Gaardian integrated all of that knowledge and applied its own superior intelligence to create superior technology.

Kieya's contribution was being able to see life on a particular planet through the eyes if its inhabitants. She could easily analyze cultures and glean valuable insights for keeping in Gaardian's memory. She could understand their ways of thinking even when she disagreed with them.

With the big felidaca now part of Gaardian's family, Kieya and Qaak began visiting some of these other planets. Qaak showed Kieya planets that he and Gaardian had already explored. They also went into previously unexplored territories. They observed conflicts on all planets that had sentient life, and they sometimes observed conflicts between planets as well.

One evening, Qaak and Kieya sat in the shade of a large plant, gazing at Red Falls far below. The falls were far enough away that it was simply a low rumble. Qaak was thoughtful. "We are observing consistency. On planets with societies involving two sexes, males and females usually assume clearly defined roles. This is true with their families, just as their roles must be clear in the workplace as well, though roles there do not have to be defined in terms of sexuality."

Kieya's purr was very soft. "I have not sought a new mate because I am letting these new Gaardian duties define who I am, what I share, and where I go. I will not be bonded to those that I police, as I am with you and Gaardian. When I take a mate, it will be necessary for our roles to be carefully defined."

"Was Tabobi your only mate?"

"No. Before the death of my previous mate, my life was very different. I was very wild. On the day I bonded with Argatta, however, our families and friends gathered with us in a large enclosure. They pressed closely against us, so that all our bodies were touching. We had a spiritual bonding sequence somewhat like worship. Then while Argatta and I continued to lean against one another, the rest stepped back and gave one another space. Those who knew us best declared to us what our roles would be with each other. It was a community contract they formed to bind us. I no longer had time to be wild or any desire to be so. Our families helped us maintain our roles and our contract from then on. After the ritual, we celebrated for seven solar cycles."

"Indeed." The triped's eyes glowed. "We also had a very physical bonding ritual on my planet. It involved the entire community."

As the evening wore on, they also discussed at length what Gaardian had mentioned in its first conversation with the new recruit. Before Kieya met them, Qaak and Gaardian had previously decided that it would be logical and useful to have a police force to deal with the larger conflicts, since none already existed in their area of the universe. Based upon their observations, they formed guidelines for planets and civilizations to follow. It took them several hundred Gaardian years. In forming that new police force, Kieya was their first recruit.

Soon other recruits followed, beginning with Doff. He was a tall, translucent being with a deep bass voice. Doff always spoke gently. Kieya found him interesting in her first conversation with him. He began by saying, "I have read much about the felidacas. I am fascinated by the makeup of your head and heart."

"Really? I would like to know more about your people as well."

Doff rumbled with a deep chuckle. "My people are easy to know. They will not be ready for interplanetary travel for many of my people's lifetimes. I know that you and Qaak recruited me because intellectually I am a genetic accident, and because I fit the other criteria that you and Qaak associated with Gaardian requirements. That is even more reason for me to know and understand you. There is no other planet in my galaxy that is even beginning to advance scientifically. I am surprised you found me."

"Yet here you are!"

Now Doff broke out of his chuckle and really laughed. "Yes! In addition, here you are. Neither of us is one who fits a mold, are we?"

Kieya purred. "No! I am hungry. Are you? Will you join me?"

"I would be honored."

They went to the mountaintop that Kieya enjoyed with Qaak and began to eat. Doff's low voice always seemed to reflect amusement. "I am intrigued by your purr. There are no creatures on my planet with that attribute."

Kieya paused eating. "That is interesting. My purr is a reflection of my emotions. I have always been happiest when my plans and potentials are fulfilled. My species purrs as a manifestation of happiness or contentment. When I accomplish something lasting, the success makes me purr. Thinking about those accomplishments afterward also gives me cause to purr. I have to strike a balance between memories that bring back purring and those that do not."

"Interesting!" rumbled Doff. Then he chuckled. "When I am happiest I sing."

"Really! Is that why I heard you singing yesterday as the sun was rising?"

"Yes!" Doff rumbled. "I understand that you are also religious, that you know that there is a Creator of everything. When I talk with the Creator I often sing."

"Yes. I think I heard you praying in one of your songs."

Doff chuckled. "The prayer in the song was taught to me by my father. It says –

Now I pray me up from sleep.

My spirit flies! Get wings my feet!
For by the grace of God above
I'm living His redeeming love.

The big felidaca chewed and swallowed. "That is a beautiful song and good thinking. I can describe my experiences this way: While happiness and contentment cause me to purr, belonging to the creator and pleasing Him gives me joy. Even when I am suffering through great difficulties – as I did when my beloved Tabobi died – talking with the Creator gives me joy and contentment. It is like a silent purr that connects me with something greater than myself and anything that troubles me."

They continued to eat and discuss whatever came to mind. That meal was the beginning of a friendship that continued for many centuries.

3. Earth

Thousands of years later, Kieya first visited Earth and saw the beauty of the planet and its solitary moon. She made that first journey alone, and she had much to do before she could enjoy Earth's mountains, hills, trees, and flowers. Kieya's planet was similar in some ways, but very different in others. Kieya later showed images of Earth to Doff and Kieya. They easily agreed that few planets they had encountered had the beauty and grandeur of Earth, though Kieya's planet was also most remarkable.

Kieya's first visit to Earth was about ten thousand of Earth's years ago. Qaak asked her to monitor the development of intelligent societies on the edge of Gaardian space. At that time, Earth held one of four such societies.

Earth's scientists divide life into two *kingdoms*. In Earth's animal kingdom, there is an order called *carnivore*, all of which eat meat. Within that order are sixteen mammal families. Kieya had a particular interest in one of those families. In terms of carbon-based life forms, the genetics were very close to those of Kieya.

During that first visit to Earth, she observed a woman holding a cat and attempting to converse with it. "Are you hungry?" asked the woman.

The cat understood the intent of the question. Its brain did not process the question in order to form a response.

"Let us get you something to eat," she said.

The cat heard the change in the woman's tone of voice, and it decided that it was going to be fed. It started to purr, and it jumped away from the woman's arms. It then followed her into a dwelling, where the woman gave it some meat. To Kieya, its purring did not seem to have a logical base. Still, she found it amusing.

During that first visit, Kieya traveled to several areas of Earth, and she found cats of various sizes. Most of them were smaller than she was. All of them had a snout, which felidacas do not have.

Tigers have a body similar in size and coloration to Kieya's, and it has similar fur. Kieya was immediately intrigued. Kieya found that, while all cats on Earth could think to some extent, none of them had advanced intelligence. The leopards and jaguars had slightly more intelligence than most cats, but Kieya knew it was doubtful their intelligence would ever advance significantly.

When Kieya returned to Gaardian after that visit, she sought the planet's counsel. "Gaardian?"

"Yes, Kieya."

"Earth has quite a number of animals that are similar in genetics to me, but none of them have more than basic thinking capacity."

"Were you disappointed?"

"Disappointed? No, I was not disappointed, but this gives fresh perspectives to our knowledge base. Please scan and record my memories."

The planet paused for a moment. "Fascinating. The dominant thinking species of Earth does not have fur to keep it warm. These beings are remarkably similar to Qaak, and to others of his species who used to occupy his home world, before it was destroyed."

"Yes. Qaak has not told me very much about that. I am curious about something."

"His name?"

"Yes."

"The name I gave him is an accident of his existence. I was traveling near his planet just before it exploded in a collision with an asteroid. My mind touched his just before the rest of his species died. The name I have called him since then reflects the sound he made when he took his first breath of my atmosphere. It was not initially adequate to support a life form such as his. I made it possible for him to breathe here, and the sound stopped. Some time passed before I asked him what name he had on his former planet. He said it did not matter, and that Qaak would do. What does your name mean, Kieya?"

"You have not scanned my mind for this?"

"No. Kieya, I never intrude where not invited. My telepathy is disciplined. I understand the need of all thinking species to have privacy."

"My name means 'Vessel of Love.'"

"Indeed. It is quite descriptive of who you are."

"Thank you, but I am not always confident that I live up to my name."

"One cannot always be what we would rather be. In all of my travels, I have not encountered another planet that can think and converse as I do. As good as the friendships are that I have with you and Qaak, I believe I would like to know another like myself."

"I understand."

The conversation continued for several days before Qaak and Doff joined them in a structure high on one of Gaardian's mountains. It had a few trees nearby where Kieya could stretch her paws and claws. Gaardian provided an occasional breeze, but it was very quiet there. Red Falls was beyond the horizon, and most of the valley below was a carpet of tall trees. With the planet monitoring and occasionally contributing, the three animate Gaardians began to talk as they made themselves comfortable.

Qaak's eyes had a subtle but steady glow. "Doff, do you need to discuss anything with regard to your activity in sector 101-A256-B1019? I am impressed with the memories you have recorded with Gaardian."

"I think not, Qaak." His voice's low rumble was quiet. "I do not anticipate the need for any further action for at least ten of their solar rotations."

"Good. Kieya, how soon will the beautiful planet you visited, or others in that sector, need a Gaardian presence?"

Kieya purred subtly. "Although there are three planets in that sector that will be ready for interplanetary travel in a few thousand years, I do not anticipate the need for a standing Gaardian presence there until then."

The others nodded as the planet spoke. "I have analyzed all the reports, and probability is low that we will need to have a permanent presence there until they are ready to venture into space. I suggest, however, that we begin to scan periodically for possible Gaardian candidates as genetic forbears."

"Agreed." Qaak's eyes glowed more intensely. "I believe that as our sphere of responsibility expands, we need to be looking for such evidence in all sectors of future expansion."

The others murmured assent.

"Gaardian." Kieya spoke quietly. "I assume that you will schedule such visits from this day forwards."

"I will do so."

A new and more powerful phase of Gaardian activity began. More recruits were now mandatory. The three Gaardians became more than a thousand in half as many years, and a second thousand were in place long before Earth had its own Gaardian.

+++

They began recording human thinking and activity in detail when they encountered Socrates and Confucius. Kieya discussed each trip to Earth with Qaak in great detail. On one occasion, Qaak looked at his friend and asked, "What's bothering you, Kieya? Did you observe something unusual?"

"I think so," she said purring softly. "I had a particularly strange experience with a human named Jesus. He has the brain configuration that we value as Gaardians, and I enjoyed listening to him teach. Yesterday he looked right at me even though I was invisible, and he nodded at me."

"Indeed!" His eyes glowed for a moment. "That reminds me of something in my planet's history, but I cannot recall it now. Perhaps someday Gaardian can help me remember."

Subsequently, several generations before Earth's society was ready for space exploration, these unseen Gaardian eyes were observing Earth's progress, along with the progress of the other two planets. Kieya enjoyed watching Johann Sebastian Bach, Wolfgang Amadeus Mozart, Ludwig van Beethoven, and Claude Debussy. On other visits, she was fascinated by the primitive scientific efforts of Leonardo da Vinci, Albert Einstein, and George Washington Carver.

Sometimes accompanied by Qaak or Doff, Kieya began looking for someone who could be trained for the job of policing Earth's sector of Gaardian space. The genetics had to be just right for his or her brain to accommodate the full scope of Gaardian life. The family background had to be fine-tuned. They watched and waited for those who would be the forebears of the Earth's first Gaardian.

In June of Earth year 1933, Edward Stephanopolos married his bride, Judi, in London at Kings College. After their wedding ceremony in the college's chapel, Edward took Judi to New Zealand for their honeymoon. Edward was asked to teach history at the University of Christchurch, and he accepted. Not long thereafter, Judi became both a church secretary and lay minister at the Anglican Cathedral of the Nativity. They both wanted many children, but it was not to be. Of their seven pregnancies, three miscarried; one was stillborn, and one boy died of the measles at the age of three. The remaining two boys kept both their own family and their church family very busy nonetheless. Arthur, born in 1938, was both strong and bright. He was good at sports and in his academic subjects. His younger brother, the future Gaardian, was born in 1942. They named him Walter.

Qaak and Kieya were there watching as Arthur was born. They both knew as they probed the baby's mind a few hours after his birth that he was not the one for whom they had been waiting for three centuries. When Walter was born, however, they knew they had their future Gaardian. When Edward and Judi brought Walter home from the hospital, a couple of giant stuffed animals were delivered from an anonymous admirer. Edward liked the tiger the best, but he thought that the three-legged one was ugly. Judi on the other hand, loved them both – *particularly* the three-legged one. They placed the stuffed animals in one corner of Walter's nursery.

The day after Walter was born, his father, Edward, walked home from the university along the Christchurch waterfront. There was a bounce to his step as he turned up along a tree-lined street and up the hill. He came around a corner to see his two-story house come into view, and he walked up the porch steps. Kieya and Qaak were already there. In the living room, Judi was on the phone. He smiled and threw her a kiss as she murmured on the telephone. He nodded as she waved and pointed at the phone.

He headed through a door to a nursery decorated in blue with a bassinet. He looked down on Walter. In the corner were the two large stuffed animals. One was a likeness of the yellow and turquoise humanoid with three legs, and the other looked like the tiger with a human face. The man smiled lovingly at his son, turned, and went back towards the living room.

As he left the nursery, the two stuffed animals started to grow and move. Kieya padded towards the crib. Quiet and intense, her tiger-like stripes rippled slightly as she walked. "He's going to excel, Qaak. Unfold that third leg of yours and come and get closer to him."

Peacefully quiet, his eyes glowed slightly as he simply responded, "Yes."

Qaak moved to the crib and touched the baby's forehead with three fingers. "Sleep soundly, Walter. We are going to have some wonderful dreams for you. When your creativity is in full bloom, and when your mind is ready for the impossible to become possible, you are going to have new friends on other worlds. Your dreams will become training for you, but now we are going to make sure you are always safe, even in this time of planet-wide war."

A pale blue glow surged through the room. As the glow subsided, identical stuffed animals appeared where Kieya and Qaak had been. Then they nodded at one another and vanished.

4. Two Environmentalists

Walter was trained for nearly a half century during his dreams as he slept. During that time, his life seemed normal to everyone on Earth. In the aftermath of Earth's second world-wide war, much of Earth's western society began making more rapid scientific and technological progress. When the Union of Soviet Socialist Republics put the first satellite into space in 1958, Qaak and the other Gaardians noted it as normal development of human society. A race to put the first human into space began, and the United States of America was determined to get into space first.

Public education in western societies began to emphasize science and math. Students who had particularly good intellectual gifts were identified and given opportunities for more rapid and comprehensive education. Some of these gifted students went on to great success in scientific and technological pursuits. A few of them were identified as being particularly adept. An even smaller number of teenaged children hardly fit into their classes at all.

Glenn Franz, for example, was an eccentric. He did not think much about how different his classes were. He was raised in a Christian home, which gave him good emotional support as well as spiritual support. His parents taught him the importance of going to church, and his Dad made a concerted effort to teach him to be honorable. Glenn gained his intelligence from his Dad, only more so – *much* much more so. Glenn was definitely different.

Before his family went to Yosemite National Park the first time, Glenn's Mom bought an interchangeable lens 35mm camera for him. She also bought an identical camera for his sister, Brittany, who was a year younger. Brittany and Glenn had picked out five lenses that they could share. Brittany used all five lenses, but Glenn shot most of his pictures with the super wide-angle lens. He was encouraged to try all the lenses, but Glenn was fascinated with all the possibilities of the one lens.

He skipped his senior year of high school. His friends thought he should spend the time getting his diploma, even if he was bored. Yes, Glenn was bored. Tall and skinny at sixteen he entered the University of Southern California. That meant that he could live with his parents and commute. He finished his bachelor's degree in physics and biology the spring before he turned nineteen. He found most of the course work easy enough, and he got all A's.

One professor, Dr. Harry Wolper, stimulated Glenn's creative juices as no other professor did. He had no classes with Dr. Wolper, but they often ate lunch together. Dr. Wolper taught at the film school, where he sometimes dreamed of innovative cameras and lenses for his cinematography students. Glenn showed Dr. Wolper many of his images taken with the wide-angle lens. Optics and associated devices interested both of them, so they had many long conversations.

After transferring to the University of California at Berkeley, Glenn decided to earn his doctorate in optical physics with a minor in chemistry. That effort took three years out of his life, which was longer than he expected, but getting that post-graduate degree pointed Glenn in the right direction. Then he made a side trip to a pawn shop and his life-changing project.

Eleven years later, and nearly seventy years after Walter was born, Glenn was entering at Yosemite National Park's South Entrance. That life-changing project sat in a case on the seat beside him. At six-foot seven, Glenn was handsome and slender, sitting tall in a rented SUV. The park ranger seemed pleasant enough. "Good morning sir. Are you by yourself?"

"Yes." A grin swept across Glenn's face.

"Have you been to Yosemite before?"

"Yes, many times." He handed the ranger a twenty-dollar bill.

"Thank you, sir. Would you like a *Visitor's Guide* or a map?"

"No thank you."

"Here's your change. Do you have reservations?"

"Yes. I'm staying at the Ahwahnee."

"Very good, sir. Enjoy your visit to Yosemite." He smiled.

"Thank you." Glenn smiled back, pulled forward, and then turned left. From there the park road led toward the Wawona hotel, and from there it went on to the valley.

Glenn knew that he was going to get some good images with the camera he had created. He planned to test it vigorously and use his laptop to analyze the results. He was approaching all of it as a scientist, but he also passionately loved photography. Still, he did not have any idea of what was about to begin in a few days.

As he approached the valley's Wawona tunnel, his mood changed. As for many people, for Glenn it was great when he was driving along in the valley with the trees whipping by. Glenn felt an incredible sense of freedom stirring inside him. It was the kind of freedom that allowed him to feel a sense of balance between his life as a scientist and his passion for life's pleasures. Glancing down at the camera's case, Glenn thought about the carefully balanced mechanisms he had built. Within him, he felt as if the different parts of himself were once again acquiring a sense of being centered. Here in Yosemite Valley, Glenn felt grounded in a way that he could not feel anywhere else. Driving along, he achieved a kind of serenity that made him open to renewal. Feeling relaxed and at peace, he did not stop to take pictures, but he simply enjoyed El Capitan on his left as he passed Bridal Veil Fall on his right. After a mile or so, in the distance he could see his first glimpse of Half Dome.

Further east, as Yosemite Falls came into view on his left, he saw its abundance of water typical of early summer. Glenn felt open and realized a feeling of both freedom and intensity, *real* intensity. The valley's extreme proportions seemed to open the deepest parts of him, and it reminded him of the things that he knew were really important and meaningful to him.

After passing the chapel, Glenn turned left across Sentinel Bridge. Winding through the trees, he came to a stop sign, and he turned right towards the village and the Ahwahnee Hotel. It was still early afternoon. The lecture series he had signed up for would not start until early evening.

After checking in, and after the hotel's bellhop helped him settle into his room, Glenn went downstairs and into the Great Room. Finding a corner out of the way from the crowds, Glenn relaxed, watched people go by, and took in the incredible scope and rustic décor of the room. Glenn had read about the architect, Gilbert Stanley Underwood, and he could readily see that the architect was truly brilliant. Glenn got out of his chair and went to the enormous fireplace. Stepping up upon the hearth, he had to stoop only slightly to stand inside the opening next to the fire.

Unexpectedly restless, Glenn wandered throughout the expansive hotel campus. Outside, he looked up at Glacier Point and pondered what images he might make there with his special camera. Looking around and upward, he could see the windows of his room, a suite that included a sitting room with a fireplace. Nearby he heard some leaves' rustling. A mule deer buck was making its way eastward across towards the cottages behind the main building. Smiling, Glenn turned and went back inside the hotel.

+ + +

Fifteen years earlier at the School for the Talented and Gifted in Dallas, Texas, the boys and girls were all smart. As focused as these boys and girls were on their studies, they also had the sense of fun of typical teenagers. The artist students were playful, but they also were very focused on their crafts. The future mathematicians and scientists were studious, but they also liked to explore things outside of their favorite field of study.

Betsy Sue Johnson had been different, almost as eccentric as Glenn, the man she would meet in a few years. Betsy Sue was highly intelligent and articulate in many subjects. She was poised, but she was not stuffy. She was also amazingly talented when seated at a piano or electronic keyboard. Typical of many other Christians on the campus, her spirit was warm, strong, peaceful, and passionate.

The boys who dated Betsy Sue knew that she was both emotionally and spiritually more mature than they were. In the eyes of many students and faculty on the campus, however, Betsy Sue was also goofy. This beautiful Texan had a nearly non-stop sense of humor that overflowed into all of her life and the lives of those around her. All the teachers had to be tolerant of the school's sometimes eccentric students, but this teenager was different.

Her sense of humor was both brilliant and wacky. At a spring concert, when the conductor of their little orchestra began making unusual gestures with his shoulders, it was not until late in the summer that it was learned who had put a chemical in the collar of the director's jacket to make his neck itch like fire. Betsy Sue had been at work.

When some boys were up to mischief in the dark basement under the auditorium, Botcy Sue set off a magnesium flare. It temporarily blinded the boys so that at first they could not find their way back to their classrooms. When her teachers did their best to keep her busy, she did not find as much time for her mischief.

When she graduated, Betsy Sue stayed in the area and matriculated at Texas Christian University in Fort Worth. Her room at Jarvis dormitory was a little smaller than she would have preferred, but she really liked her roommate. Even so, she was not there much anyway. Everywhere she went on campus, she was a fireball of energy and wacky humor – everywhere, that is, except at the Mary Couts Burnett library. Whenever she entered, she felt peaceful. Betsy Sue had learned speed reading when she was thirteen, so she decided to read as many of the library's books as she could. By the time she graduated, she had read more than 3,000 from cover to cover.

In November of her sophomore year, Betsy Sue wandered one day into Robert Carr Chapel in order to think and meditate. She noticed a man sitting nearby, who waved at her. She vaguely recognized him, so she waved back. He came over and sat down in the pew in front of her. He turned almost completely around to speak to her. "Hi, I'm J.R. Muir. I have seen you in my section of the library a lot lately."

Betsy Sue admired his abundant locks of graying hair. "Muir? John Roosevelt Muir? You're a descendent of John Muir the environmentalist and head of Environmental Sciences, aren't you? I'm Betsy Sue Johnson."

"The prankster? I've heard about you!"

She blushed. "I don't know about that. I suppose I do have a wacky sense of humor."

He smiled. "I would describe it more as goofy."

"Okay...."

"By goofy, I'm thinking of that stunt you pulled at the Fort Worth Zoo last summer to get them to do some environmental cleanup near the big cats' cages."

She smiled. "That was fun."

"They're cleaning up the area nicely, and one of the zookeepers told me that they thought your stunt was both funny and to the point. They really did not take offense. The city found a way to fund what needed to be done."

"I'm glad." She paused. "I've read several of the textbooks in the Environmental Sciences section of the library. I've not taken any courses in your department, but I may want to talk to you about a major in the area beginning this spring."

"Excellent! Finals will be over the second Friday of December. Make an appointment with my secretary for the following week."

"Okay. What are you doing here in the chapel?"

"My wife died last year about this time, so I came here to meditate. I'll be retiring in a few years – I think."

She nodded. "I remember reading about her death. I'm sorry." She paused. "I came here today because I needed to decide on a major. I think maybe that has happened." By the time they left the chapel, they had the beginning of a valuable friendship.

Three weeks later, Betsy Sue saw Dr. Muir again, and the passion of her life began to bloom. She approached her classes in environmental sciences with a zest that sometimes surprised teachers and classmates alike. After finishing her bachelor's degree, she transferred to the University of California at the Merced campus. There she began to gain recognition as a writer and lecturer while she earned her doctorate.

5. Yosemite

In Oakland, California, a black woman was kneeling on the carpeted steps at the front of the sanctuary of a large old cathedral-style church. There was lots of activity in another part of the building, but here in the sanctuary it was quiet. Although the lights were off, there was sunlight streaking through the old stained-glass windows.

Margaret was kneeling for the first time in a quarter of a century. It seemed Margaret had first started attending about two months earlier. She introduced herself as Margaret Graves at the funeral of Margaret Fields. Margaret Fields had been 92 and much loved by the congregation. She had been born up the hill at Mercy Hospital and had been part of the church all of her life.

Kneeling at the front of the church, this attractive young African-American woman who was praying appeared to be about thirty years of age. She was not. She and Margaret Fields were actually the same woman. The body they buried two months previously was a copy created by Earth's Gaardian, Walter Stephanopolos.

Margaret Fields/Graves prayed quietly. "Father, I've been talking with you since I was a little girl, but this is different. You have used Walter to give me a second chance, and I don't want to mess it up. He was my pastor for many years when I was still an old woman. I made plenty of mistakes in that first life, and I don't want to make as many this second time around."

She paused as she began to hear rain on the roof. The ceiling was nearly forty feet above her, and where she was kneeling, the sound of the rain was interrupting the silence she had grown accustomed to. She looked up into the rafters. "Lord, I'm glad we have the rain. Thank you." She paused. "What was I telling you? Oh yes, my new life. As you know, I am going to be installing a small Gaardian operating base in the vacant area above the church offices and coffee hall. Helping me will be Ann Cotter, who also works with the Gaardian crew. We are disguising it as a media development studio, so few people will ask questions."

She lowered her face to the floor. "Lord, with all the Gaardian assistance and power that are available to me, I am even more aware of how much I need you, Lord. Now that I am young again, I also want a husband again. Am I being selfish, Lord? I didn't have any kids the first time around, but I think I'd like to have a few now." She paused. "Lord, I've met a wonderful man on Walter's base on the Moon. His name is Toby. I really like him, Lord, so if you want us to be together, will you assist us? No marriage would be truly complete without you, Lord. I learned *that* the first time around with my beloved Steven. I'm sure he's in heaven with you." She paused. "I hope I don't make the same mistakes with my second husband as I did with the first." She paused again. "Thank you for everything, Lord. As always, I lift up my prayers to you in the precious and powerful name of Jesus. Amen."

Margaret got off her knees. She glanced around to see if anyone had wandered in while she was praying. She looked down at the ring on her right hand. The purple stone shimmered, and she vanished.

+ + +

At that moment, about two hundred miles east of that church, in Yosemite Valley, Betsy Sue approached the desk at the Ahwahnee hotel. "Hi."

The young desk clerk was the same one that had checked her in before lunch. "Good afternoon, Dr. Johnson." She smiled.

"Where will I be giving my lectures these next few days?"

"You'll be in the Tresidder Room for your lectures. The adjacent Tudor Lounge will be available for informal conversation, finger food, beverages, registration, and a display of your books. There is overstuffed furniture in there too. You'll also have the Colonial Room for optional space if needed."

"Is all that upstairs above the Mural Room and Winter Club Room?"

"Yes, Dr. Johnson. It is being set up now. The food and beverages will not be put out until after your first session begins at 6:00 o'clock. There will always be coffee and hot water for tea of course. This evening the food will be mostly desserts and fruit."

"Excellent. I think I'll go back upstairs and get ready for an early dinner."

"Okay. Enjoy your dinner, Dr. Johnson."

Betsy Sue did lecture weekends like this many times, though this one began on a Thursday and concluded Saturday evening. Little did she know that this would begin a new chapter in her life.

6. The Camera

Eleven years earlier, while Betsy Sue was at Texas Christian University, Glenn had needed some days off after completing his post-graduate studies. He found that sometimes he needed to relax and let his mind idle for a while. The hooding ceremony on the Berkeley campus was impressive. His parents enjoyed the whole afternoon. After dinner at Jack London Square on the Oakland waterfront, Glenn had dropped them off at the Hyatt Regency hotel. The shuttle would be taking them to the airport early the next morning. Glenn had gone back to his apartment, had taken off his shoes, and had leaned back in his recliner to watch the news. Soon he had been fast asleep, and he slept through the night. Now it was Saturday, and Glenn took a walk without thinking about where he wanted to go.

Just before noon, he stopped by a store and looked into the window. Pawn shops can be a strange experience even for those accustomed to them. Glenn had never entered one before, but through the window, he saw something in the shadows that brought back a memory from his teen days. He went in.

"Good afternoon! Can I help you?" The proprietor did not seem overly enthusiastic.

"Yes. I saw a camera in the window – one with a rotating lens. Can I take a closer look at it?"

"Certainly." The man stepped out from behind the counter and crossed over towards the window display. Unlocking a panel door, he removed the camera. "I had never seen one like it when it came in about a month ago. I had to make some phone calls to set a price for it. It appears to be in good working order."

Glenn took it from his hands and looked at it carefully. "It seems to be clean." He pulled the wind lever twice. "The advance mechanism seems to have no problems. Do you have some AA batteries, so we can test the shutter?"

"Sure." The proprietor took the camera over to the counter and reached into a drawer for batteries. After putting them in, he asked, "Now what? I don't know how this works."

Glenn smiled. "Like this." He turned a knob on the top. "I'm setting the shutter speed for an effective speed of $1/125^{th}$ second." He paused as he turned the knob and pressed the shutter release. There was a whirring sound as the lens moved. "Good. It looks like it works adequately, but I would have to calibrate it" He looked at the tag on the camera. "$1200 seems a little high since its not been professionally calibrated. I'll give you $900 for it."

"That's not giving me any profit. How about $1000 even?"

Glenn looked up at the ceiling, his face expressionless. "Okay." He handed the man a credit card.

Out on the street, walking home, Glenn was pleased. The camera was worth considerably more if calibrated, but the man had not known the camera. Glenn stopped on the sidewalk to look at it again. His mind was racing furiously as he walked home.

A half-hour later, Glenn set the camera down on his kitchen counter, took out his cell phone, and dialed. "Ralph? It's Glenn."

The voice was cheerful. "Glenn! Good to hear from you! What's up?"

"I just picked up an old Panamax 140 for a thousand bucks."

"You're kidding! That's quite a bargain! You're not into film, let alone medium format! What are you going to do with it?"

"I'm going to convert it to be digital."

"That'll be a tough nut to crack, Glenn."

"That's for sure, but we're up to the challenge, aren't we?"

"We?"

"Yeah. Remember how you built that CCD matrix array for that guy who wanted a digital four by five?"

"Sure! It took me a while, and he paid through the nose for it! But...?" He hummed softly.

"Yeah, Ralph, I know what you're thinking. This array will have to be precisely curved and a precise fit."

"I don't know, Glenn..."

"After I hang up with you, I'm going to put in a call to Mr. Kampanat in Thailand. He has some high density units for the new DSLRs. I want you to make this sensor fifty-six millimeters by one hundred forty millimeters, and curved as one hundred forty degrees of a circle. It will fit into the area where the film used to go. The sensor has to be perfectly fitted and tight."

"It would be better if I worked at the Thai factory where the resources are."

"Okay. I will liquidate some investments I have made in commodities to cover the cost. How soon can you leave?"

"How about Monday?"

"Perfect. I'll drop it by your shop this evening about 4:30."

"Great! See you then!" They both hung up.

A week later Ralph flew to Bangkok, taking the camera with him. Glenn's contact did not think it could be done, but both Ralph and Glenn were his friends, and the money was good. The women in the factory were fond of Ralph. They had worked together before. With skilled and precise craftsmanship, they installed the digital sensor right where the film used to go, just as Glenn had instructed. It required many attempts that had to be discarded. It took nearly seven months.

While Ralph was on the other side of the world converting the camera to be digital, Glenn continued to make designs and collect additional parts for the project. He modified a new and faster motor for the shutter in order to take multiple exposures rapidly. He also created a computer module to fit into one of the film compartments. Then he assembled a memory array for the other compartment. He adapted a large liquid crystal display for the camera back, and he modified the battery compartment to take a battery with higher capacity.

When Ralph returned from Thailand with the camera seven months later, Glenn was ready. Despite Glenn's extensive preparations and Ralph's precision work, it took another eleven months to assemble their first effort. Then they went out to Golden Gate Park for a trial.

That afternoon there was only a little fog towards the south end of the bridge, and there was a gentle sea breeze. Glenn set up his tripod with the camera, while Ralph stood nearby, watching. Glenn carefully squeezed the shutter release and scowled. "Nothing."

"Nothing? It has to work! We checked it just an hour ago!"

Glenn squeezed the release again, and there was a high-pitched whine. "Nothing is coming onto the display. I'll take a few more shots blind, and then we'll head back. I can process the images while you try to find out what's happening in the camera."

"Right."

Glenn took a few more shots in different locations, and then they went back to Glenn's apartment. There were no images that could be processed. Soon they realized that despite all of their previous testing, the camera was going to take a lot more work. When a year had consumed their time with the project, Glenn paid his friend and said good-bye. Ralph went home to other projects.

It took another year before Glenn was getting images that were useable. There was never a moment of labor on the camera that he was not thinking of more possibilities and modifications. The results began to amaze him.

After a total of eleven years of long days and sometimes sleepless nights, Glenn then drove into Yosemite National Park. He planned to put the camera through vigorous testing after attending a seminar. He looked forward to the sessions because he believed his camera creation would be of great value in environmental research. He had no way of knowing where the seminar and his testing would lead.

+ + +

Later that same Thursday, in the early evening, the Ahwahnee dining room was less than half occupied. The high ceiling with large windows provided a stunning environment. As the waiter brought the soup to Betsy Sue, she saw a man approaching her table.

"Good evening, Dr. Johnson, I'm Mike Howard from Yosemite Conservancy. I'm looking forward to your lectures." He felt a little off balance because of her stunning appearance. To him, she appeared to be a lot like a movie star, with her dazzling Texan looks.

"Thank you. Are you by yourself?"

"Yes. Normally, I eat at the Food Court at Yosemite Lodge, but it's easier this evening to eat here at the Ahwahnee."

"Would you like to join me? I already have my soup, but I'm sure the waiter can accommodate you."

"Thank you, I don't mind if I do." He sat down just as the waiter approached. "Hi. I won't be needing soup and salad. When you bring her main course, would you please bring me the vegetable platter? I'll have a glass of Merlot in the meantime please."

"Very good, sir." The waiter nodded and departed.

Betsy Sue was almost done with her soup. "It has been nearly a year since I was last here. I understand Yosemite Conservancy has a number of projects going right now." She looked him over carefully.

He smiled. "We've always got projects going or in preparation. It's only a matter of cash flow and manpower."

The waiter approached with a large tray, and soon they were enjoying their dinners. They were delicious. Betsy Sue looked at her watch. "I have to watch my time. I want to be upstairs before people begin to arrive."

"It probably won't make much difference to most of them. All but one of them has been here for Yosemite Conservancy events like this before. They take everything in stride."

"And the other one?"

"I've never met him. I understand that he has been coming to the park most of his life, and his home is in Berkeley. He has developed some kind of special camera. It records many aspects of the environment, and if there are people present, it records their interaction with the environment."

She put her fork down. "That's fantastic, if it does all that." She beckoned to the waiter and picked up her napkin. "Bobby, do you have my check? I need to be getting upstairs."

"Yes, Dr. Johnson, I do." The waiter reached into a pocket in his apron and handed the check to her with a pen. "Please just sign and include your room number. I will take care of it."

"Thank you, Bobby. Everything was fine." She shoved her chair back, and Mike began to stand. "Don't get up, Mike. Finish your dinner. I will see you upstairs."

"Thanks for the dinner companionship. I'll see you up there." He smiled.

She smiled back and walked briskly away. Just outside the dining room, she turned right and walked across the Great Room. At the stairs, she paused to look back at the room through which she had come. Everything about the Ahwahnee impressed her. "That massive fireplace always amazes me," she thought.

Upstairs, she greeted the few people conversing in small groups before entering the smaller area set up for her lecture. As usual, the hotel staff had everything ready. She turned on the video projector and her laptop. Other people began to file into the room carrying briefcases and steaming cups of coffee. One tall and handsome man walked in with a glass of ice water and nothing else. He nodded to her and sat down in the back row. Her heart started to be faster, and she suddenly felt warmer. For a brief moment, she forgot where she was and why she was there. She blinked as a smile crept across her lips, then she continued her preparations to start.

Minutes later, Betsy Sue began her lecture with a short video, and then she launched into her PowerPoint presentation. Everyone took notes except Glenn. She noticed. He never looked down. He kept his eyes steadily on her, and periodically glanced at the screen. She was focused on her lecture, but she still felt warm, and her heart continued to beat faster. She was conscious of his watching her and listening intently. Finishing the first part of her evening's presentation, she announced a twenty-minute break and bolted for the ladies' room, where she touched up her lip gloss and composed herself.

A few minutes later, as she emerged, she walked over to Glenn. "I understand that you have built a unique camera." She felt strangely serene yet excited as she spoke to him.

"Yes. This coming week I want to do some thorough field testing. After eleven years of work, I need to use it in a real world of wilderness and people."

"Did you say eleven years?"

"Yes. It all started when I found an old Panamax medium format film camera in a pawn shop. Initially, I was simply intrigued with the idea of converting it to be digital. I thought it would be a straight-forward process, if it could be done."

"What took so long?"

"While a custom-made sensor was being created and installed, I worked on the electronics and software. I also changed over the motor, based upon a hunch. At first, nothing worked as planned."

"And?" Without realizing it, she was becoming smitten.

"The man who helped me create the sensor had other projects to work on, so he went home. As I solved each problem I encountered I thought of new things that could be done."

She took a sip of coffee when it was handed to her. "Thanks." She turned back to Glenn. "I understand it somehow records environmental factors outside what we would consider normal images."

"Yes. As the lens rotates, recording multiple images, it also moves horizontally with the sensor. The camera is also different because instead of filtering out data outside the visible spectrum, it enhances that range. The result is an image that is three-dimensional and can record environmental factors in three dimensions. If people or animals are present, their changing relationship to where they are is recorded."

"I'd like to see that!"

"I'll be headed out Monday morning. You can tag along if you like."

"Absolutely!" She looked at her watch. "I need to finish this evening's presentation. I'll see you later."

"Okay." He stood there sipping his water while she headed back towards the lecture area. Watching her, he mumbled to himself, "She's stunning! Lord, what are you up to?"

7. The Project

Later that evening in the Ahwahnee bar, Betsy Sue and Glenn sat at a table in the southwest corner. He picked up their previous conversation, as though they had been just momentarily interrupted. "We were talking earlier about the camera." He smiled. "After I ran the first images through my software, I realized that I needed a different lens."

"Why? Did you want a different angle of view?"

"No. Every kind of glass has its own qualities. The lens that came with the camera was fine for the visible spectrum, but I wanted to record more. That meant designing an unusual lens in a different kind of mount. It took almost three years."

"Why did you need a different mount?"

"I created a lens that utilizes the piezoelectric effect."

"I'm not into physics. I focus on the life sciences." She smiled. "As I recall, the piezoelectric effect has something to do with crystals and electricity."

"Correct. I am into both the life sciences and the physical sciences. I've taught a few short courses on the relationships between the two."

She knew this was rare. He was even smarter and possibly more widely read than she was. "Without getting into the details, what's the result?" She always wanted to get to the point.

"You'll see if you tag along on Monday. You can help me make three or four images, and then we'll feed them into my computer for analysis. We should be able to make at least three images before lunch if we get started right after breakfast."

"It sounds like a slow process."

"Making the actual images only requires a few seconds, but the image files are large, and the camera's built-in computer takes more than twenty seconds to process each image."

Betsy Sue put her glass down and stared at him. "How large are the files?"

"They're just over fifty gigabytes. I put each image on a separate thumb drive." He reached into his wallet, took out a twenty-dollar bill, and began to carefully and intricately fold it.

"What are you doing?"

"Sometimes I have fun with the bar staff with my tips."

"Fun?" She took a piece of an ice cube out of her glass and positioned it in front of her.

"Yeah. When I am finished, the waitress will have a twenty dollar tip. If she unfolds it slowly, it typically takes several minutes. If she does it rapidly she'll tear it, but the money will still be good."

Betsy Sue put her thumbnail on the edge of the ice cube and pressed rapidly. The cube snapped sharply upward and landed against the bridge of his nose. "Gotcha!"

"Whoa!" he yelped, and then he grinned. "I owe you one!" He took a cube of ice from his drink, placed his thumbnails in the middle, and split the cube into several pieces. With great care, he selected two pieces of ice and positioned them on his napkin. Placing his fingers on the pieces, positioned against each other, he looked into her eyes and quickly pressed downward with his index fingers. The two pieces of ice clipped her ears.

She shrieked and laughed. "Uncle! You're better at that than I am!" She grinned as he smiled. Their friendship was growing deeper.

When the waiter brought the bill, he put both the folded twenty and a flat twenty on the tray. Then they got up and left.

+ + +

Shortly after seven the next morning, Glenn held Betsy Sue's chair for her as they sat down in the dining room. He was truly fascinated by this stunningly attractive woman. After he was seated, he looked up, and as he started to say something, she interrupted.

"I was glad to discover last night that you have a good sense of humor. I was afraid you might be just another studious scientist."

"Studious? If I could not have fun with life, I think I would go nuts with its challenges. Most of my humor is not physical, however. Where'd you learn to tidily-wink pieces of ice?"

"At the Dallas School for the Talented and Gifted, thank you." She smirked.

"That's an almost famous high school."

"I suppose. Where'd you learn that double ice missiles trick?"

"My younger sister Brittany learned it at Lakewood High School near Long Beach. She taught it to me. She called me last evening after we left the bar. I told her about you."

Betsy Sue smiled. "What did you mean by saying that most of your humor is not physical?"

"When I am teaching seminars I like to poke fun at my students. Last December I gave some physics students a true-false bluebook final. Their answers could fit onto one page of their bluebook. There were fifty paragraphs, each describing a problem, a method for solving the problem, and a solution. If there was one thing wrong in the paragraph, the answer was false. Otherwise, the answer was true."

"Wow! That sounds tough! Where was the humor?"

"Each paragraph was over two hundred words, so that they had to read it very carefully. Most of the students took all the four hours to come up with their answers. The worst of it was, the correct answer for all fifty of the questions was 'true.'"

She burst out laughing. "That's terrible! Did anyone get a perfect score?"

"Just one. I learned why a few days later. His name is Mike. He has bad eyes, and after he sat down, he realized that he had the wrong pair of glasses with him. They were for distance vision and not for reading. After thirty minutes, he had a splitting headache and knew he would never be able to read all the questions in time to finish the test. In desperation, he looked for a pattern, found it, and decided to take the risk of saying that all the answers were true. He was right, of course."

She chuckled. "He cheated! Legally!"

"Right. That is my kind of humor. A long time ago, I had a beef with the director of my high school's choir director. He always directed with his music, turning pages at the correct places, but he seldom looked at the music. His folder was sitting on the stand twenty minutes before the concert was to start, and few were in the hall. I sealed his folder shut with two way tape. The first section of the concert went flawlessly, but as he left the stage with his folder, he was sweating profusely. I had had my fun."

Again, Betsy Sue chuckled.

The waiter arrived with their food. "Will there be anything else?"

Glenn looked up at him. "No thanks. In a while, we'll need more hot water for our herbal tea."

"Right. I'll be back later. Enjoy your breakfast, folks."

Betsy Sue picked up a slice of bacon and took a bite. "Mmmm. This has hickory smoked flavor. It's delicious."

Glenn nodded. "This omelet is huge. This just might fill me up until lunch! How soon do you want to get upstairs for your final teaching session?"

She swallowed and washed it down with some grapefruit juice. "I don't think I need to be there for at least thirty to forty minutes. We've got plenty of time."

"Good. We don't have to rush." He took a large bite of the omelet. After swallowing he drank some tea. "I am enjoying your seminar. You touched on a few things we can talk about another time."

"For instance?"

"I think many of our colleagues – and present company as well – arrogantly assume that nature's mechanisms are inadequate in responding to the impact of human culture."

"I don't think so."

"I think when I get more data from my camera that the results will be surprising to many environmental activists."

Quietly, they continued to enjoy their meal, discussing minor points in the seminar. By the time they finished breakfast, their beginnings of friendship were developing rapidly. The rest of Betsy Sue's seminar went flawlessly.

That Saturday evening, after the final session, everyone expressed their appreciation and gave her high praise. Some left their cards with her for future connections.

On Sunday, Betsy Sue and Glenn went to Yosemite Chapel for worship. Betsy Sue enjoyed singing the praise songs, and Glenn complimented the piano player for his music. After lunch, they got into Glenn's SUV, and Betsy Sue got her first look at the camera. "It does not look too much different from any other Panamax except for the display on the back."

Glenn smiled. "True, but you know something of what I've put inside." He started the engine and pulled out of the parking area. "Today let's just explore and plan. We'll pick out three or four places to make images tomorrow. Today we can rest."

She nodded. "It's interesting that you never talk about taking pictures but about making images. I'm going to be really interested in what we may achieve."

Glenn drove past Yosemite Village onto Northside Drive. "Do you know anything about these diesel hybrid shuttle buses here in the park?"

"I know the Park Service paid an outrageous amount of money for them. When the first samples were here, they tried bio diesel fuel, and some said the exhaust smelled like French fries."

He laughed. "I remember! That first bus carried all kinds of testing equipment. They finally decided that low-sulfur diesel was less harmful to the valley's environment." He drove silently until they passed El Capitan. Glenn's favorite spot was Valley View, across from Bridal Veil Fall and just beyond El Capitan. He pulled into the parking area, where there were already several cars. He said, "A long time ago I was here in January while it was snowing. I climbed up on top of the hood of my rental car and leaned against the windshield. It was so peaceful!"

Betsy Sue gazed across the valley. "I love the view, but maybe we should include more foliage and possibly animal life in the image. How about off to the left there, in the midst of the trees?"

Glenn nodded. "As a teenager I used to explore the river along through there, taking lots of pictures. I still have some of them back at my apartment. I tried going down river from here to the right, but I did not get to a place where I wanted to take pictures until I got near Pohono Bridge."

"Yes. Weather permitting we might have time to make more than one image."

"Right." Glenn pulled out of the parking lot and went west until they turned to cross the river. When they reached the turnoff towards Bridalveil Fall and the south exit road, they had to slow down for traffic. "I have never been here when there has not been water in this fall."

She nodded. "Neither have I. I think there is both a lake and an artesian spring that supplements the snow melt. I would love to hike into Dewey Point again. I love the view from there."

"That's not one I've done. What is it like?"

She smiled. "Dewey Point is directly across from El Capitan. It's spectacular."

Arriving at the tunnel, they quickly found a parking space in the south lot. Locking the SUV, they headed for the stairway that marked the Pohono trail. First, they went several yards up the steep incline above the stairs and picked out a spot where they could see almost the same panorama view as seen below from the Tunnel area, including the people in the parking lot.

Glenn breathed deeply with effort required by the altitude. "This looks like a good spot.

They gazed eastward down the valley. Betsy Sue pointed. "I think it would be good if our image includes the people below. In the ultraviolet and infrared spectrums it would be interesting to compare the parking lot area with the foliage nearby.

"That's a good idea. The sensor has a fifteen-stop contrast range, so those details should show up fairly well."

"Fifteen stops? That's phenomenal!"

"It's an improvement over other digital medium-format cameras. I have helped the factory improve their technology – with Ralph's help. Are you interested in going up to Sentinel Dome?"

"Not really – there's not much in the way of environmental drama up there. The views are spectacular, but there is precious little foliage. The last tree up there died after someone carved their initials on the trunk."

"I heard about that. I think you're right. I don't think images from up there will get us enough data to be helpful."

"Right. Even down in the valley, there are some wonderful places to take pictures, but few of them would be useful from an environmental study standpoint."

Glenn was curious. "For instance?"

She answered as they started back down the trail. "For example, I love Yosemite Falls, but I don't think it is a useful area for study. Cook's Meadow and the Ahwahnee Meadow are beautiful, but panoramic views would be of little help."

Glenn chuckled. "Don't be too sure! Still, that gives me an idea. I might find a way to mount the camera on the bottom of a hang glider and make images of the meadow from above."

"Wow! I never thought of that! Along that line, I have another idea for the future. Someday you could give the camera a motor drive advance and mount it in a weatherproof housing. Then you could put it on the bottom of a helicopter and do aerial images of other areas of environmental concerns."

At Camp Curry they parked near an area where pavement work was being done. Glenn spoke to one of the workers. "Do you think our SUV will be safe here?"

"Sure! No problem! We will be here a couple more hours if you want us to keep an eye on it. There's no food in it for bears to go after, is there?"

Glenn grinned. "No way! I've seen what those big boys can do." They both laughed.

They locked the camera in the SUV and got on the next shuttle. Betsy Sue settled back in her seat as best she could. "These shuttles are much more efficient than the old ones, but compared to the initial cost, they'll never regain their investment with the money saved on fuel."

"How do these compare to the old ones?"

She looked up for a moment before answering. "The previous shuttles were straight diesel. A driver told me that those got about four to five miles a gallon at best. These hybrids get between ten and twelve he said."

"That's a significant improvement."

"Yes, but while better for the environment, these buses cost three-quarters of a million each."

Glenn whistled. As the bus slowed down for the Happy Isles shuttle stop, they got up. When the back door opened, they stepped out and paused to get their bearings. Glenn pointed. "Let's stay this side of the river and follow the path on past the rest rooms."

"Okay." They both started walking. "We don't need to stop at the Nature Center, do we?"

"I don't think so. Let's go to the end of the path, though, so we can check out the rock fall area." Glenn pointed ahead and to the right. "It's up in that area."

"Okay. Do you think we should make an image of that area?" Betsy Sue was getting a little tired.

He did not say anything for a moment. "I'm not sure. What do you think?"

"I'm not sure either. It is just ahead. Let's check it out."

At the end of the path, they spent several minutes just taking in the scene. Glenn shook his head. "I don't think it would be worth the effort to make an image here for a few more years."

"I agree. It is so desolate. I don't think the camera could reveal much that we don't already know."

"You're probably right." Glenn turned, and she followed as they headed back down the path. A hundred meters short of the shuttle stop she stopped. Glenn looked at her as he stopped as well. "What's up?"

"Maybe we need to rethink what we want here."

"Shoot." He smiled.

"What about getting a slice of just this environment? You could mount the camera low, close to the ground, so that all that is seen is foliage and trees. Then we could step back out of view a dozen meters and wait for the right moment before making the image."

"I like it! I like the way you think!" He paused and pointed. "There's a shuttle. Let's grab it!"

They walked rapidly back to the bus stop. A shuttle arrived, and they rode to the next stop.

The Mirror Lake trail offered several places where they could make images. Betsy looked up and north, pointing. "There's Washington's Column through the trees. Look how dense the foliage is. What do you think?"

"It's a possibility. There is so much traffic on the trail here I doubt we could get anything much different than what we would get at Happy Isles. Let's keep walking."

They followed the trail that skirts the shore of the lake when it is full. They stopped at the rock slide, and Glenn looked around. "The environment here is about the same as it was over near the approach. This area seems like a viable alternative if we don't get a good image at Happy Isles."

Betsy Sue nodded. "I agree. Let's head on back." They briskly walked towards the shuttle stop. "From here we could make our way to Tenaya Lake or even Clouds Rest, but the trail is dangerous. There are easier ways to get up there."

"Right. Since we have equipment to deal with as well as supplies, it would be easier to get as close as we can by car." He pointed. "There comes a shuttle. Let's catch it."

It did not take long for them to reach the SUV. As they got in, Glenn put in the key and said, "Let's head to the Ahwahnee and change our clothes and freshen up."

Betsy Sue looked at her watch. "After I freshen up, I'll meet you in the Great Room."

"Okay."

The sun was low in the sky when they got back to the hotel and went to their rooms. Glenn quickly got a shower and changed clothes. As he did, he pondered images in his mind of he and Betsy Sue throughout the day. After going back downstairs, he sat in front of the fire in the Great Room for about thirty minutes before she came down. When he saw her, he stood up. "I feel human again! You look nice!"

She smiled. "Thank you, kind sir." She did a mock curtsey. "I'm famished. Are you ready to have dinner?"

"I'm hungry too. Let's take a shuttle over to the Mountain Room. I really like the food over there."

"I do too."

Almost self consciously, he reached for her hand, and she did not hesitate. Together, they walked out to the shuttle stop like they had known each other a long time. A few minutes later, they were on their way. Getting off at the Lodge, Glenn was pleasantly surprised when they only had to wait about thirty minutes to get a table. Taking their beeper with them, they looked around in the Lodge Gift Shop until the beeper chimed.

They went back over to the Mountain Room Restaurant, and the hostess seated them next to a window on the north side. As they settled down in their chairs, water glasses were filled. As they looked at their menus, Glenn looked up at her. "What looks good to you?"

She was thoughtful. "When I teach seminars I usually just take my meals at the Ahwahnee, either in the dining room or in my room. I have only eaten here once before, and it was a long time ago. Since you've eaten here in the past, what do you suggest?"

"I must admit I prefer the food here to that of the Ahwahnee. Many of the employees prefer the Mountain Room, and I've never heard any complaints about anything here. I have not had prime rib for a long time, so I think that's what I'll have."

"Oh, that sounds good. I think I'll have the same."

A waiter approached. "Can I get you folks something to drink?"

I'll have an iced tea," Betsy Sue said with a smile. "I'm ready to order when you are."

"I'll have water with a wedge of lime." Glenn paused. "We're both going to have the prime rib."

The waiter turned to Betsy Sue. "How would you like it cooked?"

"Medium rare."

"The soup is tomato bisque or French onion."

"I'd rather have a salad, with honey mustard dressing."

"You get both, unless you'd like tomato slices instead of soup."

"I'll have tomato slices."

"Very good. And you sir?"

"Make mine all the same."

'Very good. I'll bring your salads right away." The waiter was soon gone.

"Yosemite – particularly the valley – is a great place to do environmental research." Betsy Sue was thoughtful. "I'm looking forward to seeing the images we will make tomorrow."

"I am too. We cannot analyze the results using the camera's electronics. I'll bring along my laptop so you can check out the images while I'm driving between locations." Glenn held her gaze.

"What software do you use?"

"I've created my own with the help of some programming students at Berkeley. One of them is truly gifted. He has set up a very straight forward but amazingly detailed menu system for extracting data. Another student created a snapshot tool so that we can analyze small portions of an image without constantly having to process the entire file."

"Excellent. I'm going to have to learn that menu system."

"Not a problem. I have a sample image from a garden in Berkeley with a dog in the center for including the animal kingdom in analysis. You can play with it tomorrow morning before breakfast if you like." Their salads and drinks arrived. Glenn looked up at the waiter. "Thanks."

"You're welcome." The waiter left again.

"Is there any chance I could look at that software tonight after dinner?"

"Sure. I will bring my laptop to your room after dinner. I've never been a night owl, unless I was working on the camera. Since we've a long day tomorrow, I won't be up very late."

She took a bite of her salad. "Good. Now that I'm done with the seminar I can relax and explore something new."

When their dinner came, they ate mostly in silence. After dinner, Glenn went to his room and turned on his laptop. For about a minute his hands flew over the keys. Then he closed the lid and took the laptop down to Betsy Sue's room. He knocked on the door.

After a moment, she opened the door. "Hi! Long time no see! Do you want to come in?"

"Not tonight, thanks – I need to get some sleep. The battery is fully charged, so you should be able to get a couple of hours of work on this." He handed her the large laptop.

"Thanks. See you in the morning!"

"Yes. Good night." He watched her close the door.

Inside, Betsy Sue took the laptop to a desk by her window. She paused, thinking about Glenn. After a moment, she pressed the power button and sat down to wait for it to boot. Suddenly, she had a blue screen. "Oh no!" she almost whispered. Then, in fine print in a red box, she saw the words, "Sorry, Betsy Sue. I couldn't resist...." Next, she saw a gorilla grinning, and from the speakers came an insane giggling laughter. Betsy Sue smiled. "That's one for you, Glenn!" No sooner were the words out of her mouth, when the garden image he had told her about appeared, surrounded by the window frame of the custom software.

In less than an hour, she had the interface figured out. She changed into an extra-large t-shirt and crawled into bed. Soon she had a vivid dream begin. She was taking pictures with Glenn, and they were going to many locations that she wanted to study. A voice in the dream spoke to her.

> "Sleep well, Betsy Sue. This will be a new beginning for you. In years to come, you will be both a wife and mother in addition to being successful. You will also have two children who will make a difference in the world."

The dream faded, and she slept soundly through the night.

8. Discoveries

After breakfast Monday morning, Glenn and Betsy Sue set out for the eastern end of Yosemite Valley and Happy Isles, a small group of islands in the midst of the Merced River connected by paths and bridges. Glenn loved it as a place of transition. Above Happy Isles, they could hear the river's steep and often noisy rapids. If they had gone up the trail, within a relatively short distance they would have found both Nevada Fall and Vernal Fall. From Happy Isles on down through the valley, the distance, moved more slowly and quietly. The morning sun was filtered through the trees of the islands, and the air was almost perfectly still.

They did not go far enough into the area to venture onto even one of the islands. Instead, they set up the camera so that they could see the edge of the snack bar at one end of the view. They could also see bushes and low hanging branches just to the side of the walkway leading away from the snack bar towards the islands. After doing several spot readings with a light meter, Glenn adjusted the settings to the camera. They waited on a nearby log bench, and Glenn had a remote control in his hand.

A shuttle bus pulled into the stop several yards away. As people got off, many pointed up the path in their direction. Looking towards where they were pointing, they saw a full-grown brown bear. Recognizing the danger, the people warily took pictures and kept their distance. Glenn and Betsy Sue waited. The bear began to veer towards the edge of the path as it got closer to the snack bar. As it stuck its nose into the bushes about three meters from the camera, Glenn pushed a button. When the camera's motor whined briefly, the bear looked up in the camera's direction. Not hearing any further noise from that direction, the bear looked around, took note of the people nearby, turned, and headed past the camera into the forest.

They gathered up the camera and tripod, and they ran for the shuttle just as the door closed. The driver saw them running and reopened the door. It took them past Mirror Lake and the stables before going on back to Camp Curry, where they got into the SUV. They put the camera and tripod in the back, and they covered it with a lap robe.

As they got in up front, Betsy Sue was excited. "Let's take a look at this first image before we go anywhere."

"Good idea. It is too early in the day for the light to be decent at Valley View and at Tunnel View. We should wait until well after lunch before we go to the other end of the valley."

While Glenn was talking, Betsy Sue had booted the laptop. "I'm ready for the thumb drive." She held out her hand.

"Okay." He retrieved it from his shirt pocket. "Here."

"Thanks." She inserted it into the socket. It was more than a minute before the file had fully opened. "Wow," she said, "I'm glad we shot this from a low angle." She turned so that he could look over her shoulder. She could feel the warmth of his presence close to her.

"Select the bear and the bush first, and tab it to another window."

She did so. "Amazing! The resolution is so fine, even after we have selected a small portion of the image. It is beautiful. You've designed a fantastic camera, Glenn!"

"Thanks." He paused. "Check out the infrared spectrum in the image." He enjoyed her scent as he peered over her shoulder.

"Interesting! In three dimensions, we can see not only the heat of the bear's breath, but it seems as though we can see the bush reacting subtly to the bear's presence."

"Check the far end of the ultraviolet range of the image."

"Right." She rapidly did a few keystrokes. "That's amazing too. There seems to be even more responses of the bush showing in the ultraviolet range."

"Mmm," was all Glenn could say. "Now let's do a composite."

"How?"

He reached around her with his arms either side of her and pulled down a menu she had not previously seen. "There."

"Whoa!" She paused. "This is awesome! It's going to take a lot of analysis and study!"

"Right." He slid back into the driver's seat. "Let's head over to the Ahwahnee. That projector you used over the weekend has been put in my room. We can aim it on the white wall above the bed and study the results in greater detail."

She nodded. "It sounds like a great idea, but let's wait until we have the other two images. By the time we get back to the hotel we can get an early lunch."

"Okay."

Glenn stuck the key in the ignition and started the SUV. Backing up, he steered the vehicle past the Camp Curry Gift Shop and curved right on out towards the bicycle rental area. After a stop sign, they headed across a rock bridge over the river. "This brings back some vivid memories from when I was a boy."

"Really? What?"

"On the right used to be Camp 15, a tents-only campground. Later, it became known as Upper River campground. On the left, my family used to park our trailer in what was then Camp 7, which later became known as Lower River campground."

"They were wiped out in the so-called 100-year flood of 1997, weren't they?"

Glenn nodded and pointed to the left at a sign. "You can see there on that sign how deep the river was right here."

"Wow!"

"It started on New Year's Eve and subsided almost a week later. It was the worst disaster in the park's history, except perhaps for the 1996 geological event at Happy Isles." The road began to veer west towards the village. "Have you ever seen a mountain lion here?"

"I saw one in the cliff area above the Ahwahnee Hotel three years ago."

Glenn smiled. "I once saw a mountain lion take down a buck right here on the road and drag it into the Ahwahnee meadow." He pointed to the right. "Coyotes began to howl and gather around. They were smart enough to keep their distance until the lion had had its fill. The park's visitors were not that smart. Rangers had to come and move the people further away to take their pictures."

Betsy Sue laughed. "That doesn't surprise me! Visitors sometimes check their brains at the gate!" They both laughed. "Several years ago there were some people gathered in the apple orchard at Camp Curry because a bear was in a tree munching on apples. A woman was standing under the bear taking pictures, and a friend dragged her away just in time before the bear relieved himself. The woman almost had a yellow shower!" She smiled.

They drove to the Valley View parking lot, just east of Pohono Bridge. After setting up the camera amidst the foliage along the river, they managed to get an image that included a Douglas Squirrel and a Mule Deer.

They then packed up their gear and pulled out of the parking lot and drove west to the bridge. As they crossed it, Betsy Sue asked, "Do you know where the name *Pohono* comes from?"

Glenn scowled as he thought. "I think it is related to Bridal Veil fall, isn't it?"

"Kind of. Remember how the valley used to be occupied by a tribe of Native Americans called the Ahwahnechee people?" Glenn nodded. "They believed that the fall was the home of a vengeful spirit named Pohono that stood guard at the entrance of the valley. There was supposedly a curse for anyone who looked at the fall as they left the valley. On the flip side, however, those inhaling the mist of the fall are supposed to have better marriages."

"Fascinating! I love old legends like that!" As they reached the fall, he turned right and headed up the hill. There was a slight breeze as they turned left to park at the tunnel's south lot. They climbed up the Pohono Trail several dozen meters. Both panted as they went up the stairs and the steep trail. It veered left after a few dozen meters. Then they set up the tripod and secured the camera on top.

Glenn paused to look out over the valley. "This trail continues on for twenty-one kilometers and ends at Glacier Point. Most people start at the other end because it is rather steep. I am skeptical about the potential of this vantage point. We are not going to see any wildlife from here, although we can see people below. I wonder what the foliage in the direct sun will be like in comparison to the shade foliage."

Betsy Sue nodded. "It's hard to say. There will definitely be differences in the infrared range, but I don't know about the ultraviolet range. I say 'go for it' any time you want. We'll know later if we have any good data."

On a hunch, Glenn took the camera off the top of the tripod. They then mounted the camera on the bottom of the tripod's center post, adjusting until the camera was only a few inches from the ground. Using a spot meter, Betsy Sue took readings of several parts of the scene. "There's more than a ten stop exposure range between the brightest areas of El Capitan and the deepest shadows of the foliage. This will be a nice challenge for the camera's sensor." Moments later, the camera's lens gave a high-pitched whirr.

They headed back down the trail to the parking lot. After packing their gear away, they paused to go to a fountain and get a few sips of water. After looking around and taking in the view some more, they crossed the highway to the other lot where more people were taking pictures. They wandered from group to group silently, listening to the conversations.

Thirty minutes later, with the sun getting lower in the sky, Glenn pulled out of the parking lot and headed back down into the valley. Betsy Sue looked at the last image. "There are some surprises in this last image too."

"Really?" He glanced over at her and at the laptop.

"Yes! I see!"

"So far there are no surprises in the infrared range of the people. There are some real surprises, however, in looking at a composite of the infrared and ultraviolet when I look at the foliage. On the edge of the shadows, I can see some things I do not understand. It's going to take study. Seeing it all in 3-D helps, but I need to know more." She put in another thumb drive. "Oops! I put in the drive with the first picture." She paused. "I've got an idea though. I'm selecting a section of the image where the people are against the foliage." She paused. "Amazing! I cannot be sure, but it seems as though the foliage is responding to the breathing of the people. Amazing."

"That's certainly different than I might have expected."

Down the hill and past the fall, they rolled down their windows as they drove east along the southern cliffs. With the sun getting low in the sky behind them, the cliffs took on warmer colors. They were both at peace.

Back at the Ahwahnee, neither of them was particularly hungry. In Glenn's room, they moved some of the furniture and aimed the projector at the wall. Zooming the lens out, they could project the Happy Isles scene about eight feet wide.

Glenn scowled. "I'm going to free up some memory and reboot. We need more computing power."

"Good idea. I'm going to order some food from the room-service menu. How about some finger food and hot chocolate?"

"Great! Tell them to send up a bottle of chilled champagne in a couple of hours." He did not look up from his computer.

She smiled. "I like the way you think! These images are worth celebrating."

They studied the three images into the night. There was more data there than they could have even hoped for. They could see patterns of interaction between plants and animals. They could see patterns in the air that had never before been recorded. The more they studied the images, the more excited they became. It became apparent to them that they had a new research tool at their disposal, and that they were pioneers.

At last, Glenn yawned. "It is late."

"Yes, it is." Their eyes met. He kissed her, and she kissed him back.

+ + +

Three hundred eighty-four thousand kilometers above them, Walter and his crew on the Moon base were having a late-night meeting. Walter was briefing them on the implications of current events. He told them that Qaak had decided to retire. "It was as much a surprise to me as it is to all of you. He also suggested that I be his successor as convener. That lead to a lot of discussion, which is why I've been gone for several days. I've posted new work assignments for all of you."

Walter paused and looked around the den. "That's all at present except for this. Since I am now the convener of the Gaardians, there will probably come a time when I move permanently to Gaardian Center and place someone else in my position here. I do not anticipate that happening this year or even next year, but it will happen. Good night, everyone."

He put his arm around Belinda and gave her a hug before heading for his quarters. He left behind animated conversations in the den that lasted into the night. As he flopped on his bed to join his wife Debbie, their two cats jumped down to do some exploring.

+ + +

On the planet below, Margaret Graves put her pencil down. Turning her chair around, she gazed out the second-floor window of her office. The church parking lot had only a few cars, and they were parked close to the building. In the distance, she could see downtown Oakland and, beyond that, a fog-shrouded San Francisco. The phone rang. Reaching towards the corner of her desk, she pushed a button. "This is Margaret Graves. How can I help you?"

The voice was loud and clear. "Margaret, this is Ann."

"Hey, Ann, isn't this a beautiful day?"

"Absolutely! I got a message from Asayak a few minutes ago, and we should get together and talk about some developments that we cannot discuss on the phone. Are you busy for lunch?"

"Not yet. Where do you want to meet?"

"How about there, in your conference room? I can be there in about forty minutes."

"Sounds good. I'll see you then. Bye!"

"Bye!"

Margaret punched the same button and glanced down at a gold ring on her right hand. The purple stone in its center shimmered slightly. "G-mail to Toby Ballentine."

Toby appeared next to her desk. He smiled. "Hi, Margaret! I heard that you had joined our ranks, but we have not talked since. How are you?"

"Blessed!" Margaret smiled. "Ann Cotter and I are going to have lunch here in a little over thirty minutes. Would you like to join us?"

Toby shook his head. "I'm sorry! I am headed to Washington, D.C. in a few minutes. Can I have a rain check?"

"Sure. Maybe next time!"

"Okay. Until then."

"Until then." Toby's image disappeared. "Next time," Margaret murmured in a low tone.

9. Complications

When Glenn and Betsy Sue awakened the next morning, both began making phone calls from their rooms. The first call Glenn made was to one of his colleagues at Berkeley. At the end of more than an hour of talking with Dr. Mel Huggins, Glenn realized that this was the beginning of something revolutionary in several areas of environmental research. What Glenn did not anticipate was that after hanging up, Mel Huggins began making phone calls to people he thought would be interested. Both Glenn and Betsy Sue created a stir with their phone calls across the world's scientific community and on into the political arena.

They met for lunch at the Ahwahnee dining room and greeted each other with a quick kiss. After they sat down and the waiter had supplied them with ice water, Glenn spoke. "I've been on the phone most of the morning with colleagues both in optics and in physics. I think some of them are almost as excited as we are."

"I've had the same kind of morning. I have been talking with Sierra Club leaders as well as environmental activists. Just before I came down for lunch, I got a call telling me I was going to hear from Senator Hosmer."

Glenn scowled. "I suppose that had to happen."

"Why? What's wrong?"

"Senator Hosmer is notorious for her supposedly well-intentioned supervision of scientific research. If she gets involved, our research may become a chaotic mess."

"I've met her, but she did not seem so bad." Betsy Sue was pensive.

"Let's not worry about that now. Would you like me to come along with you to the conference next weekend at Lake Tahoe?"

"I'd love to have you come along, but won't you get bored?"

"Not a chance. There's lots of wilderness in the Tahoe area. Anytime I am not with you, I will make images. I've an idea brewing about another lens. I think I am going to have my friend Ralph make another camera. He has the specs to this one. He can do all of it except the lens, and I want to do that part anyway."

Betsy Sue smiled. "If we're going to Lake Tahoe together, let's check out of here tomorrow morning and take some more images along the way. I'd like to get one or two on the Tuolumne Meadows road."

"If we're going to do that, why don't we head up to Glacier Point this afternoon? I've got more than a dozen thumb drives waiting to be filled." He grinned.

After lunch, they went to Glacier Point and took three images along the way. When hiking without the camera equipment, they sometimes held hands. Both were happier than they could ever remember. Their third image was taken near Washburn Point. They could see Half Dome and the valley through the trees.

Glenn was thoughtful. "I'm going to secure the camera to the bottom of the tripod's center column and shoot the image just above the ground, exactly like we did down near the tunnel."

"That ought to be interesting! We might catch some unusual images in the infrared and ultraviolet ends of the spectrum."

After seeing that the camera was level – though upside-down – they backed off a few meters so as not to discourage any animal life from being in the foreground of the image. He became motionless. Betsy Sue was suddenly curious. "Why are you waiting?"

"Shhh! He said quietly. I just saw some movement over there." He pointed.

He was right. Deep in the shadows of the trees and amid the foliage, there was movement. A deer? Both of them froze as a mountain lion crept towards the cliff edge and the valley. Glenn and Betsy Sue were frozen still. With no perceptible movement, Glenn pressed the remote button. As the camera whirred, the cat froze, glanced in the camera's direction, and then took off after a mule deer grazing below them.

Without waiting to see what would happen next, they gathered up their equipment and raced for the SUV up near the road. Once inside, Glenn sighed. "Wow! That was amazing! I hope the cat won't be blurred in the image!"

"I doubt it. It didn't really start to move until after the lens had spun."

"You're probably right." He paused. "I'm thinking ahead now. I want to get back up here in the winter."

"Isn't the road closed?"

"Yes, but there is winter cross-country skiing from Badger Pass to the Gift Shop at Glacier Point. The building is converted to a bunk house ski shelter for the winter."

"We'd probably have to pull a toboggan with our equipment."

"Right." He paused. "We?" He smiled, started the engine, and headed down the switchback to Glacier Point. Once there, they just walked around like all the other tourists.

Wednesday morning they checked out of the Ahwahnee, and along the Tuolumne Meadows road, they made four more images without having to hike more than a kilometer off the highway. Since making the images did not take much time, their journey that day was not difficult.

They arrived at Lake Tahoe in the early evening, and after checking into the Hyatt Regency Hotel, Casino, and Spa in Incline Village, they took a stroll. Without telling Betsy Sue, Glenn arranged for a dozen red roses to be place in their room, and he stopped at a jewelry boutique on the perimeter of the casino.

Walking along the lake a little later, Glenn stooped down like he was looking at one of the small rocks. On one knee, he looked up at Betsy Sue, his hand extended with a red velvet box and a diamond ring. Tears running down her cheeks she said, "Yes, Glenn! Absolutely! I knew you would ask me after I finished my first lecture at the Ahwahnee. I just didn't know when." They kissed.

They eloped that night, but the honeymoon was postponed. Late in the morning, while they were finishing breakfast in bed, the phone rang. Glenn picked up the receiver. "Hello?"

"Is this Glenn Franz?" asked a woman's voice.

"Yes."

"This is Senator Gayla Hosmer. I thought you two were photographing Yosemite! This morning I learned that you had left and were at Lake Tahoe. What's going on?"

"A lot. Betsy Sue has a conference here starting tomorrow, and last evening we got married." Putting his hand over the receiver Glenn whispered, "It's the senator."

"Married!! Congratulations! My best to you both! Are you going to have your honeymoon there at the Lake?"

"No Senator. Betsy Sue has a very full calendar, and so do I. I am adjusting mine so that we can stay together most of the time between now and December. We've not talked about it yet, but I'd like to return to Yosemite for Christmas."

"That sounds great! How soon can the two of you come to Washington?"

"As I told you senator, our calendar is full until after Christmas and the New Year. Why do you ask?"

"I've been getting calls from both the Department of the Interior and the EPA. Both agencies want to make use of your special camera. I think both agencies each want to have it for six months to a year."

"That's out of the question, Senator Hosmer."

"Glenn! Please."

"No, Senator! The camera is my private property and uses technology that I control. I will be more than happy to share data I acquire with the camera, but it will never be simply a Senator's toy!"

"Oh! No, no, no! You misunderstand, Glenn!"

"That's Dr. Franz to you, Senator Hosmer. I have witnessed how you abuse your power as a senator. Good bye, senator!" Glenn cradled the receiver. He turned towards Betsy Sue and gave her a wide grin. "You heard what I said. I drew a line in the sand. I hope that's okay with you. She wants to take control of the camera and act as an agent of its use for the EPA and Department of the Interior."

Betsy Sue's eyes grew wide. "Wow! I didn't realize she was such a vulture!" She grinned. "You and I are now one, my dear husband! We stand together." She paused, looking up at the ceiling. "Lord, have mercy!"

"Amen to that!"

Betsy Sue bit her lip and then turned to Glenn. "I've got an idea. How soon will Ralph be done making the second camera?"

"Probably a few days. He is still in Thailand, but we can call him. Why?"

"Why not have him make a third one like the first one, only with no electronics or software? Would that take long?"

Glenn grinned. "Brilliant! We will keep security loose on the third camera so it can be stolen by the senator's minions if she decides to stoop that low. We ought to be able to keep the first two secret and hidden for at least a while."

"Great!" She kissed him. "You call Ralph while I shower and dress."

"We can shower with each other and dress afterward. Before that, however, and before I call Ralph, let's pray together." He started to get out of bed.

"Okay," she said, as she got up and joined him on his side, and they both kneeled by the bed.

"Betsy Sue, to me prayer is a conversation with God. I'll start, and then we will be silent and see if God reveals anything to us. When you're ready, why don't you close our time of prayer?"

"Okay."

Glenn bowed his head. "Heavenly Father, you are bigger than any problem we will ever face. We confess the knowledge that, even with the intelligence you have given us, we truly need your help. Thank you for keeping us aware of your presence. Now, please provide what we need as we silently wait for you."

They silently waited in prayer for more than thirty minutes. Betsy Sue said, "Thank you, Heavenly Father, for giving us the vision to perceive your will, for giving us the faith to believe in what you have revealed to us, and for giving us the courage to trust in you and your ability to deliver us through even the most difficult challenges. We surrender it all to you in Jesus' name. Amen." She paused, and then she started to get up off the floor. "Glenn, we're going to need both cameras right away, aren't we?"

"Yes." He paused, thoughtful. "I have a friend named Mike Kuster, who has a little optics lab just north of here. He might have what I need to put together the lens I want for the second camera."

"You've got something different in mind, don't you?"

"Right." He smiled. "I'll have Ralph ship the second camera to us overnight. Then, tomorrow I will rework the lens at Mike's shop – with his help, of course. He is an optical technology genius. If he and I don't try to get any sleep, I think we can get it done quickly. Then, after your conference is over, we need to fly to Oakland, pick up the third camera, get my car, and drive to Jackson Hole, Wyoming. "

"Yellowstone! Right?" As she looked at him, he nodded. "Let's take our shower and get dressed. Then you can make that call to Ralph."

They kissed and headed towards the bathroom.

10. Yellowstone

Ralph found a Panamax 140 on the Internet, and purchased it for $1200. He mounted the third digital sensor array on the film plane, and then connected it to a usb port, which he mounted to be accessible on the back of the camera. After packing it carefully, he sent it via overnight delivery to Glenn and Betsy Sue in Wyoming. They were staying at a cabin they rented just north of Jackson Hole, within view of the Tetons.

Coming in the door of the cabin, with the package under his arm, Glenn took it to a table and quickly opened it. "It looks great!" He looked up as Betsy

Sue entered from the bathroom. "It's fantastic! It looks very useable. Except for this usb port on the back, it appears to be just like the other two."

"Where shall we hide it?" Betsy Sue had a bit of a smile on her face.

"We don't want to make it too hard to find, but not too easy, either." He paused. "How about on the shelf above the closet, behind our suitcases?"

"That might be a little too obvious." She paused, looking around. "How about those pots we don't use in the kitchenette? It will fit in that larger one."

"Good! I think that will do. It's nowhere near our secure location for our more valuable equipment."

"Right" She put the camera in the largest pot, and then she nested another smaller pot on top. Placing the larger pot on the back of the shelf, she put several other pots, pans, and skillets in front. "There! That ought to do it!"

Glenn had gone to the table and opened up their large laptop computer. Sitting down, he turned it on, and then he looked up at her. "I've been looking at that picture with the cougar again. This specially modified software is a good addition to our arsenal."

She walked over to stand behind him as he loaded the image. "What have you found?"

After the image loaded, he clicked a couple of menu items. "Watch!"

She stared, and she suddenly was wide-eyed. "Wow! I would never have imagined that being possible!"

The ground beneath them began to tremble. They looked at each other. Glenn nodded and said, "It is beginning!"

"Not to repeat myself, but WOW!"

"I think we'd better get up to Signal Mountain summit. Would you grab some snacks and drinks while I grab the cameras?"

"I'll grab our outerwear and gloves too. What about batteries?"

"I think we're okay. You might get that extra case of thumb drives though."

"Right."

As they walked out the door, the ground trembled again. Glenn reached into his pocket, stooped down, and put something near the bottom of the door. Jumping into the car, they headed out for Grand Teton National Park and Moose Junction.

At the gate, the ranger was friendly but serious. "Good morning! Have you been to the park before?"

"Yes," Glenn said, showing his annual pass. "We're headed to Signal Mountain Summit."

"Okay. Be very careful. We may be at the beginning of an earthquake swarm."

Betsy Sue leaned over Glenn. "Yes. We know! We are environmentalist photographers. Are there any roadbed problems at this point?"

"No. When Yellowstone trembles, we seldom experience any serious problems or damage. These swarms are usually low on the Richter Scale."

Glenn smiled. "Thanks! God bless you and keep you safe!"

"Thank you, sir."

Glenn put the car back in gear and headed north. Seeing a familiar sign, he turned right.

"Where are we going?"

"The Chapel of the Transfiguration is right up the road here. You'll like it, and it won't take too long." He swung the car into a parking area and put his car into a slot near the path to the entrance of the chapel.

Getting out of the car, Betsy Sue picked up her portable satellite radio and put it in her purse. After Glenn locked the car, they walked together toward the door. The wooden walkway echoed their footsteps. Just as they reached the door, the ground trembled. Betsy Sue looked the building over. "Is this safe in an earthquake?"

Glenn smiled. "It's as safe as most buildings. It is solid log construction, so the chapel is probably good up to 6 on the Richter scale. It's withstood bigger quakes than that!"

Once inside, they sat down on a rear bench. They were the only ones there, and it was very peaceful. Betsy Sue looked around at the log beams and the rustic décor. "This is wonderful!" she whispered. "I never dreamed we could find such a place here. That window behind the altar frames the Grand Teton perfectly."

"Yes." They both closed their eyes for more than a minute. Without another word, they got up, went out, and went back to the car. "And now, on to Signal Mountain!" Glenn said, as he turned the key.

Driving down the road towards the turnoff, the car's tires and shocks kept them from feeling the ground tremble with greater intensity. Betsy Sue turned on her satellite radio, and they heard a newscaster telling of the earthquakes. "I think I'll save the batteries just in case."

"Good idea." He made the turn toward the summit. "You would lose reception a lot of the time on this road anyway. We are on the north side of the mountain, so satellite reception is spotty at best until we reach the top."

For nearly a half an hour, they drove along in silence. As they neared the parking area at the summit, the panoramic scenery was stunning. "Why have I never been up here before?" This is wonderful!" Betsy Sue exclaimed.

"It's certainly one of my favorite spots. We've got great photography weather – with a few clouds but mostly clear." When he turned off the engine, the car continued to tremble. "Interesting!" was all Glenn could say.

They set up their tripods and cameras. They shifted the lenses on the cameras to take some of the sky out of the images and include more of the foliage. Glenn mounted camera number two close to the ground, and Betsy Sue set hers up at close to her own height.

After plugging in the thumb drives, they were going to make the images when the ground began to tremble and shake. It was more vigorous and sharp then they had previously experienced. Some of the other people in the area began moving back towards their cars. Glenn said, "Let's wait."

"I agree." They stood there with their arms around each other, sometimes simply holding on. Her voice was low. "These quakes seem different than the ones I've felt before."

Glenn nodded. "Growing up in California, I've felt many quakes, and some of them were severe. I have to agree with you. This seems different, but it may simply be the setting we're in and the fact we're experiencing it together." The quaking stopped.

"Now!" she said.

They pressed their remotes, and the shutters whirred. They folded up and packed up their equipment. Then, after taking one final look at the vista in front of them, they headed back to the car. After loading the equipment and getting in, they could feel trembling again before Glenn started the engine.

They noticed that they were the last car to leave the summit. Her satellite radio was still reporting the earthquakes. She shut it off as they headed down the north side of the mountain. About ten minutes later, as they were going down a straight and smooth stretch of the road, the car suddenly jolted, like they had driven over a pothole in the road. There was no pothole. The car began to shake more vigorously, and Glenn sped up. "Let's get off this road before things get worse!" he said.

"Exactly!"

When they were back on the main road, they headed south towards Jenny Lake and Leigh Lake. They stopped at the Cathedral Group turnout. Glenn turned towards Betsy Sue. "With the ground shaking this way, there's little point in using the tripods. Grab a beanbag and bring it with a camera."

"A beanbag?"

"You'll see."

At the edge of the turnout, there were two almost horizontal signs providing a map and describing what visitors were seeing. Following Glenn's example, Betsy Sue put a bean bag near the top edge of the sign. Then she set the camera on it. Standing to the side of the sign, she could see the bubble level on the top of the camera. "I get it! This is easier than I thought!"

"Right! Be sure you have your fingers on the sides and top of the camera only. Take the shot when you're ready."

The shutters whirred. On ground that was again trembling, they got back in the car. Betsy Sue was enthusiastic. "When and where did you learn that trick?"

"In Yosemite, when I was a little boy, bean bags did not have a threaded stud to mount the camera on like these do. They're great when backpacking, and you want to travel light."

"I'll be surprised if we don't get some good images today."

"I agree. Let's head back to our cabin." Once again on the road, they could not feel the Earth's trembling in the car.

Back at the cabin, as they approached the door Glenn pointed. "Do you see that piece of tape?"

Betsy Sue stooped down and retrieved a piece of brown tape, stuck to the weather strip on the stoop. "What's this?"

"I stuck that to the bottom of our door when we left. Somebody's been here in the cabin."

Inside, they went straight to the kitchenette. It looked like everything was still in place. They moved the pots, pans, and frying pans, opened the large pot, and took out the smaller pot inside. The camera was gone.

Glenn nodded. "Whoever was here was professional. We would not have looked for the camera so soon if I had not left my little marker at the bottom of the door. They probably thought we would not notice until tomorrow when we check out."

"Right. This is perfect. That camera's only a little better than its film version without the software, and without the lens modifications, they'll just get normal digital images." She smiled. "It's not usually my kind of practical joke, and it's kind of expensive, but I like it!"

"Right." He grinned. "It will probably be *at least* several days before they figure out we tricked them." He paused. "Now, here's the big question: Since we have a head start, shall we go on into Yellowstone today and make some images? We can slow the lenses down to get twilight pictures if we want."

Betsy Sue was thoughtful, looking upward. "Let's not. We can risk waiting until tomorrow. We can spend the rest of today and into tonight processing the images we already have. Tomorrow is another day."

"Okay. Let's get something to eat before we go back to work. How about going into town and getting a steak at the Snake River Grill?"

"That sounds great. First, let's secure our equipment where it's reasonably safe."

"Right."

11. The Sierra Club

Jonnie Riley put down the phone. "Have you heard about Betsy Sue Johnson?"

Jack Haddy looked up from his computer. "Wasn't she our lecturer at the Ahwahnee Hotel a couple of weeks ago for that seminar we arranged?"

"Yeah. That was about Betsy Sue. She has married Glenn Franz."

"The inventor of the special camera?" He smiled.

"Right. Anyway, right now they're trying to avoid dealing with Senator Hosmer."

"Ouch. That is tough. The senator has gotten us many appropriations over the last few years. She is pushing a bill for us right now. What's she up to with the newlyweds?" Jack got up from his desk.

"The senator wants to control access and usage of the camera. She's got both the EPA and The Interior waiting for her to supply what she claims she has." Jonnie smiled.

"What's the latest? Who was that on the phone?" Jack knew this could be serious.

"That was our special friend over at The Interior. Somehow, the senator got hold of the camera. It's a digital panorama camera all right. It has a usb connector on the back for connection to a computer. It makes nice big images, but without Dr. Franz's software, you get nothing but simply nice pictures."

Jack scowled. "We just might get caught in the middle of this. Glenn and Betsy Sue will need our help, but we can't buck the senator's wishes."

Jonnie bit her lower lip. "I've got an idea – no – two ideas!"

"What?" He looked at her intently.

"Don't worry. It is not illegal, but the less you know, the less you can spill. You deal with the senator and keep me posted on her. I will deal with Glenn and Betsy Sue, but I will keep you in the dark. Okay?"

Jack smiled. "I'm sure glad you're on *our* side!"

"I am too. As of right now, I'm taking a few personal days. Maybe I will head out to Yellowstone. I'll be back sometime next week, okay?"

"Okay." He paused. "Get plenty of rest. I want you ready to get back to work by the end of next week." He winked.

Jonnie nodded. She picked up her purse and sweater, and was quickly out the door. It was a brisk and misty day in San Francisco. Walking up Second Street, after a little over two blocks she caught a taxi.

"Where to?" The cabbie, a Chinese man she had ridden with before, was business-like.

"Take me to the Transamerica Pyramid. You can let me out at the entrance on Montgomery."

"Okay." The cab lurched forward.

Jonnie's mind raced as the cab made its way through the traffic. *I wonder how much help I can get from Ben,* she mused.

"We're here." The cabbie put down the flag and put the shift in park.

"Thanks!" She glanced at the meter, reached into her purse, and gave the cabbie a twenty. "Keep the change."

"Thanks! Do you want me to come back later?"

"Not this time – maybe next time."

"Okay. Thanks again." The cab pulled away.

Jonnie looked up. She liked this building. Even on stormy days, the crushed quartz surface kept the building looking white. A sea breeze was blowing across the steps as she headed for the entrance. Once inside, she headed for an open elevator door. She pressed thirty-two, and the doors closed.

When the doors opened, Ben Kaiser's suite of offices was in front of her. He had most of the floor. Jonnie did not know or understand even half of the business done by Tiberias Holdings, but she knew she could trust Ben. Jonnie had once told Jack, "If money talks, Ben is a sizeable chorus."

As she stepped into the plush offices and onto plusher carpeting, Ben came out of his private office. "Hey, Jonnie! Lucy saw you coming in downstairs. I can give you thirty minutes or so. What's up?" He hugged her.

She waited until they were in his office, and the door was closed before she spoke. "Have you heard about Betsy Sue Johnson and Glenn Franz?"

Ben smiled. "Absolutely. I have had people keeping eyes on them since they started doing their thing in Yosemite. It looks like they are a nice couple. Are you going to ask me to help them deal with Senator Hosmer?"

Jonnie stared at him. "Wow! You really do have your sources of information! Yes! I have a couple of ideas, and maybe you do too. I'm purposely keeping Jack Haddy in the dark on this so that he can keep us smooth with the senator."

"That's a good strategy." Ben looked up momentarily. "The senator can be very nice, but if you cross her, she can be ruthless."

"So I've heard."

"I've not met Dr. Johnson, but I spent several days with Glenn a year ago. I suspect that he is more brilliant and capable than most people in this country these days."

"Really!"

"Yes. He can wear several hats simultaneously. He is tops in a number of fields – physics, optics, biochemistry, and a few other areas. He also has a dry wit." He smiled. "I suspect that the camera that the senator has acquired is a clever ruse."

"A ruse?"

"Right. I own a major share of the company in Thailand that made the digital sensors for his cameras. They have helped Glenn's friend, Ralph, to make three cameras. The third one is now under the senator's control, but it does not have any of the features of the other two."

"Why do you think he made three?"

"The first one was his eleven-year labor of love. Once he worked with it a bit, he thought of more improvements. Instead of taking the first one off-line to make changes, he made another camera. Now, when he and Dr. Johnson are out in the field, they both have cameras to work with. It's a brilliant team effort that the senator does not appreciate."

Johnnie whistled softly. "I would imagine that the two of them can accomplish more in two days than fifty days of effort by one of the government's agencies."

"Absolutely. Do you have some ideas as to how to help them?"

"Sort of. I came to you because the senator has been decent to the Sierra Club, and I don't want us to lose those powerful and often good graces."

"Right."

"Can you keep the senator's attention diverted away from the newlyweds for a while? Once they can get some solid footing, the senator won't be able to interfere with their efforts as easily."

"I can do that. What are you going to do?"

"If I leave this afternoon, I can be in Yellowstone late tomorrow if I hurry. I'm going to call a press conference on behalf of the Sierra Club, and drop the Senator's name a few times."

Ben burst out laughing. "I have to admit, that had not occurred to me! That's great! The senator's staff will be so busy scrambling to take advantage of the publicity in an election year that she will be totally occupied with whatever you say – good or bad. She owes the governors of both Montana and Wyoming big favors. She will try to use whatever you say to her advantage. That'll be great!"

"I hope so. What about you? Have you any ideas for the newlyweds?"

Ben was thoughtful. "My lawyers are scrambling to create something new as we speak. It should not be hard. I've a hand in three things that we are going to merge together. Just outside Berkeley, I have a small optical research firm that Glenn has been associated with a couple of times. In Walnut Creek, Dr. Johnson has been associated for quite some time with an environmental research firm. She likes them and they like her. The third part of this is down in Malibu and Hughes Research Laboratories down there. I've been helping to fund several projects with them as we get ready for the next phase of our country's ventures into space."

"Wow! That's quite a mix. How are you combining them?"

"I'm not really combining them. After a lot of prayer last night, I am stealing staff from each of those three to create The Environmental Optics and Research Branch of Tiberias Holdings. I think the newlyweds will like working there. I'm going to talk with them this evening."

"That sounds great." Jonnie had a wisp of a smile. Where will this division be located?"

Ben chuckled. "As it happens, I own a large empty building complex in Fresno. Working around the clock, we will have everything up and running there in about 72 hours. The scientific staff will arrive – including the newlyweds – the first of next week. The complex is big enough and secure enough, that someone can appear to be working there even if they are out of the country. I have superb security resources."

"Good. Keep me posted, but remember that Jack and the others are not in the loop – at least not yet. Okay?"

"Okay." He paused and looked at his watch. "I know you have things to do, and so do I. I've got your cell phone, but I want you to have this." He reached into a drawer. Handing Jonnie a small device he said, "This is a secure satellite phone. Even at the highest levels of government, very few have the resources to monitor this. For right now, only you and I know that you have it, okay?"

"Great. Thanks Ben." Putting the new phone in her purse, she stood up. "I've got to pack a bag or two before heading to Wyoming, so I had better get going. Thanks again, Ben! You're a real friend to the Sierra Club and to me!" She kissed him on the cheek. "I'll call you when I arrive."

Ben smiled, as he reached for a phone on his desk. "Bye Jonnie!" Ben's secretary appeared as Jonnie went out. "Lucy, I need to talk with Glenn Franz or Betsy Sue Johnson as soon as possible." She nodded. "Also, tell Stan Mehta I need regular updates on this new division we're forming. That's it."

"Okay." Lucy turned and left.

Ben was wrong. Getting the Fresno complex ready took nearly seventy-five hours.

12. Well-Intentioned Vultures

The earthquake swarm was continuing in Yellowstone. There had been hundreds of quakes, and no one had any idea when they would stop. This was already a bigger ongoing event than both the 2008 and 2010 swarms.

Jonnie had driven non-stop when she arrived shortly after 5:00 in the morning. She checked into the same complex of cabins where Glenn and Betsy Sue had stayed. Betsy Sue had made a reservation for her. As soon as Jonnie entered the cabin, she put her suitcase down and collapsed on the bed. She slept until late morning.

+ + +

In Washington, Gayla Hosmer stared out her office window. She appeared to be relaxed and composed, but inside her mind was churning furiously. Her phone buzzed, and she touched the speaker phone button. "Yes, Peggy?"

"Dr. John Anderson on line two."

The senator scowled. She then picked up the handset. "Yes, John! How is the testing going? Is the camera going to be useful to the EPA?" She listened for several moments. "With all of our resources, don't we have software that can decipher the data?" Again, she listened, this time the voice on the other end was louder. "Wait, John! Slow down! How big did you say each file is?" She paused briefly. "I understand. What can I do to help?" She did not understand, but the fact that she did not understand helped Glenn and Betsy Sue – though she did not know it. "All right, John. I will make a call to Jack Haddy at the Sierra Club in San Francisco. With a little gentle pressure, he should tell us how to get Glenn Franz to help us." She paused. "All right, John. I'll let you know. Bye." She cradled the receiver and pressed a button. "Peggy?"

"Yes, senator?"

"Get me Jack Haddy at the Sierra Club headquarters in San Francisco. When we've got him, stay on the line and take notes."

"Yes, M'am."

In a few moments, the senator heard Jack Haddy's voice on the speaker phone. "Good afternoon, senator. I am glad you called. I've been wondering how that appropriations bill is doing?"

"Good afternoon, Jack. The bill is still in committee, but I think we will get it to the floor by the end of the month. That's not why I called, though."

"Oh?"

"I'm calling about Glenn Franz."

"What about him?"

The senator hesitated. "I called him several days ago about his new camera. I am afraid he may have misunderstood me. When the call ended, it was not on good terms. Do you know Dr. Franz?" She looked up at her office ceiling.

"I really don't know either of them. Jonnie might, though."

"Okay, let me talk to Jonnie."

Jack hesitated. "Jonnie's out of town. She needed to take some personal days off. She's not had a real break in over a year. You know how zealous she is!"

"Yes, Jack. Do you know how I can reach her?"

"She said she might head out to Yellowstone. I do not think she has been to the park in a couple of years. Even with the quakes, I think she'll be able to relax and enjoy herself."

"Okay, Jack. Is everything else going okay?"

"Yes, senator. If Jonnie calls in, I'll tell her you called and want to reach her."

"Good, Jack. I have to end this and make some other calls. Bye, Jack."

"Bye, senator." She pushed one button, then another.

"Peggy?"

"I've got it all down, senator. I'll try to find Jonnie as soon as I can."

"Good. Go to it." She pressed a button on the phone. The senator swiveled her chair around to look out the window again.

"Senator, Jonnie Riley is on Channel Five news."

The senator picked up a remote to turn on a large flat-screen television between the windows of her office. A reporter was holding a microphone next to Jonnie as she spoke.

"I drove for three days and arrived here earlier this morning. I've not been here in almost three years."

"Is there any particular reason you drove non-stop to get here?"

"I needed to take some time off, but now that I'm here, I want to find out all I can about this swarm of quakes. Contrary to a report I heard on the radio as I drove in, I seriously doubt that there is much chance of the Yellowstone caldera erupting with visible lava flow."

"Does that mean that you think there is a chance of having another Mount St. Helens here in Yellowstone?"

"As I said, it does not seem likely. The person that could assemble the right people the most quickly to analyze the situation would probably be Senator

Gayla Hosmer. I have not talked with her in several weeks, but this is right up her alley."

"Do you think she's coming here?"

"I don't know. It would not surprise me. I think she would like to see this and experience it first hand."

"You have worked with the senator personally before, haven't you?"

"Yes. She is a woman of action. I admire her tenacity."

"Thank you, Miss Riley." The reporter turned to the camera. "I've been talking to Jonnie Riley, an executive with the Sierra Club headquarters in San Francisco, California. I hope we can interview the Senator as soon as she gets here – if she gets here, that is. This is Bob Sherpa, returning you to the studio."

The senator clicked her remote to mute the TV. She scowled. She turned to see Peggy standing in her doorway. "I think she's right – I can help with this! What's my schedule like for the next few days, Peggy?"

+ + +

In Yellowstone, Jonnie thanked the reporter before getting into her car. Before she could turn the key, however, she saw a ranger approaching, so she rolled down her window. "Yes, Paul?"

"Jonnie, I heard you tell Channel 12 that you think Senator Hosmer might be coming out here. There are people in Jackson Hole that will want to be in on such a visit. They'll all want to help, but they'll probably do more harm than good. They could be like vultures feeding on a recent kill, trying to clean things up."

Jonnie smiled. "You're right, Paul. They will be like well-intentioned vultures. It cannot be helped, though. Some of those Hollywood types make big donations to the Sierra Club. You're going to have your hands full, Paul!"

"I know. I am told that Dr. Betsy Sue Johnson is here with her new husband, but I have not seen them. I think they're at the Old Faithful Inn if you're interested."

"Okay. Do you think you could forget that you know this or even that you told me for a few days?"

He grinned. "Easy! My source of that information has already left the park, and he and I are tight. It was confidential. What's up?"

"Right now, Paul, it is better that you don't know." She smiled.

"Okay. It's been good to see you Jonnie. Before you leave the park, can I buy you dinner at the Inn?"

Jonnie grinned. "Absolutely! Tomorrow evening about 7:00 okay?"

Paul continued to smile. "Great! I'll see you then." He turned and walked away as she started the engine.

Jonnie pushed the speed up to the park speed limit as she headed north towards the Inn. She had time enough to think about her approach to Glenn and Betsy Sue.

Inside the Inn, it was comfortably warm, and everything had the aroma of the wood burning in the fireplace. She approached the front desk.

"Hi, Jonnie! It's good to see you again"

"Hi David! You too!"

His voice now lower, it on took a conspiratorial tone. "I think I know who you might want to see – a couple of photographers on their honeymoon?"

"Yes, David, but you did not hear me say that."

"Just a moment." He picked up his receiver and punched buttons. After a pause, he said, "Mrs. Franz? This is David at the front desk." He paused. "Yes. This is not the woman you want to avoid. It is a woman you will want to see." He paused. "Very well." He put the receiver down. "Three fifteen – and I did not tell you that." He winked.

Jonnie nodded. "Thanks, David." She headed for the stairs.

In their room, Betsy Sue told Glenn, "A woman is coming up. David says this is someone we want to see. It's okay. I trust David. I've known him a long time."

Glenn nodded. A moment later, hearing a knock, he opened the door to an attractive young woman. "Hello! I don't think we've met." He stepped aside to let her in.

"You're right. I am Jonnie Riley from the Sierra Club. You must be Glenn."

Smiling, Betsy Sue walked over and extended a hand. "Jonnie Riley! I have heard so much about you!"

"I hope it's not been all bad!" She smiled.

"Not at all! Glenn, I've talked to Jonnie several times on the phone when she has arranged for some of my speaking engagements."

Glenn was relieved. "It's good to meet you, Jonnie. Let's sit here by the window at the table. Are you thirsty?"

"I suppose I could use some water."

Glenn nodded and walked towards another table to get refreshments.

"How did you find us?" Her voice was lower and had a curious tone.

"I think it is safe to say that we have mutual friends. I held a little television news conference about an hour ago near the South Entrance. I baited Senator Gayla Hosmer with a few carefully chosen comments. I will expect her to fly in probably tomorrow, but she probably will not be here until the next day. The idea is to keep her busy and keep her focused on other things besides you two."

"You're sure the senator won't be here before tomorrow?" Glenn was intensely concerned.

"Absolutely. Senator Hosmer is very predictable. She loves attention and publicity. She will fly into Jackson Hole and spend time there greeting wealthy supporters from the entertainment industry. She will then assemble a "fact-finding" group, and a caravan of well-intentioned vultures will drive up here. If there is some vigorous shaking while she is in Jackson Hole, she will hold a news conference, reminding people of how my little televised speech prompted her to re-arrange her busy schedule to be here where she is needed. If the governor knows she is coming, he will join her in the little expedition."

Glenn whistled. "She'll be too busy to think about us for a couple of days at least!"

"That's the idea. Have either of you heard from Ben Kaiser?" The phone rang.

Glenn went to a phone on the night stand at the other end of the room. After answering, he conversed quietly with the person at the other end of the call.

Betsy Sue was curious. "Do you think that's Ben Kaiser now?"

Jonnie nodded. "It very well could be."

"Is this the same Ben Kaiser I've dealt with from Tiberias Holdings?"

"Right. Ben *is* Tiberias Holdings. I once told Jack Haddy that if money talks, Ben is a chorus."

Betsy Sue chuckled. "I assumed that much. He gets things done, doesn't he? Do you know what they're talking about?"

"Yes. Ben and I discussed your situation a few days ago. He has been making some arrangements for the two of you."

"Arrangements?"

"Yes. Glenn can fill you in with the details. The short version is that Ben has formed a new division of Tiberias Holdings centered on environmental concerns. The main offices are in a building complex in Fresno. If you and Glenn agree, you will have a staff of two to three hundred there helping you. You will be in command of one big team."

Betsy Sue's eyes were big. "Really?!!! That is amazing. Glenn and I will have to pray about it of course, but so far it sounds great!"

"I'm glad you like the idea. I hope you understand that eventually Ben will probably make profits from this venture, but that is not his motive. Think of him as an eccentric billionaire environmentalist."

Betsy Sue nodded. Just then, Glenn hung up the phone and walked over to join them. He reached down and took a sip of water from his glass before speaking. "That was Ben Kaiser, as you may have guessed. Did Jonnie here tell you what this is about?"

Betsy Sue nodded. "Briefly. You can fill me in on the details later. Jonnie, will you join us?"

"Sure! I would love to. Instead of going back to my cabin in Jackson Hole tonight, I will just get a bed here at the Inn. The manager is a friend of mine."

"Good." Glenn stood up. "We'll see you in the dining room in about fifteen minutes, okay?"

"Great." Jonnie stood up, crossed the room, and was out the door a moment later.

Betsy Sue spoke quietly. "All that God does, God does exceedingly well!"

"Yes, he does. Let's pray, okay?"

Together, the two of them went over and knelt beside the bed. Fifteen minutes later, they went to the dining room.

13. Desperate Measures

Dinner turned into long conversations. It was late when Jonnie crawled into the bed that David had set aside for her. The night was short, however. Incessant knocking finally had her awake. In a fog, she went to the door and opened it. David was there, smiling. "Good morning, Jonnie. A woman named Lucy is here for you."

"Lucy? Lucy?" She paused. "Oh!" She scrambled to make herself halfway presentable, and in less than three minutes, she was at the front desk. Standing there were David, Lucy, Betsy Sue, and Glenn. "What time is it?"

"5:45 AM. Sorry it's so early, Jonnie." Betsy Sue had a sheepish grin. "Lucy has all of our belongings – including yours from your cabin in Jackson Hole – in a large SUV outside. Our cars will be driven to Fresno for us. Meantime, we have a private jet waiting for us just outside the West Entrance of the park. We're headed for Fresno."

Glenn nodded. "The sooner we get there and settle in, the safer we will be. Once we get to Fresno, the plane will take you back to San Francisco. Let's go." He started to move.

"Why so early? What's going on?"

As they walked toward the door and the SUV outside, Betsy Sue explained. "We've gotten word that Senator Hosmer and her caravan are leaving Jackson Hole in a few minutes. We don't want to be in the park when she comes in through the South Entrance with her brood." The ground under them momentarily quaked.

Jonnie was wide awake now. "I understand. Does Jack Haddy know?"

They were now getting into the SUV. Glenn answered, "I doubt it. Besides, I think you should hold off on calling him until after we are secure in Fresno. Okay?"

Jonnie nodded. "Right. That is the safest way. What Jack does not know cannot betray us."

The others grunted their agreement. The drive to West Yellowstone went quickly. Through a secluded gate, they went through security, and they were quickly on the plane.

As the plane's door closed, Lucy spoke. "We had a really hard time finding your remaining camera equipment, Glenn. You were truly ingenious."

Glenn scowled. "Evidently I was not ingenious enough!"

"Don't worry about it. Your new Fresno headquarters has ample security. I am told you have some special security provisions that even I don't know about. Your security chief is even taller and heavier than you. Everyone calls him 'Big John.' He is an ex-Marine who can easily take on three or four able-bodied men of more normal size. You'll like him."

As they took off, everyone was silent. Once they got to altitude, breakfast was served by a flight attendant. They ate ravenously, and then they dozed until the plane started its descent into Fresno.

The ride from the Fresno International Airport to their new home was uneventful until they got to the gate. The guard handed their driver a small rectangular box about the size of a pack of cigarettes. "Good evening folks. This is a retinal scanner. I need to have each of you hold it up to your right eye for about five seconds and speak your name. Then your identity will be associated with the scan and a matter of secure record."

One end of the little box had an eyecup like found on the viewfinder of a camera. Each of them held it to their right eye while it scanned their retina. Then the driver handed it back to the guard. The driver looked up at the guard. "That's all of us. What's next?"

The gate opened. "Please forgive the delay. Go right in." The guard waved as they passed through.

After they parked, Lucy took them to a doorway, where a retinal scanner was mounted just above and to the right of the door handle. Each of them was cleared to enter by a retinal scan that was now permanently in the system.

Inside, an armed guard greeted them. Lucy took charge. "Come this way, everyone." Going down a short hallway, they turned right and walked down a longer hallway. There was a glass wall. "This is the atrium. It will be maintained throughout the year, and always at the same temperature. Glenn, Betsy Sue, your apartment complex is down there on our left. Right now though, let's all go to the main lab." She walked briskly to the right a few steps, then two glass doors slid to the sides. The laboratory complex was about the size of two football fields, partitioned off into smaller laboratories.

Glenn whistled. "This is bigger than any lab I've ever been in! Betsy Sue?"

She nodded. "Yes! How big is our staff, Lucy?"

Lucy looked at a digital pad she was holding. "Right now you have fifty-five here in the lab complex. More are on the way and will be here within the next two weeks. There are also three secretaries, the administrator, and the security suite which has a total of seven. Your starting budget is flexible. The administrator will help you secure anything you need."

For the next two hours, they toured their complex and got acquainted with some of the staff. As the sun was getting close to setting over the hills west of Fresno, Lucy brought things to a close. "I think you've got the idea now as to what you have available to you. Jonnie, the jet is waiting for us to take us back to San Francisco. Ben is taking us to dinner at the Mark Hopkins. We'll stop at your apartment first so you can freshen up."

"Fantastic. I'll let Paul know that I'll have dinner with him another time. I am a bit tired, but I can sleep in tomorrow. Glenn, Betsy Sue, it has been great getting to know you. I look forward to seeing you soon." They walked out together to the big SUV. Lucy and Jonnie gave the other two hugs before getting in, and the men shook hands.

After the SUV was moving away, Glenn looked at Betsy Sue. "We need some rest, some food, and then some time together before we call it a day."

"Yes!" Can you believe our apartment? Did you count the rooms?"

Glenn thought for a moment. "Eleven if you count the three bathrooms."

"Yes! Lucy told me that she insisted that she be the one to unpack my things for me. That was sweet."

"Yes. I hope we will meet Ben Kaiser soon. I want to thank him."

"We can do a video conference call tomorrow morning and thank him then."

"Good idea."

Arm in arm, they made their way to the apartment.

+ + +

They slept in the next morning and had a leisurely breakfast at about 9:00. Just as they were going out their door towards the lab, Big John appeared.

His face was serious. "Senator Hosmer thinks you are here, and there are a half-dozen U.S. Marshalls at the gate with a search warrant to find you and take you to Washington. We cannot stall them long. Please excuse me and come with me." He went past them into their apartment. They followed. Going into the guest bathroom, he opened the shower door. "I'm not coming with you. That would be suspicious." He pointed downward. "Dr. Franz, flush the toilet, go into the shower, and pull down on the shower head. When the door opens, both of you go in."

"What are you talking about?"

His voice took on a tone of authority. "Just do it! Go!"

Betsy Sue flushed and stepped into the shower stall. Reaching up, she pulled down on the shower head. The back of the shower stall slid aside, opening into an inner hallway lit by LED lights along the edges of the floor and ceiling. When they were inside, the door closed silently behind them. They walked more than fifty yards down an incline. Glenn spoke. "The way this hallway slopes down, I wonder if we're going underground."

At the end of the sloping hallway, a door opened automatically. As they went inside, lights came on to illumine a large lounge. In one corner, there was a small kitchenette with a stove and refrigerator. Off in another area was a bed.

A video screen lit up near them, and the guard they had originally seen when they arrived at the front door spoke to them. "I see you've found your secret second apartment. Make yourselves comfortable. It is underground, reinforced, and insulated. You should be able to come out as soon as the marshals leave. If you do not hear from us in the next few hours, just wait. This whole thing should not take long."

While Glenn and Betsy Sue made themselves comfortable, the Marshalls searched the entire facility. The administrator and staff were all very friendly. At noon, the Marshalls were offered lunch, but they declined. Finally, at 1:30 in the afternoon, one of them made a brief phone call, and then they left.

+ + +

In San Francisco, Ben Kaiser stared out his window. There was not a wisp of fog anywhere. Though the day was cool, there was bright and warm sunshine. He pressed a button. "Lucy, get me Senator Everett Steinmetz on a video call if you can."

"Okay."

Moments later, Ben's friend appeared on the large video screen. "Hello Ben! How are you?"

"I'm blessed, Everett, and you?"

"Amen to that! What can I do for you?"

"I'm not sure that you can help, senator, but maybe you can point me in the right direction." He paused and shifted in his chair. "Earlier today, U.S. Marshals arrived at one of my older facilities that I have renovated for some environmental research. Evidently, one of your compatriots on the other side of the political aisle wanted two of my research scientists to come to Washington. Senator Hosmer thought that they were in my facility, so she secured a search warrant calling for the marshals to retrieve my scientists for her." He paused to take a breath. "They have not broken any laws, senator. What they have simply done is refuse to do what the senator wanted them to do. I'm told she was not very nice about it."

Senator Steinmetz tapped his finger on his desk for a moment. "You know, Ben, Senator Hosmer and I have butted heads on several occasions. She has a lot of power because she's been here a long time. The thing is, I was around for eight years before she got here!" He paused and Ben Smiled innocently. "This time I think she's stepped over the line, and she's gone way too far." He paused, tapping his finger. "I've got to do something about this myself, Ben. I am not doing this for you. This is simply too much! Keep your television on during the next hour!" He severed the connection.

In the doorway, Lucy smiled. "Do you think the you-know-what just hit the fan?"

Ben grinned. "It's about time!"

Fifteen minutes later, Lucy turned up the volume on Ben's monitor. Senator Steinmetz was having a press conference.

"Ladies and gentlemen, I've called this press conference because an egregious error has been committed by one of my colleagues. Every once in a while in our country's history, an elected official makes the mistake of thinking that they are above the law." He paused. "No one – no one – is above the law! A few minutes ago, I filed a written complaint with the United States Attorney General's Office. I have been informed that before the end of the day, the Office of the Attorney General will file a felony complaint for abuse of power against Senator Gayla Hosmer."

The press exploded into a frenzy of questions. "Senator, can you give us any details regarding this abuse of power?"

"Judge Andrew Miller has found that Senator Hosmer gave him false and misleading information, which in turn led to his issuing an inappropriate search warrant. Senator Hosmer then arranged for United States Marshals to execute the inappropriate warrant in Fresno, California. Other details of this sad turn of events will be forthcoming in the days ahead. That is all."

As Senator Steinmetz left the podium, U.S. Marshalls were entering Senator Hosmer's Offices. Judge Miller was sufficiently angry to have her arrested for contempt of court. Now Senator Hosmer could not pursue Glenn and Betsy Sue.

Even so, everyone in the media wanted to know more about the couple. Journalists were under great pressure to produce a story. Most of the stories had very little substance. Some of them were just plain pathetic. A few brought some laughs.

14. Winter at 2200 Meters

Life in the research complex became almost routine. After Betsy Sue made an image in the atrium with the second camera, she was excited by the result. After showing her analysis to Glenn, he had a hunch. Leaving the lab, he walked down the hall to the office area. Inside, he approached the desk of Mike Lamprecht's secretary, Joan. "Is Mike handy?"

"Yes, Dr. Franz." She pushed a button on her phone.

"Yes, Joan?"

"Dr. Franz is here to see you."

"Send him in."

Glenn smiled at the young woman. "Thanks!" He opened the inner office's door and went inside. "Hi, Mike!"

"Hey Glenn – what's up?"

"Betsy Sue and I were looking at an image she made in the atrium yesterday, and we talked about it quite a bit last evening. I've got an idea I want to run past you."

Mike nodded. "Shoot."

Glenn sat down, took a deep breath, and let it out. "Most of our environmental research done here consists of analysis of data gathered in other places and trying to duplicate phenomena on a small scale. Why not set up a larger-scale study area here at the complex?"

"What do you have in mind?"

"Most of the roof of the complex is flat with only enough slope for drainage. I'm thinking about reinforcing part of the foundation and main level load-bearing walls, then erecting a geodesic dome over a large section of the roof."

Mike nodded. "What would we have under the dome?"

"I'm thinking of a tropical environment with birds and a few small animals. We would have environmental controls to duplicate equatorial South America."

Mike smiled. "You know, it's interesting that you're suggesting this. Not long ago someone wanted to buy this property and do something similar to what you're suggesting."

"Do you think Ben might go for it?"

"I don't know, but I'll call him. It sounds like a great idea."

"Great!" Glenn got up out of the chair. "Let me know what he says. Thanks for letting me bend your ear."

"Sure! See you later."

Glenn walked out and back to the lab.

Mike called Tiberius Holdings. "Lucy, this is Mike Lamprecht. Is there any chance I can talk to Ben today?"

"Hi Mike. His schedule is pretty full today, but this afternoon...." She paused. "Wait, Ben just came in the door. He is early. Hold on a moment." She put him on hold for about fifteen seconds. "Mike, here's Ben."

"Hey Mike, it's good to hear from you. I have maybe five minutes. What's up?"

"Good morning! I will keep it brief. Glenn has had one of his brainstorms, and I think it is an excellent one. You might get a big tax write-off as a bonus."

"Shoot."

"Betsy Sue made an image in the atrium and got excited by the result. They want to expand the atrium upward, and perhaps outward. It's not in the tentative budget, but I have an idea that will help."

"Go ahead."

"I'm thinking that we could get the Fresno Chaffee Zoo involved. They have an outstanding aviary. What if we offer the zoo a research facility for plants and birds? It would expand our credibility with the environmentalists, the scientific community, and with the public."

"I like the concept, Mike. Since the roof there is relatively flat, I could have an architect design a glass geodesic dome and create a second story for that part of the complex. We would have to do some reinforcing below, but that should not be a problem."

"That sounds great – Glenn was also thinking about a glass geodesic dome. How do you want to proceed?"

"First I pray about it. If I still like the idea tomorrow, I will have Lucy put in a call to someone at the Fresno Chaffee Zoo. It would be our money but their name. We'd share some staff, and you would have to partition off part of the complex to keep them more separate from Glenn and Betsy Sue's laboratories."

"Okay."

"Let's keep this under wraps for now, but you can tell Glenn and Betsy Sue. I will have Lucy call you tomorrow and update you. Okay?"

"Okay, Ben. Thanks for your time."

"Right."

The connection was severed. Mike softly whistled, and then he lifted the receiver again and punched a button. "Joan, tell Glenn Franz I'll have news for him later." He paused. "Okay."

Glenn and Betsy Sue were taking a break in the atrium. Glenn was leaning back in a chaise lounge and sometimes sucking a straw in a glass of ginger ale. "You know, last spring we talked about returning to Yosemite in the winter for a honeymoon and for making a few winter images."

"Yes, dear, but we've been safe here from the media's eyes. We do not want any more uncontrolled publicity for a few more months. We're making some real progress!" She reached for her bottled water.

"I agree. Still, it would be useful to make some images in sub-freezing conditions. Wouldn't it be good to see winter wildlife's interaction with the weather?"

"Probably so, but how would we avoid media attention?"

"That's easy." He smiled.

"How?"

"For one thing, we'll stay away from the Ahwahnee. There is some relatively new employee housing against the southern cliffs just west of Camp Curry. Jonnie at the Sierra Club probably has friends with the Yosemite Conservancy that we can trust. We might be able to arrange for temporary housing off the beaten path. Those apartments each have a nice kitchenette, and some have a private bathroom."

She picked up her cell phone. I'll call Jonnie right now." She pressed a speed dial button. "Hi! May I please speak to Jonnie Riley? Tell her it's Betsy Sue." She paused."

In San Francisco, Jonnie was on the phone on another line when she was shown a note. She looked up and nodded. "I've got to go, Stan. I've got another call. See you soon!" She punched a button. "Hi, Betsy Sue! How're ya doin'?" She paused. "That's great. What's up?" She paused for over a minute. "Sure! That is easy! I will make the arrangements myself. There is no need to involve the Conservancy. When do you want to go?" She paused briefly. "Consider it done. I will call you if there are any snags. I'll email you with details through Mike to keep things safe, okay?" She paused again. "Great! It is good hearing from you! We'll talk again soon! Bye!" Smiling, she put down the receiver.

+ + +

It was shortly before Christmas, and the apartment was small but comfortable. The double bed was too small for them, but they managed. Sometimes they would take in a late dinner or an early breakfast at Camp Curry's Dining Pavilion. No one recognized them because Glenn had grown a full beard, and she dressed "down" as much as possible, looking almost slovenly but clean. While Glenn took a nap, late on a Sunday afternoon five days before Christmas, Betsy Sue put on her jacket and stepped out on the porch. It was snowing and peacefully quiet. Their location in the complex was nearly perfect, giving them almost total privacy unless they went to their SUV.

This particular evening, as Betsy Sue looked out over the white velvet landscape, she thought she saw movement up on the cliff, just for an instant. "A puma?" she asked herself in a whisper.

It was not a puma. In the shadow of the cliff, and in the deeper shadow of a tree, the apartment was being watched by Kieya's keen eyes. "Audio only g-mail to Walter. I am in Yosemite, watching a young couple with good scientific potential. If Asayak is available, please send him here under cloak. Furthermore, warn him that the temperature here is several degrees below zero Celsius. End g-mail."

A few minutes later, Asayak appeared, visible only to Kieya, just a meter away. It quickly flowed down next to Kieya, taking a position close to her. "Greetings, Kieya. You requested me. How may I serve?"

"Do you observe the young woman there on the porch?"

"Yes. She has a mate inside."

"Correct. I have been watching them. They have good scientific expertise, and they possibly have Gaardian potential. I need you to do some investigation. I am requesting and giving you permission to scan their minds to see what has been happening to them for the past several lunar cycles."

"I can do this." It paused. "The male called Glenn has created a technological innovation. It is a major leap even by Gaardian standards. These two people have drawn the attention of people of power and some danger. They are safe for now, but, -- what is the word? – journalists are potentially a significant distraction."

Kieya purred. "That is an understatement, Asayak. The media can cause major problems on this beautiful planet."

"Yes, it is beautiful to my senses also. We will be near here in a few days at a higher elevation, am I not correct?"

"Correct, Asayak. We will be at a re-created hotel at Glacier Point for a holiday known as Christmas."

"Yes. I enjoy this celebration. I enjoy the emotions that surround it and the experiences of intimacy with the Creator."

"Yes, Asayak. Do we have a sufficiently complete understanding of this situation?"

"No." It paused. "I need to read the thoughts of at least three additional humans if possible. They are in other locations."

"You have my permission, Asayak, to investigate where their thoughts lead you. Keep yourself under cloak and report your findings to me after your next rest cycle." She froze. "Strange."

"Agreed. I sensed it too. What was it?"

"I don't know. The hair on my back suddenly bristled, but I do not know why. There's nothing here to alert me."

"Yes. It lasted only for a fraction of a second. It was big and powerful, and it was nothing here in this park." It paused. "Shall I proceed with the investigation?"

"Yes." She paused. "I trust your discretion."

"Very well. I shall go." The creature vanished.

The big cat kept a close watch into the night and the next day."

+ + +

On Christmas Eve, Glenn and Betsy Sue were making their way along the snow covered road just above Glacier Point. Most of the time, they only heard the crunch of the snow and their own breathing. They had left their SUV in the parking lot at Badger Pass just after breakfast that morning. Glenn pulled a toboggan behind him, loaded with equipment and supplies, and Betsy

Sue followed with a rope fastened to the rear in case it began sliding out of control. It had done so more than once.

Glenn paused, his breath showing in the cold, high-altitude air. "This is where we begin our descent to Glacier Point. Why don't we trade places for a while?""

"That's okay. You go ahead and lead."

They started off again. The snow was nearly fresh powder, dropped the previous day. Ahead of them, they saw two other skiers head their way. When they reached them, Glenn spoke. "Hello! How far are we from the shelter at Glacier Point?"

"We are about a mile or so from that area. We're from the ski patrol, and I have been cross-country skiing this route for many years. The snow is deeper on the area than I have ever seen. Be very careful. I did not know anyone was going to be up here for Christmas. The snow is so deep. Have you made special arrangements?"

"Yes," Betsy Sue replied. "We have a key to the shelter from Park Headquarters in the valley."

"You must be the photographers we were told about."

"Yes."

"Again I say, be very careful. We are going to have to get going. It will be after dark when we get back to Badger Pass."

"Okay! Nice to meet you." Glenn smiled.

Betsy Sue waved. After a moment she said, "Do you think too many people know we're up here?"

"It's probably okay." They started walking.

Walking parallel to them, Kieya padded silently and invisibly through the trees a few meters away. Thanks to her special Gaardian skills, the two men from the ski patrol would not remember that they saw Glenn and Betsy Sue.

Moving downhill, they made good progress towards the point. In a short time, they could see the roof of the gift shop and shelter sticking out above the deep drifts of snow. On the downhill side, they had no problem getting to the door and unlocking it.

With power and plenty of propane for fuel, they soon made themselves comfortable upstairs in the bunkhouse. Betsy Sue began cooking some frozen entrees she had picked out for the occasion. Glenn was in the dining area, setting up their computer along with plates and forks. She called out, "You may not think so, but I think this is a very romantic way of spending Christmas Eve. Do you?"

Glenn came into the cooking area and gave her a hug. "Absolutely! I could smell turkey baking out there, but not in here. I wonder why?"

"You could not have smelled turkey! I just put it in the oven a minute ago!"

Glenn took her by the hand and led her into the dining area in the next room. "See! Smell!"

She sniffed. She sniffed again. "You're right! I think I also got a whiff of sweet potatoes, maybe even cranberry sauce! That's impossible! Kitchen smells could not rise this far from Camp Curry!"

Unknown to Betsy Sue and Glenn, the aromas were definitely not coming from Camp Curry in the valley, nine hundred eighty meters below. Just outside the building was a large snow drift. Most of its height was actually a hologram. Behind it was a re-creation of the old Glacier Point Hotel. Walter and his crew were having Christmas Eve dinner in the large dining hall. In one corner, overlooking a heavily snow-capped Half Dome, were Kieya and Asayak. As Kieya enjoyed samples of all the different foods on the buffet, Asayak swayed with enjoyment, sensing many things that no one else could without instrumentation.

Across the room, Kieya saw Walter get up from his table to cross the room and enjoy the view. He selected some dessert as Kieya approached. "Good evening, Kieya! Merry Christmas! I hope you're enjoying yourself."

"That I am!" She purred. "A few meters west of this hotel is the winter skiers' shelter."

"Yes, I know! Why do you mention it?"

"There are two scientists spending Christmas there. I have been watching them. Let's not discuss Gaardian business right now. Please touch my face and scan for my knowledge of these two people."

Walter nodded, touching Kieya's hairy face with three fingers. "Fascinating! Can you continue watching over them for a few more days?"

"I plan to. They will go back to Fresno before the celebration of New Years. If you do not mind, I will have Asayak assist me with the vigil. Can you spare it?"

"Of course! What about that strange moment the two of you had down below?"

Her purr stopped. "I don't know. I am concerned, but there has been nothing since to alert me"

"Okay. Keep me informed."

"Of course!" The big cat padded back over to join Asayak.

As he headed back to his table, Walter stopped at a table that included his Native American friend, Toby Ballentine. "Merry Christmas, everyone! Hey, Toby, I have a little project for you and Paula Rutledge. Have you had dessert?"

"Yes, thank you, I've had a few too many helpings!"

"I think Paula's finishing dessert too. Let's go talk to her."

Toby excused himself from the others at his table, and he and Walter headed towards Paula Rutledge, who was standing by the dessert table and staring down at Vernal and Nevada Falls far below.

Paula looked up as they approached. "Hi! Merry Christmas! I never tire of seeing Yosemite!"

Almost together, the two men said, "Merry Christmas, Paula."

Walter continued. "I've got a little project for you two. Tomorrow morning, wear ski outfits. A few meters west of here, there is the gift shop and ski shelter where there are two scientists. Check in with either Kieya or Asayak before they leave this evening. They are watching the two scientists. Paula, I think they will recognize you from your television days, and they possibly know that you have gone to work for me." He smiled. "You two can work out your own strategy, but I think they could use your help. Toby, you have your special resources here in this country, and so far, no one knows you work for me. You can use that advantage to the fullest. Right now, I see Kieya walking our way. She can fill you in with the rest. Keep me informed." Walter nodded at Kieya as he walked back to his table.

The big cat was purring. "I overheard what Walter told you. Both of you can touch my face, and I will fill you in with many details."

As they touched the big cat's face, they closed their eyes. Toby opened his first. "That's good, Kieya. I think we need to get Margaret Graves involved eventually."

Paula looked puzzled. "Why?"

"She and Ann Cotter are equipped to do some creative media work at a sound stage in Oakland – which is actually a small extension of Walter's base."

Kieya purred. "Good. Do not tell the couple too much too soon. That will be a good strategy for the future. Now, you two can return to the party until tomorrow!" The big cat turned and walked back towards Asayak.

+ + +

In the bright sun of the following morning, Glenn and Betsy Sue could make five images along established animal trails. Digitally, they captured a bear, a mule deer, a fox, a coyote, and a number of rodents. They also recorded the unusual wind and temperature patterns along the edge of the cliff. As they were gathering up their equipment after making an image, two skiers approached them.

"Hello! Merry Christmas!"

"Merry Christmas to you two, too!" said Betsy Sue, a little wary.

"I hope you'll forgive us," said Paula, "but I recognized you, Betsy Sue. I am no longer a journalist, but a year and a half ago I did a story on you about something you said in your annual report to the Sierra Club. This is my friend, Toby Ballentine. He helped my viewers understand your report from a Native American perspective." This was a little lie that they could live with without betraying Gaardian secrets.

"Yes," Toby said. "I've known Jonnie Riley for a long time. I have also worked with Ben Kaiser on several occasions" (Both of these statements were true.). "I think we can help you."

Glenn and Betsy Sue were now more at ease. Glenn glanced out over the east end of the valley and back at them. "How can you help us?"

"I know why Senator Hosmer is currently facing serious charges due to her attempted interference in your lives. The political heat is off of you two for at the moment, but the media are hungry for anything they can get on you."

"Yes, Paula interjected, "and if any of us here knows how to manage the media, it's me. Toby and I have discussed this briefly while we were secretly making our way out here to meet you this morning."

"You must have hiked through the night!" Betsy Sue exclaimed.

"It's peaceful up here day or night." Toby was calm. "While Paula keeps the media under control, I have ways – don't ask me how – of managing other publicity seekers. Will you let us help?"

Betsy Sue bit her lip. "It's almost noon. Will you two join us for some lunch at the shelter? We've plenty of food."

Toby looked at Paula, and they both nodded. Paula said, "Sure! We've got some food we can share as well."

They all headed for the shelter.

On the other side of the snow bank and hologram, Walter stepped out of the hotel into the sun. No one saw him as he made his way along the cliff out towards the point, where he entered the mini-shelter across the valley from Sierra Point. Standing next to the geology display, Walter gazed across the canyon and up towards Half Dome. Suddenly, a familiar glow began to fill the shelter.

> Walter, you are doing well. You must look with me towards the future. Betsy Sue and Glenn Franz are going to have fraternal twins, and both children can be Gaardians. Asayak will be a good trainer, and it can accomplish training faster than Qaak. You and Debbie have many challenges ahead, including a major challenge to Gaardian authority. Do not be afraid, for everything is unfolding as it should. I hold the future.

"What challenge?" The glow faded quickly without an answer. Walter sang several old praise songs to God. Then he began to make his way back to the hotel and to his beloved wife, Debbie.

In the nearby ski shelter, the four skiers sat around two tables they had pushed together and were eating lunch. Glenn and Betsy Sue did not see Toby's Gaardian ring shimmer as he reached inside of his large backpack. As vacuum-packed meals appeared inside the pack, he brought them out and set them on the table. Toby smiled and said, "I think we can use the microwave over there to heat these." He got up, walked behind the counter. One by one, he removed the top of each meal. Then he stuck one in the microwave. Though the microwave did not actually come on, humming could be heard briefly as his ring shimmered. He reached inside, brought it out, and put it on the counter. "Come and get it!" He then put another meal inside the microwave, followed by the others.

After everyone else had their meals, Toby brought his to the table and sat down. Glenn looked up at the ceiling. "Thank you, Lord, for this food and this beautiful day. Amen." As they all began eating, Glenn continued, "Will you two be able to help us even when we go on field trips?"

Paula nodded as she took a bite. "Yes. We will remain in touch with your lab in Fresno and keep track of your schedule. We'll try to prepare the way so that the media will have their attention diverted as much as possible from the two of you."

Glenn grunted. "I'm glad. As Betsy Sue can tell you, my mind is always thinking ahead towards new possibilities. She sometimes has to be my anchor, bringing me back to the present. Between the two of us, we strike a balance between our dreams and practicality."

Betsy Sue chuckled. "Yes." She swallowed some hot tea to wash down her food. "I have a feeling that Glenn has been thinking ahead while we have been talking."

Glenn cleared his throat. "She knows me well. Last night, as we were studying one of our images of the valley below, I realize that we have skipped a major area where we need to make images for study – the Grand Canyon. I think we should start at the east end, at the Painted Desert, and move west into the canyon. It would be a project that would take several months."

"Really!" Paula exclaimed. "Controlling the media for that would be simple. All we would have to do is grant exclusive access to just a few journalists."

Betsy Sue nodded. "I think this could be a joint venture with the Sierra Club. Jonnie would love to get involved, I think."

Toby nodded. "We'll need to get Ben involved, because I have a suggestion, Glenn."

Paula gave him a quizzical look. "What are you thinking, Toby?"

Glenn was puzzled too. "Yes, what are you thinking?"

Toby grinned. "It has to do with something Ben shared with me that I think we can keep just between us here." He paused as they all stopped eating to look at him. "A man who has been doing some work for Ben down at Hughes Research Laboratories has come up with a deep-range ground-penetrating radar that you could use in a place like the Grand Canyon or even here in Yosemite."

"How so?" asked Glenn.

"When you make one of your panoramic images of part of the canyon, we could use a sweep version of the radar to sweep the same area. With the software properly configured, the depth of penetration could be up to a hundred feet."

Glenn grinned. "Wow! If that radar is as good as it sounds, we could create composite images of large areas that show everything the eye can see plus everything in infrared, and ultraviolet, plus subsurface radar images. Incredible! I hope we can come up with software to handle all the data combined!"

Paula caught Toby's eye and gave a barely perceptible nod, and he nodded back. Their discussions with Glenn the scientists continued far into the night.

15. A Church Nook

Glenn and Betsy Sue set out the following morning, their toboggan in tow. After cross-country skiing back to Badger Pass, they loaded up their SUV and headed back to the valley. The road was somewhat slippery in the parts without direct sun, but they kept their speed at or below the limit and made their way through Wawona Tunnel.

As they came out of the tunnel, Betsy Sue pointed towards the parking lot to the left. Surprisingly, there were only three cars in the lot. "Pull over and park. I recognize that tall man by that podium map."

Glenn pulled in. "Who is it?"

"It's Marty Chen, the senior pastor of that big church we pass coming from the south into our lab complex."

"Really? How do you know him?"

"I met him once at a seminar. He is a strong advocate for good biblical stewardship of our environment. He's a member of the Sierra Club too." As they parked, Betsy Sue rolled down the window and called out. "Hey, Marty!"

Marty Chen turned, saw them, and smiled. "Betsy Sue! It is good to see you! I understand that you and your groom have made some interesting images here in the park!"

"Yes, we have." She turned to introduce Glenn, who had gotten out and approached them. "Glenn, this is Marty Chen, the pastor I told you about."

Glenn smiled. "It's nice to meet you! It's rare to find someone even taller than I am!"

Marty grinned. "Not by much – maybe an inch or so! Where are you headed?"

"We just got back from Badger Pass. We made a few images up that way."

"Fantastic! I'll bet the heavy snows make for some interesting things to study."

Betsy Sue nodded. "Yes!" She paused briefly. "We saw you as we came out of the tunnel. Are you headed into the valley?"

"Yes. My wife and I – she is in the car – are going to be staying at the Lodge. Where are you staying tonight?"

"We're over near Curry. We like the food at the Mountain Room, even better than the food at the Ahwahnee. Can we buy you dinner there this evening?"

Glenn glanced over at her, a quizzical look on his face. "Yes. How about a late dinner, say around 8:30?"

"That's later than we're used to, but since you're buying, and it's the Mountain Room, I think my wife and I will love it."

Betsy Sue smiled. "Great! We will talk later. Glenn and I just stopped to say hello. We've got to get into the valley for some other things." She turned towards the SUV.

Glenn walked around to the other side, and as he got in, he smiled. "We'll see you later!"

"Right! Bye you two!"

In the SUV, Glenn was puzzled. "Why do you want to risk dinner at the Mountain Room? There are more chances of meeting nosey people at the Lodge than at Curry's Dining Pavilion."

"I know, but I think it's worth the risk, and we haven't had a really good meal since we got here."

Glenn smiled. "I don't know! You're pretty handy with frozen entrees from Yosemite Store."

She smiled. "Thank you dear, but those meals are no substitute for a multi-course meal prepared by a decent chef."

Glenn nodded as he put the SUV in gear and pulled out of the parking lot. "So, why do we need to have dinner with them? Do we have an ulterior motive?"

"As a matter of fact, we have three reasons, as I see it. First, it would be good for us to have a church where we can worship and have a church family. Second, in a large church like Marty's, we can easily lose ourselves in the crowd if we need to. Marty's ushers might even run interference against the press for us if we ask him. He has dealt with celebrity visitors before. Third, and most important, churches have lots of nooks and crannies where things can be hidden. If Marty agrees – and I think he will if we approach it right – we can keep at least one camera hidden there. The church can be an alternative secure location, but close enough to the complex."

Glenn nodded. "I like it! If we are ever in a hurry to get in or out of the complex, that camera would be available."

"Right!"

They drove in silence from there, back to the apartment.

Invisibly above them, Kieya followed them in a small Gaardian shuttle. "G-mail to Walter."

Walter appeared next to her as a three-dimensional image. "Kieya! What have we learned?"

"Toby and Paula hiked with the couple back as far as Badger Pass. Then they went back to your base to plan strategy. Good arrangements have been made for managing the media and keeping them safe, at least in the short term. Just east of Wawona Tunnel, the scientists met the pastor of a large church. They will try to establish a relationship so that they can hide some of their proprietary equipment at the church. Frank has the layout of the church if you need it."

"Excellent. I would appreciate it if you stay with them until they are back in Fresno. Then Toby and Paula can take over."

"Agreed. I'll see you in a few days at Gaardian Center. Until then."

"Until then."

The transmission ended.

+ + +

As they drove the next day into Fresno, Glenn and Betsy Sue went past where they would normally turn off to their research complex, further on to the church where their new friend was the senior pastor. As they pulled into the parking lot, they could see empty parking spaces for upwards of a thousand vehicles. They parked right in front of the main entrance of the office complex, a small building beside a much larger one. Following some direction signs, they made their way to the entrance. Inside, it was much cooler. A man at a small desk greeted them. "Hello! I saw your SUV pull up. By any chance are you the Franzes?"

Glenn smiled. "Yes, we are!"

"I'm Steve Lyman. Dr. Marty Chen, our senior pastor, called and told me to watch for you because his secretary is expecting you. Her name is Julie. She's right down this hall, the second door on the right."

"Thank you!" Betsy Sue smiled. They walked down the hall. The second door was open, and as they went in, the secretary looked up and smiled.

Glenn cleared his throat. "Hello. We are the Franzes. Are you Julie?"

"Yes! It is nice to meet you. Reverend Chen called me this morning, and I think I have just the little nook you need. Come with me."

They went further down the hallway to the end and through some glass doors into a transparently enclosed walkway between the buildings. Passing through more doors, they were inside the much larger building. Julie said, "Down the end of this hallway is the worship area, which I'll show you in a moment." She pointed to a planter on the left. "This is something the architect installed at Marty's – Rev. Chen's – request. Do you see this small lever?" She pressed an innocent piece of wood. There was a click, and one of the panels of wood paneling opened. "This is the pastor's special door to the cloisters area."

As they stepped into the darker area, lights came on, revealing a small work area with a sink and a refrigerator. It was paneled from floor to ceiling, with an aspen colored wood paneling. Across from the sink and refrigerator were cabinets and shelving.

"This is interesting," said Glenn. "What is this area for?"

"Usually there's no one in here except for about forty-five minutes early Sunday morning and again later in the early afternoon. It is where communion is prepared for worship services and where cleanup is done after worship. That door over there," she pointed, "leads towards the altar area of the sanctuary. The door on this side," she pointed again, "leads towards the baptistery area, which is typically used about once a month. We came in the pastor's door, which few people know about. We don't want the public wandering around back here because it would create maintenance problems."

"Very nice," Betsy Lou said.

"Now," said Julie, "this is what I have in mind for you two." She walked over to the large refrigerator, which had a handle on the left. She pulled downward firmly on some molding that seemed to connect and provide a border for the paneling. A spring-loaded door popped up and open.

Glenn peered inside. "Wow!" The door was almost a meter wide and half a meter high, and it appeared to cover a compartment over a meter deep. Glenn pulled the door down to close it, and the molding popped back into place. "Smooth! What's this for?"

Julie grinned. "The architect installed a half-dozen of these compartments in various places in the complex when we built this building twenty-two years ago. He thought it would be useful to have places where things of some value could be stored out of the way and away from prying eyes."

"Brilliant!" Betsy Lou smiled, looking carefully inside. "How many people know about these?"

Julie closed it again. "The architect is now deceased, and the workers who installed them no longer live in the area, so Marty and I are the only ones who know where they all are." You two are the first people to be told about this one. Marty says it's your secret place if you want it."

Glenn looked at Betsy Sue, and she nodded.

"Good! I thought you would like this. Now, you need to know that this building is open seven days a week during the day because people like to come to the worship area to pray. There is always some light near the front. When we lock up at 8:00 PM, there is a night watchman wandering the grounds. If he sees a car come into the parking areas, he can let people in for prayers. You can have access at any time, and you can come in whether you're going to pray or not. Then you can access your secret spot when no one is looking." She paused. "Now, come this way, and you can see how this area connects to the worship area."

They entered the large sanctuary. Glenn whistled. "This is huge!"

Julie smiled. "On Christmas and Easter we fill it three times. I have to get back to the office, but you can stay if you want. It was nice meeting you both."

They all shook hands, and she walked back towards the corridor from which they had come. Glenn spoke after Julie was out of sight. "Let's go and get camera two, one of the tripods, a box of thumb drives, and the extra hard drive. After we store them, let's stay and pray a while. We need to pray all of this through."

"I agree." Hand in hand, they walked out towards the front entrance of the building.

16. Natural Beauty

At Tiberius Holdings, Francine Elliott shook her head in wide-eyed-amazed delight. "You're going to find this difficult to believe."

"What? Why?" Ben Kaiser was puzzled. In his office in the Transamerica Building, Ben had asked her to come and discuss a project for the Fresno Chaffee Zoo.

"When you said you wanted to talk about a geodesic dome aviary for the zoo, I could not imagine where it would be located on those grounds. Now you are telling me it will be located at the old Pioneer Enterprise complex. I was just out there a year ago with a realtor because he had a client who was interested in property in that area. The client wanted to build a geodesic dome atrium for botanical research."

"That was Paul Hanson, wasn't it?"

"Yes!"

"I knew that you were the consulting architect. That's why I've asked you here today."

"Wonderful! Where would you put a geodesic dome at the complex?"

"The complex has been converted. It is now a center for environmental research and optical research tools."

"I heard you had started a new division out there. You still have not answered my question. Where do you want to put the dome?"

"If you remember, near the center of the complex, there is a large atrium. What we are talking about is enlarging the atrium to include birds and possibly small animals as well as plants. It would be a bio-dome operated and maintained by the zoo. Visitors would be allowed in on special occasions and for research projects. Our current research there would be significantly expanded in conjunction with the zoo. I will finance the expansion and take a tax write-off. The zoo's gain will be shared with us as a research facility."

"What's our budget?"

Ben reached for an envelope on his desk. "Take this to Mike Lamprecht, the administrator at my Fresno complex. The details are inside the envelope. He'll show you around and maybe introduce you to some of the scientists already working there." He handed her the envelope. "After you have an initial assessment of the size of the dome you'll design, stop at the zoo. Talk to them about equipping the inside before importing the flora, fauna, and any animals." Ben's phone buzzed. "Yes, Lucy?"

"You need to get going to your other appointment. I'll see Miss Elliott out."

"Fine." He paused. "It's been good to meet you Francine." He reached out and shook her hand.

"Thank you! And thank you for this opportunity!"

"No problem. You are new talent on the architectural scene, and this can benefit both of us. I'll see you again soon."

"Thanks again." Francine stopped at Lucy's desk, as Ben walked past her, out of the door, and into an elevator.

"Ben's impressed with you. Be careful to give him your best effort. If you do, this can be a springboard that will launch your career in special ways and lead to other challenges."

"I gathered that. What is Tiberius Holdings, anyway? I did an Internet search and could hardly believe the variety of things that are associated with the company."

"Tiberius Holdings is whatever Ben says it is. He is Chairman of the Board, CEO, and CFO. The only person I have ever met who might be smarter than he is you will probably meet tomorrow. His name is Glenn Franz. He works in our Fresno facility. Let's head downstairs." They walked towards the elevators.

+ + +

Across town from Ben's offices, Jonnie and Jack were getting coffee and a morning snack in the break area at the Sierra Club headquarters. Jonnie took a sip of coffee and spoke. "I'm really concerned about our funding for next year with Senator Hosmer in so much trouble. I am fervently praying that another senator – or at least a congressman – will pick up the ball for us. "

"I've been praying for that ever since she was first arrested. I wonder if we're going to have to have a fund-raising campaign." The phone rang, and he picked it up. His eyes opened wider. "Senator Steinmetz!" We were just thinking about you!" Jack winked at Jonnie. "How are you?" He paused. "How's our appropriations bill doing?" He paused longer. "Yes, Senator. Either Jonnie or I can pick you up at the airport. What time is your flight arriving?" He paused. "Fantastic! We'll see you tomorrow." He paused. "Yes, thank you Senator. Bye!" That was Senator Everett Steinmetz. He's flying in at 11:30 tomorrow morning. Do you want to pick him up?"

Jonnie was smiling. "God does everything exceedingly well! We have been praying, and God has answered. Wow! Yes! I'll pick him up." The rest of that day seemed to pass quickly.

The next morning, Jonnie greeted the Senator with a smile and a hug. They made small talk until she had the senator and his luggage in the car, and they were on their way downtown.

The senator spoke as they got onto highway 101. "I love my home state of Colorado, but San Francisco holds special memories for me. My wife and I were married here, and our wedding night was in a bridal suite at the Mark Hopkins."

"Really! Where did you go on your honeymoon?"

"We headed up the coast through the wine country. We ended up at Crater Lake National Park in Oregon. Our first apartment was further north in Portland. That is where we first got involved in politics. We were there only until after the election, and then we returned to Colorado."

"Sounds romantic!"

"It was, but I'm not here to remember the old days. I'm glad it's you I'm seeing first. I need to pick your brain."

Jonnie nodded. "Okay. What is it?"

"My sources tell me that you have become friends with Glenn Franz and Betsy Sue Johnson." He saw her glance over at him. "Don't worry. This conversation is between us. You may not know it, but I'm a man of my word."

"Okay. Ben Kaiser trusts you, and that's good enough for me."

The old man smiled. "Yes, Ben and I have known each other since he made his first millions in his undergraduate days. It is good that we have that mutual friend. Tell me what you can about Glenn and Betsy Sue."

As they drove north on Highway 101, she crossed over through Daly City to Great Highway, which followed the ocean. Jonnie opened up, even more than she had to Jack Haddy. The senator did not take notes. He simply nodded from time to time and asked questions for details. By the time they arrived at the Sierra Club's headquarters, he knew enough.

Once inside, the senator, Jonnie, and Jack went into an office and shut the door. Senator Steinmetz spoke first. "I doubt that anyone has told you what has been going on behind the scenes in Washington on your environmental front. After Senator Hosmer was arrested, I called her staff to join mine for a powwow. I saw to it that her staff was taken care of until the Wyoming governor appointed a replacement. You will not hear anything from him. He will have enough to do keeping his head above water until the next election. He is a nice guy. His name is Jim Miller."

"We know," said Jonnie. "I've talked with him. He's okay, but he's not going to have the time, the resources, or the influence to do much good for the Sierra Club."

"Right." The senator nodded. "If you have talked to Ben Kaiser about me, you know that I use senatorial power when necessary, but I prefer the power of my tongue."

Jack laughed. "We've heard."

The senator gave him a quizzical look, and then went on. "I know that Betsy Sue and Glenn Franz are top dogs right now in environmental circles. Glenn pulled a ruse on Senator Hosmer that continues to make me chuckle."

Jonnie grinned. "Are you talking about the so-called third camera?"

He nodded. "It's possible that Senator Hosmer still has not figured out that their third converted Panalux 140 is little more than a digital conversion. It will make impressive panoramic images of extraordinary quality, but it is not a research camera. A friend of mine at NASA assures me of this."

Jack was enthusiastic. "The first camera, which they initially used in Yosemite and Lake Tahoe, produced some amazing data. I don't know about the second camera."

"Nobody does but a handful of people. Camera two is even more extraordinary. The data from camera one's images is now being spread around the scientific community, but the data from camera two is still being processed in Fresno. Hundreds of scientists want to get their hands on this data and want to use the camera – camera one – themselves. Ben Kaiser has put an army of patent attorneys to work. As soon as all the technology of the cameras and software are properly protected, then we can relax the security slightly. Meanwhile, both the optical technology and the software are being very carefully protected. If you're a Christian or a Jew, you could easily be convinced that God is watching out for those two, far beyond what Ben Kaiser has done."

Jonnie grinned. "Absolutely. It is more than you can imagine, senator. Glenn and Betsy Sue are getting data from camera two that amazes both of them. They are making discoveries every day."

"Have you heard about the project proposed to be in conjunction with the Fresno zoo?" The senator looked at Jonnie closely.

"Yes. I would imagine that the San Diego Zoo and others are probably jealous!"

The senator nodded again. "Some of the wealthy patrons in La Jolla are almost insanely jealous. Here is where I need to talk with you two. I do not – repeat, do not – want government money involved with any of this at this point. Behind the scenes, however, I am calling in some favors. Current government regulations call for an environmental impact statement to accompany this new project in Fresno. I am respectfully requesting that you two do everything you can to *legitimately* help that process along. Between you and me, as a thank you, I am pushing that appropriations bill to the Senate floor next week. We have the votes, and you will get the money you need."

Jonnie and Jack both smiled.

Senator Steinmetz's cell phone rang. "Excuse me please." The senator stood up as he answered the phone, went to the window, and talked almost inaudibly."

"We got the appropriations!" Jack was enthusiastic, but he kept his voice low so as not to disturb the senator. "This means we can go ahead with our plans and cut back on our publicity budget. I'll get our Washington contacts to monitor the passage of the bill and milk it for all its worth with the media."

"Right! You focus on that. I am going to make an appointment with Lucy to see if I can go to lunch with Ben one day and talk about Fresno. When I was a kid, the Sierra Club went to Sparks, Stuart, Wellesley, and Robertson in Oakland when it needed help with environmental impact issues. They sold their practice long ago to a firm in Daly City though."

"Good."

Senator Steinmetz put his cell phone away and approached them. "I may drop by here again tomorrow after I see Ben Kaiser. Meanwhile, you might find interesting what I learned in that call. After spending yesterday and last night along the Coastal Trail and Red Bluffs in Redwoods National Park, Betsy Sue and Glenn Franz made their way to the Prairie Creek Visitor Center this morning. While they were stopped for lunch, someone broke into their SUV and stole their equipment."

"What?!"

"This is where things get really interesting. The thieves raced away in a dark SUV, but they did not get far. The two thieves were found near their vehicle about ten minutes later. The SUV was parked just off the road. All of them were unconscious and trussed up with duct tape when they were found, and when revived, they claimed not to know anything. They had no identification, but the police found something on one of them that indicated they might have been working for a government agency. I'll find out."

"What about the equipment?"

"This is even more interesting. All five tires – including the spare – were apparently slashed with claws, and there were tracks circling the SUV. All but one of the tracks were at least partially obliterated by people checking on the equipment. The interesting thing is this: The paw prints were unlike any previously recorded animal in North America. The print is huge."

Jonnie and Jack stared at the senator, wide-eyed.

"Look at this picture of a paw print sent to my cell." The senator turned his phone towards them.

Jack whistled.

"It looks like a large print from one of the big cats, but there have been no zoo escapes in recent years. Where did it come from, I wonder? Anyway, the equipment was intact. The thieves only had possession for fifteen minutes, or maybe less."

Jonnie breathed a sigh of relief. "At least the equipment is safe."

The senator's phone rang once more "Excuse me again!" He stepped towards the window and talked softly. The call took only a few minutes, during which time Jonnie and Jack glanced at each other and at the senator from time to time. As the senator put his phone in a pocket, he turned and smiled. "That was Margaret Graves. Do either of you know her?" They shook their heads no. "She lives in Oakland and has set up an independent sound stage in some unused area of a church near downtown. I am going there this evening to make a public service announcement about people – Christians and non-Christians alike – needing to be good stewards of Earth's environment. She worked with my staff to put it together."

Jonnie and Jack showed surprise on their faces as the senator continued. "You may want to get acquainted with her. I think Glenn and Betsy Sue may find her facility both useful and very cooperative."

"Terrific!" Jack was genuinely enthusiastic. "I'll send an email to Glenn and put a note in our resource files."

The senator got up and extended a hand. "Good. I must be going now, but I'm sure we'll be talking before the end of next week." They all shook hands.

After Senator Steinmetz left, Jonnie and Jack continued to talk about the attempted theft off and on for the rest of the afternoon. They also debated whether there really could be a big cat on the loose somewhere in Northern California.

+ + +

In her apartment, Kieya purred softly as she spoke. "Report to Walter regarding the scientists I've been watching. There was an attempt to steal their technology today. Since I was available, I took care of it. The thieves are in custody, and the equipment is back in the hands of the scientists. Toby has been notified, and he will increase his surveillance. He told me that he had assisted establishing some new political connections to help these scientists. End report."

17. Consequences

The reporter stuck a microphone in the woman's face. "Senator Houser, you have been found in contempt of court and have served nine days in jail. You have been fined $65,000 for the government's cost in sending marshals to Fresno, California. What will you do now, while out on bail pending trial after the grand jury indictment?"

"The senator has nothing to say at this time," said her lawyer, a tall slender man in a thousand-dollar silk suit. As her mouthpiece paused to answer other questions, Gayla Hosmer pressed forward with a member of her staff to the street, where they got into a waiting limo. Inside, she said, "Take me home."

"Yes, Ma'am." The driver pulled away from the curb.

"Andy, how are things going for you?"

"Okay. By the time Senator Miller has his feet wet with your former duties, he will face getting elected if he wants the job. I guess a lot depends upon what happens with you."

"No, Andy, it doesn't."

"What do you mean, senator?"

"If I were to plead innocent, I'd go through a long trial that I would probably lose. I don't want that."

"So, you're going to plead guilty, ma'am?"

"Right. Publicly, I am throwing myself on the mercy of the court. Privately, there is a deal I am going to accept. Everett Steinmetz was furious with me for a while, but now, more than anything, I am an embarrassment to my party, and he knows it. He's arranged a deal for me, if the court approves."

"A deal?"

"I'm going to plead guilty, take a suspended sentence, and pay a fine. Then I am going to hold a news conference announcing that I am moving to Puerto Rico to get a change of pace and re-evaluate my future. Party leaders will let me run for office there if I wish, but I will be forbidden from returning to the states for at least four years. I will not be able to do lobbying either. I will even have to limit my press releases and public appearances. Basically, I'll be lying low for several years. My beloved husband is good with this. He and I spent a vacation there several years ago and enjoyed the island very much."

"I'm going to miss you, senator." Andy had tears in his eyes."

"I'll miss you too, Andy."

The limousine came to a halt in front of the senator's home. "I'll stay in touch, Andy. Email is easy. You can reach me by my same address. I'll probably keep my web page too." She got out. "Bye, Andy! Bye Earl!" She slammed the door.

+ + +

It was more than two weeks before Glenn and Betsy Sue learned about the deal. They heard just before they had lunch in a corner of the atrium one Friday. She was philosophical. "We shouldn't be surprised that Senator Hosmer cut a deal. She is a political embarrassment to many people in the capital."

"I guess so," said Glenn, "but I half-way wish she had gotten some time in jail. At least, she's out of sight for now."

They could hear faint noises of workers above them, working on the frame for the base of the geodesic dome. A door slid open nearby, and Mike Lamprecht walked over. "Enjoying your lunch?"

"Yes, Mike, what's up?" Betsy Sue looked up from her plate.

"I have you scheduled to make some images down in Florida's Everglades next week. Denny Singleton from the EPA wants to tag along and bring a research crew. What do you think?"

Glenn looked at his wife. "We can try it, but tell them if they get in our way or in any way give us problems that they'll never be able to work beside us again."

"Denny said he expected as much. He said he thinks you're a real pain in the butt for protecting your technology the way you do."

Betsy Sue smiled. "He can think what he likes, but until we have a blanket of patents on all of our – Glenn's – innovations, we've got a good reason to protect our stuff."

Mike nodded. "I agree. There is one more thing. Bob Hickman from the Department of the Interior wants to know if you will lend him a camera for a week. I told him I would ask you. He is someone Ben thinks we can trust. He wants to make some images at Big Sur."

Glenn scowled. "I hate to lend equipment out, but eventually we have to expand the use of our resources."

"Bob is going to give you a present in gratitude for this ten-day loan."

They both looked at him. "A present?" Betsy Sue asked.

Mike nodded and smiled. "Right. You are not going to believe this. Based upon the basic Panamax camera design, Bob let out a contract to design and build an underwater housing with an array of external controls and a display built in."

Their eyes got wide. "Who made it?" asked Glenn.

"Your friend Ralph, with the facilities and help of Bollex and Sons."

"I trust Ralph, of course, and Bollex does excellent work. This is great! I've been thinking about stopping in Biscayne National Park while we're in Florida next week."

Mike looked puzzled. "What about logistics?"

Glenn smiled. "It's no problem. Bob can take camera one while we use camera two. Only we – and our attorneys – know that camera two is much different."

"Okay." Mike turned and headed back to his office.

Glenn was thoughtful. "If we can get that housing before we leave, that will give us an extra measure of safety when using the camera in the Everglades."

She nodded. "Are you serious about Biscayne National Park?"

"Absolutely. We will need to use a higher ISO speed under water, but the sensor is supposed to be sharp up to 51,200 before significant noise becomes a problem. Ralph has said that with different software, we can probably push the ISO further. So far, though, we have only had it up to 800. It will be a good test." Glenn took one more swallow of iced herbal tea, and then he slid his chair backward. "Let's go back to work. You've been done with lunch since before Mike got here."

She slid her chair back. "I'm right behind you."

+ + +

They spent most of the following week in the Everglades. Everyone on the EPA crew was polite and cooperative, but staying out of each other's way proved to be vexing for Glenn and Betsy Sue. By the end of the week, neither of them had much sleep. They were constantly under a barrage of questions about the new technology and their use of it.

The underwater housing arrived on Tuesday, and they immediately decided to spend the following weekend at Biscayne National Park. The EPA crew wanted to tag along there too, but Glenn said no. Too many people in the water in the same area could drastically affect their images, and Glenn did not want to risk it.

With some relief, on Friday afternoon Glenn and Betsy Sue drove towards the underwater park, while the EPA crew headed for the Miami airport. They got off the Florida Turnpike at the Homestead exit, and the settled into a suite to relax. Not wanting to take chances, they had their camera case put in the hotel safe. Betsy Sue was in Homestead previously to research the environmental effects of Hurricane Andrew. After four and a half days of snack food in the Everglades, they were ready for a good meal. They went to Ruby Tuesday, where slowly and pleasantly, they had their fill. That night they slept soundly for the first time in nearly a week.

Saturday morning, they were up at six, had breakfast, and were on their way to the park by 8:00. Mike Lamprecht arranged for a boat charter and scuba gear. It was all waiting for them when they got there. Once out on the water, they did not have to go far to reach a good site. Their captain, Willard Kuster, was talkative. "Right here you'll find pristine coral reefs, but we can go to some of the sunken wrecks later if you wish. In addition to colorful fish, you'll probably also encounter dolphins and sea turtles." He stared as Glenn opened a large case, where he had already installed the camera inside of the custom underwater housing. "Wow! That looks custom made!"

"It is. I built the camera inside."

"Incredible!" Willard turned off the engine. "Since the winds are calm with clear skies, your conditions down there should be almost ideal." Reaching into a cabinet, he pulled out a rifle with a scope. When they stared at the gun, he explained. "I don't expect any problems with sharks, but I'll have this handy. I'm a crack shot. If you see a shark coming too close, head for the surface as near to the boat as you can. I'll take care of the rest."

They both nodded. Glenn and Betsy Sue took off their outer clothing, revealing their swim wear underneath. They put on their scuba gear and checked each other out. They grabbed the two handles of the camera housing and lifted it up. It was heavy.

"In the water it will be easier to handle," Glenn said. "Willard, I want to tether this to a line, just in case we need to get it out of the water quickly."

Willard nodded and reached up above their heads. "We can clip this to that anchor loop on the housing. It goes to that boom up there, and the other end is on an electric winch. Just watch." Willard pulled on a small lever, and there was a high-pitched whine. As the camera housing came up, they swung the boom out over the water. He pushed the lever in the other direction, and the camera housing began to lower into the water. "I'll release the clutch once you have control of it in the water. Okay?"

"Right!" Glenn said. Betsy Sue nodded. The two of them grabbed their masks and jumped into the water. Down there, it was a different world. Glenn had set the ISO speed of the sensor to 1600, and the shutter was set for an effective exposure sweep of a two-hundred-fiftieth of a second. Betsy Sue took a light reading and signaled Glenn to set the aperture of the lens. They had an extra-large thumb drive given them by one on the crew of the EPA. They could make up to five exposures on the one drive. They were sure that was all they would need. It was.

After almost an hour, they surfaced. Willard winched the camera out of the water as they climbed up the boat's ladder. "Did you get enough pictures, or do you want to head for the wrecks?"

"Let's head for the wrecks." Betsy Sue was enthusiastic. "It's great down there! I want to record the environment around at least two of the wrecks. I –

we – want an image of a wreck that has been here a long time. Then we want one of a wreck that is more recent."

Willard nodded. "The old wreck is easy. To see a newer wreck we will have to leave the park area and head north. That will have to be tomorrow morning." He paused as the engine came to life, and they got underway. "The newest of the wrecks is up near Port St. Lucie just outside of Bathtub Beach."

Glenn's voice was louder now, over the drone of the engine. "Could we meet you at Port St. Lucie early tomorrow morning?"

"Yes! Mike Lamprecht told me to take you wherever you want to go. He's got me booked through all day tomorrow."

"Good. We'll meet you at 7:00 AM there at the dock." Willard agreed.

The rest of the afternoon was uneventful. Back at their hotel in Homestead, Betsy Sue made a phone call to Mike. "Mike? Betsy Sue." She paused. "Yes, things have gone very well. Willard certainly knows these waters. He is meeting us at Port St. Lucie early tomorrow morning, so we can make one more image of a new wreck near Bathtub Beach. Can you arrange for a plane to fly us home from Palm Beach International?" She paused. "Great. Thanks Mike. We'll see you Monday morning." She ended the call. "You heard that?"

Glenn nodded. "We'd better retire early this evening. We'll need to get up around 4:00 AM in order to meet Willard on time." He scowled.

"Why not go up and spend the night there? We'll get some real sleep that way."

"Good idea. Let's get packing. I'll call the front desk."

Sunday went as planned. After spending the night in a hotel near the water, it was relatively easy to meet Willard and get their final image. They were back at the dock before 10:00 AM. They had time to go to church, but they skipped lunch as they rushed to the airport. Both slept during part of the flight home.

A mountain of work awaited them Monday morning. They decided to forego processing their own images until after they dealt with images taken by Bob Hickman at Big Sur with camera one. The Fresno lab had a computing power that rivaled that of the biggest government agencies. Processing images became almost routine for Glenn and Betsy Sue. This time, however, it was very difficult because of Bob. Using two keyboards, Glenn and Betsy Sue both worked using one large flat-panel monitor.

As the first of Bob's images came up, Bob explained. "I took this image down near … "Whoa!! What did you do? Let me see. … "Wow!! Why don't you – "What's that? I'm beginning to think you ought to – wow!"

Betsy Sue looked up at Bob. "We've been using this software and processing images for many months now, Bob. Why don't you just watch?"

Bob just could not stop talking about the images and what he thought they should be doing. He put Glenn on edge, and Betsy Sue began to get mad. Finally, they had processed about twenty versions of each image. Glenn transferred the data to a DVD-R disk, put it in a hard case, and handed it to Bob.

Bob was finally relatively quiet. "Thanks, Glenn."

"Okay. If you or someone from Interior makes images with our camera again, we will privately process the data and send you the results. It will be easier."

"But I like to watch you work!"

"We can understand that, Bob. The trouble is, you cannot seem to watch silently. We would have been done sooner if you had not given us a running commentary. To us, it is just data that we can study later. To you, it is your work, and you want to share it. We understand."

"Yes, Bob, we understand." Betsy Sue gave him a smile. "What you need to understand is that we are scientists, and if we need your help, we will ask for it. Okay?"

Bob nodded, sheepishly. "I apologize."

Glenn and Betsy Sue stood up, and they walked with Bob towards the lab entrance. Mike was waiting just outside the door. "I've got a video conference call waiting for you in my office, Bob. Come with me."

Bob shook hands with Glenn and Betsy Sue. Thanks again! Both of you!"

"You're welcome," they said together. As Bob walked away, they breathed a sigh of relief. Betsy Sue pointed towards the atrium, and they walked in hand in hand.

Betsy Sue spoke quietly. "You know, these past several days have been productive, but we've had some trying people!"

Glenn chuckled. "True! True! I thought some in the EPA crew were difficult to handle, but Bob was the worst!"

"Yes! At least, Willard was easy to get along with, and his boat was in first-rate shape."

"He's a good man."

Betsy Sue reached over and touched his hand. "We can look at Bob's images again at another time. We might be able to squeeze a bit more data out of them when he's not around."

"Right," He nodded. "Let's save our images until tomorrow. I have an idea. Let's heat up something from the freezer for dinner and then relax. We could both use some time in which we let our minds turn into oatmeal."

She grinned. "Turn into oatmeal?"

He smiled back. "Let's get our minds off of everything and let them idle for a while this evening. I have those old Looney Tunes collections of cartoons, and you have bought some Blu-ray movies we have not seen yet. How about it?"

"Fantastic! Let's call it quits for now." They walked arm in arm back to their apartment.

+ + +

Once the anchor area was in place on the roof, it was surprising how fast the geodesic dome went up. It took less than a month. Meanwhile, the Fresno Chaffee Zoo was well-organized and ready. During an unusually cold week in late November, the nearly empty dome began to be filled. Everyone at the complex passing by the area watched in wonder as the area above the atrium became an extension of the zoo. The atrium roof stayed in place, separating the relaxation and dining area from the newer area above. A spiral staircase went up from the center of the atrium. There was also an elevator near the edge of the dome.

On the second Friday of December, Mike Lamprect came to the doorway of the lab complex, went to a microphone clipped at a station on the wall, and announced news for the whole complex. "Can I have everyone's attention?!

The new zoological complex is now complete. When you're finished for the day, you can go up and take a tour if you like."

As it was nearly 5:00 PM, Glenn looked over at Mike. He gestured and nodded. Mike picked up the microphone once more. "Attention again! The Franzes have signaled me to have you finish what you are doing and take off the rest of the day -- and as much of the evening as you wish -- to relax. There is a buffet supper in the atrium for those who are hungry."

Arm in arm, Betsy Sue and Glenn walked into the atrium. Then they began to climb the stairs as several dozen people followed them. At the top of the stairs, they went into a glass airlock before going into the new area under the dome. As people entered, their talking was lowered to whispers.

Betsy Sue looked around in amazement. "Glenn, dear, this reminds me of one of my life lessons I got as a teenager in Dallas."

"What's that," he asked softly.

"The lesson was how important it is to read, because there are other places and other worlds."

"This time we're not just reading." He looked around in simple wonder.

"It gives me an idea, though."

"What are you thinking?"

"Why don't we create a series of interactive electronic books, so that children can study what is here electronically, seeing this place with multiple views of the same scene, just as we do as we analyze our images. We can also provide some video showing how animals and plants interact with their environment."

He smiled at her in wide-eyed amazement. "That's brilliant! It would not only help the zoo, but it could be a teaching tool used by anyone with a computer! I think Margaret Graves over in Oakland can help us with the video and sound editing."

"We can do even more. We can put it all in tablet computers designed for the purpose. All the data can be burned on ROM chips. With mass production, the cost can be kept down."

He nodded. They walked together, wandering among the plants and watching the birds, for more than two hours. Then they headed back to their apartment.

18. Meanwhile, Elsewhere

Many galaxies away, Qaak's apartment was warm and comfortable. Walter, Debbie, Kieya, Jody, and Qaak were there around the fireplace because their host had sent a g-mail to them. There were important things to be discussed.

Qaak began, "When I retired from being the convener to become just a mentor and patriarch of the Gaardians, Jody and I began visiting all the other Gaardians." He looked at his wife and back towards them. "As of yesterday, we have visited every sector. Two things have become obvious. First of all, we must find someone to replace me as the trainer."

Kieya's subtle purring stopped. "Why?"

"Eventually it will have to happen anyway, and now is a good time. I have prayed extensively about this. The Creator has pointed me in a particular direction."

"Asayak," said Walter.

"Indeed. The Creator has revealed this to you as well?"

"Yes. I have discussed the possibility with Asayak, and it says it would be honored to serve if asked."

Kieya relaxed again, and she subtly began to purr. "Does it have the ability to do what you have done, Qaak?"

"Yes it does, and more. It may well be able to complete the training for most candidates faster than I could do so in most cases. I can only mentally transfer factual content. Asayak can include emotional content as well. It could be a great advantage."

Walter nodded. "Asayak's gifts are amazing. Butch Eng has let Asayak assist him in transferring medical information to a conference of doctors of another species with full success."

"Indeed. It is very capable. I have communed with Gaardian extensively regarding this. It can prepare Asayak very quickly for its new tasks. Furthermore, Asayak is completely trustworthy. It will be a great asset to us."

Walter stared into the fire. "I do not think we need approval of the other Gaardians for this. Are we agreed that we should proceed?"

"Agreed," Kieya purred.

"Indeed."

"G-mail to Asayak." The creature appeared near them. "Asayak, we are going to send you to Gaardian now as we discussed. I see that Ann is there with you. Please communicate with Ann so that she can give us your answer."

Ann nodded and spoke. "Asayak says it thanks you and considers it a privilege to serve in this way. It is ready to be transported." Walter's ring shimmered as Asayak disappeared. Ann looked startled. "Wow! That was quick! Did you know that I'm working with Margaret Graves?"

"Yes, Ann." Walter smiled. "Anything new?"

"There's always something new!" She grinned. "Margaret and I will be helping Glenn and Betsy Sue Franz with some educational material development. We're using Gaardian technology to speed up and enhance the established technology here on Earth." She paused briefly. "It is good to see the three of you."

"We are pleased to see you as well," said Qaak.

"Yes," purred Kieya.

"I will see you soon, Ann."

"Bye."

"End g-mail," said Walter. She disappeared. "I'm glad we are all in agreement with this. What was the other thing you wanted to discuss, Qaak?"

"Simply this: Now that you are the convener, eventually you will need to have another Gaardian in your sector. Kieya has a suggestion."

"Yes," the cat purred. "As you know, I have been monitoring a pair of scientists who live and work in a town called Fresno."

"Yes, Kieya, Betsy Sue and Glenn Franz are doing some pioneering work. Both are truly brilliant."

"True. The female Betsy Sue is going to have a child, although she does not yet know it. One of their offspring will almost assuredly be a good future Gaardian candidate."

"Indeed. Yes, Walter, Kieya and I remember clearly watching your ancestors until you were born. We know what to look for in humans."

"I understand." Walter scowled. "I know we cannot seek a candidate from Keeta's planet because memories are congenitally passed on. We should, however, consider a candidate from Asayak's planet."

"Indeed not," said Qaak firmly. "Kieya, do you remember the candidate we had from that planet in sector 135-G857-D4958?"

The cat's purr disappeared. "Absolutely! That candidate seemed to be excellent. Its genetics were about ninety-six percent of Asayak's, and it had similar capabilities." She paused. "Walter, it was a very bad choice. It was a serious challenge to Qaak, and Gaardian had to rescue him!"

"Indeed! We did not realize that it could be telepathically aggressive. I was in some serious mental combat with that silicon-based creature until I sent a quick signal to Gaardian. Our beloved planet rendered the creature unconscious. That was unusual because the creature had never known sleep. While it was asleep, Gaardian removed from it all memories of Gaardians and our technology. We did not awaken it until it was back on its home planet. Since it had never known sleep, when it awoke it was simply dazed for a moment."

Walter nodded. "Do you believe there will be any problems with Asayak?"

"No. Gaardian has already done some things with Asayak. The planet has made a ghost image of Asayak's mind, which is kept in a protected area. There will be no such problems. Asayak is special. It will be a good trainer. Gaardian will determine whether Asayak can become a Gaardian. The same would be true for any other candidate from Asayak's planet."

"Kieya, are you almost certain that a child from this couple will be a good Gaardian candidate?" Walter asked.

"Yes. As with your brother, it may not be the first child. I will continue to watch and keep you informed."

"Good. This is an excellent but unnecessary confirmation. For the hearing of those here only, Glenn and Betsy Sue will have fraternal twins, and both will be suitable candidates to be Gaardians."

Qaak's eyes grew intensely bright, as Kieya's purr became more audible. "Indeed!!! The Creator has revealed this to you?"

"Yes! For now, this information is just for us. Agreed?"

They all assented.

+ + +

Coming out of the church, Glenn and Betsy Sue walked towards the SUV. Suddenly, she ran towards a nearby planter box. Bending over, she loudly emptied her stomach into the star jasmine foliage.

Glenn ran over as she was vomiting and put a hand on her shoulder until her stomach calmed down. "What happened? Do you think it was something you ate?"

"I don't know." She started walking towards the SUV again, with Glenn holding her hand. As she got in, she said, "I'm feeling better now. Let's go home. We'll see how things are in the morning."

She tossed and turned all night, getting up several times but not suffering further vomiting. At a little after 6:00 AM, Glenn called Dr. John Fagin. He was officially on tap as the physician for the whole complex. When the doctor arrived, the guard let him in and took him to the clinic, where Betsy Sue and Glenn were waiting.

"Thanks for coming so early, John." She meant it.

"That's okay. I had an 8:00 AM appointment here anyway for one of the others. I'll give you a quick once-over and draw some blood."

Glenn spoke. "We can have a messenger take the blood to a lab for you. It's not far from here."

"Sierra Medical?"

"Right."

"Good. I have worked with them many times. Other doctors in my building use them."

After her examination, Betsy Sue went back to the apartment, fixed herself some herbal tea, and relaxed in a recliner with her laptop. When Glenn came in for lunch, she was sound asleep. He did not awaken her.

In the late afternoon, Dr. Fagin called Glenn on his cell phone. "Glenn, this is John Fagin."

"Hi John. What's the news?"

"I tried to call Betsy Sue's cell phone, but it went straight to voice mail."

"I think she turned it off."

"Why don't you put yours on speaker phone so both of you can talk?"

"Okay." He pressed a button. "We're on the speaker. I'm sitting down next to her."

"Betsy Sue?"

"Hi John! What's up?"

"Well, there's good news and bad news. The bad news is that you're going to have to be more careful what you eat for a while.""

"What's the good news?"

"You're pregnant! Congratulations!"

"What???!!!"

They were both talking at once and hugging each other until the doctor's voice on the speaker phone stopped them. "Hey, you two!" They stopped talking to listen. "I'm going to email you a list of dos and don'ts. Betsy Sue. I want you to make an appointment with Dr. Susan Bell as soon as possible. She's in my building and will see you through this."

Most of that evening they made phone calls to family and friends, and they sent emails telling the good news.

19. Into the Future

Eight months later, Betsy Sue gave birth to twins in their apartment. Glenn, both doctors, and two nurses were there. Unseen, in a corner of their bedroom, Kieya and Asayak watched invisibly. It was fraternal twins as The Creator had told Walter – a boy and a girl.

Asayak stirred as the two babies were delivered. "I had forgotten this is possible with the human species."

"Yes." Kieya responded telepathically. She suppressed her purr, not wanting to be heard. "I had five in my first pregnancy and three in the second."

After some discussion, the doctors and one nurse left. Kieya and Asayak waited patiently until the babies were in their bassinets, the nurse was reading in a recliner, and Betsy Sue and Glenn went to bed. Without making themselves visible, the two approached the babies. Asayak became totally still as Kieya extended one paw to touch the boy on top of his head. A faint blue glow swept over the baby. Then Kieya touched the head of the girl with the same result. Kieya looked up at Asayak with a small fire in her eyes. The two vanished.

The atrium was empty and nearly dark except for starlight and a half moon. Kieya said, "I put them in temporary stasis so that the parents can sleep for a few hours. The nurse will not see the difference. Did you mentally analyze them?"

"Yes. It was humbling and a new experience for me. They both will make suitable Gaardians."

Kieya purred softly. "Train them both. Human twins like these remain emotionally connected throughout their lives. If they both agree to be Gaardians, it will not be the first time in our history, but it is rather rare."

The creature sank closer to Kieya's height. "I will begin taking their minds to Gaardian when they can walk."

"Good. Gaardian is now monitoring them and protecting them. Come with me up above." The two vanished from the atrium and reappeared within the geodesic dome.

The creature was moved. "This is interesting. My planet has nothing like this."

"The environment is self-contained and controlled, similar to the atrium at Walter's base on the moon above us." The cat purred more loudly.

"By Gaardian standards this is primitive, but I sense that by most standards that it is quite beautiful here. I am impressed. I do not experience this as you do, but in every way I am impressed."

"Let us commune with Gaardian before returning to our separate sectors."

"Agreed."

They vanished.

+ + +

"Twins!!!" Senator Steinmetz grinned at his secretary. "That's fantastic! Let's send them ..." He paused and looked up. "No! Call my precious Dorothy. Ask her if on Friday, instead of flying to Honolulu, if she would like to see some of the biggest living things in the world, located in Yosemite, instead. Tell her that if we do, we will have to stop on our way to bless some newborn twins. Okay?" His secretary nodded. "If she agrees, get us airfare to Fresno, housing at the Ahwahnee in Yosemite, and transportation. See if Mike Lamprecht can arrange for someone who can provide us with some security who would be willing to be our driver."

"Okay, is there anything else, senator?"

"No, ... but thank you."

+ + +

There was a knock at their apartment door. Glenn called out, "Come in!"

The door opened, and Mike Lamprecht filled the doorway. "Good morning! How are the twins this morning, and how are you two doing?"

Betsy Sue smiled from the far corner, where she was nursing. "We got a full night's sleep finally last night, thanks to Nora."

Glenn nodded, putting a magazine on the table next to him. "Yes! She is turning into a real blessing for all four of us. Having her staying in the guest room and putting the twins in there with her works out great."

Mike smiled. "Good. We're going to have a special visitor in a little while."

They both looked up, and almost simultaneously they asked, "Who?"

"Senator Everett Steinmetz and his wife will be here about 11:30 if their plane is on time."

"Isn't he the one that put Senator Hosmer in her place? I want to meet him!" She put the boy back in his crib and picked up the girl.

"Amen to that!" Glenn grinned. "He's been helping us behind the scenes for weeks now. I'm looking forward to meeting him."

"Understood. The senator says that he and his wife just want to drop by and offer their blessings on their way to Yosemite. They wanted to stay at the Ahwahnee, but it was booked. They will be staying at the Wawona. A nice suite has been arranged for them there."

Glenn nodded. "That's a grand old hotel. It's almost an hour out of the valley, but it's close to the sequoiadendron giganteum grove."

"Right." Mike turned to go. "Shall I send them to you as soon as they get here?"

"Sure!" Betsy Sue was enthusiastic. "Even if Glenn is in the lab I can visit with them here, or Nora and I can take them into the atrium."

"Good. See you later." Mike left, closing the door quietly behind him.

Glenn walked over and sat down near Betsy Sue and the twins. "Is Nora still sleeping?"

"I think so. She is just taking a nap. She will stay until after lunch. We're giving her the weekend off, so I think she can leave as soon as the senator and his wife leave."

"Good. I've been thinking." He paused. "I'm wondering. Do you think we could leave the twins in Nora's hands for a month next May?"

"A month? That's kind of soon to be gone a month, don't you think?"

"Well, I suppose you're right." Glenn was thoughtful.

"What did you have in mind?"

"While you were in the shower this morning, I got an email from Toby Ballentine. Remember, he's the guy we met at Glacier Point along with Paula Rutledge."

Her face brightened. "Yes! He's the man who made a suggestion for your proposed venture into the Grand Canyon!"

"Right! Anyway, he has been talking to Gentry Lunger, the man who developed the medium-range ground-penetrating radar. Toby helped him design a special version to compliment our camera technology." He grinned.

Betsy Sue's eyebrows went up. "How'd he do that?"

"I don't know. We will have to see it at work. According to Dr. Lunger, Toby's technology does not involve any new science. He's just improved on what Dr. Lunger was already doing."

"Isn't Toby a Native American?"

"Yes. I wrote him a little while earlier. He emailed back about ten minutes ago to tell me that he has a passion for this because of his heritage, and he enjoys helping."

Betsy Sue smiled. "If Toby can take what we've already got and help us do it better, he must have some real wisdom in that noggin of his."

+ + +

Astronomically next door, Toby was on Walter's Moon Base in the lounge. Seated nearby was Jody, Walter's chief science officer, and her 65,000-year-old husband, Qaak.

"I passed on those suggestions you gave me to Gentry Lunger. He's excited and ready to put them to use."

Jody smiled. "It wasn't hard to improve on Earth's current science and technology."

Qaak's eyes glowed subtly. "Indeed. We have also given him a little gift, embedded in the software. I created an amusing little glitch from software already on his computer. When the images are combined with the matching images produced by Glenn Franz's software, they will make some unexpected discoveries."

Toby grinned. "So we're not giving them any new science, but we're helping them assemble innovative data? I like how you think, Qaak!"

The old triped's eyes glowed more intensely. "Thank you. These two scientists are the parents of possible new Gaardians of the future."

"The twins?"

"Indeed. Mr. and Mrs. Franz are already innovators. We are simply helping them add something to their résumés. Walter suggested the possibility."

Now Jody was curious. "Why?"

"Gaardians know with certainty two things that the Franzes only surmise. We know that there is nothing too difficult for the Creator of the universe. We also know that time is not a constant, and that's part of the Creator's design."

"Right. So?"

There are many arguments on Earth regarding their planet's age and, consequently, the age of the universe."

Jody chuckled. "Now I understand what you're up to!"

"Indeed!"

Toby was puzzled. "You may understand, but I don't. I'm not a scientist, remember?"

Jody nodded. "Look at their arguments. Earth's scientists assume that they can know the age of the universe based upon what they can observe with their current science. That is understandable. They also assume that the age of the universe is directly related to the age of the Earth. That's arrogant and provincial, of course."

"Why?"

"Because God did not have to create the Earth at the same time He created the rest of the universe. God is not confined by time."

Toby stared at her. "Huh?" Qaak chuckled as his eyes increased their glow. Toby shook his head. "I don't understand. Are you telling me that Gaardians know that the Earth is a different age than the rest of the universe?"

Jody burst out laughing. "No, Qaak! What we are saying is that even with the most advanced Gaardian technology, we have no way of seeing into God's techniques. God is God."

Still shaking his head Toby asked, "Then what are they going to discover with this gift we're giving them?"

Qaak now spoke quietly as he gazed into the fire in the fireplace across from them. "Currently Earth's scientists argue the age of the Earth and the universe based upon knowledge from their own disciplines. Their problem is that their conclusions are in conflict. Added to the mix are the religious folks who look to their scriptures to see the Creator's involvement in everything."

"And???" Toby looked at the triped intently.

"As you know, thus far in Earth's development, the number of scientists who relate to the Creator is a minority. Gaardian's observed patterns of development say that such scientists will not be in the majority on Earth for two to three more generations." He paused. "Our gift to Earth's scientists is inescapable data that the Earth's age is not the same as the rest of the universe."

"Wow!"

"Indeed. The Earth is actually considerably younger than Kieya and I. We did not realize this until the Creator took all Gaardians outside of matter, energy, space, and time, to give us a glimpse of the universe as the Creator sees it. None of the Gaardians have been the same since."

Toby nodded. "That was last year, wasn't it?"

Jody held up a hand to Qaak. "Let me answer this, my love." She turned to Toby directly. "Not long ago, Toby, Qaak touched my mind with his to show me part of what the Creator had shown him. Just as surely as Qaak could not describe it to me without showing me, I cannot describe it to you. If you could see what I saw, it would not help you understand that much more."

"Okay, I trust you both," Toby paused to look at Qaak. "So you're older than my planet?"

Qaak chuckled, and his eyes glowed. "Indeed."

20. Emergency

As Betsy Sue and Glenn were planning their adventure into the Grand Canyon, Kieya resumed her duties. Once again, there was a moment when the hair on her back bristled, but when she scanned the area around her, she detected nothing unusual. "Kieya with G-mail to Walter." Walter appeared nearby.

"Hi, Kieya. What's up?"

"Just now I had another one of those strange feelings. There is nothing in this solar system that I can detect that is unusual."

"Yes, my friend. Qaak just sent me several thoughts from more than a hundred Gaardians scattered all over that had the same experience. You'll be hearing from me soon."

"Agreed. Until then." Kieya closed her eyes.

"Until then." Walter paused, thinking. "Walter to Ooza, are you available?"

The petite Quzak appeared nearby. "Yes, Walter. I felt it too. Piatek felt it even more strongly."

"That does not surprise me. Do you have some time right now that I can share with you?"

"Yes, how soon will you be here?"

Walter appeared in front of her. "How about right now?"

Even though she was startled, she smiled. "Now is good! What are we going to do?"

"We're going to the surface of your planet to see a certain child. Okay?"

Ooza was calm and looked straight at Walter. "Okay."

Walter reached out and took her hand. They vanished.

They reappeared on the southern continent of Quzak. Walter was now much shorter and had the features and skin of a Quzak male. They walked up a pathway to the entrance of a school. As they went in, a child greeted them and pointed. **"Please join me in this empty classroom."**

"Thank you," said Ooza, as they went in and sat down at a small table. "You knew we were coming, did you not?"

"Of course, Ooza. Walter, I am glad you are here as well. Even though none of us have met until now, we know each other. This is good."

Walter was calm. "You also know why we are here, do you not?"

"Yes. Gaardians will soon be facing seven beings which at first were silicon based, but which have become pure energy. For your convenience, I have named them for the seven days of the week in your English language. When you return to Ooza's satellite apartment, you will find a map on display showing where these seven beings are. Piatek is studying the map as we speak."

Ooza was also calm. "Piatek says that they must be more powerful than any other beings we have encountered until now."

The child smiled. **"Yes, they are. Each is more powerful than all Gaardians combined, but do not be afraid, Ooza. Gaardians must learn that their superior technology is not always the solution. The creation has its own solutions. You know this, Walter, better than the others."**

Walter smiled. "I hope so."

"Yes. As you will discover, the key is to trust in The Creator's grace in his grand design." He paused. **"Now, I will go back to my class. I have much to learn and to teach. Thank you for coming."**

They all got up from the table, and outside the classroom door, the child was soon gone. Walter looked around, and the hallway was empty. He and Ooza vanished back to her apartment.

As they reappeared, Piatek was still studying the three-dimensional map. There were seven globes of light scattered throughout the map of Gaardian space. As the child had said, the globes of light were labeled in English for the days of the week. Saturday was closest to Piatek. She said, "This one is a follower. That one," she pointed at Sunday, "is the leader. They can function separately, but if Sunday dies, the others will collapse from the separation. Nevertheless, this is an impossible battle the Gaardians face."

Walter studied the map. "Piatek, what do you perceive that is different about these creatures?"

Ooza pointed. "Their superior is on our side."

Piatek was confused. "Their superior?" She looked into Walter's eyes, and suddenly her eyes brightened. "Yes! I understand! Their Superior is ours as well!"

Walter touched Piatek's shoulder. "Use your unique gift, Piatek. What is special about these creatures?"

She was suddenly motionless. Softly, she spoke in halting phrases. "They have little heat . . . not like a star . . . no gamma . . . only low frequency ultra violet . . . Yes! Can we ask for Asayak's help?"

"Yes." Walter was calm. "G-mail from Walter to Asayak. Are you available?"

It appeared nearby as a hologram. "Yes. Hello, Walter, Piatek, Ooza."

Piatek was quiet. "Asayak. I know that you do not see as we do. We need your senses regarding the seven giant creatures. What do you perceive?"

"I will consider this. Please forgive a pause." The creature in the hologram stood still for almost a minute. "Amazing. I had not considered this. Will I be welcome in your apartment, Ooza?"

"Of course." Her ring shimmered.

The hologram vanished, and a moment later, it was standing near Piatek. "Since you asked the question, I invite you to use your gift and explore within this recent experience."

The two stood very still. Piatek's eyes were closed, and both swayed slightly. Suddenly, her eyes opened. "Yes!" She paused. "Walter, Ooza, a moment ago we had thought links between ourselves and Gaardian. These beings are different than anything we could have imagined. What was confusing was that these beings are somewhat like the Haydzees, only also very different."

Walter scowled. "How so?"

"The Haydzees were very small but worked together in order to think and to achieve their goals. In contrast, consider the largest of these beings, the one that has been named Sunday. It exists as a paradox that consists of both energy and thought without energy. The energy radiates because of the power of its thinking, and it is the thinking that generates the energy. It is impossible by the standards of everything else we have known."

Asayak stirred. Its telepathic voice was calm. "Nearly all the energy coming from Sunday is in the form of what you consider visible light. The range is from near-infrared to long ultraviolet. I am in awe."

Walter was thoughtful. "Asayak, I have been considering your reports regarding the two scientists now in the care of Toby and Paula. Tell me about that second camera."

Asayak seemed somewhat amused. "Glenn Franz has created a novelty that amazes my sensibilities. He has replaced one of the elements of the lens with one made of quartz instead of glass. It is connected to a small electrical source that causes the lens to change its optical qualities."

Walter chuckled. "Ingenious! That's our answer!"

Walter was calm and determined. "G-mail to all Gaardians. This is a class one call. Please convene on the surface of Gaardian at area ninety-nine for a brief meeting. That is all." He paused, "Walter to Gaardian: You know what we must do. It is time." Walter and Ooza vanished.

On the planet Gaardian, Walter stood on a raised area at one end of the assembly area, and Ooza stood nearby. In less than a minute, more than two thousand Gaardians appeared.

The planet rumbled, "All are present. Proceeding." Suddenly, the sky took on strange and varying colors. Sometimes the colors streaked, and sometimes they waved as on a multicolored ocean. There were no discernable individual stars to be seen.

Walter spoke evenly and calmly. "As you can see, we are on the move." He paused as the colors became fainter, as with twilight on earth. "Gaardian is now orbiting beyond the edge of Gaardian space. We are also in a time pocket, so that when we return, virtually no time will have passed in the planet's normal position. This is a necessary precaution."

Qaak and Kieya joined Ooza and Walter on the raised area. Qaak spoke first. "Twice before in the history of Gaardian space, our authority has been significantly challenged. In both cases, it was the Haydzees. All of you are familiar with what happened in our last encounter with them."

Ooza's voice rang out clearly over the gathering. "This current threat is exceedingly worse."

There was murmuring among the other Gaardians as Kieya padded forward two steps. "As you know, Qaak and I are the oldest Gaardians. In all these thousands of years, I did not previously imagine such a threat." She paused briefly. "I first sensed it with Asayak when we were keeping watch over two scientists on Earth not long ago. Asayak sensed it too, but neither of us knew what it meant. We do now."

Walter nodded. "I first learned about this from Kieya at our Christmas celebration in Yosemite. Shortly thereafter The Creator told me that there would be a major challenge to Gaardian authority, but to not be afraid. I trust The Creator, and that helps me deal with my fear." He paused. "Yes, fear! There are more important things than fear, however. As Gaardians, we seldom have even a twinge of fear because of our superior technology and science. This is different."

When Walter paused, Qaak spoke again. "Yes. In this case, we are not dealing with millions of coordinated energy beings like the Haydzees. In this case, seven beings think as one and act in concert. They have been named in Walter's language after the seven days in an Earth week. All of you are familiar with his language."

There was murmuring again, and then Kieya spoke. "These beings are so powerful that all of us gathered here, working together, could subdue one of them, but it would be with significant difficulty. There are seven."

"Yes!" Ooza said. "A short time ago, Walter and I talked with my planet's Arkaynee. The victory and glory belong to The Creator."

Murmuring began again, and Walter raised a hand. "It will be as though we are the bait. We do not know when they will become visible and threatening. The solution to this challenge is elegantly simple. Ooza's Arkaynee said, quote, 'superior technology is not always the solution. The creation has its own solutions.' He also said, 'the key is to trust in The Creator's grace in his grand design."

Qaak's eyes glowed brilliantly. "Indeed. You know the solution to our problem from this?"

Walter smiled. "Yes. It is in the piezoelectric effect. Gaardian, there is just beyond my sector a section of black space, with no celestial bodies for many light years. Please put a marker there so that all Gaardians can gather quartz and send it there. When there is enough quartz there equal to your weight, Gaardian, I would like you to configure it as a lens. Since the largest being is slightly less than three light-years across, make the focal length about three light years."

Kieya sat back on her haunches, and she was softly purring. "What, then, do the rest of us do?"

"Gaardian, when the lens is ready and in position, chime for us one of your beacon signals. The rest of us will make ourselves bait. We want these beings to chase us in the direction of the lens. They will see the lens as clear and not perceive it as a threat. Nothing has ever been a threat to them until now."

Qaak's eyes were shining. "I see! We must appear to pass through the lens, and we must pass through together in order to get them to follow us with each other."

"Correct. We must slow down and pass through the lens at the speed of light. We must resist the temptation to fold space and time in order to achieve greater speed."

Kieya was puzzled. "What's the point? Why are we drawing them through this lens?"

Walter smiled. "It is simple physics, not Gaardian technology – except for energy from our Gaardian rings. We do not know if they will pass through together or separately, but as they are inside the lens, all of us combined must apply ordinary electrical energy to the lens. This will change the focus of the light passing through. We cannot change their thought patterns, but we will be changing the light that is generated by those patterns, and that will feed back upon them."

Kieya was purring loudly. "It's simple! The Creator gave us our solution when He designed the universe!"

Walter paused. "Are there questions or comments, or is there a discussion?""

Doff stood up, and his deep bass voice boomed over the gathering. "I have studied what happened on Pzalop when the asteroid threatened that planet. It appeared we needed to use the same strategy. I was wrong. The Creator does everything well." He sat down.

Ooza now spoke calmly and clearly. "I was there on Pzalop. It was a great temptation to use my Gaardian ring to deal with the asteroid. It was my first experience of a crisis as a Gaardian. Now we can use our rings for a bigger problem because The Creator has provided the solution. I trust Walter, and I trust my Arkaynee."

Walter spoke more quietly now. "Is there anything more?" The murmuring stopped. "Very well. Gaardian: Take us back to your usual orbit, and send us all to our respective sectors to gather the quartz please. Then give us the beacon chime when you are ready."

The planet's telepathic voice was low but firm. "I have been monitoring all of this, both speech and thoughts. I am in awe. The Creator solved our problem before we existed and without our participation. I trust The Creator, and I will be present for this in every way."

Suddenly, the sky was swimming in colors again. Moments later, the familiar canopy of stars reappeared. Within seconds, all of them vanished to their own sectors of Gaardian Space.

21. Epiphany

At Walter's base on Earth's Moon, Walter stood outside on a promontory about a hundred meters beyond the lounge. His wife, Debbie, watched him with a slight smile. Others were gathering in the lounge to join her in watching. Walter's ring was shimmering constantly. While he gathered the quartz and sent it on its way, he tried to assume an attitude of prayer. It was difficult. Around him, there was a slight flashing, like he was under a strobe light. With each flash, a piece of quartz was on its way. Sometimes it was a chunk as small as a few kilograms. A few were the size of several metric tons. Suddenly, he vanished.

When he heard the beacon, he did not hesitate, even a fraction of a second. He was ready. Walter had traveled through space this way a few times before, but he did not particularly like it. Sunday was the closest of the beings to his position, but since he wanted all the beings to get to the lens at approximately the same time, he took his time, but he did not have to wait long. Behind him, towards Gaardian, a glow was growing rapidly. The other Gaardians were moving at even greater speeds than he was.

Using his ring as a thought amplifier, he sent a one-word thought to Sunday, not far away. "Boo!" He said.

A thunder of thought nearly overwhelmed him in response. Walter kept himself just ahead of Sunday and the others. As he approached the edge of his sector, he began to slow down. The lens was mostly obscured in the darkness beyond his sector. Now at light speed, Sunday was closing the gap between them, and he felt overwhelmed for the first time since becoming a Gaardian. Deep within his mind, without letting it become a conscious thought, Walter cried out, "Jesus! Help me!" Inside his Gaardian shield, he passed through the lens.

A moment earlier, Kieya was trailing Sunday, just ahead of Friday. The smaller being was trying to catch up. Kieya had no purr. Her eyes were filled with nearly mindless but focused fury. Instinctively, she dropped herself into a time pocket, and slipped back behind Friday. As she passed through the lens, she saw the other Gaardians, their rings starting to shimmer as hers was. It was over in a fraction of a second.

The darkness was now overwhelmed by a familiar glow, and they heard the now-familiar voice.

> "Well done, my children. I am pleased with you. The other seven beings became filled with pride and decided they did not need me. They turned away from me and rejected me, so I have cast them away. Gaardians know better. Never forget that your power and authority are blessings from me. If you continue to seek me and seek my ways, I will continue to bless you."

The glow faded, and Kieya approached Walter. "I love hearing the voice of The Creator. What do you want to do with the lens? We could drop it into a black hole."

Walter pointed into the distance. "The Creator has spoken, and our work here is done. Let's just let it vaporize in that blue star."

"Good. I agree." Their rings shimmered, and the lens disappeared. Kieya was now purring again. "This has been something I will never forget. When that light briefly enveloped me, I had a flash of knowledge of science and technology that was overwhelming. I wonder whether Gaardian will be able to process any of it."

"I'm wondering about that too. For now, though, let's go back to our sectors."

"I agree."

They vanished.

+ + +

Minutes earlier, in the Dirksen Senate Office Building in Washington, D.C., Senator Everett Steinmetz gazed out the window. "I wonder how Dr. & Mrs. Franz are doing?" he muttered. He heard a soft knock on his door. "Yes, Francine?"

His secretary came through the door. "Excuse me, senator, I was wondering if...." There was a bright flash of light. "What was *that*?"

"I don't know. Make a few calls and see if you can find out."

The senator turned back to face out the window. "What in the world?" he muttered. He went to his desk and sat down. On his right, near a portrait of the senator and his wife, was a snow globe given to him two years ago at Christmas. He picked it up and shook it. "Why do I suddenly understand things that an hour ago perplexed me?" he muttered. There was a quiet knock on his door before it opened.

Francine poked her head through the door. "News is coming in, that the flash was seen in cities all over the world. Evidently, something has happened that only our Gaardian can explain."

He nodded. "That makes sense. Thanks Francine."

"Is it okay if I take lunch now, Senator? Judy is going to be here if you need anything."

"Go ahead, Francine. I am going to be leaving anyway, and I think I will be gone the rest of the day. I suddenly understand what that arrogant Speaker of the House has been up to. I'm going to confront him and see what happens."

She smiled. "That sounds like your kind of fun, senator."

He laughed. "Yes, I suppose it is! See you tomorrow!"

She closed the door behind her as he went to the rack for his coat.

+ + +

Earlier in Fresno, Glenn and Betsy Sue were in the geodesic dome above the atrium, taking a break. Betsy Sue pointed. "I love that one! It has such beautiful plumage and flies so gracefully."

Glenn nodded. "I like that one, mainly for his call." He pointed, and there was a flash of light that filled every shadow in the dome. The birds all became quiet. "What in the world was that?" They went to the edge of the dome and walked around the perimeter, looking for clues as to the source of light from outside. Glenn became quieter. Soon, he was looking around within the dome again instead of outside.

Betsy Sue noticed that he was suddenly quiet. "What's going on inside that fertile brain of yours, Glenn?"

He looked down at her and smiled. "I've just realized something. It should have been obvious, but neither of us saw it."

"What's that?"

"The reason why Toby could do so much with configuring that ground-penetrating radar to go with camera two is because he works for Gaardian."

She smiled and nodded. "I see it too. We should have guessed because Paula has so often been associated with Gaardian activity."

"Yes. They have been unusually helpful to us, even before we would think of asking for something." He reached out towards a bird, but it flitted away.

"We could invite them to dinner, to show our gratitude. We can grill some steaks. Do you think we should tell them what we're thinking?"

"The key will be Paula. She is known to have some kind of connection with our Gaardian. We will have to think about this more before they arrive – if they come. I'll call Toby tomorrow. I wonder if..."

He nodded. "That flash of light gave me interesting feelings along with my thoughts. My head is swimming with fresh ideas."

"Yes!"

+ + +

Earlier, Ben Kaiser's soundproofed office was quiet. He liked it that way. With a wireless keyboard in his lap, his fingers flew rapidly as he recorded his thoughts in his journal. A flash of light filled both his office and the city outside. He reached over onto his desk and pressed a button. "Lucy? What was that? Did you see where that light came from?"

"No. I'll see what I can find out."

"Okay. I'll turn on my TV monitor here." Ben reached into a drawer to take out a remote. He turned it on but muted the sound. He chose a news channel, so he could watch the streaming feed at the bottom of the screen. Suddenly, the picture changed to the Palomar Observatory in Southern California. Ben turned on the sound in time to hear an interview.

"Do we know where the light came from, Dr. Jonas?"

"Not yet. These last few nights we have observed a strange glow obscuring part of the sky in seven different places. My colleagues in other parts of the world where it is currently night time tell me that those areas of glow are now gone. You can check with me tomorrow morning, when I may have an update for you."

"Thank you, Dr. Jonas."

Ben pushed the mute button, turned in his chair, and let his gaze fall upon the Golden Gate Bridge. "What's going on, Lord?" Getting up out of his chair, he went to a corner of his office where there was an antique prie dieu. He knelt on it, and as he began to pray silently, a subtle glow surrounded him.

About five minutes later, the glow subsided. There was a soft knock at his door, and Lucy stepped in. "Am I disturbing you?"

Ben got up and went back to his desk. "No, I was done. According to an interview on cable news a few minutes ago, scientists were not sure what happened yet."

"That's all I could find out too." She paused. "Do you need anything else this afternoon? I've got that appointment in Berkeley, but if you need me to stay, I will."

"No, Lucy, go ahead. I'll see you tomorrow."

"Thank you. Have a good evening."

"You too, Lucy."

She stepped out. He glanced over at the prie dieu. "Thanks again, Lord."

+ + +

Several hours later, Gaardian was in its normal orbit. Above its surface, Qaak's apartment hovered, and in it, the old triped was sipping hot liquid while staring into his fireplace with his wife Jody.

She studied her husband's face as the glow of his eyes seemed to pulsate. "This is a new one, Qaak. I can't read these emotions in your eyes."

He turned to face her. "Have I told you enough to describe what has happened?"

She smiled. "Yes, dear, but there is more going on within you, seeming to make your emotions chaotic. Can you tell me why?"

Qaak nodded. "Normally you understand me better than anyone else ever has. This is different. Indeed. This is different."

"How so?"

"All of my life I have been able to transfer thoughts and information from one being to another through my mind. This time, as Sunday passed through the lens, my mind was touched by another mind that was infinitely larger than my own. It was both frightening and thrilling." He paused, and his eyes stopped glowing for a moment. "I wonder if Gaardian was touched by any of the light. Give me a moment." He paused again. "Gaardian is inviting us to the surface. Shall we go?"

"Sure!" He took her hand, and they vanished from the apartment.

They reappeared in the community living area of the apartment complex that includes a nursery for Gaardian children.

"Welcome, my friends," the planet rumbled. "I'm glad you are present Kieya, Doff, and Walter will be here momentarily."

Kieya appeared with Doff a moment later. Then Walter appeared with Debbie. When she saw Jody, her face brightened. "Hi, Jody! I have not seen you for weeks! How are you?"

Jody grinned and crossed over to hug Debbie. "I've been great." She paused and looked at her friend. "Why don't we go for a swim in the pool below Red Falls? The others have Gaardian business to discuss."

"Good idea! Afterwards, we can come back and play with the kids."

The two women waved at the others and vanished.

Walter sat down in a recliner near the fireplace. "Gaardian, I assume you want to discuss what has happened during the last few hours."

"Yes," the planet said quietly. "May I scan all of your minds to record your experiences?" They all agreed.

Kieya stretched out on the hearth in front of the fire and began to purr. "I am glad it is all over. Despite Gaardian ring support, I feel emotionally and spiritually exhausted."

Walter nodded. "I feel the same way. I could sense God's presence as we electrified the lens. I was in awe."

"Indeed." Qaak chuckled. "It is illogical but true to say that all the Gaardians working together with the planet accomplished more than we should have been able to do."

Doff laughed aloud, his deep bass voice rumbling throughout the room. "Yes! It was amazing. All that The Creator does, He does exceedingly well. He multiplied our efforts."

Kieya's purr grew louder. "Yes! It was awesome! That is a great word! I think that is the first time I have ever used it, but it fits. Awesome!"

"It was also perplexing," said the planet.

Qaak was startled. "What made it perplexing, my friend?"

"The being named Thursday diverted its path from chasing Doff and passed over me. It was nearly overwhelming, even with all of my defenses in place. For the first time in my life as a sentient planet, I encountered a mind greater than my own."

Kieya raised her head from resting her chin on the hearth. "I think the rest of us also felt overwhelmed for a moment."

"For me, it was more than a moment. Thursday knew that my mind was nearly its equal. It lingered, and during that brief time, it was not hostile but curious. I acquired a large volume of knowledge before it moved on. For the last several hours, I have been processing that knowledge. It will help all of us in varying ways. I am..." It paused. "What is the word? The Creator said it..." It paused again. "I am pleased. Yes. That is the word. I am pleased. I have an emotion that I did not previously have. I am pleased."

"Indeed." Qaak's eyes stopped pulsating as they had been and began to have a typical and steady glow. "What was the nature of the data you acquired?

The planet did not answer immediately. After about twenty seconds, it responded. "As you know, up until this event my memory storage was less than ten percent full with all the Gaardian data since your planet died, Qaak. Now my data storage is at twenty-two percent of capacity. I am in awe."

"Indeed!" Qaak's eyes glowed brilliantly.

A few minutes passed. Then Gaardian spoke again. "Walter."

"Yes?"

"What did The Creator mean when He said that He had cast those beings away?"

Walter was thoughtful. "My answer has to be based upon the scriptures that I associate with my relationship with God through Jesus the Christ. I want to be faithful to those scriptures." He paused briefly. "What you are asking about is called judgment. God makes His ways known to His children, but He does not force them to do things His way. He wants us to do what is right because we love Him. The Creator gives us life and loves us. When a being rejects The Creator and the life and love He offers, that being cuts itself off from that life and love. As a result, the being is permanently isolated and suffers without God. Christians like me call this permanent isolation and suffering 'Hell.'"

Kieya was softly purring. "Gaardian, is this the reason you wanted to have us here today?"

"Yes."

"I'm suddenly hungry. Walter, let's call the women back here so we can all share a meal before we return to our sectors. Agreed?"

22. Mysteries and Solutions

It was then evening at Walter's base on Earth's Moon. Toby Ballentine was relaxing in the hot and cold whirlpool. A tone sounded. "There is a telephone call for you, Toby. Do you wish to take it here?"

The pool became quiet. "Yes, thank you. Hello?"

Betsy Sue's voice was clear and clean, like she was standing next to the pool. "Hello, Toby. This is Betsy Sue."

"Hello Betsy Sue! What can I do for you?"

"Glenn and I were talking earlier today, and we decided we want to do something to express our gratitude to you and Paula. We would like both of you to join us for dinner one evening this week. Is there a day that is more convenient for you?"

"I appreciate your wanting to do this for us, but it is not necessary."

"It may not seem necessary to you, but Glenn and I are really grateful for the things the two of you have done for us."

"Okay. I will check with Paula, and one of us will get back to you sometime tomorrow. Okay?"

"That's perfect. We'll look forward to you your call. Bye!"

"Bye." Toby was thoughtful. "G-mail, Toby to Paula. When you are free, we need to talk. Glenn and Betsy Sue want to have dinner with us this week. They say it is out of gratitude, but I suspect there may be another agenda. Let me know early tomorrow if you can. End g-mail." He paused. "G-mail, Toby to Kieya. Are you available?"

An image of Kieya appeared next to the pool. "Hello Toby. I see you are in the hot and cold whirlpool. May I come and join you?"

"Certainly!"

The image vanished, and Kieya appeared nearby. She approached the large pool and stepped in. "I have been wanting to do this again after meeting those light creatures."

"I heard about that. I did not know you had ever been in this pool."

Kieya began to purr as the whirlpool began to froth with steam. "Yes, I have been in this several times. I have not put one in my apartment because I like to enjoy it with others, and I seldom entertain in my apartment." She paused, purring. "Why did you call me?"

"The two scientists have invited Paula and me for a meal. She says it is to express their thanksgiving for our help. I suspect there may be another agenda. Have you or Asayak had communication with them in the last few days?"

"No. You may be right, however. I have noticed that since our confrontation with the light creatures that I have had many new thoughts and feelings. Humans on Earth may have been affected. Let me consult with Asayak for a moment." She paused speaking and closed her eyes, but she continued to purr. "Asayak will be free soon to pay them a visit. It will come here within the hour and report to us."

"Excellent. G-mail, Toby to Paula. If you are available, Kieya and I are in the whirlpool relaxing. We invite you to join us for conversation if possible."

The big cat looked across the natatorium and noted others in the large swimming pool. "I find Walter's design of his base very interesting. On my planet, when we need exercise we go out of our lairs into a forest. The trees provide limitless opportunities for fun. Evidently, Walter understands basic needs for recreation and relaxation. The areas for these activities take up as much space as the work areas. It is excellent and is very well designed."

Paula appeared at the doorway into the conference room. She waved at them, and as she walked towards them, her clothing changed to a tank swimsuit. "Good evening," she said, as she stepped into the warm water.

"Indeed," said Kieya.

"Good evening, Paula," said Toby. "I g-mailed you because you and I have been invited by the Franzes to have dinner with them."

"Dinner?"

"Yes. They say it is out of gratitude, but I suspect another agenda."

Kieya shifted to turn more towards her. "I have asked Asayak to investigate covertly. It will get back to us within the hour."

"I'm not surprised that they want to share another meal with us, but I agree – there may be another agenda. I'm not sure why I think this."

Toby was thoughtful. "We were both on Earth when we saw the flash of light across the sky. What you've just said tells me that perhaps all people on Earth may have been affected in some way."

Near the pool, Asayak appeared. "Hello everyone!" Its telepathic voice could be heard throughout the natatorium. Everyone waved to it. It glided towards the pool, and at the edge, it seemed to flow in. Its voice now quieter said, "I always enjoy this pool. It is so stimulating! I know that the rest of you find it relaxing, however."

The big cat looked up at it. "So long as you enjoy it, Asayak, that is what the pool is for."

"Yes." It paused. "I have investigated the most recent thoughts of Glenn and Betsy Sue Franz. They were in the glass dome above their apartment when the flash passed over the planet. The two of them now have what appears to be an intuition. They are almost totally convinced that Paula and Toby work for Walter."

Kieya's purr stopped. "This is more important than I realized. G-mail Kieya to Walter. Can you come to the whirlpool?"

Walter came through the same doorway where Paula had arrived. "Hello, everyone. I was in the clinic talking to Butch. He says that everyone seems to have been affected by the passage of one of the light creatures through our solar system. Is your call related?" He stepped into the water.

Kieya's purring returned, but more softly. "Yes, my friend. Glenn and Betsy Sue Franz now believe that Toby and Paula work for you. The scientists have invited them to come to a dinner of thanksgiving, but with that hidden agenda."

Walter burst out laughing. "We've got some interesting times coming in the days ahead!" The others agreed. "Let's finish up our time here in the whirlpool, and then we'll head for the lounge to talk about this." He looked up. "Frank, the standard hot and cold program."

The water began to increase in temperature, and it began to froth furiously. After thirty seconds, a chime sounded, and the temperature dropped to just above freezing. A second chime sounded. The frothing stopped, and they all got out and headed for the lounge. They were all dry, and the humans were wearing dry clothing by the time they sat down by the fireplace. Kieya stretched out near the hearth to enjoy the fire's warmth, and Asayak glided to an area nearby and sank to a lower height.

Walter was thoughtful. "Kieya, as the oldest Gaardian with the most experience, what are your thoughts?"

She rose to sit on her haunches. "There are no previous events in our history that I can refer to. My first thought is to suggest that Butch do a full physical for everyone on this base coupled with a psychological evaluation. That will give us a sample of how life has been affected in this solar system. If we do it quickly, we can pass on our conclusions to the other Gaardians."

Walter nodded, closing his eyes. "Butch, proceed with what you suggested as quickly and efficiently as possible." Walter opened his eyes. "Butch was suggesting what you just said less than fifteen minutes ago."

Asayak stirred and raised an appendage. "I am sensing very low telepathic links between all beings on this base. The links are weaker than they were yesterday after the flash."

Again, Walter nodded. "This makes sense. These are probably phenomena that are carried over from the passage of the light being through the solar system."

"Yes," it said, "this seems to be an accurate conclusion. I believe that Butch will find that some humans will be affected more than others."

Paula was very serious. "What do Toby and I do with our invitation?"

Toby nodded. "Yes! I assume we accept the invitation, but if they raise this issue, how do you want us to handle it?"

Walter was thoughtful, and then he began to smile. "This coming Sunday, most Christians around the world will be celebrating what we call Easter. I have an idea." He paused, closing his eyes. "Walter to Dawn: Will you please come to the lounge for a few minutes?"

Kieya turned her head to look at Walter. "What does your chef have to do with all of this?"

Dawn appeared in the doorway leading to the atrium. "Hello, everyone. What's up, Walter?"

"Have you been planning anything special for this Sunday afternoon?"

"Easter? I was going to put a few extra seasonal things on the menu. Why?"

"I know it's the last minute, but I also know you can handle what I am about to ask of you. I want you to plan an Easter banquet. We will have a sit-down meal for everyone on the base plus maybe a dozen special guests. Toby and Paula here can help you, I'm sure Debbie and Jody will want to help, and you can recruit as many others as you need."

"This sounds like fun! Remember that first Christmas banquet I did for you and charged you triple?"

Walter laughed. "I remember! It was a meal to remember too! Toby and Paula will join you in a few minutes. You had better get started planning. Tell Belinda to help you with anything special that you need."

"Right!" She turned and left.

Walter looked at the big telepath. "Asayak. I know that you and those on your planet do not eat banquets as we do, just as you do not breathe as we do. I also know, however, that there are unique things you do for celebrations. I will configure a particular area for you and a few others from your planet that you may choose and can trust. The area will be an extension of our dining hall."

The creature stirred. "I will enjoy this. Is there anything else?"

"Yes. Please relate all of this to Keeta. I want her to come with a few of her friends as well. I am sure that they will find food on Dawn's menu that they will enjoy."

Toby whistled softly. "This sounds like its going to be a great party, but what has this to do with Glenn and Betsy Sue?"

"Right! Paula exclaimed. "I'm confused!"

Kieya was purring more loudly. "I was confused at first, but now I know, Walter. You're making this a time of Gaardian gifting, aren't you?"

Walter nodded. Everyone's focus shifted from Kieya to Walter. "Yes, definitely, this is a time for Gaardian gifting. Glenn and Betsy Sue will come here, and they can invite a few of their friends."

23. Fellowship with Other Planets

As usual for a Sunday morning, after breakfast Walter conducted a worship service in the theater. He picked music especially suitable for Easter. They could sense God's presence as they worshiped, particularly during prayer time and during communion.

After worship, the Moon Base's kitchen was buzzing with more and more activity. Dawn and her husband James had worked together before they were married, so they instinctively knew what they had to do. Each also trusted the other to do their tasks well. Occasionally, Dawn would call out instructions to some of the day's volunteers, but all went smoothly.

A new area, about six meters by ten meters, had been configured next to the conference room, which, in turn had become the day's Easter banquet room. Belinda decorated the conference room from memories of Easter dinners at her childhood home. At Asayak's suggestion, the aromas from the kitchen were ducted through the new area before being recycled. Asayak and its five guests would enjoy the aromas and assimilate them as extra food.

When the special guests began arriving in the recreation area, many of Walter's crew were already swimming, working out, or enjoying the hot and cold pool. Toby appeared with Glenn and Betsy Sue. A moment later, Paula arrived with two other men and two other women.

Toby grinned at all of them as they stared. "I know you wanted to fix steaks for us, but I think this will be better."

"We're actually on the moon?" They all stared at first one area then another.

"Absolutely!"

Betsy Sue's mouth hung open slightly. "We're at the Gaardian's Moon Base?"

"Yes." Toby paused. "I'll give the six of you a tour of the base after dinner. Right now, would you like to take a swim?"

Glenn looked down at Betsy Sue. She nodded. "I guess so, but where do we get suits?" The others nodded.

"What color suits would you like?"

Betsy Sue looked around at the others. "I suppose a variety would be nice."

Instantly, their clothing was replaced by swim suits, and they stared up and down at each other and themselves. Almost together they all said, "Wow!" or some other exclamation.

Toby grinned again. "You can work out in the gym behind me or try the hot and cold computerized whirlpool. Right now, all of us are human, but a few aliens will be arriving in an hour or so."

"Aliens?" one of the other women asked.

"Yes. Beings from two other planets will be joining us today, both for the dinner and for the Gaardian gifts afterward. You will learn more just before dinner. If you'll come with me over here," he gestured, "I'll show all of you how the hot and cold whirlpool works."

Toby had arranged for the pool to be free when he arrived with their guests from Earth. They walked over, stepped into the water, and sat down on underwater benches. Toby said quietly, "In a moment I will start it by voice command. The water will begin to froth, the temperature will increase, and the gravity will be reduced down to Moon normal. It will stay that way for five minutes. Then a chime will ring. Within thirty seconds, gravity will go back up to Earth normal (as it is now), the water will decrease its activity, and the water temperature will drop to just above freezing. Another chime will sound, and we get out. When we do, we will be instantly dried off. Do you have any questions?"

"Are you serious?" Glenn had an incredulous look on his face, but the others just looked at Toby.

"Absolutely!"

Betsy Sue smiled. "Let's do it!"

Toby said, "Frank, normal program, please!" The water began to froth.

In the clinic, Walter sat in an overstuffed chair, talking with the resident physician. "Butch, I just want to say thanks for doing all of those extra physicals and processing so much data so quickly. You did an excellent job."

"Thanks. I understand that the same food being prepared for the banquet in the conference room is being made available in the mess hall for the rest of the crew."

"Right. You are supposed to be in the conference with the other team leaders. Your staff has to use the mess hall as usual."

"Okay. A few minutes ago, I saw Toby arrive with our scientist guests."

"Right. Glenn and Betsy Sue Franz are the environmental scientists we have been helping. The others are astronomers and astrophysicists. I've not met any of them yet."

"Some of them have physical problems. Do you want me to do anything for them?"

Walter was thoughtful. "Why not? When Toby gives them the base tour after dinner, give all of them a full Gaardian tune-up. You can take care of Keeta's guests from Biyae as soon as they arrive in a few minutes. It will be another fifteen minutes before Asayak's guests arrive. When those five gaumzas get the base tour, I leave it to you as to how you handle them and when. You can take care of the humans after the others have left. Okay?"

"It sounds good. It should not take very long anyway. Do you have any problem with my beaming down to China tomorrow to see some of my grandchildren?"

"That's no problem. Keep Frank posted as to where you are, as usual."

"Right."

Noises came from the atrium just outside the door. When they went out, Walter smiled. "Keeta, will you please assure your friends that they can trust us? It's important that we be able to see them while they are here as our guests."

A moment later, several more biyaes appeared next to Keeta. Walter smiled at them. "Good afternoon! Welcome to Earth's moon and my Moon Base. You probably recognize me from my visits to your planet as your Gaardian. You may call me Walter."

There were murmurs of greeting in response.

"In that direction," Walter pointed, "is our recreation area. That is the reason for the noises coming from there. Right now, however, Keeta is going to begin your tour here at the clinic behind me. This is Butch, our physician." He gestured towards him.

There were more murmurs of greeting.

Butch gave them his best smile. "Hello. It is nice to meet all of you. If you come with me, I am going to give each of you a gift. It will be a free and painless physical examination." He turned and walked into the clinic, and they followed.

In the recreation area, the human guests were in and around the swimming pool when Asayak arrived with its guests. Walter walked in to greet them telepathically. "Welcome. I am sure you recognize me from my visits. I am happy that you can be with us today."

Asayak gestured with an appendage. "The six of us are telepathically one right now. They wish me to speak for all of us."

"Very well. There is time, Asayak, for you to give them a brief tour of the base before the rest of us have our meal. You will then be able to observe and enjoy what we enjoy with us. Butch is expecting to see all of you in the clinic at your convenience."

"Very well. Thank you." The six of them glided off towards the atrium.

Walter went over closer to the pool before he spoke to everyone. "The Easter banquet will be served in about thirty minutes. Team leaders and all of our guests will eat in the conference room. Everyone else will have the same dishes offered to them but in the dining hall. Right now, I would like to invite Dr. & Mrs. Franz and their friends to the lounge. There is someone who wants to meet all of you." He walked towards the lounge, and the six scientists followed him.

In the lounge, Walter sat down in a large, overstuffed chair. "Please be seated somewhere here near the fireplace." After they were seated, he continued. "I have not introduced myself to all of you yet. You may call me Walter, but I ask that you not reveal that information to anyone else on Earth. I have said this to others who have visited here. If you reveal my name when you return to Earth, you will never be invited back to the Moon." He paused. "Now, starting with you, sir," he pointed, "will each of you tell me your names, please, and tell me your branch of science in which you specialize?"

"Paul Bieber; I am an astrophysicist."

"Joan Novotny; I am also an astrophysicist.

"Jill Chabert; I am an astronomer.

"Betsy Sue Franz; I'm an environmentalist and biologist."

"Glenn Franz; I'm an optics physicist, chemist, and biochemist."

"Bob Setmire; I'm an astronomer."

Walter smiled. Thank you. Glenn, Betsy Sue, you were able to figure out this last week that Toby and Paula work for me. Is that not correct?"

Glenn started to speak but had to clear his throat. "Yes. We were in the atrium near our apartment when a flash of light enveloped us. We understand that the light enveloped the entire Earth. Is that correct?"

Walter nodded. "Yes. Since all of you are scientists with an understanding of where Earth is in the midst of our galaxy, I would like to show all of you something." His ring shimmered, and the roof of the lounge rose about ten meters, sloping upward at the opposite end of the room. "You'll need to stand up and turn around to see this." As they did so, a holographic map of Gaardian space appeared in front of them.

"That is more than one galaxy, isn't it?" asked Glenn.

An area was highlighted in yellow, and within it was another area, which was red. "Yes. It is a map of Gaardian space. The number of suns that occupy Gaardian space numbers several goolgolplex."

Bob Setmire whistled. "That's far larger than I imagined. I thought Gaardian space might comprise one or two galaxies. What is that highlighted area?"

Walter pointed. "The yellow area is my sector. The red area within the yellow is our galaxy. In my little sector, there are three planets with sentient beings sufficiently advanced for space travel. Earth is one of them. Today you will meet beings from the other two planets."

"What???" Glenn's surprise brought smiles to the others.

"Yes. I will be introducing all of you at the banquet in a few minutes, so you'll learn more then." He paused. "For now, let's get back to your original question. About a month ago seven beings comprised of pure thought and manifested as light in our visible spectrum entered Gaardian space. They were a major threat to our authority. Their diameters were larger than some suns. One of them, passing through our solar system, had Earth pass through it. That was the flash you saw. We have dealt with them, and they are no longer a threat, but they affected hundreds of planets in Gaardian space." The display disappeared, and they all sat back down.

Jill Chabert asked, "Is that the reason for this private meeting?"

"No. There is someone who wants to meet all of you that will not have time to join us at the banquet. Kieya, will you join us now?"

Kieya appeared by the fireplace. "Hello, everyone. My name is Kieya."

The scientists stared and mumbled hellos.

Walter smiled. "Kieya is our second oldest Gaardian. Her home planet is many many light-years from here. She is a felidaca. Why don't you tell them a little of your history with Earth, before you tell them why you wanted Glenn and Betsy Sue to meet you?"

"Very well. I first visited Earth several thousand years ago. I explored much of your planet. As you may imagine, I found one group of Earth's animals particularly interesting because genetically they are similar to me."

Betsy Sue smiled. "Our cats."

"Yes. The first one I saw was a small one belonging to a human female who lived in an area you now call Egypt. I went further north and found animals almost identical to myself in physical size except for my face. I also found some others like me further south near the equator. As you can see, my body is larger and my head is a bit wider than any cat from Earth."

Glenn studied Kieya carefully. "So you are not related in any way to our tigers?"

"No." She paused and began to purr. "The reason I wanted you and your wife to meet me is because while you have never seen me before until now, Betsy Sue caught a glimpse of me several of your lunar cycles ago."

"I did?"

"Yes. It was winter in Yosemite Valley. You were on the balcony of your apartment one evening, and you thought you saw a puma up on the cliff."

"Yes! I remember! "That was you?"

"Yes. Walter had assigned me to watch over you and Glenn temporarily. After a few more days, I turned you over to Toby and Paula's care."

Glenn nodded. "This explains a lot. Were those paw prints yours that were found beside the SUV that was driven by the thieves who stole our equipment?"

"Indeed. It was not difficult for me to stop and subdue them."

"Thank you for saving our camera and other equipment."

"You are quite welcome."

Joan Novotny raised a hand. "Are you part of Walter's sector of Gaardian space?"

"That is a good question. No, I have my own sector. Walter and I are friends, and we communicate frequently. Now, my new friends, I must go. I have enjoyed visiting you. Until we meet again."

Walter smiled. "Until then, Kieya."

She vanished.

Walter stood up. "It's time to eat. In the conference room, I would appreciate it if each of you would take a different table. It is one of our traditions we have with our guests. If you will follow me please?" Walter walked towards the conference room, and the doors opened. Wonderful aromas greeted them as they entered. Walter signaled to his wife Debbie, and she joined him at one of the tables. Soon the conference room was full, and the six telepaths were standing in their area.

"Hello everyone! Happy Easter! Before we eat, I would like to take a moment to make introductions. Will my team members stand up briefly and sit down again when I call on you please? Beside me is my wife, Debbie. She is my chief science officer and responsible for research." He nodded to his right. "Belinda Thomas is an old friend dating back to my childhood and is this base's commander. Butch Eng is our chief medical officer. Toby Ballentine is our ombudsman. Karen Oreskovich is our communications chief. Ken Lyman is our spiritual advisor and troubleshooter. Jody Dunn is our chief engineer." He nodded to his left. "Jim Crenshaw is another of our troubleshooters here on the moon and down on Earth. Judy Valez is a goodwill ambassador for Gaardian on Earth. John Carson is our pilot when we take our ship, *The Grace*, on journeys involving a large team. Lauryn Backstrand is our recruiter and trainer. Stephanie Smith does policing work behind the scenes on Earth. Keeta is our intelligence officer and investigator. She and her species are normally transparent, but they are all visible to us today. They come from a planet in my sector named Biya, and as a species, they call themselves biyaes. Keeta, would you like to introduce your friends?"

"Because I work for you, Walter, I would feel comfortable introducing them, but to do so in this setting would violate our cultural traditions. If you wish, you may think of us as shy beings. They would rather be transparent while here, but to help with the proceedings today and to conform to your society's traditions, they are maintaining some color."

"Very well. Welcome again to all of you." He paused and sighed. "Over in a separate area of today's banquet room is my friend Asayak and five of his friends. They do not have eyes, ears, noses, or mouths as the rest of us do, nor do they breathe as the rest of us do. Their physiology is very different from ours, and they communicate telepathically. Today they are of one mind, and they all speak through the telepathic voice provided by Asayak. Will you please communicate to our gathering, my friend?"

"Yes." The voice could be heard inside of all of their heads. "We come from a planet which we had not given a name until today. We have decided that to be part of the larger Gaardian community our planet shall be called Gaumz. [GOWmz.] This is a simple decision because genetically we are known as gaumzas. [GOWm zuhs] The predominant atmospheric gas on our planet is carbon dioxide. The carbon in that gas is our food. We are eating constantly here on Earth's moon base. What appears to you as being an eye is actually an illuminating organ that allows us to see on many levels of the electromagnetic spectrum. We respect privacy, and we do not read the thoughts of others, unless those thoughts are directed to us. Thank you for inviting us today."

"Thank you, Asayak. Finally, I would like to introduce two other special guests. Xpraepostq and Saahmn come from a planet named Aegeene. Those who cannot pronounce their names call them Pixie and Sam. Pixie is the Gaardian for a sector adjacent to mine. We were educated to be Gaardians together, and we officially became Gaardians on the same day." He paused, scanning the whole room. "Now I have one more introduction to make. Dawn is our master chef, and she has prepared our food today. Dawn?"

Dawn came through a doorway leading to the dining hall. "Hello, everyone!"

There were scattered hellos throughout the room.

"I have prepared today traditional Easter dishes from many countries. This will be a seven-course meal. The appetizers are now appearing on your tables. There are nine varieties of appetizers. Please feel free to try any of the foods provided. All of them conform to the physiologies of both humans and biyaes. As I understand it, Asayak and his friends will simply experience your emotions as you eat. Enjoy everyone."

"Thank you, Dawn. It is my tradition to pray before such meals. Will you please pause with me to thank The Creator?" Walter bowed his head, and others followed. "Thank you, wondrous Creator for this chance to be together and share this food. Bless this food to our bodies' use we pray in the names of Jesus and Eiraynay. Amen."

They began eating and conversing. New friendships were formed over the next two hours. Bonds were made between them that would endure for their lifetimes.

24. Gaardian Gifts

After his third and last dessert, Walter stood up. "I hope everyone has had enough to eat." There was scattered laughter. "Dawn, will you come in here?"

"Hi. Can I get anything more for anyone?"

There was scattered laughter again. "No, Dawn, we just want to thank you." There was applause from everyone, and some of them stood up to applaud. "Thanks again, Dawn. I know that this is your job and your calling, but we are grateful for this special effort."

She blushed. "Thank you. Thank you, everyone." She went back to the kitchen.

"Our guests may like to go into the theater and relax for thirty minutes. The rest of us have preparations to make. Later, all of our guests will be transported up to the ship I mentioned a little while ago. That is the place where Pixie and I, as Gaardians, are going to give our guests their first gift for today. Meanwhile, our guests may relax while the rest of us make some preparations." Walter vanished, along with Pixie, Sam, and the other crew members except for Asayak and Keeta.

Glenn and Betsy Sue looked at each other. Then they got up and headed for the theater. Keeta, Asayak, and the other guests followed. At first, they milled about in quiet conversation. They eventually chose places to sit down.

When they were all seated, Walter appeared at the front of the auditorium. "Our first Gaardian gift for you is an easy one. Asayak's planet, Gaumz, is scientifically and technologically ahead of both Biya and Earth. At the same time, both Biya and Earth are significantly more developed than Gaumz in the area of the fine arts. Our first Gaardian gift to all of you is a concert. Some of this will be almost routine for Betsy Sue, Glenn, and their friends. I think the rest of you will see this in a special way."

Walter vanished. A few seconds later, they found themselves within a three-dimensional hologram of First Congregational Church in Los Angeles, California. For nearly an hour all of them experienced the thunderous sound of one of the world's largest pipe organs. Asayak and his friends swayed to the music, and some of the others had tears in their eyes from the music of Bach, Brahms, Mozart, and Beethoven.

Moments later, they were invisibly sailing through The Musée du Louvre in Paris, France. For most of another hour, they could see some of the world's great works of art. Next, they had a flying tour of several buildings designed by Frank Lloyd Wright and those by Gilbert Stanley Underwood. After that, they found themselves in Symphony Hall in Boston to experience its nearly perfect acoustics while they listened to Debussy's *La Mer*. Finally, they ended up in the midst of a large rock concert in the Sydney Opera House in Australia.

When it was over, Walter appeared on the stage again. "Some of you may want to freshen up before we present the final gifts, because it will take some time. I'll meet all of you in the lounge in twenty minutes." He vanished.

+ + +

Aboard *The Grace*, Walter and Pixie appeared on the bridge. "What's next?" she asked. "I assume that when I do this for the planets in my sector that you'll help me.

"Certainly, I will. Do you remember how the dining hall for this ship is directly below us?" She nodded. "I've expanded the window area to take up the entire forward wall. John knows what we have planned, so we will just talk our guests through what they are going to see. First, we will tour this solar system, then tour over to Keeta's solar system, and finally go on to Gaumz and a tour of its solar system. It also will take at least an hour to tour the stars between each system."

"Great! This will be relaxing for us. I'm glad my Saahm and your Debbie are along to enjoy it."

"I am too. We will then leave Asayak and his friends at Gaumz. Jody has prepared a vehicle for the six of them, and she and John have prepared Asayak to help them do a scientific tour of their planet from a Gaardian perspective. It will include all life forms as well as a geological analysis of the planet. Then it will do an environmental analysis. Finally, it will give them a full-scale long term analysis of their resources."

"We're then dropping off Keeta and her friends for a similar tour, and finally returning to Earth?"

"Right."

"Glenn and Betsy Sue are going to be tired when they get back to their apartment in Fresno. I don't think they'll mind though."

"You're probably right!"

John appeared at the helm. "Everybody's onboard."

"Good. I'll give you the go ahead in a few minutes." He turned to Pixie. "Let's get down to the lounge." They vanished.

+ + +

Hours later, the six scientists from Earth sat in a semi-circle, facing forward. Pixie, Saahm, Debbie, and Walter faced them with their backs to the windows. Walter spoke quietly. "This has been a long day for the six of you, and I have a suggestion. If you would like, Debbie and I would like all of you to spend the night in our guest quarters. You would be able to sleep at the reduced level of gravity of the moon if you wish. If any of you need to make a phone call to assure people on Earth everything is okay, you may do so. I request that you not tell them where you are. How does that sound?"

They all looked at each other and nodded. Betsy Sue said, "Glenn and I don't need to make a call." She looked at the others. "We live in a secure location, and our administrator knows what's going on. What about the rest of you?"

Joan looked around at the others before speaking. "The four of us have told everyone that we are on a research trip and cannot be disturbed for a few days."

Walter smiled. "Terrific! If you'll all stand up, we'll flash back down to the atrium on my base." As soon as they were standing, they found themselves once again on the moon. "Debbie, will you please show them to our guest quarters? I need to check in with Butch. I'll see the rest of you in about eight or nine hours."

+ + +

At 9:30 the next morning, Pacific Time, the six scientists sat around a large table with Debbie and Walter. The dining hall was quiet except for a few people on the other side of the room. Walter took a sip of steaming herbal tea. "I hope all of you had enough to eat."

They all affirmed they had. Paul Bieber said, "Believe it or not, I would like to have the recipe for those eggs *aux buerre noir*. They were fabulous!"

Debbie smiled. "Actually Paul, the recipe came from a Nero Wolfe mystery novel written in the twentieth century. An Internet search will provide it."

Jill Chabert put down her coffee. "I wish I had had a camera yesterday to get at least a visual record of what we saw, both in our own solar system and the others."

Walter nodded. "When you go to your bedrooms this evening, each of you will find Blu-ray disks of everything you saw yesterday and everything you will see today. They will be yours to keep and study. There will also be a Blu-ray data disk with scientific data, including data about the other two planets as well as about Earth."

Bob Setmire's eyes were big. "That will be great! Thank you!" The others also murmured thanks.

Glenn shifted in his chair. "I must say I'm curious. Why are we getting all of these gifts?"

"Let me answer this one, Walter," Debbie said. "Ever since Walter and I became one, he and I have discussed scientific progress on Earth and his Gaardian role. I have been pressing him to help the research community more. When we passed through the light being last week, we suddenly knew that we had been too conservative in our approach."

"Yes," Walter continued. "While it would be inappropriate to reveal to any of you even a small portion of Gaardian technology, we can help by providing you data that is too difficult to access, time-consuming, and challenging to separate from useless other data."

Debbie continued, "Jody and I have designed a kind of super motor home. It is almost completely transparent, and it is safe in any exterior environment you can even imagine. John Carson will drive as Walter guides you. I'll be a passenger along with the rest of you."

"Before we go, we all want to thank for everything." Joan smiled, and gestured to the rest of them. They all nodded and murmured thanks.

"We're glad to do it." Debbie gave her best show business smile. "Now, since you'll be seated in our vehicle, we can go there right now."

There was a brief soft flash of light, and they were all in the special vehicle. Walter gestured towards their pilot. "All of you had a chance to meet John yesterday."

John Carson waved. "Hi everybody! Welcome aboard!"

Walter continued. "As you can see, we are between the Earth and the Moon. We are actually about fifty-five thousand kilometers above Norway. John, before we explore our planet, I want to show a few things to our astronomers that they did not see yesterday. John, take us to the surface of the sun." He paused. "All of you have fold-down consoles at your seats. You'll see a touch-screen menu there that will give you a variety of data, depending upon what you want."

There were murmurs among the passengers as they drew closer to the sun. Paul Biber called out, "I'm amazed we don't feel more heat. It's also normal illumination in here."

Walter nodded. "If it were not for Gaardian shielding, all of us would have been vaporized long before now. John, take us towards that flare over there that's about to erupt."

They moved closer just as a moderate-sized flare erupted from the sun's surface. Bob Setmire could only say, "Wow! Incredible!"

"Okay, John. Now take us to Gaardian at pace twenty."

"Right. We'll be there in less than a minute." The stars were streaking by. There was a flash, and after that the stars were streaking again. "We more or less passed through a blue star just a moment ago folks. That can happen when we're folding time and space."

"We folded them?" Joan was incredulous.

Walter smiled. "Yes. Do not ask us how we do it. You're not ready for it." Suddenly space looked more normal. "The planet over there is Gaardian. It is sentient. Glenn, would you like to greet the planet on behalf of all of us?"

"You're serious?" Glenn was skeptical, but Walter nodded. "Okay." He paused. "Hello, Gaardian. We're scientists from Earth."

In their heads, they heard the planet's voice. "Hello, Glenn Franz. Hello also to your wife, Betsy Sue, and to Paul Bieber, Jill Chabert, Joan Novotny, Paul Bieber, and Bob Setmire. It is good to meet all of you."

The scientists' mouths all hung open slightly. Debbie laughed. "Gaardian, my friend, I think you have rendered them speechless!"

Now the rest of them started laughing. Glenn spoke up. "Gaardian, you are something – a phenomenon – that I would never have believed existed if I had not heard your voice."

"That is understandable. Your second camera is a most interesting design, considering your level of science and technology."

"Thank you." Glenn was dumbfounded.

"Walter," the planet continued, "I have two suggestions to add to your itinerary which we previously discussed."

"What do you suggest?"

"Perhaps after you have given them environmental images from all seven continents, I suggest you take them to the deepest part of the Pacific Ocean and conclude with a visit to Lake Te Anau in New Zealand."

"Thank you. Those are excellent suggestions."

"I have a request, my friend." It paused briefly. "I would like to give your guests temporary ring support and bring them to my surface. I can converse with each of them separately but simultaneously while they get some exercise and some food near Red Falls."

"I had not anticipated this." Walter paused and looked at his guests. "I have no problem with this, but if this frightens you, we can decline with no animosity from the planet."

The scientists huddled together, conversing softly. After a few minutes, Bob Setmire spoke for them. "As scientists, how can we ignore this opportunity?"

Walter nodded. "Gaardian, they agree."

Suddenly, they were on the surface, seated in lounge chairs about a half kilometer from Red Falls. Walter spoke more loudly, over the sound of the falls. "Each of you at the moment wears a ring on your right hand. Don't worry about it, but don't take it off while you are on the planet's surface, or you will die almost immediately." He paused. "We will meet back here for lunch in about an hour. Have fun, everyone!"

Debbie walked over, took Walter's hand, and then led him towards the falls. As they got close to the large whirlpool at the base of the falls, their clothing became bathing suits, and they dove in. The others watched, and then began looking around. Each talked aloud to Gaardian as they walked.

A bit later, Walter hugged Debbie and gave her a kiss. "Gaardian, let's gather everyone at the family center for lunch. Walter's ring shimmered, and he and Debbie immediately were in the lounge. The others appeared one by one during the next several seconds.

Walter's ring shimmered again, and a large round table and chairs appeared. "Let's all sit, everyone, and then after a prayer of thanks you can tell Debbie and me what you want to eat." They all crossed over and sat down. Walter bowed his head and said, "Thanks, Lord, for new friendships as well as for the food which we're about to eat. In Jesus' name. Amen." He paused. "Okay. As you can now imagine, you can have whatever you want to eat and drink. All you have to do is think of what you want while looking at the ring on your hand."

Food appeared in front of Debbie and Walter, and soon everyone had food. Joan Novotny took a bite and looked at Walter. "I wish we could keep these rings! This is amazing!"

"Absolutely!" Glenn was enthusiastic. "How long before Earth's science and technology makes this possible?"

Walter put down his fork as he laughed. "As all of you can imagine, societies develop following patterns. At Earth's current rate of development, the technology for these rings will not be available for another twelve to seventeen hundred years."

They all paused eating. Betsy Sue cried "What? Are you serious?"

Walter smiled. "As your husband said, 'absolutely.'" He took another bite.

Debbie looked up from her plate. "Did all of you enjoy your visits with the planet?"

"Definitely!" Bob Setmire was emphatic. "It did not answer all of my questions of course because we are not ready for all the knowledge it possesses. Still, it confirmed research I have been doing."

"It's amazing!" was Jill's first comment. "It told me about wandering the galaxies for a long time before it met another mind that touched it. That was a creature named Qaak. We did not meet him yesterday."

"Why not meet me today!" Qaak said loudly from the doorway. "I have an apartment here in this family complex." He walked over and began shaking hands with each guest around the table. When he got to Walter, he asked, "May I join you? I'm hungry! Your food smells wonderful!"

Debbie smiled. "Of course, Qaak. Is Jody here?"

"Yes. Permit me to enlarge the table a bit." He paused as his ring shimmered and the table got larger, making space near Debbie and Walter. "I've made extra space because Doff wants to join us as well. The children are all out playing on the other side of Gaardian. Doff does not need to baby sit at the moment."

Just then, Doff came through the doorway. "I hope I am not intruding," he said with his deep bass voice. "My name is Doff. I would be honored if I may meet our guests."

Walter grinned at his friend. "Of course, Doff. I was wondering if you might be here."

When Glenn stood up to shake Doff's hand, he found the tall and translucent creature to be nearly twice his height. "Wow! And people say that I am tall!"

Doff's deep bass laugh made the others smile as well. "I do not think of my height very much. If you are wondering why I appear to be translucent to your eyes, it is because my physiology is not carbon-based as all of your bodies are. I am silicon-based."

"Really?" Betsy Sue also stood up to greet him. "Have you spent any time in Earth's forest?"

Doff chuckled. "As a matter of fact, I have been to Walter's Yosemite many times. I particularly enjoy it when I stroll with Kieya there. Without my Gaardian ring, I cannot get nutrition there." Doff's ring shimmered, and a large chair appeared between Walter and Glenn. He sat down.

Qaak's eyes glowed subtly. "Doff and I visited Earth the first time with Kieya many of your thousands of years ago. We all agreed that Earth compares in beauty with that of Kieya's planet."

Jill gestured towards Qaak. "Sir, I'm wondering where we are in comparison to Earth, and if I may ask, why do your eyes often glow?"

Qaak chuckled, and his eyes glowed more brightly. "My eyes reflect my emotions. You met my beloved wife, Jody, yesterday. It took her many months to learn to read my emotions in my eyes."

Walter laughed. "All of you may also be interested to know that Jody and Qaak have an anachronistic relationship."

Debbie suppressed a smile. "He means that there is a major age difference between them."

"Really? How much?" Betsy Sue was intrigued.

Walter continued to grin. "Qaak is more than sixty-five thousand years older than Jody."

There was silence at the table until Doff's chuckle broke the ice. "They're perfect for each other."

Qaak's eyes glowed. "Yes. I had not had a mate in many thousands of your years when I met Jody. Then I retired from being the convener of the Gaardians, and I became lonely. The Creator helped us find one another more fully and completely." He paused. "Now, Jill, I will answer your first question. We are having lunch about twenty billion light-years from Earth."

The scientists were all silent, and people continued to eat.

+ + +

Back in their vehicle, Walter spoke to John. "Did you get anything to eat?"

"Oh yes! I ate with Kenkee and the other children. They could be exhausting!"

"Unquestionably." He looked at the rest of the passengers. "Now, let's head back to Earth at pace 20, but slow down in time for them to see Saturn and Jupiter again. Slow enough at Mars for them to see the rover, and then let's start our tour of Earth by passing through the ice of Antarctica to skirt the edge of the land mass."

"Sounds great." He moved the controls, and soon the stars were flashing by again.

"All of you heard what I just said to John. You have learned how to use the consoles by your seats. If you have questions, ask. Otherwise, I'll let you work as we travel."

Sitting next to him, Debbie kissed him on the cheek and spoke softly. "This is turning out even better than we planned." She snuggled up to Walter and put her head on his shoulder.

When they got to Antarctica, Glenn asked, "How can we pass through the ice like this without cracking it?"

Walter turned towards him to answer. "I can't tell you how, but I can tell you what is happening. At any given moment of time, the ice that our vehicle displaces is held in a buffer. The net effect is that the ice is not disturbed. There are no resulting changes in the wake of our being here."

Glenn whistled softly. "Perfect!"

Rising from the ice, John turned north to Australia. They examined the Central Eastern Rainforest, the Greater Blue Mountains area, and other areas on the continent where there were environmental concerns. Over the next several hours, they explored areas of concern in Asia and then in Europe. Turning south, they toured many areas of South America and Central America before coming into North America. They came to a stop in a jungle area just north of the Panama Canal.

Walter spoke out to all of them. "I have heard some of you wondering how we will have time to explore all these areas. I have not told you about something all of you are experiencing without your knowing it. Once again, I am not going to tell you how I am able to do this." He paused. "We are in a time pocket that I created with John just after we set out from Gaardian back towards Earth. Less than twenty seconds have passed since we left Gaardian."

"What???" Paul and Joan asked simultaneously. Paul continued. "We know theoretically that such a thing is possible but ... really???"

Walter smiled. "Yes." He paused. "From here we will explore the areas listed on your consoles. As you can see, we are going to examine nearly twenty different areas in Mexico, the United States, and Canada. When we are done with those areas, we will go under water to follow the lines of the geological plates of the ring of fire that surrounds the Pacific – the source of so many earthquakes. Then we are going down into the Marianna trench. By the way – when you get home, there will be additional Blu-ray disks waiting for you. You will have exclusive access to the disks for three months. Then copies will be distributed more widely."

When they came up out of the water and flew over Bora Bora, Betsy Sue asked, "Why is our final stop Lake Te Anau in New Zealand?"

Walter grinned. "I think it is Gaardian's way of putting frosting on the cake." He paused as they all looked at him quizzically. "Yesterday all of you have been seeing new and exciting things, and you have gained quite a bit of scientific knowledge for future study and consideration. Exploring Lake Te Anau is a bit of serendipity."

Jill smiled. "Serendipity? This is something just for fun?"

"You might or might not think that after we leave the lake. According to most reference books, the lake is sixty-five kilometers long but is rather narrow throughout its irregular span. Those same books say that its maximum depth is four hundred seventeen meters. There are some myths and legends about the lake. Some say that the lake was formed from a crack in the Earth's crust. Those same people say that there are spots in the lake that are much deeper. We are going to skirt the entire bottom of the lake. Remember how we did not disturb the ice of Antarctica and not disturbed anything anywhere else we have gone? We will not be disturbing the waters of the lake, even at the fun speed of about fifty knots!"

As Walter said this, they were approaching the lake. Suddenly, John pointed the nose of their vehicle down, and in seconds, they were traversing the bottom of the lake at high speed. With the turns, twists, and ups and downs of the bottom, it was like a roller coaster. No one was watching their console. More than once, they seemed to go deeper than expected.

Rising up out of the water, John guided them at high speed towards the United States. They came to a stop at an elevation of two hundred thousand meters above central California. John said, "Okay, Walter."

"Everyone," Walter said with a smile, "this is the end of our journey. We are no longer in the time pocket. I compressed our experience of time within the pocket, and with the help of the rings you have been wearing, you have not experienced fatigue. I have enjoyed traveling with you and sharing things with you. From this moment onward, I will periodically be helping various branches of science and technology for the three planets. Before I send all of you home, do any of you have any questions or comments?"

Glenn beaconed. "If after we study all the data we've acquired during this weekend, is there a way we can communicate with you, even indirectly?"

Walter nodded. "If it is something you consider crucially important in your research, you can leave a message for me through Paula Rutledge or Toby Ballentine. Please, remember that the names of Gaardians and my relationships with my crew is information for just the six of you and no one else. Okay?"

They all nodded. "Those are secrets we can keep," Glenn said emphatically. The others nodded agreement.

"Very well."

25. Aftermath

Betsy Sue and Glenn suddenly found themselves in the living room of their apartment. Her eyes grew wide. "That was amazing! We didn't even take any time to thank Walter and Debbie!" She looked at her right hand. "Our rings are gone."

"I know! When our Gaardian gives gifts, he is truly generous!" He looked down at his belt where his cell phone had appeared. "I had better call Mike and tell him we're home."

Nora appeared at the doorway to their bedroom. "Hi, Glenn! Hi, Betsy Sue! I thought I heard noises out here!"

"Hi, Nora!" Betsy Sue started walking towards her. How are the twins?" She gave Nora a hug.

"They're fine. Right now, they're asleep."

The two women turned to go to the bedroom as Glenn punched a number on his cell phone. "Mike? Glenn." He paused. "We got home just a second ago. It was incredible." He paused longer. "We'll tell you a little about it tomorrow over lunch, okay?" He paused. "Right. We will see you tomorrow. Bye." He closed the phone.

"Ever since that flash of light," he murmured, "I wonder what's next?"

+ + +

There was fog around the Transamerica Pyramid below Ben Kaiser's office, so he could not see the street. Above the fog, he could see the tops of a few buildings, and in the distance, he could see the Golden Gate. Going to his desk, he pressed a button.

"Yes, sir?"

"Get me Francine Elliott on the phone as soon as you can. I've got a lot to work on, but put the call through as soon as you have her and stay on the line."

"Okay."

He sat down and pulled the writing pull-out into position. He leaned back in his chair and put his feet up on the pull-out. He stared out at the top of the Golden Gate, protruding up from the fog. "Am I doing something foolish, Lord?" he murmured softly.

His phone buzzed. "Yes, Lucy?"

"Francine Elliott is on line one."

He pressed the button and picked up the receiver. "Francine? It is good to hear your voice. How are you?" He listened. "Great. I have one and perhaps two projects I want you to consider." He listened a moment. "Here's what I want you to do. Lucy is going to get you a ticket to DFW in Texas. When you get there, I want you to drive down to Ellis County and find out the current status of the property where our government canceled the building of the superconducting super collider." He paused. "Yes, I know. I want you to take the time you need to examine what was completed before the cancellation. You'll probably have to do some research in local sources there in Texas."

He took his feet down as she talked. "Yes, Francine. Once you have that information, I want you to make an appointment to see Senator Everett Steinmetz. Tell him I sent you to ask confidentially about a device he calls 'the digger.' Find out what you can, and then make an appointment to see me. You and I will need a whole day to hash out what I have in mind." He looked out the window again as she responded. "I'm not going to tell you more on the phone at this point except to say one thing. I will be asking you to spearhead an experimental project adjacent to my Fresno complex. If that experiment is successful, it will have a huge impact upon a lot of people." He paused briefly. "Yes, Francine. I look forward to seeing you next month." He paused. "Bye. ... Did you get all of that, Lucy? ... Good."

Ben stared out the window. "This will be far bigger than I am, Lord!" he murmured. "Ever since I saw that flash of light ...." He closed his eyes.

+ + +

Three hundred eighty-four thousand kilometers above Ben, Walter was soaking in the hot and cold whirlpool. His thoughts were racing as he simply closed his eyes and enjoyed the swirling warmth.

"Walter."

He opened his eyes, and standing by the edge of the pool was Asayak. "Yes?"

"May I join you? I have something to discuss."

"Certainly."

The creature flowed into the pool. "I know that Gaardians experienced the light creatures in close proximity, but the rest of us simply saw an all-encompassing flash of electromagnetic radiation coupled with thought."

"Butch analyzed its effect upon everyone here on the base. It was significant."

"Yes. Yesterday, at Butch's suggestion, we scanned those at the dinner. We did not scan for thoughts or feelings but for changes caused by the light beings. One of those beings passed through our solar system as well."

"I know, Asayak. What did you learn at the banquet?"

"When we saw that the light being had affected everyone at the banquet, we examined ourselves. We found the same effect. Creativity has been enhanced in all beings. We do not know what this will mean, but we believe it is important for you to know as Convener of the Gaardians."

"Thank you, Asayak. I will talk to Butch about this. I suggest that you and your friends analyze how the effects are affecting the population of your planet. When you have come to some conclusions, let me know."

"It shall be done. Shall I now share my findings with Butch?"

"Yes. Thank you."

"It shall be done." The creature flowed out of the pool and out of the recreation area.

"Cool-down, please." Quickly, the water dropped to near freezing, and Walter got out. Dried off, he walked towards the office complex. Turning into the first door on the right, he greeted Debbie. "Hello, my love."

She gave him a hug. "Hi! What's up?"

"We haven't spent much time just with each other in over a week. Let's plan on it this evening, okay?"

She smiled. "Yes, dear. We can look forward to it." She gave him a light kiss.

"I'm going out to Gaardian. This evening, why don't you bring Joseph with you to Gaardian? He loves playing with Kenkee. Qaak will be babysitting, so we can have all the time we want to ourselves."

"Great! It will be good to get away from here for a day or two!"

"Right! See you later!" He gave her a quick kiss, and then he vanished.

On a peak above Red Falls, Walter appeared on Gaardian. "Gaardian, I would like to converse with you today. Is Qaak in his apartment?"

"Qaak is in his second apartment on my surface at the Family Center. Do you wish to make him part of our conversation?"

"Yes."

The old triped appeared nearby and sat down on the rock ledge next to him. "Good day, Walter."

"Hello, Qaak."

"Are you here to consider the aftermath of our challenge by the light creatures?"

"Yes. Asayak made a report to me a short while ago."

"Indeed. Gaardian, has Asayak sent a report to you?"

"Yes. Consider this."

Qaak's eyes closed, but a slightly pulsating glow ensued. "Indeed. Yes, indeed! Walter, your friends Ann Cotter and Margaret Graves are reporting a query from Ben Keiser. He wants information on how to reach you."

"Interesting!" Walter was thoughtful. "Gaardian, ask Asayak to scan Ben Kaiser's recent memories to see what this is about. Qaak, Ben Kaiser is a very affluent and creative innovator on Earth. If he wants to talk to me, he must be considering something massive in scale."

"Indeed. Kieya has told me of his relationship to those two scientists, the Franzes. This may be a very important development."

"Yes," said the planet, "it is very important. An inventor in the country called Germany has developed a tunneling device that separates the output into individual elements."

Qaak chuckled. "Indeed. This development is a technological breakthrough for Earth. It will accelerate their progress for perhaps several decades."

"Fascinating! What do you think Ben Kaiser is going to do with the technology?"

The planet paused. "The man is thinking creatively, and he is considering several possibilities. He is considering both underground transportation development and mining development in conjunction with each other."

Qaak's eyes glowed. "Indeed. Walter, it is time for you to pay him a visit."

"There's more," the planet rumbled. "I am getting reports from other Gaardians. It seems that mining is a common theme. Most reports concern the mining of solids, but there are also reports of mining lakes, oceans, and other large bodies of liquid. On Pzalop and Quzak, there is a discussion of mining their atmospheres."

Walter's eyes grew wide. "Amazing! I think I know why!"

"You do?" asked the old triped.

"Those seven creatures were gathering data as they moved through space, and their processing of the data was manifest as light. For them, processing the data was like separating different kinds of thoughts and information. In a sense, they were mining information. Mining was a central theme of their existence. Now, all the sentient creatures in Gaardian space are reflecting that mindset."

"Yes," rumbled the planet. "The creature that briefly visited me tried to extract information from me, but I allowed very little."

"Indeed!" Qaak's eyes were glowing. "This all makes sense now."

Walter was intense. "Gaardian, I need to have you and Qaak communicate our conclusions to the other Gaardians. Right now, I'm going back to Earth and set up a meeting with Mr. Kaiser."

"Good!" Qaak got up from his seat. "Perhaps we will see each other tomorrow at breakfast. Jody and I are babysitting this evening at the Family Center. Until then."

"Until then." Walter vanished. He reappeared beside Debbie's desk while she was chatting with Belinda. "Hey, you two!"

"Hi," said Belinda.

"Walter! I was not expecting to see you until this evening."

"We still will see each other. Qaak and Jody are babysitting. Meanwhile, make an old-fashioned telephone call to the offices of Tiberias Holdings in San Francisco. Find out how soon I can sit down with Ben Kaiser for thirty minutes."

"I'll see you later. I've got work to do." Belinda went out as the others nodded.

A phone appeared on Debbie's desk, and she picked up the receiver. "Hello, this is Gaardian communications. Mr. Kaiser has wanted to communicate with Earth's Gaardian. How soon will Mr. Kaiser have thirty minutes available?" Debbie looked up at Walter and raised her eyebrows. "Yes, I understand. Is Mr. Kaiser available in Fresno right now?" Debbie paused and looked up at Walter. "Evidently she's talking with him in Fresno on another line." Walter nodded. "Yes. Walter will meet him in the secure apartment underneath the facility in three minutes, okay?" She paused. "Good. The phone vanished.

Debbie looked up at Walter. "It's done. In the Fresno facility we visited, there is an apartment in a bunker underneath and west of the apartment occupied by Glenn and Betsy Sue Franz. He'll meet you there."

"Good. Thanks my love." He bent down and kissed her.

Frank appeared next to them. "Ben Kaiser is in the bunker. The Franzes are talking about going down there to join them."

Walter shook his head. "No. Keep them topside. I want privacy for my conversation with Mr. Kaiser."

"Okay," Frank vanished.

"Bye, love! See ya later!" He vanished before she could respond.

26. Man with a Vision

Walter appeared in the bunker as Ben Kaiser was drinking from a water bottle. "Hello, Mr. Kaiser. I understand you have wanted to communicate with me."

"Hello." He put the water bottle down. "It's nice to meet you. Please call me Ben. May we sit down?" He gestured towards a conversation pit, and they both sat. "I've wanted to talk with you because of a rather major inspiration I have."

"I'm not surprised. You have an antique prie dieu in your office, Ben. Does Jesus dwell in your heart as your Savior, best friend, and constant companion?"

Ben's mouth dropped open, and then he closed it. "That's not a question I could have dreamed that you would ask me. Yes, as a matter of fact, He does." He paused. "May I safely assume that you are a Christian?"

"Yes, however, I ask that all of this conversation be strictly confidential. Agreed?"

"Yes."

"Then you can call me Walter. I understand that you are considering both mass transportation and mining projects that are highly innovative. Is this the reason for your wanting to see me?"

Again, Ben's mouth dropped open briefly. "Yes. I won't ask you how you know these things."

"Good. It is not a technological secret, but it is not important either. I know that Francine Locke is doing some research for you. She has worked for you before."

Ben nodded. "She designed the geodesic dome for this facility. She is a truly brilliant young architect. As you may already know, she is looking at the aborted superconducting super collider in Texas, and after that she is going to talk to Senator Everett Steinmetz about the inventor of a tunneling device that the senator calls 'the digger.'"

"I'm aware of this. Why did you want to discuss it with me?"

"Simply this: You know Glenn and Betsy Sue Franz, the scientists that lead my facility here. I have always been sensitive to environmental issues. As I've prayed about all of this, I have come to realize that doing what I envision could trigger an unforeseen environmental disaster."

Walter smiled. "It's good to be led by the Spirit, and it is good to be cautious. Since you will learn some of what I am about to tell you from Francine Locke, this will be a bit of a preview. You need to approach this project in three phases. First, invite Senator Steinmetz and his grandson, Robert, to meet you here in Fresno. Robert is the inventor of the tunneling device."

"Really! I had not made that connection!"

"You might have if you knew some twentieth-century history. A man named Charles Steinmetz was a pioneer in the early days of General Electric. He was Senator Steinmetz's grandfather. Charles Steinmetz was making and studying lightning bolts around the time of World War I."

"Wow!"

"Let's get back to Robert. Do you remember how you quietly gathered up everything belonging to Glenn and Betsy Sue and brought it here to Fresno before you brought them here?"

Ben grinned. "Again, you know things most people wouldn't know. Yes, I remember. Do I need to treat Robert the same way?"

"Yes. Tell Robert he can bring his fiancée. Gather up her things too. You have more apartments on the other side of this complex. Now you can use them."

"Okay, so what's the second phase?"

"That's not the end of the first phase!" Walter smiled. "You need to house some of your lawyers, particularly some who have engineering expertise, here at the complex – at least part of the time. That tunneling device is going to need at least as much patent protection as Glenn Franz's camera."

"Understood."

"You will find that this tunneling device involves two brand new areas of revolutionary technology. Your lawyers are going to be working on it for months, and they will have to apply for hundreds of patents. It will be expensive, but you will get it all back."

"I expect that!" They both smiled.

"I suggest you let Margaret Graves in Oakland handle and control publicity in conjunction with Paula Rutledge. Introduce Francine Locke to Margaret, and tell Miss Locke to ask for help from a man named Toby Ballentine. Senator Steinmetz knows Toby and trusts him."

"Excellent. I know about Toby Ballentine. He's been very helpful to Glenn and Betsy Sue."

"Yes. Here is another suggestion. You own some un-used office space on the west side of your floor in the Transamerica Building. I suggest that you invite Miss Locke to move her offices in there. It will save on her expenses and yours. In phase three she might end up having you as her only client."

Ben grinned. "That's an excellent idea."

Walter smiled. "She's attracted to you, just as you are to her but don't tell her I told you that!"

His eyes got bigger. "What? ... Okay!"

"You've got four hundred and twelve acres here. That is plenty of space for Robert and his crew you supply to him in order to do his research. I suggest that he and his crew do basic research here at the main facility, but that when he wants to start applying his technology, have him start using the building you originally used as a hanger."

"That makes sense."

"Now tell me your vision, no matter how outrageous you think it is."

"There are times I think I'm going crazy with it."

"That's understandable. It is probably no crazier than traveling to the other side of our galaxy in a matter of seconds. Right?"

He hesitated. "Okay." Ben took a deep breath. "This is just an example I dreamed up using what I think this new technology can do, okay?" Walter nodded. "Francine would design a train station with a parking lot here in Fresno. She would also design a train station for Yosemite Valley, next to the north wall in the area where there used to be church services on Sundays during the summer."

Walter smiled. "As a boy, I attended services there."

Ben nodded. "Robert Steinmetz's digging device would create a nearly vertical shaft at least 500 feet deep in Fresno. Next, it would go north underground until it was under the valley. There would subsequently be another nearly vertical shaft going up to the terminus in the station where I talked about. An electric monorail train would connect the two stations."

"Ben, I think you will find that you will need to go much deeper than five hundred feet for both environmental, legal, and safety reasons."

"Okay. I can also see building high speed underground monorail train routes all over the country. As I see it, it would minimize the environmental impact. What I don't know is what to do with the tailings for all of these projects."

Walter smiled. "You know, don't you, that Robert's digger includes a complex array for separating the tailings into their most elemental form."

"Yes. As I understand it, separating out the gold, silver, and other elements is highly efficient and consumes relatively little energy."

"Truthfully, depending on the material being processed, it can in reality generate energy."

"Really!"

"Yes. Robert Steinmetz has designed something that is a major jump forward in technological progress. That part of the digger will have wide-ranging applications."

"For instance?"

"I'm not going to give you very many specific ideas. That would be contrary to Gaardian guidelines. I will make one suggestion, however."

"What's that?"

"You own a waterfront operation just north of La Jolla, remember?"

"Yes."

"Have Robert and Francine design and build a separator for ocean water. See how much you can harvest from ocean water with virtually no measurable environmental impact. Then try mixing in sewage at the intake. When you see the results, I'm sure you will get other ideas and think of other applications." Walter paused. "I'll give you one other suggestion. Have Robert and Francine work together to design a gas separator. Take it to your wind generator farm east of San Francisco. Put the separator behind an air scoop, and see what profit you can make by extracting the hydrogen and inert gases from the air that flows through the separator."

"You're kidding! Those gases are such a low percentage of the air!"

"Nevertheless, your lawyers won't have to come up with a lot of additional patents for that device if they write the original ones for the tunneling device adequately. Be sure to tell them that!"

Ben laughed, but then he was sober again. "What about the potential environmental impact for the tunnels?"

"So long as your tunnels are deep enough and do not follow a major earthquake fault, there should not be problems. You'll have to arrange for sharing the profits from the mineral rights from a lot of land."

"Right."

Walter got up from his chair. "That should take care of your concerns for now. Remember that this is completely confidential. Do not make any notes of this conversation for your computer, and do not share anything I have said with your secretary. What she does not know, government investigators cannot get from her. I do not think there is another Senator Hosmer around, but you cannot take that chance. When you have other questions, shoot them past Margaret Graves. If she does not know an answer, she can get it. It's been good meeting you, Ben."

"I have enjoyed talking with you, Walter." They shook hands.

Walter vanished.

27. A Short Retreat

Joseph, Amanda, and the other children were playing with Kenkee on the water slides Gaardian had configured for them. As Kieya strolled through the forest with Doff, they could occasionally hear the screams and laughter. Doff was amused. "I remember playing hard like that when I was small, but we never had water slides like those!"

"No," Kieya purred. "We did have some wonderful mud pits, though."

"Mud pits? That sounds like fun! Gaardian, have the children ever played in mud pits?"

"They have not been suggested to me. Kieya, what do you think?"

Her purr became louder. "I think it would be great fun for them. Gaardian, you would need to monitor them carefully for safety. None of these children have my instincts."

"Understood," the planet rumbled.

Kieya and Doff climbed silently for a while into Gaardian's hills. Then Doff stopped and looked out at the forest far below them. "I understand that Walter and Debbie are on retreat for a few days."

Kieya sat down on her haunches next to her friend. "Yes. I am pleased. Walter works constantly, and it is good that he is taking time for just Debbie. She is very loyal, and they are excellent for each other. Their Joseph is here for three days. Walter and Debbie are not at the family center, however. Walter has prepared another place for retreat."

Doff sat down on a rock. "Yes. I would imagine Debbie was surprised by what Walter has done." He paused. "I have noticed that you have spent more time than usual on your planet. Is there a problem you have not reported?"

Kieya's purr grew lower and softer. "No. For the first time in thousands of years, I am playing with a highly intelligent felidaca. I may take him as my first new mate in a long time."

"Really! Do you think you will have tats again?"

"I would imagine so. I would have to set aside time each day for duties in my lair. Once my tats are weaned, my mate will take over most of the parenting duties. I will supply all of their needs. That will not be a problem."

"I too have considered such a venture." Doff's low bass voice was now even gentler than usual. "Some time ago, I chanced upon a female who was my intellectual equal. Within a short time, she surmised that I was more than I appeared. She gleaned tidbits from many conversations to conclude that I had duties not on our planet."

"Does she know what a Gaardian is?"

"Not yet. If she and I become one, I will discuss with Walter how much I will tell her."

"That's a good strategy; I will undoubtedly do the same for my new mate. Our families will join us soon."

"Congratulations! Have you told Walter?"

"I told him just before our confrontation with the creatures of light. After his retreat with Debbie, I will discuss it with him again."

They got up, and they began walking towards the Family Center.

+ + +

Elsewhere on the planet, Walter and Debbie were cuddled by a fire on a huge overstuffed sofa. Debbie took a sip from her mug of steaming hot chocolate. "That was fun! I had forgotten how satisfying it is to cook a meal from scratch over a traditional stove, taking food from a traditional refrigerator and freezer. You're almost as good a cook as I am!" She poked him in the ribs.

"Hey, I lived as a bachelor for long time before we became one." He shifted to get more comfortable beside her. "Before I was integrated as a Gaardian I had food allergies to wheat, oats, rye, dairy products, and eggs. There's no such problem now, of course."

"Right. I have been looking at the architecture of this log cabin. The logs are vertical. Why? Don't log cabins usually have horizontal logs?"

"I suppose that most do. When I was growing up, we had a cabin like this one near the town of Blue Jay in the San Bernardino Mountains of Southern California. It was a hunting lodge before my family bought it. I have reproduced it as best I can, both from the structure that still survives and from my memories. I've undone a lot of the modifications done by various owners since we sold it when I was a boy."

"You've reproduced the furniture?"

"Yes. I've also reproduced the stuffed animals, animal skins, and antiques." He paused. "The furniture is from my memories of what we had in those days. In order to furnish the place properly, my aunt bought a bunch of furniture from an auction of furnishings from an old hotel. This is like the furniture that was in the lobby of that hotel and later in our family cabin."

"Was the sofa this big?"

Walter chuckled. "I think so. Just before we sold the cabin, my brother and I slept in front of the fireplace one night on it. At the time, I was about my current adult height, and my brother was slightly taller. We stretched out on the sofa, with our heads at the two ends. Our feet never touched."

Now Debbie chuckled. "It must have come from a very large hotel lobby."

"It did. I don't know that the hotel lobby had a fireplace like this though. The fireplace in the original cabin could take logs more than one and a half meters long."

"I like the coffee table you have reproduced too."

"Thanks. I am not sure it is accurate. I remember there being a drawer in the center like this, but I can't remember the other details except for the fact that it was about two-thirds the length of the sofa."

"What about those big wing-back chairs – and the piano in the corner?"

"They're as accurate as I can make them from memory. Unlike the original piano, though, this one is in tune – and it is not electronic either. It is acoustic."

She squeezed his arm. "I'm looking forward to taking shower with you, but that shower and the tiny bathroom look a lot smaller than we're used to!"

Walter chuckled. "It will be cozy. It does not have sonic scrubbing, so we will have to scrub each other. That might be a little cramped, but it will be fun I think. If you want, we can also dry each other off with told fashioned Egyptian cotton bath towels."

"Later!" She paused. "Why did you decide to reproduce this – your childhood cabin – this time?"

"I think it might be part of the aftermath of our visit by the light beings. Creativity has been stimulated throughout Gaardian space."

"It's been amazing! I saw a video record of your conversation with Ben Kaiser. He's brilliant, isn't he?"

"Yes! The light beings evidently stirred his creativity. The technology developed by Robert Steinmetz coupled with Ben Kaiser's resources will help Earth make a technological jump ahead by several decades. Science in some areas will have to catch up. Similar things are happening throughout Gaardian space."

"Have you been keeping up with those reports coming in from other parts of Gaardian space?"

"I'm pretty well caught up, but I'm spiritually and emotionally worn out. That's why I wanted us to take a few days off."

"I'm glad we did." She kissed him on the cheek. "Let's merge, okay?"

Walter began to glow, growing brighter and brighter. His body became fluid and flowed over Debbie's. Her body was glowing too. Their bodies became one unified glowing body without human features. In the flickering glow from the fire in the fireplace, they remained within one another. Then the entire great room of the cabin began to glow with the characteristic glow of the voice.

> "Walter, Debbie, you continue to do very well. I am blessing your choosing each other for marriage. As I told you on your day of merging, your union will be long and fruitful, for I will make your union last many lifetimes.
>
> If you wish, I will bless you with more children. Long ago, I gave Gaardians authority and power, and they have made good use of what I have given them. Now, they again know who has given this responsibility. As you are working together, I am multiplying your efforts and glorifying myself as I did with the seven light beings.
>
> I will continue to be with you wherever you go so long as you let me be God and let my Son be your King. Walter, tomorrow you will again be asked to address the United Nations. They want to know about the flash of light. As before, I will be on your lips and in your heart. My creation continues. I forgive. I redeem. I make things new again."

The glow faded. The human features of Walter and Debbie returned from their combined blur, and they separately continued to glow softly, cuddling in front of the fire.

III. *The Still Small Voice*

Prologue

Earth's peoples initially became aware of the intergalactic police known Gaardians only a short time ago. The first Gaardian for Earth was (and still is) a human named Walter, who was born near the beginning of World War II. When the time had come to show himself as Gaardian, he confiscated and destroyed every gram of cocaine on Earth. Then he interrupted every television and radio station, telling Earth what he had done. He announced he was assembling a team to work with him. Millions of applications flowed in.

The term Gaardian applies to both a few thousand intergalactic law enforcement beings and to a planet. The planet, Gaardian, can think and much more. With an intellect that is greater than thousands of humans combined, it communicates with its enforcement beings across nearly countless galaxies. It can also manipulate matter and energy, so it can propel itself where it wants to go.

On Earth, Walter's first recruit was a childhood friend named Belinda, and the two of them recruited the rest of his team. When recruited, all but one were at least seventy years of age, but Gaardian technology restored their bodies to those of young adults.

As with the previous two volumes of Gaardian tales, this set is woven together to form a larger story. It begins on the planet named Pzalop, where its leader, the Suppla decides to honor The Creator in a unique way. As the leader of the Zargadetes, the Suppla was headed for a major personal change.

1. Suppla

Everyone on the planet had always known the Suppla as a tall and imposing male who was a very capable leader. The office was for life, and the planet was thriving. The Suppla's executive assistant, a male named Arooda, was the only one on the planet who knew that the Suppla was actually a female named Eibbed. She and Arooda were legally but secretly married.

Early in the morning on their anniversary, they were chatting just after they had awakened. Arooda gazed into his mate's eyes. "Of all the materials Walter has given us, I think I like Earth's *Bible,* with its prophecies and its stories about Jesus, almost as much as I like reading reports from Ooza regarding Quzak's Arkaynee. I hope we live long enough to see Pzalop's own savior." Arooda drew his mate closer.

Eibbed snuggled close into his arms and spoke softly and gently. "I also hope we will see the day of our savior. Have you recently watched the video of the Creator's hand saving our planet?"

He nodded. "Anytime I get discouraged or down, I watch it. It has been a few months now, though."

"My Suppla duties can wait. Let us watch it before we start our day. ... Computer, display the salvation video." They both again watched the video on the opposite wall carefully, beginning with the familiar scene when Walter addresses The Suppla.

"When we moved your planet to this galaxy and placed it around this sun, the approaching comet was hidden."

As Walter continued, Eibbed pointed to the display. "I was really disturbed that Walter had instructed me to gather with all of our leaders at the projected point of impact. Our population density is very high all around that little undeveloped green area." She paused. "Then I began to wonder." She pointed. "See how others of his crew are arriving – I found this provocative." In the video, she was now speaking as The Suppla.

"These are other Gaardians?"

"No, these are simply with me, and they wish to be with us here on your beautiful planet."

The Suppla was grim. "What happens now?"

"We wait for the comet to arrive. May I address your council and the others?"

In the bedroom, Eibbed beamed. "This request amused me, Arooda!"

In the video, the Suppla smiled at the deference to her position. "Proceed."

As the video continues, Walter climbs up upon a nearby boulder that is fairly flat on top. His voice seems unusually loud as he speaks.

"Greetings everyone! I am the convener of the intergalactic police group known as The Gaardians. We are the ones who moved your planet to its new galaxy as a disciplinary action."

Walter paused in the video, as there is murmuring among the crowd and several people gesture towards both the Suppla and Walter.

"I'm sure that many of you hate the Gaardians for what we did. That is understandable. We are here again now in support of your best interests. Having moved your entire planet over a distance traversing several galaxies, destroying the approaching comet would not even be a minor challenge to our power. That is not why we are here."

There was more murmuring.

"There is one that has a far greater power than all the Gaardians combined. We are here simply to witness with you what will happen."

A Zargadete approaches Walter in the video, and Arooda points to the video screen. "Isn't that Leahcim, the current council leader?"

"Yes," said Eibbed, "Many on the council began to recognize his leadership for the first time that day."

The video continued. "Are you saying that you're going to do nothing?"

"That is correct."

In the bedroom, Eibbed and Arooda watch as she steps up upon the rock as the ostensibly male Suppla of the planet. Her voice also seems unusually loud.

"Some time ago, time ago I met with this Gaardian. He gave me information, which leads me to believe without question that he wants to help us, and he wants what is best for our planet."

Watching the drama unfold, they both begin to smile as they see their friend from the planet Quzak, Ooza, climbing up on the boulder to join the Suppla and Walter.

"Many of you in the military recognize me. I was the mate of the Quzak Commander who led the expedition with you to conquer Earth. Those of you that know me know that I do not lie to anyone for any reason. Com, my mate, is now dead, and I recently made the decision to become a Gaardian. For countless solar revolutions, my people were your enemies. We joined forces against the Gaardians and failed. Though I am now a Gaardian, I am still not your enemy, and neither are the other Gaardians. Read my heart, Zargadetes! Starting tomorrow, when this is all over, I will do anything I can within Gaardian guidelines to help you have a productive and prosperous future. That is my promise."

"That was an amazing promise, especially coming from a Quzak, and she has kept it." Eibbed smiled again as, in the video, Walter looked up and then back at the crowd.

"The comet is approaching. The Creator of the universe is in command! Look!"

As he said this, Walter was facing the reddish glow where the second of Pzalop's two suns had set just moments earlier. There were cries of terror in the crowd as a huge fiery ball appeared high and off to his left. Watching the video, Eibbed and Arooda leaned forward, immersing themselves in it. Walter spoke again, but this time his voice was like thunder over the crowd.

"Don't be afraid! Watch The Creator of the universe work for you!"

Out of the darkness opposite the sunset, a fiery hand appeared, growing larger until its fingers wrap around the comet. The fingers become a fist, and it glows more and more brightly. Watching, Arooda and Eibbed hardly breathed as an unimaginably deep voice thunders out of the sky.

"Do not be afraid. I am The Creator. I created all that science knows, and all that science ever will know. I forgive. I redeem, and I make new. All of you are my children, and I love you as a parent. I have guided your growth and disciplined you because I love you. For generations, Zargadete parents have failed to teach their children about me. You must not forget. I am love. I am peace, and I am your hope. Make the most of what I have already given you, and I will be pleased. My servants the Gaardians can guide you toward fulfillment and joy. Learn from them. Teach your children and all future generations about me. I reward those who love me with life that is real and everlasting."

The brilliant glow faded, and the landscape seemed to reappear out of the glow. The hushed silence on the video as it ended was easily matched by silence of Eibbed and Arooda as the video concluded.

Eibbed spoke first. "I'm glad we watched that together again. I am going to talk to the Creator as I bathe. Would you please prepare me some food before you go to join the staff?"

"Absolutely!" He smiled and then kissed her deeply. "I think your schedule will allow us to share a special meal this evening."

"Special?" She paused. "Yes! It has been a year since we formed our secret union!"

"Yes! I'm preparing our favorite feast, and I've invited a few very special guests for just the first part of our evening."

"Who?"

"You will see!" He kissed her again, lightly, and then Arooda turned and left, leaving her speechless.

Eibbed turned and walked toward a door on the far side across the room. Beside the doorjamb, she pressed a small triangle. Using a slightly lower voice, speaking like a male and with authority, she spoke crisply. "This is the Suppla. I want council leaders to meet with me in my conference room when I arrive. Tell them to plan to remain for a meal. I will arrive shortly. That is all." Releasing the triangle, she stepped through the doorway to bathe.

+ + +

In another galaxy, a large felidaca was enjoying the warmth of her planet's sunshine. Her name was Kieya. Felidacas were superior to all the other animals on their planet. Slightly more intelligent than humans, felidacas were four-legged carbon-based animals with stripes somewhat like those of Earth's tigers. They also had ears like those of Earth's cats, but their faces were humanoid except for not having a nose. Kieya was brilliant as well as amazingly strong and agile.

On that particular day, instead of sleeping in her lair as usual, she stretched out her large cat-like body on her stomach, high on a hill. She purred softly as she felt the coolness of the soil beneath her. The sun was low on the sky, and many tats were arriving at the little school at the bottom of the hill. It was early evening. Like Earth's cats, felidacas were nocturnal, sleeping while their sun traversed the daylight sky.

She opened her eyes as she heard parents leaving their tats before departing for their workplaces. One particular mother was very stern as she spoke to her tat. "Stay away from Legere today. He just wants to bully you and fight." Now Kieya listened more carefully because centuries earlier she had a mate named Legere.

"Ahhh...."

"Stay away from him, do you understand me?"

"Yes. ... I will."

"Good. I'll see you an hour before sunrise."

"Yes." The tat licked his mother's face, turned, and went into his school."

Kieya blinked. She liked watching the tats as they played near the school. Rising, she began to pad quietly into the nearby trees. She thought about her interplanetary leader. "Kieya to Gaardian: Are there any stirrings in my sector that my crew cannot handle today?"

The planet's voice responded telepathically. "No. Your crew has everything under control. Qaak is on my surface, babysitting with his mate Jody. Walter is leaving his sector to the care of his crew today and is visiting sector 101-A256-B1019. One of the planets there will begin to explore space soon. He is doing an evaluation."

"Interesting! I have not been to that sector in several centuries. ... Kieya to Walter: May I join you?"

She heard Walter's voice inside her head. "Certainly. I think you will be interested in what is happening here."

Kieya glanced around amid the trees, and, seeing no other felidacas, she vanished.

+ + +

In another sector of Gaardian space, Eibbed had finished bathing, and had eaten a small breakfast. For the better part of an hour, she had been kneeling on a piece of furniture in a corner of her office. Although the French people on Walter's Earth called it a *prie*-dieu [French for "pray to God"], the piece in the Suppla's office had no formal name. It was a small ornamental desk chiseled out of quartz and furnished with a sloping shelf for the hands and wrists of whoever is praying. It also had a raised cushion on which those in prayer could kneel.

Eibbed was now ready for the day as she finished her prayers. "Thank you, Creator. Amen." Getting up from her knees, she stood up in the garb of the male Suppla and walked out of her office to Arooda's desk. "Have all the council members acknowledged they are attending the meeting this morning?"

"Yes, my Suppla" (He kept a formal demeanor.). "Some expressed curiosity about the meeting because they were not due to meet again for another thirty-three days."

"Let them wonder."

"Do you wish me to supervise the preparation of the meal after the meeting?"

"Please do so." She turned, and she proceeded down the long walkway to the council chamber.

2. Conference

The huge conference room had walls and ceiling forming a continuous hemisphere. In the center of the room, the council leaders gathered around a substantial circular table. Most were already seated in their plush chairs when the Suppla appeared in her chair. "Greetings!"

There were murmurs of greeting from all of them followed by silence as they waited for their Suppla to continue. Eibbed let her gaze sweep around the table, taking all of them in. On the current council, there were equal numbers of females and males, though that was not always true.

She spoke with a low, cool, calm, authoritative voice. "Earlier today I watched our planet's salvation video again, as it has become known by that name. How many of you have watched it in the last 50 days?"

Most of the females and about half the males raised a finger. Some of those raising a finger also nodded.

"Good. Most of you have had conversations with our planet's Gaardian, Puz. Many of you have also gotten to know Ooza, who has repeatedly demonstrated her friendship for all Zargadetes, which she promised on the day of Our Creator's visit in that video."

There was murmuring around the table. The older male named Leahcim, who was council leader, raised a finger. "I have seen the video again just a few days ago, and I have had many conversations with Ooza, both over video and in person. Why are we discussing all of this during council time?"

"Have Patience, my old friend." She smiled. "Eleven days ago, Ooza mentioned to me how that, while we were witnessing the salvation of our planet, a Gaardian ship was high above us all and looking down at what was happening. I asked her if there was a video record from their perspective. She has provided us with two videos. Observe!" She touched a triangle in the table in front of her.

A three-dimensional video appeared, and in it, they looked at Pzalop from space. God's hand seemed to come through an unseen opening from the darkness of space. They watched as the hand enveloped the comet, and when the hand disappeared, the comet never reappeared. As murmuring began around the table, the Suppla raised a hand for silence. "Wait! There is more. Here is a video of several Gaardians discussing us and our planet."

Another video segment appeared, showing several Gaardians gathered in a very large meeting area. They saw their Gaardian, named Puz, come onto the platform and address the group telepathically. He was a humanoid without eyes, ears, or mouth. He spoke telepathically to those in the video, and his male voice was heard as the Gaardians heard it.

"I wish I could have been there. A short time ago, Ooza and I went to Pzalop, and she introduced me to The Suppla. We have the beginnings of a good relationship. I see remarkable change in the attitudes of the leaders who were there."

They saw a three-legged humanoid named Qaak [Kuh-ACK], that some on the council had previously met, stand up at his seat.

"I do not wish to sound pessimistic, but many of them will probably forget and revert to their old ways."

Some in the conference room smiled as they saw Puz bow slightly.

"This is probably true, but I believe The Suppla is an adequate and capable leader. During his lifetime, he will keep his people on course. Zargadetes live a long time, and his office is for life. He will probably continue to be in office for another three hundred of Walter's years."

Around the table, they watched as Qaak nodded and sat down, and a large tiger-like creature sat up on her haunches to speak. Kieya's voice was feminine, and the females around the table leaned forward slightly as Kieya spoke.

"Ooza has made a difficult commitment to the Zargadetes. Puz, will this be challenging for you?"

"No. Ooza and I have had long conversations. She will assist me in the same way that Xpraepostq assists Walter from time to time."

The Suppla chuckled as the big cat now purred as she stood fully erect and spoke.

"I would like to hear from Ooza."

The Suppla held up a finger as Ooza rose. "Listen carefully to what Ooza says now," and they watched Ooza walk forward from the middle of the auditorium.

> "I have spent some time analyzing why I made that commitment. Previously, it was not part of my character. It seemed completely natural, however, to say what I did."

At this point, they heard Walter speak for the first time in the video.

> "All that God does, He does well, Ooza. The changes in your heart began when Piatek opened your mind to what I represented to the Quzaks."

There was murmuring in the Suppla's conference room as Ooza nodded and smiled.

> "I think you are right. In recent times, I have developed a much broader sense of what it means to love than I ever dreamed possible."

Several of the Zargadete council members leaned forward as still another Gaardian spoke. This one was more than twice Walter's size, and his physiology was translucent. He spoke with a profoundly deep and low voice.

> "I do not see anything in our briefings with regard to what happened to the comet."

The council members again sat back as the big cat got onto her feet.

> "I did a detailed analysis of the comet when we first detected it. Unlike most comets, it was actually like a vagrant moon and was of considerable density. If it had struck Pzalop in the valley, there was a high probability that the planet would have split or shattered. When the hand disappeared so did the comet, as though they never existed."

A tiny female stood up to speak. She was shorter than nearly all the Zargadetes watching the video.

> "That's somewhat logical. When I first looked at Eiraynay in person, he disappeared. When Eiraynay disappeared, it was as though He was never there. The disappearance of the hand and comet are on a much larger scale, but the phenomena are the same."

As the second three-dimensional video ended, the Suppla spoke quietly but firmly. "I have shared this video with you for a number of reasons. First, is there anyone here who is not in awe of our Creator?"

There was silence, until her old friend spoke again. "As well as I know you, I believe that you have a larger purpose for this meeting than that of discussing the reasons for showing us these videos. I offer a suggestion."

The Suppla smiled. "Proceed."

"I believe that we can discuss many reasons why we needed to see these videos today, but instead of now discussing your reasons — and perhaps some reasons of our own we may think of, — perhaps we can delay that discussion until we are sharing our meal a bit later. Meanwhile, I suggest we talk about what we as a council can do in response to what the Creator has done and is doing. We ourselves have witnessed to the fact that after the Creator created us and all that we perceive, that creation continues."

The Suppla nodded. "Yes. Until the Creator dispensed with that comet, Zargadetes have kept their religious beliefs very private. Now families and communities are watching the so-called 'salvation video' together. Discussions of the Creator are no longer private, though beliefs are still very personal."

A female to the Suppla's right asked, "What are you proposing?"

"If I may, I will use Qaak's favorite word, '*indeed*.' ... I have noticed that no homes are being constructed across the valley where all of us were witnesses to the Creator's glory. I propose we set aside this land as not available for development, that it be a place for quiet reflection, worship, and prayer, and that the Council construct a suitable structure where anyone there can have shelter and sanctuary."

Around the table, there were expressions of approval and support. Leahcim raised a finger. "With your permission I will see to it that a formal proposal is prepared for council approval and yours."

"Good!" She paused and looked around the table. "Now, we have a special guest. ... Ooza?"

The Quzak appeared and relaxed on a chair next to the Suppla. "Greetings!"

There were smiles and greetings all around the table. "Welcome, Ooza." The Suppla surveyed the whole council again. "I've asked Ooza to join us in case any of you have questions about either the videos or any other issues before we have our meal together."

Ooza smiled. "Yes. The only Gaardians in those videos that even some of you have met are Walter, Puz, Qaak, and me. Did any of you have questions about the other Gaardians in the video or about anything they said?"

Around the table, they took turns asking questions.

"Tell us about the big and furry creature."

Ooza smiled. "That's Kieya. She is physically stronger than anyone here by a large measure. She is brilliant, and she is the second oldest Gaardian. Most of the time, I see her as practical and powerful. I have also seen her be very gentle, loving, and nurturing."

"Who is oldest?"

"That is Qaak. He is many times older than all of us here combined."

Another asked, "Who is Piatek? We heard Walter mention a Piatek."

Ooza nodded. "Piatek is not a Gaardian; she is a Quzak, who is an old friend of mine and one of my mentors. She has a special gift where she can see far more than we can perceive ourselves. When she met Qaak for training, she was perplexed because she could see things in him that did not make sense to her at first. In turn, Qaak explained something which all of you will find difficult to believe. When Qaak's planet was destroyed, he was the only survivor. One of his ancestors, however, provided genetic material that is common to both Quzaks and Zargadetes."

"What???" The Suppla stared at her.

"Yes." She paused until murmuring around the table subsided. "Piatek was confused because she herself is unique. She is half Quzak and half Zargadete."

The Suppla and all the council members around the table stared at Ooza silently.

"Are there other questions?" asked Ooza.

The female on the other side of the Suppla asked, "What about the other two Gaardians there? The tall translucent one with the deep voice, and the tiny one, smaller than we are?"

Ooza nodded. The tall one is Doff. He is a gentle creature from a planet that has not yet begun to explore space. He is a mutant with an incredible mind. The tiny one is Xpraepostq, and since her name is difficult to pronounce for almost everyone, most of us call her Pixie, as Walter does. Because of her golden skin, she looks like a human from Walter's planet Earth, but she is not. She is from a planet named Aegeene.

A councilor directly across the table asked, "She mentioned one named Eiraynay that disappeared before her eyes. What was that about?"

Ooza nodded. "In the history of Pzalop, is it not true here that there are prophecies of one who will come and save your planet and its people?"

Ooza paused as several around the table nodded or grunted affirmation. "On her planet, Aegeene, their Savior is known as Eiraynay. On Walter's Earth, their Savior is a human named Jesus Christ. On my planet, our Savior will be known as the Arkaynee, who is not yet publicly known. Here on Pzalop, you can only hope that Zargadetes will see their Savior in your lifetimes."

There was silence. After a few moments, she turned to the Suppla. "If we eat now, I can remain before going on to other duties."

"Good. ... Councilors, let us adjourn to our meal."

+ + +

At Ooza's spherical base, invisibly in orbit above Quzak, Piatek was watching the Ooza's meeting on a monitor. "Piatek to Steve: Will you please come into my office?"

A few seconds later, Steve appeared at the door. "Hi, Piatek, what's up?"

Piatek smiled. "I've always been amused by that expression of yours, 'what's up.' It is a uniquely human idiomatic expression."

"Really? I had not thought about it."

"It is of little importance. ... I have been watching Ooza at her meeting on Pzalop. Ooza and the Suppla communicate very well with each other. I believe I will probably meet the Suppla soon. There is something within her that I've never seen before. Have you met the Suppla?"

"No."

"Did Ooza tell you why she was going to Pzalop today?"

"Yes. As you know, she has a commitment to help the Zargadetes. She and Puz are working together to help their culture in transition since the planet was relocated to another galaxy."

"I understand. ... I have another question. Do you have more volunteers who want to work with our Gaardian team?"

"Yes. I have quite a large number in our database. I will be bringing some of them here in a few days."

"Good. Thank you, Steve. I am going to examine what is happening on Pzalop more carefully when Ooza returns from meeting with the Suppla."

3. Memorial

Forty Pzalop days later, Eibbed was at her Suppla's desk. Dressed as the Suppla, she turned and stared out the large portal behind her desk. There were no real pressing needs on her agenda that day, and she was restless. A chime sounded, and she touched a triangle near the edge of her desk. "Yes?"

Arooda's spoke formally. "Council member Leahcim wishes a few minutes of your time. May I send him in?"

"Tell my old friend, I will see him momentarily. I'll signal you, Arooda."

"As you wish."

Eibbed stood up and went to the piece of furniture unique on Pzalop. Eibbed knelt on the cushion of the prie-dieu and closed her eyes. After a few moments, she stood and touched a triangle badge on her chest. "Send in Leahcim, Arooda."

"Yes."

The Suppla was returning to her desk to sit down when Leahcim walked in. "Good morning, my Suppla."

"Good morning my old friend. What can I do for you today?"

"With your approval, we will open the devotional area of The Creator's Park to everyone tomorrow. Do you have time to inspect it today?"

"Yes. Arooda has made provision in my schedule in anticipation of this. I am pleased you have achieved this so quickly, Leahcim. I will meet you there after the mid-day meal."

"Good." Leahcim smiled. "Thank you."

"Yes, Leahcim. Later."

He turned to go, and he was gone as quickly as he came in.

Arooda walked in a moment later. "May I join you and Leahcim at The Creator's Park?"

"Of course, but why?" She looked at him curiously.

"Do you remember when Walter first told us about the Earth-origin piece of furniture which you have had copied for your office?" He pointed at the prie-dieu.

"Yes."

"You talked about it with Leahcim many days ago."

"I remember." She looked at Arooda curiously.

"When designing the devotional structures in The Creator's Park, he included a variation on that prie-dieu."

"Indeed."

"I am telling you because I think it will please Leahcim very much if you take note of it and perhaps thank him for doing so. He has worked very hard on this for you as his old friend and Suppla, as well as for all of Pzalop."

She nodded. "That is an excellent idea. You can also put it in my notes regarding items for future speeches. I may want to prepare a video address regarding the park for this evening or tomorrow."

"I thought you might want to do that, and I have placed a draft in your personal file you can consider later."

She smiled broadly at her secret mate. "You know me very well, Arooda. I love you so much. We will discuss it this evening before we sleep, shall we?"

Arooda smiled. "Yes." He paused. "I suggest that you invite the other members of the inner council to the park today, including all of those that were at the meeting when we first talked about the park."

"Excellent." She paused. "Now, I want to conference with Walter and perhaps Ooza. I want privacy until our meal."

"Very well." Arooda smiled, turned, and went out to his office.

Eibbed went to her desk and sat down. Reaching under the edge of her desk, she pressed a hidden panel. A few moments later, Walter appeared three-dimensionally to the right of her desk. "Greetings!" Walter smiled. "It is good to see you. What can I do for you?"

The Suppla nodded. "Greetings! It is good to see you as well. May I have some of your time this morning?"

"Certainly. By your tone of voice and facial expression, I believe you are not consulting me concerning a crisis or other pressing need. What is your concern?"

"Shortly after mid-day here, Arooda and I are going to the area where the comet nearly struck Pzalop. Although Zargadetes have built homes and other structures up to the ridge surrounding the area, nothing has been built there until recently. One of my council members, an old friend named Leahcim, has supervised the construction of a park and devotional area called The Creator's Park."

Walter nodded. "That is very interesting. If you have video of the area, I would like to see it."

"That can be arranged, but that is not why I am communicating with you."

"Go on, please."

"As I previously indicated, Arooda and I are going there after our midday meal. We will be meeting with Leahcim and the other members of the inner council there. There will be no formal agenda. I think it would be appropriate to have one or more Gaardians there as well."

Walter was thoughtful. "Have you communicated with either Puz or Ooza?"

"No. I wanted to consult with you first. Qaak has already met all the inner council members, and though they have never met her, some are interested in meeting Kieya."

Walter chuckled. "Kieya is intriguing to a number of beings, particularly to humanoids. Qaak is retired, and he does what he chooses. When he wants to take his wife Jody somewhere with him, I excuse her from her duties at my base."

"That is interesting. I did not know that Qaak had a mate. I know that you have Debbie, and that the two of you have a son named Joseph. I also know that Puz does not desire to have a mate. Do Ooza and Kieya have mates?"

"Ooza has a man from Earth as her mate, and he is in command of her base when she is not there. Kieya has not taken a mate in many centuries. If you wish, I will transmit this conversation to all of those you have mentioned. I will leave it to them as to whether they will meet with you after midday today." He paused. "Please excuse me for a few minutes, and I will speak with Debbie." His image vanished.

On Earth's moon, Walter was sitting in front of the fireplace in the lounge. "Frank?"

The android appeared nearby. "Yes?"

"Transmit the conversation I just had with the Suppla to Qaak, Kieya, Ooza, and Puz."

"Done." The android vanished.

Getting up, Walter went out into the atrium and turned towards the offices. Walking down the hallway, he stood in the doorway and spoke to Belinda, his base commander. "Hi! I just got a g-mail from the Suppla on Pzalop."

"Is everything okay?"

"Yes. Do I have anything pressing that needs to be done over the next several hours?"

"No, but Keeta and Ken want to have dinner with us here this evening. We have not talked with them for weeks. Kenkee is as mature as a young adult now, so they can leave him there on Gaardian."

"That sounds good. The Suppla on Pzalop wants a few Gaardians there at the opening of a place called The Creator's Park. It is located where we stood when God dealt with the comet."

"Really!" Belinda beamed. "I've watched the video of that several times."

Walter nodded. "I'm going down the hall to check with Debbie and see if she wants to go."

"Okay." Belinda watched Walter turn and continue down the hallway.

At the end, Walter paused beside a large portal looking out on the moonscape. Debbie saw him through her doorway and came to join him. "Hi!" She gave him a peck on the cheek. "What are you doing over here in the land of the working?"

Walter grinned. "Slumming, I guess. In a couple of hours, I'm going to head out to Pzalop to see the opening of a park. It's located where we all stood when God dealt with the comet."

"A park?"

"Yes. It's called The Creator's Park. Do you want to come with me?"

"Sure! Could we drop Joseph off on Gaardian? Kenkee has wanted to play with him."

"Good idea." He paused, as they saw Belinda and Jody walking towards them. "What's going on?"

"Hi Walter," said Jody. "Qaak has g-mailed me about the park, and he wants me to go with him. Belinda wants to tag along because she's never been to Pzalop. Will this be too much of a crowd?"

Walter laughed. "It sounds like Gaardians are going to have quite a party, doesn't it? I think that the park is probably so big that if we brought three times as many people, no one would notice." He looked at his watch. "Frank?"

The android appeared. "Yes?"

"Several of us are going to Pzalop in about two and quarter hours. Belinda is going also. You'll be in full monitoring mode."

"Very well." The android vanished.

"We'll meet in the atrium at 3:30. Okay?"

They all nodded, and the three women turned and went back to work.

"G-mail to the Suppla on Pzalop."

On Pzalop, Eibbed was talking with Arooda at his desk when a chime sounded. Arooda looked at his monitor and pointed towards the Suppla's office. "That's a g-mail coming in for you at your desk."

Eibbed nodded and went quickly back into her office. Sitting down she said, "Yes, Walter."

Walter once more appeared next to her. "Hello again. There will be several of us joining you at the park. I need to know how many of them you would like to have mingle with you, because most of us can simply walk around and enjoy the park as other visitors there."

"Who is coming?"

"My wife Debbie will be joining us, and also from our base for the first time will be my Base Commander, Belinda, who has never been to Pzalop."

"I have not heard you speak of her before."

"She is my oldest friend. Furthermore, Qaak and Jody are coming with us. I am quite certain that Ooza and her mate, Steve, will be there. I have not yet heard whether Puz or Kieya is coming. I am sure that they will notify you themselves."

The Suppla nodded. "While you were consulting with Debbie and the others I heard from them, and both will be there. I have already notified the entire governing council of the gathering. I have told them that others will be there from other planets, and that most will come because they are curious. I have also told council members and their mates that there are to be no formal conversations. Everyone is to mingle with one another and maintain an attitude of respect for the park and what it symbolizes."

"Excellent. Once more, you have proven yourself a very capable leader. Before departing, I will inform the others on my base and the other Gaardians regarding what is intended for the afternoon. Is there anything else we need to discuss?

The Suppla smiled. "No, thank you, Walter. We will see you soon."

"Until then."

"Until then."

+ + +

Six weeks before this day, Leahcim was at an excavation site about two kilometers from The Creator's Park being developed. He sat on a rock facing seven minors, one of whom was the leader of the crew. Leahcim spoke calmly, with the assurance that comes from being a respected elder council member. "I got your message. As I understand it, you have made an unusual discovery."

"Yes. This area is normally mined for low-sulfur porous carbon for fuel. At times, we have come across small quantities of more valuable material, but never before has anyone made a discovery like this one."

"I understand you have found a crystalline form of beryllium and aluminum. How much have you found?"

"It is nearly continuous from here to The Creator's Park location, about thirty meters beneath the surface, about 50 meters wide and deep."

Leahcim's eyes grew larger. "Extraordinary! That is much more massive than anything I could have imagined."

"Yes. It seems to flow in the direction taken by the comet that nearly destroyed Pzalop."

Leahcim was thoughtful. "Can you cut pieces large enough for construction purposes?"

"Yes. A building made of this crystalline material would truly be exceptional and distinctive."

"I agree." Leahcim smiled. "Have you examined my list of construction materials for the park structure?"

"Yes. That is why we wanted to meet with you in person. We think the structure should be much larger. The current plans call for something the size of a large family dwelling. We are convinced that there is enough material available to make a structure at least ten times that size."

Again, Leahcim's eyes grew larger. "I'm not sure that such would be appropriate."

Suddenly, there was a chorus of disagreement from all the miners. The leader held up his hand for quiet. "We want to exalt the creator who gave us this crystal material. We are ready to mine it day and night, and we are agreeable to help with the obviously difficult construction using crystalline material."

Leahcim stood up. "I understand. I will present revised plans to the Suppla. You will hear from me tomorrow." He turned and walked towards the waiting hovercraft.

For the next six weeks, construction proceeded at a pace not previously seen anywhere on the planet. Leahcim did not know that in all of Gaardian space, what they were going to build would be truly remarkable.

4. The Creator's Park

Over their mid-day meal, Eibbed and Arooda discussed how rapidly The Creator's Park had been developed. Now, just outside the government complex, the Suppla and Arooda stepped into a waiting hovercraft. Eibbed touched a green triangle and spoke. "Take us to The Creator's Park and land where the water-flow enters the valley." They sat down, and the vehicle began to move. It quickly gained altitude, and they could softly hear the air rush faster as it gained speed.

Arooda shifted so that he could look at her as he spoke. "Many miners have donated time and labor to this project."

"Leahcim has reported this to me. Some time ago, the minors discovered a large vein of a nearly clear crystalline compound of aluminum and beryllium. It is almost as clear as the quartz *prie-dieu* in my office."

"Is it rare?"

"Previous discoveries of this material have been small. It seems useful for ornamentation like jewelry. Its coloration seems to vary with the light striking it. I will ask Walter about its presence on other worlds."

The soft sound of flight was now decreasing, and as the hovercraft descended to the edge of a small river, they could see the strikingly beautiful park that had been developed. As the door opened, they strode rapidly on a path through the foliage towards the center of the park. "We are early, and I want to see as much as possible before all the others get here," Eibbed said quietly.

"Good," said Arooda, his voice low, "I would love to stroll and hold your hand, but we don't dare out here in public, do we?"

Eibbed glanced down at her beloved and smiled. "No, but we can make up for it this evening."

"Yes." He paused. "These tall plants that have been transplanted here are truly beautiful."

"Agreed. They are some of The Creator's best work!"

As they came to a clearing at the center of the park, they both stopped and stared. Before them stood what Earth's Walt Disney would have described as a crystalline castle. "This is stunning. It is magnificent!" They were awestruck.

Arooda nodded. "Look how the water-flow proceeds under it and beyond."

The structure was more than 100 meters away, and still it was imposing in size. They walked towards it on a path surrounded by carefully manicured plants. Then they stepped upon onto one of the bridges and went inside. The ceilings, floors, doorframes, and window frames were a deep purple, but the walls were a cascade of subtle and constantly changing nearly transparent color. They did not climb to the upper levels. On the main floor, there was one very large triangular room, surrounded by nine smaller rooms. Each room included padded kneeling areas.

Eibbed and Arooda had been standing near the center of the largest room for about five minutes when Walter, Debbie, and Belinda appeared next to them. "Greetings!" Walter was smiling.

Together, the Suppla and her assistant said, "Greetings!"

Walter gestured towards Debbie. "I'm sure you remember my wife, Debbie."

"Hello again!" said Debbie as she shook their hands. "This is Belinda, Walter's dear friend from childhood."

Belinda was beaming. "It is so nice to meet you! This is so beautiful! How long has this been here?"

The Suppla was relaxed. "This is the first day for the public. After design modifications, it has been in actual construction for about 35 days. We are very pleased with it as well."

They began walking about in the large room. Walter touched one of the outer walls with curiosity. "From a distance I thought this was quartz, but it is not."

The Suppla went and stood beside him. "Yes, minors discovered a large vein of this crystalline material just recently. Until now, it was rare and used only for personal ornamentation."

"On Earth it is also very rare. There it is called alexandrite, and it is used for jewelry. It is quite common on Gaardian, but there it is in the form of another isotope. Both are chemically beryllium aluminate." He paused. "Suppla, would you permit me to send a small sample to Gaardian for analysis?"

The Suppla chuckled. "I always appreciate your sense of courtesy, Walter. You could have just taken as much as you wanted without asking."

"Yes, but that is not my way, nor is it yours."

She nodded. "Please proceed."

Walter's ring subtly shimmered for a brief moment. "I have taken a sample from the mine, and not from this building. I have not previously seen a building composed of gemstone material. It is amazing. Please extend my compliments to the architect."

"I could do that, but why not tell him yourself?" She pointed at her old friend Leahcim, who was approaching. "Leahcim, I believe you remember Walter, the Gaardian Convener."

"I am pleased to see you again." The old male smiled.

Walter extended a hand. "It is good to see you again as well. I understand that you designed this structure."

"Yes. I had not intended it to be this large, but the minors wanted to supply material for a structure that would glorify The Creator... It is significantly larger in area than our Suppla's main building, when all levels are included."

"It is quite stunning!" Walter gestured towards a wall. "I was just telling the Suppla that the crystalline material of your walls is also rare on Earth but is common on Gaardian. I have sent a small sample to the planet for analysis."

Leahcim nodded. "The vein of this crystal follows the direction of approach of the comet and ends under where we stand. The miners believe it appropriate that the building be made almost entirely of the crystal."

The Suppla nodded. "Leahcim, I am most pleased with what you have accomplished, especially your inclusion of the cushioned areas for prayer."

He nodded. "I'm glad you are pleased."

Belinda approached them. "Debbie and I noticed that many others are arriving. We are going to walk some of the pathways of the park, and Jody and Qaak are going to join us."

Walter smiled. "Excellent. I will see all of you later."

As Belinda walked away, Walter could see Qaak outside. There was a movement on Walter's right, and his eyes came to rest on Kieya. As she approached, Walter gestured towards his friend and introduced her. "Zargadete friends, I would like to introduce my Gaardian friend, Kieya."

"Greetings to everyone," the big cat purred softly. "I am pleased to visit your planet again." She turned to Leahcim and sat back on her haunches, facing him. Leahcim's mouth was hanging open slightly. "I understand that your name is Leahcim, and that you designed this magnificent structure. I extend my profoundest congratulations to you."

"Thank you. It was a labor of love for Our Creator, my friend the Suppla, and for Pzalop."

Kieya purred. "That is an excellent and appropriately diplomatic response. I understand why you are such a valued member of the council."

The Suppla and Arooda smiled slightly. Arooda stepped closer. "Excuse me. My name is Arooda."

"Yes, Arooda, I know you to be the capable assistant to the Suppla."

"Please forgive me if I ask a personal favor."

The cat kept purring. "I can entertain a favor, personal or not."

"Thank you. Many of us are intrigued with you. I suppose it is because you are the only non-humanoid we have seen that communicates intelligently. Will you please tell us a little about your planet and your species?"

"I am from a planet in a galaxy that your astronomers have not yet seen. We call ourselves felidacas." Others began gathering around them as Kieya spoke. "We are the dominant species of my planet, and we have social structures and norms just as you do. Our young are called tats, and I had several tats when I had a mate."

"Ooza told the inner council that you are very strong."

The big cat purred more loudly for a moment. "I enjoy Ooza. At this moment, she is conversing with other council members outside of this structure." She paused. "Ooza is correct in saying that I am strong. My species can also move and climb quickly."

The Suppla lifted a finger. "I am admiring your fur."

"Thank you. Since you are Suppla, I will allow you to touch it."

As Eibbed touched Kieya's fur, her eyes closed for a moment. "Kieya, I must confer with you at another time."

Her purr stopped briefly, and then it resumed. "Yes, I understand." She paused. "I will go to your home at mid-day in seven of your days. Will that be acceptable?"

Eibbed turned to Arooda, who responded, "I will clear the Suppla's schedule for the seventh day after this one."

The Suppla smiled. "Thank you." She paused as her gaze swept the room. She spoke more forcefully, "Please, everyone. This is a day for reflection and small conversations. Let us disburse to enjoy the park." Subtly, she gestured to Arooda, and they walked towards a far exterior wall where no one else was standing. Eibbed knelt down by the wall, and in a moment, Arooda joined her. The room grew quiet. When Eibbed closed her eyes, Arooda noticed and closed his as well. He did not see his beloved Eibbed begin to glow softly.

Outside, lying in a grass-like area, Kieya saw them. "Kieya to Walter: Are you observing the Suppla?"

Walter was about 50 meters away, sitting under a tall plant. "Yes, Kieya, I see." Around Walter, everything began to fade into the familiar glow Walter had experienced many times. Years earlier, the first few times Walter experienced this, he was frightened and nervous. Now he was at peace, as he heard the low rumble of The Creator's voice.

> **"Walter, you are my prophet from Earth. Now I am making Eibbed my prophet on Pzalop. She will not audibly hear my voice or see my glory as you do, but she will know my presence and hear my still small voice as you did when you were a pastor on Earth."**

"Eibbed is meeting with Kieya in seven days."

> **"I am going to make Kieya a prophet to the felidacas, just as I am going to make Eibbed a prophet here to the Zargadetes. In seven days, Kieya and Eibbed will begin meeting together to encourage one another in their separate faith journeys. You must teach them what it means to be faithful to me."**

"How do you want me to teach them?"

> **"Be their pastor. You have always been a good teacher. I gave you this gift."**

"Thank you, Lord."

The glow faded. Walter opened his eyes to see the Suppla and her assistant getting up from their knees. He heard Kieya's voice as she padded silently towards him.

"Has The Creator told you anything about this, Walter?"

"Yes. I will tell all of you about it later." He paused. "Walter to Gaardian: Have you analyzed the sample of beryllium aluminate that I sent to you?"

Telepathically, both Walter and Kieya heard the planet's voice in their minds. "Yes. It a similar isotope as is in Gaardian rings and in my core. Chemically and atomically, it is identical, but its subatomic particle composition is slightly different. I must continue to analyze. Will you be visiting me soon?"

"Yes," answered both Kieya and Walter.

"I will endeavor to have more information for you when you are here."

As Kieya purred, Walter nodded and said, "Thank you. We will see you soon, Gaardian."

5. Madness

Joseph and five other human children were playing with Kenkee outside the nursery and guest quarters on Gaardian. Kenkee was now nearly fully grown, but he was still young and inexperienced with life. He tried in vain to teach the other children how to fly as he could, and they had fun with their failures, just as he did with his gliding demonstrations.

Debbie and the other parents were nearby, swimming in a lake about the size of a football stadium. They were enjoying food from a barbeque where food was prepared over self-replenishing charcoal. It appeared just like many areas on Earth except the perimeter was lined with multicolored vegetation reaching into a sky tinged with green. At Walter's suggestion, Gaardian had planted vegetation similar to what is found in the World Heritage Park on South Island in New Zealand on Earth.

Inside the nearby building, Walter, Ooza, Puz, Qaak, and Kieya were gathered in the lounge. The primary subject of the day was Pzalop and the Zargadetes. Invisibly, Gaardian was telepathically part of the conversations. The planet was updating its findings on the sample of alexandrite Walter had sent for analysis. "The sample contains subatomic particles that are completely unique. The Creator has done something that is new to us."

Qaak's eyes glowed for a moment. "Are there no parallels from any other galaxy in Gaardian space?"

"No. This isotope from Pzalop does not have the same properties as does the beryllium aluminate within me and in Gaardian rings."

Kieya's purring stopped. "Does this mean that none of its properties are the same except in the area of light transmission?"

The planet was emphatic. "It does mean that, and it has the same number of protons, neutrons, and electrons, but it has at least one other property which I cannot analyze or explain. Kieya, you experienced it when the Suppla touched your fur."

Kieya was motionless and silent for several moments, and then she began to purr loudly. "Yes! It was a unique experience." She paused but kept purring loudly. "When the Suppla touched my fur, I experienced his entire being like it was an extension of my own."

Qaak's eyes glowed brightly. "You could read her thoughts?"

"No! I was reading his – or rather her – entire being."

Qaak's voice became animated. "This is unique! Gaardian, are you associating Kieya's experience with this isotope with which that structure is built?"

"It is a highly logical conclusion. There were no other new variables present reported to me."

Kieya then purred softly and gently. "Walter and I observed something else. Walter?"

He nodded. "Yes. We saw Eibbed kneeling in prayer with Arooda beside her, and she had a soft but discernable glow."

Puz leaned forward. "Have you heard from The Creator, Walter?"

Walter looked up and closed his eyes for a moment. "Yes." He paused much longer. "Yes.' He paused again briefly. " you have read Earth's Bible several times. Do you recall God saying, 'Behold. I make all things new.'?"

"It is said near the end of the final book called Revelation, as I recall. Why do you ask?"

"God is doing something new with you, and also with the Suppla."

"Why will the Creator do this with me?"

"I do not know why, but I know that you are going to become a prophet for God to the felidacas. God is also calling the Suppla to be a prophet to the Zargadetes."

"Of this you are certain?" asked Qaak quietly.

"There is no doubt. I heard The Creator's voice. I am to teach the two of you what it means to be faithful prophets. The Suppla knew it that day, though only on an instinctive level."

The planet spoke precisely. "The Creator does everything well and does not make mistakes, but I do not understand this."

Walter smiled. "Neither do I, but I have learned to trust God with anything and everything."

Puz quivered slightly in amazement. "I wonder. What implications this might this have for other Gaardians?"

Walter nodded, and then he shook his head. "I think it is much too soon for us to consider such things. I do have a request for you, Qaak."

"Indeed?"

"Indeed! On the Suppla's inner council, there is an old Zargadete named Leahcim. I would like you to visit him in his sleep as soon as possible, to evaluate him as a possible Gaardian. I do not wish to use Asayak for this."

Puz's voice was very animated. "I remember Leahcim! He is highly intelligent and extraordinarily wise. After seeing what he built there in The Creator's Park, I would assume that he is also extremely talented and creative."

Walter grinned. "Yes! Ooza, you were there along with the rest of us except Gaardian itself. Have you thought about the fact that the structure we have all admired was both designed and built in less than forty days?"

There was utter silence as Ooza began to smile. "That structure is – in your Earth's meters – 100 meters on each side horizontally and more than 50 meters vertically, made almost entirely of the crystalline material we have discussed. It is amazing even by Gaardian standards. It has beautifully designed staircases and a chamber for lifting Zargadetes up and down the structure with the power of the water-flow underneath the structure!" She paused to consider. "Did anyone notice how the cushions were made? The covers were made of a cloth woven of finely drawn platinum. The fact that the structure was even designed and built so quickly in that time frame, is phenomenal by any standard."

"Indeed." Qaak's eyes glowed steadily. "That kind of intellect and creativity is rare throughout Gaardian space. I will visit his dreams."

"This will be good, Qaak. Now that you are retired, you are not going to be doing as much training of prospective Gaardians. This time it is especially appropriate, however, due to your genetic ties to both Pzalop and Quzak."

"I met Leahcim that training day on Pzalop in the Suppla's quarters. He was interested in my physiology, particularly in how I fold my third leg to form a stool."

"I used to wonder about that myself!" Qaak's wife, Jody, walked into the lounge as she spoke. "I asked Gaardian if any of you might be hungry from some old-fashioned Texas barbeque. It suggested that I come in and drag all of you out to the pool."

Most of them chuckled. Walter asked, "Gaardian used *those* words?"

She laughed. "Maybe not exactly. Come on, Qaak, I won't eat until you join me."

"Very well."

All of them got up and began heading outside to the pool and their families.

Just outside, a chime sounded, and Frank appeared. "There is a situation you should handle yourself."

Walter turned towards him. "What is it, Frank?"

"That deranged fanatic in Asia with whom we have dealt previously has launched a missile towards the United States."

Walter scowled. "You're right. I'll handle it." As Frank vanished, Walter called out, "Debbie we have a crisis on Earth. A nuclear missile has been launched, and I'm headed home. "Do you want to come, or do you want to stay here with Joseph?"

She thoughtfully hesitated hardly a moment. "Let's leave Joseph here. I'm coming with you."

Debbie walked over and took Walter's hand. The others at the pool were waving at them when they vanished.

As Debbie and Walter appeared in the atrium at his Moon base, he looked down at his Gaardian ring, which was shimmering very subtly. "Attention, everyone. This is an emergency. We are now in mission mode. John, when all hands are on board *The Grace*, put her into uncloaked orbit above the United States, and wait there for instructions. That is all." Walter and Debbie vanished to the hanger deck aboard *The Grace while on the base everyone moved rapidly.*

"Debbie, are you up for some improvisation?"

"Sure!"

"You know how to fly a shuttle. I want you to take that shuttle," he pointed outside a portal, "and fly it at the highest speed with which you're comfortable to Washington, D.C. Go fast enough to create a fireball and a sizeable sonic boom."

"Sounds like fun! Then what?"

"The President is currently in the situation room in the White House at the moment, so land on the lawn, singeing it probably. As you step out, stride directly towards the font door. Let Frank guide you immediately to the President. Nothing and no one can stop you, and even if they try, just ignore them. Frank will do the rest. Do not identify yourself. Let him assume that you are a Gaardian, even if officially you are not. When you get into the Situation Room, walk right up to him, and look him in the eye. Tell him to cool off as politely as you can muster and be in character. Tell him to let the Gaardian handle it, or something to that effect. Use your good judgment. Then wait there with him until I get there."

"This is going to be almost fun, but I'll keep a straight face though. What will you be doing?"

"I'm headed for the enemy's camp in another shuttle, and I won't be subtle."

"God be with you!"

"The same with you!" She kissed him and got into the shuttle. He vanished into the other one. Moments later, as he entered the atmosphere at around 50,000 kilometers per hour, Walter's ring shimmered, and Frank appeared in the passenger seat. "Stay with Debbie and help her as necessary. She has her script to follow."

"Right."

"If I need you, I'll let you know. Go!"

The android vanished.

"Lord, you know my thoughts. I trust you. If you want me to do something different, please tell me now."

The air around the shuttle was glowing brightly, though the shuttle itself was cool and comfortable. The man who had ordered the launch of the missile was in a bunker below a large military base. On the base were thousands of troops, all armed, anticipating any effort to stop what was happening.

The shuttle radiated so much heat, that hundreds of troops ran away as Walter landed. As he stepped out of the shuttle, thousands of arms were cocked. Walter looked around at them, and they all collapsed to the ground, unconscious.

As he walked towards the entrance to the bunker, the doors flew off, and he walked inside. The guards inside by the elevator and stairwell were already unconscious. As Walter looked down, his ring shimmered, and he could see his target below. His ring shimmered again, and he dropped vertically until he was standing in front of the deranged leader who created the mess.

When he saw Walter, he yelled for the others to protect him, but none of them moved. In the same tone of voice, he yelled at Walter. "Get out of here! This is my base. This is my country! You don't belong here!"

Looking at an electronic display, the two of them could see that the missile was about ten minutes from its target. Walter calmly went and sat in the chair that the leader had occupied a few minutes earlier. Quietly, he said, "Everyone, sit down. Let's talk." Walter's ring shimmered, and everyone but the leader sat down. A chair near a wall slid rapidly across the floor, slamming into the back of the leader's legs, and he sat down.

Walter let his gaze slowly scan everyone in the room. "This is unacceptable." He paused. "The United States has sufficient missiles and air power to level this country without risking a single one of its soldiers. You are launching this attack on the assumption that they will not do that because they do not want to kill innocent civilians. As Gaardian, I have no such concern. Did you honestly believe that those soldiers above us could stop me from being here? Turn on your cameras above us, and you will see your army."

Someone reached to a panel, and the display showed the soldiers on the ground. The leader started to speak, but Walter snapped his fingers, and the leader was silent. The display screen was once more showing the path of the missile and its location. Walter looked at the others. "I have previously discussed your leader's insane plans with him, but he has never been willing to listen." His ring shimmered, and he pointed to the screen, where there was no signal indicating the missile's existence any longer. "As you can see, your missile is no longer on target. The men and women in this room have a decision to make."

A woman dressed in a general's uniform at the other end of the table asked, "What are our choices?"

"You have three choices, and you have five minutes in which to decide. As a first choice, your leader vanishes and is never seen again. Your second choice is this!" A cylindrical object with a tapered end appeared behind the leader's chair. "This is the warhead that was on the missile you launched. As your second choice, the warhead is detonated right here as soon as I leave."

"And our third choice?"

"Your leader is permanently deposed, and your country seeks peace with all of those whom he declared to be your enemies. You now have five minutes to decide. If you do not decide within that time frame, I will leave, and that warhead will detonate."

"What if we don't like your choices?"

"You are now wasting time." Walter looked at a watch that had appeared on his wrist.

The general took a sheet of paper from her notebook and tore it into pieces. "Each of you put a one, two, or three on your slip of paper and pass it back to me." Some of them began to grumble. "Silence! You vote with a number."

In less than two minutes, all of them passed their slips of paper to the general. She began separating them, and one slip was by itself, while the other slips were in a pile. "Lieutenant, double-check my findings."

A man from across the table went to her side and quickly checked each slip. "It's conclusive," he said. "One vote for our leader to disappear, and all the others to make peace."

The general stood up, and came over to Walter, who stood up. She extended her hand. "Thank you, Gaardian. I will do my best to see to it that we abide by this decision we have made. We have to plan strategy as to how to go about this." She shook Walter's hand. "You have my word. Would you please dispose of this warhead?"

It vanished. Walter nodded to her, and then he disappeared as well

+ + +

Walter appeared in the White House situation room, standing next to Debbie. "Hello!"

They murmured hellos. "Mr. President, everyone, the missile and its warhead are gone. Permit me to show a video."

A video of what happened appeared three-dimensionally above the center of the table. At the end, there was some applause.

Walter held up his hand and spoke directly to the president. "Mr. President, I took this action because I did not want the precedent established for this kind of behavior to be acceptable on our planet. If you or any of your minions try to score political points with what has happened today, you *personally* will have to assume the responsibility for the significant very negative consequences."

Walter looked at Debbie. They nodded, and they vanished back to *The Grace*. The two shuttles reappeared on the hanger deck there a moment later, as they reappeared on the bridge. John spoke loudly, "Captain on the bridge!"

"At ease, ladies and gentlemen. Everyone on *The Grace* and support personnel on base can stand down. Thank you for being available up here in orbit if needed and on base. Debbie, Belinda, and I will be back on base tomorrow morning." After vanishing from the bridge of *The Grace*, they reappeared by the pool on Gaardian. They both had stories to tell.

6. Prophets

Eibbed and Arooda were sitting comfortably in their living quarters and talking when Kieya appeared. "Greetings, my friends! purred Kieya. She padded over closer to them. "Tell me, Eibbed, have you been feeling like The Creator was communicating with you?"

She was not easily shocked, but Eibbed's mouth hung open for a moment. "How did you know?"

"We'll talk about that in a moment. Why do you suppose that on impulse, you said you needed to meet with me? If you are wondering this, you should know that I have the same challenge."

Arooda looked at her. "I wondered about that, but at the time I was in the role of personal assistant and not that of your mate. Your impulse to make this appointment happened momentarily after you touched Kieya's fur."

Eibbed nodded. "Yes. Kieya, you have wonderfully soft fur, but when I touched it, I felt like I was praying. It was totally illogical."

The big cat purred softly. "When you touched me, I felt at peace, which is also illogical. In your office, Eibbed, I have observed a *prie-dieu*. Do both of you use it?"

They nodded. Arooda looked at her, and Eibbed spoke first. "I do not pray at a fixed time or under certain circumstances. It is entirely spontaneous."

Arooda nodded again. "It is the same with me." He turned towards Kieya. "I have a question regarding your presence at The Creator's Park and the special structure there. Was your praise of Leahcim rehearsed?"

Kieya's purring stopped and then restarted. "No. I have seldom had experiences quite like being in that structure. I had a similar experience at the wedding of Ooza and Steve when The Creator spoke to the entire gathering in an audible voice."

Arooda was now silent, but Eibbed became more animated. "I also had a strange feeling there at the park when Arooda and I knelt to pray. For a few minutes, I lost my sense of where and who I was."

The big cat purred more loudly. "That confirms something that Walter and I observed."

"Something both of you observed?"

"Yes. Your body glowed slightly."

"Really! I was not aware of that!"

Arooda shook his head. "I did not see it."

The big cat shifted her weight slightly. "Eibbed and I need to talk alone for a while, Arooda, and we need to pray together. I have a suggestion."

Eibbed nodded. "Yes?"

"I suggest that you and I go to the structure in The Creator's Park and find a room where we can talk with each other and pray together privately. Simultaneously, I have something else to suggest for you, Arooda."

"Yes?"

"I am told you are an excellent cook, and I would like to sample the fruits of your talent. I say 'fruits' in the figurative sense because I primarily consume animal flesh and other proteins. Vegetables and fruits are acceptable as edible accessories. We could eat shortly after mid-day."

Arooda smiled. I would be happy to prepare a meal for us. Would you like me to order a hovercraft to transport you to the structure?"

"That will not be necessary. Since Eibbed trusts me, we will avail ourselves of Gaardian transportation. Eibbed, would you please place your hand on top of my head?"

She nodded as she got up from her chair. "Thank you, Arooda. We will see you at mealtime." She put her hand on Kieya's head, and they vanished.

They reappeared in a triangular room at the top of a spire. The room was smaller than the others they had seen further below. Each of the three walls was about five meters long, with a kneeling pad the entire length of each wall. At the center of the room was the top of a spiral staircase. For the first several minutes, they simply gazed in all directions because from this height of nearly fifty meters, the horizon was far away.

Eibbed sat on one of the kneeling cushions with her back against the wall, as Kieya sat down as well, facing her. "I have noticed that your purr varies significantly. Can you explain why?"

"Humanoids like yourself express your emotions through your voice, your body language, and your facial expressions. Felidacas have variations in their purr rather than body language." She began to purr. "I am going to share a video with you that probably you will find very helpful."

"Proceed." Eibbed saw the Gaardians gathered in the lounge on Gaardian. She heard Kieya first.

> "When the Suppla touched my fur, I experienced his, or rather *her*, entire being like it was an extension of my own."
>
> Qaak's eyes glowed brightly.

Eibbed leaned forward to look closely.

> "You could read her thoughts?"
>
> "No! I was reading *her* – her entire being.
>
> Qaak's voice became animated.

Eibbed sat back.

> "This is truly unique! Gaardian, are you associating Kieya's experience with the isotope with which that structure is built?"
>
> "It is a logical conclusion. There were no other new variables present that were reported to me."

Kieya's purred softly and gently, both in the tower and in the video.

> "Walter and I observed something else. Walter?"

"Yes. We saw Eibbed kneeling in prayer with Arooda beside her, and she had a soft but discernable glow."

Puz leaned forward.

So did Eibbed in the tower.

"Have you heard from The Creator, Walter?"

Kieya watched Eibbed with mild amusement. The Suppla leaned even further forward towards Walter in the video.

In it, Walter looked up and closed his eyes for a moment.

"Yes. ... Yes, He did. Kieya, you have read Earth's Bible several times. Do you recall God saying, 'Behold. I make all things new.'?"

"It is said near the end of the final book called Revelation, as I recall. Why do you ask?"

"God is going to do something new with you."

"Why me?"

"I do not know why, but I know that you are going to become a prophet, at least for your felidacas. God is also calling the Suppla to be a prophet."

"Of this you are certain?" asked Qaak quietly.

"There is no doubt. I heard The Creator's voice. I am to teach the two of you what it means to be a faithful prophet. The Suppla knew it that day, though only on an instinctive level."

As the video ended, Eibbed leaned back against the wall and closed her eyes for a moment. She opened her eyes and smiled. "This has explained many things, Kieya. Thank you for sharing this with me."

"You're welcome."

"We will need to have Walter with us from time to time, will we not?"

"There is no doubt of that. Furthermore, you and Arooda are having an unexpected influence upon me."

"How is that?"

"I have not had a mate in the many thousands of years that I have been a Gaardian. After Walter and Debbie became one, soon thereafter I observed other unions, both within species on their planets and those of differing species and differing planets. As I watched you and Arooda praying together, it occurred to me that perhaps The Creator is guiding me towards having a mate again."

"Do you spend much time on your own planet?"

"As with other Gaardians, I spend about one-third of my time on my own planet. For me, it is to supervise my Gaardian crew, along with opportunities for rest and recreation."

"Tell me more about your planet and your society. Is it similar to that of my Pzalop?"

Kieya purred softly. "It would be easier for you to have understanding of my planet if I do a direct mental transfer. If you put your hand on top of my head again, I will do so."

As I Eibbed reached out and put her hand on the big cat's head, her eyes closed. For several moments, she swayed to the rhythm of Kieya's purr. Then she opened her eyes and withdrew her hand. "Amazing! Though our genetics are greatly different, our societies are remarkably similar in character."

"Yes. With regard to our becoming prophets, I remember something Walter said that seemed very insightful with regard to this. He said, "Just as surely as a priest is someone who goes to The Creator on behalf of others, a prophet goes to others on behalf of The Creator."

Eibbed nodded. "That is a helpful summary. Doesn't a prophet sometimes get a glimpse of the future?"

Kieya stopped purring momentarily. Then she resumed. "On my planet there are sometimes parades on special occasions. If I fly above a parade, I can see where it is going. I think our Creator always sees beyond the present in that way, and often prophets are allowed to see from The Creator's perspective."

"I understand. When I saw that video, the thought occurred to me that we would have to learn how to be prophets. Now I realize that there is nothing to learn. We simply have be obedient and faithful. As Suppla, I am not accustomed to thinking about being obedient."

Kieya purred louder. "That's a good insight about yourself, Eibbed. I think that as a Gaardian, I am accustomed to sharing responsibilities with other Gaardians. As a prophet, I will simply have to let The Creator assume responsibility of a future outcome. I merely have to be faithful."

"Yes! That makes sense." She paused. "We have a lot to think about. I am looking forward to spending time with Walter and discussing this. At this time, I am growing very hungry. Shall we return to my quarters?"

"Let's pray together first."

Eibbed knelt while facing the government complex in the far distance. As Kieya sat down on her haunches next to her, she put her arm across Kieya's shoulders. They prayed as one, as one in God's spirit.

7. Training

That evening, several hours after darkness had descended upon Leahcim's home, it was time for him to rest. When he turned off the light to go to sleep, he was deep in slumber quickly. Nearby, Qaak appeared and approached him. "Sleep soundly, my friend, we have things to talk about in your dreams." Sitting on his third leg, Qaak reached over and put three fingers on Leahcim's face. Qaak closed his eyes, and behind his eye's lids, they subtly glowed.

In a very realistic dream together, Qaak and Leahcim flew high above the planet without a hovercraft. Leahcim asked, "Why are we flying, Qaak?"

"You have not seen all of Pzalop from above. It is quite beautiful."

"Most of the time when I travel, I am much lower, and I do not take enough time visually to enjoy The Creator's work."

"You are not alone. I wish I had seen more of my planet before it was destroyed by an asteroid many thousands of years ago."

"You are the only survivor?"

"Yes." They paused high above the capital. "Now I'm going to take you away from your planet, to another galaxy, to Gaardian, and to my apartment."

The sky all around them blinked. Another planet was below them, and nearby there appeared to be a large satellite. Most of its exterior was transparent. They floated towards the satellite, through its outer wall, and into Qaak's apartment. "These are your living quarters?" asked Leahcim.

"Yes. Come and sit in one of these chairs near my fireplace." They walked over, sat down, and began to enjoy the fire. "Leahcim, have you ever thought about what it would be like to be a Gaardian?"

"Yes! When so many of us waited in the valley for the comet to strike, I was fascinated both by Walter and by Ooza. I wondered what their lives were like."

"Indeed." His eyes glowed subtly. "This is good. Until recently, I always did Gaardian training because of my Creator-given gifts. Currently that I am retired, doing less of what I am doing with you at present." He paused. "At this moment you are sound asleep in your apartment on Pzalop. You and I are having this conversation in a dream I am creating for you. When I trained Walter, I did this almost every night of Walter's life for more than fifty of his planet's years. He is actually more than twice the age he appears to be. Gaardian technology renews his body as it does for all Gaardians. If you become a Gaardian, you will appear once again as you did when you were a young adult."

"Really! I have many years yet to live, but would I have enough?"

Qaak chuckled. "You may recall hearing that Zargadetes like yourself, the Quzaks, and myself share some genetic code."

"Yes. At the time, I was initially surprised. Since then I have pondered this and recognize the relatedness I share with Ooza and other Quzaks."

"Yes. Your brain and mine are configured almost identically. I can train you before this night is over, just as I did Ooza."

"Would I have to resign from the council? I have enjoyed my friendship with The Suppla."

"No. As Ooza can tell you, most Gaardians are not recognized as such on their own planets. For you, this would mean being in disguise as the Zargadete you have always been when you are on the surface of Pzalop. When acting as Gaardian, your appearance would be more than a hundred years younger, and, therefore, unrecognizable. You are the last of your family, and your friends from childhood have all died in various Zargadete wars. Your identity would be safe. Does all of this continue to interest you?"

"Yes, but I have no idea what this change would mean for me."

"This is normal. I will proceed to train you tonight, and if you decide to become our first Gaardian from Pzalop, you will awaken tomorrow with awareness of your new identity. If you decide you do not want to be a Gaardian, you will awaken with no memories of your training or of this dream. Is this acceptable to you?"

"Yes. ... What happens next?"

The next six hours were audibly silent, both in the dream and in Leahcim's apartment. Thousands of years of history and knowledge flooded his mind. They traveled throughout Gaardian space and explored Gaardian planet. His mind's eyes saw things flashing by so rapidly he was surprised he could comprehend what he was seeing.

Suddenly, Leahcim was awake and sitting up in his bed. Qaak was seated on his third leg a short distance away. "I'm glad you've decided to be a Gaardian." His eyes glowed intensely for a moment. "Indeed, both Gaardian and Walter are now aware of your decision. We will have a welcoming party on Gaardian Planet soon. That is for Walter to determine." Qaak held out a ring to him. "Put this on the fourth finger of your right hand." Leahcim did so. "That is your Gaardian ring. You can communicate with other Gaardians via g-mail at any time. I will now return to my apartment."

"It has been good getting to know you, Qaak."

"It has been good for me as well. Until then."

"Until then." Leahcim blinked when the triped vanished. Getting out of bed, he went to a window and looked out. "This is going to be amazing," he murmured to himself. Looking down at his ring, he was suddenly fully dressed. Going to a mirror, his ring shimmered again, and his appearance changed to that of a young adult Zargadete in his prime.

As the day was dawning, Leahcim vanished to the crystalline structure he had built in The Creator's Park. No one was there at this hour, so he spent some time on his knees in the large central room. As innumerable other beings on countless other worlds had discovered, humbling oneself in prayer before The Creator can expand the mind and heart of the one praying. After just over an hour of praying, he knew what he must do immediately to become an effective Gaardian.

A chime sounded, and Puz appeared next to him as a g-mail. "Good morning, Leahcim! Welcome to being among the Gaardians!"

"Good morning, Puz! Thank you! I've been praying in order to prepare for what I must immediately be doing."

"Of course. I will continue to be Gaardian for this sector for a short time. My sector will be slightly smaller at first, but you will have a large enough sector with which to start. If you wish help with assembling your team and configuring your base, you know it is available. I will come any time you need me, and Kieya has been here on Pzalop and working with the Suppla. She will help as well if called upon."

"This is very good. I am going to have to get used to the idea that my old friend is actually a female, and that I must avoid expressing knowledge of this in public." He paused. "I would like you to reflect on an idea of mine."

"Yes? How can I help?"

"Designing a base on Pzalop's nearest moon will not be a problem, of course, but I'm thinking about living quarters. Initially at least, I want to keep my current quarters on the planet, and establish an invisible time-space portal connected directly to my base on the moon. From your experience, what do you consider about advantages and disadvantages?"

"Just a moment – I'm going to come to you." The g-mail image vanished, and then Puz appeared next to him. "This is better. If you're finished praying for now, let's go to your apartment."

"Good." They vanished from The Creator's Park and reappeared in Leahcim's quarters. He pointed. "I have always kept that chair away from the wall because I used to have a pet that slept back there. As you can see, anyone can walk towards the window and then stand near that wall. I am suggesting that I make that wall a portal that can be opened and closed to move back and forth from here to my base on the moon."

"That would work. You would simply have to keep the portal closed except for transport. The risks would be minimal." He paused. "I have an idea. Your quarters here look somewhat similar to those of Walter's base on Earth's moon. I will not take you there because you need to get used to traveling on your own through space-time with Gaardian technology. With your permission, however, I will create a basic core for your base on your moon for you, with a configuration like Walter's base."

"Yes! That sounds excellent. It would give me something upon which to build."

"Very well, give me a moment to think." He paused. "All right, Leahcim, let's step through that wall." With Puz leading the way, they walked through the wall behind the chair in Leahcim's apartment. On Pzalop's nearest moon, they came through a wall between two doorways into a large multifaceted dome. "Computer, Pzalop normal gravity please."

Leahcim looked around. "I remember having a glimpse of this in my dream training." He pointed to a door on his right. "This door leads to Walter's and Debbie's quarters on his moon." His arm gestured counter-clockwise. Did you put a basic medical unit there?"

"Yes." Puz gestured further to the left. "That can go to an office complex, and that door leads to a simple lounge and recreation area like the one on Walter's moon." Sweeping his arm further left, he said, "And that door leads to a media center I've set up for you, and the door to the left of that leads to the dining area and galley. This door," he pointed just to them left of where they were standing, "leads to crew quarters when you have assembled your team."

"This will be more than adequate for now. Thank you, Puz."

"You are welcome. I have one more suggestion before I leave you and go back to my duties."

"I am prepared for *all* suggestions." He smiled.

Puz's telepathic voice was placid. "When Walter was recruited, and he had to assemble his team, no one on Earth knew about the Gaardians. You have an advantage because everyone on Pzalop knows of the Gaardian presence."

"Please continue."

"I suggest you make a video as your new and younger self, and transmit it throughout the planet. I can be with you in the video to introduce you as the first Gaardian from Pzalop, who will be taking over for me soon. I will explain that you are assembling a team, and together we can explain qualifications, requirements, and restrictions to Gaardian team members."

"This sounds like a perfect solution to what I've been pondering all morning. How soon can we do this?

"Take some time to configure your moon base just the way you want to have it. What we have here is a bare structure. You need to furnish it. When you are ready to proceed, send me a g-mail or talk to Kieya."

"This is fine. Thank you for your help."

"I am more than happy to assist you. I will see you when you are ready. Until then."

"Until then," said Leahcim, as Puz vanished.

As Leahcim walked around the interior of the dome, sometimes his Gaardian ring would shimmer, and plants would appear or changes would be made. After a brief look at the medical clinic, he left it unchanged. The lounge was similar to the one on Walter's base, and he only changed it enough to provide a place for kneeling in prayer near the view window looking towards Pzalop.

Leahcim thought the recreation area looked truly amazing. He could not think of any way to improve it. He swam in the large pool for some distance before going to the hot and cold whirlpool.

+ + +

On another continent on Pzalop, a party was concluding, and an attractive middle-aged female went to a lift. Inside, she said, "Room 3816, I am Adnil."

The lift moved rapidly, and the doors opened in the living area of her rented space. Walking across the room, she stopped at a counter and poured herself some light-blue liquid. She sighed. High above her on Pzalop's moon, was Leahcim.

+ + +

Relaxing in the steaming water, Leahcim looked up. "Computer. As I recall, Walter asked an old friend named Belinda to help him assemble his team. Where is my dear friend Adnil right now?"

A metallic voice responded, "Adnil is touring with friends on the southern continent."

"Is she with her friends at this moment?"

There was a pause. "No, she has just entered her rented domicile in anticipation of sleep."

"Excellent. Alter my appearance to that of my older self." His features changed in a moment. "Now, transport her here instantly so she is standing in front of me and facing me."

Adnil appeared in front of him, holding her glass of blue. She shrieked. "Wha ... Leahcim! ... where am I? ... where are we? ... how did I get here?" She turned, looking all around.

"It's good to see you, Adnil!"

She turned back to face him again. "It's good to see you, too, but you have not answered my questions!" She stared at him.

"I know I have startled you, but I also know we trust each other with everything. I hope I have not startled you unnecessarily."

"You've startled me, but I trust you, so please tell me what is happening."

"I will do so in a moment." He paused. "First, I'll make us both younger and change your attire so that you can join me in the pool."

Her mouth dropped open, they both appeared younger, and her clothing was changed to swim wear. She gingerly stepped into the steaming waters. As she began to relax she spoke softly. "Have you become a Gaardian?"

"Yes, obviously this is true. I am now the first Gaardian from Pzalop, and we are on our closest moon on my base."

"Incredible!"

"As my friend Qaak would say, "Indeed!"

"Qaak?"

"He's the oldest and original Gaardian, other than a planet by that name. His gift is that he can provide years of training in just moments using mental transfer."

"Really!"

"Yes. As a Gaardian, I can do a little of it myself. Would you like to help me assemble a team that will assist me with Gaardian duties in this sector?"

"Absolutely! You don't have to ask twice!"

"Good. Come and sit closer to me so that I can do a brief mental transfer." She began to move. "I will have Qaak or another being give you more knowledge at another time. This will just get you started." He put his hand on her head and closed his eyes. She also closed hers. They vanished from the whirlpool, and they reappeared fully clothed in the same pose, sitting in the atrium at the center of the base.

They opened their eyes. She smiled. "I've always loved you, Leahcim."

"And I have loved you."

"We've both had mates in the past, but we've always been friends. Do you want us to become mates now?"

"I would welcome that, if that is your desire." He smiled.

"Yes, my love." She kissed him, first briefly, and then more passionately. Still speaking softly she held him. "I think you should send me back as an old female to my friends on the tour. Tomorrow I will excuse myself to return home by hovercraft. I will come to your apartment."

"Good. Tomorrow I will find you, wherever you are, at mid-day, and we shall eat together."

"Good." He kissed her briefly. "Now I'll send you back."

"I'll see you tomorrow."

"Tomorrow," he said. His ring shimmered, and she vanished. Now alone again, he began to wander throughout the base, deep in thought. As he came into the lounge area, he looked up. "Computer: I want a fire in the fireplace from this moment onwards so long as anyone is here at the base." A fire appeared, and Leahcim sat down nearby. "Computer: Let me have an android representation of yourself."

"Do you want male or female?" came the metallic voice.

"I want a male, about the age of Arooda, with a voice slightly lower than his."

A male Zargadete appeared, about the same age and build as Arooda. "Yes?"

"Thank you. Please be seated nearby." The android did so. "I am giving you the name 'Mas.' It was the name of my father's older brother. Scan the Gaardian history banks regarding Walter's period of organization."

The android was silent for several seconds. "How closely do you wish to follow his procedures?"

"I will probably use most of them, but I may not follow all. Walter looked for possible team members from all age groups, but he ended up recruiting mostly older humans and giving them second lives. Is that consistent with most other humanoid Gaardians?"

"One moment," said Mas, pausing. "A significant majority of humanoids assisting Gaardians are usually older and wiser. Gaardians seem to appreciate the wisdom that comes with experience."

"I agree." Leahcim looked up and closed his eyes. "I need a small vehicle that looks like a hovercraft but is configured for travel at Gaardian speeds and distances. Please have it available when I return tomorrow. I am in the habit of eating at this time of day, so I am going back to my quarters."

"Your Gaardian ring eliminates your need to eat and drink."

"True, but I enjoy eating and drinking, particularly when I am with other Zargadetes."

"Very well," said Mas. He disappeared.

Leahcim walked out of the lounge, across the atrium, and through the wall into his apartment.

8. Friendly Advice

Kieya was fully aware of Qaak's visit with Leahcim, so she knew immediately of Leahcim's decision. As with previous new Gaardians, she left him alone to make his adjustments to his life, unless he asked for help.

For hundreds of years, her team on her home world had often worked without her presence for several days at a time. Kieya returned to her particular Gaardian sector and her own world after setting up a series of meeting times with Eibbed.

For several days, Kieya went back and forth between her base and Pzalop. Taking time to rest at home, she sought the quiet of a nearby forest. As she walked, Kieya made mental pictures to be possibly rendered later on the walls at her base. She changed those images frequently.

She relaxed and sharpened her claws on a number of larger plants and rolled in dirt. Kieya let a few young tabbas chase her until she was beginning to tire. It was fun. Then Kieya turned and let out a roar, which was amplified by her Gaardian ring. Startled, they turned and ran.

She stopped and closed her eyes. "Kieya to Gaardian, I want to commune with you. Is Qaak on your surface?"

Silently, she heard the planet's voice in her mind. "He is in his apartment. Do you wish him to join you here?"

"Not at first. I would like privacy with you."

"Very well. Come."

Kieya vanished, and she reappeared on Gaardian's surface above Red Falls. "Do you think it is time for me to take a mate again?"

The planet hesitated. "I am not qualified since I cannot take a mate for myself. Talk to Walter and Qaak."

Kieya purred softly, "I love them both, but I wish I could talk to a Felidaca like myself."

"What about one of your team members, such as Ydoj?" ["EE-dodge"]

"I trust him, but because he is a male it could be awkward."

The planet was silent for a moment. "You need to talk to a strong female. I consider two that could be very helpful. You have met them both."

"Of whom are you speaking?"

"On Walter's planet, Earth, there is a female who currently identifies herself as Margaret Graves. She is very wise."

"I remember her. She has amused me at times."

"The other female is Ooza's friend, Piatek. She has both wisdom and a gift that intrigues me."

Kieya purred more strongly. "Yes! I would like them to meet with me in my quarters here at the nursery complex."

"You are wise," said the planet, "I will make arrangements with Walter and with Ooza. It will be in three time periods, unless there is a problem."

"Excellent! I can walk there from here and collect my thoughts."

"Very well," said the planet, as it then became silent.

+ + +

On Earth's moon, Debbie was singing softly as she took her shower, and Walter was standing in their bedroom, looking out the portal at the Earthrise. A chime sounded. "Yes, Frank?"

The android appeared nearby. "Kieya would like to meet with Piatek and Margaret Graves in her quarters on Gaardian."

Walter looked up for a moment, and then he turned towards Frank. "I'll take care of it. Where is Margaret?"

"She is in her office in Oakland." The android vanished.

"G-mail to Margaret Graves...." A portal opened in front of him, and he could see Margaret sitting at her desk. "Hello, Margaret!"

"Hello, Walter! It is good to see you!"

"It is good to see you as well."

"What can I do for you?"

"It is early afternoon where you are. Do you have a full schedule the rest of the day?"

"I just completed a project this morning, and I was going to make a few phone calls. Why do you ask?"

"Do you remember my friend, Kieya?"

"The big cat? Of course!"

"She would like to confer with you on Gaardian planet. You would need to be free for the rest of the day and into your evening hours. Can you do it?"

Margaret laughed. "Even if I couldn't, I would! How soon are we talking about?"

"I can pick you up in about three minutes, out there by the parking lot door. Will that be okay?"

"Okay, but please make it closer to five minutes. I need to lock up and turn off the lights. I don't have Gaardian conveniences!"

Walter smiled. "Okay, Margaret, I'll be there inside of five minutes." The portal closed as the g-mail ended. "Debbie?"

She came through the doorway from the hallway to the front of their apartment. "What's up?"

"I'm going to pick up Margaret at my old church and take her to Kieya on Gaardian. Would you like to fly along?"

"Sure! Joseph's playing with Kenkee and some other children at Gaardian's nursery. It'll be fun!" She stepped towards him and put her hand on his as he held it out. In a blink, they were sitting in a vehicle looking like a Subaru SVX. A portal opened in front of them, where they could see the church and its parking lot.

They heard Frank's voice say, "It's all clear."

In a blink, they were parked in the parking lot in front of the office door. A few minutes later, Margaret appeared, and Walter's ring shimmered as a back door appeared on the car that had not been there before. She opened it and got in. Hi, Walter!" She turned her head. "I was not expecting to see you, Debbie!"

Debbie smiled, "Hi, Margaret! It's good to see you!"

Walter turned his head. "Margaret, this will be your first time traveling Gaardian style, won't it?"

"Yes! This is exciting!"

The SVX became translucent. "We're now invisible, Margaret, so we can travel without attracting attention. We have a little time, so let's have some fun!" As Walter worked the controls, the SVX flew out of the parking lot towards downtown Oakland. Passing a tall hotel, they flew across the bay at increasing speed. Flying past the Transamerica Pyramid and the Mark Hopkins Hotel, they dipped under the Golden Gate Bridge before heading across the Pacific Ocean and into space. "Since you've never been in space, Margaret, I'll take you past the other planets in our solar system before leaving our galaxy."

"I won't ask you about speed."

"It would not help if I told you, since actual speed is mostly irrelevant, and theoretical speed is almost beyond comprehension."

As they entered space, they could see the Moon far off to the right. Increasing speed, they went past Venus and Mercury before swinging past the sun to its other side. They then sped past Mars, Jupiter, Saturn, and Uranus before all the lights around them blurred with increasing intensity. There was a flash of light that filled the car. Margaret touched Walter's shoulder. "What was that?"

"We passed through a star."

"<u>Through</u> a star???"

"Yes." After two more flashes and five minutes more, the blurring began to slow down, and then a large planet loomed ahead of them. "Welcome to Gaardian, Margaret."

"Wow!"

Debbie smiled. "It's beautiful, isn't it, Margaret?"

"Yes! It's amazing! It has a turquoise sky!"

"Yes." Walter looked at Debbie. "Would you give Margaret a ring for her visit?" Walter touched some controls as they descended to the planet's surface.

Debbie reached under the dash and brought out a small ring with a purple stone. "Margaret, Gaardian gravity is considerably more powerful than that of Earth, and you would not be able to breathe the atmosphere without help. Put this on the fourth finger of your right hand." She extended the ring to Margaret.

"Thank you. It's pretty."

Walter nodded. "You can keep it and wear it from this day forwards."

"Thank you!" Her voice was enthusiastic.

"You're welcome!" Debbie smiled as the SVX slowed near the complex where the children were playing. She pointed at a small boy just beginning to walk. "There's Joseph, our son."

"He looks like his father!"

Walter laughed. "I wish I could take all the credit, but he certainly inherited his mother's great looks!"

Debbie leaned over and kissed him on the cheek. "Thank you, dear. ... Margaret, I'm going to stay here with the kids while you and Walter go inside."

"Okay."

When they got out, Walter led Margaret inside and down a hallway. A chime sounded, and they heard Kieya's voice from inside. "Come in, friends."

As they stepped inside, Margaret's eyes grew wide. "I had forgotten how big you are, Kieya."

She purred. "That cannot be helped. I am who I am."

Margaret smiled. "I know."

"Walter," the big cat purred, "this is for females-only. You and I will confer at other times."

"As you wish, my friend – I will leave the SVX here for Debbie and Margaret so that they can return when they are ready." He vanished.

The big cat wandered towards her fireplace and turned. "There is another female whom you need to meet now."

A petite pale green female came through a doorway and extended her hand to Margaret. "Hello! My name is Piatek."

Margaret smiled. "I am pleased to meet you."

"I am happy to meet you as well." She held Margaret's hand for a moment as she looked into her eyes. "You have much more pigment in your skin than Walter. I also see that you are wise and have a gift of which you are unaware."

"I have a gift?"

"Yes. I would like to ponder it for a while before talking with you about it, if you don't mind."

"Certainly. I have worked with Walter, and I have learned that in Gaardian relationships, unusual things are normal."

Piatek laughed. "That is so true!" Her smile was broad. "I like you, Margaret!"

Kieya purred as she sat down near the fire, and the two other females sat down in chairs nearby. Kieya's purr paused briefly. "Gaardian, please make yourself known to the other females."

The planet rumbled softly. "Hello. My name is Gaardian. I am the planet upon whose surface is this structure."

Margaret's mouth dropped open. "You're alive?"

"I am sentient, but I do not breathe or reproduce."

Piatek had a huge smile on her face. "Ooza told me about you, but this is truly wondrous!"

Kieya's purr grew soft. "Gaardian, I would like you to monitor our discussions here, but please remain in the background unless I ask you otherwise."

"Ladies, before I go silent, I tell you it was I who suggested the two of you as being appropriate to confer with Kieya today. Now I shall remain quiet until called."

Piatek and Margaret looked at the big cat. She blinked, and then she spoke. "The purpose of my asking you to come is simple and personal. When I was young, I had a mate, and I had several tats. Since becoming a Gaardian many – *many* - millennia ago, I have not had another mate. In recent times, I have observed several pairings of both old and young, including one pairing with a truly remarkable age difference. I am pondering whether I should take a mate again, and I have asked you here to help me consider this from both objective and subjective points of view."

Piatek nodded. "I knew this when I touched your fur a while ago."

Margaret also nodded. "This planet is wise. It knows me better than I thought possible. I will do my best to meet this challenge."

"The challenge is mine, not yours," Kieya purred.

"No," said Piatek, "it is for all of us."

Her purr paused briefly. "Perhaps." She looked up, and then she continued, shifting her gaze between them. "Before I became a Gaardian, having a mate meant focusing all of my love and emotional attention to my mate and tats. I had ample love when I was young and had good examples of how to love. There was emotional security that comes with having a mate and tats, but unlike the unions I have recently observed, there was no religious component."

Margaret interrupted, "Did you find yourself more disciplined in your life after taking a mate?"

"Yes, and I became even more disciplined after becoming a Gaardian."

Piatek looked intently at the big cat. "I gather that it was not entirely Gaardian responsibilities that have kept you from taking another mate."

Kieya became motionless and silent as she gazed back at Piatek. The old Quzak's special gift was having its effect. Kieya blinked at began to purr very softly again. "Yes. Union means sharing everything. Because my mate was very conceited, I would not have been able to trust Legere with my Gaardian activities. Without a mate, I have had the freedom to make many difficult choices on my own. Those choices might have been much harder with a mate."

"No, Kieya." Both Piatek and Margaret said it almost together.

"No?"

Margaret cleared her throat. "I have been following Jesus even longer than Walter has, and in sharing our faith we have learned and grown with each other. You are old enough to have observed Jesus. Did you?"

"Yes." Kieya's purr rumbled lower but with intensity. "I listened to him many times."

Piatek closed her eyes for a few seconds. "Yes! This is logical! I can see this in you! You follow Jesus even now, do you not?"

Kieya's purr grew soft and gentle, and she spoke more quietly. "Yes. ... Indeed. ... When Walter became a Gaardian I assimilated all of his scriptures that quote Jesus. Those words have kept my memories of Him alive.... Yes, I suppose I do follow Him."

Margaret spoke quietly. "Jesus did not take a mate, but that does not mean that you should not do so."

"Yes." Piatek's gaze penetrated Kieya's. "With Quzaks, felidacas and humans, there tends to be particular roles for both females and males. While those roles are effectively integrated, they are nonetheless separate for effectiveness."

Margaret nodded. "If you met the Apostle named Paul, you know that he said that it is a gift to be married, but it is also a gift to be single. Besides, you have an advantage now, Kieya, which you did not have when you had your previous mate."

Her purr paused. "What advantage do I have?"

Piatek smiled. "You have wisdom that comes from many experiences with many cultures."

Margaret also smiled. "Yes! Since you did not like the vanity of your first mate, you will probably try to avoid having a mate that is self-absorbed."

Piatek chuckled. "You also have your Gaardian advantage of being able to observe invisibly if you so choose."

Kieya's purr got louder. "That part of my search could very well be amusing, but I must take care not to invade other's privacy."

Margaret laughed. "Why Kieya, I think you don't need as much help from us as you thought!"

Piatek joined her laughter. :This may be true, but I still want to hear the stories of your search."

"Agreed. I will share my quests with both of you."

Their conversation continued for several hours before Margaret and Piatek went home. Feeling content, Kieya went back to her planet. Then, she began her quest.

9. Organized Power

On his moon's base in the atrium, Leahcim was looking out a portal towards Pzalop. Adnil approached and stood beside him for a moment before she spoke. "So far we have had more than 60,000 responses to the video, and they have come from all over Pzalop."

"I noticed. We must do an initial screening to pick out key leaders for our team." He turned from the portal and walked across the atrium, and then he went into the lounge and sat in one of the chairs. Adnil followed him and sat beside him. He continued, "We have to be very careful in our initial selection. In most cases, we will not be able to use applicants from government positions. Their loyalties could be divided between Gaardian concerns and those of our own planet."

"Are there any other sentient species in our sector that could be candidates?"

"Yes." Leahcim looked up. "Mas?"

The android appeared near the fireplace. "Yes?"

"Regarding the other sentient species in this sector, I think we should recruit at least one or two from that planet. Gaardian protocol is rather flexible when it comes to recruiting from planets that do not know Gaardians exist. Are there parallels in recent Gaardian history to guide us?"

The android paused. "The simplest approach is the most direct. It was used by Walter to recruit both Asayak and Keeta. Sunev's population is well organized and is beginning to venture into space, as with Asayak's culture. Walter simply selected a planet-wide challenge in each case, and as he solved their problem, he made himself known,"

Adnil smiled. "That's both ingenious and simple!"

Leahcim nodded. "Agreed. Mas, do you have a suggestion?"

Again, the android paused. "About three of their solar years ago the planet had an eruption, and the result was what Walter's Earth calls a volcano. Here, Pzalop's core is solid, so Zargadetes have never witnessed this phenomenon, which can only come from a planet with a molten core. The result on Sunev was major climate change, and the whole planet's population is struggling to survive under much lower temperatures. The ash in the atmosphere is beginning to dissipate, but very slowly."

Leahcim smiled. "By Gaardian standards, this is an easy fix!"

Adnil stared at him. "How can it be easy? Can we look?"

"Yes." A three-dimensional image appeared in front of them. They could see black clouds and storms moving all over the planet. Leahcim pointed, "Do you see those shifting patterns of grey? There is the equivalent of a large mountain in the form of fine powder floating in the atmosphere, generating storms from the moisture. I can selectively filter out the particulates and send it all into their sun."

Adnil's eyes grew large. "You can do that?"

"Yes. G-mail to Kieya: Are you available?"

A moment later, a portal appeared near the fireplace, where they could see Kieya in the crystalline building in The Creator's Park. "Yes, Leahcim, I was just going to leave and go back to my planet for the evening. I will stop at your base in a moment. ... Until then."

"Until then."

Adnil stared at the area where she had seen the big cat. "Is that another Gaardian?"

"Yes, Kieya is the second oldest Gaardian. Not all Gaardians are humanoid."

"I had not thought of that!"

Kieya appeared near the fireplace, and Mas vanished. She approached them and said, "You must be Adnil. I am Kieya." She purred softly.

"You are beautiful! I am pleased to meet you!" Adnil smiled broadly.

"I am pleased as well." She turned to Leahcim. "How may I assist you?"

"Are you familiar with the atmospheric problems on Sunev?"

"Yes. Why do you ask?"

"I want to introduce myself to them as their Gaardian by cleaning up their atmosphere."

Her purring stopped a moment, and then it continued. "I'm glad you've asked for my assistance. Excuse me a moment while I take a personal look." She vanished.

"Where did she go?" asked Adnil.

"I think she's visiting Sunev," Leahcim said flatly, as Adnil's mouth hung slightly open.

Kieya reappeared. "It is worse than I thought. We cannot simply remove the particulates. The resulting winds and sudden temperature changes would be highly destructive. I am offering my thoughts to Gaardian."

Just then, Walter appeared. "Hello, Leahcim! I am Walter," he said as he looked at Adnil and said, "and you must be Adnil." He shook both of their hands. "Gaardian has told me what you wish to do, and I like the idea, but it will take a team effort. Since you do not have a team yet, Puz, Kieya, Ooza and I will assist you."

Just then, Ooza and Puz appeared. Ooza said, "Hi, everyone!" and waved. Puz's telepathic voice was intense as well as curious. "Walter, I assume you have a plan."

"I do." He paused. "Fellow Gaardians, step over and put your hands up mine." Walter held out his hand, and the others stepped forward. Kieya lifted a paw and put it on top. Walter closed his eyes for about ten seconds, as did the others. As he opened his eyes, he said, "According to Gaardian, this approach has not been used in hundreds of years, but with God's help, there will be no problem."

Adnil came out of a daze. "God? Do you mean The Creator?"

Leahcim looked at her. "Yes, he means The Creator. I'm sorry you cannot join us this time, but the next time we face a challenge, I hope you can come along."

"Okay."

"Ooza is going to be poised over the northern pole region, with Kieya over the southern pole. Puz, Walter, and I will be spaced along the equator. When Walter signals, we will function as one, and the entire atmosphere will be clean and stable. I will then appear at their government's headquarters and introduce myself. I let you see a video later, Adnil."

Adnil was goggle-eyed. "How? ... No, it would not help if you told me since I don't know the technology, correct?"

"Correct. Walter, is there anything else we need to discuss?"

He shook his head. "Let's take our positions ... now." The Gaardians disappeared. Adnil did not see the spectacular sound and light show put on by the Gaardians until later that day.

+ + +

In the evening, as the three-dimensional video came to a close, Adnil giggled. "I think you impressed them!"

Leahcim smiled. "I suppose that is unavoidable. They now have a copy of the same Gaardian guidelines our planet's Suppla received when our planet was moved. We should start getting applications for the Gaardian team in a few days."

"In the meantime, I have a few ideas for narrowing down our selection of candidates from our own planet."

"What do you have in mind?"

"First, let's eliminate those who are currently active in the military, as we said earlier. Then, I want to follow Belinda's approach that she used on Earth. Mas has given me things to study."

"All right, Adnil, but let's get some sleep now. Tomorrow will be another busy day." In the darkness, soon they were asleep.

+ + +

In the atrium at his base, Walter walked amid the foliage. "Frank?"

The android appeared and walked beside him. "Yes, Walter. The video from Sunev is revealing. The Creator definitely assisted."

"Yes, and there was an unusual bond between us that seemed to emanate from Ooza and Leahcim. Let's have a welcome party for Leahcim in two days. Meanwhile, have Asayak make itself available to him to train both Adnil and the new recruits there at Pzalop."

"Right, is there anything else?"

"No."

As Frank vanished, Walter moved towards his apartment. Inside, Debbie was putting Joseph to bed. He put his arms around her and gave her a kiss on the cheek. "I sure do love you!"

She smiled. "I love you too. Was it interesting out there at Pzalop?" she asked, as they walked towards the living room.

"Leahcim is going to be a brilliant Gaardian. Do you remember how Belinda helped me assemble my team, and that we knew almost from the beginning that we were not going to be married?"

"Yes, and I'm glad!"

"I am too. On Pzalop's moon, Leahcim has also recruited his oldest and closest friend from childhood to help him assemble his team. The difference is, Leahcim is taking his old friend Adnil as his mate."

They sat down on a large sofa. "Really! Do you like her?"

"She seems intelligent and pleasant. I'd like you to have lunch with her one day and see if you can help her. I think she's a bit overwhelmed with the rapid and significant changes in her life."

Debbie smiled. "Do you want me to play 'Belinda' to her?"

He grinned. "Not exactly, but that's the general idea. The day-after tomorrow I want to have the welcoming party for Leahcim. It won't be at the nursery complex but at the mountain center. You could take Jody with you and take Adnil on a tour of Gaardian center while the rest of us get better acquainted with Leahcim. How about it?"

Debbie was thoughtful. "Okay. What time will we leave?"

"We'll come back together after the party, but I will already be on Gaardian when you get there. Check with the planet for the best time to arrive."

She leaned over and kissed him. "Okay. Is there any more Gaardian business right now?" she smiled sweetly.

"Why do you ask?" he smiled back.

"Since Joseph is spending the night with Kenkee and the other kids, let's create a temporary patio, grill some steaks, and have our own private party!"

"That's a great idea!" He smiled and then gave her a lingering kiss. They got up, and Walter stretched. Then, as they walked towards the Earthrise side of their living room, Walter's ring shimmered, and a patio appeared on the other side of the wall. A door slid open as Belinda's ring shimmered, and furnishings appeared. On the far left side, a brick barbeque was already shimmering with heat coming from glowing charcoal embers. They sat down in recliners.

Walter looked over at her. "Have you ever had aged beef?"

"I did once, when a producer took us to a steak house for a wrap party after we finished shooting a movie. It was amazingly tender, but I joined your Gaardian team shortly thereafter, and I don't think Dawn has ever put it on the menu."

He looked up. "Walter to Dawn. If you have a moment, come and join Debbie and I on our patio."

They heard her voice. "I didn't know you had a patio. I'll be there in a moment. I want to see it!"

A minute or so later, Dawn knocked on their apartment door and came in. As she came out on the patio she said, "Wow! You should keep this! It looks great! Is that real charcoal on the grill?"

Debbie chuckled. "Absolutely. We're ready for steaks, and that's why we called you. In Houston, there's a place called Jenai's Kiwi Steak House...."

"Yes! I've heard of that place! They're said to have the best aged beef in North America!"

"Right!" Walter smiled. "I want you to duplicate a sampling of their steaks and roasts. As soon as you have a good digital sampling, have Frank put a couple of Porterhouse steaks on our grill here."

"That sounds like a great addition to our menu. I can probably have some on your grill in less than ten minutes, okay?"

"Great!"

Dawn turned and hurried out.

+ + +

In the media room on Leahcim's base, images of twenty-two Zargadetes and five Sunevians stood on the stage. The images were life-size, and Adnil stared at the Sunevians. "I thought Walter was tall, and Kieya was huge, but these Sunevians are amazing!"

The Zargadetes were all between five feet [152 cm.] and five feet four inches [163 cm.] tall. All the Sunevians towered over them at more than six feet three inches [190 cm.]. Leahcim walked among the images, sometimes passing through them. "These two are too self-centered." As he touched them, the images disappeared. "These ..." he touched three more "have a hard time with Zargadetes that are atypical. They probably would have a tough time dealing with non-Zargadetes." He stepped off the stage and sat down next to Adnil. "That leaves seventeen Zargadetes, and that is too many for our team's core for me. Do you want to eliminate any?"

Adnil pointed. "Those two are mated, so if we take one we have to take them both. Let's eliminate them for now. Maybe we'll add them to the team after we establish the core leaders." The two disappeared.

Leahcim pointed at a Zargadete right next to a Sunevian. "I knew him when I was extending my education. He is a rebel and often questions authority. The Zargadete army rejected him because he could not follow instructions." That image disappeared as the others had. "The group is still too large, but some will probably drop out when we ask them to make a commitment. Let's look at the Sunevians. Mas?"

The android appeared. "Yes?"

"What can you tell me about the Sunevians in terms of their mental and emotional patterns?"

"The two females are fairly mature at more than two hundred of our years. The male with the red hair is also their age and is quite wise as well as stable. The other two males are considerably younger and have personalities like that of Arooda only much wilder."

"Thank you, Mas." The android disappeared as did the images of the two younger male Sunevians. "Let's invite all of these to gather in the large room in the crystalline prayer center on the bottom level in the middle of tomorrow night, and let's ask Kieya and Puz to move among them Kieya and Puz are very wise, and they may be able to eliminate some of them."

Adnil nodded. "I'll get messages out to all of them. Why have you chosen the prayer center in the middle of the night?"

"I want to see how they behave there, and in the middle of the night we will not be disturbed by anyone else. I will see to it." He paused and looked at his Gaardian ring. "Low priority audio G-mail to Kieya and Puz when convenient: Please come to the crystalline prayer center tomorrow night. I would like to have the two of you observe the possible team members to see which of them need to be rejected as candidates. End g-mail."

10. Accurate Discernment

Kieya paced back and forth in her home planet's lair. She stopped near her entrance doorway. "G-mail: Kieya to Walter."

Walter appeared beside her in a portal, slightly further into the lair. "Hello Kieya. Are you in your lair?"

"Yes. Do you have some time for personal conversation?"

"Debbie and I are on Gaardian, and she is playing with Joseph and the other children. I can be there with you in a few moments."

"Until then," she purred.

"Until then." The portal closed.

Kieya resumed pacing. After two more rounds of pacing around her lair, Kieya stopped when she saw Walter appear in the doorway. "Thank you for coming. Why don't you make yourself a chair and be comfortable?"

A large overstuffed recliner chair appeared, and after sitting down, Walter leaned back. "You sounded anxious in the G-mail, Kieya, and that is not like you at all."

"Yes, I suppose I am anxious. When you told me that The Creator said I am to be a prophet, I had no idea what that might mean. You once said that when you were a pastor that sometimes you functioned as priest and other times as prophet. What did you mean by that? As I read your Bible, I see the distinction between the two often seems blurred."

Walter nodded. "I understand. An overly simplified way of distinguishing the two is simply this: As a priest, you may intercede with The Creator on behalf of others. As a prophet, you may be called by The Creator to go to certain others and speak on behalf of the Creator." nodded. "I understand. An overly simplified way of distinguishing the two is simply this: As a priest, you may intercede with The Creator on behalf of others. As a prophet, you may be called by The Creator to go to certain others and speak on behalf of the Creator."

Kieya began to purr softly as she went to a padded area and sat down. "Thank you. I now remember you saying that previously. How do you know that The Creator has given you something to say or do, and that it is not something out of your own imagination?"

Walter nodded. "What you are asking about is called spiritual discernment. For some of us, accuracy of discernment seems to come more easily than for others. I think it is a matter of doing your spiritual homework. No one who tries to be faithful to The Creator wants to be a false prophet."

"What do you mean?"

Walter smiled a little. "Do you remember when The Creator gave us a brief opportunity to step out of time and space into The Creator's realm?"

Kieya's purr got louder. "Yes! It was truly ... amazing and memorable!"

Walter smiled more broadly. "We cannot step out of space and time on our own, of course, but we can set aside time in a place where we will not be disturbed and commune with The Creator by reading scriptures and praying."

Her purring stopped briefly and then resumed. "When you pray, do you talk with God in your mind?"

Walter nodded. "Sometimes, ... but other times I pray aloud too. When I've been angry or emotionally distraught I have even yelled at God."

"You have actually yelled at God? Is that not disrespectful?"

"God's understanding is as infinite as everything else. We cannot hurt God's feelings because He knows everything anyway."

Kieya quietly purred and blinked. "What do you discuss with The Creator?"

Walter grinned. "Truthfully, I discuss everything that comes to mind. It is very liberating. I have a suggestion."

"I'll try almost anything, if it makes being a prophet easier."

Walter nodded. "At times being a prophet can be very difficult, no matter how well prepared we believe we are. It is like everything else in life. My suggestion is that you go to Pzalop and the crystalline structure there. Find a tower area that you can isolate from the rest of the structure using Gaardian ring support. Spend some time communing with God there. If either Gaardians or other felidacas need you, there is always G-mail. That crystalline structure seems to be particularly conducive to strengthening the spiritual efforts of those seeking The Creator."

The big cat purred softy as she stood up. "Thank you, Walter. I will take your suggestion. ... You are a true friend. ... "I will see you soon. Until then."

"Until then." They vanished almost simultaneously."

+ + +

As Kieya appeared in one of the towers in the crystalline structure, some distance a The Suppla was sitting at her desk. She reached underneath and touched a hidden panel. A partition appeared on top, and she touched a button. "This is the Suppla of Pzalop. When convenient, I would like to speak to Walter."

Walter appeared on the other side of her desk, and not as a G-mail. "I was nearby, Eibbed, so I came directly. How may I assist you?"

Obviously startled, Eibbed cleared her throat. "I will not ask why you were nearby. ... Kieya has told me that she and I are to be prophets for The Creator. She also told me that you were the one to assist us in learning how to fulfill our roles. I need your council."

Walter nodded. "Just a short time ago I left Kieya after she sought me for the same reason."

"Are we congruent in our thinking?"

"Yes. God does everything well. Kieya asked me about the difference between a priest and a prophet, and we talked about the need for accurate discernment of The Creator's will."

"I had not considered a relationship between priests and prophets, even though I've read about them in your Bible and in scriptures of other cultures. Is it not true that a priest goes to The Creator on behalf of others or himself, saying and doing things on behalf of others?"

"I used almost exactly those words with Kieya. In contrast, a prophet speaks to others or does things to and for others on God's behalf. In essence, a prophet is *used* by The Creator."

Eibbed was thoughtful. "When I pray, sometimes my mind wanders away, and I begin thinking about things or people that I had not intended to be part of my prayers."

"That is common." Walter paused. "When you are praying, talk to The Creator about anything that comes to mind, whether or not you think it is appropriate. When we are praying, The Creator often guides our prayers."

"I had not considered this possibility!" She looked up, and then she looked back at Walter. "I have much to learn!"

Walter nodded. "You always will, and as we serve The Creator, we all continue to learn throughout our lives."

Eibbed leaned forward and became intense. "Earlier today, as I was kneeling in prayer on the pres-dieu in my office, I had some very disturbing images."

"Tell me about them."

"I saw Pzalop sliced into two parts like a piece of round fruit by a seemingly invisible blade."

Walter looked up, and then back at Eibbed. "Was this the first time you have seen these images?"

"No, this is the third time in three days."

Walter nodded. "G-mail to Qaak: Are you available?"

Qaak appeared nearby in a portal. "Yes, Walter? I see that you are with The Suppla. Greetings!"

"The Suppla has had a three-fold vision of the planet being sliced cleanly. Could this phenomenon be a vision of a cosmic string colliding with the planet?"

Qaak's eyes glowed brilliantly. "Possibly! Suppla, may I join the two of you and bring Piatek with me?"

Eibbed nodded. "You may."

"It will be a few moments. Until then."

"Until then." As the g-mail portal closed, Eibbed turned to Walter. "Why does he bring Piatek? Ooza says she is a Quzak friend who has a special gift. What is her gift?"

"If you permit her, Piatek will use her gift with you, or else simply explain." Walter smiled.

"This sounds mysterious. You have not previously been cryptic with me."

"I suppose that is true. I am not trying to deceive you. I simply wish to let Piatek speak for herself. She is much older than you and has a great store of wisdom."

Qaak and Piatek suddenly appeared on the other side of the Suppla's office and walked towards them. Qaak made introductions. "Suppla, it is good to see you again. This is our friend, Piatek, who is part of Ooza's team."

Piatek extended a hand. "It is a distinct pleasure to meet you. I have heard that you are a very capable leader."

"Thank you. It is good to meet you as well. I understand you have a special gift."

Piatek smiled. "I do not think of it as special, but I know of no one else that has my gift. It is unique. Qaak has brought me to you with the hope that you will permit me to use my gift with you. May I?"

"Has Qaak told you about the images I have seen when praying?"

"Yes, but that may not be relevant."

Qaak's eyes glowed softly. "May I show you something that happened with Piatek and Ooza that may help you understand?"

"Proceed."

A three-dimensional video appeared showing Ooza, Piatek, and some other Quzak females. Piatek cleared her throat. Her hair was hardly green at all.

"The young one speaks good wisdom. I am the oldest here,
but in my considerable lifetime there has never been a
greater challenge for Quzaks."

In the video, Piatek shifted her gaze around the room to everyone, and then
focused on Ooza.

"Ooza, you have special gifts that the rest of us would wish
we had if we considered it. You know my special gift,
however. I see beyond what is seen by others and sometimes
hear what will be. This is one of those times. . I have a
question for you Ooza. Think about the two encounters you
have had with the Gaardians, and consider the one you saw
both times. Can you still hear his voice?"

As they listened to the video, everyone had to listen carefully as, in a trance
Ooza quietly responded.

"Yes."

Piatek's voice in the video became softer and lower.

"Listen to his voice not with your head but with your heart.
What do you hear?"

Ooza stared straight ahead, and her eyes gradually became wider. She
blinked several times. The last time she blinked slowly.

"Thank you, Piatek! I can see! I can hear! It is a male with
extraordinary gifts that exist apart from his being a Gaardian!
There is wisdom behind him and power! There is – what is
that word – yes, joy! But, wait! There is more! He loves!
Differently than we love. It's . . . ."

Ooza blinked, and the Suppla blinked with her in sympathy. Then, in the
video, Ooza turned to Piatek, who responded.

"I know. This is a creature that does not fit any category we
have in our history or our databases."

As the video ended, the Suppla turned to Piatek. "You seem to see beyond
what others see, but you don't have to tell them about it because they see it
with you."

Piatek nodded. "Yes."

"We have just met, but I trust both Qaak and Walter. You may proceed."

Piatek smiled. "Then I shall do so." She stepped towards Eibbed, looking
directly into her eyes. "With my gift I can see that in your leadership of Pzalop,
you appear to be a male when you are actually a female." Eibbed's eyes grew
wider as Piatek continued. "Think about the images that you have been having
when you are praying. Picture them closely. See every detail." She paused. "At
this moment in time you can see even more. Now I am asking Qaak and Walter
to step closer." They came closer so that they formed a small circle. "Eibbed, I
am now asking Qaak to use his gift to receive all of this for Gaardian records.
Do you receive it, Qaak?"

Qaak's eyes were closed, glowing softly. "I see what you are seeing, Eibbed,
and I am astounded. It has been thousands of years since I have seen one of
these."

Walter's eyes were also closed as he said, "This is phenomenal, and it is a
major challenge."

As Walter and Qaak opened their eyes, Eibbed and Piatek blinked. Piatek smiled at Qaak. "I am not as old as you are, but as old as I am, I never dreamed such a thing to be possible."

"Indeed," said Qaak, his eyes glowing, "It was so long ago I had nearly forgotten." He raised a finger and closed his eyes. "Please be silent a moment." For a moment, the glow within Qaak's eyes seemed to pulsate irregularly, then he opened them. "Gaardian says it observed this type of phenomena twice before it met me thousands of years ago."

Walter's eyes had been closed but now opened them. "Eibbed, I suggest that you go to The Creator's Park to pray, and I further suggest that you take Piatek with you."

Piatek looked at Walter. "Why?"

"You will learn much when you are with Eibbed while she prays – and you, Piatek, will grow."

"I will grow? How?"

Walter smiled at them both. "You will both see." He paused. "Eibbed, do you recognize the new Zargadete Gaardian?"

She nodded. "He looks vaguely familiar, as though I have previously met him."

"You have more than met him. As Gaardian, he appears much younger than his true age. He is your old friend, Leahcim."

Her eyes grew wide. "Really! Yes, I can see it now! Yes!"

Walter smiled broadly. "I am glad that you are pleased, but you must not reveal his true identity to anyone, not even Arooda."

Suddenly, she was sober. "That is logical. I will honor him as I honor our friendship."

Walter nodded. "I am telling you this now because from this point on, when you press that hidden button on your desk, it will usually be Leahcim, as his younger self, that responds."

"I understand."

"Would you object to praying in the highest center tower in The Creator's Park? I can have Leahcim arrange for you to be undetected there any time you go there."

"This is good," she nodded.

"Walter to Leahcim, would you please come to The Suppla's office?"

Leahcim appeared nearby and took everyone in with his gaze. "Greetings, everyone!"

"Greetings," they all murmured.

Qaak walked towards Leahcim. "If you permit me, I will brief you on recent events."

"Certainly," said Leahcim.

Qaak placed three fingers on Leahcim's face and closed his eyes. It only took a moment. "Now you understand."

"Yes," said Leahcim, "I do. This is amazing. Eibbed. What are you going to tell the rest of our planet?"

"I do not know. I must pray. Please transport Piatek and me to that highest tower."

"As you wish," he said, as his ring shimmered, and they disappeared. "I will join them. When Eibbed has prayed it through, we will update you."

Walter nodded. "Very well." As Leahcim vanished, Walter turned to Qaak. "I think we're done here for now. Leahcim will let us know if he needs us."

"Indeed! Until then!"

"Until then." They both vanished.

11. The Big Picture

Kieya was pacing back and forth in her lair. "Kieya to Gaardian, after many days of prayer I can only conclude the time has come for the Felidacas learn they have a Gaardian that wants to help them. Felidacas are facing a planet-wide crisis soon."

The planet rumbled in her mind. "I will inform Walter." It paused. "It seems Walter has anticipated this from you. Do you wish to confer with him?"

Kieya became motionless and silent for several seconds. "Yes. The Creator does everything well. I will go to Walter's base."

"Very well."

Kieya resumed pacing back and forth several times. She paused near the entrance to her lair and looked out at the forest. Then she vanished.

+ + +

In the dining hall at Walter's moon base, he looked across the table at Debbie, as she fed puréed food to Joseph. Debbie paused and glanced at Walter. "I'm going to take Joseph to the pool after breakfast and see how he likes the water."

Walter smiled. "That sounds like fun! Butch was telling me that Joseph's growth and development seem to be a bit faster than that of most children." A chime sounded. "Yes, Frank?"

The android appeared next to their table. "Kieya will be here shortly. She wants to confer with you, as you anticipated."

"Okay. I'll meet with her in the media room." The android nodded and vanished. "I'd better go. I'll see you two later!" He stood up and leaned down to kiss Joseph on the forehead first. Then he kissed Debbie. "Have fun, you two!"

"We will! I'll take him with me to the office after our swim."

Walter nodded, turned, and then strolled rapidly out of the dining hall. As he crossed the atrium and walked towards the media room, Kieya appeared and walked beside him.

As they entered the media room, Kieya paused and looked around. "I do not believe I have been in here before. Is the stadium seating arranged that way for performances on the stage?"

Walter nodded. "Sometimes there are performances on the stage or three-dimensional videos. The large wall serves also as a two-dimensional video display for classic videos made on Earth."

The big cat purred as she settled on the front of the stage, and Walter sat down in front of her in the front row of seats. He waited for Kieya to speak.

She blinked. "My planet seems headed for a time of conflict. I think it is time that they learned about the Gaardians and learned of my presence."

"What prompted your decision?"

"I had a dream. One of our continents was on fire, and felidacas on the other continents did not wish to help extinguish the flames."

"I understand. It is a remarkable parallel to Eibbed's dream of her planet Pzalop being sliced apart by a cosmic string." Walter looked up, and then he looked back at his friend. "This is more than a coincidence. We must pray about this."

Kieya's purr became more intense. "I will go to a tower in that park on Pzalop. The Creator seems more intimately close there."

"It would not surprise me if you see Eibbed or Leahcim there."

"Yes, it seems to be a special place for many on that planet. Thank you, Walter, this has been brief but surprisingly very helpful. I will leave you now."

"Wait. ... Gmail to Qaak."

A portal appeared next to them, where Qaak was in his apartment with Jody. "Hello, Walter, Kieya."

"Hello, Qaak." Walter smiled.

The big cat purred softly. "Hello, Qaak."

"Qaak, in your conversations with Gaardian in these last few days, has it told you about brewing turmoil in several sectors of Gaardian space?"

"It has not told me of any particular conflicts. Why do you ask?"

"After Eibbed had a vision of Pzalop being sliced into two parts, Kieya has had a dream of one of her planet's continents on fire, with felidacas on the other continents unwilling to assist."

"Indeed. .. May I join you there in your media room?"

"Certainly."

The portal vanished, and Qaak appeared in person. He sat down in one of the theater's seats before speaking again. "Walter, why are you connecting these two visions together?"

"The Creator has revealed that they are parables. That is why I am calling a meeting of all Gaardians in about 36 hours."

The triped's eyes glowed intensely for a moment. "I am surprised that we did not anticipate this." He closed his eyes for a moment as they continued to glow. "Gaardian says that there are disturbances on several hundred planets in our space. You were the first to connect them." He closed his eyes again. "Gaardian will prepare a presentation for the meeting you have called. I will be there as you have requested, but I doubt I will have much to contribute since I am retired."

"Your presence will still be valuable."

Qaak nodded. "Thank you." He glanced at the big cat and back to Walter. "Jody loved our brief visit to the crystalline castle on Pzalop. I am going to take her there again during the next Pzalop night. I will see you and Kieya at the meeting. Until then."

"Until then," Walter and Kieya responded. The triped vanished.

Kieya stood up. "I am going back to my lair. I will see you at the meeting."

"Be at peace, my friend."

"I offer you the same." She vanished.

The media room began to fade, and the familiar glow of The Creator began to fill everything. The powerful low rumble of The Creator's voice seemed to fill Walter as well as the media room.

> Some of my children are afflicted with doubt and deception
> because they do not trust me. You understand this, Walter.
> Those who trust me experience both my peace and my love.

They thrive in the midst of adversity. Those who do not trust
me are angry because they do not have the blessings that
come with knowing me and trusting me. The visions I have
given Eibbed and Kieya are parables, as you surmised. You
must see beyond those two planets. I will help you help them,
Walter. Trust in me, as you always have.

The glow faded, and Walter sat there in the media room silently with his
eyes closed in meditation for more than an hour, hardly moving.

At last, Walter stirred. "Frank?"

The android appeared. "Yes?"

"In thirty-six hours, I want all available Gaardians to assemble at the
Gaardian Conference Center. Kieya and Qaak already will be there. Kieya and
Eibbed are not the only ones in Gaardian space that are anticipating division
and conflict. There are Gaardians other than Kieya and Leahcim that sense
some disturbances in Gaardian space. Let me know which Gaardians will not
come. I will speak to them individually."

"As soon as I have notified all Gaardians, I will inform you."

As Frank vanished, Walter stood up and stretched. Then he walked out of
the media room into the atrium.

12. Conference

The Conference Center orbiting Gaardian was glistening in the light of the
planet's sun. Gaardian's shadow covered about a third of it. Spherical, it
resembled a Bucky ball. Ten minutes before the appointed time of the
meeting, only Walter, Kieya, and Qaak were there, standing on the stage at the
front of the auditorium. Kieya got up off her haunches when Gaardians began
appearing. In the space of less than a minute, nearly two thousand Gaardians
appeared and sat down. Qaak walked off the stage to a seat in the first row.
Kieya also walked off and sat down completely, her head high and alert.

Walter stepped to the center of the stage. "Greetings, everyone, I thank all
of you for coming. Gaardian has prepared an extensive presentation for us, so
make yourselves comfortable. Gaardian?" Walter stepped off the stage and
sat next to Qaak and Kieya.

The planet's voice rumbled through the minds of those gathered, each in
their own language, as three-dimensional images of Pzalop appeared. "Not
long ago, Gaardians learned that two beings from two planets were to become
prophets, as Walter is a prophet." An image of the crystalline castle in The
Creator's Park appeared. "Our own Kieya, along with the Suppla of Pzalop,
experienced the presence and power of The Creator within this structure. Since
then, they have been learning from each other, from Walter, and from The
Creator. These two new prophets have had visions."

There were murmurs in the auditorium as the display changed to show a
graphic of a section of Pzalop being sliced invisibly away from the rest of the
planet. That was followed by a graphic of Kieya's planet, with one of the
continents in flames.

The planet continued. "Walter informed me that he had learned from The
Creator that these two visions are parables from The Creator. I have searched
the data streaming into me from all of Gaardian space. The rest of this

presentation will be regarding samples of turmoil in other sectors of Gaardian space."

For approximately three hours, the planet discussed wars and lesser conflicts from almost all parts of Gaardian space, with many disturbing images. Then the planet said, "I have done my part. Now it is time for Walter to talk to you as the Convener of Gaardians, as a prophet, and as our friend."

The last image disappeared as Walter stepped up on the stage again. His eyes swept over the assembly. "Thousands of years ago, The Creator spoke to a human named Jeremiah and said, 'Surely I know the plans I have for you, plans for your welfare and not for harm, to give you a future with hope. Then when you call upon me and come and pray to me, I will hear you. When you search for me, you will find me; if you seek me with all your heart, I will let you find me.'"

Walter paused and looked up for a moment, and then he returned his gaze back to the other Gaardians. "The Creator said this at a time on Earth when many humans were suffering in many ways, and there were many conflicts – both large and small. The humans God had set aside for special blessings had stopped trusting God. They were instead trying to trust just in themselves. The results were disastrous." He paused. "We must teach those in our sectors the benefits of trusting The Creator. Before we can do that, all of us are going to have to decide to trust The Creator ourselves."

There was murmuring throughout the auditorium.

Walter held up a hand, and the murmuring subsided. "Every single Gaardian has a smaller circle of Gaardians with whom they confer regularly for a variety of reasons. In just a moment, I want all of those small groups to meet together as groups on Gaardian's surface. There, I ask you to confer with each other and with Gaardian. Qaak and I will be available to supply your groups with whatever scientific and historical data you might need to help you work through this. When everyone in your group has made a firm commitment to trust The Creator in all circumstances, I invite you to share each other's struggles in your sectors as needed in light of this commitment. Finally, before returning to your sectors, please discuss strategies with one another for helping intelligent species in your sectors for teaching basic trust in The Creator. ... That is all for now. ... You are invited to go to the surface of Gaardian."

In seconds, all were gone except Walter and Qaak. A moment later, Pixie and Puz reappeared and walked towards Walter. Pixie smiled as she spoke. "We suddenly realized that we should be here with you, since we so often work together,"

Puz spoke gently telepathically. "Qaak, you are welcome to join us if you wish. I think we'll meet on that hill far above Red Falls."

The triped's eyes glowed briefly. "Thank you, but I shall decline and return to my apartment. I am retired. If you need me, you know where to find me." Qaak vanished.

Walter glanced back and forth with Pixie and Puz. "Let's head to that hilltop!" They vanished.

+ + +

They reappeared on the grass at the top of the hill, and they made themselves comfortable. Pixie looked at Walter. "You and I know each other very well, and both Earth and Aegeene have their Saviors. Do you want to talk about how you learned to trust The Creator?"

Puz's telepathic voice was calm. "I would be interested in this. Would it not be faster for you to do a direct mental transfer to us?"

Walter looked up briefly, and then looked at them. "Yes." Walter held out his hands, and they formed a circle, holding hands for about ten seconds.

When Puz opened his eyes, his telepathic voice was more animated. "This is amazing. I did not ever consider relating and communicating with The Creator in this way. Your followers of Jesus have a long history of this, do you not?"

"Yes, and as you now know, followers of Jesus certainly have made lots of mistakes along the way. On the other hand, God never makes mistakes. He does everything well."

Pixie nodded and smiled. "Yes, that is absolutely true. Puz, do you understand the logic upon which this conclusion is based?"

"Please explain."

"Walter, let me describe this, because I think I understand it pretty well." She turned and looked at Puz. "On Earth, Puz, a brilliant scientist named Albert Einstein once said, 'God created time so that everything would not happen all at once.' Since all of us here have had the experience of stepping outside of time with The Creator, we know that He exists apart from time. God is spirit, and the realm of the spirit is another universe parallel to ours. The Creator does not make mistakes because of seeing our existence apart from the passage of time."

Puz turned towards her for a moment, and then he turned toward Walter. He said, "Now I understand why it is logical to trust The Creator. He cannot only see my past but also my future. The Creator knows everything."

Walter nodded and smiled. "Yes!" He took a deep breath. "It appears that the two of you have joined me in trusting God with everything. We just do the very best we can and leave the rest up to Him." They nodded. "On Pzalop, the Suppla constantly has to remind everyone of The Creator's rescue of their planet. On Aegeene, you, Pixie, are going to have to get Eiraynay's followers to talk more about this issue of trust, just as Christians on Earth have always taught trusting God. You will have to find similar entries on the other planets in your sector. What about your sector, Puz?"

He was thoughtful. "I think that from this day forwards, when I am mediating conflicts, I will introduce the idea of having The Creator as a silent partner in the discussions. That will put a larger perspective on everything."

They nodded. Pixie said, "That is wise."

+ + +

As the small groups conferred all over the planet, Gaardian listened, and sometimes it was invited to participate in the discussions. Once again, the planet discovered that all of them had similar thought patterns when it came to discussing The Creator's role in their lives. Gaardian projected a thought to an apartment orbiting above the planet. "Qaak, I suggest that you and Jody come to your apartment in the nursery complex. Jody, I am learning to appreciate your love for Qaak and your role in his life. I would like you to come to my surface as well." A moment later, Qaak and Jody appeared in the apartment on the surface, and together they walked towards the fireplace in the living area and sat down.

Jody spoke aloud, "Gaardian, why did you want us here on your surface?"

"I wanted you closer to me for an extended discussion. One of the issues that has repeatedly surfaced in the group discussions has been that trusting often begins with forgiving something in the past. As a human, do you see this in the same way as Qaak does?"

Jody was thoughtful. "Yes, but since you are a planet and do not have biological processes, I can understand why this issue may perplex you."

Qaak's eyes glowed. "I have tried to explain the importance of forgiveness to Gaardian many times, but it sees forgiveness simply as a logical necessity. I have not been able to explain to Gaardian why some beings find it difficult to forgive."

Jody nodded. "Gaardian, when humans are either physically or emotionally hurt, healing takes time. Do you understand this?"

"Yes. When Qaak grieved for the death of his planet, all I could do was wait, while I was observing his healing process."

"That's good. When humans do not forgive those that hurt them, they keep remembering the pain as well as the injury. That emotional pain generates chemicals in their blood flow that is detrimental to their health. Simply stated, when humans fail to forgive, it is as though they are taking poison while waiting for the others to die."

Qaak chuckled, and his eyes glowed. "That is brilliant! That is a most excellent way to describe it!"

"I now understand," the voice of the planet rumbled. "Thank you. Do most humans understand this?"

Jody shook her head. "No. Sadly, most people do not."

The planet continued, "Trust is precious, and when it is lost it is difficult to regain. Is this not true?"

"Yes, it is very true, Gaardian."

Qaak looked at Jody intently. "You once told me that you trusted Walter from the very beginning. Was it because you had to, because you became part of his Gaardian team?"

"That's not entirely true, my love. Let me show you a video I've kept in my files just for fun." Her ring shimmered. A three dimensional video began in front of them. It showed Jody and Karen emerging from a lift aboard *The Grace* and walking into the lounge. Jody was speaking as they entered.

> "I asked Qaak if Walter knew all the stuff I knew. He said that he had taught me enough to get me started, and I in this instance I had learned about six percent of what he had taught Walter in my field of expertise."

The video showed the two women stopping for drinks at the synthesizer station and going to a window where Debbie, Stephanie, and Toby were already relaxed watching stars go by. Debbie appeared mellow.

> "Hey, strangers! What have you two been up to?"

Jody appeared still excited.

> "We've been having meetings of our minds with Qaak. I met with him before the meeting with Walter in the hanger, and Karen just now finished."

Debbie laughed.

"Isn't Qaak a trip? If he weren't a few thousand years too old for me, I think I might try to seduce him!" They all laughed.

"Well! Look who's coming to join the party!"

Butch was approaching with a smile and a chocolate sundae.

"Easy, Debbie! You and I can flirt another time! Right now, I want to indulge myself for a few minutes before getting back to the clinic."

"Speaking of getting back," Jody said, "I'd better get back to engineering. Now that I have Qaak's training to back me up, I need to start rehearsing various scenarios. See ya later!" Jody ambled off to the trans-lift.

Debbie was still mellow.

"I'm still thinking about what Jody said. If she knows only six percent of what Walter knows regarding engineering, his training must have been long and rigorous."

Butch paused between spoonfuls of his chocolate sundae.

"You've got that right. Walter's training was all night while he was sleeping every night, starting when he was a little boy until a short time ago."

Debbie whistled softly and smiled.

"The more I hear about that man the more he interests me - and not just as our leader."

"You'd better get in line, Karen said, smiling. Belinda has known him for most of her life. They met in grammar school and did not separate until after high school. If she wants him, she has the edge."

Debbie was thoughtful and had a wistful smile.

"Maybe, maybe not. Belinda is not out here while we are on *The Grace*. That could give one of us the edge - at least while we are out here

As the video concluded, Jody said, "What you did not see at that point was that Walter was very loving towards all of us, and we responded with trust. Since real love is completely trusting, it follows then that trust breeds trust."

The planet rumbled, "I will add this to my understanding of emotions. I seldom if ever experience emotions, since I have no chemical basis for them. I simply observe and analyze what I see in others." The planet paused. "Many Gaardians are now departing and returning to their sectors. Much has been accomplished. If the two of you wish to remain, some of them may pause for a meal before departing. I will supply food here in the lounge."

Qaak's eyes glowed. "Shall we stay, Jody?"

"Why not?"

13. Facing Reality

The Suppla once again sat at the large table with her Zargadete council. "I have one more issue to discuss with you before we conclude. ... Tomorrow I am going to broadcast a video planet-wide. While praying for Pzalop and all Zargadetes I have discerned some unrest that used to be properly handled by our military. I want all of you, as members of the council, to support this. Earlier today, we discussed the controversies and minor conflicts that have been dividing our communities. It has been more than a year since I last made a planet-wide address. What I will say in the video will reflect the consensus we have achieved today. I depend upon all of you to be supportive and not change your mind regarding the issues. Now, let us be adjourned."

The Suppla left for the office complex while council members talked quietly. One of the youngest members said unobtrusively, "I'm not sure a planet-wide address will do any good."

Leahcim, appearing as his older self disagreed, saying, "I don't think you realize that this will not be a political speech. Our Suppla has many gifts. That is why he is an effective leader. You will see, my young friend."

"I hope so."

As she went into her office, Arooda followed. Would you like me to help you prepare your speech? I can have summary notes of this meeting within an hour."

"No, Arooda, not this time. The Creator has given me what I must say. I will have you activate the recording system in a short while. We will then edit if necessary before supplying it for broadcast this evening."

"The Creator has spoken to you?"

"In His non-vocal voice, yes."

"How is The Creator's voice non-vocal? I don't understand."

Eibbed smiled. "Walter says that in his Christian scriptures, it is called 'the still, small voice.' When I first heard him use that expression, I was puzzled. Now I have spent time in prayer at The Creator's Park, and I understand. Let me have some time to prepare. I will call you when I am ready to record."

Arooda nodded. "I'll be in my office." He walked out.

Eibbed went to her desk and sat down. When she closed her eyes, a subtle glow surrounded her. She meditated for a much longer time than she anticipated. It was well past mid-day when she touched a triangle on her desk and spoke. "I'm ready to record now, Arooda. I want you at the control console while I speak."

"I will be right there."

As he entered, Arooda went to the far wall and pressed a short lever. A control console for both audio and video recording slid out of the wall. Cameras appeared in three locations, and a tiny microphone array rose from the surface of the Suppla's desk. He worked the controls for a moment. "I'm ready when you are."

Eibbed sat up a bit straighter and gazed into a camera about three meters from her desk. She closed her eyes for a moment, and then she cleared her throat. "I'm ready." She paused.

"Zargadetes, I have spoken to you many times as your Suppla. All of you know that we live in Gaardian space now because we were relocated to this solar system in this galaxy several years ago. Not long after, The Creator delivered our entire planet from death when He snatched a comet out of the sky while we watched. Recently, The Creator's Park was set aside by the Governing Council, and a place of sanctuary and prayer was created within it.

"On the opening day at the park, I was one of many Zargadetes who were there, and there were Gaardians there as well. I had two unusual experiences. First, the convener of the Gaardians introduced me to another Gaardian named Kieya. She is a felidaca – a large creature with stripes but with a face somewhat like ours. When I touched Kieya's fur, I had a sensation of peace and wholeness unlike any other experience I could have imagined. When I talked to Kieya about it at a later time, she said that she had a similar but slightly different experience.

"The second unusual experience that day happened when I knelt for prayer. It is difficult to find words to describe what happened. Two Gaardians who saw me praying said that I had a slight glow surrounding me. For a few moments, it was as though I were no longer on Pzalop or anywhere else in time and space. Simultaneously, I felt warm, calm, and safe. Several days later, the Convener of the Gaardians named Walter revealed something to me. The Creator told him that Kieya and I are to be prophets, each for our own planet.

"Several Gaardians in Gaardian space have had disturbing dreams, and I too have had a troubling dream. In my dream, I saw Pzalop sliced apart by a cosmic string fragment. The dream was repeated two additional times. Other Gaardians have had similar dreams of planetary division. The dreams are symbolic.

"We are a divided planet. Several times since The Creator delivered us from death, conflicts have arisen in some of our communities. These conflicts have had little or no merit. As a prophet, I must now speak to you about these conflicts. The Creator is watching over us, supplying all of our needs. When we fight over things we do not need, it is wasteful. The Creator has used the Gaardians to place Pzalop and the Zargadetes in a place of peace and wholeness. The Creator is being true to His promises made that day we were delivered. He started us down a new and more productive pathway.

"In spite of when our times become exceedingly difficult and threatening, we don't need to fear anything. This is because The Creator is watching over us as a parent watches out for children. We are being supplied abundantly even while our former enemies are having difficulties. The Creator is repeatedly supplying us with encouragement along our new path. We are being supplied with lifetimes of love and care.

"On the day we were delivered from the comet, The Creator said, "I forgive, I redeem, and I make new." If you have watched the so-called 'salvation video' recently, you know that The Creator loves us and wants the very best for us. The Creator is our hope. It was no accident Gaardians were here with us when we were delivered from death. It was no accident when the Quzak named Ooza promised to help us in any way she can. It is no accident that we now have one of our own, a Zargadete, as our Gaardian. We have been saved from ourselves, and we are being shown how to respond to that salvation that we saw as a hand in the sky. I am determined to do all I can to live a life worthy of what I have been given, both as a Zargadete and as your Suppla. I call upon all Zargadetes to pursue better relationships with The Creator and with each other. ... That is all."

Arooda worked the controls. "It sounded very good. Do you want to redo any of it?"

"I think I can make it more concise. Let's get something to eat, and then we can watch it and critique it."

"Good." Arooda stepped out from behind the console." I'll fix us something to eat, but first let me check to see if there are any messages." He went back out into his office."

+ + +

Felidaca day alliances had existed for as long as any males – or females – could remember. The closest equivalents on Earth were private clubs. Typically, male felidacas gathered in a secluded area of a forest for entertainment, swapping stories, and drinking edaem. There were several varieties of edaem available, prepared in various locations on the planet. All were made from fermented mixtures of sap and pollen varieties. Most felidacas that went to these day alliances were interested in relationships, either short-term or long-term. Some had mates, and some did not. Almost always, a few would drink too much edaem, and they would be escorted back to their lairs.

Kieya had not visited day alliances very often when she was young. Her previous mate, Legere, she met during intensive training exercises. They purred in concert together from that first day. Now, thousands of years later, Kieya was searching again for a mate. Margaret suggested she find a day alliance near her lair. She began exploring beyond her immediate neighborhood. It was not long before Kieya found a popular day alliance only a few thousand meters away.

As she approached, her Gaardian ring shimmered slightly, and she became invisible. Almost every felidaca there had a container of edaem. None of them were in the branches of the trees, so Kieya climbed up and found a comfortable place where she could relax and watch.

Her ring shimmered softly again as she sent a thought message to her governing planet. "Gaardian, please tune into my eyes and ears so that I may share this with you."

"Indeed," the planet's voice rumbled in her head. "It has been many centuries since I have observed felidaca social activity. ... Do you notice the male near the blue foliage that just purchased more edaem?"

"Yes."

"He appears to be a descendent to Legere's family, though not a descendent of one of your tats."

Kieya purred a bit louder. "He is beautiful, but I am not looking for a replacement for Legere."

"Are you not? Why is that?"

"Legere knew he was beautiful, and it was his vain arrogance that got him killed. I do not wish a repeat of that history,"

"I understand. What then are you looking for in a mate?"

"I am not sure." Kieya's gaze shifted to rapid movement nearby, just below her perch. "I wonder what he is doing."

"Indeed. I have not previously observed such skill combined with such great speed in any other creature in Gaardian space."

Kieya stared, as if transfixed. "Again, I ask, what is he doing? There appears to be debris flying in all directions, and no other felidaca seems to notice his work."

"I am fascinated. In a moment, you will see that this male is an artist. On your planet, sculpture is not a common art form."

"Sculpture? Of wood?" Indeed!"

Debris was no longer flying. Between this male's paws was an amazingly detailed sculpture of a felidaca about a half-meter long, and it bore a remarkable resemblance to Kieya. The male picked up his artwork in his mouth. He looked around. Not a single felidaca on the ground noticed that he was there. His body's stripes rippled rhythmically as he began to move away from the others.

Quietly, Kieya made her way down the trunk of the tree and followed. With them both on the ground, Kieya examined him more carefully. He was about the same size as she was, only he was less muscular. His stripes were not as pronounced as hers, and he was not well toned. Although she did not find him particularly attractive physically, his fur was clean and well maintained. Kieya was intrigued.

From time to time, as they walked, he would look back over his shoulder, sensing Kieya's presence but not seeing her. Kieya was suppressing her purr to near silence. After they crossed a river, Kieya let herself become visible, and she approached him.

He stopped, put the sculpture down, and looked over his shoulder at her. "You've been following me for a long time. I could sense your presence but could not see you. You have truly accomplished stealth!"

Kieya sat down on her haunches a few meters away. "I was very impressed with your speed and skill as I watched you carve that image. You are an amazing artist."

His purr grew louder. "Thank you. Where were you as you watched?"

"I was above you. I am interested in why your claws are not harmed or at least worn down by your artistic efforts."

His purr paused briefly as he stared. "I coat my claws with a special resin. I am amazed! It did not occur to me that anyone drinking edaem would venture higher into the foliage."

"I was not drinking. I was simply watching."

He looked down at his sculpture and back up at Kieya. "This has not happened ever before. As I was carving, I had an image in my mind. Evidently, my mind could see you."

"Indeed! ... I am growing hungry. May we eat together?"

"I would enjoy that. My home is towards the setting sun, some distance from here. I will need to eat before I make the journey."

"Excellent. Let us proceed. My name is Kieya."

"Mine is Icnivad ["IK-neh-vahd"]." He picked up the sculpture again in his mouth, and he started padding towards the sun.

14. Friends

Two days after the Suppla's planet-wide broadcast, the news capsules were still offering short segments of Eibbed's speech. Most of the council members had made public announcements the day after the speech in support. Small crowds now were appearing at The Creator's Park nearly every day.

Leahcim, as an older council member, identified the Suppla as a prophet. Since he was so well known and highly respected, this helped Eibbed to thrive in that role, as various Zargadetes sought the council of the Suppla.

At his base on Pzalop's moon, Leahcim lingered over breakfast with Adnil. "I want to bring our first recruits here today. We need to start training them."

"I hope I'll get some further training myself!" She smiled.

"Yes. Once we have them fully committed and present here at the base, I will bring in a Gaardian trainer to train all of you at once."

"How long will that take?"

"It will not take long. The trainer can give any Zargadete the equivalent of twenty years of training in just moments."

"You are serious!"

"Yes. We also need to evaluate how our planet's population is responding to the Suppla's new role as a prophet. Our analysis may have implications for other Gaardians in other parts of Gaardian space."

"I had not considered that."

"When we're finished with breakfast, we're going to a party."

"A party? Where?"

"It is on Gaardian, the planet. The party is a celebration of my becoming a Gaardian. There will be other Gaardians there, and you are invited."

"What do I need to do to get ready?"

"This is not a formal party. It should be fun, so just relax. Walter told me that you are my 'wife' now – the human term for a committed 'mate' – so we need to get used to doing things together as a couple."

They got up from the table. "Do you need further training too?"

"No. My training as a Gaardian is complete for now." They started moving towards the atrium. "How soon will you be ready to go?"

Adnil looked at her ring as it shimmered. Immediately, she was wearing more colorful clothing. "Thanks to support from my ring, I'm ready."

"Let's go out towards the recreation area." They started walking. "I've a special hovercraft waiting for us outside."

"Outside?" In a blink, they were in the hovercraft, seated near the front. "This does not look like any hovercraft I've ever flown in, Leahcim."

"This is true." His hands moved over the controls. "We'll be at Gaardian planet in a few moments. It's in another galaxy."

She stared out the windows, transfixed, as stars streaked by. "This is so beautiful."

"Yes." The stars stopped streaking, and a large planet loomed in front of them. "This is Gaardian. I think you'll like it." His ring shimmered, and they were standing beside a swimming pool near a large structure. Others were standing nearby, and they walked towards them. Leahcim began the introductions. "Adnil, I am sure you remember Walter. This is his wife, Debbie."

"I'm so glad to meet you, Adnil," Debbie said as she smiled. "This is Jody, one of my coworkers on Walter's moon base, and her mate, Qaak."

Jody beamed. "I'm glad to meet you."

Qaak's eyes glowed. "As I am, to meet you, Adnil."

Adnil looked at him curiously. "I understand you are the oldest and original Gaardian."

"Indeed. In terms of Pzalop years, I am slightly more than 46,000."

Adnil's eyes grew wide. "Amazing!"

Ooza and Puz approached. "Hello Adnil, Leahcim. It is good to see you both again."

"Yes." She smiled. "We met when you helped clear the atmosphere on Sunev. Hello Puz"

"Hello again," his telepathic voice rumbled. "The pleasure is mine. It is my privilege to introduce both of you to Gaardian, the planet on which we are standing. Gaardian, please offer your greeting."

"Hello, my friends, and welcome," the planet rumbled.

Adnil's eyes grew wide. "You are sentient?"

"Indeed."

Adnil's mouth remained slightly open as they all moved towards a large table with food.

A dark-haired woman approached Adnil and took her hand. "Hello, my name is Belinda. I am an old friend of Walter's. It is good to meet you."

"Hello, Belinda. Are you a Gaardian?"

Belinda smiled. "No, I am Walter's base commander, trouble-shooter, and friend. We have known each other since we were children."

"Leahcim and I have also known each other since we were small."

"So I understand. After we eat, I want you to join Jody, Debbie, and I for a bit of planetary exploration. As we get to know each other, we can talk about what it means to be the wife or mate of a Gaardian."

Adnil reached for a plate. "That sounds like fun. At this time, I find I am suddenly quite hungry. Shall we eat?"

"Of course."

+ + +

It was the middle of the night on Pzalop when Eibbed stepped out of the hovercraft at The Creator's Park. A few minutes earlier, she had left Arooda while he was sleeping soundly in her apartment. Eibbed dismissed the hovercraft and started walking down a path towards the crystalline castle. Though there was no moonlight, the path was lit by countless dots of light that lined the path's edges. Carefully hidden floodlights softly illuminated the park and the crystalline castle from the hilltops surrounding the valley. As she walked, she could see no other Zargadetes. As late as it was, she did not expect to see any.

Entering the castle, she proceeded directly to the large room in the center. She liked its spacious atmosphere, and looking upward, the crystalline lines of the structure formed beautiful patterns.

Certain of being alone, she prayed aloud. "I have been trying to be the prophet you have called me to be," said Eibbed. "The people of Pzalop have been watching the salvation video but not learning from it. They have been fighting over trivial things, and some have assaulted those who defend me. I am here in this place to commune with you." Outside, it began to rain, and rivulets of water began flowing over the crystalline castle. She watched for several minutes "Rain was not anticipated by our atmosphere scientists today, O Creator. Is this from you?" The rain became torrential, and wind began to blow from one direction, then from another direction, but Eibbed still felt alone. She was completely motionless for several minutes more. "Please, Creator, why is this happening?" The wind and rain became more violent, and the crystalline structure began to vibrate in a musical way. Now she was calm and at peace. She simply enjoyed the sound. "Creator, this has to be from you! I've at no time before seen a storm like this! I've not at any time in the past heard my surroundings sing! Is this you?" The ground began to quiver, and the entire castle began to vibrate at lower frequencies than those created by the wind. Eibbed fell to her knees in the center of the room. "It's you, isn't it Creator! It's you!" It was a symphony of sound, and it continued with waves of sound accompanied with flashes of lightning directly above.

Suddenly, all was quiet except for a whisper of wind she could barely hear. The rain stopped. "Thank you, Creator. Thank you!

Behind her, Eibbed heard Kieya's soft purr, and her voice quietly responding, "Yes, Creator! Yes, Jesus! Yes, Eiraynay! Yes, Arkaynee! Yes, Holy Spirit! Yes! Yes!"

Eibbed slowly turned towards her friend. "How long have you been here with me?"

She purred a little louder. "I was praying when the rain began. I looked all around and saw you below me. I transported here, but for some reason, I stopped breathing until the rain stopped. As a Gaardian, I am seldom in awe. This gives a new definition to the term."

"Yes. What were you praying about, Kieya? May I ask?"

"Certainly. I have been speaking in small gatherings as a prophet, but not to my entire planet as you have. I have also found a male felidaca that I want to get to know. I was talking to The Creator about the male named Icnivad and about the felidacas that will not listen to what The Creator has given me to say."

Eibbed nodded. "This is interesting. I know that all Zargadetes on Pzalop hear me when I speak, but I am not sure how many listen."

Kieya stretched out her front paws, putting the rest of her body on the cool floor. "The Creator does everything well. When we are given things to say, we say them, but we must leave the rest to the Creator."

Eibbed got off her knees to sit facing Kieya with her legs folded and crossed in front of her. "Yes. I learned long ago that though I have the power as Suppla to order things to be done, I have no control over my people's emotional reactions to me or to what I say."

The big cat paused to think, and then she resumed purring. "You lead by example and with the power of your voice as well as the authority of your office. I have not had a leadership role in my planet's government or society, and I do not seek this kind of role. It is enough to be a Gaardian, but The Creator wants more of me. I am honored by that call."

"Yes! It is more than enough for me to be Suppla, but The Creator asks more. It is a new kind of burden, and you are correct in identifying it as an honor. Tell me a little about this Icnivad of whom you spoke."

"I went to a social gathering not far from my lair. I chose to watch the others invisibly from up in a tree, and below me, nearby, was a male whose paws were moving with incredible speed, causing debris to fly in all directions. Gaardian was watching through my eyes and informed me that this furiously fast activity was artistic."

"He is an artist?"

"Indeed. When he stopped, between his paws was a wooden sculpture of me, about a half-meter long. He had not yet ever seen me, yet there was the sculpture."

"I am amazed. He did this with his paws? What were his tools?"

"They were his claws. Just as many humanoids coat their fingernails with colors for adornment, felidacas often coat their claws. He has invented a coating that is harder and stronger than titanium. His coat is clean and well maintained, but he is not exceptionally muscular. By felidaca standards, he is not notably attractive, yet I am fascinated by him. What drew you to Arooda?"

Eibbed smiled. "I am not entirely sure. I have trusted him and liked him since the moment we met. Love came slowly. He did not know I was a female until I told him. I would not have told him ever, if it were not for Walter revealing to me that he is totally trustworthy and loves me unconditionally. In a sense, Walter and Debbie helped bring us together."

"I am not sure whether I will seek Icnivad as my mate. We seem to be naturally moving in that direction. I need to discuss him with some friends on Gaardian planet."

+ + +

On Gaardian, Adnil, Belinda, Debbie, and Jody were standing on a cliff at the top of Red Falls. Adnil spoke louder because of the thunder of the falls. "I'm feeling better now about being the mate of a Gaardian. I have loved Leahcim all my life, and it is like fulfillment of a dream."

Belinda smiled. "That's great. That's why Walter wanted us to spend time together today. Now, Adnil, would you like to do something really, really fun?"

"What?" She almost yelled.

"Look at your Gaardian ring and think of your favorite swim wear.""

Immediately, Adnil was in a dark-blue bathing suit. "How's this?"

"Great! Do you see that whirlpool just beyond the base of the falls?"

Adnil nodded. "Yes!"

"At the count of three, we'll all jump into the whirlpool!"

"Are you serious? From this height?"

They all looked at each other. "One...two...three!"

They jumped. Plunging downward, they all screamed. The whirlpool was like a giant carnival ride. As they sank into the bottom, the planet transported them upward to a lake high above the falls. They all swam to the shore. Adnil watched as the others got out of the water. They walked a few steps towards the trees, and they were immediately dry and dressed in the casual clothes they had worn when they arrived.

Adnil followed and did the same. "What is next?"

Debbie pointed down into the valley far below them. I think that the others are about done with their welcoming party. We might as well go back and join them.

Adnil grinned. "That looks like quite a hike!"

"Not necessarily!" Jody responded. A small vehicle appeared next to them, and they got in. Jody suddenly sat up straighter. "Before we go back, why don't we do a quick tour?" The others, except Adnil, nodded.

"What kind of tour?"

Jody took the controls. "Watch."

They sailed up higher and higher, until, in space, they started moving towards a large, multifaceted ball. Debbie pointed. "That's the Gaardian conference center. You might as well take a quick look while you're here, Adnil."

A few moments later, they passed through a force field and landed in front of the entrance. Belinda grabbed Adnil's hand. "Come on in!"

Just inside they stopped, and Belinda gestured, taking in the entire cavernous room. "This is where all the Gaardians meet periodically. There are more than two thousand of them. At our current rate of growth, there will be three thousand within a few more decades."

Jody pointed. "Do you see that aisle in the middle? When Ooza and Steve got married, this hall was filled to overflowing with creatures from all over Gaardian space. The wedding party marched down that aisle – followed by Ooza of course. Now, Adnil, we've got one more stop to make."

"Where?" asked Adnil.

"To save time, we'll go there Gaardian style, okay, Debbie?"

"Sure!" Debbie's ring shimmered, and all of them were immediately in Jody's and Qaak's apartment satellite.

"This is my home." Jody pointed out and downward. "Down there is Gaardian planet."

"It's beautiful! What a view you have!"

Debbie smiled. "On Earth, it is appropriate to offer a toast on special occasions. Adnil, hold out your hand like you're holding a glass of liquid like this." Debbie held out her hand, and the others followed. Champagne glasses appeared with champagne in each of their hands. "I propose a toast to Leahcim and Adnil, the newest members of our Gaardian team!"

"Yes!" The others said.

"Thank you! This has been a truly memorable day!"

"Absolutely!" Jody beamed. "Now, once again Gaardian style, let's go back and join our mates."

In a blink, all of them appeared on the planet's surface, and they rejoined the others.

15. Checking

The atrium at Walter's Gaardian base on Earth's moon was quiet. In the dining hall, a few were quietly finishing dessert after dinner. The clinic was quiet. About fifty of Walter's team were watching an old Marx Brothers movie called *Duck Soup in the media room.* In the recreation area, some were working out, some were swimming, and a few were in the hot and cold whirlpool.

Kieya appeared near the center of the atrium and silently padded towards the lounge. There, Margaret and Piatek were seated near the fireplace and chatting quietly. As Kieya entered, Piatek said, "I love that whirlpool! I'm going to talk to Ooza about having one at our base!"

"Hello, my friends," said Kieya as she walked in. I understand this works out best for us this time."

"Yes," Piatek nodded, "Walter wanted me to meet with some of his crew to use my gift, and he wants to know more about Margaret's gift after we have met regarding a mate for you."

"Yes," the big cat purred. She settled down on the floor. "I am intrigued with a felidaca by the name of Icnivad."

Margaret nodded. "I want to hear the whole story."

Piatek got comfortable in her chair. "As do I."

"It was your suggestion that I find a gathering near my lair. I found one only a few thousand meters away." She paused briefly. "When I found it, I chose to be invisible as we discussed. I had Gaardian, the planet, observe through my eyes and ears. As I told it, I had already decided that I did not want another mate like Legere. I loved him, but his vanity got him killed. I did not know what kind of mate, if any, was in my future. Gaardian called my attention to an indirect descendent of Legere, but I did not consider him."

Margaret gazed at the big cat. "Did you wander about among them?"

"No. Most of them were consuming various amounts of edaem. I did not wish to have one of them bump into me accidentally because I was invisible. I found an almost level branch of a tree about ten meters above the ground and made myself comfortable."

"What is edaem?" asked Piatek.

"It is an intoxicating beverage brewed with various blends of sap and pollen."

She nodded. "Continue please."

"I noticed some rapid movement almost directly below me. Looking through my eyes, Gaardian had as much difficulty as I did in determining what he was doing. There was debris flying everywhere from where he was working. It tuned out that he was an artist and, in this case, a sculptor. When he stopped, the completed effort was a half-meter statue of me." Kieya's purr was louder.

"But you were invisible!" Margaret was fascinated.

"Later he told me that he had an image in his mind of what he sculpted. He said he had never had that experience before."

Piatek was curious. "What kind of blade did he use? After all, with your paws I would think it difficult to hold a knife or chisel combined with the speed you described."

"Indeed. The material he carved is quite dense and hard, yet he did it all with his claws."

"What?" The women asked almost simultaneously.

Kieya purred steadily. "Yes. I too was truly amazed. Let me finish my story, and afterwards question me please." They nodded as she continued. "After he finished it, he picked it up in his mouth and started to leave. I followed. With some effort, I suppressed my purr to be almost inaudible, and I remained invisible. After we crossed a river, I made myself visible, and we began to walk and talk. After introductions, he complimented me on my stealth skill and asked where I had been in the gathering. Later, I learned that he coated his claws with a formula that he himself had developed. That is the basic story of how Icnivad and I met. He and I have talked frequently since then." Her purr was soft and steady.

Margaret held up a finger. "Do felidacas coat their claws just as humans used fingernail polish?"

"Yes. In this case, there was no change in color. His formula is synthetic, and it is both harder and stronger than titanium. I looked at his claws that day, and I could detect no wear, scratches, or other problems with the coatings. His formula is almost as remarkable as he is."

Piatek gazed at the big cat. "Please let me use my gift. Just look at me and relax."

"Very well, I can do this."

"I want you to describe your impressions of Icnivad. Don't talk about what either of you said or did. Just talk about your impressions of him as a felidaca."

Kieya's purr continued to be steady, but it grew very soft. "Icnivad is not appealing physically. His fur is well-groomed, but his muscles are not well-defined."

Piatek's gaze was steady. "His stripes are not as well-defined as yours. His eyes are large."

"Yes. He is ... brilliant ... articulate ... confident ..."

"Icnivad is lovable ..."

"Yes. He is loving ... totally trustworthy ... truthful ... responsible ... honorable ..." Kieya blinked and sat up straighter. "I see now! He could even be a Gaardian!"

Margaret watched the two of them, fascinated. "There is more about Icnivad, isn't there, Kieya!"

Kieya's purr was now strong and steady. "Yes, definitely, there is more. I truly loved Legere, but I love this felidaca differently, perhaps more."

Piatek sat back and relaxed. "Yes, Kieya, he is your intellectual and emotional equal, isn't he?"

"Yes, and I did not think that possible in a felidaca. That was my pride." She paused. "Kieya to Asayak: Are you on the moon base?"

Only Kieya could hear its response in her head. "Yes."

"Would you please come to the lounge?"

"Yes."

"Ladies, Asayak will be here in moments. I do not believe you have met it. Asayak speaks telepathically and has amazing gifts."

The seven-foot tall creature glided into the lounge. Piatek noticed that its smooth translucent green skin was a similar color to her own, but that it seemed to glow subtly. As Margaret looked it over from top to bottom, she saw that it had lots of long hair mingling with the glow, with four arms that swung somewhat. It also had an array of finger-like appendages at the ends of its arms. Piatek was fascinated with what appeared to be an eye near its top, but she knew instinctively that the 'eye' was an illuminating organ of some kind. There was no evidence of ears or mouth. It moved smoothly across the floor with no legs. They heard its voice say, "Greetings, everyone. How may I serve?"

Margaret and Piatek murmured greetings in response. Kieya purred as she said, "Asayak, I am glad you are present and available. Please scan my mind for our conversations since we got here today."

Asayak settled lower, with some of its body going out behind it. "This is unique. It fascinates me. Piatek, your gift is similar to one of mine, but it is also different. Margaret, I hope Piatek helps you explore your gift. Kieya, how may I assist you?"

"Asayak, my friend, do you remember the time I asked you to explore the lives of two scientists on Earth?"

"Of course, I do. Do you wish me to perform this type of examination with regard to Icnivad?"

"Yes, my friend."

"One moment please." It paused about twenty seconds. "Walter says I am to take what time I need for this today."

Margaret stared. "I don't think Walter is on this base. You just spoke to him?"

"Yes. I have discovered a way to communicate telepathically across several galaxies."

Piatek's mouth dropped open. "You can communicate across galaxies?"

"Yes. I am able to do it with Gaardian ring support. Now I must proceed with the task given me. It has been a privilege to meet you, Margaret and Piatek. I hope to see you again."

Margaret nodded, and Piatek said, "We hope so too."

"Until then." It vanished before the others could respond.

Piatek was emphatic. "That is an amazing creature! Is it from Walter's sector of Gaardian space?"

Kieya relaxed against the floor again. "Yes. It has become our principal trainer since Qaak retired. Thank you for letting me share this with you today, and thank you both for your input."

Margaret nodded. "You're welcome, Kieya. Will you keep us apprised of what happens with you and Icnivad?"

"Yes. I will be pleased to do so," Kieya purred. "Piatek, I will send you back to Ooza's base now, unless you have anything else to do here."

"That will be fine, Kieya. Good by, Margaret!" She turned and gave her human friend a hug. Then, as Kieya's ring shimmered, Piatek vanished.

"Margaret, do you have other business here at Walter's base?"

"I think I'd like to stay here long enough to enjoy one of Dawn's dinners. I'm sure someone can get me back to Oakland."

"Very well, Margaret, I will probably see you again soon. Until then."

"Until then."

Kieya vanished. Margaret stood up, stretched, and headed to the dining hall.

+ + +

Together, Walter and Debbie walked along the shore of a cobalt-blue lake on Gaardian. Debbie looked up at her husband. "Did you get a telepathic message a moment ago?"

Walter smiled and looked down at her. "I'm sorry! Was I gone long?"

She poked him in the ribs with a finger. "No, you seemed out in space just for a moment. Was it important?"

"It's important to Kieya. She has found a felidaca that may become a mate for her. She's not had one for thousands of years."

"What happened to her previous mate?"

"He was killed in a senseless fight with several other felidacas, and the killers were never caught."

She nodded. "So what was it you had to deal with?"

"Kieya is asking Asayak to do a detailed and complete assessment of this male felidaca. I gave Asayak permission to take whatever time it needs to do it. It's similar to a background check, only it is much more detailed and personal."

"Do you know anything yet about him?"

"At this point, what I can say for certain is that he is very different from her previous mate, and he is an artist."

"If he is an artist, that could very well make things interesting for Kieya. After all, you married an artist too!"

He squeezed her hand. "That I did!" Let's go back to the apartment and nursery complex and pick up Joseph. I think its time we went home, don't you?"

She nodded. "Yes. I can't complain about the on-demand food we have here on Gaardian, but I still enjoy Dawn's home-cooked creativity and variations."

"Amen to that!" His ring shimmered, and they were on the patio of the apartment complex. "I think Joseph is in the nursery. Gaardian, can you bring him out, please?"

"Certainly." As Debbie held out her arms, Joseph was there immediately.

"Gaardian, we are going back to Earth."

"Very well."

The three humans vanished.

16. Gifts

Leaving her car, Margaret walked past the memorial rose garden to the west door of the church. She put her hand against a scanner to the left of the door, and she heard the lock click open. It was 7:00 AM, which was much earlier than usual. Down the short entry hallway she turned left, went straight to the stairway door, and stopped. She felt a tingle on the back of her neck. "Frank, is everything okay?"

Walter's android appeared next to her. "No, Margaret, I will take care of it. Go ahead upstairs. I will take care of this."

As Frank vanished, Margaret went through the stairway fire door and started up the stairs. Just before the door clicked shut behind her, she heard some men yelling. She smiled. Those men did not know what they were up against. At the top of the stairs, she went through the stairway fire door, down the hall, and into her office.

Just after she sat down at her desk, Frank appeared again. "I'm here only to let you know what happened. There were two men there on the ground level and two others in the basement. I detected an empty cell at the jail downtown, and I put them in it so that they were wearing nothing but their underwear. One wasn't wearing underwear, so I supplied a pair of briefs. All the things that they looted I put in their van, along with their clothing and weapons. If anyone other than a police officer tries to gain access to the van, there is a surprise waiting." By this time, Margaret was smiling broadly. "I'm sure this is somewhat comical to you, Margaret. I sent an email to the police, detailing all of this with Walter's signature. I told them that by chance these men encountered one of Walter's agents who was patrolling the area on another matter."

"That's great, Frank. Thank you"

"You're welcome." The android vanished.

Margaret picked up her phone handset and punched a number. It rang twice before a connection was made. A female voice said, "Hello?"

"Good morning, Ann, this is Margaret."

"Good morning! Are you at the office already?"

"Yes. You know I like to get started early in the day. Do you still have an appointment with Ben today?"

"Yes, but I am not going to his office. He is coming to the church at 10:00. He's bringing Senator Steinmetz with him."

"Good! I've been wanting to meet that man. Are you going to get here about nine, as usual?"

"No, I'm just now getting ready to go out the door. Why do you ask?"

"We had some unwanted visitors here when I arrived this morning. Frank took care of them."

"Really!"

"Yes, so if you see police cars here when you arrive, just be prepared."

"Okay. I'll see you in ten or fifteen minutes."

"Right." She hung up. A chime sounded, and she turned and looked out the window and down to the parking lot. A police car was there, parked next to her car. Margaret pressed a button. "Yes? May I help you?"

A female voice said, "This is the Oakland Police. May I please come in?"

"I can see your car in the lot. I will be right down to let you in." Margaret chuckled after releasing the button. She went downstairs much faster than she had come up. She smiled as she approached the door and let the officer in. "Hello. I am Margaret Graves. What is the problem?"

"The church was burglarized this morning, Ms. Graves."

"Really! This is a large building. I entered from this door and did not see anyone."

"That's understandable. They entered on the other side, off of twenty-ninth street."

"I did not see any damage on the level above us. Why don't you walk with me across the main level, and we'll see if there are any problems on this level before we go downstairs."

"Thank you. Please lead the way."

Margaret kept a straight face as she walked down the hallway. They looked into the large hall on their left, but she knew there was no damage there. The kitchen door was locked, so they proceeded into the worship area. She pointed. "It looks like they stole our communion ware and the microphones." The officer wrote in her notebook. Going on across, they went down the enclosed stairwell, past the custodial apartment and the rest rooms, and there were no evident problems.

As they entered the basement, Margaret pointed to the other end of the large hall. "That stage curtain is normally closed. They may have gone back there to steel some of our equipment."

"Yes, we think they did." She wrote more down in her notebook."

Margaret stepped into the kitchen and pointed again. "I can see that a number of our appliances and larger pots are missing."

"Okay." She wrote it down.

Another officer came into the kitchen. "Hello. I'm officer Peterson." He turned to the other officer. "Karen, have the two of you looked things over upstairs?"

"Yes. I've written down what she's told me. This is Margaret Graves. She works upstairs."

"Okay." He turned to Margaret. "We have a van full of stuff, but how much of it belongs to the church we don't know yet. You or someone else from the church will have to come down to claim things after we've finished our investigation."

Margaret kept a straight face as she asked, "I did not call the police. The alarm did not go off. Why are all of you here?"

Now he smiled. "I wish we could get help like this more often. Evidently, one of the Gaardian operatives was in the neighborhood, for some reason. He took the suspects into custody and placed them into one of our jail cells. We never saw him. Chief Williams got an email from the Gaardian, informing him where the suspects were held, where the church was, and where the van was. With the suspects already in custody, all we have had to do is investigate. We're getting lots of fingerprints, so assuming the prints of the suspects are in the van, in the church, and on the evidence, we've got a good case."

Margaret nodded. "Good. Please give the church a call when necessary. If you will excuse me, please, I have to get back upstairs." She looked at her watch. "We have an appointment with some very important guests in a little while, but that will be in the area of my office, on the other side of the building, away from your crime scene. I would appreciate it if you did not disturb us again until this afternoon – unless absolutely necessary of course."

"Yes, Ms. Graves. We will do our best. Thank you."

"Thank you." Margaret went back upstairs. On the other side of the building near the parking lot, she saw Ann Cotter as she was coming in. "Good morning again, Ann."

"Good morning. I saw the police at work over on the other side. I guess they'll be here for a while.""

She nodded. "Yes. Frank left them all the evidence they needed for a good case. The rest is up to the court and the lawyers."

They parted to their separate offices. As Margaret sat down at her desk, she saw a light flashing on her phone. Picking up her handset, she punched numbers for her voice mail. As her message was about to play back, Piatek appeared in a g-mail next to her desk. "Good morning, Margaret."

"Good morning, Piatek."

"Would it be convenient for us to meet at your apartment this evening? I know you've been wanting to discover and explore your gift."

"I would like that, Piatek."

"Good. Until then."

"Until then," Margaret smiled.

+ + +

As the flight attendant opened the plane's door, Senator Everett Steinmetz rose from his first-class seat. With his briefcase in his left hand, he extended his right hand to a flight attendant at the door. "Thank you for your helpful service on this flight," he said, smiling.

"You're welcome, Senator Steinmetz."

He walked out the door and proceeded up the gangway at San Francisco International Airport. There was a small crowd at the gate, but no one seemed to recognize him. He walked briskly until he saw Jonnie Riley, who was waiting for him just beyond the security gate. As she waved, he smiled at her.

She was as effervescent as usual as she greeted him. "Good morning, Senator Steinmetz! Did you have a good flight?"

"It was smooth except for the early approach into here. Did you hear that your appropriations for the Sierra Club are approved?"

"Yes! Thank you!" They started walking. "After we pick up your bag, I have my car waiting."

"I don't have a bag this time. My secretary shipped my bag ahead to the Mark Hopkins yesterday."

"Good."

Less than ten minutes later they were driving out of the airport and going north on highway 101. The senator adjusted his seat to lean back slightly, and he relaxed. "Jonnie, how well do you know Margaret Graves?"

"I've worked with her several times, senator. Ben Kaiser has been using her services too. He thinks she's great."

The senator nodded. "Ben has told me about her, and he does his homework. Her background seems to be okay, and her work seems to speak for itself."

"She will meet us in Ben's office after lunch. I'm taking you to the hotel first."

"That's very good, Jonnie. My body is in the eastern time zoon, so I want to stretch out and take a nap."

Jonnie chuckled. "Are you ever bothered with jet lag?"

"Not very often, but today I have a little. I've been bouncing between the coasts a lot lately. My grandson is doing some work for Ben over in Fresno."

"Speaking of Fresno, isn't that dome they've built for the zoo amazing?"

"Yes! I've been very impressed." He became quiet for a few miles, then he spoke quietly. "Have you ever heard anything more about a big cat up in the redwoods' area?"

Jonnie shook her head. "I've made a few discrete inquiries, but if anyone knows anything, they're not telling the Sierra Club."

"That's interesting. I still wonder about that. According to a veterinarian I know, the size and depth of those paw prints indicate a cat weighing somewhere close to seven hundred pounds [317 kilograms]."

+ + +

Kioya was sound asleep in her lair when she was awakened by a chime. "Yes?"

The planet Gaardian spoke to her telepathically. "You wanted to know more about the gift that The Creator has given Margaret Graves. She is meeting with Piatek soon in her apartment, and she has told Walter she would like you to be there."

The big cat purred. "This is excellent. I am enjoying my friendship with those two human females. I will be there. Please arrange to inform Margaret."

"It shall be done." The planet became silent.

Kieya looked at her ring on a finger of her right front paw. "Attention felidaca team members. I will be away from our planet for the next two to three solar cycles. Follow your usual procedures. Thank you." She paused and breathed deeply as she purred. "Gaardian, where is Leahcim located?"

"Leahcim is at his base, in the clinic."

"Thank you. Kieya to Leahcim."

A portal opened next to her, where the newest Gaardian appeared. "Hello Kieya."

"Hello. Are you now fully organized, or is Puz still helping you?"

"Puz is available, but I am endeavoring to work independently. Things are going as well as I could have expected."

"Good. Do you remember the piece of furniture in Eibbed's office where she prays?"

"I do, of course. It inspired me to put kneeling areas in the crystalline structure in The Creator's Park."

"Yes, I remember. Have you considered having such a piece of furniture in your apartment, made from the beryllium aluminate from that vein of crystal?"

"That is an excellent idea! Would you like me to design something similar for you, only designed for a felidaca such as yourself?"

The big cat purred more intensely. "Indeed! That would be excellent. I liked the platinum cloth covering on the praying pads in The Creator's Park. I would like a large, low bench, large enough for two felidacas to recline upon it, and padded as on Pzalop in the park."

"This is an easy request. Shall I transport it to your lair?"

"Please. I will not be in my lair for a few days, but you may proceed as needed."

"As you wish, it shall be done. Perhaps we will see one another soon. Until then."

"Until then." The portal closed.

"Kieya to Ooza." Another portal opened, and the petite Quzak female appeared.

"Hello, Kieya. As my Steve would say, 'What can I do for you?'"

"Hello, Ooza. Is Piatek there with you?"

"No, Kieya, I have already transported her to Margaret's apartment. Are you going to be there?"

"Yes, Ooza. Would you like me to transport Piatek home after our meeting with Margaret?"

"Yes, thank you, Kieya. I'll see you soon. Until then."

"Until then." The portal closed, and Kieya vanished.

17. A Unique Gift

Crossing over from the door to the kitchen, Margaret walked with Piatek to a sofa in the living room, and they sat down. Margaret straightened a pillow behind her back and said, "I'm expecting Kieya any minute."

They sat silently for a moment, and then Kieya appeared near the front door. "Good evening! It is pleasant to see you both."

Margaret stood. "It is good that you are here, Kieya."

Piatek nodded. "I agree. It is very good, Kieya."

As she sat down again, Margaret pointed to a space near her television. "I think there's enough room there for you to be comfortable, Kieya."

"Indeed, it is." She went there as directed and sat down.

Margaret turned slightly towards the Quzak. "How shall we proceed, Piatek?"

"It amazes me that you are now in your second lifetime, this time working for a Gaardian, and you still do not recognize your gift as a gift. You can do something that comes naturally to you, but which is unique in my experience. I discussed this briefly with Gaardian, and it says that it does not know of any other being that can do what you do. I would like to help you demonstrate your gift."

"You have me mystified. Please proceed."

"Turn and look directly at me, and while doing so describe our last meeting in as much detail as you can."

"Kieya began by telling about the gathering near her lair."

"Yes. Don't tell us about what anyone said. Tell me your impressions."

"Okay. ... As Kieya described going to the gathering and finding a place in a tree from which to observe, she purred softly. ... She felt comfortable, and at peace."

"Kieya mentioned not wanting another mate like Legere, and she purred less. ... She had mixed feelings about her memories of Legere."

Piatek nodded. "Kieya was intellectually curious about those consuming edaem. There was no purr."

There was a subtle blaze within Kieya's eyes as she focused upon the two females and their conversation.

Margaret spoke quietly and clearly. "As Kieya's gaze had shifted to the rapid movement below her, her purring became intense. It was a purr unlike any she had had in centuries."

"Yes. Her purring was not entirely her own. It was in concert with the felidaca below her."

"Agreed. As Kieya began describing to you his impressions of Icnivad, you became very pleased with Kieya's description. As Kieya described Icnivad, her portrayal brought back a flood of emotions to you from your own distant past. Right now, you are having difficulty focusing on what I am reporting because you are again being flooded with memories."

Piatek did not blink. "Continue."

"As Kieya began to report more about Icnivad and compare her love for Legere with her love for Icnivad, her purr was beyond her control. Her love is real. She could think of no one else in that moment."

"And when Asayak came into the room?" asked Piatek.

Margaret took a slow breath and sighed. "Asayak is a beautiful and humble oroature. It's thoughts are wild, going in many directions at once and yet totally disciplined."

Piatek blinked, and she blinked again. She sat back against the sofa and sighed. "This was amazing Margaret."

Margaret took the pillow from behind her back and sank more deeply into the sofa. "Yes."

Kieya hummed briefly. "Margaret, I now understand the nature of your gift. You don't merely see the emotions of other beings. You can experience their emotions with them. Unlike one who has total empathy, you can control how much you experience the emotions of others, can't you?"

Margaret looked at the big cat. "Yes. Can't others do this?"

"No. ... I have a question. Could you experience the emotions of others in your first life as Margaret Fields?"

"Yes! However, I always thought that other people could experience my emotions just as I could experience theirs. It never occurred to me to ask, however."

Piatek chuckled. "That might have been a good thing!"

Margaret nodded. Kieya's purr became more pronounced. "I have two additional thoughts. It does not seem to matter the species with whom you interact. You could share not only my emotions, but Piatek's and those of Asayak. Is this sometimes overwhelming?"

Margaret shook her head. "Not since my early childhood. When I tried to explain to my mother how I could experience the feelings of others, she was amused and thought I had a vivid imagination. You are right. I can control it."

"Indeed. My other thought is of a broader perspective. Our planet, Gaardian, has often stated that it cannot experience emotions, so it simply tries to understand them. I am wondering if you and Piatek could work together to teach the planet how to experience emotions, even if it is only the emotions of others."

Piatek sat up straight. "That is an intriguing idea. Margaret, would you be willing to try this?"

"I don't know. I need to pray about it first."

"Indeed," the cat purred. "I agree. Piatek, do you wish to go further with this during this meeting?"

"No, I think not. Will you send me home, Kieya?"

"I can do this."

"Margaret, this seems to have gone even better than I had hoped. I hope now that we will get together again on Gaardian."

"Perhaps. Until then?"

"Yes, until then." She looked at the big cat. "Kieya?"

The cat's ring shimmered, and she was gone. Kieya purred softly. "Margaret, I have enjoyed your hospitality, and thanks to you, I have seen something unique this evening. I look forward to our next meeting. Until then?"

"Until then."

The big cat vanished.

+ + +

Kieya appeared just outside her lair in the shadows of twilight. Instead of going inside, she began to walk. At first, she was not sure where she wanted to go, but soon she realized she was following the last glow of sunset. "Walking will take too long," she murmured to herself.

In a blink, she was in the midst of some deep foliage, just outside Icnivad's lair. "Icnivad?"

He appeared in the doorway. "Kieya!" He stepped forward and rubbed his cheek against hers. "Please come into my lair."

Inside, much of his lair was furnished with things he had created. They walked about, purring together in concert. "It is all so beautiful. I draw images on my walls, and you create three-dimensional images."

"Yes. I am glad you are here. May I offer you some edaem? I make a special blend myself."

"Certainly. I will be pleased to try some of your edaem." He went into an adjacent room. He came out, walking on his hind legs, and carrying the edaem. Vertically, he was about the same height as Kieya. "Enjoy!"

For several hours, they relaxed and drank his edaem. Finally, he asked, "It is time you told me why you have come to visit me."

"Yes. Have you considered whether we should become mated before your family?"

"I have thought about little else in recent days. Do you not want your family present?"

"My family is very distant. Instead, I would have friends present. Before we commit to one another, however, there is something important that you need to know."

"I will listen carefully."

"Do you listen to news each day?"

"Yes, definitely, I do, because many of my sculptures are based upon events in the news."

"Have you noted the news that we are in what is now called 'Gaardian Space?'"

"Yes. This news is difficult for me artistically, because of trying to conceive things beyond our planet."

"I understand. I trust you completely, Icnivad, so from this day forwards there will be things I will tell you that you can tell no one else. I am the Gaardian of this sector of Gaardian Space."

His purring stopped momentarily, and then it resumed, but louder. "This explains many things! Tell me more!"

"I could do that, but there is a faster and easier way. I assume that you trust me. Am I correct?"

"You are absolutely correct."

"With your permission, I will bring an alien being to your lair, and he will teach you many things with great speed and little effort. Will you permit this?"

"I am intrigued! Yes! Of course, yes!"

"Kieya to Asayak: If you are available, please come and join me at this location, and you will meet the felidaca who is to become my mate."

A moment later, Asayak appeared on the other side of the room. "Greetings!" They both heard its voice in their heads.

As Kieya purred softly, Icnivad said, "Taaaa!" His mouth hung open slightly.

She rubbed her shoulder against his. "Relax, dear one. This is Asayak.

It flowed forward, extending an arm with a few appendages. "I am pleased to meet you. I speak telepathically, so that is why you hear my voice inside your head."

Icnivad went up on his hind legs and extended a front paw. "I am pleased to meet you as well. I am an artist, and I am trying to imagine how I could carve an image of you in wood."

"I would like that. That is an interesting idea." It turned slightly. "Kieya, have you brought me here to train him?"

"Yes, my friend, I would like you to tell him what he needs to know about me, and about the Gaardians, so that he can function comfortably with the knowledge of who I am."

"I am pleased to serve." It turned back to Icnivad. "I believe you will be more relaxed if you are on all four of your legs. I will flow down to your level."

As Icnivad went down, Asayak flowed downward to the same height, extended the rest of its body behind it. Icnivad said, "What else will I have to do?"

It extended one of its arms and said, "Just press the side of your head against my arm and close your eyes."

As Icnivad did so, the two of them were enveloped in a soft glow for less than three minutes. He had no purr, but as Asayak flowed away slightly and lowered its arm, he purred strongly. "This is amazing!"

Kieya stepped forward and rubbed her cheek against his. "Yes, indeed it is! Thank you, Asayak."

"You are most welcome. It has been pleasant to see both of you."

"You also," they said almost together.

It vanished.

"If you wish, we can celebrate our union somewhere in a forest. One or both of us must move our possessions. Do you need to live in this location?"

He shook his head. "I would rather we find a new location." He looked around at his lair. "It is going to take some time to move all of this."

"Think. I am a Gaardian. The moving will take virtually no time. I will let you do the arranging. Since I spend two-thirds of my time away from this planet, I will let you choose a location. Then I will configure us a lair using my Gaardian techniques. It can be as large as you wish, and it can be in any configuration you wish. It can be in the middle of a population area, or it can be in wilderness. It will make no difference to either of us. I will see to that."

Icnivad began to purr more intensely. "There is a small community in the mountains above the large lake we visited together once. It is on the sunrise side. Can you picture it?"

"I can do better than that. Put one paw on top of my shoulders." He did so, and in a blink, they were among trees on the edge of the little community he described."

He took his paw down and stared at the little community. Then he turned to her. "This is amazing! You did that so easily!"

Kieya purred with him. "Yes. It is simple for me." She turned and pointed. "Do you see that cliff above us? There is no cave in it, but I can create a large lair within the cliff and the mountain. Would you like that?"

He looked around. " sun's light on the cliff is constant, and there are never any shadows. It would be good for both the weather and the light."

"Come, my mate, let's start a home." She started walking up the hillside, and he followed. At the base of the cliff she asked, where would you like the entrance?"

Icnivad pointed upward. "I like that overhang there. Can we put the entrance under it?"

He did not see it, but Kieya's ring shimmered as an opening appeared at the base of the cliff, under the overhang. They walked towards the entrance of their future home.

+ + +

At Walter's former church in Oakland, Margaret was upstairs in her office, looking out the window overlooking the parking lot. In the distance, she could see downtown, and just beyond the parking lot, there were apartments for seniors on a fixed income. She closed her eyes for a moment. "Lord, it seems as though Kieya finally has another mate after all these thousands of years. Will I have another mate? Is Toby to be my mate?"

She opened her eyes, turned, and as she left her office, she turned off the light. Closing the door and locking it, she went down the hall and down the stairs. Outside the stairwell door, she turned left instead of going towards the parking lot. Down a long narrow hallway, she entered the sanctuary. High and behind her, the afternoon sun was streaming through the stained-glass windows. She walked to the center and knelt on the carpeted steps leading to the chancel.

"Master, what shall I do?" For nearly a half hour, she was motionless, listening for God's still, small voice. Then she stood up and looked down at her Gaardian ring. "Margaret to Gaardian: If you will arrange for Piatek and I to be on your surface, I have a gift for you."

She heard its voice inside her head. "You have a gift for me? How can this be? What can you give me that I cannot get for myself?"

"With Piatek's help, we can help you learn to experience emotions."

"Indeed! I am intrigued. I will have Walter make arrangements for you and Piatek. Until then."

"Until then."

+ + +

The joining ritual for Kieya and Icnivad would be in seven solar cycles. Her eyes swept a chaotic scene. "The contents of both our lairs are here now. Are you sure you still want to do all the arranging?"

"Yes. I know you must go to your duties."

"True." She rubbed her face against his and licked his chin. "I will be back in less than two solar cycles, unless I communicate with you."

"I understand. Until then, I wait to see you."

"Until then." Kieya vanished.

+ + +

She reappeared in her apartment in the nursery complex and went to the community living area. "Gaardian. You wanted me present now. I do not know why."

"Margaret and Piatek will be here momentarily," rumbled the planet. "Margaret said she has a gift for me. She said you could explain."

Kieya began to purr louder. "Scan my mind for a meeting with the two females at Walter's base."

The planet paused. "Indeed."

Voices could be faintly heard out in the hallway, then Piatek and Margaret came in. "Hello, Kieya," said Margaret. "I'm glad you're here for this."

"Hello, Kieya," said Piatek.

"Greetings! This is your effort, Margaret, so the initiative is yours."

"Actually, Kieya, it was your suggestion, but it was The Creator who revealed to me what I must do, with Piatek's assistance."

"Indeed!"

"Gaardian," asked Margaret, "you know how to propel yourself through space by manipulating matter, energy, space, and time. Is this not correct?"

"Correct."

"In order to do such things, you have your own form of sensory perception, do you not?"

"Yes. I can sense such things as inertia, movement, and direction."

"Are there forms of matter and energy beyond yourself that you can detect, and to which you can respond?"

"Yes."

Margaret looked at Piatek, and the old Quzak nodded, saying, "All of these things you are describing are your ways of feeling the space, matter, and energy around you, Gaardian."

"That is logical, so proceed."

"When this information is put into your consciousness, you, in turn, respond in ways you choose to be beneficial."

"Yes."

Piatek closed her eyes. "Gaardian, I want you to recall a recent and powerful experience. As you do, I do not want you to recall the specific data you received, nor do I want you to recall the approach of this being of pure thought or what it did. Just remember those moments when it was here, and the way in which your mind processed the presence of that being."

"As the being named Thursday passed over me my mind was almost overloaded. I defended myself. It's power was larger than mine. It's intellect was greater. For the first time, I felt pleased."

"Yes, Gaardian," said Piatek, "and there was more, wasn't there? ... You felt fear."

"Yes ... and more important than my fear was the presence of The Creator."

"You sensed The Creator?"

"No. Not with my senses, but The Creator was here."

Margaret's voice rang out. "Gaardian, scan my mind to see what I perceived in you these last few minutes while you were in dialogue with Piatek."

There was silence. Margaret and Piatek did not breathe. Kieya stopped purring. Motionless, they remained silent for more than three minutes.

18. Danger

High in a tower near the center of the crystalline structure in The Creator's Park, Leahcim was walking rapidly around the top of the spiral staircase. He stopped to gaze at the last streaks of pink faded into beginning the night. He fell to his knees. "Creator, you have called me to this new life of service. It seems your telling me there's something wrong. Do I perceive this correctly? Gaardian technology says everything's okay."

Leahcim waited. After several minutes, he looked down at his ring. It shimmered subtly, and he was in the atrium of his base. "Leahcim to Gaardian: Are there any disturbances in my sector of which I am not aware?"

"I have not received any such information. Is there a problem?"

"I have just come from The Creator's Park. As I was praying and meditating in one of the towers, I sensed something was wrong, but I could not detect scientifically anything to verify my hunch."

"This is understood. I will notify Walter."

"Thank you."

"You are welcome."

Leahcim heard some faint sounds, and he walked towards the recreation area. Seeing Adnil, he walked toward her, where she was conversing with another member of the base team. "Hello, Adnil."

She stood up and gave him a hug. "Hello, Leahcim."

"What has been happening today?"

"Asayak was here to do training of our team's core leaders. Tomorrow we'll begin phase two, training the rest of the team."

"Has there been any communication from either Pzalop or anywhere else beyond the base?"

She looked at him directly. "No, there has not. Is there something wrong?"

"Probably there is not, but I have a hunch I cannot shake. I asked Gaardian, and it said it did not know of any problems detected in our vicinity. ... I'm going to go see the Suppla. You know how to reach me if necessary." Before she could reply, he vanished.

Appearing in the empty council meeting room, Leahcim walked briskly towards Eibbed's office. Arooda saw him coming and stood up. "Arooda, is the Suppla engaged in anything important?"

Arooda looked down and pushed a triangle on his desk. The Suppla's voice came a moment later. "Yes, Arooda?"

"Our Gaardian is here, my Suppla."

"Send him in."

When a door slid open, Leahcim walked through briskly and on into the office. "Good day, Suppla."

As the door behind him slid closed, she smiled. "Hello my old friend. I probably should have expected you." She pointed to a chair in her conversation pit. "Please sit down." When they were seated, she continued, "By any chance are you sensing an unseen danger?"

Leahcim nodded. "For the last few solar cycles, I have had an uneasy feeling. I have inquired of Gaardian, but it had no information to help. Have you had any further visions?"

"No, but I have been following Walter's advice regarding prayer."

"Which advice is that?"

"Walter says that when we are praying, if our mind begins to wander to another subject, or if we have an image in our mind, we should discuss it with Tho Creator. Everything that happens during genuine prayer is worthy of discussion with The Creator."

"How has that advice been helping?"

"I have been praying about many things, but my mind keeps straying to the cosmic string I saw in my vision."

Leahcim nodded again, and now he spoke slowly and intensely. "I have been considering this. I would like you to come with me briefly to Gaardian. You will not be able to tell Arooda where you are going because it is best that he not know."

"I understand." Eibbed rose and went to her desk. She pressed a triangle there. "Arooda, our Gaardian and I will be unavailable for a short time. I may be back before another day begins, but if not, you know how to handle things."

Arooda's voice came from a hidden speaker. "I understand. Be safe, my Suppla."

"I will."

Eibbed returned to the chairs, and Leahcim was standing. He reached into a pocket and extended a ring with a purple stone to her. "Put this ring on the fourth finger of your right hand. It will help you cope with the different conditions on Gaardian."

"Thank you." She slipped the ring on, and looked up. "It is rather pretty. Now what?"

Leahcim held out his hand. "Put your hand atop mine." When she did so, they immediately vanished.

+ + +

When they appeared on Gaardian next to Red Falls, Leahcim was secretly relieved. He had not transported directly to Gaardian before in this way. Pointing, he said, "That is known simply as Red Falls. It is one of my favorite places. I'm going to take you into a more traditional structure for our meeting, however." Taking Eibbed's hand, he said, "Come this way." As they walked, she felt like a tourist for the first time since when she was a child. She had a child-like sense of wonder. He led her to the community structure containing the nursery, Gaardian apartments, and other rooms.

Turning left, he led her to a doorway that led directly into the community room with the large fireplace and lounge furniture. She could see the eating area on the far side of the room. Still full of wonder, she asked, "What is this place?"

Leahcim smiled. "We have not really named this place. We created it when one of Walter's team members had an unusual pregnancy. Gaardian created a nursery here with an attached apartment for the parents. That quickly led to apartments for some of the Gaardians, and then this community room was built. On the far side of the structure, there is an outdoor recreation area with a swimming pool and provisions for eating. It is an extra home for several of our Gaardians, and there are also guest rooms for those who want to visit with Gaardian."

"You talk about the planet as though it is alive."

Leahcim nodded. "Gaardian does not breathe or reproduce, but it is sentient. ... Gaardian, this is my old friend, Eibbed, and she is the Suppla of Pzalop. Please introduce yourself."

His voice rumbled through both their heads. "Welcome, Eibbed, I am pleased to meet you."

Her mouth dropped open, and she quickly sat down on a nearby chair. "I am not easily shocked. ... I am pleased to become acquainted with you. Are you this entire planet?"

"Yes, Eibbed, I am. Leahcim, please tell me why you have taken this unusual action today. She is not Gaardian personnel or family, as you well know."

"Yes, Gaardian, I ask you to please scan our minds for our activities for the past seven solar cycles on Pzalop."

"As you request, I shall do so." There was silence for about five seconds. "Indeed, I understand why you have brought the Suppla here. She is functioning as a prophet as well as Suppla. This is a good strategy."

Leahcim spoke carefully. "Gaardian, may I suggest additional beings for this conference?"

"Of course, but I assume you wish for Walter and Kieya to be here. Who else do you suggest?"

Eibbed cleared her throat. "I have a suggestion."

"Yes?" the planet rumbled.

"Ooza made a commitment to Pzalop and the Zargadetes. I believe she will want to be here."

"I agree. ... Leahcim, do you suggest others?"

"Yes. I suggest Asayak, and I believe Qaak will be interested due to his history with us on Pzalop."

"I will inquire of these. Please wait."

"Leahcim, this ring is pretty, but how is it helping me cope with being here?"

"I cannot explain the technology to you, but please understand that the gravity here is several times greater than that of Pzalop, and the atmosphere affects everyone differently. It is not exactly poisonous to Zargadetes, but it has a differing density."

Qaak appeared a few meters away. "Hello, my friends, I am the first one here because I have an apartment orbiting the planet."

Eibbed smiled as they shook hands. A moment later, Walter appeared with Asayak, followed by Kieya, and then by Ooza. All offered greetings.

Eibbed was transfixed by Asayak. She looked up at the illuminating organ near its top and asked, "Are you the one called Asayak?"

"I am the being called by that name. I speak telepathically, just as the planet does." Chairs appeared for the others, and all sat down in a rough circle. Asayak oozed down to about Walter's height.

Leahcim began the discussion. "I brought the Suppla of Pzalop here because she is a prophet as well as the planet's leader. Gaardian, have you briefed everyone before asking them to come?"

"Yes. There is probably a cosmic string moving into your sector of Gaardian space, Leahcim. As suggested by Asayak, there is a way to modify known Gaardian technology to detect and monitor the movement of the string. Until we investigate further, we do not know whether or not we can change its trajectory, let alone alter the string itself in any way."

Walter turned to his friend. "What are you suggesting, Asayak?"

"Long ago, before several of our planet's cycles around our sun, our scientists succeeded in artificially forming a very small cosmic string in a laboratory. With the planet's permission, I can show it how this was done."

"Please do so," the planet rumbled. There was silence for over four minutes. "Indeed. That is amazingly creative. Eibbed, with your permission, I will send both you and Asayak into that large crystalline structure in the recently created park on your planet. Leahcim, I want you to go with them. Eibbed, as you kneel in that structure, I want you to not form any words. Simply focus on remembering the visions you previously had of your planet being sliced. Asayak, while there, I want you to monitor every aspect of her mind, body, and spirit."

"I do not know how to monitor a spirit."

"Indeed. Kieya, please step closer to Asayak, and teach it how felidacas love their tats to sleep."

Kieya purred strongly as she rose. "This is fascinating! I had never considered this a spiritual activity!" Standing next to Asayak, she closed her eyes. Asayak's body began to spread out over the floor until it filled all the space within the circle of chairs. Its illuminating organ went dark. Then it oozed back upward to its full height, and the organ began to glow again. Its voice was very soft. "That was an amazing experience! I have not slept that deeply or completely since the day I came into being with my progenitors. Gaardian, I now understand what you are asking me to do for Eibbed."

She sat up straighter. "I am ready for this, but I request that Ooza go with us. I think I need her presence."

Ooza looked at her. "Are you sure of this?"

"Yes, my friend, I am sure."

Leahcim stood up. "Gaardian, Ooza and I can transport them to the structure."

"That is logical," the planet rumbled.

Leahcim, Ooza, and Eibbed rose, and they walked over to stand with Asayak. Ooza looked at Leahcim and nodded. The four of them vanished.

Kieya moved towards the fireplace. "We might as well relax. We don't know how long they will be gone."

"Indeed." Qaak's eyes glowed intensely.

19. Teamwork

On Pzalop, it was the middle of the night in The Creator's Park. Other than Eibbed and Leahcim, the nearest other Zargadetes were beyond the ridge that surrounded the valley. When they appeared with Ooza and Asayak, they were in a hovercraft staging area near the edge of the park.

Leahcim spoke first. "We are not detected. Since I am not needed inside, I will monitor the perimeter of the park."

Ooza pointed to an entrance to the structure. "Eibbed, shall we go to the large center hall?"

The Suppla nodded. "Yes." She started walking, and the others followed. Along the pathway towards the entrance, there was dew on the foliage, and there was a chill in the night air.

Asayak's illuminating organ seemed to surge in brightness as the door slid open, and they entered the hallway leading inside. The others could hear its telepathic voice as it commented. "There has never been anything like this in all the experiences of all of us on my planet. To the rest of you, this is a beautiful structure, and you feel your spirits being enhanced. I am experiencing patterns of energy here unlike anything else known to Gaardian space. I am in communion with Gaardian planet as well as the three of you. It is a mystery of bewildering proportions."

As they entered the large, triangular hall, Eibbed closed her eyes for a moment. "Asayak, please ask Kieya to join us. She must join me in knowing what the Creator is revealing."

At the center of the hall was a water-powered lift, which was surrounded by a large, spiral staircase. When Kieya appeared near the bottom of the stairs, she started padding towards them. She stopped, went down on her belly, and placed her chin on the crystalline floor. She continued to purr softly, and deep in her eyes there was a subtle fire. Eibbed, seeing the large cat, went closer to the her and she lay prostrate on her face. Ooza went to her knees, and she put her face on them. Asayak stood taller, and it made no movement whatsoever. It's illuminating organ dimmed.

On Gaardian planet, it sensed what was happening. "Through Asayak I sense great power at the crystalline castle."

Walter closed his eyes for more than a minute, as the others became silent. "Walter to Pixie, to Puz, and to Waagere: This is a priority call for you to come to Gaardian as soon as possible." He opened his eyes. Within a minute, all three of them appeared, joined the circle, and sat down in chairs that appeared. "Gaardian, please give a telepathic update to the three that have just joined us."

There was nearly thirty seconds of silence. Pixie looked around the circle. "Okay, Walter, we know each other very well. Why are the three of us chosen for this?

Walter looked at his tiny friend. "When you and I spent some personal time together many months ago, I became aware of a particular gift you have, though you seldom use it. You have a sensory organ just behind your eyes that no other Gaardian has. With that gift, you will be able to see the cosmic string that is approaching Leahcim's sector of Gaardian space. No one else can, not even Gaardian itself."

She nodded. "When I was a small child, my parents took me to see through a large telescope. When I looked at the nearest galaxy at sector 129-H857-C4901, I saw a cosmic string within it. When my father looked, he said he saw it too."

Walter nodded. "Yes, Pixie, that is why you are here. Waagere, you are present because of a natural unity with Pixie, and she will need your support. Puz, you are here because Pzalop used to be part of your sector, and for some mutual reasons, you and Ooza think alike."

Walter scanned the circle. "Qaak, you are retired, so you may not wish to be involved in what we are about to do. The choice is yours."

His eyes surged brightly. "Do you have a plan?"

"Yes. When I prayed a few minutes ago, I saw images of what we must do."

They heard Puz's voice telepathically. "I have no eyes, but I easily see in three dimensions. How may I be of assistance?"

"Pixie, move over and sit next to Puz." She got up, and then sat down next to him. "Now, Pixie, take Puz's hand and meld your hand into his." Their hands became one. "Now, Pixie, let Puz see the cosmic string you saw when you were a child." They were silent for about ten seconds.

Puz's telepathic voice was now animated. "Amazing! I will be able to see one-dimensionally as well as two, three, and more! I will see this string as Pixie does!"

Walter nodded. "When we are ready, I want each of you to assume a position in separate sectors adjacent to Leahcim's sector. I will stay with Pixie and Waagere. Qaak, I want you to be with Puz. He and Pixie will serve as the eyes for the rest of us."

Pixie nodded. "How will we then proceed?"

"We will not know exactly what we need to do until we know the position, direction, and speed of the string."

The planet's voice rumbled, "When this operation is completed, I hope we will know more about the origins and properties of these rare strings."

"I hope so too." Walter stood up. "We must remain in constant telepathic communication." He looked up. "Heavenly Father, all that we are and have comes from you. Please guide us and multiply our efforts I ask in the name of Jesus. Amen." Walter nodded, and all of them vanished.

+ + +

As they assumed their positions, Pixie and Puz could immediately sense the presence of the cosmic string. Connected to Gaardian, their calculations were completed almost instantly. Pixie's voice was calm. "The trajectory appears to collide with that of Pzalop, as we anticipated."

Puz was equally calm. "Its orientation is perpendicular to the planet, moving sideways at about one hundred twenty-five thousand kilometers per second."

Qaak spoke with confidence. "It will be easy for us to move Pzalop out of the way temporarily."

"No." Walter's voice was emphatic. "We must not do that this time. This planet has a special history, including the instance when The Creator delivered it from the destructive path of the comet. That is our example."

Pixie's voice was now very animated. "I see now what we must do! We can fold space-time to turn the string. It will then become like an arrow. Gaardian, when we do this, where will the string strike Pzalop?"

"Indeed," The planet rumbled, "I have calculated it thrice. It will strike the center of the crystalline castle. All The Creator does is done well."

"Yes, Gaardian, God does everything well." Walter paused. "Now, everyone, we must move quickly to aim the string. Please make us of one mind, Gaardian."

As five Gaardian rings shimmered simultaneously, the string became an arrow. "Audio only message to Kieya, Leahcim, Ooza, Asayak, and Eibbed: Whatever you do, make no move until you see what happens."

In the valley on Pzalop's surface, Leahcim was about fifty meters from the crystalline castle, watching it. A perfectly straight beam of light pierced the sky like a bolt of lightning, striking the structure, and it in turn emitted a brilliant flash of purple light. An instant after, there was a clap of thunder that undoubtedly was heard for many kilometers.

Leahcim sprinted down the pathway and into the castle. As he rushed into the central, triangular chamber, the other Gaardians were arriving. Everyone was excitedly talking at once, except for Asayak. It stood, motionless, and taller than usual. Walter noticed, and he stopped talking. He walked over to stand next to the creature, and he touched one of its arms. "Asayak, are you okay?" By now, the others were quiet.

The creature oozed down to Walter's height, and its voice was unusually soft and gentle. "Please forgive. Much has happened that I cannot understand, let alone explain. Has anyone noticed the castle? It has subtly changed."

All of them except Asayak began moving about, examining the various features of the structure. Leahcim was the first to speak aloud. "When I designed this, originally I planned the center of the staircase to be as a source of illumination instead of as a lift. Now it is both, but I cannot see the source of power that illumines it."

"I can." Pixie walked over to an outer wall and touched it. When she did, some of the structure's glow washed over her. "The cosmic string has become an integral part of the castle. Power flows from the structure to its center, which then is manifest as visible light."

Kieya padded over to an outside wall, placing her large front paws on the kneeling pad. She pressed her face to the crystalline window, and light began emanating from within her. Her purr was amplified. "My Gaardian ring has no effect upon the flow of this energy."

Qaak walked over to next to Kieya, and reached out to touch the crystalline window. His eyes immediately glowed intensely. "Indeed! Yes, indeed!" He withdrew his hand, and Kieya stepped away. "When I put my hand on the window, I could instantly see the thoughts and prayers of everyone who has been here! This is quite remarkable! Yes, very striking. Are you seeing this, Gaardian?"

"Yes," the planet rumbled from far away, "I sense all of this. I will be considering all of what has happened through many days into the future. Zargadete scientists have been here to see the structure and to pray. In your brief touch, Qaak, I gained some scientific knowledge that was previously unknown to me. I am in awe."

"Indeed," Qaak said as his eyes glowed. "Indeed, I am in awe as well."

Pixie walked over to stand by Walter. "I see the one-dimensional string within the three-dimensional crystal. It is somewhat like the Haydzees we captured in the Gaardian isotope of alexandrite crystal. Puz, do you see the string?"

His voice was unusually soft and gentle. "Yes, I see the string. It is all in every single segment of crystal."

The planet rumbled, "Pixie, please examine the vein of beryllium aluminate that is the source of the materials for the crystalline castle. Are the strings found there?"

She vanished, and when she reappeared, she was holding a piece of the crystal about the size of Walter's fist. "Yes, Gaardian, the string – or at least an image of it – is contained here as well."

"Please send it to me for analysis." The crystal vanished.

Ooza was sitting on a platinum mesh cushion at the base of another window. Her hands were turned upward, and her eyes were closed. When she opened her eyes, she stood up and pointed outside. Speaking loud enough for all to hear she said, "I think all of this has gotten the attention of other Zargadetes." On the hills surrounding the park, Zargadetes were gathering. Some were simply standing there and gesturing towards the crystalline castle. Others were starting to come down the hill. Still speaking rather loudly, Ooza said, "I think it is probably time for us to leave."

Walter looked at her. "I agree." He walked over to stand next to Asayak. "I will take you home, my friend. ... Okay, everyone, let's go home." All of them vanished.

20. Romance

In his office, Ben Kaiser looked out his window. Wisps of sunset-pink fog were touching the Golden Gate Bridge, but his eyes did not see what was in front of him. Softly, he prayed, "Master, I've taken lots of risks, and you have rewarded my efforts graciously countless times. I've never taken a risk like this before. I truly hope that this is the right time to do this."

He turned and strode purposely out of his office. Passing his secretary's desk, he said, "Lucy, I'm not coming back before tomorrow morning. You can leave as soon as your done."

"Okay, Ben. Good night."

"Good night." Walking out the door of Tiberias Holdings, he did not stop at the elevators. Instead, he strode down the hall to the other offices on his floor of the Transamerica Pyramid. On the plain and simple door was simply a name and title: Francine Elliott, Architect. As Ben approached, the door slid open silently. Inside, the girl at the desk smiled. "Hi, Mr. Kaiser, is Francine expecting you?"

"She probably does. She knows me pretty well."

"You might as well go on in. She's just mulling over some changes for her next proposal to you."

Ben smiled. "Thank you, Carol." He opened the door and went in. Leaning over her desk was the woman who had been filling his thoughts for months whenever he was not working. He had never known another woman like her. "You can't work through the night, Francine. Are you ready for dinner?"

She looked up, came from behind her desk, and threw her arms around him. "Absolutely, I am famished!" As they walked out the door she said, "Carol you can lock up whenever you're ready. I'll see you tomorrow!"

"Thank you, Miss Elliott."

"You're welcome. Good night, Carol."

"Good night."

They walked down the hall to the elevators and pressed the down-arrow button. It was less than a minute before the doors opened. "What's on your mind, Ben?"

"I'm just thinking about you. I'm taking you to a place recommended to me by Margaret Graves. She's the woman who did that great multi-media project that is a teaching tool we offer over in Fresno."

Francine smiled. "Those little pre-programmed video books are great! I have bought one for my nephew for his next birthday."

The elevator doors opened, and they went out and down to the street, where there was a taxi waiting. "Hi there, Josepha! You're right on time! Francine and I are having dinner at The Dry-Aged Steer."

"I've heard about that place. Make yourselves comfortable." She put up her flag and pulled into traffic. "From what I hear, The Dry-Aged Steer is probably well beyond my budget. It's right on the water at Jack London Square. It always seems to have plenty of customers."

Ben looked at Francine. "Carol said you're working on some final revisions. Are there any major challenges?"

She nodded. I don't want to talk about it tonight, but I'm going to propose something to you that's never been even attempted before architecturally. When Toby Ballentine suggested it, I thought he had taken leave of his senses at first. I'm glad he's your friend. He's brilliant."

Ben smiled. "Yes, he certainly is. You told me a couple of days ago that you're calendar is free for this coming weekend. Have you kept it free?"

"Yes, why?"

"I've got a few surprises headed your way. This is only Wednesday, so you'll have plenty of time to finish that proposal." They rode silently for a while.

The taxi came to a stop, and when he opened the door, the aroma of the salty sea air greeted them, mixed with the aroma of broiled beef. "Thanks, Josepha. If you come back here in two hours, just put up your flag until we come out. You know I'm good for it. Thanks for waiting for us in front of my office." He handed her enough cash to include a large tip.

"Thank you, Mr. Kaiser."

"You're welcome. We'll see you later."

As they approached the door, a big muscular man held the door for them. Ben looked him in the eye. "Thanks for doing this overtime work, John. Stay available, but not too close, unless there's a problem."

"I'm glad to do it, Mr. Kaiser. I'll be handy if you need me."

"Good." Ben and Francine went inside. When the receptionist looked up, he said, "Ben Kaiser. Reservations for two on the water."

"Yes, Mr. Kaiser, right this way please."

Soon they were seated next to a narrow walkway that followed the edge of the water. A waiter approached and filled their water glasses. "May I get you something else to drink, sir?"

Ben looked up at him. "In your wine cellar, do you have any Domaine Romanée-Conti?"

"Yes, sir, our sommelier acquired some last week."

"Bring us a bottle."

"That's excellent, sir." He walked away, and they looked at their menus.

When the sommelier came, he opened the bottle and offered Ben a taste. "Excellent!" Then the man poured two glasses for them and departed, leaving the bottle.

Francine tasted it, and her eyes grew wider. With raised eyebrows, she said, "You're right! This is excellent! What is the occasion for such a fabulous wine?"

"It's just this." He extended a small red velvet box to her. "I did not want to wonder about this all through dinner." As she opened it, tears began rolling down her cheeks. He said, "I love you more than I could have ever dreamed possible, Francine. Will you marry me?"

She nodded. "Absolutely! I love you too!" They stood up, and they kissed over the table. She slipped the three and a half carat emerald-cut solitaire onto her ring finger. Sitting down, she murmured. "It did not have to be this big, silly!"

He grinned. "Why not, I can afford it. If you want to incorporate it into a combined wedding band, we can do that."

"We've got lots of time to talk about it."

"You once told me that you don't want a big, fancy, public wedding. Do you still feel that way?"

"Yes, Ben, I do. A marriage is not about the way it starts, but about the way it thrives and lasts."

"I agree. I've got a wedding license, if you want to get married this weekend." Her mouth dropped open. "How many people do you want to invite?"

"Wow. This is like a whirlwind! I like it! I only want my parents and my brother. For friends, I'd only like to invite the Franzes from Fresno, Senator Steinmetz and his wife, and maybe Toby Ballentine. Where will we do this? I trust your judgment, and location doesn't matter to me."

Ben's eyes felt like they were swimming in hers. "That will be a surprise, okay?"

"Of course its okay. I know you have good taste: You picked me!"

They both smiled.

+ + +

Margaret Graves closed and locked her office door, and she started down the hall. After a few steps, the stairway door opened, and Toby Ballentine came through. "Good afternoon, Margaret!"

She beamed. "Hello, Toby! This is a great surprise!"

"I've been in the area today. After meeting with Jonnie Riley of the Sierra Club this morning, I met with Francine Elliott earlier this afternoon. She is an architect on the same floor of the Transamerica Pyramid as Ben Kaiser. After a bit of sightseeing, I'm hungry. Do you have any plans for dinner?"

"I was going to fix something at home. Where do you want to eat?"

"Ben Kaiser is having dinner at The Dry-Aged Steer down in Jack London Square. Let's not take a chance on disturbing their dinner, though. I'd like to try something different, at least for me. Since you're an African-American, where is the absolute best place in Oakland to get authentic soul food?"

"The best place is not in Oakland. It's in San Francisco, just a few blocks west of the Civic Center."

"Really! I'll drive if you'll navigate." Silently, they went down the stairs and out to the parking lot. Toby held the door for her, and then he got in himself. "Is the easiest way to go to just cross the Bay Bridge?"

"Right! When we get near the Civic Center I'll start to navigate."

The engine started, but she did not see him put a key in the ignition. Her focus was on Toby. "I'm glad you came by. It will be good to get out of Oakland for a pleasant dinner."

He pulled out of the parking lot and headed down the hill. "When was the last time you were over in Fresno to the geodesic dome? Didn't you help develop video material for the electronic children's books?"

Margaret nodded. "Yes. I enjoyed doing that. I was there a couple of months ago. Why do you ask?"

"I'm going to go over there on Friday. Ben has a new project that is almost ready to go public. Would you like to go with me?"

"Sure! If we're going to go there Gaardian style, you can pick me up at my apartment."

"That sounds best. I'll pick you up there about 6:00." He pointed. "Can't we take the BART from here?"

"Absolutely. Why not?"

He parked a few steps from the entrance. "Actually, we don't need the BART, but we can get to where we're going from here."

"Gaardian style?"

"Gaardian style." Going into the station, he pointed towards a door between the rest rooms. "We'll go through there." He opened the door for her, and she saw what appeared to be a lighted hallway. As the door clicked shut behind them, Toby said, "I think I know where you want to go. When we step through this doorway, if I'm wrong, just tell me, and we'll turn around and go back out." He opened the door to the glorious aromas of soul food she anticipated.

"This is the place!" She took him by the hand and led him to a table. He held her chair, and then he sat down himself. A server appeared and delivered glasses of water and menus.

"Can I get you folks anything to drink besides water?"

Margaret smiled at her. "Bring both of us large glasses of Dr. Pepper."

"Okay." She headed off.

Toby looked at her. "I'll have whatever you have. The evening is yours."

Margaret did not let him down with her choices. For the next three hours, they feasted on turkey necks, soul-smothered chicken, roasted okra, collard greens, mayonnaise biscuits, Louisiana red beans, and other delicacies, filling up on some of the best California Soul Food fixed anywhere. Their friendship grew.

+ + +

The next morning, Jonnie Riley at just sat down at her desk at the Sierra Club headquarters when her phone rang. She picked up the receiver. "Sierra Club headquarters, this is Jonnie Riley. How may I help you?"

"Hi, Jonnie. This is Paul Jackson."

"Paul! It's great to hear your voice! How are things in Yellowstone?"

"As far as I know, everything is fine there. I'm on vacation, though. Right now, I'm visiting some friends in San Jose. I still owe you a dinner. Do you have plans for this evening?"

Jonnie smiled. "Let me look at my calendar. Looking up in prayer she whispered, "Thank you, Lord!" Then she said, "I'm free, Paul. This is a great surprise."

"Fantastic! I'm glad we can get together. Do you want me to pick you up at your office at 5:00, or shall I pick you up at your apartment there on Mission?"

"Let me go home and change clothes first. Make it about 6:00, okay?"

"Great! I'll see you at 6:00! Bye, Jonnie."

"Bye, Paul! See you then!" She hung up. "Yes!"

The day went quickly because there was so much to do, and Paul picked her up promptly. He held the door for Jonnie to get into the car, and then he wont around and got in himself.

"We've waited a long time to have this dinner, haven't we?"

"It was last year in Yellowstone when you asked me, but working with Ben Kaiser got in the way."

"Speaking of Ben Kaiser, he asked me to take a position in Fresno, and the money was much better than I get from the National Park Service. I'm not money oriented, however. A few days after that I got a call from Washington, asking me if I'd like to work in Sequoia instead of Yellowstone. I prayed about it, but I had to tell them no." He turned south on highway 101.

"Is that why you're out here for vacation?"

"I suppose that's partly it, but I wanted to see you again." He glanced over at her, and she was smiling." The other day I drove into Sequoia, and I'm glad I did not take the job. It's just not what I want. I'm thinking about driving in to see the Wawona Grove in southern Yosemite tomorrow. I'll probably drive into the valley too."

They drove for a while in silence, and then she said, "I've got friends in Fresno who have spent quite a bit of time in Yosemite."

"Are you talking about Glenn and Betsy Sue Franz?"

"Yes. Oh – that's right! They were visiting Yellowstone when we last saw one another!"

"Right."

Several miles after they passed San Jose, he turned into a winery a short distance south of the city. As he parked, he said, "A cousin owns this winery. They not only have award-winning wines, but they serve great food in the restaurant."

As they walked from the car she said, "I had not thought about finding a winery and restaurant this far south on 101."

He held the door for her. "They also brew excellent fruit wines here."

After they were shown to their table, a waiter served them ice water and asked, "While you're looking at the menus, would you like something else to drink?"

Jonnie looked up at him. "He was just saying that you brew some excellent fruit wines here. What is your personal favorite?"

"Our most popular fruit wines are cherry, plum, and strawberry. My personal favorite, however, is apricot."

Paul looked up. "That sounds excellent." He looked at her. "What do you think?"

"Let's try a bottle."

"Very good." The waiter left, and they began to look at their menus.

The waiter came back with the wine, opened it, and offered Paul a taste. He smiled. "This is amazing!"

The waiter poured each of them a glass, and they enjoyed it both before and during dinner. They maintained nearly constant eye contact as they ate. For dessert, they had an apricot cobbler.

As they left the winery, Paul took Jonnie's hand, as they walked to the car. When he opened the door for her, she turned to him, thanked him, and reached up and kissed him on the cheek. He wrapped his arms around her and kissed her deeply on the lips before she got back into the car.

Although it was a cool evening, Jonnie felt very warm there in the car as she waited for him to get in. He smiled at her as he started the car, and then they were on their way back north.

After a few minutes, Jonnie asked, "When will you leave for Yosemite tomorrow?"

"I'll probably leave around 6:00 in order to miss most of the traffic. Would you like to come along?"

"I'd love to. I can take a long weekend." She paused. "I have a suggestion, though."

"What's that?" They were rapidly moving north on highway 101.

"Why don't we go by way of Fresno. I can give you a personal tour of Ben Kaiser's environmental operations there, particularly the geodesic dome built as an extension for the Fresno Zoo."

"Why don't we say that it depends upon how much you like it – and me."

"That last part is already a given." He looked at her and gave her a quick smile.

+ + +

In the Ahwahnee Hotel dining room in Yosemite, Senator Steinmetz's voice carried to everyone there. "That's great! I'm glad to hear it!" He looked at his wife, Dorothy, and then back at Greg Laraway, the Park superintendent. "It's hard to believe you're ready to retire! Is there somebody out there that's as good as you are?"

"Actually, I know a man who would be absolutely perfect here. His Dad and I are old friends. He's a bit young to be appointed a park superintendent, but there's nobody who could do the job better. Right now, he is assistant superintendent in Yellowstone. His name is Paul Jackson."

"With that kind of praise coming from an old grunt like you or me, that's high praise indeed. ... Excuse me, my phone is vibrating." He reached into his inside coat pocket and brought out his phone. "Yes, Francine? ... No, that old buzzard can wait. You know how to stall him. ... No, don't worry about that. So long as you've called, I want to start the process of pulling some strings. Check our sources and find out what you can about a Paul Jackson, who works for the Park Service in Yellowstone. He may just be the perfect replacement for the retiring Greg Laraway here in Yosemite. ... Right. ... No, keep it discrete until I talk to this Paul Jackson, okay? ... Right. I'll see you Monday, or Tuesday at the latest." Bye." He put the phone away.

His wife touched his sleeve. "Yes, Dorothy?"

"Why don't we head over to San Francisco on Sunday afternoon? We can fly back to Washington on Monday evening."

He nodded. "That's a good idea! Maybe we can get our honeymoon suite again at the Mark Hopkins!" She smiled.

"Greg, do you want to approach Paul Jackson, or shall I?"

"Well, there's a slight complication we have to consider."

"What's that?"

"New Year's Eve this last January, he and I talked on the phone. We'd both had a couple of beers, and he confessed that he's was in love with Jonnie Riley at the Sierra Club."

"Jonnie? She's a terrific lady!"

"When Jonnie was in Yellowstone because of that earthquake storm, Paul asked her to dinner, but the plans got nixed because Ben Kaiser had to rescue Glenn and Betsy Sue Franz from the hands of Senator Hosmer."

The senator nodded. "I'll remember that little drama the rest of my days."

"Anyway, I know Jonnie very well, and she's been in love with Paul for as long as I can remember, and neither one ever let on to the other."

Dorothy Steinmetz grinned. "I love it! That's straight soap opera material!"

The senator laughed. "Right you are, my dear!"

Greg smiled. "I'm telling you this because I talked to Jonnie early this morning. She called me to tell me that last evening, she and Paul went out to dinner at a winery just south of San Jose, and romance is blooming. She and Paul visited Ben Kaiser's environmental labs this morning, and right about now they are touring the Wawona Sequoia Grove. Then they're going to do a quick visit to the valley before going back."

The senator was thoughtful. "Greg, have everyone be on the lookout for them. Dorothy and I will be at the chapel for the wedding of a couple of friends of mine. Afterward, I'm treating them to a small reception here at the Ahwahnee in the Winter Club Room."

"I'll make a few calls. I hope to see you tomorrow before you and Dorothy leave."

"We'll look for you."

"Enjoy the wedding!" Greg shook their hands, and then he headed out of the hall.

22. It's Who You Know

Steve Leonard liked doing weddings. There were typically at least three hundred weddings each year in Yosemite Chapel, and Steve did most of them. This one had been easy because it was small. Now it was a matter of straightening up and cleaning up, so that the chapel was ready for its next function, which in this case was going to be another wedding on Sunday evening.

Senator Steinmetz and his wife, Dorothy, were standing at the top of the front steps when he spotted Jonnie Riley walking up the sidewalk with a man about her own age. He knew it was probably Paul Jackson. "Jonnie!" he called out, and he waved.

She waved back. "Senator! What are you doing here?" She and Paul came up the steps. "This is my dear friend, Paul Jackson. Paul, this is Senator Everett Steinmetz and his lovely wife, Dorothy."

They all smiled and shook hands.

"Paul, it seems you have a significant friend here in Yosemite."

"Do you mean Greg?"

"Yes! He is retiring in a few months, and he says that you are the best man for this job. Would you be interested?"

Paul smiled. "I'm pretty young to be the park superintendent, particularly for one of the jewels in the National Park Service crown."

"Paul, we've just met, so we don't know each other yet, but I've known Greg since he was little more than a teenager. If he says you're the ideal man for the job, I trust his judgment. You have not answered my question. Would you be interested?"

"I'd have to pray about it. I would love being out here closer to where Jonnie is based with the Sierra Club, and I do love Yosemite."

"Young man, in Washington I prefer to make things happen with the power of my tongue. I'm a pretty good judge of manhood at my age, and I think Greg is right. Now, if you're smart enough to marry this pretty young woman next to you, I have no doubt that if you were park superintendent, you could find space for her to open a branch office of the Sierra Club here in the park. As a senator who finagles appropriations for places like this, I think that might be very good for the Sierra Club. Pray about it, Paul, and let me know within the next week or two, okay?"

"Yes, sir, I'll pray about it."

Dorothy started maneuvering her husband towards the steps. "Come on, dear, let's get started on the road to San Francisco. We can be there for dinner."

He gave an obvious wink to Jonnie and turned towards his wife. "Have you forgotten? We're putting on a little reception over in the Solarium at the hotel. We'll stay for an hour or so, and then let's get on that road. We'll take highway 140. It's quicker to San Francisco than highway 41. Meanwhile," he looked at Jonnie and Paul, "why don't you two join us at the reception. You don't have to stay long, but I've paid for a beautiful cake for them." Before they could answer, he said, "See you at the Ahwahnee." They made their way down the stairs and the sidewalk to their car, where their driver was holding the door. They waved before they got in."

Paul and Jonnie went inside the chapel, where Margaret and Toby were just getting ready to leave. Margaret looked up at the couple approaching them. "Jonnie! I didn't think we'd get to see you! I see you've got Paul on your arm."

"Do you know each other?"

"We've met. Margaret has signed on to help us arrange for some new high definition videos of Yellowstone." As Margaret continued to talk, Toby excused himself when his cell phone apparently rang. He stepped into the restroom across the breezeway from the chapel. "Yes, Walter?"

"Tell Margaret we watched your wedding in the media room in three-dimensional video. If the two of you get back here in the next hour, you can enjoy a party that Dawn has put together."

"Thanks, but Senator Steinmetz and his wife are putting on a reception at the Ahwahnee for us. You can play it as a video at your party."

Walter laughed. "That sounds like a plan. I'll see you when you get back to the base after your honeymoon."

+ + +

In their satellite apartment orbiting over Gaardian, Qaak and Jody sat in front of a fire in their fireplace, with two big cats. Qaak's eyes glowed subtly as he looked at his oldest friend. "Kieya, I'm glad you brought Icnivad to join us. Did you originally plan for him to become part of your crew?"

Her purr was steady, in concert with that of her mate. "No, that was not part of my thinking. Then I saw how successfully Leahcim incorporated Adnil into his life, and it made sense for me to do the same with Icnivad."

He stopped purring briefly, and then he resumed. "Jody, I understand that you are a human. I am quite taken with your appearance. May I make an image of you?"

Jody smiled. "Why, thank you, Icnivad, I think I would like that. When would you like to make it?"

"I can do one right now. Kieya, would you please provide a suitable piece of wood about a meter in each direction?" The block of wood appeared between Jody and the big cat. He stood up. "Kieya, another request, please. Would you please arrange for the debris to go into the fire?"

"Certainly. I will enjoy watching."

Sitting back on his rear haunches, Icnivad's front paws began flying over the block of wood at an amazing speed. About half of the time, he focused upon Jody without looking at his work. In less than fifteen minutes, his efforts were complete, and he sat down. "I hope you like it."

Qaak went and picked up the sculpture. His eyes glowing softly. "Indeed. This is an amazingly precise likeness, down to that tiny wrinkle in your forehead."

Jody got up and stood by her husband, looking at it carefully. Tears began to roll down her cheeks. "It is truly wonderful, Icnivad." She went over and planted a kiss on top of his head. "I hope it is acceptable to you that I show that human expression of affection. I am delighted. Again, thank you." She smiled broadly, and she put the bust on a table.

"Kieya, much has been happening in Gaardian space, and much of it has been good."

She purred. "Yes, I have seen full records of what was accomplished at Pzalop while I was in the crystalline palace with the others. I now have a mate and valued partner on my team. I believe Leahcim will be a good friend as well as a Gaardian. Piatek from Quzak and Margaret from Earth, though they are not Gaardians, they are valuable parts of Gaardian life, as is Asayak. This has been a most satisfying time."

Jody leaned forward as she spoke. "As the oldest Gaardians, are you two happy with Walter's leadership as convener?"

Qaak's eyes grew brighter. "Yes. He is valuable to me as convener, as a prophet, and as my friend. Yes."

Kieya stretched. "Yes. He is very good. He is not better or worse than you, Qaak, but he is different. That is as expected."

Qaak closed his eyes for a moment. "Gaardian, have you any comments?"

They all heard the planet's response, including Icnivad. "Everything seems to be unfolding naturally. Margaret Graves, the human, has given me a wondrous gift. For the first time, I can say with conviction that I have a feeling of contentment. It is good. Kieya, I believe you need to explain who I am to your new mate, Icnivad."

Kieya looked at her mate. He had stopped purring, and his eyes were wide. She put a paw on his shoulder. "Icnivad, as hard as you may find this to believe, Gaardian, the planet below us, is mentally aware and can make things happen. It is not a threat to any of us. Gaardian is one of my two oldest friends."

He began to purr again. "Gaardian, you can think and communicate?"

"Indeed, I can."

"I trust my Kieya, so please continue with what you were saying. You were saying you were feeling contentment. Are real feelings new to you?"

"Yes, they are. A human named Margaret, with the help of a Quzak named Piatek, have opened a door to an aspect of reality that is new to me. You take feelings for granted. For me, they were only a concept until recently."

"This is fascinating. Please continue with what you were saying."

"Thank you, Icnivad. I felt an uneasiness when Gaardians dealt with a cosmic string for the first time. I am analyzing the apparent images formed in the crystals on Pzalop. It is entirely possible that their composition may hold some additional surprises. This is a new area of science, and it will take time to analyze properly what has happened."

Qaak's eyes glowed softly. "Walter has told me that all too often the scientists on Earth come to premature conclusions because they do not deal with their assumptions appropriately. I agree. I have seen this same phenomenon on other worlds."

Kieya stood up. "Qaak, Jody, thank you for your hospitality." Icnivad stood up beside her as she lifted a paw to point at the planet. "Before we go back to our own planet, I am going to take my mate for a walk on Gaardian. I've given him basic ring support. I will probably see you in a few days. Until then."

"Until then," said Icnivad.

Qaak and Jody nodded. "Until then." The big cats vanished.

IV. Conclusion: *Stepping Beyond*

Prologue

In previous Gaardian tales, it was established that Gaardian is a planet located in a galaxy so far away that Earth's scientists have not yet seen the galaxy in which it is located. The planet is sentient, and its intelligence is beyond measure. Over a great length of time, it learned it could manipulate its own mass and gravity, and it could propel itself through space from galaxy to galaxy at great speed.

For many thousands of Earth's years, Gaardian thought it was the only thing in the universe that could think. In its travels, it finally came upon a planet where there were telepathic humanoids. Gaardian began by reading the minds of one particular humanoid and his family. It quickly learned that the planet upon which they lived was about to be destroyed by an asteroid. As the collision was about to take place, Gaardian decided that it wanted further communication with this humanoid.

As the other planet exploded, destroying all life there, Gaardian rescued this one humanoid by transporting it to its own surface. Based upon the first sounds made by this guest on Gaardian's surface, it named him Qaak. Gaardian quickly adjusted its own gravity and atmosphere so that its guest could survive.

That guest, Qaak, learned that Gaardian was sentient because its core was made up of a unique isotope of beryllium aluminate, which on Earth is valued as a gemstone called Alexandrite. With a piece of this special version of the gemstone mounted on a ring on his finger, Qaak was empowered to do many amazing things that the scientists from his home planet had considered impossible by any stretch of their imaginations.

All of this happened 65,000 Earth years ago. The being that Gaardian named Qaak was a turquoise-edged yellow humanoid, with huge ears and three legs. He could fold any one leg like a chair and sit on it to rest.

Qaak was amazingly patient. As he and Gaardian traveled through various galaxies, and they studied plants, animals, and cultures. From time to time, they picked up other beings to join them in their quest. Qaak could teach through direct mental contact, and he could also teach other beings to communicate without spoken language when desired.

It has also been established in previous Gaardian tales that the second being to join Qaak on Gaardian's surface was Kieya. She was a four-legged creature with stripes, somewhat like a tiger, but with a human-like face. On her planet, they called themselves felidacas, and they were slightly more intelligent than humans. Kieya was stronger than a half-dozen humans combined. On all fours, Kieya was just over 9 feet 10 inches [3 meters] long and weighed nearly 510 pounds [230 kilograms]. She could run as fast as a cheetah over great distances. She also could jump nearly ten meters into the air. Kieya and all other Gaardians wore Alexandrite rings like that of Qaak.

When Kieya joined Qaak on Gaardian, she had been without a mate for several years, and she remained single for many thousands of years. Recently, she became a prophet and acquired a mate who was an artist. He helped her by being in command of the base on their planet when she was not there.

Early in their lives together, Gaardian, Qaak, and Kieya had recognized that there needed to be an interplanetary policing force. As more beings joined their group, they created laws to govern the beings in the galaxies in their part of the universe. They acted as intergalactic police and called themselves Gaardians.

The first visit to Earth by a Gaardian was centuries before the birth of Christ. Kieya thought Earth to be almost as beautiful as her own planet. When Jesus Christ was teaching his followers, Kieya was invisibly and silently there on a number of occasions.

By the beginning of Earth's 18th century, Gaardian space encompassed the Milky Way, along with many other galaxies. Since humans would begin to explore space within a few hundred years or so, Qaak and Kieya began to visit Earth more often, seeing if a potential Gaardian would emerge from the population.

They narrowed down their search to one family, and after a few more generations, they had their candidate. Walter Stephanopolos was born during World War II, and just after he began to walk, Qaak began training Walter in his dreams as he slept.

After a little over a half century, Walter became the first Gaardian from Earth. As a follower of Jesus, he had a different perspective on Gaardians and Gaardian power. Soon after becoming a Gaardian, God made him a prophet.

Walter had a close friend he called Pixie. Her actual name is Xpraepostq, and humans other than Walter cannot pronounce it, so Pixie is her handle. She, like Walter, became a Gaardian on her planet, Aegeene, at the same time he became a Gaardian on Earth. When on Aegeene, she witnessed her planet's equivalent of Jesus living a life similar to that of Earth's Savior. Walter helped her put it all in perspective, based upon his decades of experience as a pastor on Earth. Her planet's savior was named Eiraynay.

Not long after that, in another galaxy, the savior was born for the beings of another planet known as Quzak. A new Gaardian native to Quzak named Ooza noticed strange phenomena, and she notified Kieya. Upon investigation, they saw that the phenomena pointed towards Ooza's home planet.

Quzak had three continents. The western and eastern continents were much larger than the southern continent. A peninsula from the southern continent pointed into the ocean between the east coast of the eastern continent and the west coast of the western continent. There was a great expanse of water separating all three of Quzak's continents. At the northern pole, there was an ice cap. The southern continent also had the appearance of a vast frozen wasteland.

When Ooza and Kieya landed on the southern continent to investigate the phenomena that they had seen from space, at first they thought they were landing on ice, but that was an illusion using images from the northern ice cap of the planet.

Getting past the illusion, they found a large settlement of scientists and explorers. At the southern rotational center of Quzak, the Gaardians Ooza, Qaak, and Kieya found the baby named Haissem. Like the wise men with Jesus on Earth, they brought him gifts. In the case of this planet called Quzak, the gifts were made of spun gold, spice rocks, and fragrant oil.

That happened about three decades ago. As these final Gaardian tales begin, that baby is fully grown. Haissem will soon become known planet-wide as their Arkaynee, which in the Quzak language means *savior*. This volume begins with a first glimpse of the Arkaynee's adult life.

1. Savior

Less than a year after he legally became an adult by Quzak standards, Haissem the Arkaynee moved to the southwestern corner of the eastern continent with his parents. As it happened, they made their home in the same small town where that planet's Gaardian had been born and educated. The town's name was Melasurej ["MEL-uh-surge"], and its roughly 25,000 inhabitants were situated at the base of some foothills along the shore of Quzak's ocean. High above the planet was the satellite base for that sector of Gaardian space.

A typical Quzak female, Ooza the Gaardian was slender and just over 5 feet [1.5 meters] tall. She had gray skin with a pale green tint. As a Gaardian, she became well-accustomed to her duties. Her human husband, Steve, was about the same height and very strong. One particular morning they awakened and, as usual, they prayed together before getting out of bed. While Steve was in the sonic shower, Ooza got dressed and received her morning bulletins from Bahna, the android representation of her Gaardian computer.

The android spoke without emotion. "While you and Steve were sleeping, Haissem and his parents finished moving from their home on the southern continent to Melasurej, where you spent your childhood."

"Really! Do we know why they chose Melasurej?" She smiled.

"No. He is an adult now, and Quzaks in the community are rapidly becoming their friends. They have been welcomed as neighbors. Haissem, along with his parents and siblings, received a large amount of assistance for getting settled. While Haissem lives with his parents, his siblings and their mates have established other homes in the same vicinity."

At that moment, Steve walked in, and stopping next to Ooza, He put his arm around her. "I could not help overhearing! If he is now an adult and in a new location, this probably means that Haissem is going to begin his Quzak calling as the Arkaynee. Perhaps we should begin active monitoring of his life and keeping records."

"Yes!" Ooza beamed, and she kissed Steve on the cheek as Bahna vanished. "Do you have any ideas how we should do this? Gaardians did not visibly monitor your Jesus on Earth."

Steve was thoughtful. "Kieya was sometimes there, but not visibly. We've got half-dozen new recruits we've not assigned yet. Two or three could follow him around."

Ooza nodded. "I like it. I know Kieya invisibly followed Jesus at times, but not throughout his life. If we do this, it will be useful for Quzak's future." She paused. "Tomorrow morning, before sunrise in Melasurej, I'm going to go down and talk with Haissem before the others are awake. I met him several years ago, and I'd like to see him again." [For that meeting, see *Starlight Adventures*.]

Steve nodded. "I wonder. ... I hope this is wise."

They turned to facing each other, and she nodded. "I know what you're thinking. This might be the one and only time I can speak with him again during his time on Quzak." She kissed her husband. "I must be obedient to him. ... Curious! ... it feels more than slightly strange when I talk about obedience as a Gaardian."

"I trust you to do the right thing."

"Thank you, love." They hugged.

Later that morning, as Ooza appeared in the semi-darkness of dawn's early light, Haissem walked out of his home nearby and joined Ooza under some trees. **"Good morning, Ooza, I'm glad you decided to pay me a visit at the beginning."** He hugged her. **"You know of course that this might be the last time we converse before I give my life. Do you understand?"**

A tear rolled down Ooza's cheek. "I understand, my Arkaynee. May I have one or two of my crew follow your movements and record events of your life and your teachings?"

He nodded. **"I have expected your request. One of your new recruits is a female named Euteekus ["YOU-tee-cuss"]. Please release her to me, and I will allow her to send you reports."** He put his hand upon her head. **"You are the first Quzak to address me as your Arkaynee, so receive a measure of my spirit. I will never leave you or forsake you."**

She smiled. "Thank you, Haissem, -- my Arkaynee. You are very gracious."

"Now go. Our Father in heaven will be with you."

Ooza vanished.

Haissem reached into the branches above him, picked a piece of fruit, looked at it carefully, and began to eat it. He smiled and walked back into his home.

Inside, his mother was putting hot food on a table. "Good morning! Let us eat together. Your father is already working. I have news for you, though you may already know."

He sat down across the table from her. **"Is this about my cousin, Nodge?"**

"Yes. My sister says that her son is immersing Quzaks in water, saying that he is washing away offenses against The Creator." They ate in silence a moment.

"Yes. Nodge is fulfilling prophecies from centuries ago. I am going to the waters' edge today to meet Nodge and do my part."

"You will do your part?"

He paused and chewed a few bites before he answered. **"Yes. He has been preparing Quzaks for what is certainly to follow in me. You of course remember the time, just after my birth, when three visitors brought spun gold, spice crystals, and fragrant oil?"**

"Of course, course I remember, my son. The spun gold helped pay for many expenses associated with raising you and educating you. We kept a few of the spice crystals for enhancing our home. The fragrant oil was of such high quality it lasted a long time."

Haissem nodded. "Do you remember what was said at that time, by the one from this eastern continent?" When she nodded, he continued, "Now is the time for me to begin fulfilling what has been prophesied. I will return this evening for dinner." They continued to eat in silence. After their meal, he rose, gave a slight bow to her, and turned and left.

Just outside, he noticed Euteekus in the shadows of the nearby foliage. Haissem walked towards her and into the shadows. "Good morning, Euteekus."

"Good morning, my Arkaynee. It is an honor to meet you."

He nodded. "Ooza has released you to me, and I expect your obedience. You must never reveal here on Quzak your association with Gaardians, and when you make your reports, you must not identify yourself within the reports. I will allow you to be close by, and I am your friend unconditionally, but these restrictions must be honored. Do you understand?"

"Yes, my Arkaynee."

He smiled at her. "Good. For now, you must keep your distance. I will call you into our public friendship when it is time."

As Euteekus smiled and nodded and stood under the foliage, Haissem walked rapidly towards the ocean. Moments later, Euteekus followed him at a distance.

+ + +

When Walter became a Gaardian, he decided to put his base on Earth's moon, near its horizon. He sold his condominium in Oakland, California, and used the proceeds to buy land in Franz Joseph, New Zealand. He never regretted his decision to put his base on the moon, and the furniture from his condominium was initially the furniture in his moon base apartment. The house in New Zealand was unknown to that country's government, and it was an excellent place for retreats for Walter and his crew.

His first recruit was his oldest friend, Belinda, who at the time was dying of terminal cancer before he restored her. Belinda then helped him recruit his core leadership team. After that, they all worked together to make the base and its occupants what it was.

The center of the base was a large atrium filled with a variety of plants from Earth, at least initially. Later, their chef began growing a variety of herbs and spices both from Earth and elsewhere. The atrium had a transparent ceiling that was more than fifteen meters in height. At first, it had not been this high, but as the plants had grown, the atrium accommodated the additional height needed for the plants. It would be many decades before the two redwoods achieved their full height.

The base's atrium was surrounded by an office complex, living quarters, a dining hall with kitchen, a medical complex, and a recreation area. There were large portals in each of the areas that looked out on the moon's surface below a canopy of stars. On one side of the base, the Earth hung just above the horizon.

In recent years, Walter became the Convener of the Gaardians. When there were issues facing the Gaardians that encompassed more than just one or two sectors of space, Walter had the responsibility to coordinate the appropriate Gaardians to handle such challenges.

It was quiet in the lounge at the beginning of this final Gaardian tale. Deep in thought and seated on a large sofa, Walter stared at the fire. His wife, Debbie, was reading a book. Walter seemed not to hear either the voices or the sounds of activity from the recreation area just beyond an open doorway. His base commander and oldest friend, Belinda, poked her head through the door. She was about to say something when she noticed Walter deep in thought and shifted her gaze to Debbie. "Psst!"

Walter's wife turned her head and raised her eyebrows. Belinda crooked a finger, asking her to come to the door. Debbie quietly got up from the sofa, went to the doorway, and stepped through to just the other side. "What's up?"

Belinda scowled. "I was just going to ask you what's bothering Walter. I've known that man for most of a century, and I know when something big or important is happening."

Debbie shook her head. "He's been real quiet these last few days. I'm not pressing him because I've learned that this mood says he's in his emotional man-cave. I hope he's about ready to come out. I'll keep you posted, my friend."

"Okay." Belinda turned and walked to the rear towards the pool area. Debbie turned back into the lounge, sat down on the sofa, and began reading her book again. She glanced up at Walter a couple of times, but he was staring into the flames in the fireplace.

Though a senior citizen by human standards, Walter looked like a young adult. He was a Gaardian, with advanced technology keeping him fit and healthy. He shifted, sitting deeper on the sofa, and he drew his legs up until they were folded and crossed in front of him.

Debbie had returned to reading the paperback she had picked up on her visit to Earth three days earlier, and she kept quiet. Before joining Walter's Gaardian team, and long before she married him, she was a world-famous actress with a home in the Hollywood hills of Southern California. Though now a senior citizen at this point, Gaardian technology kept her looking as young and fit as her husband. She had no desire to go back to her first life, but once in a while, she had opportunities to use her acting skills. Appearing calm right now, while Walter was in turmoil, meant she was using those skills.

Aside from being Walter's wife, on the Gaardian team Debbie headed science and research. She finally looked up from her paperback. "You seem both absorbed in thought and restless. That's not like you, Walter. What's going on?"

He was very still. "There are creatures on the edge of Gaardian space that we have not dealt with before, and while sitting here with you, I've been discussing possible procedures telepathically with Gaardian planet."

She nodded, and thoughtfully she responded. "We haven't been to Gaardian in a few weeks, and I'm sure Joseph would like to visit with Kenkee. Why don't we go there and spend a few days?"

Walter looked at her and nodded. He unfolded his legs, put his feet back on the floor, and turned to her. "That's an excellent idea. Dawn and James soon will be serving lunch, so why don't we plan on going after we eat?"

"Okay." She got up. "I'm going to go soak in the whirlpool and relax before we eat. Want to join me?" She put the book down.

"I'll join you in a few minutes. I want to g-mail Kieya, Qaak, and Asayak first."

"Okay." Debbie turned and strode out of the room.

Walter was thoughtful and looked up. "Frank?"

His android interface with his computer appeared next to the fireplace. Frank always had the appearance of a central European male about forty. "Yes?"

"We need more information about the Buuds ["boo'OODZ"]. I'd like to meet with Kieya, Ooza, Piatek, and Asayak on Gaardian this afternoon. Let them know and keep me posted as to your progress."

"Right." The android vanished.

Walter got up and walked towards the door where Debbie had gone earlier. As he entered the large recreation area several of them called out, "Hi Walter!" Some were swimming in the pool, and others were working out nearby in the gymnastics' area. Walter waved at them as he walked towards the large whirlpool where Debbie was soaking with two others. As he approached, his clothing changed to a swimsuit. He stepped in and sat down next to Debbie, with the water nearly up to his neck.

She smiled. "We've been waiting until you got here before we run the hot-cold program."

"Good! I'm getting hungry, and that will probably stimulate our appetites."

Debbie looked up. "Run the program, Frank." Immediately, the water began to froth more vigorously. Gravity in the pool adjusted downward from Earth-normal to Moon-normal, and the temperature of the water increased. For about five minutes, they all floated in the water's very warm bubbles. A bell chimed, and in less than ten seconds, the temperature plummeted to nearly freezing. After thirty seconds, the frothing of the pool ended, and gravity returned to Earth-normal. Debbie smiled. "I don't think I'll ever get tired of that!"

Walter nodded as he stood up. "I agree." Holding hands, Walter and Debbie stepped out of the pool, and as they did so, they were immediately dry and back in their regular clothing. "Why don't you go get Joseph and meet me in the dining hall, okay?"

Debbie reached up and gave him a quick kiss on the cheek. "Okay. See you in there."

+ + +

While Walter, Debbie, and Joseph were having lunch, in a distant galaxy on Gaardian planet, Qaak and Jody sat comfortably near the edge of a cliff overlooking Red Falls. Looking down they could see the rain forest that filled the canyon at the base of the falls. Though the colors of the forest were brilliant oranges, reds, and yellows, unlike autumn on Earth the colors were permanent.

Qaak was retired from his duties as Gaardian Convener but still involved in many Gaardian activities. Jody was a human on Walter's Gaardian team, who was about Walter's age. Like all humanoid Gaardians, they both appeared to be about thirty. It was Jody's first marriage, and she was his second mate. His original died when his planet was destroyed thousands of years earlier.

Sitting on the edge of the cliff, Red Falls was far enough away that they could talk quietly and enjoy the day. Jody said, "As Walter's chief of engineering, I can't imagine what we could design to help us deal with these new creatures. What do we know about them?"

Qaak's emotions glowed through his eyes briefly after her question. "We do not know much about them at all. They can move through space-time and manipulate matter and energy without any of the technological assistance that Gaardians use with our ring support."

"Really! What do they look like?"

"They are shape shifters, so they take whatever form they choose. Furthermore, as with the energy beings we dealt with recently, they have a communal consciousness, though they all behave as individuals. I can identify with that, since on my home planet we also had a collective consciousness. So far, we do not know how many Buuds there are."

Jody was thoughtful. "Have they always lived in Gaardian space?"

"No." He paused. "I understand Walter is going to tell us about a conversation he has had with The Creator regarding the Buuds."

There was movement nearby as Ooza and Piatek appeared. Piatek was on Ooza's Quzak team. As with everyone else on their planet, Piatek was about Ooza's height. While both these females had grey skin with a slightly green tint, the Quzak males' tint was grey with a faintly blue tint. Piatek had a unique gift that enabled her to link with the minds of others and see beyond what they could see in their own.

Jody and Qaak stood up to greet them, and Jody threw her arms around Ooza and gave her a hug. "Hello, my friend!"

"Hello!" Ooza smiled. "I'm glad you've joined Qaak for this."

Piatek offered a hand to Qaak. "Hello, friend. It is very pleasant to see you."

Qaak's eyes glowed. "It is for me as well." He paused to take them all in. "I think it is time that all of us assemble in the family center. Walter, Debbie, and Asayak should be here shortly."

Qaak's ring shimmered. Instantly, they were in the lounge of the family center, and they made themselves comfortable in a rough large circle.

Piatek looked around the room. "I like this place. It is comfortable beyond a physical comfort. Thank you, Gaardian."

"You are welcome," the planet's low voice rumbled in their minds telepathically. "I enjoy having all of you here on my surface. Asayak, Walter, and Debbie have arrived with Joseph. As soon as Joseph leaves to go on a hike with Kenkee, the others will be here in this room with you."

Qaak's eyes glowed. "Thank you, my friend. Have you acquired any knowledge of the Buuds since we last talked?"

"No," the planet rumbled. "I will be as attentive to this meeting, as you will."

"Indeed."

A door opened. "Hello, everyone," said Walter as he walked through the door." Debbie came through the door with him, and everyone greeted one another.

A creature about seven feet tall glided in behind Walter and Debbie. It had smooth translucent green skin that almost glowed. It also had lots of long hair mingling with the glow, with four arms that swung slightly, and an array of finger-like appendages at the ends. Near the top, it appeared to have an eye, but there was no evidence of ears or mouth. It glided across the floor without legs. Named Asayak, it moved in and found a space in the circle. It then flowed down to a lesser height, extending part of its mass behind it.

Like Gaardian, Asayak spoke telepathically. "Greetings, everyone, and greetings to the planet Gaardian."

The others murmured greetings. Walter looked around at the group. "I'm glad we could all be here for this, because this is a new territory for both Gaardian planet and all Gaardians." He paused. "Before we approach the Buuds, we need to know more about them."

The planet's voice was quiet. "All we know thus far is this: They can assume any form that they wish. They can move throughout space-time at will, and they can manipulate matter and energy without technological assistance. They also have a collective consciousness even while they function independently. Their powers seem nearly equal to that of Gaardians with ring support assistance."

Walter nodded. "In my one brief encounter with one of them three days ago, I gathered that they see themselves as god-like, and they treat all other life forms they encounter as beneath them."

Asayak stirred. "This is not good."

Qaak's eyes glowed. "No indeed, it is not." He looked at Walter. "Are we able to track them?"

Walter nodded. "Yes, in a very basic way. Gaardian?"

"Yes. At the moment, the nearest Buud is in sector 859-T720-G5640, just beyond Leahcim's sector."

"I apologize for being late," said Kieya as she padded quietly into the gathering. "It could not be avoided." She sat down next to Asayak.

"We were at this moment getting started, Kieya," said Walter. "As Gaardian was just reporting, there are no Buuds in this vicinity presently."

"Indeed," the planet rumbled. "They do not thus far seem aware of us."

Asayak waved one of its arms. "I have a suggestion."

Walter raised his eyebrows. "Yes?"

"Gaardian and I can communicate over great distances without encumbrance, detection, or possible interference."

"Yes."

"Is there a planet in that sector that has at least moderately intelligent life?"

The planet's voice was slightly more animated. "Yes. There is a planet with humanoid population that has not yet begun significant scientific development. It is just beyond the far edge of Leahcim's sector."

"This is excellent," said Asayak. "If you transport me there, Walter, I can be there invisibly and relay the thoughts and emotions of the beings there that are encountering the Buuds. I will send their thoughts directly to Gaardian, where we can process what we learn."

Walter nodded. "I like your suggestion, Asayak, but with one modification. I want Leahcim to go there with you, to be there for you as full Gaardian support."

Qaak's eyes glowed. "Indeed! I like this!"

Kieya purred. "I agree. Kieya to Leahcim. Are you available?"

A three-dimensional image of Leahcim appeared next to her. "Yes, Kieya?"

"Are you available?"

Leahcim nodded. "In a few minutes, yes. Is this about the Buuds?"

"Yes."

"Excellent. When I was praying this morning, The Creator's silent voice said I would hear from you. I will be there shortly." The image vanished.

Kieya turned to Walter. "You have had a conversation with The Creator about the Buuds, have you not?"

Walter nodded. "Yes. As soon as Leahcim gets here, I will share all of it with you."

As if on cue, Leahcim appeared on the other side of Kieya from Asayak. "Hello, friends!" Everyone murmured greetings in response.

Walter looked around the circle. "A few days ago, the Creator spoke to me about the Buuds. They must learn to live within the parameters of civilized Gaardian space and not be a law unto themselves. The good news is that the youngest one has been born with an active moral compass. She is troubled by the amorality of the others. She is our key to success."

Leahcim scowled. "Why am I suddenly made part of this meeting? I am the least experienced of all the Gaardians."

Walter nodded. "There are two reasons. The first reason is simply one of Gaardian protocol. Some of the Buuds are just beyond your sector of Gaardian space, which places this challenge officially in your jurisdiction, so you need to be part of any strategies we devise. The second reason is a physical one. You were the architect of the crystalline structure in The Creator's Park. Tell everyone here about the security measures you built into the structure."

Kieya's purr halted. "Security measures?" Have I missed something?"

Walter smiled. "Yes, Kieya, but it is not surprising. I noticed them quite by accident that first day we went to see what I like to call the crystal castle. Leahcim, I must compliment you again. These measures are brilliant in design, amazingly effective, and almost totally unnoticeable unless you are looking for them. I have to say again, 'well done!' Now, please tell everyone."

Leahcim nodded and spoke quietly. "When the miners practically insisted on building the larger structure, I decided that I had to design security measures in keeping with the peculiar design and the construction material."

Qaak's eyes glowed more intensely than usual. "You're talking about the crystalline sheets composed of a unique isotope of beryllium aluminate."

"Yes. As I was considering possibilities, I remembered a peculiar expression I had read in literature from Earth – 'hidden in plain sight'. I realized that since most of the construction materials were transparent, that any security measures had to be hidden in plain sight. Thus, at each doorway, there are transparent security panels that can slide into place under the same water pressure that moves the elevators. As a second security measure, I embedded force-field generators deep beneath the soil both under and around the structure. The power source is secure and well hidden."

Walter smiled again. "As I said earlier, all of that was brilliant, but then I noticed something even further beneath the surface that I'm sure was perplexing to the miners."

Leahcim chuckled. "Yes. Scientists on your Earth call it a Leyden jar. On both Quzak and on Pzalop it is called a Peqqui bey ["PECK-ee-bay"]."

The planet's low voice rumbled. "Indeed! This is another stroke of genius, Leahcim. The natural flexing of the structure due to thermal variations stores energy in the Leyden jar, and it can either be discharged within the structure to stun the occupants, or it can be discharged back into the structure itself, causing a momentary pressure pulse within. As Walter said, 'well done!'"

Leahcim nodded. "Thank you. Walter, why are these security measures important?"

"Simply because, if one or more Buuds were inside while these security measures were in place, they would be powerless, because your force field is opaque. With no energy entering the structure, their abilities are suspended. Furthermore, because of the unique alexandrite material, the Buuds outside the crystal castle cannot telepathically see what or who is inside – and vice versa. The Creator revealed this to me."

Qaak's eyes glowed. "Indeed! Getting them into the structure would be difficult, but this information may be of use in some other way in the future."

Walter nodded. "True. ... Leahcim, until now, I planned to send you with Asayak to that class L5 planet where the Buuds are exploring. I've changed my mind." Walter turned. "Kieya, do you remember when I had you hold Keeta in security while she explored the Quzak ship that ultimately turned itself into dark matter?"

Kieya purred softly. "Yes. ... Yes, I see what you are suggesting. I can keep Asayak in security while it telepathically explores the area and sends reports."

"Yes, Kieya, and you can supply physical backup to Asayak if needed as well. What about the rest of you? Questions? Comments?"

Piatek made a low noise in her throat. "I think it would be best if I went with them. Kieya, could you fully protect both of us?"

"Yes," Kieya purred, "but why?"

Ooza nodded. "I know Piatek, and she would be perfect for this." She smiled. "I could disguise her as one of the beings native to the planet. She can look beyond the sight of both the natives and the Buuds. She will let Asayak see what she sees, and it will relay what she sees to Gaardian."

Kieya purred more strongly. "I like this! There will be minimal risk, since Asayak will always be able to assess the thoughts of all beings in the vicinity. If there is an emergency, I will take all three of us to Pzalop. Gaardian, you can hide one of your own crystals within the structure built by Leahcim, where all of us can hide if necessary until the danger has passed."

"I can do this," rumbled the planet, "but the structure itself will provide protection. The extra Gaardian crystal can serve simply to be there, if needed. Is everyone in agreement?"

They were affirmative.

Jody waved at Leahcim. "Would you please give me your personal tour of the crystal castle? I want to see some of these things you have engineered."

2. Baptisms

Several galaxies away, on Quzak, Haissem was walking across the top of a hill. He could see a crowd gathered down near the water. He could faintly hear his cousin Nodge's voice, which was powerful and carried well. Haissem's cousin's appearance was almost repulsive. Nodge was roughly covered with animal skins, and he had a rope of skin around his waist.

Nodge was scrawny because he ate only what he could gather from his wilderness environment. As he breathed in, his ribs showed. He spoke forcefully, "Some of you know that out in the desert east of here I have been saying that everyone should get ready and straighten out their lives."

As Nodge spoke, Haissem looked around at the crowed. Euteekus also looked at the crowd carefully. Thousands of Quzaks from the Melasurej area were there, but additionally many more were there from larger communities to the north and south.

Nodge's voice seemed to grow more powerful minute by minute. "Now I say the same about changing your lives at this moment in this great water. It your time for you to regret your crimes against Our Creator and change your ways. You live in your own empires of desire, while the empire of The Creator is among us. I call upon all of you to acknowledge your crimes and turn back. After that, allow me to put you under the water as though you are buried and dead. When you come out of the water, you will be a new Quzak, and you must then walk in The Creator's ways. Symbolically, it will be as though the water washed away all of your offenses against The Creator."

Nodge stepped out into the water until it was up to his waist. One by one, Quzaks came forward to him, and after they confessed some of their offenses, Nodge put them under the water. When they emerged, they appeared joyous and happy. Haissem was smiling, as was Euteekus a short distance away.

Nodge's critics were incensed, and they turned and walked off through the crowd. Nodge continued to put Quzaks under the water after hearing them acknowledge their offenses against The Creator. He also continued to speak to the crowd loudly. "I put you under water to wash away your offenses, but there is a Quzak coming after me who is much greater than I am. In fact, I am not worthy to be his servant. He will immerse you in the spirit of The Creator and with fire. He separates the good from the bad. He will deliver the good Quzaks and protect them, but the bad he will release to fiery destruction."

The crowd was now much smaller, and of the hundreds Nodge had immersed, a few were remaining and listening. Haissem stepped out into the water to be immersed as the others had been. Nodge recognized his cousin, and he hesitated. "If anything, you should immerse me, Haissem."

The Arkaynee shook his head. **"This needs to be done this way now, in order to fulfill what The Creator declares to be right."**

"As you declare it, so it must be." Nodge immersed his cousin in the water.

As he lifted Haissem from the water, a portal in space-time opened above them. Out of the portal, a white bird flew down and perched on Haissem's shoulder. A voice like thunder came from the skies, saying,

> **"This is my son, whom I love dearly, and he pleases me immensely."**

Haissem smiled at his cousin. **"Thank you for fulfilling The Creator's plan today."**

As Nodge nodded, tears rolled down his cheeks.

Haissem walked out of the water and started proceeding northward along the shore. When he was away from the crowd, he made his way inland and started climbing the range of hills that separated Ooza's small town from the large city that was some distance further northwards.

Filled to overflowing with The Creator's spirit, Haissem was guided by that spirit into some rugged wilderness. For more than five weeks, he stopped eating and was tempted by evil that appeared as another Quzak. When

Haissem got hungry, the evil one spoke to him and said, "Since you are The Creator's son, turn one of these rocks into food so you can eat."

Haissem shook his head, saying, **"Quzaks do not have to live dependent upon food alone."**

In a moment, the wicked one took him high above Quzak, so he could see the entire planet. The evil one said, "I will give you authority over all of this glorious planet, because it is mine to give if I choose, if you worship me."

Haissem answered, **"Wise Quzaks of old times have said, "You shall worship and serve the Creator, and only the Creator."**

Without hesitation, the wicked one took Haissem to the top of the highest spire of the Quzak government capitol complex, so that Haissem was balanced on its tip. The evil one said, "If you are the Creator's son, feel free to throw yourself down from here. Did not those wise Quzaks also say that the Creator will command his army to protect you in all circumstances?"

Haissem looked at him and said, **"Those wise old Quzaks also said that we should never test the Creator."**

In an instant, they were back in the wilderness. The evil one glared at Haissem for a moment before vanishing until there would be another opportunity.

+ + +

Meanwhile, on the planet called Pzalop, in the semi-darkness just before dawn, the Suppla was kneeling in prayer in the large center room of the crystal castle in The Creator's Park. The Creator had made her a prophet, and she took on that role with every fiber of her being. Her body had a very subtle glow as she prayed. For a long time, this had been an early-morning routine that she followed almost every day. Sensing that something was about to happen nearby, she stood up and turned so that she was facing the center of the room.

Her old friend Leahcim appeared with a taller blonde female. As they walked towards the Suppla, Jody extended her hand in greeting. "Hello. My name is Jody. We met some time ago when you dedicated this structure. I am Qaak's mate, and I am a member of Walter's Gaardian crew."

She smiled. "Yes. I remember you." She turned. "Hello, Leahcim."

"Good morning, my Suppla. Jody is Walter's chief of engineering, and she has asked me to show her some of the special features I have built into this structure, the security features in particular."

"I have not observed any security features."

"That is good, my Suppla, because they are hidden in plain sight."

"If you are showing Walter's engineering chief, I would like to observe as well."

"Certainly. First, come with me to that doorway." He pointed, and they walked to one of the main entrances to the structure. Pointing down at the sill, he said, "You will notice that the sill has three divisions. When this security is needed, that center section rises to block the doorway utilizing the same water pressure that propels the elevators."

The Suppla smiled. "It is ingenious!"

"Thank you." He pointed outside. Do you see…?"

"Excuse me," said Jody, "but before we look at that, would you mind if I examine the mechanism beneath the floor here? It will only take a moment."

"Of course."

As Jody's ring shimmered slightly, she dropped rapidly into the ground and disappeared. The Suppla's mouth hung open. Moments later, Jody reappeared. "Thank you. That mechanism is fascinating. I made some mental notes for future use. Now, you were saying?"

Leahcim again pointed. "Do you see how there are trees of that one particular variety with long needles? Do you see how they seem to form a perimeter around this entire structure?" They both nodded. "There are force field generators fifty meters beneath the surface forming a circle around us. There is another row of generators, not as deep, about 100 meters further out. When activated, the generators create an opaque force-field that would be difficult to penetrate even with our best military weapons. ... Before you ask, my Suppla, these generators cannot be made portable, so they are not useful to the military."

The Suppla nodded. "I can understand that, but I would think it to be good to have such generators around our primary government buildings."

"I already did that some time ago. Ask your assistant about the enlarged security features there. He can show you the file."

"Excellent. As we speak of this, I realize that my first meal of the day is probably waiting." She touched a triangle on her chest, and a hovercraft suddenly approached and stopped nearby. "It has been good to see you again, Jody. Please give my best to Qaak and to Walter. You also, Leahcim."

They nodded as she stepped into the hovercraft. In a moment, she was but a dot in the distance.

Leahcim turned to Jody. "I would imagine you would like to see the Leyden jar or Peqqui bey."

"Yes! I am curious." They started walking back into the building. "Why did you engineer such a jar when you could simply use a bank of capacitors?"

Inside, when the door closed, Leahcim's ring shimmered, and they vanished. They reappeared in a large cavern. "The reason is simply this!" With a sweeping gesture, he pointed out the size of the cavern. "We are *inside* what amounts to a Leyden jar or Peqqui bey. It is roughly fifty meters in diameter with a thirty meter ceiling. From here, all connections to the structure and all the controls are hidden. Theoretically, given enough time, this jar could store sufficient static electricity to generate a lightning bolt several kilometers long with many trillions of volts of power."

"Nice! The Creator provided the planet with a gift, and you're making the most of it!"

+ + +

While Leahcim was showing Jody the security features of the crystal castle, the Suppla flew in the hovercraft back to her apartment in the government complex. Outside of that apartment, she was the Suppla, an imposing male with great leadership skills.

Stepping into the apartment, the door closed, and the outwardly male Suppla became a female named Eibbed. Her mate, Arooda, greeted her warmly. "Good morning, my love! You prayed a bit longer at the Park this morning! Did the Creator reveal anything new to you?" He put his arms around her.

They stood there together in each other's arms for a moment before she answered. "Actually, today I prayed about as much as usual, but just before I finished, I saw Leahcim and the blonde human woman named Jody, who is Qaak's mate."

"I remember her! She was there the day we opened the park and the crystalline prayer center."

"Yes. ... I'm very hungry this morning. What have you prepared?"

He took her hand, and started leading her to their dining area. "Come and see."

As they came through the doorway, she could see an abundance of food, still showing some steam. "That looks delicious!"

Arooda looked up. "Thank you, Creator, for Eibbed, our marriage, and for this food."

"Yes! Thank you, Creator!" They sat down and began to eat. After eating for a few minutes, she looked up at Arooda. "Eibbed was showing Jody the security features of the crystalline structure, which are amazingly well hidden. I told him we should have similar security around these government buildings, and he said that it was done previously. Do you know about this?"

Arooda swallowed and nodded. "There's a file I'll be happy to show you after our meal. The force-field generators were installed just before the cosmic string struck the structure in the Creator's Park."

"Why didn't you tell me about it?"

"Actually, I did, but you were preoccupied with the glow of the crystalline structure. Don't you remember my saying that we had improved security while you were occupied with other things?"

She paused from eating for a moment. She nodded. "Yes, I remember now. I think I assumed that they were minor improvements since we had never had any significant security issues."

"I wonder why Jody was interested?"

"Jody is Walter's 'chief' of engineering. I suppose she was here simply because it is her area of interest."

"Perhaps." They went on eating.

+ + +

On Earth, Walter and Debbie were at their home in New Zealand. Many years earlier, Walter created a retreat home on a bluff near the town of Franz Joseph. Since the house and facilities were hidden behind holographic generators, no one even in the nearby town of Franz Joseph had ever known they were there. Sheep were grazing as usual in the adjacent fields, with the Southern Alps rising beyond. Seagulls and other birds were also flying about. On the town side of the holographic generators, people could see the open fields with the sheep and birds, with the sea shimmering beyond them. Behind the generators, it was a different story.

Walter and Debbie went there for a few days of relaxation regularly. They were relaxing on their patio, having decided not to go back to work at least until after sunset. Debbie put down her paperback and looked at Walter. "Do you think it's about time we came up with a little brother or sister for Joseph?"

Walter grinned. "I'm ready whenever you are! I'll try to be around for the birth this time. I promise!" He crossed his heart.

She laughed. "I know you couldn't help it when Joseph was born."

He nodded. "I appreciate that, but I want to be there for you, if at all possible."

"I know you'll try."

They heard a chime, and a 3-D image of Dawn, their cook, appeared beside them. "Hi! Sorry to disturb you, but Frank told me you might be back on base before dinner. I've got baked potatoes and a nice salad prepared, along with some fresh veggies. Would you like me to grill up an aged steak or two for you?"

"Hmmm," said Debbie. She looked at Walter, who nodded. "We'll be back home on our apartment patio there on base in fifteen or so, okay?"

"I'll be ready." Dawn's hologram vanished.

"How soon does the Buuds reconnaissance operation begin?"

"Kieya did some scouting a few hours ago. She found a cave in a nearby cliff where she and Asayak can observe unseen, while simultaneously Piatek will engage in some minor commerce on the beach below. The area is almost like a tropical small town like Havana, Cuba was in the 18th century. The inhabitants have some conveniences, but they will not even have advanced to Earth's equivalent pre-World War I society for another 100 to 125 years. Piatek has worked with Ooza and Bahna to come up with a variety of clocks of various sizes to sell. They are making maximum use of the technology currently available there."

She nodded. "Interesting. I enjoy Piatek. ... On another subject, I'm thinking maybe we should have our annual Christmas party down here in New Zealand for a change. We have spent the last several Christmases on Glacier Point in Yosemite, hidden behind a snow bank in that re-creation of the old hotel. I love it up there, but it might be nice to have a warm Christmas for a change. Seven years ago, if you remember, I sold my house in the Hollywood Hills, where I hosted those first parties. Now, our home here is a logical choice."

Walter was thoughtful. "You've got a point. We can have fun in that temporary hotel any time there's enough snow up there to hide us. This year the snow pack is much smaller than usual. Some environmentalists are arguing that it's because of world-wide climate change, but it's simply because of the cycle of seasons that's about four decades long."

She nodded. "That volcanic eruption last year distorted the cycle of seasons for a few years, but even so, it's better not to have the party at Glacier Point this year.

He smiled. "Okay, let's have it here. There's some excellent snow pack at Queenstown for anyone who wants to do snowboarding or skiing."

She smiled. "We could create a toboggan run between here and the beach, no matter what the weather! I'll talk to Dawn about snacks before and after the big Christmas feast."

He nodded. "When Dawn brings our steaks in a few minutes, you can tell her. While we're down here for Christmas, she and James might like to re-create their honeymoon." He stood up and held out his hand. She took his hand, and when she had stood up, they vanished and reappeared in their apartment at the base on Earth's moon.

She let go of his hand. "Joseph's with Belinda, helping her with some things. I'll go and get him."

"Okay. I'll check on our project's progress." As Debbie went out the door Walter said, "Frank?"

The android appeared in front of him. "I assume you want a report. Kieya has finished her preparations. Ooza is completing Piatek's transformation. She is practicing her walk and other movements because she is much taller now, appearing as a namuh ["NAY-moo"] does on that planet. Right now, Asayak is enjoying the aromas in the kitchen because it knows it may be several days before it can be back here to enjoy them again. When Piatek's preparations are complete, Kieya will launch the mission."

"Very good. Thank you, Frank. That's all for now."

The android vanished just as Debbie returned with Joseph in tow. "Hey Dad!" The boy rushed towards Walter, who hugged him.

"Hey yourself, Joseph! Your birthday is next week?"

"I'll be seventeen!"

"Are you hungry!"

"Always!"

"Okay. You've gotten taller even faster than I did. Go in and wash your hands, and then come out to the patio."

"Okay!" He ran off.

Debbie walked over and put her arms around him. "When Joseph's asleep later, maybe we can get started making him a little brother or sister."

Walter raised him eyebrows. "Why not both?"

She hugged him. "I like the way you think!"

The apartment bell rang. Debbie called out, "Come in, Dawn."

Their cook walked in with three sizzling platters on a tray. "Good thing I was a waitress before I was a cook!" She put the tray down on the table in the patio and pointed. Your salads are in the fridge, and your other stuff is in the steam table. I can beam some dessert to you from the kitchen when you're ready. Enjoy!"

"Thanks Dawn!" Debbie gave her a hug before her old friend walked out and back to the kitchen.

Joseph walked out onto the patio. "Oh boy! That smells good!" He sat down and reached for his fork.

"Hold it! Wait for us, little man!" Debbie sat down as Walter held her chair.

After sitting down, Walter held their hands around the little table, saying, "Thank you, Lord, for this food and for your mercy. In Jesus' name, we pray. Amen."

While Joseph wolfed down his food like he was starving, Walter and Debbie ate more slowly.

A chime sounded, and a holographic image of Kieya appeared next to them. "Good evening, Walter, Debbie, and Joseph. I am sorry to disturb your meal. I am informing you that we are now proceeding to the planet named Waysad ["WAY-sud"] to work among the namuhs. Please tell Dawn that on my next visit to your base, I would like to enjoy one of her large aged-beef porterhouse steaks, uncooked. I'll want to eat it privately, so I do not have to pay attention to table manners!"

Walter laughed. "You'll have one, my friend! If you bring Icnivad, Dawn can have a steak for each of you."

"Excellent! I'll be sure to bring him!"

"Keep everyone safe, including yourself."

"I plan to. Until then."

"Until then"

"Until then, Kieya." Debbie smiled.

The holographic image disappeared.

+ + +

On Gaardian, the planet rumbled some final instructions. "I have placed a supplementary Gaardian crystal in the crystalline structure on Pzalop. I will monitor all of you constantly. There will be no privacy for you at any time. Is this understood?"

As her much taller self, Piatek nodded. "Privacy for an operation such as this is neither required nor expected." The others nodded agreement. "I have designed some time devices to sell in their market that make the most of their current technology without giving them anything really new. If an appropriate opportunity comes to me, I will ingratiate myself with one of them as a healer. I won't do anything fancy, but I can be helpful. What do you think, Kieya?"

"Just do not draw attention to yourself by doing something miraculous. If a miracle or two is needed, we can supply them as we leave."

Asayak gestured with an appendage. "This appears to be a good strategy. I will monitor and assist as needed, Piatek."

"Thank you. ... Gaardian, is there anything else we need to discuss before proceeding?"

There was a moment of silence. "No. I think not. Proceed."

Asayak flowed closer to Kieya, and Piatek put one hand on Kieya's shoulder. They vanished.

3. Watching

On Waysad, it was early morning, and the outdoor market was mostly deserted. The tents were only a few dozen meters from a bay surrounded by a large curved beach, all at the foot of some high bluffs. Piatek had a little tent store, with a table in front of the door, just like dozens of other tents in the market. Not far above her in the cliff were Asayak and Kieya. Seen from the market area, the cliff seemed to rise continuously to the top, but part of it was a holographic image, projected to disguise the cave.

Once in the cave, Asayak settled itself against the rear wall, employing all of its telepathic skills. It covertly scanned the minds of every intelligent being on the planet, including the minds of the two Buuds conversing on the other side of the planet. After sending images of all the minds to Gaardian, it scanned out into the solar system and its galaxy. No other Buuds were in the immediate galactic area at the time. From that moment, anytime there were Buuds on the planet's surface, all the thoughts of those Buuds were being recorded by Gaardian, several galaxies away.

Though hidden by a holographic image of rock, both Kieya and Asayak maintained invisibility because they did not know enough about the two Buuds that sometimes walked among the tents of the merchants below them. As the twin suns rose higher off of the horizon, more merchants opened their tents. More customers began to wander through the market.

Several years earlier, Walter had asked Asayak to do something that it did not know it could do, and now that skill was being utilized again. It laid down a shield around both the cave and Piatek's tent that did not allow sentient energy to penetrate. If the Buuds were telepathic, both Piatek and the cliff were blank to them, without discernable thoughts.

Next to Asayak, Kieya crouched low without purring, her eyes taking in the scene below without blinking. Deep within her eyes appeared a faint fire. Suddenly, the hair on her back rose slightly, as down below she could see Piatek become wary. Both Asayak and Kieya were motionless as a female Buud approached the market from the ocean. Everything that was experienced by the Buud was seen through Piatek's gift of second sight, and Asayak transmitted everything Piatek experienced back to Gaardian.

The Buud paused from examining a piece of jewelry to look around. It was a young female whose gaze paused briefly on Piatek. When she did not detect much intelligence, her eyes moved on to examine others. She put down the jewelry and walked down the street beyond Piatek, who, with sight beyond normal sight analyzed every movement and gesture for everything beneath.

In the distance, an older male Buud was walking towards the female. Since they both appeared to be just like the others in the market, the only ones who recognized them as Buuds were the three from Gaardian. The male stopped to converse with the female. For a moment, the female appeared frightened. After displaying that moment of fear, the female moved on and out of the market area. The male paused by Piatek's table, but she remained silent, observing her "customer." The male grunted and moved on.

Throughout most of the day, Piatek was busy, although the Buuds moved out of the market and beyond her ability to see them. Asayak monitored them, however. Piatek sold several items, and a number of the namuhs placed orders with her to be picked up the next day or soon thereafter.

+ + +

Two months passed by. On Earth, Walter was relaxing with Ooza on the patio of the home he had created in New Zealand near the little town of Franz Joseph. As Debbie came down the spiral staircase, Walter glanced up and smiled. Then he looked back at Ooza. "We are learning much of what we need to know about the Buuds, but before Kieya brings everyone home, we need to talk about strategy. How much do you trust Piatek's wisdom?" As he asked, Debbie sat down beside him.

Ooza looked directly at Walter. "I have always trusted her abilities, and I suppose I have also equated those abilities with her wisdom. Until now, I've not thought of the two as separate. Why do you ask?"

Suddenly, the room began to glow. Ooza started to stand, but Walter put up his hand to tell her to remain where she was. The details of their surroundings began to fade, and Walter slid off of the sofa onto his knees. Debbie quickly joined him at his side on her knees. Not knowing what else to do, Ooza followed their example and went to her knees. The powerful rumble of God's exceedingly low voice began to be heard.

> I have put a suggestion into Piatek's heart, Walter, and she is using it well. I am pleased with what Gaardians are accomplishing on Waysad. ... I will use you, Walter, when I cause the female Buud to step beyond time

and space. Afterward, she can get to know the
Gaardians in the park called by my name on Pzalop.
Stay within the crystal structure. ... Ooza, your
friendship with Piatek will be her greatest need when
she returns from her mission. You and Steve must be
patient with her. ... Debbie, you must bring Joseph to
meet the Buud female. She will see Joseph's special
gift and know she can trust both Walter and you as
well as Joseph. ... Walter, I will guide and empower you
as I always have. None of you need to be afraid. I am
with you. I am faithful.

They remained on their knees in stunned silence until the glow faded. Ooza
said, "That's the first time I've heard the Creator's voice since my wedding day
with Steve." She got off her knees and sat back in her chair. "I forgot the
power that we feel from that voice. For me, it is so powerful that I do not think
of being afraid until afterward – like now. The Creator fills me with awe!"

Walter smiled. "Centuries ago, God spoke to Jesus, and some people in the
crowd said that it thundered."

"Yes!" Ooza's voice rose. "Yes! The Creator's voice is both low in pitch
and..." she paused. "It is so powerful it is overwhelming."

Walter chuckled. "To this day, Earth's entertainment industry tends to
depict God with a voice like that of a gentle grandfather. They haven't a clue!"

Debbie and Walter rose. She asked, "I wonder what Joseph has to do with
all of this?"

With a slight smile, Walter replied, "I don't know, but I trust God with
anything and everything."

Ooza's eyes got bigger as she too got up off of her knees. "Have you always
totally trusted God?"

Walter shook his head and scowled. "No, and I'm sorry to have to admit
that. If I had trusted God more completely, my first life would undoubtedly have
been less stressful. When The Creator initially spoke to me with that power, I
clenched my fists and jaw so tightly they ached. Gradually, as I accepted my
role as a prophet, I began to be more at peace in that powerful presence."

Debbie smiled. "God is always present, though."

"True, but when I was young I used prayer more as an escape route or
routine, rather than as a lifestyle. Even as a pastor I did not pray as much as I
should have. Since becoming a Gaardian, prayer is now integrated into me as
constant part of who I am."

Ooza spoke more quietly. "Why do you think The Creator wants you to take
the female Buud beyond time?"

"Actually, I can't take her outside the universe. Only God can do that. God is
probably doing it because it's the ultimate equalizer. None of us except God
has any control whatsoever when we step beyond time and space, out of our
universe. I believe the female Buud is to be the one because she has twice
shown a moment of fear in the presence of another Buud. When God takes her
beyond time, none of the other Buuds can follow her, or even find her. Then, in
the crystal palace, her Buud powers are neutralized, for some reason. Frank?"

The android appeared at the end of the sofa. "Yes?"

"Do not summarize this past half hour here but provide a full video and audio transcript to Gaardian. Leave nothing out. In addition, find a convenient time for Dawn and James to come here to New Zealand with Debbie to plan the Christmas festivities. Finally, consult with Kieya when she gets back regarding having others from her Gaardian team join us for Christmas. ... That's all for now." The android nodded and vanished.

"Ooza, you probably had better get back to your base. Have you and Steve taken any time off together lately?"

"No, we have been too busy."

"Your marriage is too important to be so busy that you can't take time just for yourselves. I said the same to Kieya and Icnivad. You need to take some time away from your base, from Quzak and from Gaardian stuff at regular intervals, even if only for a short time. Debbie and I are going to stay here for a while before we insert ourselves again into the mission to the Buuds."

"Do you have a suggestion as to where Steve and I might go?"

Walter was thoughtful. "Neither of you have spent much time on Aegeene, have you?" She shook her head. "It's truly beautiful. Let Pixie know that you are coming, and she'll probably have a specific suggestion for the two of you."

"Thank you." Ooza stood up. "I'll see you soon!"

Walter and Debbie nodded. "Until then."

Ooza vanished.

Debbie looked over at Walter with a twinkle in her eyes. "What do you say we have some dinner and then start working on enlarging our family?"

Walter winked. "Sounds like fun!"

+ + +

On Waysad, it was the middle of the night without moonlight, and Kieya was continuing to keep watch. All the namuhs on their side of the planet were asleep. Asayak stirred. It's low voice spoke quietly in Kieya's mind. "We have a message from Walter. He says that the next time we see that female Buud, we are to inform him. God will take the Buud beyond time to join Walter, and when that happens, the three of us must simultaneously vanish back to Gaardian. We must be ready."

The big cat softly purred. "I will be ready. Inform Piatek."

Asayak paused. "I have informed Piatek." It went back to monitor all namuhs, along with the two Buuds on Waysad.

+ + +

On Quzak that very evening, when Haissem had returned to his home in Melasurej, his mother had already gone to sleep. In the dark shadows of the nearby trees, Euteekus observed with keen interest as a visitor appeared in the semi-darkness of the moonlit night. He was a prominent Quzak government leader named Sumedocin ["SOO-muh-DOE-sun"]. After Haissem invited him inside, they sat down in a corner and got comfortable. Outside, Euteekus quietly sat down below the window. There was a small light on a table nearby. A spice crystal was in a dish under the lamp, and as it reflected many colors while giving off its fragrance, the two Quzaks began to talk.

Sumedocin spoke quietly and clearly. "About the time you completed your education, I heard you speak to a large gathering of other students, indicating your intention to teach Quzaks about the Creator. Earlier today I heard a voice from above saying of you, 'This is my son, whom I love dearly, and he pleases me immensely." I believe that you are a special Quzak that the Creator intends to use powerfully.'"

Haissem nodded. **You are absolutely correct. Believe me when I say: Unless a Quzak is born from above, neither female nor male can possibly understand what I teach about the realm of the Creator."**

Sumedocin looked at Haissem carefully. "No adult Quzak can be born a second time, can they? Would they have to ask their mothers to repeat what they did at their birth? That cannot possibly be what you mean!"

Haissem smiled. **"Listen more carefully. I will say it differently. Unless a Quzak surrenders to their original created moment, receiving fresh breath flowing over them and into them, invisibly immersing them in new life, that Quzak cannot enter the Creator's realm. Consider a newborn Quzak, when it is just a body that the parents can touch. The Quzak that develops within that body is a living spirit. Do not be astonished that you have to be born from beyond Quzak – this planet. You know how wind blows through trees and foliage, where you do not always know its direction. In the same way, those born from beyond Quzak move in the direction and power of the Creator's spirit."**

Just outside, Euteekus invisibly listened carefully. Using her Gaardian supported ring, she transmitted both sound and three-dimensional video to Bahna, high above at Ooza's Gaardian base.

Sumedocin asked, "What does this mean and how does this occur?"

Haissem looked at him intently. **"You are an elected and highly respected Quzak government officer, but do you not know the ancient and wise teachings about the Creator? Hear me truthfully say this, based upon my own education and experience: All of this knowledge is readily attainable by you, if you do the research. You have more than enough evidence, and despite this, you hesitate and ask questions. If I tell you these things which are common Quzak knowledge, and you do not believe me, what would be the point in my telling you things about the Creator that have been hidden until now?"**

Sumedocin nodded. "I am listening."

"No one has ever gone into the presence of the Creator except the one who has come from the Creator, the son of a Quzak. Do you not realize how much the Creator loves all of Quzak? There is so much love that the Creator has sent His son, with whom He is immensely pleased, and who loves him unconditionally and passionately. The Creator has done this so that no Quzak will be lost. Any Quzak who believes in the Arkaynee and follows him will have a life of love in eternity."

"Eternity?"

Haissem nodded. **"In our universe, we have time, along with matter, energy, and space. When time is unlimited, we speak of it as 'forever.' In the parallel universe that is the realm of the spirit, there is no time. There is eternity."**

"Are you also saying the Creator loves all of us, and wants all Quzaks to be saved? That is our choice?"

"Yes. The Creator has no need to accuse anyone. He wants Quzaks, male and female, to confess their offenses, change their lives, and follow their Arkaynee into eternity."

Sumedocin nodded again. "I am beginning to understand."

"This is a good start. Anyone who trusts in their Arkaynee to save them is automatically forgiven. Otherwise, Quzaks are under a death sentence because of their offenses."

After this conversation, Sumedocin went back to his office in the capital. There, he talked privately with friends and colleagues. They agreed that their support of the Arkaynee would remain a secret for the foreseeable future. Haissem went back into his home and slept until dawn.

That next morning, Haissem kissed his mother good-bye after eating, and set out on foot. As he was walking from town to town beyond Melasurej, he taught any Quzaks who would listen. Along the way, a handful of other Quzaks became his daily companions, and Euteekus finally joined him publicly.

4. Party Time

On Waysad, for six days Piatek and her Gaardian support team did not actually see any Buuds, but they knew that the Buuds were nearby, in other communities on the planet. More and more namuhs visited Piatek's tent storefront because of the quality of her wares.

Early one morning, just after Piatek opened for business, she sensed the previous male Buud nearby. High above her in the cliff, Kieya was watching. The male approached Piatek and said telepathically, "This device shows very unusual craftsmanship."

Piatek paused before looking up. Looking at his face, she said, "Greetings! May I assist you with something?"

"This time measuring and reporting device is very sophisticated and well made."

"Your compliment is appreciated," said Piatek, carefully using the style of communication common to Waysad.

"Did you make this yourself?"

"Yes. I finished it three solar cycles previously."

"How much time was required for you to make it?"

"Three season-cycles and some."

"Is that the reason for the high value on the label?"

"My skills are as valuable as my time. Do you wish to purchase it?"

The Buud looked at her carefully. "No." Abruptly, he put the clock down, turned, and walked away.

When the Buud was almost out of sight, Piatek heard Asayak's telepathic voice say softly, "The Buud tried to probe your mind, but I received his probe and transferred it to that of another vendor about two hundred meters from you. I also made an instantaneous image of the Buud's mind and transmitted it to Gaardian."

Piatek appeared to continue with her tasks as she thought to Asayak, "Good. Tonight I will reveal to you what my gift perceived of him, so I may add to the report."

A female namuh approached her, and Piatek said, "Greetings! May I assist you with something?"

"Yes! I admire that same time device examined by the male who was just here. I regret I do not have the resources to purchase it. I also like this smaller one, so I want it."

Piatek nodded. "Would you like to bargain for the larger time device?"

"No, I could not afford more than two hundred yan."

"Two hundred yan would not provide me with much profit. Is your purchase for yourself or for another?"

"It is not for me, but for my youngest male descendent, recently declared of prime age."

"Then you have offered me an excellent bargain." Piatek held out her hand for the coins, and when she had placed them in a box, she handed her customer the larger time device. "Your business is appreciated."

"Your consideration is noteworthy. I will send others to do business with you."

Piatek nodded, and the female walked away.

As the next two days passed, Piatek's "business" began to thrive even more. The quality of her wares was being noticed as previously, but now her willingness to offer real bargains made her noteworthy throughout the market. On the third day, the same Buud male she saw previously returned. High above, Asayak and Kieya watched closely. Briefly, Asayak connected to the community mind of the rest of the Buuds and sent an image of their thoughts to Gaardian.

As the male Buud approached her, Piatek greeted him saying, "Greetings! May I assist you with something?"

The Buud looked around at Piatek's wares. "I was here three solar cycles previously and admired a large time device. I no longer see it."

Piatek held his gaze for a moment. "I remember your curiosity. I sold that particular time device to a female, but I have another that is similar to the one you examined." As Piatek turned, she could feel the Buud's gaze trying to penetrate her, but Kieya and Asayak protected her. She reached up to a shelf and brought down a slightly larger time device. "This one is similar. It took me longer to craft it, and I think it is better."

The Buud looked at it from all sides very carefully. "Yes. It has been crafted with great skill. I will pay the additional cost." Putting the time device under his arm, he offered her a handful of coins. "This is more than worth the additional cost. Your skill is appreciated."

"Your compliment is as welcome as your business."

The Buud turned and walked away rapidly.

Later that evening, Piatek relaxed in the cave with Asayak and Kieya. "He is going to examine what I sold him to try to detect advanced technology. He will not find any because I took great care to use only the technology and skills available on this planet."

Kieya purred softly. "This is excellent. Gaardian has examined the image of the Buud's mind that you sent two days ago. We have learned a lot more about them."

Asayak stirred. "Today was an interesting challenge, Piatek. When you turned your back to the Buud, it tried to probe you for further knowledge. While Kieya shielded you from his mental probe, I diverted it to the same female whom I had used previously when this male was here. Then, as he left the village and passed the other female, I kept him from detecting her presence in that part of the village."

Piatek smiled. "You and Kieya make a good team."

"We have worked together many times."

For the next three days, none of the Buuds were anywhere on Waysad. Still, all three sent from Gaardian stayed alert.

+ + +

On Gaardian planet, in the family center, several Gaardians and their mates were taking time to relax, and they gathered for casual conversation. Sitting there in the lounge were Walter and Debbie, Qaak and Jody, and Ooza and Steve. Leahcim was there and was content, mostly to listen. A few other Gaardians were swimming at the base of Red Falls.

Walter was relaxed. "I wanted all of us here today because of what has been transpiring on Quzak. Pixie and Saahmn, her mate, will join us in a moment because they will probably have some insights."

Just then, the petite Gaardian from Aegeene appeared at the doorway with her mate. Pixie smiled and greeted all of them, "Hello!" She went up to Walter as he stood up, and she gave him a hug. "Hello, my dear friend!"

"Hi, Xpraepostq."

After greeting everyone, Pixie and Saahmn made themselves comfortable in the semi-circle around the fireplace. Walter then continued. "Have all of you been seeing the marvelous reports from Euteekus?"

Ooza nodded. "She is going to be an excellent asset for me after she is done with the Arkaynee. Her reports are even more than what I have expected of her. I was particularly taken with what Walter calls the baptism scene. Until then, I did not have a clear concept of what Walter calls the trinity."

Pixie smiled. "I have enjoyed that scene as well."

"Yes," said Qaak, his eyes glowing. "We now see that Haissem the Arkaynee is traveling on foot, teaching, and often healing Quzaks without the available technology. This seems to be parallel to the experiences of the saviors of the other planets. We can more clearly see it now. I remember Kieya following Jesus from time to time during the Christ's three years of teaching and healing on Earth. Now it seems to be beginning on Quzak."

Pixie nodded. "Yes. Unfortunately, I did not notice Eiraynay's presence on my beloved Aegeene until the last few weeks of his ministry on my planet. I'm glad I got to meet and talk with him before he returned to heaven. ... Yes, Qaak, there seem to be strong parallels beginning on Quzak."

Qaak's eyes glowed subtly. "I remember very little about Qapoku on my home world. It was in my first life on my home world, when my given name was Semaj."

Jody giggled. "I cannot begin to imagine calling my beloved husband 'Semaj.' It just does not seem to fit!"

His eyes glowed more intently. "As I think about it, in that first marriage more than 60,000 years ago, the mother of my children was simply my mate who I learned to love. In this life, Jody is much more than that. She is my best friend, nearly constant companion, and soul-mate. It is indeed appropriate that I have a different name." He winked at her, and she smiled.

Debbie was thoughtful. "Walter and I did not know Jesus while he was physically on Earth, but we were married in the presence and power of God, and we heard His voice bless our union. I've observed videos of Pixie interacting with Eiraynay, and now I am watching the Arkaynee on Quzak. It is wonderful."

Ooza smiled. "This morning, just before coming here with Steve, we saw the latest report from Euteekus. The rest of you will find it in your Gaardian mail a little later. As you may have noticed, he now has a solid inner circle of friends who travel everywhere with him. More than half of them used to earn their livelihoods within a short distance of my childhood home in Melasurej. One of them was a kind of religious fanatic while he lived in the capital, but now he is rather quiet and loving, according to Euteekus. Another one was a wealthy investments manager, and he is the unofficial treasurer of the little group. While Haissem is not married, all the others but Euteekus are, and their mates sometimes travel with them. They don't see their children as often as they would like to, but they visit through video every day. Euteekus is assisting with that, but she is not allowing her relationship with me as Gaardian to be known."

Walter was thoughtful. "We've been getting these reports for nearly half a Quzak year now. Did any of you see any patterns worth discussing or applications to yourselves?"

Saahmn cleared his throat.

Walter looked at him. "Yes, Saahmn? This discussion is for everyone, not just Gaardians."

He nodded. "Good. When I listen to the Arkaynee as he teaches, it gives me material for sharing the good news about Eiraynay with others on Aegeene."

Walter grinned. "Excellent! That's how it should be! Gaardian, do you have any observations that would be of interest to this discussion?"

The planet's low telepathic voice rumbled quietly in their heads. "I am detecting a powerful glow from Haissem the Arkaynee at all times. He often withdraws to be by himself to pray at night, where his glow cannot be seen by others. It seems to be similar to the identical but lesser glow that I at times detect in the Suppla of Pzalop when she prays, particularly when she is in the crystalline worship center. Although Kieya is unaware of it, the same glow is in her when she prays in that crystalline structure."

Leahcim smiled. "This explains a phenomenon that I previously noticed. When I am praying at home, I sometimes fall into a deep sleep. I never sleep when I am in the crystalline castle."

Debbie smirked. "Why, Leahcim! I always knew there was something else I loved about you! I sometimes fall asleep when I'm praying too!"

They all laughed. Steve was grinning. "This is a relief! I was feeling a little guilty sometimes when I realized I had fallen asleep while talking to God."

Saahmn nodded. "Sometimes, when I fall asleep when praying, God gives me dreams that prepare me for what lies ahead."

"Yes," said Walter, "sometimes our dreams can be prophetic."

"Mom? Dad?" Joseph was at the doorway.

Debbie turned towards him. "Joseph? What do you need?"

"We don't need anything, but Kenkee, the other kids, and I were wondering if we can go swimming?"

Debbie looked at Walter, and he said, "Sure! Have fun! Keep track of the time, though. We'll have dinner in an hour or so."

"Okay! Thanks!" He went back outside.

Ooza nodded to Walter. "I have an idea, and I want to see what the rest of you think."

Walter nodded. "Go ahead!"

She paused, thinking. "For the last several years, we have had an anniversary celebration of the relocation of our planet. At first, I thought it was strange to do so, but I asked Piatek to give me some input. She says that most Quzaks now realize that the relocation – as traumatic as it was – was the best thing to happen to our planet at least in recent memory."

"This is good!" Kieya purred.

"Yes. Most families have a feast for the celebration, which is nine of our days henceforth. Haissem and his followers have no common home anymore because they are constantly traveling. Haissem himself has only returned home to his mother in Melasurej once since his baptism."

Walter began to smile. "Are you thinking of using Dawn and James?"

"I'm thinking that we can give Dawn and James the personas of wealthy retired land owners with a home right along the route of Haissem and his group. They can invite Haissem and his followers to feast with them. We can have a hundred or so Gaardian personnel there pretending to be Quzak guests from the other continent, who don't know anyone in the area. Haissem and his followers can fit into the larger celebration. What do you think?"

Qaak's eyes glowed intensely. "I like your idea, but I would offer a variation in addition."

"What do you have in mind?"

"Make the Gaardian personnel part of a traveling entertainment group. Kieya and Icnivad can provide invisible security for the event. We will set up a large structure made of canvas, like an open tent. All of us here know talented humanoids who can take on the appearance of Quzaks and entertain Haissem and his friends. The next day, when they continue their journey, the entertainers will appear to be traveling in another direction, but will, in fact, simply disappear. Before, during, and after, Dawn and James can provide the feast that you suggested."

"I like this, Qaak." Walter was enthusiastic. "What do the rest of you think?" The others expressed agreement. "Qaak, do you remember John Carson, one of my team leaders?"

"Indeed! Before he got a second life on your crew, he was a professional entertainer, wasn't he?"

"Yes. This is the kind of thing John would love to organize. We've more than a week to prepare, and that's generous by Gaardian standards! Let's do this!"

Jody stood up. "I agree. We can talk more about this over dinner. Let's join the kids outside and fix some dinner!"

Ooza shook her head. "Wait!" They all stopped to look at her. "I must communicate with Euteekus first, and ask her to convey this idea to the Arkaynee. I want his approval."

Soberly, Walter nodded. "Very good, Ooza. As soon as you know from Euteekus, send us a g-mail."

"Agreed."

As they walked outside, Walter touched Pixie's shoulder. "Have you talked to Ooza recently?"

"No, why?"

"Ooza and Steve need to take some time off together, and when they asked for a suggestion, I suggested Aegeene. I told Ooza you might have a suggestion or two for her."

She nodded. "Since she's here, I'll ask her if she and Steve would like to take a vacation on Aegeene. There's a place that Saahmn and I go to fairly frequently."

"Good."

+ + +

"Are you kidding?" John Carson was amused, standing with Walter in the dining hall. "Of course! I'd love to. I've been working with Ken and Keeta, and they have a great ventriloquist routine they're working on. Additionally, I've been trying to get Qaak and Jody to work up a dance routine, but so far they've declined. Maybe this is just the venue for them!"

Walter shook his head. "I doubt it. I can't even imagine Qaak dancing with his three legs in conjunction to Jody's two. It's ... the idea is mind boggling!"

John laughed. "Do you know any talent that we have not tapped?"

Walter was thoughtful. Then he grinned. "Belinda may have all but forgotten, but she learned to play the clarinet, and I learned the bassoon when we were in junior high school." As John's face lit up, Walter shook his head. "No, John, it would be much too time-consuming to learn something again on the bassoon."

"Are you sure?"

"Yes, John, but Belinda just might perform, depending upon her mood." He paused. "I think Butch learned to play the piano before he went to medical school. You might ask him. Moreover, when Jim Crenshaw played major league baseball, he had a juggling act where he juggled balls and bats both separately and together."

John laughed. "That sounds like something fun to watch. Anyone else?"

"Yes. Judy Valez was an award-winning script writer. She might be able to help you put together a melodrama or an overdone comedy skit or two, and Karen would be your best choice of a director."

"Great! You've given me some excellent ideas, but we've only a few days to get ready."

"True, but I know you can pull it off. Talk to Ken Lyman. I think he'll love the idea of producing something with an unlimited budget in three days!"

John laughed. "Right! Ken and I have done things together before!" They started out the door of the dining hall. "See you later!"

As John started sauntering towards the office complex to find Belinda, Walter walked in the direction of the clinic. "Later!"

He stopped and turned a moment to look at an area where Dawn and James, their chefs, were growing herbs and vegetables in the atrium. He smiled and studied them a moment.

Then he walked on across the atrium and into the clinic. Butch Eng was sitting at his desk, studying a screen in front of him, and he looked up. "Hi Walter! What's up?"

He went over to a small seating area, and they both sat down. "Debbie and I are trying to get pregnant. She probably told you. Still, when I think about having another child, I cannot help but think about Joseph. He's almost seventeen. I think his hormones are going full tilt!" He smiled.

Butch nodded. "Full tilt and then some! He has his full height now. Didn't you say you grew nearly a foot in the seventh grade?"

Walter chuckled. "Oh yeah! Belinda and I blossomed the same year. She and I were in junior band together, and we'd walk home with each other while carrying our instruments. She learned clarinet that year, and I learned the bassoon."

"The bassoon? I haven't seen one of those in years!"

"That's not surprising. It's a difficult and rather expensive instrument. Anyway, what's your overall assessment of Joseph?"

Butch was thoughtful. "Physiologically, everything is normal, of course. Emotionally, he's a bit more mature than most boys his age. You've probably noticed that when you and Debbie take off for a few days to Earth, girls are drawn to him like a magnet."

Walter nodded. "I trust him. He's got his head on straight. Debbie and I are hoping to have another child soon. We're definitely having fun trying. I love being married to a woman who's not only smart but knows how to make the most of what she has. I'm a man truly blessed!"

"Amen to that."

5. Disappearance

On Waysad, when nearly three days went by without seeing any Buuds, Piatek and the Gaardian team began to wonder. Previously, Asayak could sense their presence nearby, but for nearly three full days, there were no Buuds anywhere in the astronomical vicinity of Waysad.

Late on the third day, however, both the male Buud and the young female previously seen suddenly appeared just outside the village and began walking into the village at the end opposite to that of Piatek. It was nearly dusk, and a breeze came over the water and into the market as the two Buuds walked through the village.

Asayak saw them through Piatek's eyes and sent a message to alert Walter, while Kieya's gaze very carefully watched everything below. Piatek found herself becoming tense as they walked in her general direction.

The two Buuds seemed to be walking along calmly, conversing quietly. About fifty meters from Piatek's tent, the male suddenly raised his right arm, pointing to the sky. Black clouds formed within seconds, and lightning began flashing across the sky. Most of the vendors in the village closed their tent flaps as rain began to pour down.

The young female Buud yelled at the older male and tried to get him to lower his arm, but he would not. No one could hear what they were saying over the loud claps of thunder that were coming more frequently and intensely with each lightning bolt. Rain was heavily pelting the tents, along with anyone not under shelter.

Piatek closed and secured the flap of her tent. As she stood up, Kieya transported her back up to their cave. "What are they saying?" asked Kieya.

"I don't know, but their argument seems to be rather violent -- matching the weather."

As the sounds of thunder faded, the interior of the cave began to glow. Everything in the cave disappeared except Asayak, Kieya, and Piatek, and they began to hear the low powerful rumble of The Creator's voice.

> "Do not be afraid. I am your creator. Everything is unfolding as it should. You must go to the crystalline structure on Pzalop and wait. I am taking the young female Buud named Refinnej ["ruh-FIN-edge"] outside my created universe. She will be there with Walter. Be patient with her and love her as I know you can. I am her creator as well as yours."

The glow faded quickly, and Kieya's purr started again. "Piatek, is there anything in your tent below that you wish to keep?"

She shook her head. "No."

"Then we are going to Pzalop and the crystal castle." Kieya's ring shimmered, and the three of them vanished from Waysad. The holographic image of rock covering the mouth of the cave vanished as well. Below the cave, the tent previously occupied by Piatek and her wares was then as totally empty as the cave.

The male Buud stared at the spot where the female Buud had been standing before she vanished. He looked puzzled, turned, and looked in all directions. When he could not sense her anywhere on Waysad, he used his natural gifts to search the rest of that galaxy, but she was not there. Over the community mindset, he notified all the other Buuds. Within minutes, dozens of Buuds were searching for the female who had vanished, but The Creator had taken her out of the universe.

Several galaxies away, Asayak scanned their thoughts as they searched. It was amused but wary, and it continued to report to Gaardian planet, who was still highly alert to the Buuds.

+ + +

At that moment, Walter was on Earth's moon, in his quarters. Everything began to glow in a way he had seen many times. He fell to his knees and waited as the features of his quarters disappeared into the glow.

> Walter. I have taken the Buud female Refinnej out of the universe. I am taking you to be with her. Listen carefully to all that is said. Then both of you will be placed upon Pzalop with Kieya, Piatek, and Asayak.

Immediately, Walter was in an amazing symphony of colors and sounds that surrounded him. Refinnej was seemingly nearby, and when she saw Walter, she stared. Walter nodded and smiled at her but was silent as the Creator's low voice thundered.

> Refinnej. I am your creator and the creator of all of what you know of the universe. For this moment, you are not a part of time and space. You are simply in my presence.

She looked around in wonder. "Where am I?"

> You are not located anywhere. Moreover, you are not in the presence of time. You are simply with me and with one of my other children, whose name is Walter.

> You will be talking with him when I put you back in my creation.

She was getting mad "Who is this Walter?" she asked resentfully. "Why is it that I cannot be a Buud with all my powers here?" she asked rebelliously.

The answer came with incredible power, as the Creator's voice thundered.

> I supply your powers, and I can take them away. I am your creator. Before your progenitors created you as their child, I knew you, and I made plans for you. Walter can answer your other questions when I return you to time and space. Now you must listen, my child.

Awestruck, her response was much softer and humbled. "Yes."

The Creator's voice continued to thunder, but more gently.

> You are unique among the Buuds because you have chosen to use the moral compass I give to all Buuds. You are the youngest of your kind, and you will be a teacher and prophet for the others. Live within my love. Just as I have spoken, I will stand with you. I am faithful. I will not forsake you.

There was a brilliant flash of light, and Walter appeared with Refinnej in the large room high in the crystal castle at the center. Nearby stood Kieya, Asayak, and Piatek – who now had her normal appearance as a Quzak.

She looked at Walter, and when he took her hand, she looked down at his touch. Then she looked back at his face, and he was smiling. He led her to the others. "Refinnej, first I would like you to meet Kieya."

Kieya lifted a paw, and instinctively Refinnej took it in her hand. Kieya purred. "I am most pleased to meet you at last. Twice I have previously seen you, but you have not seen me."

Refinnej looked at Kieya with wonder. "The honor is mine, but I do not know why I am here." Releasing Kieya's paw, she waved her hands above her head several times. "I do not have my powers in this place!! How is that possible?"

Walter looked at her. "In time, you will understand everything, Refinnej." He gestured to her right. "This is Asayak."

At its full height, it was an imposing creature. It telepathically spoke and said. "I am pleased to become acquainted with you. As with Kieya, I have beheld you, but you previously have not seen me."

Refinnej nodded as Walter gestured again to her right. "This is Piatek. She is a friend who has a special gift, and I will ask her to share it with you at another time."

Piatek stepped towards her and extended a hand. "I am fascinated to meet you, and I look forward to getting to know you."

Refinnej was puzzled. "Thank you, ... I think."

Walter turned to Kieya. "Please thank Leahcim for engaging the security measures for us. Tell him he can lower them either at dawn or when the Suppla arrives."

"Agreed."

"For now, please take Asayak and Piatek to their quarters, as I believe they are overdue for some rest and relaxation." Walter stared into the distance. "Gaardian, please continue to monitor our proceedings. When you believe it appropriate, send Debbie and Joseph here." He looked towards the big cat again.

"Excellent," Kieya purred. "Refinnej, all three of us will see you again. Until then."

She nodded. "Until then."

The team from Waysad vanished silently.

Walter paused a moment, then he turned to the young Buud. "There are many things for you to learn and consider between now and when the sun rises on another day here. You asked a question earlier about why you do not have your powers. This crystalline structure that encloses us is made of a unique isotope of beryllium aluminate. The Creator supplied it to this planet on a special occasion. This crystalline material, along with some security measures that protect us, will not allow you to have the energy you need to employ your powers or the ability to communicate with other Buuds."

Refinnej went to a transparent wall and touched it. She jumped back, as though it were hot. "It is strangely cold to me and yet extremely hot. It is fascinating." She paused. "Normally, I have a constant telepathic connection with all other Buuds. I don't have it here."

Walter's ring shimmered, and two overstuffed chairs appeared. "That is correct." He pointed, "Let's sit down." As they did so, he continued. "So long as you are within this structure, there is no way another Buud can detect your presence here, or communicate with you. The structure feels different to you because you do not have your powers. That is why it seems both cold and hot when it is neither."

"Understood. Am I a prisoner?"

Walter was thoughtful as he held her gaze. "My most accurate answer is to say that you are temporarily confined here while you are informed of some things you need to know and simply must learn."

She hesitated. "Since you say this confinement is temporary, I will willingly comply. Strangely, I trust you because I trust the Creator."

"Excellent. As the Creator told you, my name is Walter. I am the Convener or leader of a group of beings known as Gaardians. I am also one of the Creator's prophets. This means that sometimes the Creator uses me to communicate with other beings on the Creator's behalf. The Gaardians are an intergalactic policing organization. You and I heard the Creator say that you were chosen for this day because you have made a choice not made by other Buuds – to use your moral compass to guide your conduct."

"The Creator also said that I was to be a prophet, like you are. Tell me more about this."

"We are created in God's – the Creator's – image. Since God is spirit, it is our spirit's image that is like that of God and not our physical appearance. Since you, as a Buud can appear in any bodily form you choose, do you not find it interesting that you and I have a common spiritual image?"

She nodded. "I am still trying to understand what I – what you and I – saw when we were outside this universe. Were we in another universe?"

Walter nodded. "That is one way to think of it. God is spirit, and everything in God's realm is spirit. It is useful to think of the realm of the spirit as a parallel universe."

"Fascinating! You and I were there! If we want to go there, how do we proceed?"

Walter shook his head. "God is in total control of the realm of the spirit. No one outside that realm can decide on their own to go there, but God can take us there."

"But when and how?"

"In that realm, there is neither 'when' nor 'how.' The 'how' is solely through God and His will, and in that realm, there is no dimension of time, so there is no 'when.'"

She was thoughtfully silent for a few moments. "I'm beginning to understand. Tell me more about the Gaardians."

Walter answered that question and many others as they continued to chat for most of the night.

+ + +

On Earth's moon, Frank explained to Debbie and Joseph what Walter was doing on Pzalop. "The Buuds are potentially very dangerous to Gaardians. They can do almost anything a Gaardian can do, only they can do it naturally without technological assistance."

Joseph's eyes were big. "Wow! When will Dad be back?"

Debbie turned towards her son. "Good question, but we really can't know!" She turned to Frank. "Is Walter in danger?"

Frank shook his head. "No. The danger is minimal because they are within the crystal castle, which in turn is behind a security shield that prevents the young Buud from using her powers or contacting other Buuds. She is quite youthful, Joseph, perhaps nearly as young as you are."

"Wow! What does she look like?"

"Later, you will see, when you and your Mom go to the crystal castle."

Debbie was incredulous. "What? We're going there? Both of us?"

"Yes. The Creator has made it clear to Walter that the two of you will be meeting the young Buud in a few hours."

Joseph smiled. "If I'm going to meet a girl – no matter what she looks like – I think I'd better get a shower." He turned and walked towards the rear of the apartment.

Frank stood there waiting while Debbie sat down. "This is scary! If it were just Walter and I, that would be one thing. I don't know how I feel about exposing Joseph to this."

Frank sat down across from her. "Walter has instructed me to say that if you appeared scared for any reason, I am to remind you that, quote, 'God does not make mistakes, and we can always trust Him,' close quote."

Debbie looked at the android. "You're right, Frank – Walter's right. Thanks. How much warning will Joseph and I have before we're transported to Pzalop?"

"Probably not more than a moment or so. I will let you know when dawn is approaching there, because that is the time frame that Walter has set."

"Okay, Frank. Thank you."

"You're welcome." The android vanished.

About an hour before dawn on Pzalop, Debbie and Joseph arrived at the crystal castle, appearing across the room from Walter and Refinnej.

He smiled. "Refinnej, my wife and son have arrived. Let me introduce you to them." They got up from their chairs and walked towards the others. "Refinnej, this is my wife, Debbie, and my son, Joseph."

Though frightened, Debbie put on her best Hollywood actress smile. "How nice to meet you, Refinnej." She took Refinnej's hand. "Normally, I would be more intimidated, but God is in command, and I trust Him with everything."

"I am pleased to meet you as well!" She turned slightly. "I understand that your name is Joseph?"

His eyes locked with hers. "That's right. I understand that you are fairly young, by Buud standards. I am too. I am seventeen Earth years old. How old are you?"

Her eyes were locked on Joseph's, as she replied, "Let me think. ... My age is eighteen of your Earth years. Does that make me too elderly for you?" She smiled, her eyes still locked on his.

His eyes held hers. "No, you're ... you're perfect. You are stunningly beautiful, Refinnej."

"Thank you. As a Buud, I can assume any form I choose when my powers are available, but this is my natural appearance because the Creator brought me here. This is my normal height, slightly shorter than Walter and you, Joseph, but taller than Piatek and Debbie. You are different, Joseph, and not just because you are attractive to me. You have a gift which I do not understand. Perhaps it is because I do not have my powers."

Joseph cocked his head to one side. "This is interesting. The Creator told Mom and Dad that I have a special gift, but none of us know what it is yet."

"Interesting!"

Walter smiled. "The Creator told me to include Joseph in our dealings with you and with the other Buuds. I'm sure we will all know more in the Creator's good time. Right now, I think it is time for Kieya, Asayak, and Piatek to return." He looked up. "Gaardian, will you please send them?"

A few seconds later, the three of them appeared nearby, and chairs appeared. Walter gestured towards them. "Piatek, in a moment I will have you sit down here, but before you do, I'll alter your appearance so that Refinnej can know what you looked like on Waysad."

As Walter's ring subtly shimmered, Piatek grew in height and took on the appearance of the vendor Refinnej had met in the tent on Waysad. Refinnej smiled. "You were the time device artist!"

Piatek nodded. "Yes." She shrank down, and her appearance was once again that of a Quzak. "I am going to sit in this chair. Would you please sit down in that chair opposite me?"

Refinnej sat down. "I agree to this, but why?"

"As Walter told you earlier tonight, I have a unique gift. With your permission, I will use my gift to help you."

She nodded. "You have my permission." She looked directly at Piatek as Piatek looked closely at her. Refinnej began to sit taller, but she was also very relaxed.

Piatek spoke softly. "As you look at me, consider all Buuds together and separately. You are not mentally connected to them, so you can look at all Buuds objectively."

Refinnej was also quiet, her voice soft and peaceful. "Buuds are powerful ... and wasteful ... we have no discipline. ... we have no ... purpose. ... we ... we wander aimlessly, looking for meaning. ... meaning ... meaning ...."

Piatek held her gaze. "Now, consider the Creator, who you encountered beyond time and the rest of our universe."

As the others looked on, Refinnej's mouth opened, then closed, then opened again to speak. Joseph stared at Refinnej, almost transfixed, as the young Buud spoke again. "I am ... I am afraid – no! ... I am ... in ... awe! ... Overwhelmed! ... All Buuds together are as nothing before the Creator. ... The Creator has and controls all power. ... The Creator has all authority ... knows everything ... is wise beyond wisdom ... is everywhere at once ... sees beyond time ... is filled with ... is filled with joy ... is faithful and disciplined ... is ... is loving – no, more! ... the Creator is love!"

Piatek nodded and continued to gaze into Refinnej's eyes and beyond. "Now consider those gathered here in this crystal castle with you."

Refinnej stares silently for several moments. "Kieya is wise ... powerful ... loving ... brilliant." She swallowed. "Asayak has different sight ... different life ... is humble ... is all it can be, but more ... because of the Creator's call upon it."

She took a deep breath and let it out with a sigh. "Debbie ... nurtures others ... encourages others ... draws others out to be themselves ... loves God ... and Walter ... and Joseph and the ones forming within her. ... Walter ... Walter loves God ... Debbie ... Joseph ... has one named Jesus in his core ... loves ... loves me ... but I do not understand." Her lips curved up a bit. "Joseph is ... belongs to God ... is somehow mine ... He sees beyond me ... sees more of me." She blinked once. Then she blinked again. "Thank you, Piatek. Perhaps someday I will share what I see in you as well."

Walter smiled. "It appears you gained a great deal in your session with Piatek."

"Understated, but, yes! That was phenomenal!"

"Excellent. ... Now, I will send Debbie, Joseph, Kieya, Asayak and Piatek to their homes, while you and I remain here to talk about the immediate future." He paused. Piatek nodded, and Asayak rose to its full height. Walter's ring shimmered, and they vanished.

She looked over at Walter. "Now what?"

+ + +

On Earth, an extraordinary genius named Robert Steinmetz was standing in a small air-conditioned building on the northeastern edge of Fresno, California. He was excited. "I know that all of this works, but I'm still in awe as to how much we have accomplished in this short length of time." Linda, Robert's girlfriend standing next to him, looked up at him and smiled.

Facing them, Ben Kaiser nodded. As a billionaire industrialist, he had financed all that they would experience that day. "I agree. I'm sure your grandfather here is proud of you, Robert."

"Absolutely!" Standing next to him, Senator Everett Steinmetz beamed. "I know the three of you have made the trip a time or two, but I'm glad to be the first person outside the project to take a ride on this. As I understand it, this subway is more than a quarter mile underground, even near the beginning of the run here in Fresno. You've done very well – and faster than your grandma and I dreamed."

Robert Smiled. "Thanks, grandpa, and thanks, Ben, for all of your support. Did the lawyers get their work done?"

Ben nodded. "I've got the paperwork on all the patents in my office. After we take this first 'official' ride from here to Yosemite Valley and back, your grandpa can call a press conference. There'll be a lot of people that will want to meet and interview you, but we'll control the media as we did for Glenn and Betsy Sue when their new technology became known to the world. ... now, let's take a ride, shall we?"

As Robert nodded, he touched a down arrow button, and sliding doors opened. They stepped into what appeared to be a very large elevator with cushioned seating. "Grandpa, I know this looks kind of like an elevator, but it is actually a train."

"Really!" Everett Steinmetz sat down with them. "Is that why there is a door over there?" He pointed.

"Yes. If you'll recall, here in the train station, there appeared to be three elevators, but the other two sets of doors did not open this time because it's just us." The doors closed. "Right now, now we feel a little like we're on an elevator because we're traveling vertically, but our movement will become horizontal as we accelerate." He pointed. "If you want to know where we are, just look at that display. The red dot is traveling down now at about a thirty-degree angle. The train cars are always level, while their undercarriages may slant upward or downward."

Ben looked around the car. "Our engineers have done an excellent job of keeping this quiet."

The senator nodded. "I'm impressed too." He pointed at the display. "I see we've leveled off, but I did not feel a change. That's great engineering too. Are we still accelerating?"

Ben pointed. "Yes. Look at the upper left corner. That's our speed in kilometers per hour, and the number in the upper-right corner is in miles per hour." They rode in silence for several minutes. "By car, normally this trip involves a two-hour drive, winding through the foothills and on into the Sierras. This subway system makes the trip in just over twenty minutes."

Linda, snuggled closer to Robert. "When I was growing up, our family flew into Fresno, where we rented a car and drove in by way of Oakhurst."

He nodded, "That's when we first met."

Linda smiled. "We had a long-distance relationship until this project started. ... thanks again, Ben, for letting me live in the complex while all of this has been happening."

The senator looked at her. "What were you doing while Robert was at work on the project?"

She smiled. "I'm almost done with my Juris Doctor program in Fresno. I've been working with some of Ben's lawyers, clerking for them and helping all of this get properly patented and otherwise protected."

Robert kissed her cheek. "She also came up with a trade-mark," he pointed at a logo above the door, "and it is an umbrella trademark over all of our efforts with similar technology."

The four sat back and relaxed. They watched another display that showed the same route as though being taken on the surface. In it, they appeared to be flying over the hills and through the trees. After coasting for about ten seconds, the train began subtly to slow down.

Ben looked over at Robert. "I'm glad we decided to put the actual train station underground in the valley and let people walk to what will soon be the valley shuttle stop. You may remember that, at the last minute, we changed the opening to the shuttle stop so that it faces away from the road. The person who suggested that little change is waiting for us at the shuttle stop."

Robert raised his eyebrows. "Who is it?"

"You'll see. None of you have met him before now, and you won't recognize him. He's unique."

The senator looked at Ben. "Unique? What do you mean?"

Ben chuckled. "You'll see. His wife is a brilliant engineer, and she is fascinated with what we've done with this project."

The train came to a stop, and the doors opened. The three let Linda get out first, and then they followed. The tunnel leading to the shuttle stop was relatively short and well-lit.

Against the bright sunlight, at first they could not see the faces of two others waiting for them near the entrance. The others came into the tunnel a few steps to greet them. "Hello, everyone. My name is Qaak, and this is my wife, Jody."

Ben and Everett smiled. Robert and Linda stared at them. Robert noticed his third leg and said, "You're a Gaardian!" He shook Qaak's hand.

Linda was enthusiastic as she greeted Jody. "I remember you! You played the girlfriend in that wonderful May-December romantic adventure with Jimmie Stewart!"

Jody laughed. "You remember that?"

"Absolutely!"

"That was long ago in an earlier life!"

Qaak looked at Robert. "You've really accomplished something here. I understand that you and Linda have become friends with Glenn and Betsy Sue Franz."

He nodded. "Yes! Glenn and Betsy Sue are making arrangements for Linda's and my wedding reception after our wedding next month."

Jody pointed. "Let's get back into the tunnel a ways everybody. Qaak and I have arranged for lunch for all of us at the Ahwahnee. We're going over there Gaardian style."

As they stepped back deeper into the tunnel, Linda asked, "What's Gaardian style?"

Qaak's ring shimmered, and in a blink they were in a private dining room, upstairs in the Ahwahnee Hotel. Jody pointed, "Out through those windows we can see Glacier Point. We've got this room for a private meeting, and we won't be disturbed. Walter's chefs, Dawn and James," she pointed, "standing over there, will see to it that we have plenty to eat."

They all sat down around a large rectangular table, and they were served fruit salads. Qaak looked across the table at Ben. "You're a man of your word, Ben, and you and Francine have made a terrific team."

Ben grinned. "I think so too. She would have enjoyed this!"

His eyes glowed, and he nodded. "That can be arranged. Give me a moment." Ben stared at him as Qaak closed his eyes, which glowed beneath his eyelids. After about ten seconds, he opened them. "Francine will be here in a few moments. As you know, right now she's in a meeting with Toby Ballentine. Toby works for Walter, and he's sending Francine."

As if on cue, Francine appeared, standing behind Ben's chair, and staring all around the room. "Amazing! I've been here before, only downstairs. ... Hi, Ben, everyone!" Chairs shifted so that Francine could sit down. Dawn brought her a fruit salad. "Thanks! That's a beautiful salad."

Dawn smiled. "You're welcome." She moved back over to the serving table.

Qaak looked at her. "Walter is Earth's Gaardian, and I recruited him. This is my wife, Jody, who is Walter's chief of engineering." They exchanged hellos. "Francine, I was just telling Ben that the two of you make a great team."

She nodded. "We think so. ... so, why are you and Jody here today?"

He chewed and swallowed a forkful of fruit salad. "Walter met with Ben many months ago, before this project was started, and Ben has kept that meeting secret. Ben was concerned about environmental issues, and Walter shared some guidelines and suggestions with him. Ben can tell you more about that later. Walter is on another planet as we speak. Jody and I come to visit Yosemite frequently with Walter and his wife, Debbie. This project is significant to all of us, though I'm sure it is not as important to us as it is to all of you."

Jody took a swallow of water. "I have been fascinated with the way you have engineered all of this. Walter wanted to meet with all of you to facilitate periodic connections, and Qaak and I are filling in."

Ben cocked his head to the side. "Periodic connections?" James and Dawn were taking away the salad bowls and putting down bowls of soup. They stopped talking while the soup bowls were all at their places.

"I'll answer your question now." Qaak's eyes glowed subtly "There are times, like the one with Ben, when Gaardians can be of help to major technological and scientific efforts. Gaardian guidelines preclude our giving you any new science or technology, but we can make suggestions for inquiry as Walter did with Ben. Conversely, there can be times periodically, when we might ask a favor of one of you."

Francine put down her fork. "Can you provide an example?"

Qaak's eyes glowed more brilliantly. "We monitor a lot of what is happening here on Earth. If we were to see that you were going to make a public pronouncement about something new and revolutionary, we might suggest an approach to the media, or a way to present your material to them. We will never tell you what to say or when to say it, but rather we will make suggestions that we think would be mutually helpful. Walter has already made a few suggestions to Ben regarding how to handle the media frenzy when this project becomes public."

Light conversation ensued through the rest of the meal. After dessert, Jody and Qaak stood up. Jody smiled. "We've enjoyed meeting all of you." Qaak's eyes glowed brightly, and there were murmurs of agreement from the others.

Qaak lifted a hand in farewell. "Our paths will cross again." Qaak, Jody, Dawn, and James vanished, along with all the food service and refuse.

6. Time to Think

In the crystal castle, Walter looked at the young Buud. "You've been given a lot to think about in a short length of time, Refinnej. It is nearly sunrise, and I am a man of my word. When I lower the force field, you will be able to see outside, and you will have all of your Buud powers. Until you leave the castle, however, you will not have a mental connection with the other Buuds, and they will not know you are here."

She was thoughtful. "I know now that all of us – the Buuds – must conform our behavior to Gaardian intergalactic rules when we are in Gaardian space, … and beyond as well. The others will not like this. The Creator wants me to be a prophet and teacher for my kind, but I don't think they will accept me in that role because I am the youngest and least experienced. Some could band together and destroy me."

Walter nodded. "That is logical from your point of view, but God equips us to do what He wants us to do."

"Do you always refer to the Creator as 'God?'"

"I do so most of the time."

Again, Refinnej was thoughtful. "What do I have now that I did not have before? How am I equipped for this? When you lower the force field, I will remain here until I am ready to face the other Buuds."

Walter looked up and closed his eyes. For a moment, he was totally motionless. He opened his eyes. "Very well." Suddenly, off to her left, the pink of early dawn began to shine through the castle. Walter smiled, but he watched her carefully as she stood up.

"It is good to feel normal and complete again." She paused, and then she looked at Walter. "I have a request."

"You wish to speak with Joseph again."

Her eyes grew wide. "Yes, but you did not read my mind. How did you know?"

"The Creator just told me."

She stared at him. Her mouth opened, then she shut it again. Then she spoke softly. "I promise you I will never harm him."

Walter smiled. "I know."

"You know," she said with fascination. "Yes, you know. I perceive you are wise. Understandably, you know your son, but I do not understand how you know me after this short time."

"God knows each of us better than we know ourselves, and I trust God with anything and everything, no matter what. Joseph and Debbie do too. Would you permit me to do a mental transfer of my experiences of God's presence and power?"

"Yes. I would appreciate that."

Walter stood up, stepped towards her, and placed his right hand on top of her head. He closed his eyes for a moment, and when he opened them, she stared at him. He said, "Now do you more fully understand?"

She nodded. "Yes. Yes, I certainly do."

"Walter to Debbie."

Debbie appeared next to them as a hologram. "Hi! How are things going?"

"Very well, I think." He looked at Refinnej.

She nodded. "Yes, I have been nearly overwhelmed by all of this, but yes, things are going well."

"Where is Joseph right now?" Walter raised his eyebrows.

"He's finished his studies for today and is swimming. Do you need him?"

"Yes. Have Frank send him as soon as he dries off."

"Okay. Will I see you for dinner this evening?"

Walter nodded. "Probably."

"Okay. Until then."

"Until then."

The hologram vanished.

Refinnej was curious. "What is swimming?"

"It is a physical activity where you propel yourself by your own strength through a liquid – in this case water."

"Interesting! I will have to try it."

"For many beings, it requires some practice in order to be done well."

Just then, Joseph appeared nearby. "Good morning, Dad. Good morning, Refinnej."

Walter nodded as Refinnej said, "Good morning, Joseph! May I approach you?"

"Of course!"

They walked towards each other.

Refinnej looked down as she took his hands in hers. She then looked up intently at his face. "Walter, your son is an amplifier."

"What does that mean?"

"He can use his gift to amplify the efforts of other beings. Buuds have always known this is possible, but Joseph is the first actual example. His own power is as limited as that of most humans, but with his gift, he can help others by amplifying their efforts. ... Joseph, may I scan your mind?"

"Sure!"

Refinnej closed her eyes briefly. "Astonishing! This partnership with God that you call prayer is amazing. Your Dad has taught you far more effectively than any other humanoids I have encountered."

Walter's ring shimmered, and as a third chair appeared, all three of them sat down. "Thank you for the compliment." He smiled. "I try to be a good father as well fulfill my other roles in this life."

She nodded. "Understood. I would like to converse with Quzak's Arkaynee named Haissem."

Walter closed his eyes for a moment, and opening them, he said, "It is an hour before dawn there. Haissem has awakened and will be here momentarily. He will not stay long."

Haissem appeared nearby and walked towards them. They all stood up as he spoke. **"Before you ask, Refinnej, I have had plans for you and Joseph before either of you was born. If you decide to pursue the life I have prepared for the two of you, I will help you thrive in the midst of your apparent defeats as well as in the midst of your victories. If this is what you want, just accept me as your Savior, Refinnej, and I will be with you always."**

"What about Joseph?"

"He received Jesus as His Savior some time ago, didn't you, Joseph?"

"Yes." He swallowed hard.

"It is your decision to make, Refinnej."

Haissem vanished.

Refinnej stared. "There was no evidence of transport, either when Haissem arrived or when he left!"

Walter laughed. "Of course not! God does not need transport!"

Joseph chuckled. "Refinnej, I understand that the Buuds have a collective mind as well as individual minds. Until now, have you ever been truly alone with your thoughts?"

She shook her head. "No. ... Thank you, Joseph. I think that is what I need to have right now. I want to stay here for a full day. Will you please leave me alone now until the same time before dawn tomorrow? Then, I would like both of you, with Debbie, to return. Is that acceptable?"

Walter nodded with his son, and he put his hand on Joseph's shoulder. "Until then."

She smiled. "Until then."

They vanished.

For the first time in her relatively short life, Refinnej felt truly alone, and she knelt in prayer on a pad by a window.

+ + +

On Quzak meanwhile, much was happening on the home planet of Ooza, Piatek, and Haissem. Along with his intimate circle of friends, Haissem was sitting under a tree, resting after they had stopped to refresh themselves. He took a drink of water from a canteen, and, after swallowing he said, **"Today is a feast day for most of our planet, and some of you have talked about wanting to be with your families. Our group is a little larger this day because those of you with small children have had them join us. In a short time, we will be just east of Melasurej. A tent has been erected there, and a traveling group of entertainers are hosting a feast. We have been invited. It should be a very enjoyable celebration."** He stood up. **"Let us move more quickly and make the very most of this day!"**

They began walking as rapidly as they could with the children with them. As they did so, others who saw them joined to make a small crowd. In about a half hour, they came to the top of a hill and saw the tent in the valley below them. Some of the children shrieked and started to run. The rest of the Quzaks could smell the aromas of Dawn and James' cooking, and they quickened their pace. In a few minutes, they joined several dozen others who were gathered under the tent.

Soon the celebration was in full swing. Debbie and Walter took on the appearance of Quzaks, with their heights and skin colors adjusted for the evening. Near one of the serving areas, Dawn approached Debbie. "I hardly recognized you two, but I guess James and I are hard to recognize as well!"

Debbie's voice was almost a perfect match for Ooza's, who was observing invisibly with Kieya and Icnivad. Debbie looked at Dawn. "I feel so very different at this lower height! ... the food smells delicious!"

"Thanks! This is a nice challenge for James and I. The Quzak palate is much more spicy – and tart too – than our human diet. There are a couple of things we prepared this evening that I'm going to put on our regular menu at the moon base."

"Walter and I will probably try a little of everything. We'll have time to do it. Quzak celebrations usually go at least halfway into the night."

"That's what I hear. ... I've got to go and replenish some things. See you later!"

"Later!"

Walter smiled. "There's not a cooking challenge that your old friend can't meet, is there?"

Debbie nodded. "She's always been amazing. God has truly gifted her. When she married James and we paid for their honeymoon, they discovered that their skills were complimentary. Her weaknesses – as few as they are – are his strengths, and vice versa. When they're doing something like this, it seems as though both know what the other is thinking, and everything comes together naturally. ... Look! Here comes Euteekus."

As per Quzak custom, the conversation was between the two women, but it was for the benefit of Walter. Euteekus nodded to Debbie. "I'm glad you're here. Do you like my reports? Is there anything I should do differently?"

"You're doing a marvelous job, Euteekus. While you listen to me, Walter is doing a mental transfer of a conversation some Gaardians had a few days ago. I am keeping talking, but you will remember their conversation later. We are pleased with your work."

"Thank you, both of you. I will possibly see you again soon. Until then."

"Until then," said Walter and Debbie together. They started walking towards the other end of the giant tent, which was more than 200 meters long and about 100 meters wide.

Near one end of the long tent, Haissem sat in a large chair, teaching lessons about the empire of the Creator. There were many Quzaks of all ages sitting on the ground around him, listening with rapt attention.

Invisibly, Keeta moved among them, looking into the eyes of each one as they listened to their Arkaynee. Her husband Ken stood nearby with rapt attention equal to that of the Quzaks. When she had looked into the eyes of each Quzak, Keeta went and wrapped her arms around Ken and held him tight. Though his wife was totally invisible, he could not help but smile as he looked down towards where she held him.

While nearly everyone near Haissem faced that end of the tent and Haissem, behind them, on the other side of a row of relief facilities, some entertainment was being put on by John Carson and his troupe for a smaller crowd. John was dressed as a clown with only light makeup, and he introduced the various acts and cracked jokes in between. All the 'real' Quzaks were laughing along with the others. John did his homework very well, as usual.

Because this was a Gaardian event, they never ran out of food or drink, and no one got physically tired until Walter nodded at John an hour or so after midnight. At that point, Gaardian energy support was lowered, and everyone began to get sleepy.

John got on the stage one last time. "I see that everyone is starting to get sleepy. If you look off towards the sea, there are three tents equipped with comfortable sleeping pads supplied by local friends. This main tent with the food and entertainment will probably be gone when you awaken tomorrow. We hope you enjoyed this feast and celebration, and we hope to see you again sometime."

Many of the Quzaks cheered, and then as Euteekus began to make her way to the sleep tents, the others followed. Standing nearby, Walter softly said, "Frank, start the dampening field slowly. When all are asleep except Haissem, we'll end this program."

"Right!" came Frank's voice in Walter's ear.

"My Father and I bless you, Walter."

He turned, and Haissem was standing next to him. "I'm glad we could serve, and that you're pleased," Walter said.

"I am indeed. I have spoken to Ooza, even though she thought I could not see her. I am pleased with all of you. Thank you."

"You're welcome!"

Walter watched as Haissem walked into the night towards the other tents and disappeared. Those sleeping tents were now quiet. As he turned back towards the main tent, it disappeared along with all the "temporary Quzaks." As everything else disappeared, Kieya, Icnivad, Steve, and Ooza walked towards Walter.

The petite Quzak was beaming. "I'm so glad we did this! The Arkaynee spoke to me while I was invisible. I am still in awe!"

Steve laughed and turned to Walter. "When you gave me that assignment years ago to work with Diane to watch Ooza, not only did I not dream I would marry her, but even less could I have imagined something like this!"

Icnivad raised a paw. "Walter, please shake my paw. It has been a privilege to serve for this, and I will carve many images of what we saw here tonight – including Qaak and Jody!"

Walter's eyes grew a little wider as he took the cat's paw. "I did not see them – or, at least, I did not recognize them!"

The big cat purred a little louder. "They sang a duet together and did a dance I had not previously seen. You must watch a video later!"

Walter laughed. "I will do that! I think both Debbie and I will want to see it!"

Softly, Kieya said, "It has been a rare privilege to be part of this. Even though we were invisible, Icnivad and I have grown closer this night. Praise the Creator!"

"Amen!" Walter smiled and turned to Debbie. "Would you like to go to Fresno with me? I want to meet with Glenn and Betsy Sue. I'm sure she'd like to chat with you after I meet with them, and meanwhile, you can play with their twins."

Debbie grinned. "I've been wanting to see those twins ever since Kieya told me about how Asayak is training them in their sleep."

"Good! Shall we go?"

As she nodded, they disappeared from Quzak, and they reappeared in the atrium of the Fresno complex. She looked around. "It's so beautiful! Before I go see the twins, I think I'll climb up to the upper level and explore the bird sanctuary."

"Okay." He gave her a light kiss. "See you later." He vanished from the atrium, and he reappeared in the secure apartment underneath the facility.

Walter walked over to one of the sofas and sat down. Looking at his ring, it shimmered briefly before he said, "Phone call to Glenn and Betsy Sue."

He could hear the phone ringing, and Glenn answered. "Hello?"

"Glenn, this is Walter Stephanopolos, the Gaardian. I'm in the secure apartment underneath you. I'd like to visit with you and Betsy Sue. Would you permit my wife, Debbie, to come to your apartment there and baby-sit the twins while I meet with you and Betsy Sue?"

"Just a moment."

Though they did not know it, Walter could clearly hear them whispering in the background. "It's Walter, the Gaardian. He wants to visit with us downstairs."

"The Gaardian? What's he doing here?"

"He hasn't said. His wife Debbie will baby-sit the twins up here while we go downstairs. What do you think?"

Walter could not see her nod. Glenn said, "Okay. As soon as your wife gets here we'll come down. What did you say her name is?"

"Debbie."

"Okay. See you then." He hung up.

"Walter to Debbie. I need you to knock on their apartment door, and when they answer, for you to baby-sit for a while. Okay?"

Walter heard her answer in his head. "Okay."

Walter held his hand out, and a can of decaf Pepsi appeared. He drank about half the can before he heard Glenn and Betsy Sue coming down the ramp into the secure apartment.

He stood up as they entered. "Betsy Sue! Glenn! Good evening!"

"Good evening," they said almost simultaneously.

"I apologize for coming without warning."

Betsy Sue smiled, as the two of them sat down. "That's okay. We were just watching an old rerun of "M*A*S*H.""

Walter chuckled. "I haven't watched one of those episodes for quite a while, but they are certainly always entertaining. ... Glenn, I understand that you're interested in applying some of the technology you used in your cameras to an optical telescope. Is that correct?"

Glenn tipped his head to one side and scowled. "I have no idea how you know that, but yes, it is true. Why do you ask?"

"Remember when I gave planetary and brief interplanetary tours to you and your colleagues?" They both nodded. "You probably also remember the fact that similar tours were provided to representatives of two other planets in my sector with intelligent life."

Betsy Sue smiled. "I had an interesting conversation with two scientists from one of the other worlds. They were brilliant, and they were almost totally transparent."

He nodded. "I have someone from that planet on my team. She's married to a former television producer."

"Really!" She grinned.

"Glenn, I believe you had a telepathic conversation with one of the big creatures without sensory organs as we know them."

Glenn smiled. "Telepathic communication is amazing! We could cover a couple of hours' worth of discussion material in less than five minutes! It was not all verbal. We exchanged data like living computers. I loved it!"

Walter nodded. "I'm glad that was a good experience for both of you. All of that happened in response to the visit of the light creatures to Gaardian space.

Did you notice that, for about a day after all of you went your separate ways, that you still felt like you were communicating with each other?"

"Yes!" Betsy Sue was enthusiastic. "I wish that had lasted longer!"

"Good, because what you shared with the others regarding electrified lenses made of quartz and other crystals was amazing to them. Neither scientific community had ever explored the piezoelectric effect as you have."

Glenn nodded. "I realized that."

Walter looked at them. "Here's where things get either complicated or innovative, depending on your perspective. For thousands of years, Gaardian guidelines have strictly controlled the dissemination of scientific data to cultures so as not to interfere with a scientific community's development and advancement. In other words, I can't give you Gaardian technology, because that would create an unnatural push in our planet's scientific development and advancement."

Betsy Sue nodded. "Glenn and I have talked about this. Sometimes we wish we knew what Gaardians know, because that would make our scientific research easier – and provide shortcuts. We realize, however, that it's probably never a good idea for that to happen." Glenn looked at her and nodded.

"I knew that you both would understand. Here's the challenge. When the light creatures passed through Gaardian space, gathering information as they went, they caused an intermingling of scientific knowledge between planets previously never seen. At quite some length and with many details, Gaardians have been discussing this privately."

Glenn nodded. "So what's all this to do with Betsy Sue and I?"

"First, Gaardians are obviously not going to provide Earth's scientists with the knowledge necessary for interstellar travel – at least not yet. Furthermore, we are not going to provide you with total communication between the planets in my sector." Walter paused.

"Here's what I am going to do. I am going to allow limited questions and answers between the planets. For safety and other reasons, these communications will be monitored. I hope Earth's scientists will not get greedy and try to get too much help from the others too soon. You will need to respect one another, and you will need to respect Gaardian guidelines. There can't be any abuse of privileges. I do not want my team to have to redact any of your communications."

"Betsy Sue and I will honor the restrictions, but I can't warranty the behavior of other scientists."

Walter smiled. "Of course not. That's why there's going to be double filtering. My team will filter first. Then, you and Betsy Sue will look for violations. Now, the Biyae – that's the transparent humanoids – they would like a schematic of your second panorama camera, along with a schematic of the waterproof housing you used down in Florida. As a follow-up, the Biyae will probably later ask you for some of your research data. Tomorrow morning, you will get a Gaardian-secured email from Margaret Graves. You will be communicating through her using that enhanced security. Do you have any questions?"

They both shook their heads.

"Okay." Walter stood up, and then they stood up. "Let's go upstairs, and you can show me the twins. Each of you put one hand upon mine."

They put their hands upon his, and in a blink, they vanished.

7. Everett

While Refinnej was still praying, in another galaxy Haissem and his followers went across the sea to the western continent of Quzak. They landed at Rahcys ["RAW-sis"], a small village about a day's walk from the city of Airamas ["AIR-eh-muss"]. An artesian spring fed a large fountain there just a short walk from the port. Haissem stopped and rested there, while the rest of his followers explored the town and got supplies. It was the middle of the day.

In the Capitol, the son of Quzak's Prime Leader was very sick, and all the medical efforts to cure him were failing. The doctors told the father of the young Quzak that his son appeared to be dying. When the Prime Leader heard that Haissem had landed at the port, he took a transport and landed, not fifty meters from where the Arkaynee was sitting by the fountain.

The leader approached Haissem, who stood to greet him. **"Hello, Prime Leader, would you care to sit and drink some pure water with me?"**

He nodded. "Thank you." He sat down and accepted an offered cup of water. "I came to see you because my son is dying. I am hoping you will help him."

"With respect, Prime Leader, it has become common for everyone to expect miracles associated with me. Quzaks refuse to receive me for who I am, unless they are somehow dazzled by something impressive."

"Do not push me away, please, and come with me. It is a matter of death or life for my child."

Looking directly into the Prime Leader's eyes, Haissem said softly but firmly, **"Go home to your family. Your son is fine."**

He sat up straighter and nodded. The Prime Leader believed him. He touched a disk on the center of his chest. "My beloved, our son is well now, is he not?"

His mate answered excitedly, "He sat up a moment ago, and he is getting off of his bed! He seems fine! Come home!"

He stood up, and Haissem stood up with him. With tears in his eyes, the Prime Leader could hardly speak. "Thank you!" As Haissem nodded slightly, the visitor turned and walked rapidly back towards his transport.

As the transport took off, Haissem's followers were returning from their errands. "What did he want?"

Haissem smiled. **"He made a simple request on behalf of his son."** He looked at them. **"Sit down and rest! Do you have some food to share?"** He looked over at Euteekus, who was standing under some nearby foliage. "Come! Join us! You must be hungry too!"

She nodded and walked to the fountain.

+ + +

At that moment, Margaret Graves watched the latest video from Euteekus with keen interest in her office in Oakland, California. As she turned off the video with her remote, she turned to Toby Ballentine. "I wish I could put these videos on DVDs as evangelism tools."

"Most of humanity is just beginning to cope with the idea of our Gaardian presence on Earth. I doubt anyone is ready for videos about a Savior on another world in another galaxy. Besides, I'm sure that most clergy believe that Jesus was totally unique to God's creation. This would be beyond their thinking."

"That's true, I guess. I'm making video masters of all of these reports for future use, though." She glanced down at her screen. "I've got an email from Fresno."

Toby nodded and looked at his Gaardian ring. Toby to Paula Rutledge."

As Margaret worked with an email from Glenn Franz, Paula appeared in a g-mail portal next to Toby and Margaret. "Hi, Toby! Hi, Margaret! What's up?"

"Have you watched any of the video reports from Quzak regarding their Arkaynee?"

"No, I haven't, but I overheard Walter and Debbie talking about Quzak yesterday."

Margaret smiled as she continued to type at the keyboard. "You really should see all of them, Paula, from the beginning. I'm making video masters for possible use in a few decades here on Earth."

"In a few decades? Why so long?"

Margaret finished and clicked a button to send. "If you see them and continue to watch them as they come out, I think you'll easily understand why."

"Okay. ... Toby, I'm having Senator Steinmetz over to my apartment for dinner this evening, and I'm wondering if can you join us."

"Sure! Why?"

"Walter has given the okay to explain the paw prints made by Kieya a few years ago. The senator is becoming more frail, and he's wondered about those prints for years now. In Yosemite, Qaak and Jody noticed that he put on a good act, but his health is not strong."

Toby smiled. "This ought to be an interesting evening. What time?"

"Let's make it 7:00 PM local time, okay?"

"Got it! See you later!" The portal closed.

Margaret looked at Toby. "What paw prints are you talking about?"

Toby chuckled. "A few years ago, when Glenn and Betsy Sue Franz were starting out together with his special cameras, the first camera was on loan to someone from the Department of the Interior. Some thieves drove off with all of that exceptional equipment belonging to the Franzes. Walter had asked Kieya to keep watch over them while Paula and I were helping them in other ways. Kieya intercepted the vehicle, and she disabled and trussed up the thieves. In the soft soil around the car, there were a couple of clear paw prints, which could not have been made by any feline in North America."

Margaret grinned. "I don't remember reading anything about such an incident."

"That's not surprising. The incident was not a total secret, but Ben Kaiser offered a couple of provocative stories of his own to get the story of the prints buried further into the news that same day. It was mentioned in the Oakland Tribune in a short paragraph at the bottom of the fourth page of the first section without a picture. Ben arranged for the picture to be too late in getting to the paper before they went to press, and then it was never used."

Margaret nodded. "Getting back to the videos, I'm expecting the next one on Thursday. Would you like to watch it after dinner then?"

He smiled. "Dinner and a video with you? Of course!"

+ + +

While Margaret and Toby were talking about Kieya's paw prints in Oakland, across the bay in San Francisco, Ben and Francine Kaiser were at the Cliff House restaurant on the western side of the city, watching the sunset as they sipped some Domaine Leroy Musigny Grand Cru from crystal wine glasses. Francine smiled at her husband. "Don't you think this is a great place for our anniversary?"

He grinned. "Absolutely!" He looked into his glass. "Normally, we both prefer a Cabernet to a burgundy, but when I learned that the Cliff House had a few bottles of this available, I wanted to try a glass." He paused, took a sip, and rolled it around in his mouth before swallowing. "This is amazing! I love it!"

She nodded. "I do too." She took a sip. "I got a call from Paula Rutledge this afternoon."

"Really! "Neither of us has talked with her in months. What's up?"

"She said that this evening, she and Toby Ballentine are meeting with Senator Everett Steinmetz to give him an explanation about some paw prints. Paula said you knew the story. What paw prints?"

Ben smiled. "A few years ago, I used my influence to keep a story off the front pages of the California news papers. This place is too public for me to tell you about it here. That meeting is going to be this evening, about the time we're going to be having dessert. When we get home tonight, I'll tell you all about it."

"Why would paw prints be a story in the papers? As I understand it, they were found in a forested area north of here. It's an area with all kinds of wildlife."

Ben chuckled. "It was only a story because the print was seemingly from an animal not native to California." He gazed at Francine, directly into her eyes, and shook his head. "I love you Francine. ... Let's talk about it later."

"Okay."

+ + +

Everett Steinmetz leaned back into Paula' plush rocking chair. "That dinner was delicious. I know my late wife would have loved it too. At this point in the evening, she would be asking you for a recipe or two."

Paula smiled. "I'm glad you enjoyed it, senator."

He nodded. "You're a pleasurable hostess and an excellent cook, but did you invite me here just to feed me?"

Toby smiled. "No, senator, ... we know that for years there has been a mystery that has perplexed you, and we're going to solve that mystery for you this evening."

"A mystery? I've had several in both my personal and professional life, ... but the biggest mystery for me has been..." he paused to look at Toby directly "... are you talking about the paw prints?"

"Yes, senator."

The old man was thoughtful. "May I assume that what you're going to tell me I have to keep to myself?"

Paula smiled. "Yes. You're probably wondering why the two of us have the answer to your big mystery while none of your best sources have been able to help you."

His eyes twinkled. "I was thinking about it last year, while my beloved Dorothy was completing her final days here on Earth. Since my sources could come up with no reasonable scientific explanation for those two prints, I have – just for myself – concluded that only a Gaardian or one of his employees can explain it to me. Am I even close?"

Toby grinned. "You're very close, senator. Before I continue, however, let me re-affirm to you that this conversation stays here in this apartment. Okay?"

"Of course! Both of you work for our Gaardian, don't you?"

"Yes, senator." Paula smiled.

"Right. The configuration of the print was similar to an extremely large tiger, but how would such a tiger get loose in northern California without alerting all kinds of agencies, both federal and state, and how would such a huge cat get here in the first place without someone ..." He paused, and then he grinned. "You're smiling a little too much, Paula, and Toby, why are you shaking your head?"

"Senator, do you trust us? I mean, do you *really* trust us?"

The old man was thoughtful. "Yes, I believe I do. Why do you ask?"

Toby spoke quietly. "With your permission, we would like you to see – actually, meet – the animal that made those prints."

The senator's eyes grew wide. "You're not kidding around with this old man, are you?"

"No, senator. If you do not wish to meet our friend, we will not insist, but she would like to meet *you*."

"Meet me?" He paused. "She won't eat me, will she?"

Toby and Paula burst out laughing. Paula said, "Her name is Kieya, and while she is extremely powerful, she is also brilliant, gentle, and loving."

"Brilliant? Now I definitely want to meet this Kieya."

The big cat came around the corner from Paula's bedroom. "I wish to meet you as well, senator."

Senator Steinmetz's mouth hung open for a moment, but he did not get up. "I am not easily rendered speechless, but ... I am pleased to meet you. You're name is Kieya?"

"Yes," she purred softly. My name is Kieya. I am a felidaca, from a planet that is in a galaxy quite some distance from here. I am a Gaardian whose base is in that other galaxy. Earth's scientists could find my galaxy with some help, but your scientists do not yet have the technology to detect my planet at this distance."

The senator cleared his throat. "Please forgive me for not getting up. I feel a bit overwhelmed."

"May I shake your hand, senator?" She approached him and lifted a paw.

"Certainly!" He took it and looked at it. "It is my honor to meet such a beautiful creature."

"It is my honor to meet you, Senator." She sat down. Sitting at his feet, the top of her head was above his knees as he relaxed in the chair. "As I told you a moment ago, I am not the Gaardian from this sector of Gaardian space, but you have seen Earth's Gaardian. His name is Walter. He is elsewhere as we speak and would like to meet with you. Meanwhile, Walter has an invitation for you."

"An invitation?"

"Yes. May I call you Everett?"

The senator grinned. "What an unexpected and delightful request! Of course, you may! May I call you Kieya?"

"Certainly," the big cat purred. "The invitation is simply this: Walter would like you to come and work for him."

"How can I work for him? My beloved Dorothy has already died, and I am in failing health. How could an old man like me possibly work for a Gaardian?"

"Do you remember seeing Walter when he appeared before the General Assembly of the United Nations?"

"Yes."

"How old do you think Walter is?"

"He appears to be in his early thirties."

Kieya's eyes looked straight into those of the senator. "He is older than you are, senator."

The senator's mouth dropped open, then he closed it. "I had forgotten. He told the assembly that Gaardian technology had allowed age regression for those who worked for him – or something like that."

"Essentially, you are correct. I will give you an example. When Walter became a Gaardian, he recruited an old friend named Belinda to help him assemble his team. At the time, Belinda was in hospice, and if she had not gone to work for Walter, she would have died within a few hours. Today she appears to be about Walter's age. By the way, in terms of Earth's years, I am more than twenty thousand of Earth's years old."

Again, the Senator's mouth opened, but this time he closed it more quickly. "I have been almost looking forward to joining my Dorothy in heaven these last few months. Now I'm being offered a second life. Am I correct?"

Paula smiled. "That is absolutely correct, senator."

"Call me Everett"

"Okay, Everett. ... I will tell you something. I have learned to trust Walter and his decisions. He makes very few mistakes."

"In his position, I would imagine that if he makes a mistake it's a lulu!"

Toby laughed. "Right! As a Native American and also a Christian, I will tell you that for Walter, Debbie, and most of Walter's crew at the base, prayer is not an escape route – it's a lifestyle. As a result, most of the people who work for Walter are of one mind, like a well-knit team. Walter's inviting you to join the team."

"Give me a minute or two, okay?" The senator closed his eyes.

Kieya looked away from Everett and up at Paula, and then she turned her head towards Toby. She winked. Toby was startled, and he raised his eyebrows, as did Paula. Kieya resumed looking at the old man.

He opened his eyes. "Yes! Yes! How can I say no? What is next?"

Kieya realized that she had stopped purring while Everett prayed. Her purr resumed. "First, you need to meet Walter's base physician, Butch Eng. ... Kieya to Butch."

Butch appeared next to Kieya in a hologram. "Hi, Kieya! Hi Paula! Toby! And aren't you Senator Steinmetz?"

Paula and Toby waved, and the senator simply stared at the holographic image. Kieya's voice was slightly softer. "Butch, Everett here has agreed to join your team. His health is failing, so I'm going to bring him to the clinic. Can you take him right now?"

"Absolutely! I see you in a moment." He disappeared.

The senator blinked. "In a moment?"

Kieya purred more loudly. "If you would prefer a tour of the solar system before we restore your health, I doubt that you would enjoy it as much as getting your health restored first. Is that agreeable to you?"

Everett nodded. "Okay. Now what?"

"Paula, are you staying here tonight? What about you Toby?"

She shook her head. "I want to go back to my quarters on the base. I have lots to do there tomorrow. Toby?"

"Me too. Ken Lyman left me a message to check with him tomorrow."

Kieya stood up. "Everett, can you get out of that chair without assistance?"

"Sure!" Moving slowly and deliberately, he got out of the chair.

"Just put your hand on top of my head, Everett. We'll be there in a moment."

Hesitantly, Everett reached out and put his hand onto the soft fur of Kieya' head. Kieya's Gaardian ring subtly shimmered, and all of them were standing in the atrium on Walter's moon base, at the entrance to the clinic.

Butch smiled and extended his hand to greet his new patient. "Welcome! I'm the base doctor, and everyone just calls me Butch."

The senator took his hand off of Kieya and extended it to him. "It's nice to meet you, Butch."

"The gravity is adjusted to being the same as that of Earth, in case you are wondering. Come on into my clinic. It's this way." They started walking in.

Paula called out. "See you later, Everett."

"See you, Everett!" said Toby.

Everett turned and waved, and then he continued going into the clinic. "Did you say you adjusted the gravity? Is that possible?"

Toby smiled. "One of the perks of living on Earth's moon is that we can sleep in Moon-normal gravity if we wish, but not if we don't want to. It took me a few nights to get used to it, and now the only time I sleep with greater gravity is if I'm overnight on Earth. You'll be learning lots of new things in the days and weeks ahead." He stopped and pointed to a small vertical partition. "Please stand next to that partition while facing me."

The Senator went over and stood where he was directed. The partition rose until it was about the level of his chin. Then two more partitions rose around him to the same height.

"Senator, your clothing is going to disappear, so that's the reason for the partitions."

"Really?"

"Look over here at this screen, Everett." He pointed. "The red areas are diseased or cancerous tissues. The orange areas are those of tissues that are weak or otherwise unhealthy."

"Man! I'm even sicker than I thought."

"Right! It's hard to say how long your body would have held out if you hadn't joined the team, but not more than a few weeks. ... Now, Everett, put your hands on top of the partition in front of you and hold on. You may feel a bit weak for a moment."

He closed his eyes. "Ooo. ... Hmm." He opened his eyes again. "I feel a lot better. In fact, I feel amazing!"

"Good. Now. A lot of my new patients want to slip into the whirlpool or take a swim first. If you don't I'll have someone give you a quick tour of the base before showing you your quarters. What would you like to do first?"

"I think if I got into a whirlpool I'd fall asleep. How about that quick tour?" A blue jumpsuit appeared on his body.

"Great! Toby?" The partition around Everett lowered into the floor rapidly.

"Yeah!" Toby walked into the clinic. You look great! What's first for you, Everett?"

He smiled. "Thanks! I'd like a quick tour. Then I think I'll be ready for a good night's sleep. I've not had one in months!"

8. The Trap

The same morning that Haissem talked briefly with Refinnej at the crystal castle, the Arkaynee returned to his home in Melasurej, and news was passed that he was there. A crowd gathered, blocking the doorway so no one could get in or out. He was teaching in his living area, and Euteekus quietly stood just outside the window. They brought a paraplegic to him, carried by four males. When they were not able to get in because of the crowd, the four males removed part of the roof and lowered the paraplegic on his stretcher to lie directly in front of Haissem.

Impressed by their bold faith, he said to the paraplegic, **"Son, I forgive your offenses against the Creator."**

Some scholars who were students of the ancient ones were sitting there, and they started whispering among themselves, "He can't talk that way! That's a terrible offense against the Creator! The Creator and only the Creator can forgive offenses against the Creator."

Haissem knew immediately what they were thinking, and said, **"Why are you so doubtful? Which is easier? To say to this paraplegic, 'I forgive your offenses against the Creator,' or to say, 'Get up, take your stretcher, and start walking'? ... Well, ... just so it's clear that I'm the Son of a Quzak and authorized to do either, or both..."** he turned his head and looked at the paraplegic. **"Get up. Pick up your stretcher and go home."** He did it. He got up, folded up his stretcher, and walked out, with everyone there watching him. They rubbed their eyes, incredulous—and then praised the Creator, saying, "We've never witnessed anything like this!"

+ + +

At the crystal castle on Pzalop, Leahcim's security of the crystal castle had been lowered the day before. High up in the center of the castle, one triangular room was still occupied by Refinnej, who was praying, and she was thinking about all that she had learned.

She was confused regarding Joseph. She asked herself, "Why is Joseph so different?" Based upon the thoughts Walter transferred to her mind along with her reading of Joseph's mind, she recognized that she and Joseph were *friends*. This was a new experience, and she liked the feelings that went with friendship. She was pretty certain that if she pursued this thing called friendship with the others she had met, that the results would probably be positive. This was strangely exciting, and she had not exercised any of her Buud powers. It was both thrilling and amazing. "Does using my Buud powers prevent me from establishing more friendships?" That question intrigued her.

There were more questions that fascinated her: She had asked Walter and Joseph to return after a day, and she now asked herself, "Why did I ask for Debbie to come as well? What was I thinking? Will there be a need for Debbie to be here? Why?" Somehow she knew that it would be important, and she got back on her knees to pray. Then she paused to ask herself, "Why am I on my knees?"

As she knelt to pray, one of the other Buuds was silently and invisibly looking for her not far from there. The male with whom she had argued the day before was zealously searching Pzalop for her, totally unaware of her presence in the crystal castle. As he was doing so, Piatek, Asayak, and many of the Gaardians began to sense Buuds appearing in various parts of Gaardian space as they looked for her. Asayak monitored the locations of the Buuds and informed Gaardian.

+ + +

The day after Haissem returned to Quzak from the crystal castle, He made his way unnoticed deep into the forest near his home to pray. Then he walked up a hill nearby and sat down on a rock. In the distance, he could see the port and the beginning of the day's activity there. His inner circle of friends who spent the night outside his mother's home now saw him on the hill and joined him. They greeted one another warmly.

A military officer approached him and said, My Arkaynee, my best friend is sick. The medical scientists cannot determine what is wrong with him. He cannot walk, and he is in excruciating pain."

Haissem said, **"I will go with you and heal him."**

No, please," said the officer. "I don't want my Arkaynee to change his plans. Just say that my friend is healed, and he will be healed. As an officer, I give and take orders as part of Quzak life. If I tell a soldier to say or do something, he does what I tell him. When I give an order it must be done, and you are our great Arkaynee."

Startled, Haissem said, **"This is the first time I have witnessed such simple faith in all of Quzak. This officer is the forerunner of many Quzaks from both continents who will soon be coming from all directions on both continents. All will share in the Creator's grace and mercy. Those who are adult Quzaks, who learned the wisdom of our ancient ones but did not gain their wisdom, will be separated from the rest. They will wonder why my followers are joyous, and they are not."**

Haissem turned to the officer and said, **"Go. What you believed should happen has happened."** At that moment, the officer's friend was totally healed of body, mind, and spirit.

+ + +

All night, Refinnej was praying both on her knees and standing, high in the crystal castle. She did not expect to hear the Creator's voice again, nor did she expect to see the Creator's son, Haissem – Quzak's Arkaynee. Since she did not have the collective mind of the Buuds for a dialogue with her, she found that praying aloud helped her to think. With each question she asked, she paused silently for anywhere from a few minutes to over an hour.

"Why, Creator, did you choose me?"

"Why do the other Buuds not have active moral compasses?"

In her mind, she had a flash of memory of being with Walter outside of the universe with the Creator. Remembering their arrival at the crystal castle, she recalled Walter taking her hand to lead her towards the others in order to meet them. *That was a new experience.*

"Why was Walter so patient and kind to me? ... I guess he was being a *friend* to me like his son Joseph."

"Friend ... this experience of having friends, Father ..."

"Father? The humans seem to call you father. I just called you father. It seems natural. I saw that in both Walter's and Joseph's minds. That means more to me than *everything* else I have learned about you. Father ... Father. You are truly more father to me than my progenitors."

As she continued to pray, images crossed her mind of her first encounter with Joseph. "Father, what did your son mean when he talked about a life for Joseph and I? Does this mean a singular life? A life together?"

On through the night, she prayed. Images began to flash before her that reminded her again of what she saw outside the universe. As the sky began to glow before the dawn, Refinnej sensed movement in the crystal castle below her. Then she began to hear a soft purr, as Kieya was otherwise silent. Her paws treaded the stairwell silently as she padded up the stairs. "Hello, Kieya."

"Greetings, Refinnej. I hope I am not disturbing you."

"No, you are most welcome to join me up here. I welcome your presence."

"Thank you. I need to report something to you by way of Asayak. The other Buuds are becoming extremely angry that they cannot find you. They seem to be blaming one or more Gaardians for your disappearance, which is indirectly true." She paused. "The Creator kidnapped you, but you have been in our care." Her purring paused. "Perhaps I should bring Asayak here."

Refinnej looked up and closed her eyes. When she opened them a moment later she looked at Kieya. "No, Kieya, the one I really need is Joseph."

Kieya's purring grew louder. "Indeed! Walter told me that you might request him, and Debbie agreed. I will bring him here immediately." She disappeared.

Again, Refinnej looked upward. "Father? For some strange reason, I sense that you are leading me, though I do not know how. Thank you."

Kieya and Joseph appeared next to her. Joseph smiled. "Hello, Refinnej. I am glad to see you again."

Refinnej's heart beat faster, and she suddenly felt warmer. "Hello, Joseph. I am glad to see you."

Kieya continued to purr. "The two of you do not need me, and I am going down below to join the Suppla in prayer and prophecy. Joseph, Refinnej can take you home at the appropriate time."

Refinnej looked at the big cat. "Thank you, Kieya, we will be fine. Before the Creator formed us, He knew us and had plans for us. We will see one another again soon. Until then."

"Until then." Purring softly, the big cat padded silently down the stairs."

Joseph took Refinnej's hand and turned her to face each other. "This morning I read a chapter by a man named Paul, who wrote to people in the town of Corinth on Earth many hundreds of years ago. Paul defines love in a way that may be useful to you. Please read it in my mind."

She looked into his eyes. "Yes! Yes! I do not understand how what you and I actually have is possible, but we cannot deny the Creator's bringing us together."

He nodded. "We must trust one another unreservedly, and we must also love one another unconditionally. I can do this because I have witnessed it, and because I have been taught to practice it. Can you do the same?"

"I can do so because you can amplify all my efforts."

"Amplify? You said before that my gift is to be an amplifier. What does this mean?"

"Let me demonstrate, okay?"

Suddenly, they were outside of the crystal castle, with their backs to the glow of dawn. She squeezed his hand. "Do you see that star? Look through my eyes!"

Joseph looked at the star, and suddenly they were flying towards it, with all other stars a blur. Like a firefly flitting between leaves on plants, for several minutes the two of them darted between galaxies in a seemingly random way.

Then they were back inside the crystal castle, standing next to Kieya and the Suppla. Joseph continued to smile as he looked at Refinnej, and he said, "Kieya, we need your help."

The big cat's purr stopped. "How may I help?"

"Do you know how to trigger the security devices of this structure?"

"Indeed. I know how."

"We've only moments to work with. Please send the Suppla to her apartment. I'm sorry, Suppla, I will explain later." As Kieya's Gaardian ring shimmered, the Suppla vanished. "Just now, Joseph and I visited several galaxies. I tried to make it look random, but I got the attention of all the other Buuds. As we went past them, I sent a thought to them that I would meet them in this crystal structure and explain everything to them. The next time I say your name, please leave us and trigger the security."

Kieya's purr returned. "Excellent! How much time do you need alone with them?"

"Give us a day and then return."

"Done."

Suddenly, more than a hundred other Buuds began to arrive, and within seconds, the large triangular room at the base of the crystal castle was very crowded. Refinnej looked at the big cat. "Thank you, Kieya."

As Kieya vanished, suddenly all was dark except for the low glow of interior lighting. There was chaos, with all the other Buuds trying to communicate at once.

Refinnej pressed her forehead to Joseph's. "Since you and I are one, Joseph, your power will amplify my efforts while all of us are trapped in here. I hope you trust me."

"I do."

With a voice louder and more powerful than she ever knew was possible, Refinnej called out, "Silence everyone!" Suddenly, all the Buuds were silent. "Thank you. First of all, we Buuds do not have our powers here, so do not waste energy trying to use them. We will be in this place for one full rotation of the planet, and then we will all leave. Does everyone understand?"

An older Buud male nearby said, "Why are you speaking to us in this way? You are the youngest and least experienced Buud. You have no right to speak to us this way."

Refinnej nodded. "I have learned a lot during these recent days while you were searching for me, and I have much to tell all of you. Standing next to me is Joseph, my life's partner. He is from a planet called Earth, and he is approximately my age, but he is a human and not a Buud. His gift is that he is an amplifier. He exponentially amplifies my powers. I ask that you withhold your questions for most of this planet's rotation. If any Buud is determined to interrupt or interfere with my efforts here, I will deal with that offense appropriately." She turned to the older Buud, who had raised the question. "Are you, at least for now, satisfied with my answer?"

"Proceed."

For most of the night, Refinnej did all the talking.

+ + +

In orbit miles above Gaardian planet, was the Conference Center. Its main meeting hall was large enough for meetings of all Gaardians when necessary. That particular day, more than half of all the Gaardians were there, with the others connected by three-dimensional video.

As Walter stepped up onto the stage, the hall grew quiet. "All of you have received the reports regarding the Buuds. As I am speaking at this moment, all the Buuds are trapped in the structure on Pzalop designed by Leahcim, which I call the crystal castle. In a previous report, you learned of the special nature of the beryllium aluminate structure and its security features. In a brilliant maneuver, the Buud known as Refinnej – with the help of my son, Joseph – drew all the other Buuds into the castle. Once they were there, she signaled Kieya, who left them there and triggered the security features. Gaardian is monitoring everything within the castle, without the knowledge of any of the Buuds."

Kieya stood up. "I have some observations."

"Certainly."

The big cat padded up onto the stage and turned to face the other Gaardians, sitting down on her hindquarters. "I observed Joseph and Refinnej as I brought them together in the crystal castle, and moments later I saw them step out of the castle and start moving from galaxy to galaxy. They moved more rapidly than I have ever seen a Gaardian move, and faster than any Buud." She paused. "I do not know if Walter and Debbie have anticipated this, but it would not surprise me if Refinnej and Joseph became husband and wife." There was murmuring in the hall as Walter smiled.

Kieya continued, "I saw their spirits function as one, as with other Gaardian couples. I also offer a surmise. I believe that within the crystal castle, Refinnej is more powerful than all the other Buuds because Joseph amplifies her power."

Walter was puzzled. "I've wondered about what Refinnej meant when she said that Joseph's gift was that he is an amplifier."

Kieya lifted a paw. "Our Gaardian rings take our thoughts, amplifies them, and turns them into reality. Joseph amplifying Refinnej's efforts goes much further." She put her paw down. "Walter, when you pray, one of the things you do is surrender to God's will. God's unlimited power becomes available, as your will and God's will become one. As a very limited metaphor, and in a much more crude way, when Refinnej and Joseph surrender to each other, the power unleashed is greater than those of their own individual powers combined." The big cat returned to her seat, and there was murmuring in the hall.

Walter scratched his head. "It appears that Joseph and Refinnej are actually functioning as one. Even with all that God has revealed to me, the possibility that my son would be married so soon had not occurred to me." He smiled. "I'm sure that Debbie and I will be discussing this!" There was some scattered laughter. Walter held up a hand. "Today we need to focus on the current situation. Prior to Refinnej's strategy, the other Buuds decided that Gaardians are responsible for Refinnej's disappearance, and they were becoming angry. We can be reasonably sure that this was the reason for Refinnej and Joseph drawing them into the crystal castle. I believe that if Refinnej had not acted, Gaardians might have had war with the Buuds. Asayak reported to us that such thoughts were going through their minds." Again, there was murmuring among the Gaardians in the hall.

Just then, Qaak appeared and sat down next to Kieya. He gestured to Walter, and Walter stepped off of the stage to confer with him. Qaak's eyes glowed subtly. "I have been conferring with Gaardian and with Asayak, and I have an unusual suggestion."

Walter nodded. "This morning, God spoke to me and informed me that you would have a useful if unusual suggestion. Why don't you go on stage and present it?"

"I am no longer convener – you are."

"Yes, but your wisdom and experience are highly respected. The suggestion should come from you."

His eyes glowed more brightly. "Indeed! Very well!" The old triped ambled up onto the stage, and the hall grew quiet. "I have been conferring with Gaardian and with Asayak, and I have two observations and a suggestion."

Qaak folded one leg and sat on it like a stool. "We Gaardians are not inhibited in our actions by either the crystal castle or its security. This gives us an advantage over the Buuds. Furthermore, both Asayak and Gaardian are able to scan the minds of the Buuds without detection. This has been confirmed, and it is important that both maintain their anonymous roles."

He closed his eyes for a moment, and then opened them. "If I go into the crystal castle, there would be little physical danger to me, and I can teach them all they need to know in order to behave appropriately in Gaardian Space. I can do so in a matter of moments. Furthermore, as strange as this suggestion may sound, I believe that we should make Refinnej with Joseph a Gaardian pair, not to a sector of space, but to the Buuds as a species."

Walter stepped closer to Qaak. "Since this is a very unusual suggestion, let's take time to consider this and discuss it. Let us adjourn for one hour." He turned to Qaak. "Let's go to the surface and confer with Gaardian together."

Qaak nodded. Their rings shimmered, and they vanished. A moment later, they appeared on Gaardian on a hill high above Red Falls. A moment afterward, Kieya appeared. "I hope you don't mind my joining you, but I am assuming we need to confer with Gaardian."

The planet's voice rumbled, "I'm glad you came. Walter, do you consider your son wise for his age?"

"I have not given it much thought, I must admit."

"Your wife Debbie has."

Kieya purred. "Indeed, Walter. Knowing Joseph had a unique gift which none of us had been able to identify, I have observed him carefully as he has developed. He is a faithful image of his parents."

Qaak's eyes glowed. "Indeed! You and Debbie have done well. He has also benefited from the rapid maturity and growth of his friend and mentor, Kenkee."

Walter's eyes grew wide. "Kenkee? His mentor?"

The planet's voice was emphatic. "Yes. Though they are approximately the same chronological age, Kenkee was developmentally an adult before Joseph approached adolescence. Do not forget the fact that Kenkee's mind was imprinted with all the knowledge of his mother's species when he was born, and he gained some of his father's knowledge and wisdom as well. Kenkee and Joseph have been good for each other."

Walter nodded. "This puts a different – and better – spin on all of this. Qaak, I think you need to go to the crystal castle, while the security systems are still in place. Refinnej and Joseph will have your back."

Qaak chuckled. "This is original. In all my years, this is the first time that the son of a Gaardian and his life-mate will have my back!"

Walter smiled. "His life-mate?"

Qaak's eyes glowed softly. "It seems all but certain to happen soon, if not already in terms of their emotions. You should be prepared to be supportive of their decision."

"I'll pray about it."

"That's advisable. Let's return to the Conference Center." The three of them vanished to join the others.

9. Stepping Beyond

Refinnej's voice was firm. "All of you need to learn the guidelines that govern all of Gaardian space."

"We are Buuds. No one needs to teach us anything!" All the others were murmuring their agreement.

From the perspective of all the Buuds in the crystal castle, suddenly their Buud existence became surreal. They could no longer see the castle or one another. The voice of the Creator thundered around them.

> I am your Creator. Before your physical existence was
> possible, I knew you and made plans for you. I gave
> you your lives, and I gave you your abilities. I can just
> as easily take both away.

In a brilliant glow, the Buuds then saw more than all the thousands of years of their existence all at once. There were fleeting images, along with sounds like that of wind through treetops. They saw how Haissem, Qapoku, Eiraynay, and Jesus affected their entire lives. They saw that they were about to meet Qaak, and how Joseph and Refinnej would lead them. The glow was suddenly gone. They were back in the crystal castle. For a few moments, they just breathed deeply.

In the eyes of Joseph and Refinnej, all the others were gone but for a moment. Into the silence, Refinnej spoke quietly. "The Creator has shown us how we look to Him. In that moment without time, you saw a glimpse of a creature named Qaak. He will be here in a moment."

As if on cue, Qaak appeared on the other side of Joseph. "Greetings, everyone. My name is Qaak." His eyes glowed softly, as he turned to Refinnej and Joseph. "Refinnej, it seems the Creator has taught them their lesson. You and Joseph have done well. I will now teach all of you what you need to know. Joseph, please stand on the other side of me. You already know what I am about to teach."

Joseph smiled. "It's good to see you, Qaak. I knew you would come."

The glow in Qaak's eyes was soft. "It is good that all the Buuds have a collective consciousness. What I am about to teach you, Refinnej, all of you will learn. You will learn Gaardian regulations, a summary of Gaardian history, and some things that The Creator wants all of you consciously to know." Qaak paused, and he moved closer to her.

"Refinnej, I am going to place three of my fingers on your face. I suggest that you close your eyes while I do so." He turned to the others. "I suggest the same to the rest of you."

Qaak extended his hand and touched Refinnej's face. As he did so, her eyes closed, and all other eyes of the Buuds closed. Joseph watched, fascinated. The glow in Qaak's eyes brightened and dimmed several times over a period of about ten minutes.

Withdrawing his hand from Refinnej's face, he turned to face all the other Buuds. His voice seemed much larger and powerful. "Do all of you understand?"

There were nods and murmurs of agreement.

Qaak paused and turned to Refinnej and Joseph. "I will place this structure in a time pocket. When sufficient time has passed within the time pocket, the pocket will be removed, releasing all of you. The two of you are behaving wisely, and you have a decision to make that is separate from the decision to be made by the other Buuds. It is good that they hear what I am about to say to you."

"What must we decide?" asked Joseph.

Qaak spoke gently, and his eyes glowed softly. "If the other Buuds decide to live under Gaardian guidelines, and the two of you are indeed to be life-mates, Gaardian and Walter are offering you the opportunity to be a Gaardian pair, whose primary jurisdiction will be over the Buuds. It is a major decision, since it is for life. Do you understand?"

Tears rolled down Refinnej's cheeks. "Are you serious? How is this possible?"

Qaak chuckled. "In my 65,000 Earth-years of living, I have observed repeatedly that with The Creator, all things are possible."

Joseph smiled. "You have always liked that old rabbinical tale that my Dad told you, haven't you?"

Qaak nodded. "Indeed. If you and Refinnej accept the offer, Asayak will teach both of you the many things you must know as Gaardians." He paused. "I will now leave you in the time pocket. Send a thought to me, Refinnej, when the time is right. Until then."

Together they nodded and said, "Until then."

Qaak vanished.

+ + +

Far away on Quzak, Haissem spent the day visiting towns on the southeast coast of the western continent, teaching and healing. It was now late, and they were eating a small meal by a fire on the shore. **"We have all had a long day, my friends. The crowds are now back in their homes. I need to spend time in prayer, but I want all of you to go back to Melasurej, across the sea. I will join you there tomorrow."**

"We could wait for you here until you have finished praying, could we not?" asked a male named Nomis ["NAW-mus"].

Haissem shook his head. **"No. Most you have your families waiting for you in Melasurej. If you leave now, you will be back there before dawn. I have arranged for that boat over there,"** he pointed, **"to take you tonight. I will see you tomorrow."**

Haissem's friends gathered up their things and walked towards the boat, while he turned and went up a nearby hill. As he knelt down by a rock to pray, in the distance, he could see the boat pulling away from the shore.

He prayed, **"Father. The time will soon come when you will glorify me that I may glorify you. I have mixed feelings about what I am facing. I know I must do what you have sent me to Quzak to do, but I do not look forward to the pain, the abandonment, and the rejection."** While Haissem prayed, he saw images of what had already taken place, and they discussed everything. Then the Creator showed him images of what would take place in the days ahead.

Haissem prayed, **"I am praying for them. I am not praying for Quzak, but for those whom you have given me, for they are yours. All my friends are yours, and I am glorified in them."** He went on to pray for each of them by name.

After praying, Haissem went down the hill. He could see that the wind had arisen, and the surf was more than two meters high. He decided to join them in the boat, so he started walking on the sea towards his friends.

They did not see Haissem until he was only about a dozen meters away. When they saw him, they thought he was some kind of spirit, and they cried out in fear.

Haissem raised his hand and said, "Do not be afraid! It is me! It is Haissem."

When he climbed into the boat, they gathered around him and clung to him, still afraid.

He raised his arms to the heavens and cried out, "Be quiet! Be still!" The sea became totally calm, and they stared at him in awe.

+ + +

When Qaak vanished from inside and reappeared outside the crystal castle, his ring shimmered again, and the castle had the inner glow of the time pocket. On his left, the faint glow of early dawn was beginning. Nearby, a hovercraft approached. When it stopped, the Suppla stepped out and pondered the crystal castle a moment. "It looks strange. What is going on, Qaak?"

His eyes glowed intensely. "Inside are dozens of alien beings, held inside a time pocket, behind the security barriers."

"What is a time pocket?"

"In this case, it is an area within which time seems to move at a normal pace, but compared to what is outside it, time passes within the pocket much more rapidly."

"Fascinating! How much longer will they be in there?"

Qaak shook his head. "It is strange. I thought I would have a signal by now. In their time frame, more than a week has passed while a few minutes have transpired here outside the crystal castle." He paused. "I will be just a moment." He vanished.

Inside, Qaak reappeared. "I am ready for your report. If you please, I want to hear all Buuds respond as a single voice, telepathically."

There was a moment of silence, and then they all responded. "Yours is an interesting request, one which we did not anticipate, and for which we were not prepared, but now we speak as one."

Qaak's eyes glowed as he nodded. "Good."

"We Buuds are powerful, but we have been wasting our gifts of power and using them frivolously. We have been wasteful of who we are because we have not exercised any self-discipline. Until now, we have not had any sense of purpose or any perspective beyond ourselves. We have wandered aimlessly."

Qaak's eyes glowed more intensely. "Indeed."

"Yes. That is a good word. 'Indeed.' It has taken us much time within this time pocket of yours to become more focused. In considering the Gaardians, we were stunned by both your sense of purpose and your self-restraint. It has taken us even more time of discussion to realize that until the Creator showed us ourselves, we had no sense of meaning or of purpose."

Qaak nodded. "Yes."

"It will take us much more time to deal with these new things, but we have decided, and we are of one mind, that we agree to Gaardian guidelines. In this first phase of our relationship with the Gaardians, we will stay mostly outside of Gaardian-controlled space, until we know confidently that we can do what Refinnej and Joseph call *behaving ourselves*."

Together, Joseph and Refinnej said, "Good."

Their voices as one continued. "For the first time in our collective memory, Buuds have experienced fear. We are fearfully in awe of our Creator. As Refinnej has said, we are nothing in comparison to the Creator. We know that the Creator has all authority and knows everything. We are overwhelmed, which is another new thing for us. We are overwhelmed by the knowledge that the creator is wise beyond all our wisdom, that the Creator is everywhere at once, and that the Creator is beyond time. Beyond all this, there is no doubt in our minds either separately or collectively, that the Creator is for all practical purposes the very definition of love. When we returned from beyond time, we experienced a kind of residue of the Creator's joy."

Qaak nodded, and he turned to Refinnej and Joseph. "Have you two made your decision?"

Joseph nodded. "I have asked Refinnej to marry me, and she has said yes."

Qaak's eyes glowed brightly. "Congratulations!"

Refinnej smiled. "Thank you, Qaak. We have also decided to accept the offer and be a Gaardian pair. What happens next?"

"Excellent! Indeed!" His eyes continued to glow brightly. "When I release the time pocket, everyone but you two will be on the larger moon of Waysad, just beyond Leahcim's sector, where you first met Piatek as a timepiece vendor." He turned to the others. "Are the rest of you prepared to be disbursed to Waysad's larger moon?"

As a single voice, they said, "Yes!" They vanished, and all the security features were deactivated.

Qaak chuckled. "This has gone very well indeed. You two have done extremely well!"

"Thank you!" Joseph was smiling. "I'm glad that's over!"

Refinnej hugged him. "I am too!" She looked at Qaak. "Where do we find Asayak?"

Qaak's eyes stopped glowing for a moment. "He's been here all this time, actually. Follow me."

As he started ambling towards the water-powered elevator, the Suppla came through the main entrance. "Greetings!"

Qaak stopped and turned. "Greetings, Eibbed. You might like to meet one of the aliens of which I spoke. Eibbed, this is Refinnej. She and Joseph here are going to be a new Gaardian pair."

"Joseph, are you not Walter's son?" She shook Joseph's hand.

"Yes, Eibbed. This is my fiancée, Refinnej."

"It is a pleasure to meet you, Refinnej."

"It is also my pleasure. I am a Buud, from outside this galaxy."

Qaak's eyes glowed briefly. "Eibbed, I am sure we will see one another again. You are here to pray, and I must take these two on the elevator lift to an upper level. Please excuse us."

"Certainly. It is excellent to have met both of you, and it has been pleasant to see you again, Qaak. Until another time."

"Indeed." Qaak ambled towards the water-powered lift. Once the three of them were inside, Qaak pressed a green triangle, and the lift began moving upward.

Joseph looked at the triped. "Why are we using the lift? We can transport wherever we want to go."

As the lift stopped, the green triangle popped out of the panel into Qaak's hand. The other two stared. Qaak chuckled and said, "Come."

They stepped out into a three-sided room at the top of the center of the crystal castle. Chairs appeared to circle around a triangular table. Qaak put the green translucent stone on the table and sat down. "Asayak has been here all the time. Just as the security features of this crystal castle are hidden in plain sight, Asayak has been hidden here in plain sight in this beryllium aluminate crystal." Qaak's ring shimmered, and Asayak appeared between Qaak and Joseph.

"Greetings, friends," said Asayak telepathically.

"Hello Asayak," said Joseph.

Refinnej was smiling broadly. "Well done, Qaak, I would never have thought to look inside a crystal for a spy."

Qaak's eyes glowed. "There was not just one spy, Refinnej, but two. Another one of Walter's crew is here with us, standing near the stairs."

Refinnej turned her head. "What do you mean, there's just us here."

Keeta allowed a pale yellow tint to reveal her transparent body. "Hello, friends."

Refinnej's eyes grew wide. "I was not able to see you even with all of my Buud powers just now. You are amazing!"

Asayak flowed down to their height. "One might say that Keeta and I have been spies, yes, indeed. Qaak, thank you for this unique experience. When Keeta moved about, looking into the eyes of the Buuds and sometimes into the eyes of Joseph, she could see things that I could not. I could look through her eyes and send images to Gaardian."

Keeta walked over to Refinnej. "You have a beautiful and gentle spirit, Refinnej. You will be a great asset to the Gaardians, and you are the perfect mate for Joseph."

"Thank you, Keeta. It is a pleasure seeing you in addition to hearing your voice."

Keeta smiled. "When you go to Gaardian, I hope you will meet my husband, Ken, and our son, Kenkee."

"I will look forward to it." She smiled.

Asayak stirred. "When the time pocket was in place, I experienced both the passage of time within the pocket and the seeming non-passage of time outside of it. Now it will be my privilege to train the newest Gaardians."

Joseph tilted his head quizzically. "It took my Dad more than fifty Earth years to be trained as a Gaardian, and my human brain is no different than his. How can you train both Refinnej and I simultaneously?"

Qaak chuckled. "I will let you answer that question in a moment, Asayak. In the meantime, I am going back to Gaardian to discuss all of this with Walter and the others. I will see all three of you soon. We normally have a welcoming party on Gaardian for new Gaardians. If you two want to, I suggest you consider combining that welcoming party with a wedding reception, if you are going to be wedded in the future.""

Refinnej squealed. "Amazing! I'm going to really like being married to a human! Let's get our training first, and then we'll talk about it."

Qaak's eyes glowed. "Until later."

"Later, Qaak," they said.

He vanished.

Asayak stirred. "To answer your question, Joseph, I perceive that you two have already bonded in a unique way through your gift as an amplifier. My training thoughts will go through Refinnej to you, where you will amplify them and return them to her from a human perspective. The two of you will always be able to see through your separate and combined perspectives."

Refinnej and Joseph nodded and got comfortable in their chairs. The training did not take long.

10. Resurrection

A Quzak male was in very poor health. His name was Surazal ["SIR-uh-zal"], and he was a friend of Haissem. His sister, Ahtram ["AH-trum"] sent to the Arkaynee, telling him that his friend Surazal was near death.

Strangely, when Haissem heard it, he said, "His illness does not lead to his death. It is for the glory of the Creator, so that the son of a Quzak can be glorified through this."

Haissem loved Ahtram and Surazal. Nevertheless, when he heard that his friend was ill, he stayed two days longer in the place where he was. After doing so, Haissem said to his inner circle of followers, "Let us go to Melasurej again."

One of them said to him, "Haissem, our planet's leaders were just now seeking to execute you on false charges, and are you going there again?"

Surprising them, Haissem answered, "Is not each day the same length? If a Quzak walks in the day, he does not stumble, because he sees the light of this planet on which we live. However, if a Quzak walks in the night, he stumbles, because the light is not in him."

They all seemed puzzled.

Then Haissem said, "Our friend Surazal has fallen asleep, but I go to awaken him."

Another of his followers said to him, "Haissem, if Surazal has fallen asleep, he will recover."

He was speaking of Surazal's death, but his followers thought he was talking about sleep.

Haissem told them plainly, "Surazal has died, and for your sake, it is good I was not there, so that all of you may have faith. Let us go to him."

When Haissem came, he found that Surazal had by now been in the crypt for four days. Many of the Quzaks had gathered around Surazal's sister, Ahtram, to console her, for Surazal was very young when he died. When Ahtram heard that Haissem was coming, she went and met him.

She said to Haissem, "My Arkaynee, if you had been here, Surazal would not have died. I also know that whatever you ask of the Creator it will be given to you."

Haissem said to her, "Your brother will live again."

Ahtram said to him, "Almost all Quzaks know that he will live again in the resurrection on the last day. The ancient ones have said so."

Haissem said to her, "I am resurrection and life. A Quzak who believes in me, though he dies, shall again live, and every Quzak who lives and has faith in me shall never die. Do you believe what I am saying?"

"Yes, my Arkaynee, I believe that you are the Savior, the Son of the Creator, who has come to Quzak."

Haissem had not yet come into Melasurej, but was still in the place where Ahtram had met him. After walking some distance, they came to the burial site. As she began to weep, Haissem was deeply moved. He asked, "In which crypt is he lying?" As she led him to a large structure, Haissem wept with her.

He said, "Take off the cover." Ahtram said to him, "My Arkaynee, by this time there will be an odor, for we did not have him embalmed."

Haissem said, "Did I not inform you that if you had faith you would see the glory of the Creator?"

She motioned to some Quzaks standing nearby, and they took away the cover. Haissem looked up and said, "Father, thank you for hearing me. I know you always hear me, but I am saying this on account of the Quzaks gathered here, that they may believe that you sent me."

Looking at the crypt, he said with a powerful voice, "Surazal, sit up and climb out."

He sat up and climbed out, but his hands and feet were bound with strips of cloth, and his face was wrapped as well. Haissem said to the Quzaks that had removed the lid, "Unbind him, and let him go."

Many of the Quzaks, who had gathered there and witnessed what he did, believed in him, but some went to the planet's leaders and told them what Haissem had done.

A large number of political and religious leaders gathered in a secret meeting. The leader of one of the largest cities said, "What are we to do? For this Quzak does amazing things without the assistance of science and technology. We cannot let him go on like this. His influence upon all Quzaks will soon be greater than ours."

One of the priests said to them, "You know nothing like that. Look at the writings of the ancient ones. Do you understand that it is better for our planet that one Quzak should die for all Quzaks? All of that for which we have worked should not perish." Without realizing it, what he said cleared the way for ancient Quzak prophecies to be fulfilled. So from that day on they made plans to put him to death.

+ + +

A few days later, Joseph, Refinnej, Walter, and Debbie were sitting around a small table in the atrium at the moon base above Earth. Joseph spoke quietly and said, "Refinnej and I have talked a lot about when and where we want to get married."

Refinnej nodded. "Our marriage is not only a union of ourselves and our families, but a union of much more in the galactic sense."

Debbie smiled. "Your father was a bit surprised that the two of you are getting married so soon, but I saw that this would happen when the two of you met in the crystal castle, and your eyes locked on each other."

Joseph smiled. "Right! That was totally unexpected for both of us! It was amazing!" He looked at her.

Refinnej put her hand on Joseph's, and leaned over and kissed him on the cheek. "I thought Buuds had seen just about everything, but that was both unique and special."

Joseph squeezed her hand and looked at his parents. "We want to have our wedding on a little uninhabited and unnamed planet in Kieya's sector. She told us that she and Icnivad often go there to relax and have fun. There is a kind of veldt there that is about two thousand meters across. Dad, we'd like you to perform the ceremony, with just the four of us, standing at the center of the veldt. Gaardians and Gaardian crew members can sit on the veldt around us, and Buuds would be there among us appearing as their natural selves."

Refinnej raised one finger. "We have a request, but we do not know who to ask."

Walter looked at them quizzically. "What do you mean?"

Refinnej was very serious. "My mind is partly connected to a collective consciousness made up of all Buuds. Other Buuds are aware of this conversation. There is nothing I can do to stop it. The only place I have ever been where I have been disconnected from it was in the crystal castle."

Debbie grinned. "So do you want to have your honeymoon in the crystal castle?"

They all laughed. Walter shook his head, and more seriously was thoughtful. "That might be okay with Leahcim and the Suppla, but that would not solve your larger problem. Would you mind if I ask Leahcim to join our conversation for a moment?"

Joseph smiled. "I like Leahcim! Sure! Why not?"

Leahcim appeared next to their table in a three-dimensional image. "Hello, Walter! Hello Debbie, Joseph, and Refinnej, what is the occasion?"

Walter asked, "When construction of the crystal castle was complete, was there any of the beryllium aluminate left?"

"Certainly! There's enough for several more structures the same size. Why do you ask?"

"Joseph and Refinnej have privacy issues that could be solved with a base surrounded by sheets of that crystal. It would not have to be large enough for a crew, since they will not need one. Still, they will need ample space for themselves."

Leahcim nodded. "I understand." He was thoughtful. "I can use Ooza's base in orbit above Quzak as a model. Where would you want it to be, and would that be the right size?"

Refinnej looked at Walter. "If you will excuse me for a moment, I will take a quick look at Ooza's base. She vanished for about five seconds and reappeared. "Leahcim, if you could assemble a sphere about twice that size made of that crystal material, I can furnish the insides and its capabilities. Having it larger will make it like having a small moon to ourselves."

Joseph nodded. "Leahcim, as for location, assemble it wherever it is convenient to you and to the minors. We can locate it wherever we want it."

Leahcim nodded. "How soon do you need it?"

Refinnej smiled. "The sooner you can assemble it, the sooner we can have our wedding!"

Leahcim laughed. "I'll tell the minors that it will be a wedding present for a couple of Gaardians. They'll like that! I'll get back to you in a few days. Until then."

"Until then, Leahcim," said Walter.

Leahcim's image vanished.

+ + +

On Pzalop, Kieya was walking in The Creator's Park, which surrounded the crystal castle. She stopped to sharpen her claws on a large plant. Her purr stopped while she stretched her legs, and then as she relaxed her purr resumed. There was a faint chime, and she heard Leahcim ask, "May I join you?"

"Certainly." She continued her stroll as Leahcim appeared and walked beside her. "How are you my friend?"

He smiled. "I am well, of course. I'd like your help with something."

"How?"

"Refinnej and Joseph need a place where they can have privacy."

"What does that have to do with us?"

"I'm going to have the minors cut more sheets of crystal, enough for a sphere about twice the diameter of Ooza's base in orbit above Quzak."

"Ingenious! Whose idea was this?"

"Walter's."

"How can I help?"

"I will work with the minors as my older self. I would like you to transport the materials into space above Pzalop to assemble and fuse the panel edges together. For fusion, the temperature required will be less than 2500 degrees Kelvin."

The old cat was thoughtful. "That is well below the melting point of carbon."

"That is true, but what is your point?"

"I can put a sphere of carbon in orbit here above Pzalop. The minors can cut the gemstone in any convenient sizes and shapes. You and I can simply melt it to cover the sphere in orbit. Once it is of sufficient thickness, we can remove the carbon from the inside. It will look like a giant version of the toy marbles that Walter and other humans play with when they are children, only it will be hollow."

"Should we install some Gaardian security?"

Her purring stopped briefly, and then it resumed. "That's a good idea. A Gaardian gem of only a few grams will be enough to maintain basic security. We can hide it in plain sight." She paused about ten seconds. "Yes, Gaardian agrees. When we're done, we'll put it in orbit above that little planet in my sector where Joseph and Refinnej will have their wedding."

"Agreed. I think we can start tomorrow. Until then."

"Until then." They both vanished.

+ + +

"Your wedding dress?" Refinnej's eyes were huge. You are willing to let me wear it?"

Ooza grinned. "Absolutely. I've even got an android version of the original designer to help fit it to you. His name is Bob Mackie."

"I'm a Buud. I can do it."

"I'm sure you could, if you had any experience with dress fitting. Besides, I have three breasts, and you have two. That alone will require some adjustments!"

Refinnej grinned. "I think you are right! This just might be fun!"

"Yes! ... Bahna?"

Her android appeared. "Do you wish Bob Mackie again, along with the dress?"

"Yes. Let's have a platform here for Refinnej to stand on while she is fitted."

When the platform appeared, Refinnej stepped up upon it. Suddenly, she was clothed in a Bob Mackie original that had been fitted to Ooza several years earlier. It was short, however, and did not touch the floor as it had for Ooza. "Oooh! This is amazing!"

Ooza smiled, as the Bob Mackie android appeared. "Hello ladies! Wow! Even improperly fitted, you're stunning, Refinnej!"

"Thank you."

"You will be easier for me to fit since your body is closer to that of a human and taller. Bahna, let's adjust the length so that the dress flows naturally behind her." There was a shimmer, and the dress was longer in length. "Okay, Bahna, now let's adjust the bodice to form fit her." Again, there was a shimmer. "Okay, now its nearly perfect. Bahna, in your database you have that drawing I made of how I thought the soon-to-be Princess Diana could look when she was to marry Prince Charles. Let's take those embellishments and add them to this gown."

As the features shimmered into place, Ooza was stunned, and she sat down on the floor beside the platform. "That's the most amazing gown I've ever seen, Mr. Mackie!"

"Thank you. Now, Bahna, put a mirror in front of Refinnej."

As the mirror appeared, she gasped. "I could not have imagined this. I have not dreamed such art! Thank you!"

"You are welcome." He vanished.

The dress was ready. Other details were being worked out.

+ + +

A few days later, in the center of the veldt on a planet in Kieya's sector, stood a transparent crystal platform. If jewelers had looked closely, they would have seen that it was actually a giant emerald-cut diamond, standing about three meters tall and four meters in diameter. The sun had set, and above the veldt was a canopy of stars shining brilliantly, and the planet had no moon. The platform was illuminated from above from hidden sources. As a surprise to the couple, John Carson had suggested a special source of music, which he designed and Walter implemented. The perimeter of the veldt was surrounded by just over 12000 pipes ranging in size from a few inches to 64 feet in length.

As the guests began appearing all over the veldt, a pipe organ began playing the ending to "Tocatta," from Charles-Marie Widor's Symphony for Organ Number Five. Next to a 64-foot pipe stood Asayak, Kieya, and Icnivad. "I cannot hear sounds as you do," said Asayak, "but I experience this organ in a profound way that does not come from any other source of sound."

As she watched, Kieya's eyes hardly blinked. "This organ music has more purr than all felidacas on our planet combined!"

"Agreed," said Icnivad. As the music concluded, Joseph, Refinnej, Walter, and Debbie appeared on top the platform. Icnivad's paws were flying at lightning speed over some wood in front of him, with chips flying, as he created a sculpture of the ceremony. He finished his work at about the time the ceremony was over.

When Walter said 'amen,' everyone on the diamond platform vanished within seconds, and a moment later, so did the guests.

+ + +

A few weeks later, everything seemed almost routine on the Gaardian base on Earth's moon. In the recreation area, the frothing of the hot-cold whirlpool simmered down and stopped. As Walter, Debbie, and four others stepped out, they were dressed in normal clothing again. Earth's Gaardian and his wife walked with their arms linked into the lounge.

They sat down and made themselves comfortable. Joseph and Refinnej suddenly appeared. While Joseph seemed more serious than usual, Refinnej's face was streaked with tears. Debbie got up and gave Refinnej a hug while Walter shook Joseph's hand, looking carefully into his eyes. They all sat down.

Joseph was the first to speak. "The Creator appeared to us a few hours ago, and Refinnej was told to call all the Buuds to Quzak. Invisibly, we watched the execution of Haissem, Quzak's Arkaynee. It was ghastly! Do you remember Sumedocin in one of the early videos?" Walter and Debbie nodded. "Sumedocin and a friend of his on the High Council voted against the execution, but they were outnumbered. After the execution, they took Haissem's body, wrapped it, and put it in Sumedocin's friend's crypt."

Refinnej nodded. "I only met Haissem that once, in the crystal castle, so why is his death affecting me in this way? Buuds have observed death before, but it is not part of our existence. Buuds do not die. Why? ... Why?" She looked at Walter, to Debbie, and back to Walter.

He spoke quietly. "I will answer you, but you may not understand all of it right now. ... I know my son will be patient with you, because he knows the story of Jesus."

"Why did The Creator want us to witness his death?"

"Do you remember stepping beyond time just before you met Joseph?"

"Of course."

"Look carefully at that memory. Did you see all the Buuds through all the time you witnessed?"

Refinnej closed her eyes. She opened her eyes and her mouth opened, but at first she did not speak. Then, she said quietly, "No."

"Buuds live a long time, and none of you have witnessed the death of another Buud thus far, but it will happen. Gaardians use technology to live almost indefinitely, but a few have already chosen to stop being Gaardians and have allowed themselves to die."

"Remembering that episode outside the universe, I realize now that all Buuds must eventually face death, as with every other living being."

"That is correct. It is probable that one of the reasons you have been crying is because witnessing Haissem's death serves as a reminder of that limit to your life."

"One of the reasons?"

Walter nodded. "The other reason will begin to become evident in a couple of days. In the meantime, I'd like to give you – and by extension to the other Buuds – some knowledge that you will definitely find useful."

"What knowledge do you speak of?"

"Haissem was and is the savior of all Quzak's who will let him save them. That's why he had the title of Arkaynee."

"Save them from what?"

Joseph smiled. "Death."

"What? This cannot be possible!"

Walter nodded. "Nothing is too difficult for the Creator! Please permit me to give you some knowledge from several planets scattered throughout Gaardian space."

She nodded and closed her eyes, and Walter touched her face for a moment with his fingers. She opened her eyes and said, "Those are amazing stories!"

Joseph touched her hand. "They are all true stories!"

Refinnej stood up, and Joseph stood up with her. She said, "Mom, Dad, I'll need to think about this. You have not seen our new home, and I know my husband is hungry. Will you come with us to our home and have a meal with us?"

Debbie grinned. "Great! We've been waiting for you to invite us!"

Walter nodded. "Frank?"

The android appeared. "Yes?"

"You're going into Gaardian monitor mode. Tell Belinda that Debbie and I are going to spend an evening in Joseph and Refinnej's home. Tell Dawn we'll be back tomorrow."

"Done!" The android vanished.

Refinnej smiled, and the other four vanished as well.

11. Victory

The four of them appeared in a large round room. With a central spiral staircase going both up and down, furnished around the perimeter were three conversation areas. One had a fireplace. One had a table surrounded by plush chairs, and the third was more sparsely furnished with molded furniture. The perimeter wall and ceiling were white, and the carpeting was a deep green.

"I like it!" said Debbie.

"Me too!" said Walter.

Joseph pointed at the stairs. "With this configuration, above us are sleeping areas and gardens. Below us are recreation areas and miscellaneous working areas. Of course, we can change things instantly as needed. Watch!" As he spoke, the entire wall all around them disappeared, and they could see the Earth on one side of them and the Moon on the other.

Walter smiled. "Very good. I assume that you have a security force-field outside the crystalline ball."

Refinnej nodded. "Yes. The force-field also adjusts the color temperature to provide for coloration. Moreover, it creates the illusion that we are an asteroid. When I go outside, even with my Buud abilities, all I see is an asteroid. ... Let's sit down over here."

They sat down near the fireplace, and logs inside it burst into flame. Debbie again looked around. "I like your taste. It's a good space."

They both smiled. "Thanks," said Joseph. "On our honeymoon, we took the sphere to Aegeene, and we embedded the lower third of it into the soil there, just below the floor of this level. We went outside and explored Aegeene a few times, but we enjoyed ourselves here inside as well."

Refinnej winked at him, and he blushed. "Xpraepostq and Saahmn came and visited us once." She shifted in her chair. "They are an amazing couple. I hope that Joseph and I will have as good a relationship as they do."

Walter nodded. "You do already, with God's help."

She smiled. "That has been an amazing experience as well. I am beginning to sense what Joseph calls 'the still, small voice.' Up until recently, it never occurred to Buuds that there is a Creator. Now, wherever we go, we look for evidence of His presence. It is like having a hunger I cannot satisfy."

The room began to glow. Refinnej, startled, started to stand up, but Walter and Debbie motioned her to remain seated. All the features of the room began to fade into the glow. They heard the powerful and low voice of the Creator.

> I gave you that hunger, Refinnej, so that you would draw closer to me. It is time for you and the other Buuds to witness my son Haissem's victory over death. It is nearly dawn on Quzak. Have the Buuds gather invisibly on the planet, particularly in Melasurej, where

> my son Haissem spent his childhood, and where he is
> buried. Remain there on Quzak one full solar cycle.

Refinnej spoke softly. "Why must we go to Melasurej? Why is it important to the Buuds?"

> You will see Haissem gain victory over death for all
> Quzaks. His victory is also for those Buuds who allow
> him to save them, and give those Buuds victory over
> death.

As the glow quickly faded, Walter spoke quietly. "The two of you should go immediately. Debbie and I can explore your home with you another time. The next time we get together, you can tell us about it." His ring shimmered, and Walter and Debbie were gone.

Joseph and Refinnej stood up. He took her hand, and he nodded. They vanished.

+ + +

On that first day of the week on Quzak, Buuds were scattered all over the two main continents. Several of them were in Melasurej, just outside the cemetery area.

Two of them invisibly followed Euteekus as she came to the crypt early. She saw that the cover was taken away from the crypt. She touched a small button on her shirt and said, "Euteekus to Steve and Ooza. Haissem is not in his crypt. I'm going to go tell the others, and I'll report later."

She ran and went to the Quzaks that had become Haissem's inner circle of friends. They were gathered in the home of Nomis, the most outspoken of the followers of Haissem. One of the Buuds that had been standing at the entrance of the burial area had followed her invisibly and ran with her.

Euteekus was breathless when she arrived at the large dwelling. Euteekus said to them, "They have taken our Arkaynee out of the crypt, and I do not know where they have taken him."

Nomis and his brother went out, and they sprinted toward the crypt. Peering into it, they saw the burial wrappings. At that point, they did not understand the ancient writings, that the Arkaynee must rise from the dead. They went back to their own homes. Invisibly, the Buuds that lingered in the burial area were joined by most of the others, and they waited to see what would happen next.

Euteekus stood weeping next to the crypt, and as she cried, she stood up on a stone to look down into it. It was empty, with only the burial wrappings inside.

Looking up, she saw two Quzaks clothed in brilliant white, standing opposite her on the other side of the crypt.

They said to her, "Quzak, why do you weep?"

She said to them, "They have taken away our Arkaynee, and I do not know where they have taken him."

Silently, the Buuds communicated in their communal mind. "Those were not Quzaks. How did they get here? They were not present, and now they are. Look! Now they are gone. We did not detect where they came from, and we cannot detect where they are gone. Are they from the Creator? Yes!"

Sensing someone behind her, Euteekus turned around and saw Haissem standing there, but she did not know that it was him.

Again, the Buuds were fascinated. "We saw him die, yet he is alive. Where did he come from? How did he get here?"

Haissem said to Euteekus, "Quzak, why do you weep?"

Supposing him to be someone who maintained the cemetery, she said to him, "If you have carried him away, tell me where, and I will take him and bury him properly."

Haissem said to her, "Euteekus."

She turned and said to him, "My Arkaynee!" She threw her arms around him.

Haissem said to her, "Do not cling to me, for I have not yet gone back to the Creator; nevertheless, you should go to my brothers and say to them, 'I am ascending to my Father and your Father, to my Creator and your Creator.' Tell my friends to stay in Melasurej until they receive spiritual power." Haissem once again vanished.

As she left the crypt and the cemetery, Euteekus went and announced to the Arkaynee's inner circle, "I have seen Haissem," and that he had said these things to her.

The communal mind of the Buuds was active and clear. "The Creator wanted us to see this. ... The Creator wanted us to stay on this planet throughout its day. We shall obey. It is new to think of obedience! Yes!"

+ + +

In orbit high above Quzak, Ooza, Steve, and some of her crew watched from the Gaardian base. Additionally watching were Asayak, Walter, Pixie, Joseph, and Kieya. In three dimensions, they watched the video of the burial area, and they heard everything as well. In addition, Asayak tuned into the communal mind of the Buuds and transmitted their voices to Gaardian, to be part of the permanent records.

Walter looked at Ooza. "Gaardian is recording the thoughts of the Buuds as well as the rest of this, with Asayak's help."

Ooza nodded, her eyes moist. "I'm glad. It was so hard watching him be executed and put into the crypt. Now, to see Haissem alive again is incredible!"

Pixie touched her hand. "I went through your emotions a few years before I met my Saahmn and married him. He persecuted Eiraynay's followers until the Creator spoke to him, just before I met him."

The video stopped as Euteekus left the burial area.

+ + +

A week later, Walter's moon base was empty except for Frank, who kept watch, along with Walter and Debbie's cats, Tiger and Tammie. All of Walter's crew was in New Zealand for Christmas. Debbie and Walter were sitting on the bench of the concert grand piano in their living room, while more than a hundred guests stood around them in their great room. Even more were out on the patio. While softly playing "Silent Night," Walter said, "Thank you, all of you, for worshiping with us and once again, and for making Christmas so special for all of us. Dawn will spread the food on the table out on the patio in a few minutes. Tomorrow, or even after dinner if you wish, there is a toboggan run and a luge track down the bluff between here and the Tasman Sea. Many of you have already gone swimming or diving, so I don't need to tell you about the pools on the east side the house. If you want to ski or go snowboarding in

Queenstown, there are passes to those areas if you want them. Meanwhile, let's eat!"

As they stood up from the piano bench, Debbie whispered in Walter's ear, "We've been working hard all day for everyone else. Why don't we go upstairs and take a shower together before we eat?" She winked.

"I don't think they'll miss us do you?" He smiled as they looked out over their sea of guests, milling around.

As they walked up the staircase, she said, "I've got a surprise for you."

He looked at her quizzically. "A surprise?"

As they walked into the bedroom she said, "Butch confirmed it yesterday, but I told him not to tell you."

Walter grinned. "When?"

"In about seven and a half months, we'll have triplets."

Walter's eyes grew huge.

Downstairs, Dawn and James called out, "Okay, everyone. Dinner is served for as long as anyone is hungry!"

The patio appeared to grow ten-fold in size in order to serve everyone. On the buffet, in addition to traditional Christmas turkey dinner dishes, there was less conventional fare. On the south end of the balcony was a table with varieties of seafood, from Earth, Quzak, and Pzalop. On a separate table on the north end were varieties of meat, including prime rib, lamb, and two varieties from Aegeene. Next to that table was a small cooler. Kieya took Icnivad to the cooler and opened it. "Indeed!" She purred. "Dawn knows us so well! My beloved mate, I introduced you to beef a few weeks ago. I have tried the less fully cooked prime rib that we can get from the steam table, and I recommend it, but you should try one of these steaks from Aegeene!"

Icnivad's eyes gleamed. "I shall sample the rare prime rib later. Right now, these bemal steaks from Aegeene look wonderful. What about the other felidacas?"

"Good idea." Kieya's ring shimmered slightly, and several of the steaks in the cooler vanished, and they reappeared on a rock down on the beach in front of six other felidacas from their base. The two big cats each took a two kilogram steak, and they found a quiet place below the patio on the bluff to enjoy their feast.

Standing near the doorway into the house stood Asayak. As Dawn and James walked by, he looked at it and said, "Asayak, are you enjoying yourself?"

"Indeed," the creature's voice rumbled in his head. "You and Dawn have prepared a wondrous feast of aromas to enjoy here. I also like all of this country called New Zealand for the feast of aromas of its unusual plants and animals. I particularly enjoy the scent of the Kiwis. I do not think Walter and Debbie are aware of the large nest of Kiwis near this house."

"We're glad you're enjoying yourself, Asayak." James moved on out onto the patio to converse with other guests.

As Qaak and Jody moved into the house with their plates, they looked up and saw Walter and Debbie, who were smiling as they came down the stairs, arm in arm.

Qaak's eyes glowed. "Did Debbie surprise you, Walter?"

Debbie's eyes grew big. "You knew?"

Qaak chuckled. "Not until this moment, but I suspected."

Jody looked at her husband. "What did you suspect?"

"Debbie is pregnant with a child."

"Actually, Qaak, there will be three."

Jody softly screamed. "You're going to have triplets?"

People standing nearby began to applaud.

Walter waved and said, "Thanks everyone. Get back to the feast!"

Joseph walked up, with Refinnej. "So I am going to have three siblings?"

Walter grinned. "So it seems, son, so it seems!"

Refinnej hugged first Debbie, then Walter. "Congratulations, Mom; congratulations, Dad."

Debbie smiled. "That's the second time I've heard you call us Mom and Dad. I like it."

Refinnej nodded. "I was conceived and raised without love. The two of you are truly my parents in so many better ways."

Debbie hugged her again. "I'm glad to have you as a daughter, Refinnej." She looked across the room. "Come with me, there's someone you have not met yet that you should.

Kieya and Icnivad were coming in from outside the house as Debbie approached them. "Kieya, I don't think that Icnivad and Refinnej have met yet."

She purred. "Indeed. Icnivad, this is Refinnej. She is the Buud that is our latest Gaardian, along with Walter's son, Joseph. Refinnej, this is my mate, Icnivad. He is a sculptor."

Refinnej took his paw. "It is indeed a pleasure to meet Kieya's handsome mate. Kieya is a dear friend to me. I have already met the other felidacas from your team that are down on the beach."

"The pleasure is mine, Refinnej."

Debbie smiled at both. "Icnivad, I would like you to do me a favor. I would like you to take a good look at Refinnej and later create a bust of her for Joseph."

"It will be my delight to do so for you, Debbie. If you like, I will make a smaller sculpture of the two of them for you and Walter."

Debbie grinned. "Yes, Icnivad, I would like that very much."

Refinnej smiled. "Joseph and I will look forward to seeing it."

12. Fishing

The next morning, most of the guests were gone before dawn. Joseph and Refinnej were in the guest bedroom across the hall from the master bedroom for Walter and Debbie. As Joseph opened his eyes, Refinnej was on her side, looking at him. "Good morning, my handsome husband!"

"Good morning my love. What shall we do today? There are no Buuds in this galaxy, and none of them are up to mischief. What shall we do?" He thought for a moment. "I know!" His Gaardian ring shimmered.

She looked down at herself as they at up on the bed. "What is this clothing I am suddenly wearing? It clings to my body like no other clothing you've created for me. What are we going to do?"

He grinned. "Take my hand!" As she did so, they vanished and reappeared by one end of the Olympic-sized swimming pool just east of the house. Joseph looked at her. "You once asked me what swimming was. I'll demonstrate, and then you try it." He did a shallow dive, swam a basic crawl to the other end, reversed, and came back to her.

"That looks easy enough!" She made a belly-flop, partially sank, and came up coughing and gasping for air. "What happened?"

Joseph grinned, and she began to laugh. He said, "I told you it takes practice. Come here."

She vanished out of the pool to stand beside him. He said, "Touch your head to mine and I'll give you the head knowledge." They touched their heads and closed their eyes for about ten seconds."

She stared at him. "This looks like a fun thing to learn. Let me try again."

This time, when she dove in, she made a perfect shallow dive and duplicated what Joseph had done earlier. Then she did two laps each of the back stroke and the butterfly.

Crawling out, she was enthusiastic. "I'm going to make a pool like this for us on our lower level at home. I love doing that butterfly stroke!"

Joseph hugged her and kissed her. "That's my girl. I was hoping you would enjoy it."

"I do. ... Why is that other pool over there separate from this one?"

"That pool is mostly for diving. It is much deeper."

"Show me."

"Okay." They walked over to the diving pool. "The first time off of that upper platform, just jump in. Don't try to dive."

"Why?"

"Because if you hit the water at a bad angle it can be very painful."

"I've had almost no experience with pain. I didn't like the feel of my first shallow dive in order to swim. I won't like more pain, will I?"

"Most beings don't."

"Let's touch heads again so you can teach me diving lessons."

Joseph smiled. "Okay." It took about the same length of time. "Remember what I said. Just jump in the first time. A belly flop from that height would be very painful."

"You go first."

"Okay." He vanished and reappeared on the top platform. Going to the edge, he let his toes curl over it slightly. Then he went three strides back, turned, strove forward, and did a pike. He swam to the edge of the pool where she was and crawled out. "That was a forward pike dive. It wasn't perfect, but not bad. Now, do you want to try a jump?"

She nodded, disappeared, and reappeared at the top of the upper platform. She ran off the platform, and when she landed in the water, she was nearly flat on her back. She swam slowly to the edge where Joseph was standing and crawled out. She lay on her back, breathing deeply. "*That* was even more painful than I imagined."

"Are you okay?"

She grinned. "Of course, but I don't think I want to do that ever again!"

"Good dives are fun to watch as well as to do."

"Show me."

"I'm not an expert, but Dad knew an Olympic diving champion named Ken Sitzberger. We can have an android version of him demonstrate a few dives."

"Okay."

Joseph's ring shimmered, and a replica of Ken Sitzberger appeared on the top platform. "First, here's a forward 4-1/2 somersaults dive in the tuck position."

As they watched, Refinnej's eyes grew wide. "Wow! That's amazing!"

Ken again appeared on the platform, and he did a back 2-1/2 somersaults dive in the pike position. They both smiled. Joseph loved watching Refinnej watch the dives almost as much as the dives. "Wow!" He looked at his wife. "Let's see if our computer can come up with a women's champion diver. Ken! Who was the women's champion in Tokyo?"

"Lesley Bush"

His ring shimmered, and a representation of Lesley Bush appeared next to Ken.

"Hi!" Leslie smiled." As Refinnej and Joseph nodded hellos, she looked at Ken and gestured toward the diving boards. "Shall we?"

For the next hour, Joseph and Refinnej watched many of the dives used in the Olympics. Refinnej liked the dives from the platforms best, but Joseph preferred the springboard dives. It was a continuation of their unique romance.

The next day, when they went back home to their artificial moon, they first appeared in their living area. Joseph was the first to see it. "Look!" He pointed.

Refinnej just stood there, staring. Then she turned and put her arms around Joseph. "It's beautiful! It's from Icnivad, isn't it?"

"Yes." They just stood there, holding each other, for several minutes.

She walked over and touched it softly. "This is some kind of wood?"

"Yes. I would guess from the grain it is one of the hardwoods from their planet." He reached out and touched it. "It looks so real and so detailed!"

She looked into Joseph's eyes and smiled. "We must do something for them."

"Yes. Let me think." He held her again. "I've got it!"

"What?"

"Picture the Christmas party in your mind. Do you remember the small cooler at one end of the porch where Icnivad and Keiya got their meat for the feast?"

"Yes!" She was quiet. "That was not synthesized, was it?"

"No."

"This is where being a Buud has its advantages. Don't move. I'll be back in a moment." It seemed to Joseph like she was gone less than a second. "Done."

"What did you do."

"I bent time-space a few times. After finding out where Dawn gets the aged beef for the steaks that Kieya and Icnivad like, I went back to the time when the beef was being put into the smokehouse, and I put an extra side of beef in it. Then, just before the beef was to be removed from the smokehouse, I harvested my side of beef, and I prepared it as a butcher would before cutting steaks. Then, I delivered the entire side of beef to the cool storage in the home of Kieya and Icnivad."

Joseph smiled. "That was a lot of effort."

She nodded. "Perhaps, but this sculpture is amazing, and I love Kieya."

+ + +

At his base on Earth's moon, Walter was jogging in the recreation area. In their apartment, Debbie was holding a sculpture of Joseph and Refinnej. "Frank?"

The android appeared. "Yes?"

"When I came into the apartment a few minutes ago I found this sculpture of Joseph and Refinnej on the bed. I'd like you to configure a little niche in that wall," she pointed, "where we can put this." A niche appeared. "Make it a little larger, Frank, and a few inches up higher from the floor." It changed. "Good, Frank. Thank you."

"You're welcome," he said, and disappeared.

Carefully, Debbie placed the sculpture in the niche, and she stepped back to look at it. "Debbie to Belinda, can you come to the apartment for a minute or two?"

Belinda's voice answered from an invisible speaker. "Sure."

Debbie continued to study the sculpture in the niche. Less than a minute later, Belinda walked in. "Knock-knock!" She saw what Belinda was looking at. "Wow! When did *that* come?"

"It was waiting for me when I walked into the apartment a few minutes ago, and I had Frank create a niche for it. What do you think?"

"I think that's a great spot for it. Icnivad does such amazing work, doesn't he?"

"He sure does. I'll g-mail him a little later and thank him."

Belinda was thoughtful. "I was just quitting for the day and headed for the rec area when you called. Do you want to join me?"

"Sure! Walter's already in there, jogging I think. Let's go." They walked out of the apartment, across the atrium, and straight towards the recreation area.

Walter was still jogging. Nearby, Refinnej was practicing some dives, as Joseph watched her every move. Frank appeared and jogged next to Walter. He kept looking straight ahead as he asked, "What is it, Frank?"

"You wanted Euteekus to watch and see what Nomis and the others did after the resurrection. Nomis and five of the others are going to the sea to go fishing."

Walter stopped and closed his eyes. A moment later he opened them and spoke loudly. "Attention everyone. Those of you who wanted to see a resurrection appearance by the Arkaynee on Quzak, go to the theater. We're going to have a live three-dimensional feed."

As Frank vanished, nearly everyone stopped what they were doing and headed towards the theater. As they entered, Debbie joined Walter, and they sat down as a family with Joseph and Refinnej near the back.

Frank appeared at the front on the stage. "Haissem's circle of closest friends have been in Melasurej, waiting for spiritual power to come to them as Haissem had promised. You're going to see a large Quzak, who has begun to lead them merely with the force of his personality. His name is Nomis. About ten hours ago he said he was going fishing. Some of the others joined him. They used a boat, but during the night, they did not catch anything. Now it is nearly dawn." Frank vanished.

Refinnej turned to Joseph. "Isn't fishing the capturing of aquatic animals for consumption? It seems like a waste of time. Such flesh can be bought in a market on most planets."

"Catching the fish can be hard work, or it can be entertaining and-or relaxing. It can also be profitable."

"Interesting...."

"Shhh!" He pointed to the action appearing on the stage area.

Just as the day was breaking, Haissem stood on the shore; however, the disciples could not know that it was Haissem standing there because of the darkness.

He called out to them, **"Friends, do you have any fish?"**

They answered him, "No."

Haissem said to them, **"Cast your net on the right side of the boat, and you will find some there."** So they cast it, and because of the huge quantity of fish, they had difficulty hauling all of them in.

In the theater, Refinnej leaned forward slightly, watching the Quzaks strain their muscles with the effort. She turned to Joseph and said very softly, "They enjoy their work, don't they?"

Joseph nodded.

As they watched, they could see that Nomis was much stronger than the others. His muscles rippled with the effort, and even in the cool of the early morning, his skin glistened with sweat.

One of the others said to Nomis, "It is the Arkaynee!" When Nomis heard this, he put on a shirt and jumped into the water. Quickly, he began a powerful crawl stroke towards the shore.

The others came in the boat, whose engine had rumbled to life. They simply dragged the net full of fish, for they were not far out, but only about a hundred meters from shore.

When Nomis and the others got to the shore, they saw hot charcoal burning under a large grill, with fish already laid out with bread.

Haissem said to them, **"Bring some of the fish from the net."**

Nomis went and hauled the net ashore, full of large fish. Though there were many, the net was not torn.

Haissem said to them, **"Come, Quzaks, let us eat."** By then, all of them recognized him.

Haissem looked up and said, **"Thank you father for these my friends and for this food. Please bless the food and bless us as we eat."** Then he began to pass out the fish and bread to them.

As they ate, they looked around at each other. Whenever they wanted more, they went to the grill and helped themselves. Without anyone tending to the grill, there was always enough to eat for all of them.

Behind Refinnej and Joseph, Dawn nudged James and whispered, "I think God is replenishing and tending the grill!" James smiled and nodded.

Walter whispered to Debbie, "This is not the first time that Haissem has appeared since his execution and resurrection."

Close to his ear, she whispered, "I know! Frank told me that he has appeared to more than a thousand Quzaks, meeting them in several places."

On the shore, when they had finished breakfast, Haissem said to Nomis, **"Do you love me more than these other Quzaks?"**

Nomis replied, "Yes, my Arkaynee, you know that I love you."

He said to him, **"Supply their needs."** Then Haissem said to Nomis a second time, **"Nomis, do you love me?"**

He said, "Yes, Haissem, you know that I love you."

He said to him, **"Watch over our friends."**

Refinnej leaned over to speak to Joseph, but he shook his head and pointed at the drama unfolding in front of them.

Haissem said to Nomis a third time, **"Nomis, do you love me?"**

Nomis looked sad because he had been asked the same question three times. "My Arkaynee, you know all there is to know, so you know that I love you."

Haissem said to him, **"Feed our friends. ... "Beyond doubt I say to you, from the time you were a young Quzak, you have been accustomed to doing everything for yourself and go wherever you wanted, but when you are older, you will no longer have your freedom, and you will be executed as I was executed."**

The audience in the theater watching the drama unfold was totally silent. No one whispered, and all were focused upon Haissem, who then said, **"Follow me."**

Nomis turned and saw Euteekus, and said to Haissem, "My Arkaynee, what about her?"

"If it is my will that she remain until I return, what is that to you? You follow! Soon the Holy Spirit will come upon you, and you will accomplish even more of the miracles you have seen with me." After saying this, Haissem rose into the sky until he had disappeared from their sight.

After silently looking around at one another, Nomis and the others got up, doused the charcoal with water, and went to their net to sort the fish. The three-dimensional drama on the stage concluded.

Walter stood up. "Debbie and I were just talking about the fact that Haissem has appeared to more than a thousand Quzaks since his resurrection. Just as in this instance, they did not merely see and hear him, but they also ate and drank with him." He paused. "Now, if watching them eat fish and bread has made anyone hungry, I'm sure there are some desserts we can get in the dining hall."

The rest of them stood up and began walking out. Joseph said, "Up until now, when the videos have come in we've been able to start and stop them, discussing them as we watched. This live feed from Quzak was so very different!"

Refinnej nodded. "Yes. As we watched, the other Buuds were observing through my eyes. Some of them are talking about Haissem's victory over death, and a few were talking a moment ago about how important it is to see Haissem alive after witnessing his death."

Debbie smiled. "It was crucially important for all Buuds to witness the death, burial, and resurrection of Haissem the Arkaynee."

Walter raised his eyebrows and nodded. "Yes, definitely."

They walked into the dining hall. After sitting down, Walter asked, "Do you mind if I order for all of us?"

They shook their heads.

"Frank, strawberry shortcake for all four of us." As soon as the desserts appeared, they started eating. Walter asked, "Refinnej, do you have any thoughts you'd like to share about the drama we witnessed this evening?"

She ate a spoonful of whipped cream with a strawberry before answering. "It is almost overwhelming." She swallowed. "A few months ago I did not know there was a Creator, let alone the Arkaynee. Since then, I have met all of you, I have become a Gaardian, and I have witnessed things that have radically changed the lives of all Buuds." She took another bite of shortcake. "Of course, those same events have changed the lives of all Quzaks now and forever."

Walter smiled. "Does my question come too soon?"

She shook her head. "My current thoughts now, and those of other Buuds, will undoubtedly change in the days into years ahead, but I'll say what we are thinking, okay?"

"Good."

"As I understand it, Haissem died on behalf of all Quzaks – and Buuds – so that all of our offenses against the Creator will not be held against us. The punishment that should be ours, Haissem has taken upon himself."

Walter, Debbie, and Joseph nodded.

"The Creator raised Haissem from the dead. For those of us who accept Haissem's sacrifice on our behalf, he died so that, in a very real sense, we do not have to die."

Walter smiled. "I tell people who will listen that we will all eventually leave these physical bodies behind, but our spirits will live beyond time, either with God if we let our savior save us, or suffering alone."

Refinnej was thoughtful. "When we are with God, we are in heaven, but if we do not accept our savior's sacrifice, our spirits will be forever alone, without light, warmth, love, or hope."

Walter nodded. "God has given of us a glimpse of his realm, but we really could not comprehend it because we are still in these temporary physical bodies."

For a fraction of a second, the four of them disappeared, then they reappeared. In that moment outside of time and space, God spoke to them, as all around them was brilliant white.

> On each planet where I send my Son, I provide guidance for records to be kept. Trust in my ability to achieve my plans through your lives. Soon Joseph will have two sisters and a brother. Everything is unfolding as it should. Tomorrow before dawn, Haissem's friends will be gathered by the shore near Melasurej on Quzak. Once more, all Buuds should gather there with the Quzaks, with Quzak appearance. I am faithful. I am your Creator.

After they reappeared in the dining hall, all of them blinked. Frank appeared beside their table. "The four of you were gone for a moment. What has happened?"

Walter looked up at the android. "Everything's fine, Frank. The Creator spoke to us. I'll make a report before Debbie and I go to bed."

"Understood." The android vanished.

Refinnej was thoughtful. "Walter, do you know why, or what is going to happen tomorrow morning?"

Walter shook his head. "No. I can only guess, based upon past experiences." He paused. "Just before Haissem ascended, he spoke of the Holy Spirit. I suspect that tomorrow morning, the gathering of Quzaks will be much larger than merely Haissem's inner circle of friends. He has made many other friends during the past three years from both continents." He looked at Refinnej. "I truly hope that the Buuds will be able to cease their communal chatter tomorrow morning. I suspect that what is about to happen will be startling, if my surmise is correct." Walter paused. "Tomorrow the Holy Spirit will come with its power."

"Okay. I guess time will tell." Refinnej smiled. "Dad? I just realized something."

"What's that?"

"When the Creator spoke to us just a moment ago, all Buuds everywhere in the universe heard what The Creator said. This is how I will function as a prophet to the Buuds, just as the Creator said."

Walter nodded. Debbie said, "God is faithful."

13. Power

Overnight, hundreds of Quzaks sailed from the western continent to Melasurej. In the semi-darkness before dawn, they joined other Quzaks from all over the eastern continent. They set up chairs at the shore and sat down quietly. Within the crowd, in disguise, came Ooza, Steve, Piatek, and all the others on Ooza's Gaardian team.

Every Buud came to Melasurej. In the shadows before dawn, they took on the appearance of Quzaks, and they walked with the others to the shore. Refinnej, now shorter with the pale green gray skin of a female Quzak, walked towards the shore with Joseph. He was much shorter than his usual self, and he had the pale blue gray skin and appearance of a male Quzak. Silently, they looked for Ooza, and when they spotted her, Joseph caught her eye and winked. Ooza blinked, and then she and Steve made room so that the four of them could sit together.

As the first rays of sunlight began to warm them, Nomis began singing, and the others joined him, repeating each line together after him.

> Haissem the Arkaynee ended death!
> Children of Quzaks angels say,
> Raise your joys and victories high!
> Sing, O universe, and Quzaks answer!
> Love's transforming work is done!
> He fought the fight, and won the battle!
> Death unsuccessfully buried him!
> Haissem opened eternal life!
> Now He lives again, our king of glory!
> Where is the throb of death?!
> Dying for us he saved us all!
> Where is the triumph, O crypt?!
> Now we fly where Haissem has led us!
> We follow him!
> Created like Haissem, like him, we rise!

There's no crypt but just the skies!
Hail the Arkaynee of Quzak and heaven!
Praise to him is given by both!
You we greet triumphant now!
Resurrected now we bow!
Reign of glory, spirit's bliss!
Everlasting life now is this!
You know us, your power's above!
Now we sing, and you, our Arkaynee, we love!

Without warning, the entire sky became white, blotting out the sun. There were claps of thunder, but there was no lightning or even clouds. Between claps of thunder, there was the sound of a raging wind, yet the air around them was calm and peaceful.

As the Buuds looked around, they realized that Buuds and Quzaks alike were of one mind, as though all were talking at once and all were listening at the same time. They looked at one another with fascination. As though synchronized, Quzaks and Buuds alike naturally fell to their knees and put their faces to the ground. Buud life was the same as Quzak life. Every Quzak knew every other Quzak as though they were brother or sister. Quzaks caught glimpses of the other planets where Buuds had lived. Buuds had glimpses of the homes of the Quzaks. Through all of it, neither Quzaks nor Buuds made a sound, yet the song that had the Quzaks had just sung was heard by all of them like one glorious angelic choir.

Just as suddenly as it all began, the sky returned to looking like a normal clear day. There was silence except for some quiet expressions of joy with tears. As everyone got off of their knees, they silently scattered in all directions.

+ + +

In all Gaardian-controlled space, Gaardians and their crews watched all of it happen as a live three-dimensional feed. Above Pzalop, Leahcim and his crew watched with fascination in the little theater at Leahcim's orbiting base.

On the planet below them, at the crystal castle within The Creator's Park, it was the middle of the night. Without signaling each other, all the Buuds left Quzak and gathered in the Creator's Park. Refinnej and Joseph sat down on a large boulder on the eastern hillside facing the crystal castle. The other Buuds sat down just below them. They were all now in their normal humanoid form, looking remarkably like humans from Earth. Though all of them were smiling, many of them had tears rolling down their cheeks.

An older Buud, named Samoht ["sah-MAWT"], stood up. "Refinnej, you are a prophet to the Buuds. Explain to us what has just happened to us."

Refinnej spoke quietly. "Last evening, I asked my Dad – Joseph's father – about this. You saw and heard his response through me."

"He spoke of a "Holy Spirit."

"Yes. My husband has experience with this. Will you listen to him as you listen to me?"

Samoht nodded. "Yes. That is acceptable."

Joseph cleared his throat. "I am young – even younger than Refinnej, but I am a follower of Jesus, and I have heard my Dad teach these things many times. I will do my best." He paused. "Quzaks and Buuds are in a transition period. When Haissem returned to heaven, he told his followers to anticipate receiving the presence and power of the Holy Spirit. Today, all of those who have accepted Haissem as their savior has received a measure of the presence and power of the Holy Spirit."

The old Buud nodded. "I felt something happening, but other than hearing that song from beyond our universe, I do not seem different within myself."

"There will be times when you will know the difference. I will give you a spectacular example, but in most instances, what Haissem's followers will experience will not be this obvious." Samoht nodded, so Joseph continued. "This planet, Pzalop, and the planet called Quzak, where we were earlier, used to be in another galaxy. To move them required the combined efforts of several Gaardians. To move the planets without damage to any life on either planet required massive genetic mapping. In the few previous times when such a thing was done, the genetic data was transferred to Gaardian, where the mapping was done, while a planet was moved, and after the mapping was complete, the creatures were relocated from Gaardian to their new location. It would take several time periods."

Again, Samoht nodded. "If the Buuds were to do such a thing, with all of our combined efforts, that mapping process would take six Pzalop days or seven Quzak days. Are you saying that when these two planets were moved that it did not take that long because of the power of this Holy Spirit?"

Joseph smiled a big smile. "My Dad and his crew sent the genetic data to Gaardian, and moments later placed the two planets in orbit in two entirely different galaxies. What was distinctive was this: The genetic code was received by Gaardian as already completely mapped, and the peoples of the two planets did not realize anything had happened until the beginnings of their next days."

"The data was already completely mapped?"

"Yes. Instantaneously."

"That's impossible by any standard."

Joseph shook his head, still smiling. "With the Creator, all things are possible."

"How do we access this power?"

Joseph shook his head. "We cannot make that happen. When any of the Creator's children molds their own will to be congruent with the will of the Creator, all of that power is available. I'll put it another way: When you want what the Creator wants, the Creator backs you up."

Refinnej put her hand upon Joseph's, and together they stood up. "For those of you who have accepted Haissem as your Savior, I have a suggestion. Within the crystal castle, if you are in a room by yourself, you are isolated also from the Buud communal consciousness. In that total privacy, you will find it easier to commune with the Creator than if you have other Buud voices constantly part of your life. That option is yours. Right now, Joseph and I are going home, unless there are more questions."

Out of the communal mind came, "We need to learn more about this Holy Spirit. Can you arrange it?"

Refinnej nodded. "That is a reasonable request. Tomorrow I will provide an answer." She looked at Joseph, who was holding her hand. As he nodded, the two of them vanished.

+ + +

A few hours later, a meeting was held in the family center on Gaardian. Asayak was intrigued with the request. Gaardian was not. The planet was emphatic. "We do not yet have a basis for knowing if you will be safe when providing them with the requested information. I am preparing a set of files regarding the Holy Spirit from seventeen planets that have written as well as media records on the subject."

Walter was thoughtful. "I think there is a way to assure Asayak's safety to a reasonable degree. If Refinnej can be the presiding Gaardian, with Joseph as the amplifier. With that combination, Refinnej's powers are amplified a thousand fold."

"No. Joseph can be trusted to amplify, but Refinnej does not have enough experience and maturity to handle the possible tactics of one or more Buuds intent upon doing damage."

Asayak oozed down lower to get more comfortable. "The planet has a valid point. Refinnej has the best of intentions, but she lacks experience and wisdom. Joseph is an excellent choice as part of my team, but even you, Walter, might not be the best choice instead of Refinnej."

"Why not?" Walter shook his head.

"With respect, my friend, you are Joseph's father, so you cannot use your son's gift objectively."

"Agreed," the planet rumbled, "the accompanying Gaardian must be one that is both brilliant, like you, Walter, and cunning. The choice is clear."

"Kieya?"

"Yes. Unquestionably."

Asayak rose to its full height. "Yes! Kieya and I know each other very well. I like this!"

Walter closed his eyes, and he was motionless almost a full minute. "Yes. The Creator will use the three of you very effectively." Walter paused. "Asayak, do the Buuds know that you can monitor them from intergalactic distances?"

"No. There is nothing in their communal mind to suggest this, and I have chosen to hide this fact from Refinnej."

"Good. Are there currently any Buuds within this Gaardian sector?"

"Refinnej and Joseph are at home, nearby, but that isolates her from the other Buuds."

"Kieya," rumbled the planet, "is engaged in some disciplinary work in her sector, but she will be available within less than an hour."

Walter nodded. "Good. Walter to Joseph." A few seconds later, Joseph appeared in a hologram.

"Hi Dad! Hello, Asayak! What's up?"

"One of the Buuds made a request, which your wife passed on to me. We need to have a meeting in your home with the two of you. Kieya will also join us. Are the two of you free for a few hours?"

"A few hours?" Joseph looked off to the side, and Refinnej joined him in the hologram.

"Hi, Dad. Are we going to need all of us to fulfill the request?"

Walter shook his head. "No, but all of us need to discuss it. We'll be there in forty-five minutes or so. Kieya is busy until then. Joseph didn't answer my question."

She nodded. "We're free, barring emergencies of course."

"Of course. Until then."

"Until then." The hologram vanished.

"Asayak, I'll have you stay here on Gaardian. I'm going home to bring Debbie up to speed on what is happening. I'll see you in about forty minutes."

"Understood."

Walter vanished.

+ + +

In Joseph and Refinnej's home, they met in a large atrium which Walter had not seen before. "Your Mom will want to see this atrium after all this is over. Don't get rid of it too quickly."

Joseph nodded. "I like it too. Did you talk to Mom about this?"

"Yes. At first, she was not enthusiastic with how we are proceeding. Then she stopped and went into our bedroom to pray. When she came out, she said to tell you that she won't worry about you because she trusts us and trusts God."

Joseph looked over at Refinnej and back to his Dad. "Thanks, ... so why are all of us necessary for this?"

"At first, we talked about having the two of you go with Asayak as its backup while it teaches the Buuds who are curious. The planet pointed out that Refinnej, as the newest Gaardian, is relatively inexperienced and is just beginning to gain wisdom. If I were to go instead of Refinnej, with you, Joseph, there is the concern that my judgment might be affected by my being your Dad, and that I might not be able to use your gift with total objectivity if necessary."

Refinnej looked intently at Walter. "Is that why Kieya is here?"

Walter nodded. "The planet pointed out that, of necessity, this operation requires a Gaardian that is brilliant, experienced, and superbly cunning when necessary. That's Kieya."

The big cat purred. "I don't have to be cunning often, but it is a useful strength in felidacas like myself."

Refinnej continued to study Walter. "Why might cunning be needed?"

"Look at it this way. Have you not told me that there are a few Buuds who are being slow to adhere to Gaardian guidelines and prone to mischief?" She nodded. "With your communal mind, they will know what is going on. One or more of them could decide to be disruptive."

"I could discipline them just as easily as Kieya."

"Yes, my daughter, but your first momentary instinct would be to protect Joseph and exercise the discipline, while possibly leaving Asayak vulnerable."

Her mouth hung open for a moment. Then she blinked. "You're right, Dad. I might make a mistake in judgment. Kieya, would you handle it differently?"

Her purr grew softer, but it was steady. "Asayak and I have worked together several times, and in some ways, we can function as one. We both use our individual gifts constantly, monitoring the environment in our astronomical vicinity, communicating our findings continuously, and responding appropriately with total trust in each other. You are still young enough to have less experience in functioning with someone as a team. You are at the same time getting used to working with your husband in a team effort."

Refinnej nodded. "You also have thousands of years of experience that I do not have. ... I understand." She turned to Joseph. "Do you trust Kieya enough to let her use your gift without limits?"

He laughed. "I've trusted Kieya all of my life. She was my baby-sitter in my early years when I could not take care of myself. By sheer will, she can put a child into stasis for hours."

Her eyes grew wide. "Really? Is that possible, Kieya?"

"Yes. Do you remember Keeta?"

"The transparent one?"

"Yes. I taught her to do it with Kenkee, and then we worked out some interplanetary cooperation so that I could teach others from her home planet. Her species did not know that they had the capacity to do it."

"Could you teach me to do it?"

"Only if you have the capacity of doing so. We can try it sometime after this is all done."

She nodded. "Okay. I have a suggestion as to where this education project should take place."

"Where is that?" asked Asayak.

"There is a solar system just beyond Leahcim's sector that has ten planets revolving around a double star. Gaardian has already talked to Leahcim about annexing the system into his sector of Gaardian space."

Walter looked at Refinnej. "I have a request of you, both as your Dad and as Convener of the Gaardians."

"What is that?"

"I want you to stay here in your home during this operation. It should not take more than a Gaardian day."

"Why?"

"The reason is simple. If you are outside of your home sphere, mischievous Buuds might try to draw you into a conflict through the Buud communal mind."

She nodded. "That's true, I guess, I'll be bored silly, being here by myself all that time."

Walter laughed. "I'll be here, but would you like Debbie to keep us company too? We could probably get Qaak and Jody to come also. They haven't seen your home yet."

Refinnej got up and gave Walter a hug. "Dad, I like your style! Have them all come!"

Asayak stirred, and its voice was clear and solid. "I have communicated with the three of them. In a few minutes, Frank will send Debbie, and Qaak says that he and Jody will also be here soon."

Refinnej turned and gave Joseph a hug. "Stay safe, my husband. Keep Kieya on a short leash!"

Kieya blinked, her purring stopped. Then as the purr started again she spoke. "I have never been on a leash. I am not sure that I would like it, but it is an amusing thought!"

"I did not mean any offense, Kieya."

"I know. I did not take offense." She turned. "Asayak, as soon as we are on the planet, send out the invitation we talked about. Joseph, take a handful of my mane, and don't let go."

"Right."

The three of them vanished, and Refinnej blinked. "Walter, this is the first time I've been without Joseph since we got married!"

As Walter nodded, Debbie appeared, walked over to them, and then gave each of them a hug. "Thanks for the invitation! Where's the sculpture that Icnivad sent you?" Refinnej pointed to a table. "Wow! That's beautiful, but then my daughter-in-law is beautiful!" Debbie went closer to examine it more carefully. "It's an amazing piece of work."

"Indeed! It is magnificent!" Qaak and Jody had appeared a moment earlier and behind her. "Jody, come look at this!"

Jody walked over. "It's wonderful." She looked around. "Refinnej, I know you can reconfigure this at any time you choose, but for today, can you give us the grand tour?"

Refinnej smiled. "I'd be happy to!"

14. Interruption

Kieya, Joseph, and Asayak appeared on the distant planet in the midst of an area with many large plants, somewhat like a dense forest on Earth. While Kieya and Joseph configured a substantial transparent structure and an assortment of furniture, Asayak sent out the planned invitation. In seconds, dozens of Buuds began appearing in various shapes and sizes.

Kieya was not amused. "If you want to play games, assuming the appearance of differing species, that is your choice, but we are not here to play games. If you are serious about learning about the Holy Spirit, please assume your natural appearance."

In a blink, all of them were humanoids. Samoht was sitting nearby. "Where is Refinnej?"

Kieya's purr stopped momentarily, but then resumed. "Refinnej is not an expert in the Holy Spirit. She is not a seasoned teacher, and she is not an experienced Gaardian. With regard to the latter qualification, I am quite experienced. My name is Kieya. You are all familiar with the time measurements of a planet called Waysad. I have been a Gaardian for twenty-four thousand three hundred forty-two Waysad years. You already know Joseph, Refinnej's life partner. He is here to amplify my efforts and those of Asayak, the master teacher standing beside me. Asayak, I suggest you greet our Buud friends."

It's telepathic voice was low and powerful. "Hello, friends." Several of the Buuds murmured hellos.

Kieya looked at the first speaker. "As I understand Refinnej's description of you, your name is Samoht. I ask you, are all these Buuds here because they genuinely want to learn more about the Holy Spirit?"

"To the best of my knowledge, yes."

"Good. If we did this through a single Buud and his or her communal connection to the minds of other Buuds, this training could take months. Doing it this way, we can get it done in a day. We will begin with giving all of you a large amount of raw data. Then we can entertain questions and discussion. As a preliminary, I must tell you this: If there are any significant interruptions or distractions, I will halt these proceedings without saying why and continue them at a more opportune time. Is this understood?"

Samoht nodded. "You are direct and to the point. It is good. We understand."

"Very well. The transfer of data will be telepathic at high speed. Get comfortable in your chairs. This phase can seem exhausting if you try to control it. Just relax and close your eyes."

As the Buuds closed their eyes, Joseph knelt beside Kieya. "They can't hear us, can they?"

"No, but be alert. This seems a little too easy."

As Asayak started to transfer the data to the minds of the Buuds gathered there, it sensed the approach of two other Buuds at high speed. A glimpse of their thoughts indicated hostility. In an instant, the hair on Kieya's back bristled. It was time for a fast exit. Kieya, Joseph, and Asayak vanished along with the structure. They moved at speeds that were utterly amazing as they bounced from galaxy to galaxy.

Passing the Gaardian sector containing Refinij's sphere and those in it, Asayak sent a thought to Qaak. Without hesitation, and without telling the others, Qaak and Walter transported Joseph's and Refinnej's home to the same solar system as Earth, and into the asteroid belt between Mars and Jupiter. Then the sphere was another asteroid among the countless others.

+ + +

A moment later, Kieya, Joseph, and Asayak were back inside the sphere, exactly where they had left. Qaak's eyes were glowing intensely. "It is well that we anticipated this!"

Walter nodded, as Refinnej hugged Joseph. "What happened, Asayak?"

The big creature oozed down to their level as they sat in their chairs. "As I was transferring data, I sensed two other Buuds approaching at high speed. I signaled Kieya. A quick scan of the emotions indicated hostility. The Buuds in our structure were totally peaceful. I again signaled Kieya, and she extracted us."

The big cat purred. "My conversation with Asayak lasted less than a second. I had warned Joseph to be alert, so the rest was easy. I must say, Joseph, that your amplification of my efforts were astounding. In all my years as a Gaardian, I have never traveled that fast nor folded space-time so deftly." She paused and looked to her left. "Qaak, my friend, we passed through twenty-three galaxies and changed directions as many times in less than four seconds."

His eyes glowed intensely. "Indeed. That is even faster than that initial apparently random tour done by Refinnej with Joseph their original time, when the lured the Buuds into the crystal castle."

Joseph laughed. "Refinnej, my love, if you had been along for the ride, I think even you would have been impressed."

She blinked. "Really?"

Kieya turned her head towards her and gazed directly at her. "It was a matter of keeping Joseph safe as well as Asayak and myself. Did you know that this sphere of yours is no longer in the same galaxy that it was when Joseph and I left?"

She stared at her. "No! Where are we?"

Qaak chuckled. "Relax, Refinnej. As Kieya was bouncing them around from galaxy to galaxy at high speed, when they passed near us, Kieya sent me a thought through Asayak, and I told her where we would be. Walter and I did the rest."

Refinnej's mouth was open slightly. She closed it. "So where are we?"

"Since your sphere looks like an asteroid, we are now in the asteroid belt not far from Joseph's home planet, Earth. In this solar system, there are two planets closer to the sun than Earth, named Mercury and Venus. Beyond Earth are Mars and Jupiter, and more planets beyond. Between Mars and Jupiter is an asteroid belt containing nearly countless asteroids ranging in size from a fraction of a millimeter to that of a moon or small planet. The asteroid in which we reside at this moment is one of hundreds about the same size."

Asayak stirred. "Even if one of the Buuds saw the general direction we finally headed in, which they most likely did not, they would have great difficulty finding us amidst all of this space debris."

Refinnej sighed and looked down, and everyone was quiet for a few moments. She looked up. "I honestly did not expect any of the other Buuds to betray us. ... I'm sorry! In the back of my mind, I think I was upset that Kieya did this instead of me." She turned to the big cat. "Thank you, Kieya. I know now I probably would not have handled that as well – and as skillfully – as you did."

Kieya looked at her directly. "Are you sure you are okay with all of this?"

A tear rolled down Refinnej's cheek. "Yes, my friend, I am." She looked at Joseph and smiled. "Was it fun?"

He grinned. "Yes, but it would have been even more fun if you had been with us."

She shook her head. "Maybe, but I don't think things would have gone so smoothly." She paused. "Dad, what's next?" How do we proceed?"

Walter scratched his head. "Actually, I think the initiative is with Samoht and the others. When they are ready, they will contact you.

She was grim. "I'll want to give them a piece of my mind!"

Walter shook his head. "No. It's not the fault of Samoht or any of the others who want to learn, that some spoilers want to create mischief. I have a suggestion."

"What?" Joseph put his arm around her.

Walter nodded towards her. "After you both have gotten some sleep, the two of you can bounce this asteroid around some more – from the inside, not outside – until you have it back where it was before."

"Why?" they both asked, almost together.

Once you're in place, step outside of your asteroid, find Samoht, and bring him inside, where he is separated from the communal thoughts of the other Buuds." As Refinnej began to smile, Walter continued. "Talk to Samoht as the wise leader he is becoming. Ask him for suggestions with regard to discipline. Point out to him again the fact that, with Joseph as your amplifier, you could simply exterminate the erring Buuds, but you do not want to resort to that. Such extremes must be reserved for truly serious offenses, and then after consultation with other Buuds. Before you meet with him, you and Joseph can plot some variations and potential strategies."

"Thanks, Dad." Refinnej hugged Walter.

"Indeed." Qaak and Jody stood up. "We are going to go home and get some rest ourselves. I will file a full report with Gaardian, and then I will take Jody to your moon base."

Jody smiled. "I have gotten behind on some of my work, and I don't want to get even further behind. Qaak is going to visit the Suppla on Pzalop. He promised her some help a few weeks ago, and it is time."

Qaak raised a hand. "Farewell, my friends!"

Jody waved, "Bye!" They vanished.

Kieya stood up. I'm going to depart as well. It has been too long since Icnivad and I spent some alone time with each other. I hope we can spend several days together before duties call. Now that I have a mate again after so many thousands of years without one, I want to make sure that I give our marriage the attention it deserves. I'll drop off Asayak at your base on my way home."

Walter nodded. "Thanks, Kieya. God does everything well, my friend."

"Agreed."

Refinnej walked over and put her arms around Kieya's neck. "Thank you again, Kieya. Enjoy yourself."

Joseph waved. "Good night!"

"Good night!" She and Asayak vanished.

Refinnej took Joseph's hand and looked at their parents. "Mom, Dad, come on! We'll show you your bedroom suite!"

They started up the spiral staircase. Debbie was amused. "Did you say 'suite?'"

Joseph grinned. "Yep! Right this way!" A door slid open, and they walked into a sitting room about six meters by eight meters, with a fireplace and overstuffed furniture. Through the next doorway, they entered a bedroom about the same size with a king-size bed. Joseph pointed. "Through that doorway is a bath suite with a shower and whirlpool bath with other necessities."

Walter and Debbie both smiled. Debbie hugged Refinnej. "It's beautiful! We'll see you in the morning!"

Refinnej kissed her on the cheek. "Until then!"

Walter nodded, and she hugged him too. Good night, Dad!"

Walter shook Joseph's hand. "Good night you two!"

The next morning, as they were finishing breakfast, Refinnej said, "When Joseph and I woke up earlier we decided to get our moving business out of the way, so outside we're back where we started yesterday."

Debbie swallowed some juice. "Good. I was wondering about that. As soon as we're done here we'll go back to our base and get caught up on some things."

Joseph looked at his Mom. "Are you starting to slow down a little because of the triplets?"

Debbie shook her head. "Not yet. Since it is triplets, Butch says to expect some slow times for a few months or so, but we're not there yet."

Walter nodded. "I'm going to do everything I can to be there this time. I wasn't there for your birth, Joseph!"

He grinned. "So I've heard!"

Refinnej smiled. "I'm really enjoying being married into a human family!"

Debbie slid her chair back from the table. "Walter, I think it's time for you and I to get going so that our children can get on with their day."

As he stood up, Walter nodded. "I agree. Keep us posted as to how things are going. I know it may seem a bit tedious at times to keep Gaardian informed of things, but it's the way we keep things running smoothly."

Joseph smiled. "It's cool, Dad. See you soon." He shook his hand.

Refinnej hugged them both. "See you soon!"

Debbie looked around. "You can be proud of this. You've made yourselves a real home!"

"Absolutely!" Walter smiled. "See you soon!" Walter and Debbie vanished.

In a blink, the dishes and remaining food were gone. Refinnej took Joseph's hand. "Let's go find Samoht."

Appearing with Joseph on Quzak at the southern rotational center, Refinnej listened to the chatter in the Buud communal consciousness. She kept her mind as quiet as possible. Joseph relaxed, watching the sun move horizontally around the horizon.

Samoht appeared next to them. "We are sorry, Refinnej. They must be disciplined."

She looked at him carefully. "I agree. Will you please come with us and be our guest?"

"Yes. I will come."

In a flash, the three of them were inside of the asteroid-appearing sphere. Joseph smiled and pointed. "Make yourself comfortable. Have refreshment if you like." A beverage appeared in Joseph's hand, and then beverages appeared in the hands of Refinnej and Samoht.

As they sat down, Refinnej said, "We asked you here because this is one of two places in Gaardian-controlled space where Buuds are disconnected from their communal mind."

Samoht looked around. "Is this bounded by that isotope of beryllium aluminate?"

"Yes. I like the quiet here. Do you?"

He thought for a moment. "I believe I am beginning to enjoy it. Yes, thank you."

Joseph spoke quietly. "If I may, I would like to point out that you are rapidly becoming what we might call a wise leader of the Buuds. Do you think that is fair?"

"I don't mind being thought of as a wise leader, but why?"

Refinnej looked at him directly. "I am young and inexperienced, but I have been given a great responsibility. I do not think of this responsibility casually."

Samoht smiled for the first time in Refinnej's memory and looked at her. "I have recognized for quite some time that, while you can enjoy yourself like any other Buud, you do not take life itself as frivolously or lightly as many others Buuds have done."

She returned his smile. "Together, Joseph and I have the power to exterminate with regard to truly serious offenses, but for smaller offenses, such power is problematical at best. We Buuds have mostly lived very undisciplined and meaningless lives until now."

"Yes. In recent times, many things have changed. Gaardian guidelines now give us behavior boundaries. As adults, we can no longer act without control or discipline. When you drew us into that crystalline structure, and we suddenly were stripped of our Buud abilities, it was life-changing."

"For me, discovering there is a Creator, who made us all we are, and who provides all we have, was even more life-changing. It was an answer to a hunger that I did not know I had."

He nodded and turned to Joseph. "You may know the answer to this, but you may not. Do you know the nature of that force-field that stripped us of our powers at the crystalline structure?"

Joseph shook his head. "I am not an engineer, but I know the Zargadete that designed that force-field system."

Samoht nodded. "Excellent! It seems to me that, intentionally or not, your friend has provided a solution to our discipline problem. I have been trying to find a way to duplicate that isotope of the crystalline material, but with my most judicious use of Buud powers, I have been unable to do so. Evidently, it is only something that the Creator of the universe can create."

Refinnej leaned forward. "Did you say that there is a solution to our discipline problem?"

"Possibly, yes. It could be at least a provisional solution. To me, the obvious brief solution is incarceration in a place specially prepared for Buuds."

She nodded. I can learn how to prepare such a place and, as a Buud, prepare it instantly. You and I have no mental barrier between us. It seems as though you envision apartments, each with a singular source of light with minimal non-visual energy. Food would be synthesized by external sources and delivered automatically. During incarceration, they would have no exposure to other life forms."

Joseph raised a finger. "Total solitary confinement would have to be relatively brief."

Refinnej nodded. "Details will have to be worked out in terms of distinct levels of punishment for different kinds of offenses. ... Thank you, Samoht. Now, I have one further question: Was the brief experience of education with Kieya a positive or negative experience for those who were there?"

Samoht laughed. "Even though the training barely began, we all loved it. We were so angry with those two that approached us that we chased them, and they raced away, whimpering, into hiding. As soon as you prepare a place for incarceration, let's put them in it for three days, telling them that it is for three periods of planetary rotation."

"Joseph and I will pray about how long they should be in our little jail. As soon as we have a place for imprisonment, we will put them there. I think it best that we not attempt further education until after those two have experienced their incarceration. I hope that it will discourage them from disturbing the class again."

Samoht stood up. "This sounds like a good strategy. I will wait to hear from you." Joseph nodded, and as his Gaardian ring shimmered, Samoht vanished.

Joseph looked at Refinnej and chuckled. "If I acted that way around my parents I would have suffered for it!"

She smiled. "Really? You needed to be punished?"

"Yes! Our Mom and Dad are gentle but firm, and they would not take anything disrespectful from me."

"Wow! I haven't seen that side of them."

"That's because they see you as an adult over whom they have no jurisdiction. Now that you and I are married, they see me as an adult as well. I'm only seventeen, and you're just eighteen, so we are both very inexperienced with life. I don't take their treating us like adults lightly. I respect them too much for that."

15. Future Bound

It did not take Leahcim long to design the prison, but determining a location was up to Refinnej. She and Joseph discussed it in their hot tub one evening. "When I have to discipline one of the Buuds, their physically suffering the consequences of their actions is not as important as their thinking about the consequences of what they have done."

Joseph nodded. "Right. On Earth, there was a time when a prison was called a 'penitentiary' because of a desire to make prisons a place for repentance from sin, or offenses against God. More commonly, Earth's history is full of examples of prisons used for political purposes to control one's enemies."

She shook her head. "I'm not interested in restricting anyone's freedom, so long as they treat others with respect. For far too long, we Buuds were narcissistic. We were enslaved to our own desires and hungers. We cared for no one but ourselves. ... We are in new territory, thanks to the Creator making Himself known to us."

"So let's talk about where to put this installation. We want a stable environment that requires little maintenance of either the installation or of the prisoners."

She got out of the hot tub and held out her hand. "Okay. Let's go planet shopping. It has to have a stable, moderate climate without intelligent life."

He stood up and walked up the steps out of the tub. Fully dressed, he took her hand. "Okay, let's go."

Since most of the Buuds decided to live on Waysad or near that planet, that's the direction they headed. Arriving there, they went to the town where Refinnej had been kidnapped by the Creator. They appeared in the cave in the bluff above the town. Looking down, Refinnej smiled. "This really is a pretty little planet, isn't it?"

He nodded. "This is Waysad?"

"Yes."

After staring downward a few moments, Joseph locked his eyes with hers. "Let's go to the crystal castle."

"Okay." In a blink, they were there. It was night, and they had the large center room to themselves.

"Now what?"

"We needed privacy from the communal mind while we're talking about this."

"Yes." She was thoughtful. "I was just thinking, as we stood there in the cave, what if we located the installation inside that planet?" She looked at him. "We don't want prisoners to have access to energy anyway. The internal temperature of the planet would provide the installation with a livable temperature. What do you think?"

"Let's look at it." His Gaardian ring shimmered briefly, and a hologram appeared so that they were looking out the mouth of the cave and they were looking downward. Joseph pointed. "As we were standing there, I looked all around. Let's take a look underground at that cavern we could see below the cave."

The hologram changed views, and immediately they were there in the cavern by way of the hologram. Refinnej pointed, and the ceiling of the cavern subtly began to glow. "Do you sense any moisture?"

He shook his head. "Not really. There has not been an underground lake there for a long time I don't think. How deep is it?"

Refinnej looked carefully. "It looks like nearly two thousand meters by Earth measurement. This is excellent! The area there is bigger than several sports stadiums side by side, and that ceiling is more than a hundred meters high in places. A one-level installation will fit in easily."

He looked at his Gaardian ring. "Gaardian, scan our minds and our conversations for the last hour. We need your input."

There was a pause of about ten seconds. Then they heard the planet's telepathic voice. "Yes. Waysad is not currently in Gaardian space, but is in Buud space because so many have chosen to live in that vicinity. Geologically, the planet is stable. Because of the crystalline construction designed by Leahcim, and because of his force field design, Buuds would not be able to detect other Buuds inside the prison in the planet." Gaardian paused. "Yes. Gaardians can monitor and maintain the interior of the facility with a secure relay. ... Yes. You have made a good choice."

Refinnej nodded. "Thank you, Gaardian. Joseph and I will install the facility in a few minutes. Then we will transfer our first two prisoners into it. If Samoht or other Buuds inquire about those two Buuds, simply tell them that I have secured them in a punishment area."

"Agreed. Keep me informed."

"Yes."

Joseph looked at her. "Let's go do our thing!"

She put her hand upon Joseph's shoulder and gestured with her other hand. As they appeared in the cavern, she gestured, and the ceiling began to glow. The prison was there a moment later. "Now for the force-field generators." She gestured again. "I have ovenly spaced them in all directions."

Joseph took her hand. "Let's go inside." They walked into the entry area, and a door slid closed behind them. "Let's test this thing. Try communicating with other Buuds."

She shook her head. "Good. Refinnej to Gaardian. We are inside of our installation. How soon can you install a Gaardian relay here?"

The planet's telepathic voice was clear. "I have used Joseph's Gaardian ring to install the relay. You are in the entry area, and there are three cells without doors or windows, though the entire facility is transparent. As you planned, you will have to transport prisoners in and out of the cells yourselves."

She nodded. "Good. Thank you. ... Joseph, let's go get those mischief makers."

With Buud speed and power amplified by Joseph, they rapidly captured and restrained their prisoners. While their captives were unable to see and hear, hastily the two were placed in separate cells and released within them.

Refinnej stood with Joseph in the entry area facing them. The two Buuds looked around, and then they began pressing against the crystalline walls. They jumped back when the walls felt both hot and cold simultaneously.

They ran around in their cells, grunting as they pressed against the walls of their cells. The one named Saduj ["sah-DOOGE"] was furious. "You can't do this!"

When he looked at her, Refinnej held his gaze. "We just did, so be quiet and listen!"

Both the prisoners stopped.

"You know why you are being punished, and your punishment so far will be minimal. You will be here for seven rotations of this planet. At the end of those seven rotations you will be returned to where we got you. Meanwhile, if you are hungry or thirsty, state your request, and the facility will provide you with food or drink. Do you understand?"

The other prisoner, named Mot, slapped his hand against the wall. "Where are we?"

She shook her head. "That is something you do not need to know. These are the consequences for interrupting the training session provided for other Buuds at their request. This is your first offense. If there is another offense, the punishment will be more severe."

She looked at Joseph and nodded. As they vanished, the light level in the cavern dimmed so that the prisoners could barely see one another.

+ + +

A few days later Margaret Graves picked up her cell phone and dialed in her office in Oakland, California. It was an early Friday morning just before dawn, and from the parking lot below, no one could see that she was there – at least she did not think so. Below her, at the parking lot entrance, Samoht appeared in the semi-darkness. He pressed the doorbell button.

"Yes?" asked Margaret from above.

"Hello. My name is Sam, and I am a friend of Walter's, who I understand is secretly your boss."

There was silence for several seconds. "Very well. Please enter, turn left down the hallway, and go up the stairs. I will meet you on the next floor."

"Okay. Thank you."

Margaret pressed her Gaardian ring's stone firmly against her finger, and Frank appeared. "He's a Buud. It is unlikely that he is a danger to you, but be very cautious of what you say. I am informing Walter." Frank vanished.

Margaret got up from her desk, and walked out to meet 'Sam.' Seeing him through the window in the door, she opened it and admitted him. "Good morning! I am told that you are a Buud. Please come into my office."

Samoht nodded. "Thank you." As she pointed to her office door, he went in. "I hope I have not startled you. Since you know that I am a Buud, please also know that I am not a threat to you."

They both sat down. Margaret offered a weak smile. "Thank you for saying that, but I cannot avoid feeling intimidated."

"I understand. My real name is Samoht. I am one of the oldest Buuds. A few weeks ago, some of us requested education regarding the Holy Spirit. A creature named Kieya came to us, accompanied by Walter's son, Joseph, and another creature named Asayak."

Margaret pondered what he said, and she began to relax. "I have met Kieya, and I have known Joseph since just after he was born. Why have you come to me?"

"While each Buud has his or her own mind, we also share a communal mind. What one of us learns, we all can eventually learn. We know you as a woman who can connect with Walter through a data device of yours called email."

Margaret closed her eyes for a moment. When she opened them again, Walter appeared in the other chair by her desk. "Good morning, Margaret." He turned to the Buud. "Good morning, Samoht. I must say that I am impressed. You have approached Margaret with restraint, with care, and with diplomacy. The Buuds have learned a great deal in a short time."

"Yes. So we have. I have been impressed with you in the past as with now, and I am impressed with your friend here." Margaret smiled but said nothing.

Walter nodded. "May I assume that you are here regarding further training on the subject of the Holy Spirit?"

"Yes – for that reason and more. Two Buuds are currently incarcerated by Refinnej and Joseph. I have been told by Refinnej that they will be in their cells for two more days. Neither the prisoners nor any other Buuds know where the prison is. Refinnej and Joseph are going to take me blindly to see the prisoners in a few hours." He paused and looked down. "One of the things I have noticed from the very beginning is that Gaardians treat everyone with dignity and respect, unless they are provoked or Gaardian rules are violated. That is important to us. I doubt that either of you can comprehend how the boundaries provided by the Creator and the Gaardians have provided us a sense of meaning and purpose in life."

Margaret cleared her throat. "I think I actually do understand."

Samoht looked at her. "Please explain."

She hesitated a moment. "In order to explain it to you, I need to make a comparison, and I do not wish you to take offense."

"None will be taken."

"What I have learned about the Buuds thus far is this: Before you encountered God – the Creator – Buuds were powerful but totally wasteful. You had no discipline or purpose, and you wandered about the universe aimlessly, looking for meaning in your existence."

Samoht now had a small smile. "You are accurate in your understanding."

"Forgive me for saying so, Samoht, but that description also fits small human children. All the human kids I have known in two lifetimes have resented discipline and conformity. At the same time, children always feel safer and have a sense of direction and purpose when they know where their boundaries are. Does that not describe the Buuds?"

Samoht chuckled. "Yes indeed! We have discussed it. It seems strange to think that beings with our power feel safe now, but it is true – especially after witnessing the death, burial, and resurrection of Haissem."

Walter nodded. "All of us are God's children, and God does everything well."

"Yes. The other reason I wanted to talk to you was this: I understand that the term 'Gaardian' refers to both a title for the enforcers of Gaardian guidelines and also for a planet as well. May I see this planet?"

Walter nodded. "Yes, but please be patient. I think it appropriate that the Buuds first learn more about the presence and power of the Holy Spirit. Talk to Refinnej, and she will arrange it."

"Thank you." He stood up. "Thank you for your time, Walter." He turned. "I have enjoyed meeting you, human Margaret. I hope we can talk with one another again." He vanished.

"Walter to Refinnej."

A hologram appeared where Samoht had been. "Hi Walter! You must be Margaret! I recognize you from an image Joseph showed me."

Margaret smiled. "It's nice to meet you, Refinnej."

Walter nodded to her. "Refinnej, connect to Gaardian and review the conversation that just took place here." Refinnej disappeared for about 30 seconds.

When she reappeared, she was nodding. "I'm impressed. He is becoming very capable as a leader. When I take him to see the two prisoners, do you want me to set up the Holy Spirit class afterward?"

Walter nodded. "I will leave that up to you and Kieya. She can retrieve Asayak when you're ready."

"Thanks for letting me know about this visit to Margaret. Did he scare you, Margaret?"

She smiled. "I was intimidated at first, but once I got used to him, he was very charming."

"Good. ... Anything else, Walter?"

"Just let me know how the class goes."

"Okay. Bye you two!" As Margaret waved, she vanished.

+ + +

Three days later, Kieya, Joseph, and Asayak appeared again on the distant planet in the midst of the same area with the sizeable plants as they did in the first attempt to hold the class on the Holy Spirit. Kieya and Joseph configured the identical transparent structure and the assortment of furniture. Asayak sent out the invitation. In seconds, Buuds began appearing. This time, they were all in their natural humanoid form.

Kieya purred softly. "It seems all our previous students are here, and there are a few more. That is not a problem. We had barely begun when we were previously interrupted."

In the front row, one of the former prisoners spoke. "My name is Saduj, and this is Mot. We apologize for interrupting your first session. It will not happen again."

"Very well. As I said the first time, if we did this through a single Buud and his or her communal connection to the minds of other Buuds, this could take dozens of sessions. Doing it this way, we will get it done quickly. You will begin with getting raw data. Then we will entertain questions and discussion. Refinnej will get a separate session with Asayak."

Samoht, who was also sitting in the front row, nodded. "We understand. Much has happened since our first attempt at this."

"Very well. The transfer of data will be telepathic at high speed through Asayak. Get comfortable. This can seem exhausting. As I said before, do not try to control it. ... Now, relax and close your eyes."

Joseph created a chair and sat down next to Kieya. Her eyes were unblinking and intense, and she had no purr. Joseph understood.

Twelve minutes later, Asayak stirred, and the Buuds opened their eyes. Samoht spoke first. "When we met the Creator, I realized that He does everything well and does not make mistakes. It seems obvious that the Gaardians have the guidance of the Holy Spirit available to them. This is very well organized. Kieya, I understand that the Creator has made you a prophet, just as Refinnej is a prophet to the Buuds. Do you often get visions of the future?"

Kieya's purr resumed. "I asked Walter the same thing a long time ago because he was a prophet before me, and he still is. When the Creator uses a prophet, we are given a glimpse of things from the Creator's perspective. Since that perspective is without time, God's perspective seems to be of the future. Instead, it is simply a much broader perspective of our lives than we can see otherwise."

The Buuds closed their eyes. When they opened them, Samoht spoke again. "We know that you planned for discussion and questions at this point, but we need to discuss all of this among ourselves. What we have learned today has given us an even greater understanding of the Creator and His ways. We have much to consider together, and we are grateful that the three of you came again. We bid you farewell." The Buuds vanished.

Joseph and Kieya stood up, and Asayak stirred. It said, "I will have much to report for Gaardian records. I would like for us to go to Gaardian."

Kieya's purr paused momentarily, and she blinked. "Indeed. Yes, we should. Joseph, take a handful of my mane again."

The three of them flashed rapidly through space, until they were in the lounge of the family center. The planet spoke first. "I have asked Walter to assemble this meeting in the crystal castle, in the triangular room at the top of the center area. Refinnej will also be there." The three vanished again.

It was mid-afternoon on Pzalop at the castle when they began assembling there as the planet suggested. When the teaching team arrived, Refinnej gave Joseph and Walter hugs before all of them made themselves comfortable. The planet's voice was strong and firm. "Refinnej, you need to hear all of this, but how much of what we say here that you will discuss with the Buud community will be up to you."

She nodded. "I understand."

Asayak raised an appendage. "As I transferred the data on the Holy Spirit, I listened to each individual Buud mind and noted their emotions. I can report the entire twelve minutes as a mental transfer data stream in about one-fourth of that time. Will that be acceptable?"

Walter nodded. "Proceed, Asayak."

For a little more than three minutes, hardly any of them stirred. When Asayak was done, they all looked around at each other.

Refinnej was astonished. "I would not have thought this possible. It must be the Creator's work."

Walter nodded. "Yes, indeed yes! Amen! Praise God!"

Kieya's purr was audible throughout the room. "Refinnej, it appears that the Buuds have become a mature civilization in a matter of weeks. The Creator does indeed do everything well! May I ask about the encounter between the prisoners Saduj and Mot when they met with Samoht?"

Refinnej grinned. "I do not know the details because all three of them have refrained from discussing it in the community. I have only impressions from them. I will say this to all of you even though I find it difficult to believe myself. Saduj and Mot have been different Buuds since Samoht finished talking with them. They cling to him and try to learn from him. Of course, we have no way of knowing whether or not it will last."

Asayak spoke quietly. "Based upon my reading of their emotions as the talk with one another, I would say that their transformation is real."

Kieya purred softly. "Indeed. As I looked into the eyes of those two, I saw no hostility as I did before. I saw gentle compassion. That is a true transformation."

Walter nodded. Quietly, he said, "As good as this appears, my friends, let's not be complacent, and let's not deceive ourselves."

Refinnej looked at her Dad with pain in her eyes. "Why?"

Joseph nodded. "I know, Dad."

Refinnej looked at him. "You do?"

He nodded. "No matter what part of the universe we are from, all intelligent life forms are God's sinning children. Right, Dad?"

Walter smiled. "Right. As scriptures from many planets testify, 'all have sinned and fallen short of God's glory.' None of us is perfect except God. We make mistakes. We commit offenses against our Creator. However, God graciously loves us and wants us to want Him. This is the pastor in me talking, which at least Joseph expects. Right, son?"

"Right."

"Centuries ago on Earth, God had hundreds of thousands of unarmed people trapped against a body of salt water, trapped by a large army. God created a dry pathway across in the midst of the water. The people went through, and the army that chased them was drowned. For a generation, the people remembered what happened. Later, they began to ignore what God had done for them. Refinnej, you and the other Buuds have witnessed the death, burial, and resurrection of Haissem, and right now they are highly impressed with The Creator. After some time passes, it is likely you and they will regress."

Refinnej's eyes were moist. "Has that kind of thing happened elsewhere in Gaardian space?"

Walter looked at her. "Certainly it has, ... repeatedly. You can ask Gaardian to show you many records. Face this squarely, okay? You and Joseph are Gaardians to the Buuds for *a reason*, and God has made you a prophet for *a reason*. The Buuds still have growth to experience ahead. There will be difficulties, and there will be challenges. They may not entirely forget, but at least some of the progress will be lost. That is an integral part of the lives of all Gaardians and of all civilizations."

"Okay. I guess I understand, Dad."

"I have one more piece of advice for you two, and Kieya can bear to hear it again. One of the things that the Creator stresses to all of his children is that they must take time for rest routinely. Kieya and Ichnivad are taking time from Gaardian duties for each other and for their union regularly. Your Mom and I take time out with each other every week. Joseph, you've seen us do this all of our lives. Scheduled rest is just as important as the work that you do, because it pleases God and makes your work more effective."

Refinnej nodded. "I will not reveal to the other Buuds the fact that Asayak read all the Buuds individually while it was teaching them. The rest of all of this they will need to know eventually."

After a few moments of silence, Kieya stood up. She purred louder, and her voice was stronger. "There's one more thing we must do right now. While we have been having this meeting here on Pzalop, others have been gathering on Gaardian. Refinnej and Joseph, it's too late for you to have a wedding reception, but we've not had our welcoming party for our newest Gaardians. The party is waiting, so Joseph, grab a handful of my fur, and we'll all go at once!" As Joseph's fingers touched Kieya's mane, all of them vanished.